THE
EMPIRE
OF
ASHES

BY ANTHONY RYAN

Raven's Shadow
Blood Song
Tower Lord
Queen of Fire

The Draconis Memoria
The Waking Fire
The Legion of Flame
The Ashes of Empire

THE
EMPIRE
OF
ASHES

THE DRACONIS MEMORIA: BOOK THREE

ANTHONY RYAN

www.orbitbooks.net

ORBIT

First published in Great Britain in 2018 by Orbit

1 3 5 7 9 10 8 6 4 2

A CIP catalogue record for this book
is available from the British Library.

HB ISBN 978-0-356-50644-9
C format 978-0-356-50645-6

Printed and bound in Great Britain by Clays Ltd, Elcograf S.p.A.

Papers used by Orbit are from well-managed forests
and other responsible sources.

MIX
Paper from
responsible sources
FSC® C104740

Orbit
An imprint of
Little, Brown Book Group
Carmelite House
50 Victoria Embankment
London EC4Y 0DZ

An Hachette UK Company
www.hachette.co.uk

www.orbitbooks.net

Dedicated to the memory of my uncle Bill—
formerly Sgt. William McNamara of the Royal Scots Dragoon Guards—
in recognition of the price he paid for fighting the good fight.

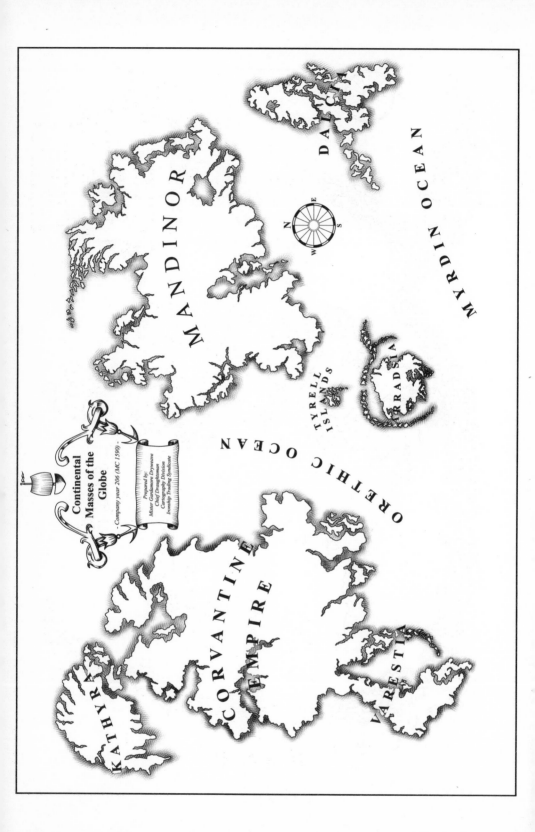

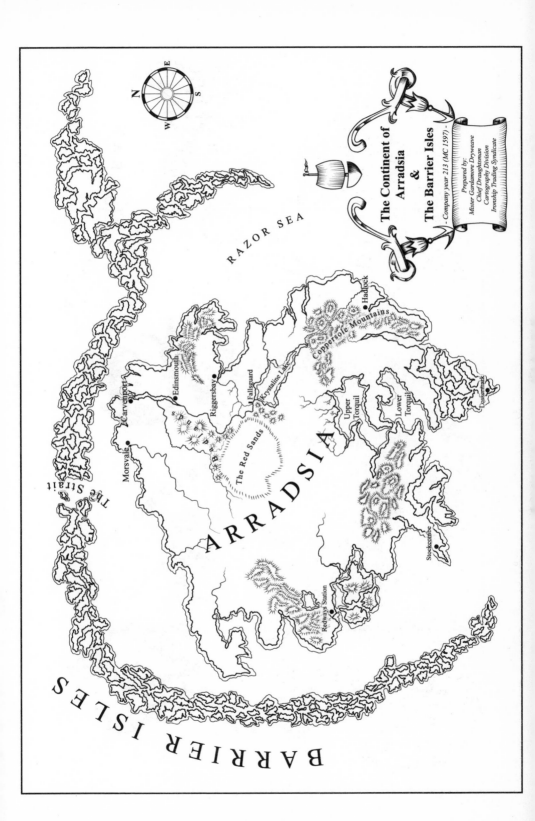

The Continent of Arradsia & The Barrier Isles

- Company year 213 (MC 1597) -

Prepared by:
Mister Gardamore Dryweave
Chief Draughtsman
Cartography Division
Ironship Trading Syndicate

RAZOR SEA

ARRADSIA

BARRIER ISLES

The Strait

Coppersole Mountains

The Red Sands

Morsvale

Carvenport

Edinsmouth

Riggersbay

Fallsguard

Krysaline Lake

Upper Torquil

Lower Torquil

Hadlock

Dossermark

Stockcombe

Redways Station

CORVANTINE EMPIRE

SUBARISK

MELKORIN

SAIRVEK

TAKMARIN'S LAND

SABIRAS ARCHIPELAGO

THE RED TIDES

VARESTIAN PENINSULAR

THE SEVEN WALLS

ISKAMIR

THE HIGH WALL

ORETHIC OCEAN

N
W E
S

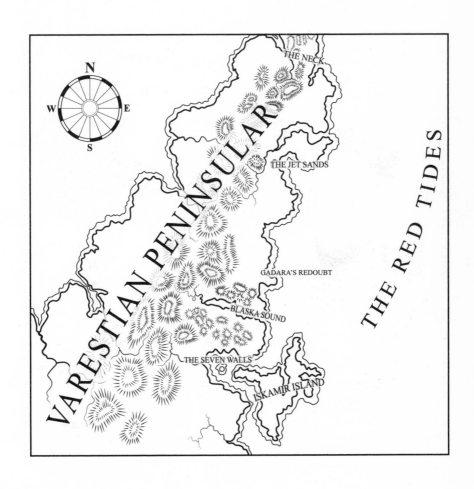

I

THE ARTISAN'S SHADOW

From the Journal of Miss Lewella Tythencroft—
Sanorah, 27th Termester 1600 (Company Year 211)

I awoke from another dream of Corrick, as is my wont most mornings in
these troubled times. If, as the infrequent responses to my many letters to the
Maritime Protectorate insist, Lieutenant Corrick Hilemore is most likely
dead as opposed to merely missing, he appears to have left behind a very
busy ghost.

My humour is misplaced, I know. Cruel even. To myself if not the memory of the man I loved (still love, at least be honest with yourself, Lewella).
But I find it preferable to the weeping and mewling expected of my sex.

The dream was different again. My erstwhile fiancé's nightly visits are
rich in variety if not clarity. I would dream of him before of course, especially
during those long awful months of separation thanks to his slavish service to
our corporate overlords. Even more so during the unjust Dalcian slaughter
the Syndicate chooses to call an "emergency." But those dreams were more
like memories, my mind seeking his company in somnolence when it was
denied me in the waking hours. Walks in the park, stolen hours of intimacy
away from my parents' ever-prying gaze, our many, many wonderful argu-
ments. I used to cherish my dreams of him, but now I dread them, for I always find him in danger.

This time he was somewhere cold and very far away. The images are
always vague but his face remains clear, and just lately it is the face of a man
troubled by a terrible weight of guilt. Corrick is not a man given to excessive

introspection but, despite his professional calling, he does have a greater capacity for feeling than many might imagine.

There I go again, the present tense. But, like my misplaced humour, I find I can't help it. In my soul, if not my mind, I know him to be alive . . . and somewhere very cold.

I endured another breakfast with Mother and Father, he hiding behind his copy of the Intelligencer, *as per usual, whilst she filled the silence with inane gossip. Just lately, as the news from home and abroad grows ever worse, I have noticed a certain desperation in her chatter. Her myriad tales of petty scandal, announced engagements and barbed comments regarding my own singular lack of prospects in that regard are spoken with a somewhat shrill note and an over-bright cast to her eyes. At times I think she is trying to weave some form of magic spell, as if this verbal frippery will banish the encroaching threat through dint of sheer, mundane normalcy. But the threat is real and shows no sign of abating.*

"Feros Falls Silent" proclaims the Intelligencer *in characteristically bald terms. As yet, however, the reason for the city's silence remains unexplained, if much speculated upon. The interior pages relate more lurid details of the latest Corvantine Revolution, this one apparently successful. "Entire Corvus Aristocracy Slaughtered in a Single Night," "Mock Trials See Hundreds Hanged," "Self-Proclaimed Ruling Council Led by Notorious Criminal Dictatress," and so on. Many of my Voterist friends insist these stories are lies concocted by the corporate-controlled press to stoke fear of just rebellion. Personally, I'm not so certain all these horrors are in fact imaginary. The Corvantine people suffered centuries of cruel oppression at the hands of a hideous, blood-soaked Regnarchy. Is it so surprising they would act with a vengeful heart now?*

Other stories speak of riots in many North Mandinorian towns, an increased desertion rate amongst Protectorate soldiery, and, perhaps most worrying of all, a collapse in the corporate bond and share markets. I noticed Father's hands take on a small tremor as he turned the page to this particular report causing me to ponder just how much of the family wealth he has invested in market speculation over the years. But of course, any question I might raise in regard to financial matters would be met with either cold indifference or a suggestion that, if business interests me so much, I should give up my radical hobbies and find corporate employment. So I said nothing, washed my toast and boiled egg down with a gulp of tea, kissed Mother on the cheek and set off for the offices of the Voters Gazette.

As has become somewhat routine the morning editorial meeting soon degenerated into a political discussion and thence a full-blown shouting match. Mr. Mantleprop, the photostatist, nearly came to blows with Mr. Mityard, the foreign affairs correspondent, over the latter's "blatant bias in favour of vindictive beastliness" in his reporting on the Corvantine Revolution. Lately, in my capacity as acting editor-in-chief, I have been sorely tempted to simply dismiss every correspondent on the staff. Given that I write at least two-thirds of the words in every issue whilst my supposed subordinates spend their hours in fruitless argument, it would hardly be a greater burden to run the paper as a solo enterprise. It would also make for a much more peaceful working environment. But, as this periodical—being the official organ of the Voters Rights Alliance—*was constituted as a co-operative rather than a private entity, I lack the power to dismiss anyone without a majority vote of the editorial board.*

I would normally have made efforts to calm the atmosphere and force some semblance of order on the meeting, but today found myself too wearied by my troubled sleep. So instead I took my note-pad and pen and set off for the dock-side district, leaving my colleagues to their strife. Any experienced correspondent will know that the docks are always a useful source of information, most particularly during troubled times. Sailors from all corners of the globe can be found in any dock-side tavern and they are ever a talkative breed, especially when encouraged by a young and not unattractive woman willing to spend a few scrip on a round of ale or two.

Today, however, it transpired that such machinations would not be necessary, for I found the docks in a state of considerable excitement. Several weeks before, the so-called Blessed Demon had forsaken her reign of terror in the Marsh Wold to inflict fiery destruction on the dock-side district before mysteriously vanishing. The damage has been only partially repaired and many warehouses remain in a blackened and ruined state. However, Syndicate authorities were efficient in restoring the cranes to the wharf and rebuilding the many wooden jetties which had been burned down to the water-line.

I found the quayside a-throng with Protectorate soldiers and constabulary, several senior officers amongst them. Beyond the broad waters of the harbour itself I could see smoke pluming from the great engines that operate the huge doors in the guard-wall. Usually, only one door is raised after the morning tide, but today all three doors were being drawn up at once.

Naturally, my questioning of the Protectorate officers on the scene produced either a bland but polite "no comment" or a frosty suggestion that I seek grist for my "Voterist propaganda" elsewhere. Consequently, I was compelled to elicit information from a more willing source, albeit reluctantly.

I found Sigmend Talwick midway along the wharf, his lanky, poorly tailored form perched on a crate as he scribbled in his note-pad. "Miss Tythencroft," he said upon noting my approach. His broad smile would have been taken for warm and welcoming if not for the poorly concealed carnal interest he simultaneously displayed in surveying my person. "How are things at the Gazette? I hear your circulation is booming, almost breaking four figures last month."

"Five figures," I lied, as I often do in Mr. Talwick's presence and find it scarcely tweaks my conscience at all. "I must congratulate you on the Intelligencer's latest issue," I went on. "For a periodical given to vulgar and tasteless reporting, your paper truly outdid itself today. Corvantine rebels are roasting and eating aristocratic babies, apparently."

He stiffened a little, his smile fading. "I am merely a correspondent, miss. Not the editor."

"Quite so, sir." I turned and nodded at the rising harbour doors. "Might I enquire if any of your Protectorate friends have enlightened you as to the meaning of all this?"

"No," he replied, somewhat archly. "They haven't, but one doesn't raise all three doors for a single ship, does one?"

"A fleet then. And not composed of enemies."

"So it seems. But from where does it hail is the question. Care for a wager, Miss Tythencroft? My money's on a flotilla of Dalcian mercenaries, hired by the Protectorate to augment the Northern Fleet."

"I leave the financial speculation to my father, sir. However, I doubt the Protectorate could find many Dalcians willing to take their scrip after the Emergency."

"Varestians then. In the pre-Colonial era they'd fight for anyone if the price was right."

Just then the harbour doors reached their full elevation, as signalled by the chorus of steam-whistles that sounded from the top of the wall. A short while later the dark, slow-moving shape of a vessel appeared in the central entry-point to Sanorah harbour. I immediately recognised it as a small steam-ferry, the type normally employed in carrying passengers around coastal regions. However, from its appearance it seemed to have been at sea for many days. The vessel's paint-work was besmirched with soot and her paddles were missing some blades, making only partial purchase on the water as she moved sluggishly to one of the near by jetties.

Mr. Talwick and I quickly made our way to the jetty as lines were thrown between ship and shore. I could see a large crowd of people on the ferry's fore-deck, mostly women and children and all possessed of the kind of grey-faced silence that comes from prolonged privation. As we drew nearer I could see many weeping, either in relief or sorrow. I couldn't tell.

"A fleet to be sure," Talwick commented, jerking his chin at the opened portals through which several more similarly bedraggled vessels were making their way. "But composed of refugees, not mercenaries."

We were close enough to make out the lettering on the ferry's hull: IRV Communicant—Rg'd Feros Harbour, 03/06/177. "Sailed all the way from the Tyrell Islands in a thirty-year-old coast runner," Talwick said with a note of admiration.

A gangway had been manoeuvred into place and people were disembarking the ferry, most moving with a stooped, unsteady gait that bespoke near exhaustion. Some of the older passengers were being aided by their younger compatriots, and many were still weeping. As they began to congregate on the quayside my gaze was drawn to a particular figure who stood straighter than the rest. She was a tall woman of South Mandinorian colouring and, from the way the other refugees responded to her, seemed to enjoy some form of authority.

"Joya," she called to a slender girl who, along with a pale-skinned woman wearing oddly garish face-paint, was helping a man with bandaged eyes navigate his way down the gang-plank. "Bring him here. We need to keep all the patients together. Molly, when you've settled Mr. Adderman get y'self back aboard and retrieve all the medicines you can find. Ain't rightly sure how generous our hosts are gonna be."

"Good day, madam." Talwick, always possessed of a keen eye for the best source of information, walked up and greeted the tall woman with a bow. "Sigmend Talwick, chief correspondent of the Sanorah Intelligencer. *Might I enquire as to your name?"*

"Surely," the woman replied, moving away. "It's Mrs. Mind Your Own Seer-damn Business."

Talwick straightened with an aggrieved sniff but, never one to be distracted in his quest for a story, immediately began questioning the other refugees. I, however, felt there was more to be had from Mrs. Mind Your Own Seer-damn Business, and pursued her through the crowd for several minutes until she consented to notice my presence.

"You another correspondent?" she asked, glancing up from inspecting a wound on a child's arm. The infant seemed to have lost the energy to cry, merely sitting quietly in her mother's lap and gazing at the stitched red-and-blue mark in her flesh with wide, incurious eyes.

"Of a sort," I replied. "I represent the Voters Rights Alliance." I looked around at the growing throng of beggared people, finding I had to cough away the sudden catch in my throat. "I assure you I only want to help."

"*Good.*" *She tied a fresh bandage around the girl's arm, then tweaked her small chin. The girl merely blinked and settled deeper into her mother's arms.* "*These people need medical care,*" *the woman went on, rising and turning to me.* "*And those on the other ships will need places to live and food to eat. Can your Alliance help with that?*"

"*Yes,*" *I said, possessed of a sudden conviction.* "*I'll return forthwith to our offices and start organising a relief effort.*" *I extended my hand.* "*Miss Lewella Tythencroft.*"

"*Mrs. Fredabel Torcreek.*" *We shook and a faint, grim smile played on her lips, presumably as she read the feelings evident in my features.* "*Guess this is a new sight for you, hun?*"

"*Yes.*" *I coughed again, standing straighter.* "*Please, before I go. You were at Feros, yes?*"

"*That's right. And it's gone. Drake and Spoiled came out of the sea and sky and took it, doing a whole lotta killing in the process. Us former Carvenporters and a few others managed to get away, but we left a good many folks behind.*"

"*I . . . have a friend,*" *I began, hating myself for the way my words stumbled from a faltering mouth.* "*My former fiancé in fact. A Lieutenant Hilemore. He's been posted as missing presumed dead. I wondered . . .*"

"*Hilemore?*" *Mrs. Torcreek stared at me for a moment then let out a laugh.* "*Firstly, I believe it's Captain Hilemore these days. And he ain't dead, hun. Last I heard he's very much alive, though he's probably freezing his ass off alongside my kin just now.*"

CHAPTER 1

Clay

It was like drinking liquid fire, the heart-blood sending a searing bolt of agony through him the instant it touched his tongue. Somehow he managed not to lose his grip on the vial, keeping it pressed against his lips until the entire contents had made a fiery progress from his throat to his gut. He convulsed as the pain blossomed, thrashing in the water as it grew, banishing all other sensation, turning his vision grey then black. He wondered if the pain would kill him before Last Look Jack could send a stream of flame down to boil him as he thrashed. Either way he knew with absolute certainty he had barely seconds to live.

Then it was gone. The pain vanished in an instant. Clay blinked and the black void filling his eyes cleared. He was still in the water, floating weightlessly below a shimmering surface. The water was cold but the chill was muted somehow, a distant thing beyond the confines of his body, a body he quickly realised had grown to huge proportions. The view ahead was a mélange of colour, cool azure shades shot through with smudges of orange and the occasional small flutters of deep red. *They see heat rather than light,* Ethelynne Drystone had said when she shared memories with him in the ruined amphitheatre. Once again, he was seeing the world through the eyes of a drake.

He saw that these colours were not so vibrant as those captured by the doomed Black all those centuries ago, but any sense of limited vision was more than dispelled by the sound that filled his ears. It was a constant vibrating echo, varying in pitch from one second to the next. It meant little to him but he could sense an understanding somewhere in his mind, an instinctive knowledge possessed by the one who had captured this memory.

The conclusion was as inescapable as it was terrifying. *I'm trancing with Last Look Jack.*

The view shifted as the soundscape changed, a sharp pealing cry cutting through the echo. The shimmering surface above blurred as Clay was propelled through the water, moving with a speed that was beyond any human engine. He could feel the great drake's pulse quicken from a steady, ponderous thrum to a rapid drum-beat as the pealing cry came again. It was plainly a distress call, shot through with panic and terror. Clay could sense Jack's increasing alarm as they raced through the water, the understanding afforded by the trance enabling him to recognise it as parental concern. Somewhere his child was suffering.

Abruptly the distress call rose to a scream, piercing enough to send a shiver of pain through Clay's mind, then it was gone, cut off in an instant. Another sensation seeped through his consciousness as the scream faded, not a sound this time, a scent. It was a smell that would usually stir hunger in the belly of this monstrous predator, but now stirred only despair. Blood, but not prey to be hunted down or a drifting whale carcass to be scavenged. This was the blood of a Blue drake.

Last Look Jack gave voice to a cry of his own then, a deep throaty roar of grief that seemed to shake the sea. His speed remained undiminished, however, his massive body coiling with furious energy to propel him on. The scent of blood grew more intense until Clay saw a dark billowing red fog ahead, cooling to pink as the warmth leeched into the water. Jack slowed as he neared the cloud, Clay making out a dark matrix amidst the billowing warmth, a net stretched tight around something large and limp. He could see the dark barbs of several harpoons jutting from the dead Blue, a juvenile judging by its size. Blood bloomed with fresh intensity as the net shifted and the body rolled in its snare as it was drawn up towards the surface. Jack's gaze followed the black lines of the hauling ropes, finding two long dark shapes interrupting the surface above. He knew these shapes, knew they brought danger and normally the sight of them would have caused him to dive for the security of the depths. But not today.

He tore the net apart first, triangular, razor-like teeth tearing it to pieces, freeing the slaughtered juvenile inside. Jack paused to regard the slowly descending corpse, falling away into the cold black depths in a shroud of blood. A new memory filled Clay's mind. A small Blue struggling free of her mother's womb to coil against her father's massive flanks as he curved his body around them both in a protective embrace, voicing a soft song to soothe her distress.

The memory faded and Clay found Jack's gaze had returned to the two dark shapes above. He roared again, his despair merging with rage. It was a rare emotion for a Blue, conserved for the mating season and defending territory from aggressive young males. Now it bloomed to unprecedented heights, filling every fibre of Jack's body. Clay felt something give in Jack's mind, a jolting shock that banished his last vestiges of reason. The great Blue's roar died. He had no need to voice his rage now. He was rage.

The two dark shapes had begun to move, the water on either side of them frothing white and a rhythmic thrum sounding through the ocean. Clay saw soft yellow globes burning in the centre of each shape as the Blue-hunter's engineers stoked them high. Unnerved by the sudden loss of their catch, these sailors had clearly opted not to linger. It wouldn't save them.

Jack made for the shape on the left, making a steady but unhurried approach from below. Although the rage still boiled in his mind, his predatory instincts held true and he knew the wisdom of preserving his energy for the final rush. When he was some fifty yards from the spinning blades of the Blue-hunter's starboard paddle, he struck. A single thrash of his massive tail shattered the paddle-blades into splinters, causing the ship to veer off in a ragged circle, tilting from the force of Jack's blow. Small, dark figures plunged into the water around him, sailors cast from the deck of the stricken vessel. Jack took his time, snapping each struggling figure in half and spitting out the remnants, finding he disliked the taste of these tiny monsters. Their blood was bitter and their flesh too full of bones. In any case, he was not here to feed.

He thrashed his tail again, an explosive release of power that propelled him free of the sea. The ship passed beneath him as his massive body soared over it, sailors gaping up at him in terror then screaming as he opened his jaws wide and unleashed a torrent of fire. The flames swept the ship from stern to bow, incinerating men and fittings alike, flooding the holds and setting light to anything that would burn.

Jack plunged back into the welcoming chill of the ocean, circling the ship as it burned and killing the charred and barely alive sailors peppering the surrounding waters. A sudden, hard vibration pulsed through the sea as something gave in the ship's vitals, probably a stock of gunpowder from the size of the explosion. Jack watched it break in two and slowly subside into the depths, trailing a dark cloud of blood from its sundered holds. The scent of his kin's blood stoked Jack's rage to even greater heights, Clay feeling the already fragile structure of his mind crumble yet further.

The huge Blue returned to the surface, raising his head above the waves to see a second ship several miles to the north, smoke billowing from her funnels and paddles churning as she piled on the steam. It wouldn't save her.

The trance fragmented then, Clay experiencing a jolt of pain as the shared memories flitted through his head in a kaleidoscope of wrecked ships and slaughtered sailors. Jack's existence had evidently become an unceasing epic of vengeance, days and nights consumed by the hunt, the endless search for more monsters to kill. He preyed upon whales or giant squid only when his hunger grew into pain; otherwise, he scoured the oceans for ships, destroying all he could find, but there were always more.

Then came a change, a shift in the torrent of rage and tireless hunting. Jack had shunned the company of his own kind for years, ignoring their songs of greeting whenever he passed close to a pack. He knew on some basic level he was no longer one of them, their songs of bonding and play or the joy of the hunt were echoes of something forever lost; Jack had only one song, the rage song. But then came the day he heard something new, not a plaintive cry drifting through the depths, but a song within his mind.

Clay felt another jolt of pain as the song enveloped him, alien and dislocating, and yet dreadfully familiar. *The White.* The depth of malice was unmistakable, although he found it impossible to fully comprehend the intricacies of the beast's thoughts. But he could feel them, the new sense of purpose seeping into Jack's mind, merging with his rage. Clay could sense the Blue struggling against this intrusion. He had a purpose of his own and wanted no other, but the White would not be denied. Soon a fresh torrent of images accompanied the sensation, another ship viewed through the eyes of another Blue. This ship was different however, a warship judging by its guns. Also, it had no paddles. *The* Superior, Clay realised, watching a young woman raise a pair of revolvers on the deck below. *Loriabeth, the day the Blue attacked us.*

The image changed as Loriabeth's bullets struck home, filling it with a red mist that obscured much of what came next, although Clay was able to discern the sudden halt in movement, recalling how he and the Varestian Blood-blessed had used Black to hold the Blue in place whilst Captain Hilemore and Lieutenant Steelfine readied the cannon. There was a flash amidst the red mist and the vision turned instantly to black.

The sense of purpose flooding Jack's mind altered, becoming an implacable command as the image of the *Superior* reappeared. This time Clay was able to discern a clear meaning in the White's thoughts: *Go south . . . Kill them.*

Clay reeled in shock as Jack's memories swirled around him. *It sent him after us. It knew where we were going. How?* The answer dawned swiftly, accompanied by a tinge of self-reproach at his failure to realise it sooner. *Silverpin.* The remnant of her consciousness had been living in his head since her betrayal and death beneath the mountain. *It followed her scent, forced poor mad Jack to hunt us down.*

Another tumble of memories: Jack finding himself part of a pack once more, although the Blues he swam with sang no songs. The destruction of Kraghurst Station and his repressed but still-evident relish at the sight of so many small monsters burning. Jack chasing the *Superior* through the channel between the Chokes and the shelf, the crushing weight of the huge wedge of displaced ice bearing him down to the depths, so far down the pressure threatened to crush his mighty body like paper. But he hadn't died, somehow struggling from under the descending weight and straining damaged muscles as he sought the surface. Soon exhaustion claimed him, leaving him limp and drifting on the current. He would have subsided back into the depths had the pack not found him, coming together to bear him up to the surface and the salvation of the air. Still, he was wounded, needing time and sustenance to heal. The other Blues brought walrus and whale-meat, starving themselves so he might eat. Had he still been capable of such things, he would have sung the song of thanks. But they were not truly his pack and such songs were a distant murmur of who he had once been.

He ate, he healed, he waited, and then came the great upsurge of heat from below, fracturing the ice and allowing him to hunt down the monsters that had wounded him. He marshalled his silent pack, sending them out into the newly sundered ice, ranging far until one found his quarry. A new ship, one with no bloom of heat within its hull, but with monsters roving its deck. Jack, though mad, was far from stupid. Having recently suffered at these creatures' hands, he opted for a more cunning approach, sending his pack to bear the brunt of their terrible, unnatural defences. He watched the sundered, flailing Blue bodies fall one by one, clamping down on his rage, forcing patience into his damaged mind. Only when the last of his pack had slipped into the depths, trailing a cloud of gore from the rent in its neck, did he determine to strike.

Then a new distraction, a fresh bloom of heat from below accompanied by a great cloud of bubbles as something rushed towards the surface. Jack had no notion of what this thing was, his vision unable to penetrate the hull to discern any heat sources within. But, as it bobbed to the surface and he watched four monsters clamber out, he knew he had found his first easy prey for a long time. A shallow dive then an upward rush was enough to leave the creatures struggling in the water. Jack made for the closest one, grunting in momentary pain as one of the monsters on the ship cast something at him, small but possessed of enough speed to tear a hole in his scales. But it was a familiar sting, his scales bore the scars of many such irritations, and with the prey so close he paid it scant heed.

The creature struggling in the water below stared up at him with its tiny, bead-like eyes, its claws fumbling for something about its neck. A weapon, perhaps. As if anything so small could threaten him . . .

Clay watched the image of himself struggling in the water freeze and then shatter, leaving him in a formless, multicoloured fog. Mist swirled around him, coalescing into dense, vibrantly hued clouds then breaking apart. Here and there he caught glimpses of firmer memories, Blue bodies drifting, dismembered sailors, burning ships. This then was the mindscape of Last Look Jack. Beneath the horror Clay could feel a deep weight of confusion pressing in on his own consciousness, shot through with a growing anger.

You can feel me in here, can't you? Clay asked, hoping the drake could discern some meaning in his thoughts. The surrounding mist shimmered, reddish forks of lightning crackling as evidence of Jack's burgeoning rage. *Well, you're stuck with me, for now at least. So let's talk.*

The lightning flashed again, blood-red tendrils reaching out from the fog to envelop Clay, lacerating him with implacable, utter rejection. He steeled himself against the sensation, fighting off the waves of nausea and confusion that threatened to end the trance. *I know you got good reason to hate me and my kind,* Clay persisted as the nausea blossomed into an ache. *But the White . . .* He choked off as the ache transformed into an abrupt burst of agony, deep within his being. The mindscape shimmered again and he felt the imminent loss of the trance as Jack exerted all his will to cast out the hated intruder.

Bargaining won't work, Clay realised, reasserting his own will, the mindscape flaring bright about him, revealing yet more scenes of death and fire. *He's just too crazy.* He struggled to remember everything Ethelynne had said about the effects of drinking heart-blood, how it had enabled her to control Lutharon. *No,* he reminded himself. *Not control. A "mutual understanding," she called it.* But how to birth understanding in a mind damaged by so many dire memories? He paused as more of Ethelynne's words came back to him: *Drake memory does not die with the individual, but rather accumulates down the blood line over many generations.*

He scanned the surrounding chaos, reeling amidst the fury of Jack's continuing efforts to drive him out. *Lutharon remembered the White,* Clay thought. *Even though he'd never seen it.* Maybe one of Jack's ancestors caught sight of it too. But if so, what then? The experiences of Jack's forebears could hardly be sufficient to restore his sanity. Then something Silverpin's ghost had said popped into his head, a small nugget of insight that reminded him she had been more than just the White's vassal: *What are people, anyway, if not just a collection of memories?*

Clay summoned all his will then unleashed it in an instant, blasting away the surrounding fog. He felt Jack shudder under the impact, his rage momentarily quelled by the burst of mental strength. *Must be the heart-blood,* Clay decided. *Gives extra power in the trance.*

He focused on the remnants of memory now drifting around him in an otherwise black void, finding fragmentary glimpses of yet more bloody, flame-soaked vengeance. Reaching out to one, a tight ball containing a vision of the attack on Kraghurst Station, he exerted his will again, forcing it into a tiny bead before crushing it to fragments. He moved on, roaming Jack's mindscape and crushing all the traumatic memories he could find. Jack fought him, red lightning lashing out again and again, but with diminishing force as his memories died. Clay couldn't get them all, some were too formless to be captured and others just snippets of barely remembered carnage. Here and there he encountered odd moments of serenity or even joy, mainly concerning Jack's life before the raging insanity of his vengeance. These Clay left alone, though they were few and far between and certainly not enough to return this beast to sanity.

Confusion reigned in the mindscape as Clay crushed the last of the major horrors: the death throes of a Blue-hunter Jack had tormented for days, rearing up every few hours to roast a sailor or two before diving down to let the survivors ponder their impending fate. Humans, it seemed, had taught him the pleasures of sadism. All Jack's resistance seeped away as the memory crumbled, leaving only the vaguest sense of who or what he was. *I could just leave now,* Clay knew. *End the trance and let him wander the ice, mind broken forever.* But what use was there in that?

Let's see what your ancestors left you. Clay reached into his own memory, summoning the most vibrant image of the White he could find, that final glimpse beneath the mountain as it raged amongst the swarm of its newly hatched kin. *Remind you of anything?* he asked Jack, who failed to provide an answer. Clay expanded the memory, filling the surrounding void with it. *Come on, must be something in here, something buried deep.*

He saw it then, a faint glimmer in the void. Clay exerted his will, drawing the glimmer closer, feeding it with the memory of the White so that it grew, blossoming out into a view of a broad sky above a choppy grey sea. Blues churned the water on all sides, long bodies knifing through the waves, whilst above a battle raged. Drakes, Red and Black, wheeled below grey-white clouds, casting flames at each other or locking together in an ugly tangle of thrashing tails and snapping jaws. Drakes plummeted into the sea with grim regularity, either sinking immediately or struggling on the surface as their wounds leaked into the water. The Blues ignored the stricken Reds and swarmed over the Blacks with streaming fire and gnashing teeth. Clay could sense the blankness of the mind that had captured this memory, largely devoid of thought and filled only with a purpose not its own. *Kill them,* it commanded, the image shifting as the owner of these ancient eyes fixated on a maimed Black near by, trying vainly to take to the air with one undamaged wing. *Kill them a—*

Then it was gone. The purpose, the command. Vanished from the Blue's mind and allowing an inrush of sensation. The Blue halted its charge as the urge towards combat faded, instead circling the struggling Black, casting out curious songs of greeting as its strength gave out and it slipped beneath the waves. The Blue cast its gaze to the sky, seeing that the warring factions had now separated, the Reds formed into a loose pack and striking out towards the north-east whilst the surviving Blacks made for the west. Clay managed to make out the dim but unmistakable figure of a human rider on at least one of the Blacks before they slipped into the cloud and were gone from view.

The end of the war, he realised. *The first one. The White rose before and they defeated it, somehow.*

He pushed the question aside, for it was clear the answer didn't lie in the mind of this long-dead Blue. He sorted through the memories, finding it a far simpler creature than Jack, its songs joyous and possessing only the smallest tinge of rage. *A simple soul,* Clay thought, fighting down a pang of guilt. *Not sure you're gonna like your new home.*

The chill gripped him like a steel fist the moment the trance faded, forcing out a gasp that would have been a yell if he had the breath for it. He bobbed in the swell as the huge Blue sank back into the water, retreating a short distance to hover close by, its head barely above the surface with one wide eye fixed on Clay. He could feel its song thrumming the water, rich in distress. It seemed the trance had left him with an understanding of Blue-song.

A splash drew Clay's gaze to the left, where he found Kriz and Loriabeth struggling to keep Lieutenant Sigoral's head above the water. The Corvantine's face was bleached white and his one good eye dimmed. A series of splashes came from the right, accompanied by the overlapping whine of multiple bullets and the faint crackle of rifle fire. The distress song from the Blue that had been Last Look Jack rose in pitch as he recoiled from the hail of projectiles, sinking lower in the water.

"Stop—!" Clay shouted, twisting about to face the ship, his words choked off behind chattering teeth. He could see a row of armed men at the rail, Uncle Braddon among them. Preacher stood tall in the crow's nest, rifle at his shoulder. More worryingly, Lieutenant Steelfine and Captain Hilemore were frantically trying to manoeuvre a cannon into place. The gun had clearly suffered some damage, its barrel thickly wrapped with rope, making Clay wonder if the act of firing it would pose more of a danger to the crew than to Jack.

Clay dragged a deep breath into his lungs and called out with all the volume he could muster: "STOP FUCKING SHOOTING!" The words echoed across the intervening water, heralding a pause in activity on the ship. Clay saw Hilemore straighten from the cannon in evident confusion.

"Clay!" Loriabeth gasped and he turned to see Sigoral slip from her grasp. Clay swam towards them and dived, managing to grab hold of the Corvantine's jacket before he sank beyond reach, dragging him back to the surface. Kriz and Loriabeth closed in, the three of them kicking frantically to bear Sigoral up. A series of shouts came from the ship, Clay craning his neck to see Hilemore directing a party to lower a boat into the water. *Won't be enough time,* Clay knew with a grim certainty, turning back to regard Sigoral's bloodless complexion. It was also clear that Kriz and Loriabeth were fast approaching their limits as the water's chill sapped their reserves of strength.

He turned to where the huge Blue still loitered twenty yards off, casting out his plaintive distress call. Clay concentrated, summoning the memory of the remade mindscape he had crafted in the beast's head, filling it with a distress call of his own. The Blue's response was surprising in its immediacy, propelling himself towards them with a single swish of his tail before rolling over to present his back spines.

"Grab on," Clay told the others, reaching out to grasp the nearest spine. He took a firm hold of both the bony protrusion and Sigoral's jacket before hauling himself closer. Kriz was obliged to help Loriabeth, who seemed to have lost the ability to raise her arms above the water, the older woman wrapping an arm around her chest and pulling them both towards the drake's huge flank. Once they had all taken hold the Blue rolled again, lifting them clear of the water's deathly chill before bearing them towards the ship.

As they surged through the water Clay caught sight of something bobbing on the surface, his pack, kept afloat by the bulbous cargo it held. *Slow,* he told the Blue, who obligingly reduced his speed, allowing Clay to reach out and reclaim the pack. *Don't worry, young 'un,* he silently comforted the egg. *Carried you way too far to leave you behind now.*

He looked up as the deck of the ship loomed above, finding a row of gaunt and stunned faces. Uncle Braddon was the sole exception. Any astonishment he may have felt was clearly drowned by the joy of seeing his daughter again. "Got y'self a new pet, I see," Braddon said, his heavy beard parting in a broad smile.

"More like a new friend," Clay replied.

"That there's Last Look Jack," one of the crew said. It took Clay a moment to recognise Scrimshine's face under the fellow's scraggly beard. The former smuggler clutched a rifle in his bony hands as he stared down at the Blue's massive body, eyes large in his emaciated skull. "We should kill it, Skipper!" he went on, turning to Hilemore with shrill insistence. "Kill it right now, I says!"

Hearing the murmur of agreement from the other crewmen and noting the severe doubt on the captain's face, Clay said, "That name don't fit him no more. This"—Clay leaned forward to pat the broad scaly space between the Blue's eyes—"this is Old Jack now. And he's gonna get us out of here."

CHAPTER 2

Lizanne

"Nothing at all?"

Sofiya Griffan shook her head, loose red tresses playing over the pale skin of her forehead. She had maintained a largely silent and downcast demeanour since the *Profitable Venture* sailed from Corvus, her inexperienced mind no doubt crowded with the horrors she had witnessed during the capital's fall. However, now she seemed on the verge of some form of mental collapse, her husband reaching out to clasp her hands as they trembled in her lap.

"Nothing," she said, eyes flashing at Lizanne in resentful accusation, as if this turn of events were somehow her contrivance. "Feros is silent. That . . . that has never happened before."

"You have an alternative point of contact, do you not?" Director Thriftmor asked, the inevitable brandy glass in hand. "In Sanorah?"

Sofiya's head moved in a sharp, nervous nod. "A scheduled emergency contact in Northern Fleet Headquarters. I tranced with them less than an hour ago. They've had no contact with Feros since yesterday, nor with any fleet units in the harbour. Blood . . ." She faltered, closing her eyes to stem an upsurge of tears before continuing, forcing the words out. "Blood-burning patrol-craft have been dispatched but it will be several days before they report in."

Silence reigned in the ward-room as each person present digested the news and the Director took the opportunity to refresh his glass. It was Captain Verricks who broke the silence, his only evident sign of discomfort a slight twitch in the impressive grey whiskers that covered the lower regions of his craggy face. "My orders remain clear," he said in a gruff tone that said much for his ability to convey a sense of unflappable authority even in times of great uncertainty. "The *Profitable Venture* is to transport Director Thrift-mor and Miss Lethridge to Feros following the completion of their mission to the Corvantine Empire. I intend to fulfil these orders. Trance or not."

"Feros has fallen," Lizanne told Verricks, the certainty in her own voice more than a match for his. Her imagination had seen fit to crowd her mind with a plethora of dreadful visions concerning the likely fates of those she had left behind to pursue her Corvantine adventures. *Aunt Pendilla, Jermayah, Father . . . Tekela.* Guilt and self-reproach roiled in her breast as she met the captain's gaze. *I should have gotten them on the first ship to a Mandinorian port.* But she had had no notion the White would be able to strike so far north so quickly, and Feros was one of the most well-defended ports in the world.

"My orders . . ." Captain Verricks began but she cut him off.

"Your orders came from a Board which is now most likely dead or enslaved." The harshness in her tone drew a frightened sob from Sofiya, but Lizanne ignored her, stepping closer to Verricks to emphasise her point. "We should hope for the former, since I do not relish the prospect of our adversary learning their secrets, as it surely has if it captured any alive."

Verricks blinked, his gaze switching back and forth between her and Thriftmor. "In that event," he said, and Lizanne could see the distasteful curl of his lips beneath the whiskers, "Director Thriftmor would appear to be the sole remaining authority."

Thriftmor's brandy glass halted its progress towards his mouth as all eyes turned to him in expectation. Besides Lizanne, Verricks and the Griffans, the ship's senior officers were also present at this conference. It was clear to Lizanne that Thriftmor didn't enjoy the scrutiny of such a sizable audience.

"I . . . ah," he said, lowering his brandy glass and inclining his head at Verricks. "I believe, in times of crisis, it is best to defer to military judgement." He coughed and forced a tight smile in Verricks's direction. "Your advice, Captain?"

A derisive scowl momentarily creased the captain's forehead before he turned his gaze away from Thriftmor to address his officers. "It's highly likely the *Profitable* is closer to Feros than any Protectorate patrol-craft. Our first duty must be to the Syndicate. We will approach in full battle order and endeavour to carry out a fulsome reconnaissance of the Tyrell Islands. Once the current situation at Feros has been established, Mrs. Griffan will convey the intelligence to Northern Fleet Headquarters with a request for further orders."

Had Lizanne still held to her operating parameters as an Exceptional Initiatives agent she would have protested, perhaps even leveraged her status to force the captain to sail immediately for northern waters. She had endured weeks in the stink and danger of Scorazin, the Imperial Prison City, to free the Tinkerer and the precious knowledge he possessed. Then there had been the great tribulation of the revolution and the fall of Corus, all the time wondering when the Electress would choose to settle her score. All just to get the Tinkerer aboard this ship. Making for Feros threatened to rob them of whatever advantage his secrets might hold. But the guilt still roiled and she found she had to know what had befallen those she had left to face the storm. So, she stood and said nothing as Captain Verricks reeled off a string of orders to his officers.

"In the meantime, Miss Lethridge," Verricks said to Lizanne when the room had cleared, "it might be best if you compiled whatever report Exceptional Initiatives is expecting of you. It can be communicated by Mrs. Griffan before we close on the Isles."

"Sadly," Lizanne replied with a sigh, making for the ward-room door and sparing a glance at Thriftmor now busily refreshing his brandy glass, "it's not quite that easy."

"You promised security," Tinkerer said in his usual colourless voice. He glanced around at the spartan cabin he had been given and Lizanne wondered if he was pining for his books and diagrams. "This isn't it."

"I promised escape from Scorazin," Lizanne returned. "And I delivered. My end of the bargain is fulfilled." She held out a vial of Blue. "Now it's time for yours, sir."

"Bargains can be renegotiated," he said, making no move to take the vial. "Especially when the value of the item under negotiation has increased . . ."

He fell to an abrupt silence as Lizanne took a revolver from the pocket of her skirt and levelled it at his head. The cylinder clicked as she cocked the hammer. "I am in no mood for your particular manners, sir," she informed him in slow, unmistakable tones. "Up until this point have I given you any reason to doubt my word?"

His face remained impassive as he replied with a fractional shake of his head.

"Good. Then trust me when I say that you will either surrender your secrets now or I will decorate this cabin with your brains." She held out the vial once more. "As I say, I am in no mood."

He lifted one of his deft, slim-fingered hands and plucked the vial from her grasp. "One trance won't be enough," he cautioned her, removing the stopper and drinking half the contents. "The amount of information is considerable and complex."

"Then it's all the more important that we make a start," Lizanne replied, retrieving the vial and drinking the remaining product. She lowered the revolver and they matched stares. For several seconds nothing happened, the expected trance failing to materialise. It occurred to her that Tinkerer's singular personality might prohibit any trance connection, it required some form of emotional bond after all, however slight. But she recalled that he had made at least one friend in Scorazin, although even the unfortunately deceased Melina felt obliged to punch him in the face at one point.

"Perhaps a stronger dose," she began, reaching for her wallet, but then Tinkerer blinked and the cabin disappeared.

The vision that greeted Lizanne was amazingly detailed, possessing a clarity and exactitude she had never before seen in a Blue-trance. Even the most vivid memory was inevitably altered by the mind that recalled it, insignificant elements rendered vague or omitted completely. For Tinkerer, however, it appeared nothing was insignificant. Every cobble of the street beneath their feet caught the dim sunlight peeking through the slowly drifting grey clouds above. Every brick, timber and pane of glass that formed the surrounding houses was fully present as was the tinge of horse-dung that combined with wood-smoke and a faint tang of salt to stain the air.

A port, Lizanne decided, trying vainly to conceal the sense of wonder that leeched from her mind as she surveyed her new surroundings. She spied a tall tower poking above the roof-tops to the south, a spire that closely resembled the oracular temple in the Morsvale park where she had hidden with Tekela and Major Arberus. Thoughts of Tekela immediately quelled her amazement. *We have a task,* she reminded herself, turning to Tinkerer who stood a few feet away, expression as blank as ever.

Where is this? she asked him.

Valazin, he replied. *I was conceived here.*

She had never been to this city but knew Valazin to be the largest port on the Corvantine Empire's north-eastern coast. Once an independent city-state it had been incorporated into the Empire some six centuries ago. She remembered from her many briefings on Corvantine politics that the port had been the scene of some of the worst outrages of the Revolutionary Wars. The inhabitants had unwisely taken advantage of the chaos to resurrect archaic notions of reclaiming long-lost sovereignty. A series of brief battles and prolonged massacres, undertaken by the three now-extinct legions of the Household Division, had put paid to any such illusions. Judging by the fact that many of the houses in sight were of recent construction, and the numerous Imperial posters pasted onto the walls, she deduced they were viewing Valazin some years after its subjugation.

Tinkerer strode across the street and halted before a shop-window decorated with the words "Eskovin Toys & Trinkets—Finest Toymakers in Valazin Since 1209." Lizanne moved to his side, peering through the glass at the interior where a diminutive figure could be seen at a work-bench. Peering closer, she saw that it was a woman, perhaps twenty years old, engaged in wrapping a small wooden box with brown paper. Lizanne took note of the woman's bulging belly. *Your mother.*

Yes. This was my family's shop. Grandfather taught Mother how to make the toys and Father took the shop over when he died.

If she had expected to see some flicker of affection as he gazed upon his mother she was to be disappointed. His face retained its usual impassivity as the woman finished wrapping the box, tying the covering in place with a length of string and a small knot. The woman placed the box under her arm and exited the shop, the bell above the door jingling as she stepped out onto the cobbles. Lizanne was struck by the resemblance to Tinkerer, her pale features a feminized mirror of the man standing next to her, and similarly vacant of expression. The emptiness to the woman's gaze told of a failure to fully perceive the world, as if she were drugged. As the door swung closed Lizanne caught sight of a man's body lying face-down next to the work-bench, a recent and broad patch of blood spreading across the tiled floor.

Father tried to stop her, Tinkerer explained. *She stabbed him in the chest with a screwdriver.*

She and Tinkerer followed the woman on a southward trek through winding streets and alleys. She moved with an automatic precision, turning this way and that without pause as if locked into a pre-set course. Eventually she emerged from a narrow walkway onto the broad wharf of the Valazin dockside. She side-stepped the many carts and barrows with unconscious ease, making for a large three-storey building Lizanne recognised as the port's Custom House. Tinkerer's mother walked up to the uniformed guard on the door and presented the box, Lizanne catching her soft precise tones as she said, "I was told to give you this."

The guard's face broke into a puzzled smile as he bent to accept the box. The expression abruptly turned to consternation when the woman turned on her heel and walked briskly away. The guard had time for a half-shouted command to stop before the box exploded. Lizanne was impressed by the woman's skills, somehow managing to cram so powerful a device into such a small container. When the smoke cleared there was little left of the guard save a red smear surrounding the ruined Custom House door. Tinkerer's mother stood a short distance from the carnage, hands folded over her fulsome belly and an oddly satisfied smile on her lips. When a squad of constables descended on her a few moments later she said, "Free Valazin, death to the Empire" with all the conviction of a child reciting a poorly remembered rhyme.

Why? Lizanne asked as the memory faded into a grey mist. *She hardly seemed the radical type.*

She was told to, Tinkerer answered as the surrounding mist formed into a more familiar scene.

Scorazin, Lizanne thought in sour recognition. This vision possessed the same clarity as the first memory, made all the more disconcerting by being an unwelcome reminder of her time within these walls. They looked out on the prison city through a part-shattered window, more roof-tops than she remembered just visible through the familiar haze of smoke fumes. Tinkerer had managed to perfectly capture the signature scent of sulphur, coal and death she had hoped would never again assail her nostrils.

She turned at the sound of a small plaintive cry behind her, seeing a man cradling an infant beside the bleach-faced body of a woman covered by a filthy blanket. Stepping closer, Lizanne confirmed her suspicion that it was Tinkerer's mother, face even emptier now having been slackened by death.

They sent her here, Tinkerer said, moving to stand by the man with the infant. *As he knew they would. Even a pregnant woman can expect no mercy if the crime is treason.*

Lizanne looked closer at the crouching man, seeing a stocky, bald-headed fellow in his thirties, his face possessed of the sallow hardness that marked those who spend years within the walls. He stared down at the child in his arms with what appeared to Lizanne to be cold animosity, his face betraying not the slightest twitch as the baby raised a tiny hand to his unshaven cheek. *Who is he?* she asked.

You met him once before, Tinkerer said. *But he was dead by then.*

Lizanne recalled the chamber beneath Tinkerer's quarters in the cinnabar mine, the fourteen corpses that had included the long-dead Artisan. *He brought you here,* she realised, her mind stumbling over the implications with unaccustomed confusion. *How?*

The trance, Tinkerer replied. He stepped back as the man got to his feet, moving with the infant to the window.

Lizanne frowned in consternation, this all being so far outside her experience. How could a man compel a non-Blessed soul to such extreme action via the trance? She remembered what Clay shared with her about Silverpin's revelation when they discovered the White's lair, about there being more to the trance than just shared memory. *Blue is a remarkable product, your kind understands only the barest fraction of its power.* Somehow the blade-hand had compelled the rest of the Longrifles to keep searching for the White long after it became obvious the most rational course would be to return to Carvenport. Also, she had been able to bind Clay somehow, forcing him to confront the sleeping White. But they had both been Blood-blessed whereas Tinkerer's mother couldn't have been.

He had the blessing, Lizanne said, nodding to the man who now stood cradling the infant as he stared out at the prison city. *As do you. But your mother didn't. The blessing is not hereditary.*

What is the mind if not a means of controlling the body? Tinkerer said. *To share a mind is to share control, or surrender it to a greater will. He had been searching for me for a long time, or one like me. Sending his mind out far and wide until he snared a Blood-blessed infant still nestling in its mother's womb. The mind of an unborn child is blank, easily claimed, and through it, so is the mother. Later, he saw fit to share the memory of the act that had brought her here, the crime he had forced her to commit. I believe he hoped it would distress me. Instead I found it fascinating.*

The man at the window spoke then, his voice low and croaking, the rasp of a guilty soul. "You poor little fucker," he said as the child squirmed in his arms. "If I was any kind of a man I'd strangle you right now."

The memory shifted again, swirling into another darker space. *His home in the mine,* Lizanne realised, looking around at the rough-hewn rock. Tinkerer was at least ten years old by now, though his slightness of frame may have made him seem younger. He sat on a stool next to a bed, holding a cup of water to the lips of a barely conscious older girl. Though apparently in her mid-teens the girl was so tall her bare, soot-covered feet protruded off the edge of the bed.

"Can't stay," a raspy voice said and Lizanne turned to see the man from the previous memory standing unsteadily in the chamber entrance. His countenance had become even more sallow and sunken in the intervening years and his eyes were dark reddish holes in his face. A half-empty bottle dangled from his hand and Lizanne could smell the acrid stain of whatever concoction it contained on the man's breath. "Can't have her here," the man went on, voice loud and slurred as he waved the bottle about. "Shouldn't've brought her."

The young Tinkerer barely glanced at the man, continuing to hold the cup to the girl's lips and speaking in a flat voice he would carry into adulthood. "I expected you to have expired by morning. Your organs must be close to failing by now."

The man responded with a snarl which sounded somewhat half-hearted to Lizanne, as if he had long exhausted all anger for the boy he had condemned to this place. "Always the fuckin' same," he growled. "Ever since you were old enough to speak. There's no soul in you, boy." He took a long drink from the bottle, his throat working with greedy, desperate gulps that told Lizanne this was a man engaged in a protracted suicide attempt. "We'll sell her to that bitch who took over the Miner's Repose," he added upon draining the bottle. "Once she's healed up, and all."

"No," Tinkerer said, setting the cup aside. "You will be dead soon, and I require assistance."

The girl on the bed groaned and shifted a little, Lizanne noting the marks of a recent and severe beating on her face. Despite the discouration and the swelling, it was still possible to recognise Melina's high cheek-bones and strong nose, although at this point she evidently retained possession of both eyes. Lizanne had liked her, as much as it had been possible to like any inmate of Scorazin. Melina, although brutalised by her years within the walls, had at least possessed a straightforward fairness and lack of duplicity that set her apart. Lizanne found she couldn't suppress a twinge of guilt at the woman's eventual fate, shot in the head during the first chaotic charge into the wreckage of the citadel, itself a spectacular distraction Lizanne had orchestrated to facilitate her own escape.

Your regret is misplaced, the older Tinkerer told her. *She would certainly have killed you had she survived. Forgiveness was not a trait she possessed.*

As interesting as this all is, Lizanne replied, *you have yet to show me what became of the Artisan.*

He became him. Tinkerer nodded at the sallow-faced drunkard, now glowering at the boy in impotent rage. *In time, so did I.*

Another shift in the vision, the setting switching to a much darker place. The young Tinkerer had sprouted several inches in height in the interval. He crouched at the drunkard's side, holding up his ingenious lantern so the focused beam could fully illuminate the man's face. The drunkard had lost much of his body-weight by now, his features gaunt and skin resembling old yellowed paper in the lamplight. It was clear to Lizanne he had only a small amount of life left to him. His eyes were half-closed and his lips moved in a faint murmur. The young Tinkerer leaned closer to catch the sibilant rasp, "You're the last, y'know that?"

"The last of what?" the youth enquired, a rare frown of puzzlement on his brow.

"These . . ." The dying man's hands jerked and Tinkerer turned the lamp to illuminate the bodies, thirteen in all and soon to be joined by one more. "All of these . . . lived wretched lives trapped in this place . . . just to bring you here." He managed to lift a shaking hand and extend a finger, Tinkerer's lamp following it to reveal the oldest corpse, the one chained to the wall. "That one . . . began it all. Fucker!" The man coughed out the insult and began to jerk spasmodically, breath catching. "Started it . . . Called the first one, found her in the womb . . . just like I found you."

Tinkerer turned the lamplight back on the dying man, head angled in curiosity. "Why?"

The man fumbled for something in the pocket of his besmirched clothes, coming out with a small glass vial. "It's time," he rasped, holding the vial out to Tinkerer. "She'll be coming . . . soon. Need to be ready."

Tinkerer took the vial, Lizanne recognising the hue as he played the lamplight over it. *Blue.*

"Ready for what?" Tinkerer enquired, his voice betraying only mild interest, which Lizanne suspected concealed a raging curiosity.

The man grunted out a wheezing laugh, baring half-rotted teeth in what was probably his first smile in decades. "Escape . . . you little shit. What else?" He held out the vial. "Drink."

Lizanne watched Tinkerer take the vial and lift it to his lips then hand it back to the dying man. "If you do happen to find the Artisan's ghost one day," he said, tipping the remaining Blue down his throat, "give them my undying hate."

He leaned forward then, grunting with the effort, staring into Tinker-er's eyes. The trance shifted again, the chamber fading into a black void, absent of light or sensation. Lizanne had experienced shallow minds before, mostly lacking in thought or imagination, but nothing as completely empty as this. She searched for Tinkerer but found nothing. Somehow, he had been removed from a memory in his trance. Then she saw something in the dark, a small bright glimmer in the void. It grew as she went to it and she saw it to be a metal box, spinning in the darkness, a box of gears and cogs that caught the non-existent light as it spun and spun. A box she had seen before. The solargraph-cum-music-box that had once belonged to Te-kela's father. The work of the Artisan's very own hand that had set her and Clay on this path. The mystery they had spent many hours trying to unlock in Jermayah's workshop.

The trance vanished. Lizanne found herself blinking into Tinkerer's blank gaze. For a long moment neither of them said anything.

"Well?" Lizanne demanded as the silence stretched.

"That is all I can give you."

"For your sake, I hope that is a lie."

"I showed you all that I can."

"There has to be more."

"There is. But it is behind a lock I cannot undo. But now you know the key."

The solargraph, she thought. *The solargraph is the key. Everything always comes back to that damned box.* "You know how it works?" she said, jaw clenched as she bit down on her frustration.

"No. But if you want the memories in my head, you will have to find it and make it work."

Lizanne swallowed a hard, bitter laugh. "All those tales you had to tell me," she said. "Of his days in Arradsia, his many discoveries. Of the women he loved and the men he hated. You don't actually know any of it, do you?"

"No more than educated guesses." He angled his head, frowning in marginal confusion. "I would have thought someone in your profession would appreciate creative dishonesty when demanded by necessity. You were always my only means of escape."

She turned away from him, clenching her fists to stop herself reaching for her revolver. "You were expecting me," she realised after taking a series of calming breaths. "That man, he said, 'She'll be coming soon.' He was referring to me, wasn't he?"

"I expect so. I believe it was a vision shared with him by his predecessor. But not one he chose to share with me. Out of spite, I suspect." Tinkerer paused, raising his gaze to the cabin roof as a loud pealing cry sounded throughout the ship. "What is that?" he enquired.

"The ship's siren," Lizanne said, refusing to be distracted. "How could he possibly have known I would be there?"

Tinkerer's eyes narrowed slightly in a gesture she had come to recognise as bemusement at the stupidity of others. "A question I pondered briefly until the answer became obvious, once all other possibilities had been discounted."

Lizanne winced as the ship's siren came again, three long blasts. *He didn't know,* she thought, striving to concentrate. *The Artisan knew, centuries ago* . . . "The future," she said as the answer came to her in a rush. "He saw the future."

"Yes. Though quite how I do not know. I suspect the answer is locked away with the other memories."

But she already knew the answer. *White blood.* Lizanne experienced a small moment of inner triumph stirred by at least knowing one thing he didn't. *The Artisan must have drunk White blood.*

"That sounds urgent," Tinkerer said as the siren sounded again.

"Stay here," she said, rising from the bunk and moving to the door.

"What does it mean?" he enquired.

She paused to glance back at him, wondering if it might be better to get him to a life-boat whilst there was still time. But she knew it to be a desperate notion; they would scarcely be any safer adrift on the high seas than on a Protectorate battleship.

"Enemy in sight," she replied. "If the guns start up, lie down on the deck. If the White's forces seize the ship, I advise you to find the most efficient means of killing yourself." With that she hauled the door closed and started off along the passageway at a run, making for the bridge.

CHAPTER 3

Sirus

Slaves we may be. Monsters we may be. But if we can be merciful, can we not love too?

Katrya's words drifted through his head like the whisper of a morning breeze, kept deliberately faint by the fear he used to cloud the image of her death whenever it arose. But still it was hard not to dwell on the sight of her scaled, despoiled features, so vibrant at the end, glowing with triumph during that last instant before his bullet tore through her head. *We can be merciful . . .*

The words felt like the distant echo of a bad joke as he surveyed the city below, the view being preferable to the spectacle unfolding behind him on the roof-top. He could see neat columns of Spoiled moving through the streets towards their billets in the dock-side warehouses. Smaller parties were engaged in a methodical search of every house, workshop, shed and sewer for any Feros citizens who had survived the assault and so far escaped capture. Many of those doing the searching had been citizens themselves only days before and Sirus wondered how many sons or daughters had been dragged from their hiding-places to find themselves staring into the distorted visages of their parents.

He stood atop the imposing fortress-like tower that had been, until very recently, the headquarters of the entire Ironship Syndicate. The White had chosen to nest on the building's broad flat roof, along with its clutch of adolescent kin. Also present was the Blood-blessed Mandinorian woman who had inexplicably arrived on a passenger liner the day after their seizure of Feros. So far, she was the only one of her kind not to face near-immediate slaughter upon entering the White's company. Instead she had received instant elevation to the pinnacle of this monstrous army, something that Sirus found piqued his pride in no small measure, much to his self-disgust. Morradin had been quick with his taunts, sensing Sirus's resentment with grating ease. *General no longer, eh? Victory, it seems, brings no reward in the Legion of Flame.* For such a self-interested soul the former Grand Marshal had a remarkable facility for divining the feelings of others.

Sirus's mind churned with questions regarding this woman. *Who is she? Why does the White dote on her as if she were one of its own? Why didn't it kill her like the others?* But the biggest mystery of all was the fact that the woman's mind remained her own, unshared and impenetrable. However, this didn't prevent her from invading the minds of other Spoiled.

What are you looking at?

He turned to find her standing at his side, head angled in faint curiosity. The torn and scorched dress that had barely covered her when she first arrived in Feros had since been exchanged for a formal attire of dark blue, the kind usually worn by women of the corporate managerial class. Adorning the otherwise plain jacket were four silver shareholder pins, each one taken from the corpse of an Ironship Board member. *With one more to come,* Sirus thought, resisting the impulse to look over his shoulder as another scream sounded.

"The search is proceeding well," he said aloud in Mandinorian, choosing to maintain his custom of speaking rather than thinking. He was curious to see if she objected to spoken communication. Besides, with this one there was no obvious indication she had absorbed any thought he might share. He sent a subtle probe her way as she followed his gaze, hoping to detect some faint leakage of emotion. But as usual there was nothing. Trying to touch her mind was like jabbing at a wall fashioned from cold unyielding iron. He wondered if his inability to reach her thoughts was somehow related to the fact that she was only partially Spoiled. Instead of the spines and discoloured scales of his fellow slaves, her brief exposure to the Blue crystal's light had left her with a mostly human appearance. A cluster of scales had appeared around her eyes and a series of barely perceptible bumps marred the otherwise smooth perfection of her forehead. The eyes themselves showed the most change and were another unique and mysterious facet of her story. Instead of the yellow eyes with which they had all been afflicted, hers were like two red coals set into black orbs.

"He let me choose," she said, surprising him by speaking aloud. "I always liked the combination of red and black. It used to drive my dress-maker to distraction."

He blinked as her unnatural gaze lingered on him, his surprise height-ened by the fact that she had spoken in Eutherian. "Such a lovely tongue," she went on. "So much more elegant than Mandinorian, don't you find?"

Her tone and flawless accent put him in mind of the casual and mean-ingless chatter of the Corvantine noble class. This was the kind of exchange he used to stammer his way through whenever his father had forced him to attend a social gathering. Somehow he knew that this woman would have felt entirely comfortable in such company.

"In some ways," he replied, also in Eutherian. "Though it remains overly archaic in many instances, and the strictness of its grammar resists adaptation to the modern world."

"Spoken like a true technocrat." She inclined her head, revealing slightly elongated eye-teeth with a smile. "And it's Catheline, by the way," she added, with a shallow curtsy. "Since you were wondering. Catheline Dewsmine of the Sanorah Dewsmines. At your service, sir."

"Sirus Akiv Kapazin, miss," he replied with bow. "Former Curator of Native Artifacts at the Morsvale Imperial Museum of Antiquities."

"Once a curator, now a general." She pursed her lips in apparent admi-ration. "You've risen high for one so young."

"I thought you were the general now."

She surprised him again by laughing. She had a rich laugh he knew other men had assuredly once described as delightful. "Oh, I wouldn't dream of stealing your honours, good sir. Not when you've done such ster-ling work in our wondrous cause. Your stratagems are so much more ele-gant and effective than that Corvantine brute. Where is he, by the way?"

"Mopping-up operations," Sirus said. "Some survivors are lingering amongst the inland hill-country, most of them refugees from Carvenport."

"Carvenport, eh? Will we find our elusive quarry amongst them, do you think?" There was a sardonic twist to her lips that told him she already knew the answer.

"I very much doubt it, miss."

"Catheline, please." She stepped closer, looping an arm through his and steering him away from the edge of the roof. "And I will call you General, since you seem so attached to the term."

"Sirus will suffice . . ."

"Nonsense." She tweaked his nose with a finger. "I think we should accommodate some customs from the old world, don't you?" She turned her focus on the ghastly tableau before them, smile broadening. "Since so much of it is about to vanish forever."

The spread-eagled body of Madame Gloryna Dolspeake, Chairperson of the Ironship Board of Directors, was suspended in mid air by virtue of each of her limbs being clutched firmly in the jaws of an adolescent White. Her silver-grey head lolled as she voiced an exhausted scream that was more of a high-pitched gasp. A surprisingly small amount of blood leaked from the jaws of the Whites, the youthful beasts having been careful not to inflict fatal damage, as yet. It would have been a simple matter to convert the woman and pluck the secrets from her head, but it seemed Catheline had a preference for complication, at least insofar as the Ironship Board were concerned.

"Pardon the interruption, madame," Catheline apologised, switching smoothly to Mandinorian. "Please do go on. You were telling us all about the fascinating Miss Lethridge and her recent mission to the Corvantine Empire. A perilous endeavour to be sure, and all to decipher the workings of an old music-box."

Madame Dolspeake gave no immediate response, continuing to sag in apparent exhaustion until the juvenile Whites tugged in unison, the woman's slight form convulsing and a fresh yelp erupting from her lips. "Yes!" she grated through clenched teeth. "The box . . . the Artisan's box."

A low, inquisitive rumble sounded above and Sirus raised his gaze to see the White lowering its massive head. Prior to this the beast had regarded the interrogation with apparent indifference, but mention of the Artisan seemed to have piqued its interest.

"Quite so," Catheline said. "And what exactly is in this box, pray tell?"

"Answers . . ." Madame Dolspeake whimpered, her body seeming to thrum with pain. "A key to . . ."—her gaze took on a sudden animation, eyes flashing at the huge drake looming above her—"defeating this . . . monstrosity!" She shouted the final word, pain-wracked features moulded into a mask of defiant hate. Sirus couldn't suppress a pang of admiration at this, something which drew a sharp glance from Catheline.

"You find something noble in this wretch, General?" she enquired, her arm tensing against his. Although she was not fully Spoiled, he could feel the strength in her, and added to that was the worrisome awareness that she was also a Blood-blessed.

"Allow me to assure you this woman is not worthy of your regard," Catheline went on, fixing her gaze on the unfortunate Ironship luminary. Sirus could see the naked hatred shining in Catheline's red-black eyes, her lips taking on a wet sheen as she continued, "This woman and her kind have enslaved those like me for generations. But for my family's influence they would have had me labour in their service like some slum-born slattern. Once my family would have been great and powerful, standing high in the court of the Mandinorian Empire. Now, for all their wealth they are beggars, grubbing for crumbs from the corporate table like every other slave in this world of greed, a world they created. It is they who are the true monsters. They who have raped an entire continent in their avarice and would have raped the whole world."

She unhooked her arm from Sirus's and moved to crouch at Madame Dolspeake's side, leaning close to murmur in her ear. "Tell me, madame. What were you going to do when all the product ran out? When you had wrung the last drop of blood from the last withered drake? What were you going to do then?"

Madame Dolspeake met Catheline's gaze, matching the enmity she saw in full measure. "I . . . remember you," she said in a thin whisper. "A spoilt little bitch . . . born to a family of wastrels. You'd spread your legs . . . for the merest chance at a gossip-column headline." Somehow the woman managed to laugh, though it emerged from her throat as more of a choking sob. "At least . . . now your looks match your character."

Catheline's lips drew back in a snarl, nails extending into claws as she clamped a hand to Madame Dolspeake's throat. A short grunt came from the White and Catheline froze, the snarl fading as she jerked her hand away as if it had been burned. Watching her retreat a few steps and take a calming breath, Sirus was compelled to wonder at the viciousness of a woman who had to be restrained by one such as the White. After a moment Catheline straightened, smoothing her hands over her skirt before staring down at the older woman with cold determination. "The Artisan's box," she said. "Where is it?"

For a moment Madame Dolspeake said nothing, but soon began speaking in a rapid babble as the juvenile Whites tightened their grip. "Reported lost at Carvenport, though Bloskin was certain Lethridge had placed it in her father's hands. He chose to leave it there in the hope the man could unlock it, then seize it when he had."

"Ah yes, Taddeus Bloskin," Catheline said. "The esteemed Director of Exceptional Initiatives who had the good sense to blow his brains out when the city fell." She paused for a moment, frowning in recollection. "Lethridge's father. Presumably that would be the famous Professor Graysen Lethridge, genius inventor and denizen of this very port." She turned a questioning glance in Sirus's direction.

"He's not amongst the captives or the new recruits," he reported promptly, hoping a steady current of fear would mask the memories provoked by the name Lethridge. Tekela slaughtering the Greens with that infernal repeating gun, the balloon taking her away. As ever, the daughter of the late Burgrave Artonin retained an effortless capacity to haunt his thoughts. His disastrous wooing in Morsvale. The sight of her adorned with the ancient sapphire necklace, twirling in delight in the museum vaults, probably the only time he had managed to make her laugh. Then the moment only three nights ago when he stood naked in her sights. *Out of bullets,* she had said with a shrug. "I'll have his home searched," Sirus added, flooding his mind with all the horrors he could muster before turning his attention to the collective memory of the Spoiled.

He was careful to scour the collective minds of the recent captives for the address before issuing a thought-command to a troop of Spoiled. It wouldn't do for Catheline to question why he already knew of the location. The search-party shared their findings as they tore through the domicile of Professor Lethridge, finding no sign of the man or the elusive musical box. Also, no sign of Katrya's body, which Sirus had buried in the port's largest park. He put her close to the flower-beds, thinking she might have liked that.

"Gather every scrap of paper and machinery," Catheline ordered. "Examine them yourself, General. I think this is a task for our keenest mind." She paused as one of the searchers cast their gaze at the workshop's ceiling, finding it mostly absent. "No fire damage," she observed. "Why would the professor remove his own ceiling, I wonder?"

Sirus was aware of her close scrutiny as he sorted through the mélange of images captured by the collective mind of the army the night of Feros's fall. He had hoped the escape of Tekela and her companions might have been missed altogether. Unfortunately, it transpired that several sets of eyes had glimpsed the balloon craft as it soared over the roof-tops towards the northern shore of the island. All of those who had seen it had died in the fighting, but not before their memories had been shared with others. The vision was dull and misty, as was often the case with memories formed during combat, but clear enough to make out the dimensions of the novel conveyance and its three occupants.

"A dirigible aerostat," Sirus said, speaking aloud once more. "I've read of experiments with such craft in northern Mandinor, but all were said to be at a very early stage."

"Then the professor must be a man of even greater talent than his reputation allows," Catheline replied. She looked up at the White who gave a throaty rumble before turning its massive head in the direction of a neighbouring building. A dozen Reds immediately rose from their perch atop the building's roof, Sirus recognising Katarias amongst them. The huge Red took the lead as they adopted a northern course, wings sweeping in rapid arcs.

"Ingenious as it is," Catheline said, "it didn't strike me as the fastest of vehicles. We'll have them soon enough. Now then," she added briskly, clasping her hands together and returning her attention to Madame Dolspeake, "let us discuss the strength of the Protectorate Northern Fleet."

Katarias returned two days later, appearing on the northern horizon as the sun began to fade. The Red's wings moved in sluggish half sweeps that barely caught the cooling evening air. He glided over the harbour wall to land on the quayside, head slumped and eyes dimmed with exhaustion. Catheline ordered he be fed immediately and a trio of captives were duly dragged forward to be feasted upon. They were all in their early teens, too young to be worth converting but kept alive for the amusement or nourishment of the drakes. Madame Dolspeake had at least been spared such a fate, though Sirus doubted she saw much mercy in Catheline's decision to cast her broken but still-living body from the headquarters roof-top.

"I would have you join us, dried-up old hag though you are," Catheline told the Chairperson, lifting the woman's spindly form above her head with effortless strength. "Your experience and insight might have been useful. But I find that I simply can't stomach the thought of your mind touching mine. Any wisdom or defiance to share at the final moment?"

Madame Dolspeake raised her head, a stream of blood falling from her mouth as she tried to speak. The words were too soft to hear and Sirus doubted the woman was still capable of forming a rational thought in any case.

"Oh, never mind," Catheline said, casting the Chairperson away. She stood watching her plummet to the ground, arms crossed and expression reflective rather than triumphant. "I doubt it would have been one for the historians anyway."

"The other Reds died," she explained to Sirus now, seemingly deaf to the screams and breaking bones behind her. "Flew until they couldn't fly any longer then fell into the sea." There was a curiously mournful tone to her voice, as if she were speaking of cherished comrades lost in a noble cause. "Thankfully, he alone managed to stay aloft and caught sight of this."

She pushed a memory into Sirus's head, a small bulbous speck on a far horizon. "It appears the winds carried them west. He followed for over an hour but was forced to turn back lest he share his brothers' fate. It was long enough to discern that the professor's marvellous contraption is losing height."

"Then the sea will claim them," Sirus said, concealing a wince as Katarias tore the last of the captives in two with a loud snap of his jaws. "The problem would appear to be solved."

"We have to be sure," she replied, shaking her head. "The box must be destroyed. Along with any who might unlock it. All other considerations are secondary."

She turned to survey the ships within the harbour walls. Their appearance was decidedly unimpressive, each one blackened by fire or scarred by explosions. Of the Protectorate warships at anchor in Feros at the time of its seizure, only six could be said to be fully operational. The rest were undergoing extensive repairs and those beyond saving were being cannibalised for weapons and parts. Sirus estimated the full strength of the White's fleet would be some twenty-five vessels once the work was complete. Added to that were another two dozen merchant vessels and Blue-hunters, which would be used as troop-transports, once their next destination had been made clear.

"I so wish to sail north, General," Catheline said with a wistful air. "How I long to see Mandinor burn. But sadly we have more pressing matters. It's time for you to add the title of 'admiral' to your collection."

CHAPTER 4

Hilemore

"Who is she?"

"Told you who she is, Captain." Clay gave Hilemore one of his signature, punch-inviting grins. Hilemore wasn't sure whether to take some comfort from the fact that this young man had retained an effortless ability to annoy him despite his recent travails.

"Her name doesn't tell me a great deal," he replied, striving to control his burgeoning ire. "And, given our circumstances, I find my patience in short supply. So I will ask you again." He put both fists on the desk and leaned closer to Clay, meeting his gaze with unmistakable intent. "Who is she?"

They were in the captain's cabin aboard the *Dreadfire*, Clay nursing a cup of something hot Lieutenant Steelfine had managed to concoct in the galley. Lieutenant Sigoral was being tended to by the youngest Torcreek, though Loriabeth herself seemed close to collapse from exposure. Despite that she continued to nurse the Corvantine Marine and proved deaf to her father's stern and repeated order to rest.

Then there was the woman. The woman named Kriz, who had not been a member of their party when they entered the Spire, and yet had now somehow been retrieved from the depths. She had nodded a greeting when Clay introduced her but seemed reluctant to utter more than a few words, her Mandinorian spoken in an uncannily perfect Carvenport accent. She sounded like someone raised in the Blinds, the notorious slum where Clay had spent his childhood years, but Hilemore knew instinctively that couldn't be the case.

He felt an overriding sense of strangeness when he looked at her. Judging by her colouring he would have taken her for a South Mandinorian, but there was an angularity to her features that made him doubt it. Added to that was her manner, the way she stared at every fixture on the ship, eyes wary but also hungry for detail. Then there was the hour or more she had spent on deck staring at the sky and the surrounding ice-floes, her face occasionally breaking into a smile of unalloyed joy. The smile disappeared, however, the instant Hilemore attempted to talk to her, at which point she pulled her blanket tight about her shoulders and disappeared belowdecks. Hilemore couldn't help the feeling that, although he had witnessed something unbelievable in Clay's taming of Last Look Jack, this woman represented something far more incredible.

"Her full name is Krizelle," Clay said, hesitating before gulping down some of Steelfine's beverage and continuing in a tone of forced matter-of-factness. "Last survivor of the Philos Caste. She's about ten thousand years old and was the first Blood-blessed born on this planet." He sipped from the mug again, smacking his lips in appreciation. "This is really good, whatever it is." The humour faded from his face as he glanced up at Hilemore's silent, glowering visage.

"Alright," Clay said with a sigh, setting the mug down on the desk. "But you better take a seat, Captain. This is a long story."

"It's true," Loriabeth said. "Every word of it." She jerked her head at Sigoral's slumbering form on the bunk behind her. "You can ask him when he wakes."

She had curtained off a section of the hold to use as a sick bay and hadn't strayed from the lieutenant's side since. Sigoral had been dosed with a small amount of their remaining stock of Green, Loriabeth also applying a diluted tincture of the product to his wound with a compress. Judging by the state of the damage, Hilemore entertained serious doubts the Marine would ever recover his sight in that eye. The pain had clearly left a deep mark for the man fidgeted in his sleep, hands jerking repeatedly as if he were clutching his carbine.

"An entire enclosed world down below." Hilemore shook his head in a mixture of awe and incredulity. "It's a hard tale to swallow, miss. And not one the Board will easily believe."

"They can believe what they like." She gave a pointed glance at where Kriz sat conversing with Clay at the galley table. "Besides, it ain't like we got no proof."

Hilemore nodded his thanks and moved away, pausing to regard the ancient woman who appeared only a few years his junior. She and Clay spoke in a language Hilemore didn't know, an oddly inflected tongue of elongated vowels and soft consonants. *The language of the past,* he assumed. *Learned by Torcreek in the trance along with many secrets he no doubt chose to keep back.* Lengthy as the young Blood-blessed's story had been, Hilemore's experienced eye picked out several instances of slight hesitation accompanied by the fractional aversion of the eyes that told of a lie or deliberate omission. *It won't do,* he decided, starting forward with a purposeful stride. *I must know all of it to decide our course.*

His purpose, however, was soon interrupted as the *Dreadfire's* deck suddenly heaved beneath his feet, coming close to pitching him flat on his face. Hilemore grabbed a beam to steady himself, holding on as the deck lurched again. Cutlery and plates cascaded from the galley table as the ship seemed to revolve, swaying as if borne up by a heavy sea. *But the weather's calm,* Hilemore thought, peering through the nearest port-hole.

"Blues again, Skipper?" Scrimshine asked, eyes wide and bright in his cadaverous face.

"Not with Jack so close by," Clay said, making an unsteady progress to Hilemore's side with Kriz following close behind. "Reckon we got some fresh trouble, Captain."

The ship settled and Hilemore rushed for the steps to the upper deck, emerging to see Steelfine and a pair of crewmen leaning over the rail to stare at the water below. Moving to the Islander's side, Hilemore followed his gaze to see that the sea was churning, large bubbles rising to the surface and bursting all around.

"Seer's balls, what a stink!" one of the crew exclaimed, wafting the air from his nose at the miasma rising from the roiling sea. It was a potent stench to be sure, sulphurous and thick enough to clog the nostrils with an acrid sting.

"The fault in the sea-floor," Hilemore realised as more bubbles rose, once again causing the *Dreadfire* to sway. "It must still be coughing out a great deal of lava. An annoyance but hardly an obstacle. Mr. Scrimshine!" he called to the former smuggler. "Take over the helm if you please, keep her heading north."

"Aye, Skipper!" Scrimshine gave one of his less-than-regulation salutes and ran to the tiller, pushing the previous helmsman aside with an urgent shove.

"Stop!"

Hilemore turned as a hand tugged at his sleeve, finding himself confronted by Kriz. "We need to stop," she said in her clipped, street-level Mandinorian.

"You may have noticed, miss, but time is against us." Hilemore politely disentangled himself. "Our food stocks being what they are . . ."

"Gas!" she interrupted, pointing towards the ship's prow. Hilemore followed her finger, frowning at the haze ahead. It was thin but definitely there, a soft grey vapour drifting amongst the bergs.

Kriz said something in her own language, raising her finger to point at the distant fiery bulk of Mount Reygnar. When Hilemore blinked at her in incomprehension she gave what he assumed was a highly simplified translation. "Poison gas. The fault extends all the way to that volcano. If we sail towards it everyone on board will be dead within the hour."

Hilemore went to the prow, training his spy-glass on Reygnar's slopes. The eruption that had begun days ago continued unabated, huge chunks of molten rock spouted from the mountain's gaping summit in a plentiful torrent. The lava-stream made a sluggish but irresistible progress to the sea where great billows of steam occluded what he assumed to be a rapidly growing new island. Although his education in geology had been confined to a few classes at the Protectorate Maritime Academy, he knew another side-effect of so much of the earth's innards being released into the sea would be the production of various gases, none of which were conducive to longevity.

"Trim sails!" Hilemore ordered, sending the sailors scurrying. "Mr. Steelfine, see if you can get the anchor lowered. Boiling some oil to melt the ice on the chains might do it."

"I'll see to it, sir."

"We can't wait this out," Kriz said, moving closer to Hilemore and speaking in a low voice. "The eruption could go on for days. As you said, we don't have the food."

"There is but one navigable channel through this ice," Hilemore said, pointing to the winding course ahead. He felt a resurgence of his earlier anger, the sensation of having no good options was never a comfortable one for a captain. *We sail on we die, we stay we die,* he thought biting down on a sigh of frustration.

"There is a way," Kriz said. "But I'll need a particular substance in as much quantity as you can provide."

"What substance?"

Kriz gave a doubtful frown, as if unsure the word she was about to speak was the right one. "Piss," she said with a bland smile. "I need a great deal of piss."

Scrimshine proved the most productive of the crewmen, filling two large pickle-jars to Hilemore's one. "Reckon I can squeeze out a few drops more, Skipper," he offered, britches still undone as he hovered splay-footed over a steaming jar. Hilemore wasn't sure what smelled worse, the gas or the product of Scrimshine's bladder.

"I think that'll do for now," he said, averting his eyes as the helmsman buttoned himself up. There were some sights even a seasoned sailor couldn't abide.

In addition to the urine, Kriz had Steelfine roast as much coal as could be crammed into the galley stove. The scorched bricks were then pounded into a fine powder. "Two layers will provide better protection," she explained laying out a strip of their thinnest fabric on the table. In addition to the *Dreadfire's* meagre sails her hold had yielded a number of flags, all dating back to the pre-Corporate age. Hilemore assumed they were souvenirs of the long-dead Captain Bledthorne's brief pirating career. He had thought they might be worth something to an antiquities dealer should they ever return to civilisation, but was happy to surrender any potential profit in the circumstances.

Under Kriz's instruction the flags had all been sliced into strips six inches wide and twelve long. "Carbon absorbs most gases," she said, spooning about a quarter-pound of the powdered coal onto the fabric. "But not all. Hopefully," she continued, laying another strip on top of the layer of coal dust, this one having been dipped into one of the steaming buckets, "urine will filter out the rest. Stitch them together and you have a basic respirator."

"Hopefully?" Hilemore asked, receiving a helpless shrug in response. He resisted the urge to ask more questions. There were no other choices and this had to be risked. "Let's be about it, lads," he said instead, sending the crew into motion. "Two masks each. Just like she showed you. Stitch them tight and be quick."

He drew Kriz aside as the crew got to work, speaking softly. "How long will they last?"

"It depends on the thickness of the gas. If we run into a dense concentration they'll become saturated fairly quickly."

"At our current speed it will take at least a day to reach the mountain and another to get clear of it."

"Then we need to sail faster."

"We've barely enough sheets to keep her moving as it is."

"Pardon me, Captain," Clay said, appearing at Kriz's side. "But we don't need the wind to get this old tub moving. Just a lotta strong rope."

They used the *Dreadfire*'s only boat to string the rope out in front of the prow. Hilemore, Steelfine, Clay and the elder Torcreek took on the task, the crew displaying a marked reluctance to place themselves in proximity to the monster whose spines were frequently glimpsed cutting through the surrounding waters. Hilemore knew the sailors were unlikely to disobey a direct order but thought it best not to fray their already threadlike nerves further. Steelfine, of course, appeared to have no nerves whilst Braddon assumed a mantle of steady surety, though Hilemore caught the wariness in his gaze whenever it alighted on Jack's spines. By contrast Clay exuded only a cheerful calm as they rowed away from the ship's hull, playing the rope out behind. It was really three ropes in one, the thickest hawsers they could find braided into a single cable thicker than a man's arm. It had been fashioned into a loop some thirty yards long, both ends fixed to the anchor mountings on either side of the rotted figure-head on the *Dreadfire*'s prow.

"Reckon this is far enough," Clay said and the boat slowed to a gentle drift as Steelfine shipped oars.

"What now?" Hilemore enquired as Clay focused his gaze on Jack. The Blue loitered only a stone's throw away, one great eye poking above the surface to regard them either with curiosity or hunger. Hilemore couldn't tell.

Clay's response was soft and cryptic, his expression now one of studied concentration as he stared at Jack. "Now I get to see if I could've made Miss Ethelynne proud," he murmured.

For a full minute nothing happened, Hilemore and the others looking at Clay in frigid expectation. The Blood-blessed's brows creased and uncreased several times, his lips twitching all the while, and Hilemore knew he was witnessing direct communication between a human and a drake. Finally, the great eye blinked and disappeared below the surface, the beast's tall spines frothing the water as it twisted its body and dived.

"Let it go, Uncle," Clay told Braddon and they released the rope in unison. It subsided below the surface with a soft splash that soon transformed into a white explosion as Jack's head erupted from the water barely a second later, huge jaws clamping down on the cable. The resultant swell sent their boat into a spin, Hilemore coming close to tipping over the side before Steelfine used his oars to steady the craft.

Hilemore's gaze was drawn by the sound of Clay's laughter. He stood at the boat's stern, head shaking and grin wide as he regarded the sight of Jack waiting patiently with the rope lodged firmly in his mouth. "He gets it," Clay said and laughed again. "He really gets it."

"Six knots, do you think, Mr. Steelfine?"

"Closer to seven, sir." The Islander's voice was muffled by his mask and he was obliged to shout to make himself understood. "Think he might get up to eight when the channel straightens."

Hilemore cast his gaze over the *Dreadfire*'s much broader and deeper wake then back at Last Look Jack, or Old Jack as Clay insisted on calling him now. The Blue seemed tireless as it towed the ship northwards, his huge body coiling in a steady unchanging rhythm. Thanks to Jack they had covered more miles in an hour than in the previous two days. Whatever dire results the gas may have inflicted on an unprotected human didn't seem to affect the beast at all.

"It's a creature that breathes fire," Clay explained when Hilemore raised the issue. "Probably got all manner of poison swirling about his lungs already."

Pleasing as this was, any elation Hilemore might have felt was quelled by the thickening stench which was detectable even through the nostril-stinging barrier of his makeshift mask. So far the masks had worked, none of the crew having succumbed to the miasma, though a couple had displayed signs of confusion and unsteadiness. As an added precaution Hilemore ordered the bulk of the crew belowdecks and all hatches and port-holes sealed. He knew it was scant protection; although the *Dreadfire* was a remarkably sturdy old bird she had more holes in her than a Corvantine deserter after a court martial. But a crew needed to be kept busy, especially in times of crisis.

More worrying than the gas was the looming sight of Mount Reygnar. They were little over two miles away from the volcano now and what had been a fiery spectacle was fast becoming an ominous danger. The ice surrounding the mountain had disappeared entirely, creating what was in effect a large warm-water lagoon of churning currents which even Old Jack might have trouble navigating. Added to that was the unpredictable violence of the eruptions, Reygnar vomiting forth chunks of molten rock at irregular intervals. They would ascend to a great height before plunging down into the surrounding lagoon, trailing smoke like fire-balls cast by some ancient and massive catapult.

Initially the currents proved more of a danger, Jack swimming headlong into a swirling eddy that sent the *Dreadfire* heaving to starboard and threatened to rip the cable from the prow. "Look lively at the helm!" Hilemore barked at Scrimshine, who was busily spinning the tiller in an effort to counter the current and maintain the correct angle to the tethered drake.

"The beast needs to slow down, Skipper!" Scrimshine returned, grunting with the strain of hauling the wheel to midships.

"Mr. Torcreek," Hilemore said, moving to where Clay stood at the very apex of the prow. "A tad slower, if you please."

Clay gave a distracted nod, keeping his gaze fixed on the Blue. A moment later the ship began to slow to about two-thirds her previous speed. Hilemore extended his spy-glass and trained it on the waters ahead, finding just a wall of drifting smoke and steam, no doubt rich in a plethora of lethal gases. "Five points to port, Mr. Torcreek," he ordered, drawing a bemused glance from the Blood-blessed.

"That way," Hilemore bellowed through his mask, pointing to the left.

"I'll tell you when to straighten her out. We need to keep close to the edge of this expanse."

Clay nodded again and Jack soon altered course, hauling clear of the fast-approaching fog. Hilemore turned his gaze to the mountain, now a dark mass in the roiling smoke, glowing lava threading the slopes' flanks like veins of fire. Even more unnerving than the sight of it was the volcano's voice, a constant thunderous roar accompanied by the occasional boom as lightning flashed in the billowing black clouds that crowned the summit.

"Sir!" Steelfine gave an urgent cry from the starboard rail, pointing at the mostly black sky. Hilemore saw it immediately, a flaming ball of lava reaching the apex of its flight. He had a fraction of a second to judge its course, but a life aboard warships had left him with an instinct for gauging the trajectory of dangerous projectiles.

"Hard to starboard!" he said, clamping a hand on Clay's shoulder and pointing to the right. "Fast as he can!" Hilemore whirled away and sprinted towards Scrimshine, joining him at the wheel to help spin it to starboard so the drake's abrupt change in course wouldn't rip away the tether.

The fire-ball came streaking down barely a second later, throwing up a great geyser of steam and displaced water as it impacted within pistol range of the *Dreadfire*'s port side. The old ship hadn't been built for such violent manoeuvres and Hilemore felt the aged timbers beneath his boots thrum in a groan of collective protest. *Keep together, old girl,* Hilemore implored her, running a hand along the oaken wheel. *Not much longer now. Then you can rest.*

As if in response the ship settled, Hilemore tracking Jack's course as Clay steered a more gentle track back towards the fringes of the lagoon. It was then that Hilemore realised he was alone at the tiller. He began to voice a rebuke at Scrimshine then saw the former smuggler lying prone on the deck, eyes red and bulging above his mask as he convulsed.

"Mr. Steelfine, take the helm!" Hilemore called out, rushing to Scrimshine's side. The man's gloved hands scrabbled at Hilemore's arms, white froth appearing at the edges of his mask as his choking and convulsions intensified. Hilemore hooked his arms around Scrimshine's chest and dragged him to the hatch leading to the hold, stamping on the planking until Skaggerhill heaved it open. Together he and the harvester dragged Scrimshine to the galley table, laying him out. His spasms were weakening now, though his eyes were still bright and full of pleading as they stared up at Hilemore. *Don't let me die, Skipper.*

"The filters must be saturated," Kriz said, coming forward with a fresh mask. She took hold of Scrimshine's face and turned his gaze to hers, speaking in firm tones: "Hold your breath, keep still." She waited for him to master himself, then swiftly undid the ties on his mask, tossing it aside to fix the replacement over his mouth and nose. "Don't breathe too deep," she cautioned as Scrimshine heaved, doubling over on his side, eyes shut tight in pain as he issued forth a rich stream of muffled Dalcian profanity.

"Pretty thick out there now, huh?" Skaggerhill asked, casting a worried glance at the open hatch.

"Not much longer," Hilemore said, speaking with what he hoped was sufficient volume and clarity to reassure the onlooking crew. "Need another hand at the tiller, if you're willing," he added, climbing the ladder to the upper deck.

They were obliged to dodge two more fire-balls over the course of the next hour, the second one streaking down close enough to leave a good portion of the upper works ablaze. Hilemore had begun shouting orders to muster a fire-fighting party from below when Old Jack paused in his towing to thrash his tail. The resultant curtain of water was sufficient to both drown the flames and subject all on deck to a thorough soaking.

"The damage could have been worse, sir," Steelfine reported after ascending the rigging to inspect the masts. "But we'd be lucky to rig more than a few yards of sail after this." The Islander glanced at the prow where Clay maintained his unerring vigil over Old Jack. "We'd best hope his pet monster doesn't get tired."

Another crewman came close to succumbing to the gas as the journey wore on, Braddon managing to get a fresh mask on the man before he suffered lasting damage. After that Hilemore ordered everyone to replace their masks. He could tell from the increasingly fetid air leaking through his own mask that it was close to saturation. Finally, as the day slipped into evening the miasma began to thin. Mount Reygnar became a dim, thunderous bulk at their rear as Jack dragged the *Dreadfire* clear of its deadly atmosphere. It wasn't until the last vestiges of smoke had cleared and they were once again amongst the bergs that Hilemore saw fit to remove his mask, taking a short experimental breath that he thought might be the sweetest air he had ever tasted.

"Take them off, lads," he told the crew, heralding an outpouring of relief.

"Thank the Seer for that," Skaggerhill said, drawing in several deep luxurious breaths as he tossed his mask over the side. "One more whiff of piss and I think I might've preferred the poison. No offence, miss," he added, nodding in Kriz's direction as she emerged on deck.

She replied with a placid nod before turning to Hilemore, speaking with a hesitancy that reminded him she was very much a stranger to this company. "Your man," she began. "The helmsman."

"Scrimshine," Hilemore said. "What about him?"

She gave an apologetic sigh. "He's dying."

"This is all of it, sir," Steelfine said, placing the last flask on the table. "Every drop of Green on board. Some of the lads had private stocks secreted about their person."

"Had to shake it loose of them, I suppose," Hilemore said.

"Actually no." Steelfine inclined his head at where Scrimshine lay on his bunk, normally sallow features now rendered pale as candle wax as he convulsed with another bout of coughing. "Scoundrel he may be, but the lads know we'd all have perished long since but for his hands on the tiller."

"Will it be enough?" Hilemore asked Kriz.

"I have no idea," she replied. "I suspect my people knew less about the medicinal properties of drake blood than yours."

"He'd need at least three full vials by my reckoning," Skaggerhill put in. As harvester and ad hoc healer to the Longrifles he was the closest thing to a medic on board. "We've got"—he played a stubby-fingered hand over the assembled product—"maybe two, at most."

"And no knowledge of what lies ahead," Braddon added, meeting Hilemore's gaze. "It's a long way back to civilisation, Captain, and odds are there'll be plenty of dangers betwixt here and there."

Hilemore concealed a wince as Scrimshine coughed again, a deep, wet retch full of pain. *The man's a rogue,* he reminded himself. *Smuggler and pirate both, no doubt with a good deal of blood to account for, not to mention cannibalism.* The decision was obvious and swiftly reached.

"Give it to him," he told Skaggerhill. "All of it. Mr. Torcreek, Miss"—he went on nodding at Clay then Kriz—"please join me in my cabin. I believe it's time we had a serious and honest discussion."

CHAPTER 5

Lizanne

"Crow's nest reports twenty vessels so far, sir," an ensign related from the speaking-tube. "Bearing south-south-west. Man-o'-war in the centre, all the rest appear to be freighters. Pennants are raised but the distance is too great to make out any signals."

"Speed?" Captain Verricks asked, standing with his hands clasped behind his back with barely a twitch disturbing his whiskers.

"Estimated at eight knots, sir," the ensign related a few seconds later.

"A somewhat sedate pace for an attacking fleet," Verricks mused, turning to Lizanne with a questioning glance. She had entered the bridge without permission but the fact that she hadn't been ordered to leave said much, for the captain valued her advice.

"The White will have captured a large number of ships at Feros," she pointed out. "It could be a ruse. Approach at a slow speed to lure us close then spring the trap." She nodded at a spy-glass on the map table. "May I?"

"Be my guest, miss."

She moved to the front of the bridge, taking a vial of Green from her wallet and drinking a small amount. When first viewed through the lens of the spy-glass the approaching vessels were little more than grey smudges cresting the horizon, but soon sprang into sharp clarity as the vision-enhancing effects of the Green took hold. The first one to come into focus was a Blue-hunter, clearly heavily laden judging by how low she sat in the water, her paddles labouring as smoke belched from her single stack. Lizanne tracked the glass along the line of ships, stopping when a familiar sight came into view. She had only ever seen this ship through Clay's eyes but the lines were unmistakable, as was the Ironship Protectorate flag and friendly greeting signal flying from her mast.

"The IPV *Viable Opportunity*," she told Verricks. "This is not an enemy fleet, Captain. Though I would caution you that you may be about to experience a very trying interview."

"Trumane."

"Verricks."

The two captains exchanged nods. They were alone in the ward-room apart from Lizanne; Director Thriftmor, who was engaged in a thorough hunt of the room's cupboards, presumably for more brandy; and a woman of Dalcian appearance who had accompanied Captain Trumane. The captain looked much the same as she recalled from Clay's shared memories, his uniform an impeccable buttoned-up contrast to Verricks's open jacket and misaligned necktie. But there was a new pale hardness to Trumane's face. Always a stern character, albeit with occasional displays of conviviality during moments of personal triumph, he appeared to Lizanne to have lost whatever vestiges of affability or humour he had once possessed. She doubted his crew had enjoyed their time under his command since Lieutenant Hilemore's desertion in Lossermark harbour.

Lizanne would have described the Dalcian woman as elegant but for the tattered seaman's jacket she wore and the numerous wayward strands of hair escaping from her otherwise severe bun. "May I present Madame Hakugen," Trumane said, extending a hand to the woman. "A senior executive of the Eastern Conglomerate and former Comptroller of Lossermark Port."

"Welcome aboard, madame," Verricks greeted the woman with a formal bow which was returned in kind.

"And I am very pleased to meet you, Captain," she said with a note of relieved sincerity.

"Your reputation precedes you, Captain Verricks," Trumane went on. "So I won't waste time with petty demands for the date of your commission."

Verricks gave a slight incline of his head. "Appreciated, Captain. It therefore behooves me, as senior officer, to request your report."

Trumane hesitated, his eyes flicking to Lizanne and Director Thriftmor.

"Your pardon," Verricks said. "May I present Mr. Benric Thriftmor, Ironship Syndicate Board member and Director of Extra-Corporate Affairs."

"Delighted, I'm sure," Thriftmor replied, straightening from an empty cupboard with a distressed cast to his eyes. "Captain Verricks, I wonder where I might . . ."

"I had it tipped over the side, sir," Verricks told him. "All other liquor on board is now under lock and key, and will remain so for the duration of our current difficulties."

Thriftmor stared at the captain, tongue tracing over his lips in an unconscious display of desperate thirst. "Oh," he said. "Well, as important as this meeting is, I find myself suddenly quite unwell and will adjourn to my cabin . . ."

"I had it searched and all the bottles disposed of," Verricks told him, then pointed to a chair. "Sit down, Mr. Thriftmor. The steward will bring you some coffee presently."

A range of emotions passed over the Director's face, from defiance to anger before subsiding into resentful acceptance as he sank into a chair, gaze lowered.

Trumane afforded Thriftmor a brief and plainly disgusted glance before nodding at Lizanne. "And this lady?"

"Miss Lizanne Lethridge," Verricks introduced her. "Of Exceptional Initiatives."

Trumane stiffened a little at that, as did Madame Hakugen, though they both greeted Lizanne with a polite nod. "By any chance," Trumane said, "would you be related to . . ."

"Professor Graysen Lethridge." Lizanne didn't bother to keep the weary irritation from her voice. Mention of her familial connections just now was certain to worsen her mood. "He's my father."

"And my valued colleague," Trumane said. "His insights were of great assistance when designing the refit of the *Viable Opportunity*."

"Then I hope you paid him. It would make a pleasant change from the norm. I believe you have a report to make."

"My report is somewhat lengthy," Trumane said after a moment of bemused irritation. "As yet I haven't had time to compile a written version."

"A verbal report will do very well, I'm sure," Verricks said, moving to the table and pulling out a chair for Madame Hakugen. "Let us all please sit. Refreshment is on the way."

Trumane related his tale over coffee and sandwiches, Lizanne noting the enthusiasm with which the former Comptroller consumed the food while the captain maintained an air of restraint. She already knew much of what he had to say, particularly regarding the desertion of Lieutenant Hilemore along with half the crew of the *Viable Opportunity*. "A vile and outrageous breach of contract," Trumane said, some colour returning to his face. "I intend to petition the Sea Board for the ultimate penalty at the court martial, in the unlikely event the swine ever returns from his mad venture."

"There will be no court martial, Captain," Lizanne said, instantly drawing a fierce glower from the captain.

"I beg your pardon?" Trumane asked.

"Lieutenant Hilemore will face no charges," she said simply. "In seizing the Corvantine ship and sailing for southern waters he acted on the instructions of an Exceptional Initiatives agent, as you should have done."

"What Exceptional Initiatives agent?"

"Claydon Torcreek and the Longrifles Independent Company are contracted employees of my division."

"Contracted for an insane expedition to the Interior from which they returned with a pack of fairy stories."

"Their expedition bore fruit, bitter though it turned out to be. The answer to our current difficulties may well lie amidst the southern ice. It was your duty to find it, a duty Lieutenant Hilemore undertook instead. Therefore, as I say, he will face no charges."

The reddish tinge to Trumane's face deepened as he continued to glower. "I will not stand for this," he grated. "When the Sea Board reads my full report . . ."

"If Torcreek and Hilemore fail," Lizanne cut in, matching his glower with an intent stare, "within a few months there may well be no Sea Board to read it."

Trumane began to speak again but stopped at a cough from Captain Verricks. "A matter for another time, I think, Captain," he said. "I have little doubt that once this . . . confused state of affairs has been rectified there will be a full enquiry. Any charges you wish to bring against your subordinate will receive due consideration then. As for now, I should like to hear how you came to be in command of such an unusual fleet."

Trumane took a moment to master his anger before turning away from

Lizanne, addressing himself solely to Verricks. "The *Viable* was the only warship in Lossermark. With no cargo arriving and the Interior closed to foraging parties Madame Hakugen and I agreed that an evacuation had to be attempted."

"So your fleet carries the entire population of Lossermark?" Verricks asked.

Trumane remained impassive but Madame Hakugen's coffee-cup paused on its way to her lips, Lizanne noting how her hand trembled as she set it down. "Lossermark is a large port," she said, staring straight ahead. "There wasn't room for everyone. Mothers with children were automatically allotted a place, as were the Conglomerate Levies. All others had to be chosen by lot, myself included. The situation . . ." She faltered, blinking rapidly. "The situation deteriorated alarmingly on the day of departure."

"Bunch of headhunters and other scum tried to storm their way onto the fleet," Trumane elaborated. "A few salvos from the *Viable* put paid to that mischief." He sipped his own coffee and Lizanne saw that his hand didn't tremble at all. "To the Travail with the lot of them, I say," he added. "Worthless cowards."

Watching Madame Hakugen dab a napkin at her welling eyes, Lizanne recalled her own fraught days leading the resistance at Carvenport. As bad as things had gotten towards the end she had at least been spared the burden of making such a decision. "I'm sure you did your best, madame," Lizanne told the former Comptroller. "These days it appears we have nothing but hard choices ahead of us."

"Any incidents during the voyage north?" Verricks asked.

"We lost one ship to a storm three days from port," Trumane said. "An old coal hauler barely fit to sail. Another two took off on their own course a day later. I wasn't going to waste time hunting them down."

"No drake attacks?" Lizanne asked.

Trumane gave her a frosty sideways glance and shook his head. "Never caught sight of one during the whole voyage. Makes me wonder if all these tall tales of rampaging drakes and conquering Spoiled are just that."

"Sadly, they're all true," Verricks assured him, whiskers bunching in a grim smile. "Feros has fallen silent. We have been unable to trance with them for two days."

"There could be any number of reasons for that," Trumane said. "An outbreak of influenza amongst the trance staff for instance."

"Indeed. Which is why I intend to sail there forthwith. Your command is hereby ordered to join us."

"There must be thousands of civilians in those ships," Lizanne said. "You're asking them to sail towards the very thing they're trying to escape."

"Thirty-two thousand civilians, to be exact," Madame Hakugen said. "Who have been at sea for far too long already. Our supplies are not copious and Feros is the nearest port." She inclined her head at Captain Verricks. "We will be happy to sail under your protection, sir."

Verricks gave a small huff of discomfort that told Lizanne all she needed to know about his intentions. "Captain Verricks is not offering protection, madame," she said. "He intends to form company with the *Viable Opportunity* and sail for Feros at the best possible speed. The *Viable* is a blood-burner and there are three Blood-blessed on this ship, which means the engines of both vessels can be fired to full capacity. Do I miscalculate, Captain?"

"Military necessity, miss," Verricks sniffed. "As you said. Nothing but hard choices."

"If you abandon these people," Lizanne told him, speaking every word with great precision, "the report I will write to the Board regarding your conduct will make Captain Trumane's report on Lieutenant Hilemore seem like a love-letter in comparison." She held his gaze, seeing the stern resolve of a professional and long-serving Protectorate officer.

"Much as I respect the advice of an Exceptional Initiatives agent," Verricks replied, "command of this vessel rests with me . . ."

"She's right."

They turned to Director Thriftmor, both elbows resting on the table as he massaged his temples. An untouched cup of coffee sat beside him. "Leaving thousands of refugees to fend for themselves in the middle of the ocean is an unconscionable act," Thriftmor went on, lowering his hands to regard Verricks with tired eyes. "One I can't support or, more importantly, justify to a public whose passions will no doubt have been inflamed by a hostile press. You may have command of this ship, sir, but I am a Board member and senior shareholder of the Ironship Syndicate. To all intents and purposes this is my ship and so is"—he waved a hand at Trumane, trying and failing to remember his name—"his."

Thriftmor turned away from Trumane's glare to offer Madame Haku-gen a smile. "Your ships will join with us, madame. Together we will sail for Feros where, if fortune favours us, safe harbour will be found." He got to his feet and made a slump-shouldered progress to the door. "I'll be in my cabin. Please knock only in the direst emergency."

She found Makario at the rear of the mid–upper deck, following the sound of the flute he had somehow obtained during the voyage. Meet-ing here had become something of a nightly ritual. Since first meeting him in the odorous pit of Scorazin she had noted his aversion to serious con-versation, something she now welcomed as a reprieve from the worries crowding her head, as was his music. It transpired that Makario was as accomplished with the flute as he was with the pianola and she had no difficulty in recognising the tune.

"Illemont again?" she asked, moving to rest her arms on the rail beside him. The long-dead Corvantine composer had been a particular favourite when Makario played for the largely unappreciative patrons of the Miner's Repose. "One might suspect you of nurturing an obsession."

"One would be correct," he replied, lowering the flute. "But what is love, if not obsession?"

Makario pointed the instrument at the ships following the *Profitable*, the many freighters and Blue-hunters arranged in two long rows that ex-tended for at least two miles. "I didn't know we were expecting company."

"We weren't." Lizanne cast her gaze over the darkened hulks of the refugee fleet. Whatever misgivings Captain Verricks might harbour about taking charge of this rag-tag collection of vessels hadn't prevented him from issuing strict and sensible orders regarding its organisation. All lights were to be doused and each ship appointed a slot in a prearranged sailing formation. Every ship had also been strictly forbidden to stop for any rea-son. "I don't care if the skipper's grandmother falls overboard," Verricks had said. "I'll shoot any captain who stops their engines."

"Keep playing," Lizanne told Makario, keen for the distraction. "Please."

Makario gave a gracious bow and raised the flute to his lips. Soon the lilting interlude from Illemont's supposedly lost "Ode to Despair" was drifting across the warship's pale wake.

"Have you finished it then?" she asked when the flute fell silent. "Your reconstruction of the great lost work?"

"I doubt if it can ever be finished. All I can do is record my guess-work and perhaps in time more talented souls will take it further." He fell silent, face uncharacteristically sombre as he gazed at the following ships.

"Wishing you'd stayed behind?" Lizanne asked.

Makario gave a short laugh and shook his head. "We both know I had little choice. The Electress would have settled accounts with me sooner or later. It's not in her nature to forgive a betrayal. Besides, I always had a yen to see the rest of the world, even if it is about to catch fire."

"You never told me how you ended up in Scorazin. Your presence there seemed so incongruous."

"I was a thief." He shrugged. "Thieves go to prison."

"Not to Scorazin. Not unless they've somehow offended the Emperor."

Makario looked at the flute in his hands, slim fingers playing over the keys. "My obsession, as you call it, has always been more of an addiction, and an addict will go to extremes to sate his need. That old student of Illemont I told you about lit a fire in me, a fire that could only be quenched by seeking out everything I could find that the great man had written or touched in his lifetime. Sadly, amassing such a collection requires a great deal of money and my parents had selfishly conspired to ensure I was born poor. My talent brought money in time, and a modicum of fame in certain circles, but it was never enough to quench the fire.

"It was small things at first, an item of jewellery from a box left carelessly open the evening I had been contracted to play for the amusement of the lady of the house. Then there was a pocket-watch taken from the drawer of a viscount who had probably forgotten how many he owned. Many of the more valuable trinkets were not so easily plucked of course, but my access to the homes of the nobility enabled a first hand reconnaissance before a stealthy night-time intrusion.

"It transpired I had a facility for climbing; musicians tend to have strong hands and I have always been fairly spry. I found a delightfully awful old reprobate in one of Corvus's seedier quarters who was more than willing to teach me the finer points of lock picking, as long as I kept him well supplied with ale and opium.

"Thanks to my new-found skills I soon had sufficient funds for a fine and growing collection of Illemontaria, and a decent fortune to go with it. I also had a name for my larcenous alter ego, the Moonlighter they called me. Corvus society was publicly alarmed and secretly delighted by his exploits. Ladies harboured entirely misplaced fears of being ravished in their own beds and servants were denied their meagre sleep ration to keep armed watch on the great houses lest the Moonlighter come calling. There was a lot of theatre to this, of course. Half the valuables that went missing during this period were never stolen by me, if they were stolen at all. And any family who did fall foul of the Moonlighter's attentions found their cachet suddenly enhanced, invitations to grand occasions and exclusive dinners would follow. Everyone wanted to hear more about the Moonlighter. There was even a series of vulgar periodicals about him which I fervently hope the Cadre have since seized and burned. The prose was dire and the illustrations terrible, but even the nobility bought them.

"The wealthy are a strange breed, dear Krista. Like children in many ways with their pettiness and susceptibility to flattery, and there are few creatures in this world more susceptible than a once-handsome man of privilege. Burgrave Erbukan wasn't a bad man, not really. Just bitter about getting old and fat, and he was far too trusting of the many artistic young men he invited to his home, a home which happened to contain one of the largest collections of original sheet music in the world. He was happy to show it to me, encouraged by an enthusiasm I, for once, didn't need to fake. The collection had been inherited from his late wife, a woman in whose company he spent as little time as possible. It was clear the old dullard had no notion of what he had. Original handwritten sheets penned by some of the greatest composers who ever lived, and there amongst it all, not even properly catalogued, no less than four previously undiscovered pages from Illemont's 'Ode to Despair.' I had to have them and, once the Moonlighter paid a visit to the Burgrave's mansion the following night, for one precious week I did."

"You should have waited," Lizanne said, voicing the critique of an experienced burglar. "Your visit was too fresh in his memory, it was inevitable that he would connect you to the theft."

Makario voiced a faint laugh. "It was just too tempting, you see. Like dangling a full bottle of best brandy before the eyes of a hopeless drunk. But it was a wonderful week alone with those pages, almost like being in the presence of Illemont's ghost. I barely rose from the pianola, so lost was I in the music. I'm not claiming it was worth all those years in Scorazin, but it was worth a great deal nonetheless."

"The Burgrave was well connected, I assume?"

"No, but his wife had a smidgen of Imperial blood and some of the other pages I stole had been gifted to her by the Emperor himself. The Moonlighter had offended the Divinity and could no longer be tolerated, however entertaining his skulduggery might be. The Burgrave received a visit from the Cadre, who didn't take long to piece it all together. I suppose I should be grateful they didn't amputate my fingers before throwing me into the great smokey pit. But then, I would never have met you, dear Krista, and I feel my life would be much poorer for the omission."

"Lizanne," she corrected. "As I've told you many times. My real name is Lizanne."

"Oh," he said with a wistful smile, raising the flute to his lips once more, "you'll always be Krista to me. It was her who set me free, after all."

She was woken by the ship's siren sometime around dawn. The signal, two short blasts followed by two long, wasn't one she had heard often and it took a moment to place it: "vessel in distress sighted." She dressed quickly and checked that the vials in her Spider were fully loaded with product before strapping it to her wrist. She made her way to the bridge where the duty officer had his glass trained on something about thirty degrees to port. Through the bridge window she could see an ensign haranguing a squad of sailors on the lower deck as they manoeuvred a launch over the side.

"What is it?" she asked the duty officer, who obligingly handed over his spy-glass. She had no need of Green to make out the target, a bulbous shape silhouetted against the red morning sky, bobbing as it made an irregular but inexorable descent towards the waves. Realisation dawned instantly. This could be only one thing, a thing she had seen the designs for a few months before, and there were very few people capable of constructing it in so short a time.

"Distance?" she asked the duty officer.

"Just over a mile," he replied.

Lizanne kept the spy-glass to her eye for a moment longer, tracking from the aerostat to the sea then back again as she gauged how long it would be before the craft completed its descent. It was too far, she knew. The launch wouldn't get there in time.

"Keep the ship at dead slow," she told the duty officer, handing back the spy-glass and making for the door. "Steer thirty degrees to port. On my authority if the captain has any questions," she added before stepping outside.

Lizanne moved to the walkway in front of the bridge, depressing a button on the Spider to inject a full vial of Green. She took a second to steady herself as the product flooded her system before vaulting over the walkway railing and making her way down the cruiser's upper works via a series of spectacular leaps before landing next to the boat party. They had succeeded in getting the boat over the side and lowered so that it bobbed on the swell. The wind was up this morning and the sea choppy, adding yet another level of difficulty to her task.

"You." Lizanne pointed to the ensign in charge. "Take the tiller. You and you." Her finger jabbed at the two burliest sailors in the party. "Get in. The rest of you stand away."

She leapt over the side and landed in the middle of the boat where she immediately sat and hefted a pair of oars into the rowlocks. "Hurry up!" she ordered, seeing her three chosen crewmates staring down at her. The ensign reacted first, barking a command at the two sailors who had them following him down the netting on the *Profitable*'s hull.

"Don't bother," Lizanne told the two sailors as they began hauling the oars into place. "You'll just upset my rhythm. Ready?" she asked, turning to the ensign who had obediently taken position at the tiller. He gave a tense nod and Lizanne raised the oars. "Hold tight," she said, and began to row.

CHAPTER 6

Clay

"You have maps?" Kriz's expression was guarded as she asked the question, and she avoided the hard, inquisitive gaze Hilemore afforded her before moving to where his pack lay in the corner of the captain's cabin.

"The southern ice-shelf and the Chokes," he said, extracting a rolled-up sheet of waxed parchment and laying it out on the desk. "The only one I was likely to need once we disembarked the *Superior*."

Clay watched Kriz survey the map then shake her head. "No. I need a map of . . ." She paused and he knew she had been about to voice a name from her own era. "Arradsia," she finished, a slight roll to her eyes giving an indication as to what she thought of the continent's modern-day title.

The captain's jaws bunched a little in evident impatience but he said nothing as he opened a desk drawer. "Captain Bledthorne may have been a poor pirate," Hilemore said, extracting a sheaf of papers, "but he was a decent enough seaman to recognise the value of charts. I suspect he stole most of them. The condition is surprisingly good, something to do with the sterility of the atmosphere I assume."

"Freezing temperatures kill most of the corrupting agents in the air," Kriz said, her attention fixed on the charts as she sorted through them. "Here," she said, pointing to a small map that Clay recognised as a rendition of south-eastern Arradsia. Although he had little notion of what Kriz intended, he was unsurprised when her finger alighted on a familiar landmark.

"Krystaline Lake," he said.

"My people called it 'The Divine Mirror.'" A sad smile of recollection played over Kriz's lips. "On calm nights the surface would reflect the stars almost perfectly. It was a place of pilgrimage during the summer months where the Devos would gather to give thanks to the Benefactors."

Hilemore let out a soft grunt, clearly irritated by what must sound to him like gibberish. "And the importance of this place today?" he enquired.

"There's something there." Kriz's hand went to the small crystal she wore on a chain around her neck, the one with which Zembi had tried to kill her. So far she hadn't revealed its significance to Clay beyond a single word: *memory*. "Something important."

"Miss," Hilemore said in a tone of controlled anger, "as previously stated I have no more tolerance for vagary or obfuscation. Speak plainly and tell me exactly what is at Krystaline Lake and why it is so important."

Kriz looked at Clay, clearly seeking support, but his own desire for answers was at least a match for the captain's. "I don't see any more reason for secrets," he told her.

"The knowledge I hold is dangerous," she said, eyes switching between Clay and Hilemore. "Dangerous to you, your whole civilisation . . ."

"We have a more pressing danger to deal with," Hilemore cut in. "As Mr. Torcreek has told you."

"The White." She nodded, closing her eyes, face downcast. "I know, and you are right to fear it. We never dreamed it would be capable of so much . . . hatred."

"Then you probably shouldn't have bred the thing," Clay said. "But since you did I'd say it's up to you to put it right." He tapped a finger to the map. "Let's start here. There's an old legend about a marvellous flying treasure ship that came to rest at the bottom of Krystaline Lake. I'm guessing your item of importance has something to do with that."

"I assume so, but it wasn't a ship." She opened her eyes and Clay noticed her knuckles were now pale on the crystal shard. "It was an aerostat, like the one we used to escape the enclave below. It was stolen by my brother when he made his own escape thousands of years ago."

"Your brother?" Clay asked. "You mean one of the other Blood-blessed kids."

"Hezkhi." She nodded. "He grew up to be our best pilot, and probably the most impetuous soul amongst us. I don't know all of it, not yet."

Clay's hand traced along the chain around his own neck in unconscious mimicry of Kriz, pausing on the vials beneath his shirt. One contained heartblood, scavenged from the corpse of a slain Black beneath the ice. The other held a small, congealed amount of blood from the diseased White that Kriz had reduced to ash with her bomb-throwing gun. *Could save a whole lot of trouble,* he thought. *One sip could show us the way.* He discounted the notion almost instantly, remembering the intense disorientation of his first experience in harnessing the power it held. It seemed to him that a human mind simply wasn't attuned to perceiving the future and feared for his sanity should he try it again. Added to that was the deep sense of uncertainty it engendered. Once, he would have assumed such a gift would banish all doubts, provide answers to all problems. Instead it only raised endless questions.

Letting his hand slip from the vials, Clay nodded at the shard in her fist. "I guess that's got the whole story, huh?"

"Zembi's memories," she said, opening her hand to show them the dagger-like length of crystal. "But I'll need what's on the aerostat to access them. Hezkhi escaped the enclave, and whatever killed the others and made Zembi into that . . . thing. That's what he told me as he lay dying. Hezkhi flew away and he took something with him." Her fingers traced over the irregular elongated arrow-head form of Krystaline Lake. "There's another crystal there . . . a black crystal. And if anything can defeat the White, it's that."

Jack towed them clear of the bergs a day later. Clay could feel the drake's burgeoning exhaustion as he dragged the *Dreadfire* out into the Whirls, the broad stretch of water that formed a minor sea between the Chokes and what had been the solid ice-wall of the Shelf.

Let it go, he told the Blue, standing on the prow as had become his custom over the past few days. He sent an image of a slackened cable along with the thought and Jack immediately opened his jaws. He rolled as the hawser slipped from his mouth, Clay sensing his joy at the release. He could also feel Jack's hunger, something that had grown to alarming proportions as the voyage through the ice wore on.

Go, Clay told him, sending images of whales and walruses he had found in Old Jack's memories. *Hunt. Come back when you're strong.*

Jack lingered on the surface for a moment, his eyes bobbing above the surface. Clay could sense his reluctance to be separated from their connection. *Distance don't matter,* Clay assured him, uncertain whether the beast could understand the concept. *I'll hear you however far you go.*

Twin columns of smoke issued from Jack's nostrils as he grunted in apparent assent before disappearing from view. Clay followed him for a while, sharing the sensations of the hunt as the Blue dived deep, his incredibly sharp ears tuned for any betraying echo that might lead him to prey. Within seconds he had it, a series of faint splashes and muted barks that told of a seal pack several miles east. Clay withdrew his thoughts as Jack sped off in pursuit.

"We seem to have lost our engine, Mr. Torcreek."

Clay turned to find Hilemore and his hulking second in command standing close by. The captain's demeanour towards him had become less suspiciously judgemental during the voyage, but the Islander's expression told of an unalloyed mistrust. Such an attitude should have made Clay wary of the man, he was even taller and broader across the shoulders than Cralmoor, another dangerous Islander of Clay's previous acquaintance. However, he took comfort from the sense that Steelfine was incapable of doing anything unless ordered by his captain.

"He's hungry," Clay replied. "He'll be back soon enough."

"Whilst we drift on the current in the meantime," Steelfine pointed out.

"Got an anchor, haven't you?"

Clay moved away, ignoring the Islander's ominous scowl as he descended the steps to the hold. He found Loriabeth at Sigoral's side, a spot she had rarely strayed from since coming aboard. Clay was relieved to find the Corvantine awake, though his face appeared worryingly gaunt as he drank the thin broth Loriabeth had concocted from the ship's rapidly dwindling stores.

"Good to have you back, Lieutenant," Clay told him, surprised by his own sincerity. The man was a Corvantine Imperial Officer of somewhat duplicitous nature, and therefore technically an enemy. However, Clay knew he and his cousin would most likely have died beneath the ice but for Sigoral's skill with a carbine. Also, he was a Blood-blessed and therefore too valuable a companion for the trials ahead to allow any lingering resentment.

"I had a dream in which I was drowning in piss," Sigoral replied, grimacing as he took another spoonful of broth. "It tasted better than this." He shrank back as Loriabeth aimed a swipe at his head.

"That was the mask," Clay said, taking a seat on a near by barrel. He went on to explain about the gas and Jack's role in hauling them clear of Mount Reygnar. "We had us an eventful voyage so far. And it ain't over."

"Have you told the captain . . . ?" Sigoral trailed off, affording both Clay and Loriabeth a questioning glance.

"That you're a lying, double-faced Corvie shithead?" Loriabeth said. "Sure, we told him."

"Needed to know there was another Blood-blessed on board," Clay added. "It's his ship after all, such as it is."

He turned as a stream of muttered gibberish sounded from the neighbouring bunk. Scrimshine had sunk into a semiconscious state after Skaggerhill dosed him with all their remaining Green. His colour was better and his bouts of coughing had abated, but he showed little sign of waking save for the occasional bout of babbling in an unfamiliar Dalcian dialect.

"I bet Skaggs twenty scrip he don't make it," Loriabeth said, the callousness of the remark contrasted by the softness of her voice.

"You'll lose," Clay told her. "Seen his kind before, they only ever die old. It's like life just ain't mean enough to kill them."

Jack still hadn't returned by nightfall, although the images of reddened waters and dismembered seals told Clay he had at least partially sated his hunger. The crew shared a sparse meal of soup, Sigoral joining them for the first time. He wore an eye-patch over his still-unhealed orb and Clay saw how his features tensed as he fought to control the repeated spasms of pain. Conversation was muted and frequently interrupted by Scrimshine's delirious outbursts.

"Least he's got the energy to swear," Loriabeth observed after another lengthy Dalcian diatribe.

"He's not cursing, miss," Hilemore told her. "He's praying."

"You know Dalcian, Captain?" she asked.

"A little. I spent a year or so in Dalcian waters before the Emergency. It's a difficult tongue to pick up, there being so many variations between islands. But prayers to the ancestors are always spoken in the same holy language, which also serves as a common tongue for commerce."

"I had heard, sir," Steelfine said, "that there was much fine combat to be had in the Dalcian Emergency. I'm aggrieved to have missed it, I must say."

"There was combat, Lieutenant," Hilemore said, his face taking on a grim aspect. "And plenty of it, to be sure. But I wouldn't call it fine."

"An alliance of pirate clans attempted to seize corporate holdings," Sigoral said. "And were soundly defeated. At least that's what we were told."

"Curiously the Dalcians have no word for pirate," Hilemore replied. "Whether a vessel is to be taken, sunk or allowed on its way is determined by a complex array of clan loyalties and unsettled feuds. They call it the 'Mehlaya,' which roughly translates as 'a web of many spiders.' It's what they have instead of written law and proved remarkably effective at keeping some semblance of order for centuries, until the corporate world came calling, of course."

"The old will always fall to the new," said a rarely heard voice. All eyes turned to Preacher, who finished the last of his watery soup before getting up and making for the stairs without another word.

"Seer scripture," Braddon explained after Preacher had ascended to the upper deck. "Seems the only thing he speaks these days. If he speaks at all."

"Silent or verbose," Hilemore said. "I'm still grateful for his eyes."

Scrimshine's muttering had abated into a sibilant whisper by the time a new sound came to them, a faint whoosh and boom from outside followed by a hollering from the look-outs on deck.

"That cannon?" Braddon asked as they scrambled to their feet.

"Signal rocket," Hilemore said. "It appears we have company and it might well be friendly."

Clay joined the rush to the upper deck and the starboard rail where one of the look-outs was pointing into the darkness. "About thirty points off the bow, sir," the crewman told Hilemore, who was busy scanning the gloom with his spy-glass. After a short interval there came another whoosh and Clay saw a thick stream of sparks ascend into the night sky before blossoming into a bright yellow flower followed a heart-beat later by the flat thud of combusted powder.

"Light torches!" Hilemore ordered, Clay seeing a grin play over his lips as he lowered the spy-glass. "All hands step to it. Quick as you can, lads."

Soon every crewman had a blazing torch in their hand. Hilemore instructed them to stand along the rail and wave them high whilst shouting as loud as they could. Within moments two shapes appeared in the gloom some two hundred yards off, a narrow, sleek warship moving wraith-like through the placid waters and a markedly less elegant Blue-hunter with paddles that churned the sea white as it drew closer.

Clay heard Hilemore give a soft sigh as he murmured, "I told her not to wait."

"You look like a drake ate you up then shat you out," Zenida Okanas greeted Hilemore. They had rigged a gang-plank between the *Superior* and the *Dreadfire*. As was apparently custom, the captain had been the last to leave the old sailing-ship.

"Then I must look better than I feel," Hilemore replied, before giving a formal bow and adding something in Varestian. Clay only spoke a few words of this tongue but noted a certain gravity to the exchange that followed, almost as if they were observing a ritual of some kind. Zenida said a few short lines then gave a bow and moved aside, Clay recognising the last sentence she spoke as Hilemore stepped from the gang-plank and onto the frigate's deck: "Welcome home, sea-brother."

Hilemore cast a glance around the *Superior*'s deck and upper works, nodding in approval. "Glad to see you've kept her in good order."

"There wasn't a great deal else to do," she said before inclining her head at the *Farlight*, which was anchored a short distance away. "Apart from a small matter of mutiny."

"Mutiny?"

"Seems about half the *Farlight*'s crew weren't too keen on honouring our bargain once they'd blasted a channel through the Chokes. That old captain managed to save his skin thanks to your Mr. Talmant, though the lad was obliged to take a pistol to the ship's bosun. We happened upon them when we were making our way out, persuaded Tidelow to come back with us, not that he needed a lot of persuading. I think he didn't like the notion of sailing north alone with so many of his crew locked in the hold. I offered to cast them overboard but he wouldn't have it."

"I recall instructing you not to linger."

Clay saw the woman avoid Hilemore's gaze as she pointed at the distant glow on the southern horizon. "Took it as a sign we should wait awhile longer. Besides, Akina thought it was pretty."

Clay saw the pirate woman's daughter hovering near by, though her eyes weren't fixed on the volcano but on Kriz. She had placed herself close to Clay's side, her expression a mix of guarded uncertainty and fascination as he drank in the sight of the *Superior.*

"Who's this?" Akina demanded, stabbing a finger at Kriz, small features bunched in suspicion. "She's new, and she looks wrong."

Clay saw the girl wasn't alone in her fascination, several of the *Superior's* crew were also staring at Kriz.

"I'd guess you didn't find her at Kraghurst Station," Zenida said to Hilemore.

"Her name's Kriz," Clay said, matching the stares of the crew. "She's with me." *It's different,* he realised, watching the uncertainty on their faces. Mostly they displayed a basic fear of the unfamiliar mixed with a desire for this long, wearisome expedition to end. Before it hadn't been like this, they had all followed him across miles of ocean through many perils without any real question or reluctance. Now he saw many of them were asking themselves why.

He had seen Hilemore and the others exhibit the same diminished faith in him on the *Dreadfire* and had put it down to the extremity of their situation, but now saw it went deeper than that. *Didn't you ever wonder why they were so willing to follow you?* Silverpin's ghost had asked, making him understand that somehow he had cast a spell over these people, just as Silverpin had cast a spell on the Longrifles during their search for the White. Now that spell was gone. Now he was just an unregistered Blood-blessed from the Blinds who had returned to them with something impossible.

The answer came to him as Hilemore stepped forward, casting out a string of orders that had the crew rushing off to their allotted tasks, albeit with many a suspicious or baffled glance at Kriz. *Silverpin,* Clay thought. *Part of her lived on in me, the part that could compel the un-Blessed to follow me on the promise of little more than a waking dream. And I killed it when I killed what was left of her.*

"Are you alright?" Kriz asked and he realised his face must have betrayed his thoughts.

"Just fine," he lied, forcing a smile. "But I think we got us a long and trying trip ahead."

"Krystaline Lake?" Zenida's face betrayed a curious mix of amusement and foreboding. "That's where we're going?"

Hilemore had convened a meeting in the *Superior*'s ward-room. He stood at the map table, face scraped clean of his previously copious beard and wearing a fresh uniform. Although Clay thought the captain had weathered the depredations of the ice better than all of them, the uniform still hung loose in several places, though Hilemore stood as straight as ever. Braddon and Kriz were the only others present besides Clay and Zenida.

"You know it?" the captain asked the Varestian woman.

"I know of it, as I should. My father died there." Zenida gave a rueful grimace as she surveyed the map, a more detailed rendering of the south Arradsian coastal region than that offered by the antique maps of long-dead Captain Bledthorne. "The last of his many foolish and expensive jaunts in search of mythical treasures. I never knew what truly became of him. He went off exploring and never came back. I hoped to go looking for him myself one day but the pressures of commerce always prevented me. And I had a daughter to think of."

Clay opened Scriberson's note-book as something chimed in his memory. Thanks to the leather binding, the pages hadn't been ruined when he dropped his pack in the sea. "Mr. O.," he said after finding the series of entries that corresponded to their journey across the lake. "The *River Maiden* was charted by a Mr. O."

"For Okanas." Zenida frowned at him, her gaze fixed on the note-book. "What is that?"

"A dead man's journal," Braddon said before going on to relate the story of their time on Krystaline Lake. "It was Dr. Firpike who had the most interest in it. Pity we left all his papers in the grave where we buried him in the Coppersoles."

"Looks like Scribes took plenty of notes," Clay said, continuing to leaf through the book. "Guessing he didn't trust Firpike to share what he knew later on." He stopped as he came to a particular notation, a line of text underscored with the words "Translated Dalcian text—Early Satura Magisterium." "'A vessel of wonder,'" Clay read aloud. "'Unbound by earth or sea, come to rest with precious cargo 'neath the silver waters.'" He raised his gaze to Zenida. "You have any notion what it all means?"

"Relations between my father and I were . . . poor in the three years before his disappearance. I know that he spent the better part of two years paying out a good portion of his wealth to an artificer. A renegade Corvantine who had a design for an apparatus that would enable a man to breathe underwater. So whatever he was after will not to be easy to reach. The location would be marked on one of his many maps, but they are all locked away in the family archive at the High Wall."

"Firpike said the story came from a Dalcian legend," Braddon said, brow creased as he strove to recollect the details. "Close to three thousand years old, he said."

Clay turned to Kriz. "Seems too recent to be Hezkhi."

"The legend may be three thousand years old," she said. "But the story that inspired it could be much older. And we don't know exactly when he woke. He could have been sleeping for centuries."

Clay sighed as Zenida and Braddon squinted at Kriz in bafflement. "It's . . . a really long story," Clay began.

Kriz yelped and shrank back as the flames consumed the candle in one fierce blast of heat, leaving a patch of dripping wax on the stern-rail. "I don't get why you ain't better at this," Clay said, watching her straighten quickly, smoothing a hand through her hair in an effort to cover her embarrassment. "You can fashion a crystal into a rose but you can't light a candle with Red?"

"Red plasma was never my speciality," she said, somewhat stiffly. "The blessing, as you call it, was only marginally understood in my time. Your people have had centuries of practice. As for the crystals, they were much more easily manipulated than other material. It was almost like they wanted to be altered."

"We'll try again." Clay took a box from his pocket and extracted a single match. "Something smaller might work better," he said, setting it down on the rail and stepping back. "Concentrate on the head. The fire goes where your eyes go. You can feel it, right? The Red in your veins. Try to think of it as a barrel, full of power. You only need to let out a little at a time."

Kriz kept her gaze locked on the match, frowning in concentration. Clay was soon gratified to see a slight heat shimmer appear between her and the rail just as the match-head flared into life. The fire was still too fierce, consuming the match in a fraction of a second to leave a speck of black ash on the rail, but it was her most controlled effort so far.

"I want to try again," Kriz said. "Something bigger."

"The captain's got us on a strict product ration," Clay said. "No more than a few drops at a time, just for practice."

"This ship truly runs on Red plasma?" she asked, casting her eyes over the frigate's upper works.

"Didn't think we had just sailing-ships, did you?"

From her slightly chagrined expression he saw that she had in fact been thinking that very thing. Although they had shared much in the trance, it was clear they still understood relatively little about each other and the eras that had produced them. *Contempt, Mr. Torcreek,* Sigoral had said during their sojourn through the strange world down below. *That's what she thinks of us. To her we are just useful primitives.*

"It's called a thermoplasmic engine," he said, watching closely to gauge her reaction. "Just a vial or two of Red is enough to shift this whole ship at a right old lick, and she's a tiddler compared to some."

"Remarkable," Kriz murmured, though her gaze darkened as it alighted on the rear gun-battery. "So much progress, and yet you're still fighting wars."

"It's a big world. Guess there's a lot to fight over."

They both turned in unison as an upsurge of shouting came from the deck of the *Farlight* moored some fifty yards to port. It was still early as Hilemore wanted to wait for a fully risen sun before commencing the voyage north. However, there was ample light to make out the tall spines cutting through the Whirls towards the three ships. Although the Blue-hunter's crew had been warned that Jack no longer posed a threat and might appear at some point, it seemed their long-held instincts were not so easily assuaged. Clay saw a group of sailors feverishly loading the ship's forward harpoon cannon as others formed up along the side with rifles in hand.

"Lesson number two," Clay said, opening his wallet and extracting a vial of Black. "How to stop a missile in flight."

The harpoon cannon fired just as Jack raised his head above the water, blinking in apparent bemusement at the sight of the huge barbed length of iron as it hovered in mid air a few yards away. Clay knew he was showing off and burning more product than he should, but it wasn't just Kriz who needed to learn a lesson. The harpoon gave a loud squeal as Clay twisted the arrow-head point back at a sharp angle. The crew on the *Farlight* could only stare in shock and then duck as he hurled the projectile back at them. It slammed into the Blue-hunter's stack with sufficient force to leave a sizable dent.

Clay cupped his hands around his mouth, raising his voice to full volume. "Any of you fuckers casts so much as a nasty look in his direction again and I won't blunt it next time!"

He heard a faint hiss of steam and turned to see Jack letting out a contented puff of flame as he slipped below the water.

CHAPTER 7

Lizanne

She exhausted most of her Green rowing to the aerostat, the oars blurring like paddles as they propelled the launch through the choppy sea. By the time they reached the craft it had settled on the waves, the boat-like gondola bobbing on the swell and sinking ever lower as water lapped over its shallow sides. Above, the elongated gas-filled balloon swayed in the wind, threatening to twist the ropes that bound it into a tangle that would no doubt see it fall and the whole craft subside along with it into the ocean. It appeared to have been fashioned from overlapping panels of silk, which fluttered as the gas inside grew thinner by the second. There were three people in the gondola and the sight of them flooded Lizanne with a relief that made her pause in her labour, though it was shot through with an awful realisation. *Father, Jermayah, Tekela . . . No Aunt Pendilla.*

"Get a rope over there," she commanded the two burly sailors at the front of the launch. They duly cast a weighted rope to the gondola as the ensign at the tiller steered them alongside. The last of Lizanne's Green gave out as she closed the distance between the two craft. She slumped in her seat, chest heaving thanks to the effects of burning so much product so quickly. So she barely heard the thump and clatter of feet on the boards, sitting with her aching head bowed and chest thumping like a drum.

"Lizanne."

She raised her head as a pair of soft hands met her cheeks, looking up to find herself confronted by a familiar, doll-like countenance, albeit one that seemed to have suddenly become much more womanly in expression if not form. "It is very good to see you again, miss," Lizanne said with a tired smile.

Tekela's face blossomed into a smile of her own, tears welling in her eyes, and she pressed a kiss to Lizanne's forehead before pulling her into a tight embrace. Lizanne swallowed, her throat hard and tight. "My aunt?"

Tekela drew back, tears falling as she shook her head. "I'm sorry. It was horrible . . ." She trailed off, face clouded with confusion and unwanted memories. "Sirus . . . Sirus was there."

"What?"

"He was there. Changed, Spoiled. But it was him. He saved me."

The resurrection of a youth Lizanne had last seen strapped into a chair and apparently dead in a Corvantine torture-chamber was a singular mystery, but one that would have to wait. As would her grief.

"The box," Lizanne said. "Do you still have the box?"

Tekela had deposited two bulky objects on the deck of the launch. One was wrapped in waxed canvas against the damp but Lizanne could make out a familiar if much-reduced shape under the covering. *Jermayah's been busy, I see.* She turned to the other object, also concealed in canvas. Tekela crouched and pulled the wrapping away to reveal a familiar, shiny, box-shaped device of numerous cogs and gears.

"Good," Lizanne said. "Keep it close."

Tekela's eyes widened in surprise. "You want me to look after it?"

"You seem to have done a fair job so far. I assume that thing works," she added, nudging the other object with her toe.

"Six hundred rounds a minute on the slowest setting," Tekela replied, face suddenly grim with no doubt ugly remembrance. "It works very well."

"No, young man, I will not abandon this craft." Her father's voice tore her gaze from Tekela. Jermayah had already clambered onto the launch but the esteemed Professor Graysen Lethridge stood resolute on the rapidly descending deck of his latest invention. "Do you have any notion of the import of this device?" he demanded of the ensign. "I insist you see to its salvage."

Lizanne stood, moving on unsteady legs to slump against the side of the boat, staring at her father until he met her gaze, not without some reluctance. She saw his resolve falter, but not completely. "It's important," he said, a faint pleading note in his voice. "Surely you can see that."

Lizanne gave an involuntary roll of her eyes which she knew must have made her resemble a sulky adolescent, but found herself too weary to care. "He's right," she told the ensign. "Lash the launch to it then use your flags to signal the *Profitable* for more boats." He began to protest but she waved a dismissive hand. "Exceptional Initiatives. Just get on with it, unless you'd like to be posted to a research station in the northern polar region."

She assumed either Verricks put a great deal more weight on her authority than she really deserved or Director Thriftmor intervened again. In either case the *Profitable Venture* soon came to an almost complete stop, raising flags and blasting her sirens to order the rest of the convoy to follow suit. Within minutes the cruiser's twenty-foot steam-powered pinnace had been lowered over the side and was making a steady progress towards the floundering aerostat.

Her father and Jermayah used a valve on the balloon's underside to vent the remaining gas, provoking a worried question from Lizanne as the pinnace drew alongside. "Isn't it flammable?"

"Helium," Jermayah said. "Take more than a spark to set it off. Tried a few experiments with hydrogen but they nearly burned the shop down."

"Helium is more plentiful in any case," her father added. "And cheaper."

Soon the balloon was just a flaccid sprawl of wet silk on the water. Professor Lethridge ordered it gathered up whilst Jermayah oversaw the recovery of the gondola. "Not so much the carriage we need," he said, slapping a hand to a bulky cylindrical apparatus at the rear of the gondola, "it's the engine."

"Thermoplasmic?" Lizanne asked, recognising the tell-tale pipe-work visible through a gap in the engine's carapace.

"It's a hybrid," Jermayah replied and she saw the glimmer of professional pride in his eyes. "Kerosene or blood. Both burn in the same combustion chamber. She'll give out more power if you feed her Red, of course, but kerosene is fine for basic manoeuvring."

"Speed?" Lizanne enquired receiving a reply from an unexpected source.

"I had her up to thirty miles per hour using kerosene," Tekela said. "We hadn't yet managed to conduct a trial with blood."

Lizanne scowled at Jermayah. "You let her fly this thing?"

"She's our test pilot," he answered with a grin far too lacking in contrition for Lizanne's liking. "We weren't too sure about the lifting properties at first, needed someone who wouldn't weigh her down. Tekela volunteered. Got a right good feel for the controls too."

Lizanne shifted her baleful gaze to her father. "I told you to find her a decent school, not subject her to your experiments."

"We did," Professor Lethridge replied. "Miss Hisselwyck's Finishing Academy. She wouldn't go. Your aunt tried to march her there but she fought her off, then threatened to run off and live in the refugee camp."

Lizanne rounded on Tekela, who met her angry visage with a shrug and a purse of her lips. "I'm too old for school anyway."

"And too young to be careening around the sky in one of his mad contraptions."

"Well, you gave him the plans." A small vestige of the old Tekela appeared then, pouty and defiant in the face of legitimate concern. At this juncture Lizanne wasn't sure if she preferred that Tekela to this one. *At least the brat had been predictable, up to a point.*

Lizanne took a calming breath and turned back to her father as he helped drag the last of the depleted balloon onto the fore-deck of the pinnace. "If you're quite finished we need to return," she said. "You'll also have to provide a full account of Feros's fall to Captain Verricks and Director Thriftmor. It seems we have some more hard decisions to make."

Soon the pinnace had closed to within about a hundred yards of the *Profitable*. The helmsman steered hard to port to bring the craft alongside as a group of sailors gathered at the lower-deck rail, ready to cast off their securing lines. It was then that Lizanne felt a small hand clutch at her arm and turned to see Tekela, face pale and eyes wide as she pointed at something in the sky.

The drake was high enough to be out of range of the *Profitable*'s guns, but the angle of the sun drew a faint red glitter from its scales as it banked and turned for the east. Lizanne went to the junior lieutenant commanding the pinnace and demanded his spy-glass before training it on the eastern horizon. An "enemy in sight" signal was already blasting from the *Profitable*'s sirens by the time she picked out the tell-tale silhouettes resolving through the morning mist. *Warships.* There were five of them, all either frigate or sloop class. She saw what at first appeared to be a thick pall of smoke rising from each of the ships then realised it to be a swarm of drakes.

"Change of orders," Lizanne said, returning the spy-glass to the lieutenant. "Make for the *Viable Opportunity*. Tell Captain Trumane to head east at best possible speed and signal the rest of the fleet to follow. He is not to linger for any reason."

She stared at his blanched, near-panicked features until he gave a nod of assent. "What are you doing?" her father asked as she moved to the prow of the pinnace.

"I left something behind."

Lizanne climbed onto the prow and took out her wallet, extracting a vial of Green and exchanging it for the exhausted one in the Spider before injecting all of it along with a quarter vial of Red. She would need it to ward off the chill. She glanced back, seeing Tekela struggling in Jermayah's grip as she sought to follow. "Take care of her," Lizanne said before diving into the sea.

The *Profitable*'s main batteries were firing as she scaled the stern anchor mounting and vaulted onto the lower deck. The cruiser's guns fired according to a pre-set sequence so as not to buckle the ship's structure with the release of so much energy at once. The resultant roar was therefore continuous and deafening, drowning out the cacophony of shouted orders as the crew scrambled to their battle stations. The *Profitable*'s bloodburners came on-line when she made her way onto the mid-deck, the ship lurching into accelerated motion as Mr. and Mrs. Griffan lit the product in her dual engines. Apart from their brief and distressing sojourn through the revolution-torn streets of Corvus, neither of the Griffans had been in battle before and Lizanne had to suppress a pang of sympathy for what they were about to experience. *They are not your mission.*

She was obliged to struggle past a throng of rushing sailors to get to the officers' quarters, opening the door of Tinkerer's cabin to find him lying on the deck just as she had instructed. He stared up at her with bright eyes, though his face was typically lacking in animation. She noticed he also had a small bottle clutched in his hand. "I stole it from the ship's medical bay," he explained, following her gaze. "Potassium chloride. You said to seek out the most efficient means."

"Best hold on to it for now," she said. "Get up. We're leaving."

She led him to Makario's cabin where she found the musician playing a surprisingly jaunty tune on his flute. "Thought I'd prefer my death to be accompanied by something cheerful," he said.

"It'll have to wait. Follow me, and don't dawdle."

She led them both to the corridor leading to the middle of the ship where they could scale a ladder all the way to the lower deck. They were halfway down the ladder when the ship gave a sudden, violent shudder. A loud high-pitched groan of protesting metal echoed all around.

"That doesn't sound good," Makario observed, holding on to the ladder with a white-knuckled grip.

"She's been hit," Lizanne said, continuing to climb down. "And it won't be for the last time. Keep going."

On descending to the lower deck she started for the stern, dodging around sailors laden with equipment and ammunition. The ship heaved several times as they made their way aft, Lizanne deducing that Captain Verricks had thrown the *Profitable* into a series of evasive manoeuvres. Even through the thick iron bulkheads and continuing roar of the main batteries she could hear a familiar rapid percussive thump and growl. *Secondary armament,* she realised. *The drakes must be close.*

The pale rectangle of an open hatch appeared ahead and she started forward at a run, then came to a sudden halt as the ceiling buckled, the metal tearing open to flood the corridor with smoke and flame. Thanks to the Green in her veins Lizanne recovered quickly, the ringing in her ears and blurred vision subsiding after only seconds. Makario and Tinkerer were not so lucky. The musician required several hard slaps before he regained enough sensibility to stand whilst Tinkerer remained unconscious, though mercifully free of injury.

"Did you have to bring him?" Makario enquired as Lizanne hauled the artificer's slight form onto her shoulders.

"Just be grateful I brought you."

She was obliged to step over the mangled remains of several sailors before reaching the hatch, stepping out into the open air to find the stern of the *Profitable Venture* in shambles. It appeared the cruiser had been hit by at least four shells from a salvo of five. One of the rear batteries was a complete wreck, the armoured housing shattered and the gun-crew transformed into charred lumps of flesh. Two large holes had been punched into the deck from which smoke issued forth in copious amounts. The surrounding ironwork glowed a deep red as the inferno beneath raged unchecked. It was clear that her original plan to make for the aft life-boats was now out of the question.

"By the souls of all the emperors," Makario breathed as a large winged form soared through the smoke. The Red gave a brief squawk before opening its talons, allowing something to tumble free of its grip, a man-sized, man-shaped something.

The Spoiled landed directly in front of Lizanne, no more than three feet away. Time seemed to slow then, thanks to the Green, which had a tendency to increase perception in times of great stress. Therefore, Lizanne was able to discern a great deal about the Spoiled in the space of the next few heart-beats. She saw that it was male, stood an inch or two over six feet in height and appeared to be wearing a greatly modified version of a uniform normally worn by Protectorate infantry. Various trinkets had been sewn into the uniform's tunic, cap badges from Protectorate and Corvantine regiments along with what were unmistakably human teeth and other more fleshy tokens. It also carried a .35 Dessinger long-barrel service revolver in one clawed hand and a tribal war-club of some kind in the other. She even had time to look into its eyes and be left with absolutely no doubt that it was about to do its best to kill her.

"Catch," Lizanne told the Spoiled and threw Tinkerer's unconscious body at it. Doing the utterly unexpected was a tactic that had worked for her in the past and so it proved now. The Spoiled nimbly caught Tinkerer in its arms then wasted a few precious seconds staring at Lizanne, its spined brow creasing in bafflement. She drew her revolver from her skirt pocket and shot it in the eye.

At least they die like a human, she thought, bending to retrieve Tinkerer's body. "Take that," she told Makario, nodding at the Spoiled's fallen revolver.

"I . . ." Makario was blinking rapidly, face white with shock. It seemed even the depredations of Scorazin hadn't prepared him for this. "I don't like guns."

"Just pick it up."

She turned and carried Tinkerer towards midships, keeping to the walkway that fringed the lower starboard deck. She passed several Thumper and Growler batteries, the crews casting a flaming torrent of tracer into the sky at the Reds that now seemed to be everywhere. She had the satisfaction of seeing one drake torn apart by a concentrated blast from a Thumper before it could deposit the two Spoiled in its claws on the deck. Sadly, the Thumper crew's cheers were short-lived as another much larger Red swooped down through the cloud of gore left by its fallen brother and doused the jubilant sailors in a thick stream of fire. Lizanne closed her ears to the screams and ran on.

On reaching the ladder that led to the starboard life-boat derricks they were confronted by the sight of a vicious hand-to-hand mêlée between sailors and Spoiled. At least twenty were assailing each other, rifle-butts and bayonets against war-clubs and hatchets. Lizanne was struck by the unnaturally coordinated movements of the Spoiled as they fought, one ducking a swinging rifle-butt whilst its comrade stepped forward to dispatch the sailor who had delivered it, whereupon they both stepped aside in unison to dodge a bayonet charge. It was like some form of dreadful murderous dance and proved dishearteningly effective. Within what seemed like seconds all the sailors lay dead or dying whilst the Spoiled had only lost three of their number.

Lizanne heard Makario let out a shocked gasp as the Spoiled all turned to regard the pair of them. There were a dozen, uniform in their silence if not their appearance, but betraying slight head movements that indicated inner thoughts. *Not thoughts,* Lizanne decided, seeing the Spoiled suddenly take on a more purposeful stance as if some unspoken decision had been reached. *Communication.*

"What do we do now?" Makario asked as the Spoiled started forward.

"Fight. What else?" Lizanne shrugged Tinkerer from her shoulder and pushed him into Makario's arms. "Guard him."

She had time to inject half a vial of Red and Black before the Spoiled closed, fanning out with pistols raised. Lizanne released most of her Black at once, blasting the Spoiled off their feet, then rushed forward to methodically shoot five of them in the head in quick succession as they lay on the deck. The remaining seven were up quickly and immediately began their deadly dance, circling her with frustrating speed and loosing off shots with their revolvers that forced her into a leap. She tumbled in mid air over the head of one of the Spoiled, unleashing Red as she did so. The Spoiled's mismatched garb of Corvantine uniform and Island tribal gear caught light immediately, though his scaly hide proved more resistant to the flames. He swung his war-club at her as she landed, forcing her to back-pedal and use all her remaining Black to propel his flaming body over the side and into the sea.

Another Spoiled loomed out of the smoke left by his comrade's departure, pistol levelled at her head, too close to dodge. Something boomed behind Lizanne and a hole appeared between the Spoiled's eyes as a crimson plume exploded from the back of his skull. Lizanne darted forward to retrieve the fallen Spoiled's revolver, then turned to see Makario hunched against the bulkhead, flaming pistol in hand. The musician held Tinkerer's inert form to his chest in the manner of a human shield, meeting Lizanne's gaze with a tremulous grin.

"I said I didn't like them," he told her. "Not that I couldn't use them."

Lizanne whirled away, feeling the whoosh of a war-club as it passed close to her head. Sending her assailant reeling with a blast of Red at his eyes, she followed up with a quick shot to his chest then leapt again. Bullets buzzed around her as she twisted in mid air, Green-enhanced reflexes given full rein as she targeted each of the remaining Spoiled, felling them all with single shots to the head before her feet met the deck.

She crouched, shuddering as the last of the Green faded from her veins, then looked up at the thump of several large bodies hitting the walkway. She let out a tired groan at the sight of what now confronted her. It appeared the Reds' cargo didn't just consist of Spoiled. The trio of Greens spent a brief moment sniffing the smokey air before fixing their gaze on her and immediately charging, jaws gaping wide as they summoned their flames. If there had been any Green left she might have been able to leap over the drakes at the last moment. But there was no Green so all she could do was inject her remaining Red and Black, hoping to match their flames with her own but knowing it wouldn't be enough.

Flames began to blossom from the mouth of the leading Green as it closed to within a dozen feet, whereupon it was lifted off its claws and propelled into a near by iron support beam with enough force to break its spine. Flames engulfed the two remaining Greens as they whirled to the left to meet the new threat, Lizanne turning to see a slender, soot-covered figure emerge from a hatchway.

Sofiya Griffan seemed to have suddenly acquired a demonic aspect, her face like a mask of white and black and her unbound red hair flowing as she advanced on the Greens, the air around her shimmering with unleashed heat. Lizanne marvelled at the amount of Red she must have ingested, far more than was normally considered safe judging by the intensity of the fire she cast at the Greens. The heat was sufficient to blacken even their fire-resistant hides, causing both to scamper back, squealing in distress in a manner that was almost piteous. Mrs. Griffan, however, appeared to have lost all capacity for pity.

Having forced the pair of Greens to the edge of the walkway she unleashed her Black, tearing the limbs from their torsos, their screams multiplying as the unabated flames met exposed flesh. Even then she wasn't done, advancing to stand over the writhing creatures as she tore ever more flesh from their bones until the screams finally fell silent and they were no more than blackened, twitching husks on the deck.

Sofiya collapsed as Lizanne rushed to her side. She was saying something, lips moving in a faint whisper as she sang a soft tune Lizanne recognised as an old Mandinorian nursery rhyme. "Eat, eat, eat it all up, or you'll get no pudding today . . ."

"Mrs. Griffan," Lizanne said, shaking the woman's shoulder.

There was no response save the continual repetition of the same whispered words. "Eat, eat, eat it all up, or—"

"Sofiya!" Lizanne shook her again, hard enough to force the other woman to turn. Sofiya Griffan blinked at her blankly for several long seconds until recognition dawned.

"Miss Lethridge," Sofiya said, her voice possessed of a calm that seemed completely out of keeping with their present circumstance. "They ate my husband. Ate him all up."

Lizanne glanced back at the hatch from which Sofiya had emerged. It led to the engines, but from the thickness of the smoke billowing from below Lizanne had serious doubts anyone would still be alive down there. She rose, peering through the acrid, billowing fog at the sea beyond the walkway. She could see one of the enemy ships burning, a frigate drifting in a lazy circle as tall flames consumed her superstructure. From the speed at which the wreck passed by the *Profitable*'s starboard beam it was clear that whatever conflagration raged beneath the cruiser's decks, her blood-burners were still operating at full power.

Lizanne went to the rail and leaned out, squinting at the sea beyond the bows. Through the haze she could see two more warships, bright flashes on the fore-decks and the whine of approaching shot indicating they were still very much in this fight. The fact that the *Profitable* was heading straight for the ships told her the cruiser was still answering the helm and Captain Verricks was resolved to see this through to the end.

He's buying time, she realised, turning about and shielding her eyes to scan the eastern horizon. The refugee fleet were dim shapes in the haze now, growing dimmer as they piled on the steam to complete their escape. *Time for them but none for us.*

"Come with me," she said, moving to grasp Sofiya by the arm, pulling her upright and tugging her along. Lizanne found Makario propping Tinkerer up against the bulkhead. "I think he's coming round," he said, catching sight of Lizanne.

"Let's see." She delivered a hard slap to Tinkerer's jaw, provoking a groan and a vague blink of his eyes. Several more slaps were sufficient to return him to consciousness.

"Please stop that," he said as Lizanne drew her hand back for another blow.

"We can't carry you any farther," she said. "Follow and stay close."

Fortunately, Sofiya seemed to have subsided into a state of dumb compliance which made it easy to lead her to the ladder and down to the life-boat derricks. "Oh bother!" Lizanne exclaimed, viewing the shattered and blackened remnants of the boats she had hoped to find.

"There!" Makario said, pointing to the end of the row where a single boat, smaller than the others, lay apparently unscathed if somewhat charred. They rushed to it and climbed in, Lizanne checking to ensure it was equipped with oars before turning her attention to the lowering mechanism.

"Won't someone have to get out and wind it?" Makario asked, his tone indicating a marked reluctance to volunteer.

From above came the grinding whistle of an approaching shell followed by a deafening explosion. "I doubt we have the leisure for that," Lizanne said, pulling Sofiya into a protective huddle as debris rained down about them. When the cascade stopped she focused her gaze on the ropes from which the life-boat was suspended. "Hold on!" she said and used the last vestiges of her Red to burn the ropes away. The life-boat plummeted ten feet to the water, impacting with sufficient force to tip Tinkerer over the side, though Makario was quick to catch hold of his flailing arms.

"Do you have any Green?" Lizanne asked Sofiya after she and Makario had hauled the sputtering artificer back on board. Mrs. Griffan offered a blank stare in response before shrugging her slim shoulders. "Never mind." Lizanne turned to Makario and Tinkerer. "Take the oars. I'll steer."

Their two male companions proved to be inexpert but enthusiastic rowers, their efforts spurred on by a series of explosions that wracked the *Profitable* from end to end as they drew away. Lizanne set the tiller to an easterly course then turned to watch the *Profitable* as it closed on the two enemy frigates.

The huge cruiser's forward guns kept up a steady barrage as she charged on, Lizanne estimating her speed at close to forty knots. Shell after shell tore into her upper works, transforming much of the superstructure into a mangled mass of twisted smoking metal. Judging from the bodies littering the sea the ship's Growlers and Thumpers had taken a fearful toll on the attacking Reds, and only half a dozen remained to torment her, swooping down to cast their flames at the sailors who fought back with rifle fire to little effect. Still the *Profitable* came on, her return fire becoming more accurate as the range diminished. One of the frigates took a full salvo amidships, birthing an instantaneous explosion that tore the warship in two. The stern section sank almost immediately whilst the bows rolled over and lingered on the surface for a short time, Lizanne seeing the ant-like figures of men clinging to the hull.

Not men, she reminded herself, watching the wreck sink beneath the waves amidst a roiling froth of foam and hoping every single member of her inhuman crew drowned along with her.

The *Profitable* changed course, angling her stern towards the sole remaining enemy ship, sirens blaring a salute to what Lizanne knew would be her final act.

CHAPTER 8

Sirus

He could feel them drowning. Over two hundred Spoiled were on the *Losing Proposition* and most of them survived the explosion that ignited her magazine and tore her in two. So Sirus was given a fulsome education in the experience of convulsive gasping as salt water invaded throat and lungs. Even amongst the Spoiled panic would take over at the end, subjugated human instincts reborn at the instant of death. The resultant blossom of terror and desperation should have been repugnant, something to slam his mental shields against. Instead he drank it all in. Fear, he had come to understand, was a precious commodity. He could use this. Constant exposure to a life of horrors was creating an ever-thicker callus around his soul, eroding his capacity to feel anything. When his own reserves of fear were depleted now he could summon the memories of the dead to guard his mind. This he did now as he sent a silent pulse of thanks into the fading minds of the Spoiled as they slipped into the depths.

The *Losing Proposition* had been the fastest and least damaged ship in their small fleet, her original name of the *Negotiator* scraped from her hull and replaced by something more to Catheline's liking. It transpired that the Blood-blessed woman had a flair for the ironic. Sirus's command ship, a heavy frigate once dubbed the IPV *Position of Strength*, was now the *Imminent Demise*, a name that seemed increasingly appropriate as the huge Protectorate battleship loomed ever larger in the bridge window.

"Hard to starboard!" he commanded aloud to the Spoiled at the helm, simultaneously sending a thought-command to the engine room: *Reverse starboard paddle.*

The *Imminent Demise* veered away as the battleship came on, paddles turning the sea to foam on either side of her hull. Despite the damage that had wrecked much of her upper works, the fire of the battleship's forward batteries continued unabated. Sirus had ordered the guns seized by the Spoiled the Reds had deposited on the ship but resistance from the Protectorate crew had been ferocious. Consequently, all but a handful from an assault force of over fifty had been killed. They had succeeded in dispatching over twice their number in the savage fighting that raged throughout the ship, but a vessel this size had plenty of crewmen in reserve. Sirus felt sure that one of his squads, all veterans of the Barrier Isles campaign, would have succeeded in silencing the guns if they hadn't encountered the Lethridge woman.

Sirus's mind had been fully occupied with marshalling his fleet against the battleship and her fearsomely accurate guns, but the rush of recognition experienced by the Spoiled boarding party had cut through the competing morass of image and sensation. Lizanne Lethridge's face had been plucked from the memory of one of the few Exceptional Initiatives agents captured at Feros and seared into the mind of every Spoiled by Catheline herself. The image had been accompanied by an implacable instruction: *Kill this woman on sight.*

They had certainly tried, Sirus taking charge of the squad and orchestrating an assault that should have left Miss Lethridge a bullet-riddled corpse. The notion of summoning a burst of fear to mask his mind and allow her to escape fluttered through his head, but he resisted it. Recognition of this woman had spread throughout the fleet and across the many miles to Feros; Catheline would know.

In the event, no subterfuge was necessary. Sirus had faced many formidable people in battle before, wickedly skilled Island warriors, the Shaman King and grizzled Protectorate veterans during his warship-seizing operations. But watching this woman as she leapt and shot, utilising her powers with an economy and ferocity that was truly frightening, he knew he was looking upon the most dangerous individual he was ever likely to meet.

He had come close, however, his sole remaining Spoiled might actually have done the deed if Lethridge's companion hadn't intervened. The woman's face disappeared into instant blackness as the bullet tore through the Spoiled's brain and Sirus felt a painful howl of frustration filling his mind. The connection to his fellow Spoiled was lost as the howl continued, accompanied by a lacerating fury as Catheline gave full vent to her feelings.

Sink that fucking ship, Admiral, her mind boomed in his head. *Whatever the cost. I want that bitch dead!*

He had organised his ships into a broad semicircle, the two more lightly armed sloops at either end and heavily armed frigates in the centre. The whole affair would have been over fairly quickly if a sufficient number of Blues had been with them, but it transpired the aquatic drakes were unable to keep pace with steam-powered ships for more than a few hours at a time. Consequently, their accompanying force of two dozen Blues were nowhere in sight when the Protectorate fleet hove into view, obliging Sirus to fight the battle with the forces on hand.

He ordered the two sloops to use their superior speed to dart close to the battleship, loose off a rapid salvo then withdraw so as to divide the enemy's fire whilst the frigates' barrage did most of the damage. All the while the Reds conducted harassing dives on the battleship, sweeping her decks with fire. It had been an effective if costly tactic so far, most of the Reds had fallen to the battleship's deadly repeating guns and a sloop and a frigate had been destroyed thanks to sheer weight of gunnery. But it was working. The big ship could only take so much more, despite her captain's impressive manoeuvring and the desperate courage of her crew. All they had to do was draw back a mile or so and let her exhaust her reserves of product before closing in for the kill. But with Catheline's command the time for tactical niceties was over.

Sirus ordered his three remaining ships into a tight formation and launched them head-on at the battleship. The other sloop went down first, striking out in the lead only to be caught by a mixture of heavy and light armament when she drew within four hundred yards of the enemy. Both her paddles were wrecked within minutes and her boiler exploded as she foundered. The *Losing Proposition* went next, felled by a lucky plunging shot to the magazine, which left the *Imminent Demise* to face the dying monster alone.

"Midships," Sirus ordered as the frigate's bow swung north. He sent a command to the engine room to set both paddles into forward motion but a glance through the side-window told him it wouldn't be enough.

The battleship loomed over the smaller vessel as the two ships closed, the repeating guns on the Protectorate ship raking the *Imminent Demise* from stern to bow. Sirus dived to the deck as cannon shells and bullets tore the bridge apart, showering him with shattered glass and timber. He felt the ship heave to port and looked up to see the helmsman lying near by. A cannon shell appeared to have punched clean through the Spoiled and he lay gazing at the smoke rising from the hole in his chest, yellow eyes curious rather than afraid.

Sirus tore his gaze from the sight and scrambled upright, lurching towards the wheel in the vain hope he might correct the ship's course whilst she could still make headway. He was propelled off his feet before he could reach it, the entire ship wracked by a mighty shudder as the battleship rammed into her port beam at full speed. Ironwork screamed in protest as the huge ship's prow tore into the guts of the *Imminent Demise*, steam exploding up through the sundered deck as her boiler burst. For a moment it seemed as if the battleship would slice the frigate clean in two but then her velocity suddenly diminished, Sirus assumed due to her blood-burners finally exhausting their fuel.

He had been thrown clear of the wrecked bridge and found himself clinging to the starboard railing. The sea seemed to be heaving around him and he realised the two ships were now locked together in a mad dance. The frigate's starboard paddle was still turning and the battleship had brought her auxiliary engines on-line, forcing the two vessels into an erratic pirouette as neither had sufficient power to break free of the other. However, a quick scan of the minds of his remaining crew told Sirus the *Imminent Demise* would soon live up to its name. The impact had torn a gaping rent in the port hull plating and several tons of water had already deluged the hold and the ballast tanks. She would go under in minutes.

Sink it! Catheline's voice in his head, shrill and undeniable in its compulsion. *Kill her!*

Sirus found a pair of Spoiled crewmen attempting to shore up the hull and sent them to the magazine instead. He also found a drowning Spoiled trapped beneath an iron beam in engineering. The man had been an armourer on a Protectorate vessel before his capture and it was an easy matter to pluck the required knowledge from his head before the rising waters claimed his final breath. Sirus instantly shared the knowledge with the two Spoiled in the magazine. They completed the task with the kind of efficiency only the Spoiled could display, pushing the detonators into the sacks of propellant and rigging the fuses in a scant few minutes.

Sirus clambered back onto the listing deck of his short-lived command, gazing up at the prow of the battleship above. *The* Profitable Venture, he read from the iron-lettered plate behind the great ship's anchor mounting. *Not today, it seems.* A bullet ricocheted off the bulkhead a few feet away as a Protectorate marksman tried his luck. Sirus ignored it, instead focusing his gaze on the tallest figure he could see amongst the riflemen assembled along the battleship's rail. Whether the man was the captain, or even an officer, he couldn't tell, but Sirus straightened and offered a perfect salute nevertheless. It seemed only polite.

He never knew if the man returned the salute for at that moment Catheline's thoughts pushed their way into his. *Very noble, I'm sure, Admiral. But we still have need of you. Time for a swim.*

This command was no more resistible than the others and Sirus turned and sprinted for the starboard rail without pause, chased all the way by Protectorate rifle fire. He leapt over the rail and dived into the sea, plunging deep and staying below the surface as he swam away. The magazine blew when he had covered perhaps twenty yards. The blast wave would probably have killed a non-Spoiled, forcing the remaining air from his lungs and propelling him to the surface, his back arched like a bow.

Air flooded his lungs as he reared up out of the water, floundering for a brief time before his instinctive panic receded. He let the fear linger as he bobbed on the surface, gazing at the final moments of the two warships. The explosion had torn the *Imminent Demise* free of her ugly embrace with the larger vessel and she foundered quickly, Sirus once again sharing the final agonies of a drowning crew.

The *Profitable Venture* took longer to die. The explosion had torn away most of her prow, revealing the corridors and compartments of her innards. Smoke and flame gouted from deep within her then died as the decks flooded. Her stern reared up as the forward section became inundated, her massive rudder turning this way and that like the tail of some huge, wounded fish. The battleship emitted a last, forlorn groan as she sank, men dropping from her flanks like flies escaping a submerging corpse. Then the rudder slipped into the patch of frothing sea and she was gone.

Night seemed to fall quickly, though his sense of time slipped away as delirium took hold. As disciplined as his mind was it remained susceptible to the depredations of persistent cold, thirst and hunger. A short exploration of the surrounding water had discovered a shattered piece of life-boat. Sirus clung to it, managing to keep the upper half of himself out of the water to stave off the deadly chill. From the diminishing screams of the Protectorate sailors not far off, it seemed most of them had not been so lucky.

The temptation to let go of his fear was strong, his resolve leeching away with every passing hour. *What does it matter now?* he pondered, too numb to feel the pain of the all-encompassing chill. *Let her see it all. The last testament of a dying man.*

For some reason Katrya's face came to him as his mental defences began to erode, threatening to reveal his scheming, his desperate desire for release from this bondage. It was Katrya who stopped him. Her face was not the one she wore when he killed her. This was her human face, the pale, frightened visage of the young woman he had sheltered with in the Morsvale sewers. *Why are they doing this?* she had whispered to him then as they huddled beneath a drain cover listening to the horrors unfolding in the streets above. *What do they want?*

He had no answer for her then, but he had one now. *Because they hate us, and they want everything.*

He let out a shout as consciousness returned, thrashing in the water and nearly losing his grip on the wreckage. *Hold on to the fear!* he commanded himself, summoning the sensations he had stolen from the drowning Spoiled. It was possible there were others in the army who had learned how to mask their thoughts in the same manner and he was determined not to allow Catheline to learn the secret. *Give her nothing. Even if you die here.*

So he clung to his flotsam, shivering in fear and cold as the night wore on until the first slivers of sunlight snaked through the clouded eastern sky. Finally, the last of his strength seeped away and his hands lost purchase on the wreckage. He lay back as the swell carried him off, waiting for the sea to claim him and staring up at the dimly lit clouds . . . Then blinked as a large black shape soared into view, folded its wings and dived down towards him, claws extending.

Katarias, Sirus thought as the Red plucked him from the water and beat his wings to strike out on a westward course. Before Sirus slipped into unconsciousness he entertained the notion that the drake had found him hours before but delayed his rescue, curious to see how long he would last.

His new flagship was a diminutive mail-carrier recently renamed the *Fallen Stock*. She had a single paddle at the stern driven by the most recent mark of steam engine. Sirus recalled from the inventory provided by Veilmist, the Island girl turned mathematical genius, that this craft was the fastest civilian vessel they possessed. It seemed he had Catheline to thank for ordering the mail-carrier to follow the ill-fated battle fleet as added insurance.

Katarias had dumped his inert form on the fore-deck before taking perch on the small ship's bridgehouse. The drake's weight was sufficient to buckle the ceiling and cause the ship to dip several inches. Sirus spent a day in delirious slumber belowdecks, being fed broth by his Spoiled crewmates until he returned to full consciousness. Once again he found himself marvelling at the fortitude of his remade body. An ordeal that would certainly have killed his human form was now little more than a daylong inconvenience.

Welcome back, Admiral, Catheline's thoughts greeted him when he made his way to the bridge the following morning. *May I say how gratified I am by your survival, sir. This whole enterprise would be much less entertaining without you.*

You do me too much credit, miss, he replied. *My orders?*

Sadly, it seems your mighty efforts proved in vain. She pushed a vision into his head. It showed an eye-level view of the sea, the waves swept by gusts of thick smoke. The vision kept fading to grey before springing back into clarity, from which Sirus deduced it had been captured by an injured Spoiled near the point of exhaustion. *There,* Catheline said, freezing the memory and dispelling any extraneous detail to focus on a vague shape in the smoke. Spoiled eyes were capable of capturing much more detail than human vision so even through the haze it was possible to discern the shape of a life-boat. Catheline magnified the image, revealing the slim form of a woman seated at the stern of the boat.

Lizanne Lethridge, Sirus commented, stoking his fear to conceal the twinge of admiration for the woman's resourcefulness.

Isn't she just so appallingly aggravating? Catheline replied. *The poor fellow who saw this didn't last much longer, I'm afraid. But it seems the boat was heading west. It's possible the sea may claim her before she finds rescue, but I doubt our luck is that good. Follow her, my dear faithful Admiral. Find out her destination then await us. We are coming. All of us.*

CHAPTER 9

Lizanne

"What is that?" Makario said, peering at the western horizon. Lizanne followed his gaze, regretting the lack of Green to enhance her vision. Spending the better part of two days in this life-boat with no provisions or product had left them all in a state of chilled lethargy, apart from Sofiya Griffan, who maintained the same rigid and silent posture throughout. Lizanne found her vision blurring as she tried to focus on the small speck in the distance, hoping not to discern the flap of wings as it drew nearer. However, it was Tinkerer who solved the mystery

"An aerostat," he said, his brow furrowed as if trying to recall something out of reach. "I don't know how I know that."

"The Artisan knew it," Lizanne said. "It seems not everything is locked away after all."

It took an hour for the aerostat to draw close enough for Lizanne to make out its two occupants. A diminutive figure sat in front manning what Lizanne assumed were the contraption's controls whilst a person of considerably bulkier proportions tended to what appeared to be some kind of flaming brazier situated in the middle of the gondola.

"A caloric oil burner," Tinkerer observed. "Hot air is a reasonable alternative to a chemical lifting agent. Though the design is crude."

"I'd advise strongly against telling him that," Lizanne said.

She waved her arms as the aerostat slowed to an uneven hover a hundred feet above. The propeller on the single engine at the stern spun fast enough to blur its blades but seemed to be having difficulty making headway against the prevailing westerly winds. She saw Jermayah lean over the side of the gondola and drop something. It splashed into the water a few feet shy of the life-boat's bows where it bobbed on the surface until Makario retrieved it with one of the oars. It was a tarpaulin sack rigged with floats, quickly opened to reveal a large flask of water, some loaves and cured ham and, to Lizanne's great relief, one small vial of Green.

She looked up as Jermayah shouted something from above, the words mostly swamped by the noise of the engine and the wind but she was sure she caught the word "back." She saw Tekela give a wave before returning her hands to the controls whereupon the aerostat turned about and flew off towards the west. It seemed to Lizanne that its departure had been much swifter than its approach.

"Couldn't they have taken us with them?" Makario asked around a mouthful of bread. Lizanne had noted that his usual decorum, and refined accent, had slipped somewhat during their time in the boat.

"I doubt it can lift more than two persons at a time," Tinkerer replied, eyes locked on the receding craft and head presumably filling with numerous design improvements. Lizanne wondered if her father would welcome the artificer's input and found herself doubting it. Though the prospect of their meeting did fill her with a certain guilty anticipation.

She retrieved the flask of Green from the sack and sat beside Sofiya. Removing the stopper, she held the flask up to the woman's nose in the hope the scent of product might provoke her into some kind of animation. Instead, she was rewarded with only a small nose wrinkle.

"Drink," Lizanne said. "It'll restore you."

That drew a response, Sofiya turning her head to regard Lizanne with a vacant stare. "Can you restore my husband, Miss Lethridge?" she asked, her tone light and conversational. "The father to the child I carry. Can you restore him?"

Lizanne saw it then, the way the woman's hands were clasped over her belly in a tight protective shield. "Emperor's balls," Makario muttered. "Just what we need." He fell silent as Lizanne shot him a warning glare.

"No," she said, turning back to Sofiya. "I cannot." She reached out to prise the woman's hands apart, placing the vial in her palm. "But I can keep you both alive. Don't you think he would want that?"

Sofiya stared at the vial in her hand then put it to her lips and took a small sip, Lizanne taking some gratification from the faint colour she saw blossom in the woman's cheeks.

"So what now?" Makario asked.

"We eat," Lizanne said, reaching for the sack again. "And await rescue."

"It may have escaped your notice, miss," Captain Trumane said. "But, since Captain Verricks and Director Thriftmor can no longer be counted amongst the living, command responsibility for this fleet now rests with me. I'll thank you to leave decisions regarding our course in my hands."

They were alone in his cabin, Lizanne having been granted an interview only after the most strenuous insistence. Captain Trumane, it seemed, had none of Captain Verricks's pragmatism when it came to advice offered by an Exceptional Initiatives agent.

Lizanne hadn't been offered a seat but took one anyway, slumping into the chair opposite the captain's desk and running a weary hand over her forehead. It had taken three hours for the *Viable Opportunity* to appear and rescue them, and most of that time had been taken up with coaxing Sofiya into eating something. She was in the care of the ship's doctor now, a highly capable and affable man named Weygrand Lizanne recalled from some of Clay's memories. Glancing up at Trumane's arch, imperious visage above his steepled fingers, she couldn't help but wish events had conspired to keep this man in a comatose state, which would have placed the good doctor next in line for command.

"As a matter of professional courtesy," she began with all the politeness she could muster, "what is our present destination?"

She saw Trumane's face twitch in an unconscious expression of discomfort. It was probably some effect of his prolonged coma and it told her a great deal. *Wherever we're going, he's not happy about it.*

"Given our current fuel stocks, not to mention the supply situation," Trumane replied, "there is only one viable course." His face twitched again and he let out a small cough before continuing. "Varestia," he said. "Specifically the Red Tides."

Lizanne stared at him, her lips curling as she contained an incredulous laugh. "I know only a little of your career, Captain," she said. "So please correct me if my memory plays me false. Is it not the case that for most of your active service you have been engaged in antipiracy operations?"

Trumane coughed again. "Quite correct."

"So, it would be a fair assumption that your name and reputation will be well known amongst piratical circles."

"A fair assumption indeed."

"Then please explain to me why sailing into the most pirate-infested region in the world at the head of an unarmed fleet of civilian vessels is such a good idea."

"There is nowhere else!" Trumane slammed his hands onto the desk, face twitching with renewed intensity. He glared at Lizanne for a long moment before composing himself, leaning back and straightening his uniform as he added, "Not unless you think it wise we try our luck in a south Corvantine port."

This was a point Lizanne was forced to concede. There was little prospect of finding safe harbour in one of the ports on the southern Corvantine coast. The region was a hotbed of Imperial loyalists and the chaos caused by the as yet incomplete revolution would surely make for a hostile reception from the local authorities. But the welcome they would receive in Varestian waters might well be worse.

"The *Viable* is the only warship in the fleet," she said. "Even with two Blood-blessed on board to fire the engine and augment the defences, it won't be able to protect every ship from seizure by pirates."

"Not all Varestians are pirates," Trumane replied. "Though they do tend to be universally greedy. They formed a government of sorts after the Empire lost control of the region, the seat of which is located at the Seven Walls. We will sail there and seek asylum in return for suitable compensation from the Ironship Syndicate."

"The Seven Walls sits at the heart of the Red Tides," Lizanne pointed out. "That's a considerable distance to cover without drawing unwelcome attention, regardless of what agreement we might want to make."

Trumane's brow furrowed as he spent a moment in silent calculation, before his expression brightened fractionally. "Then we have your esteemed father to thank for providing the means of sending an advance party," he said, the first smile Lizanne had seen him make appearing on his twitching face. "Miss Lethridge, please do not worry that I might dissuade you from volunteering for such a mission. I feel that keeping you cooped up aboard ship would be a singular waste of your talents."

"It's supposed to have a frame."

Lizanne smothered a laugh as she watched Tinkerer unceremoniously pluck the pencil from her father's hand and begin sketching lines on his blueprint. From the look on the professor's face she deduced he was simply too shocked to voice an objection.

"A rigid envelope allows for more capacity and durability," Tinkerer went on, the pencil moving in swift, precise strokes across the diagram. "And stronger fabric. Silk is far too fragile." He stopped drawing and stepped back, turning to regard her father's rapidly darkening countenance.

"And why," Professor Lethridge began, voice possessed of a distinct quaver, "should I take any advice from the likes of . . ."

"Three concentric rings connected by diagonal cross-beams," Jermayah broke in, lips pursed as he surveyed the altered blueprint. "You know, that might actually work, Professor." He raised an eyebrow at Tinkerer. "Materials?"

"In the absence of a bespoke composite alloy, hollow copper tubing would be the best substitute."

Professor Lethridge gave a snort but, Lizanne noted, failed to voice any further objections as Tinkerer went on to make additional modifications to the design for an improved aerostat. "The control surfaces are too small . . . Increased lifting capacity will allow for the addition of a second engine . . ."

Lizanne left them to it, deciding to check on Makario's progress with the solargraph. Captain Trumane had ordered a good-sized portion of the *Viable*'s hold cleared for use as a makeshift workshop. This included a curtained-off section where the musician had some measure of privacy whilst he attempted to decipher the device's musical mysteries. It sat on the work-bench, its various cogs and wheels gleaming in the lamplight. During the siege of Carvenport they had taken the first steps to unlocking a few of its secrets, such as the fact that it was powered by music, or "kinetic resonance," as Jermayah termed it. However, to Lizanne it remained as unknowable and frustrating an enigma as when she first set eyes on it in the office of the unfortunate Diran Akiv Kapazin. As yet, despite Makario's efforts, it had signally failed to reveal any clue as to how it might unlock the secrets in Tinkerer's head. She had asked Tekela to assist, hoping the girl's musical insights might yield some progress, as they had in Jermayah's workshop.

"Wrong," Tekela said as Makario finished tapping out another tune on the device's exposed chimes. "I doubt the Artisan would have chosen something so ugly. He had far too much taste for that. Try this." She went on to sing a short melody in her fine, accomplished voice. She seemed oblivious to Makario's baleful stare which Lizanne fancied was at least a match for the one her father had directed at Tinkerer. The tune was wordless, formed only of notes into something both pleasing and haunting to the ear. It reminded Lizanne of "The Leaves of Autumn," the tune that had first caused the solargraph's gears to turn in Jermayah's workshop, in feeling rather than composition.

"I don't recognise it," Makario grated when Tekela fell silent.

"You wouldn't," she replied. "I made it up."

"If this infernal thing is powered by music, it will be by a composition from the Artisan's era. May I point out, miss, that only one of us is an expert in musical history."

Tekela made a face and arched an eyebrow at Lizanne. "He's just jealous because I have perfect pitch."

"Perfect pitch is just a trick," Makario stated, bridling as his face darkened further. "I once saw a monkey with perfect pitch in a circus."

"Try it," Lizanne said before Tekela could give voice to a no-doubt-vicious rejoinder. "We've tried every other tune the Artisan might have heard in his lifetime and all they do is cause the levers to turn, which describes the orbits of the three moons but fails to convey anything actually meaningful. There is more to this thing than just astronomy. It has another secret to tell and we know the Artisan was scrupulous in guarding his secrets. He may well have used a unique composition, one known only to himself."

Makario huffed but dutifully raised the silver spoon he had borrowed from the officers' mess and tapped out the notes of Tekela's song on the chimes. "See?" he said, moving back as the tune faded. "A fruitless . . ."

He gave a start as a soft click came from the solargraph. It was faint, but definite evidence that somewhere within the complex array of components that formed the device's innards, something had responded to the tune. Makario immediately repeated the sequence, all animosity replaced by a steady-eyed concentration. This time, however, the solargraph failed to respond.

"The main theme from 'The Leaves of Autumn,'" he said, reaching for pen and paper and scribbling down a series of musical notes. "What else?"

"'Dance of the Heavens,'" Tekela said. "The second movement. Also, the choral melody from 'The Maiden's Fall.'"

Makario wrote down all the notes from each piece, one beneath the other. "Now your little tune," he said, setting the notes out at the bottom of the page. He stared at it for a moment then let out a soft laugh. "See it?" he said, holding the paper out to Lizanne. Music had never been her subject and she had only a bored child's understanding of musical notation so immediately passed the page to Tekela.

"I don't . . ." she began after scanning the notes, then frowned as comprehension dawned. "A descending scale," she said. "They all share the same descending scale, but at different tempos."

Makario nodded and tapped a series of notes onto the chimes. This time the response was much more prolonged and impressive. All three of the solargraph's levers turned at once, moving with more energy than Lizanne had seen before whilst several of the cogs along its sides spun fast enough to blur. It lasted for no more than three seconds then stopped after which the solargraph emitted a series of notes of its own. It was the same melody Makario had tapped out, but at a much slower tempo, and also followed by several more notes. To Lizanne's ears the tune possessed much the same melancholy flavour as "The Leaves of Autumn" and the other centuries-old tunes the device had so far responded to. She could also tell it was incomplete, the final note cutting off abruptly as if the solargraph had been silenced in mid-conversation.

"I do believe we might have made some progress," Makario said. "Perhaps our fellow former inmate can shine some more light on it."

"Not yet," Lizanne replied. "I'd rather his energies were concentrated on the new aerostat, for now at least." She nodded at the solargraph. "Do you think you can get it to play the whole tune?"

"With time and"—he cast a reluctant glance in Tekela's direction—"some further assistance. Music is a code after all." He nodded at the page of notes he had scribbled down. "At least now we have the beginnings of a key, and thanks to the additional notes it played, a clue as to where to look next."

"So what are you calling this one?" Lizanne enquired as Jermayah crouched to undo the ties on a canvas-wrapped item on the deck. "Do you have a new Whisper for me? I must say I miss the old one."

He gave a soft grunt, shaking his shaggy head as he stepped back to reveal his latest invention. "This one doesn't whisper. Could call it the Shouter, if you like."

At first glance it appeared to be a standard-issue Silworth .31 lever-action repeating carbine, albeit modified with a slightly longer barrel and more elaborate fore- and rearsights. The wooden stock had also been augmented with a brass shoulder plate and spring arrangement. However, the strangest modification was that the upper half of the breach mechanism had been replaced by glass instead of the usual iron.

"Something occurred to me during that business in Carvenport," Jermayah began. "Takes a keen eye and a skilled hand to kill a full-grown drake with a fire-arm. It's one thing for a Contractor to do it on a hunt through the Interior, different matter in the midst of a battle. The Thumpers and Growlers are fine and good, but you need a whole crew to work them. The mini-Growler I built in Feros could do the job but it eats up a huge amount of ammunition and takes too long to manufacture. If we had a mass-producible small-arm that could do the job with only a few shots, seems to me things might go better for us."

Lizanne cast a doubtful gaze over the carbine. "This can kill a drake?"

"Surely can, provided you load it with the right ammunition." He produced a cartridge from his pocket and tossed it to her. It was about a third longer than a standard carbine round with a more pointed bullet featuring a slight indentation at its base.

"This isn't steel," she said, touching a finger to the tip of the bullet. Military-grade rounds were usually formed of a lead core surrounded by a hard-steel jacket. Jermayah had apparently crafted something new in this one.

"Titanium," he said. "Hard enough to punch through the hide of any drake. Your father had a small stock of it set aside, but couldn't remember what he was going to use it for. He also had some magnesium and mercury. So you have a titanium-tipped projectile which collapses on impact to set off a composite explosive charge. Took a little experimenting but I think you'll find the results impressive."

He hefted an empty brandy-keg the ship's galley no longer had a use for and made ready to toss it over the side. Lizanne bent to retrieve the carbine from the deck, finding it marginally heavier than a standard-issue model, but not enough to be unwieldy. She slotted the cartridge into the tubular magazine below the barrel, worked the lever to chamber the round and put the stock against her shoulder.

"Very well," she said. "Have you ranged the sights?"

"Fifty yards," Jermayah told her before heaving the keg into the sea. "Put some whitewash in to illustrate the effect."

Lizanne stepped to the rail, tracking the keg's progress towards the stern. The *Viable Opportunity* was maintaining a slow speed to keep pace with the rest of the convoy so her target took a moment or two to drift the required distance. When she judged it to be about fifty yards away she raised the carbine's barrel, centring the fore- and rearsights on the bobbing keg. The wind was slight today so she didn't need to account for it as she exhaled and squeezed the trigger. The sound of the bullet's leaving the barrel did indeed resemble a shout, though the recoil was less severe than she might have expected. The stock seemed to pulse against her shoulder instead of the usual hard shove and the foresight deviated from the target by only a few degrees. Consequently, she had a fine view of the brandy-keg as it transformed into a cloud of white vapour. There wasn't even enough left of it to litter the surrounding water with debris.

"One, maybe two to stop an adult Green," Jermayah mused. "Three for a Red. Blue's a different matter of course, but you should still be able to do some serious damage. It'll also fire standard rounds if you need to shoot a Spoiled."

Lizanne lowered the carbine and ejected the spent cartridge with a smooth motion of the lever, catching it before it could fall to the deck. It was hot, but not enough to burn and leached a thick foul-smelling cloud of spent propellant.

"Had to mix a variety of agents to get enough power behind the bullet," Jermayah said with an apologetic wince. "Couldn't make it smokeless."

Lizanne grinned and blew the fumes from the bullet before tossing it over the side. "Then I'll call it the 'Smoker.'" She tapped the glass covering the upper portion of the breach. "And this?"

"That's for an old friend." He produced another cartridge from his pocket, holding it up for inspection. This projectile was more elongated than those she had used in her Whisper, but still recognisable from the viscous liquid she could see inside the glass cylinder.

"Redball," Lizanne said, remembering the various forms of carnage she had inflicted with the product-fuelled round.

"Three times the range of the pistol version," Jermayah said. "Could only buy enough Red to make a dozen though, so best forgo the test firing, eh?"

She nodded, reaching out to take the cartridge. "And the explosive rounds?"

"Just thirty. I had just bought enough magnesium and mercury to make a hundred but . . ." He trailed off, face darkening.

"Did you see it?" Lizanne asked. "My aunt?"

He shook his head. "It all happened so fast. It was Tekela who woke us, told us we had to get in the aerostat and leave. Your aunt didn't believe it, or didn't want to. She went outside to look for herself. Not an easy thing to just fly away from the place you've lived all your life, I suppose. It's my belief she locked the workshop doors so the drakes couldn't get in when she saw what was happening. Even then." He paused and gave a sad, helpless shrug. "If your ward hadn't gotten her hands on the mini-Growler we'd certainly have shared your aunt's fate."

"We'll need more of those before long." Lizanne hefted the carbine. "And more of these."

"Only so much we can do on this tub. Not a lot to work with."

"I'll see about rectifying that. In the meantime"—she shouldered the carbine and started towards the ladder to the crew quarters—"I have a long-delayed call to make."

Do you believe it? Clay asked as the last images of his journey through the world beneath the ice folded back into the grey hues of Nelphia's surface.

Lizanne took a long time to reply. Absorbing such a quantity of new and incredible information left her own mindscape in an unusual state of disarray. The whirlwinds twisted and entwined with the kind of energy that only came from confusion and indecision. Neither were sensations she enjoyed.

I don't wish to cause offence, Mr. Torcreek, she told him after managing to straighten some of the more fractious whirlwinds. *But I doubt you are capable of constructing memories of such . . . remarkable variety and precision.*

Got plenty of wild tales of your own, he observed and their joined minds shared a brief instant of empathic humour. *Bringing down the entire Corvie Empire. Quite a feat, miss. Even for you.*

A house built with rotten timbers on shaky foundations was always bound to fall. My concern is what they'll build in its place.

Think we got more pressing concerns than that.

She took a moment to calm her mind yet further, forcing the whirlwinds into a reasonable semblance of order, before sending him a pulse of agreement. *You're certain of this woman's motives? You believe she only wants to help?*

I believe she wants to put right what her people did wrong. But I'm pretty sure there's a good deal she hasn't shared yet. I'm hoping I'll get some answers at Krystaline Lake.

Returning to Arradsia at this juncture seems excessively risky. It's likely the entire continent is now under the sway of the White.

Maybe not. It ain't there just now, don't forget. And there are limits to what it can do. Silverpin showed us that. Besides, I'm all out of other options, lest you got something to share.

Tell Captain Hilemore to sail for Varestia. We will join forces. It was a suggestion that would have carried more weight when spoken aloud, but in the trance she knew he could sense the reluctant insincerity in it. They were both fully aware he would sail to Arradsia and then journey on to Krystaline Lake, whatever the cost.

Guess that settles it, he observed.

So it seems. However, I feel it would be better if Captain Hilemore stayed with his command this time. Given the fate of the Corvantine main battle fleet he now commands possibly the most advanced warship in the world. An asset we'll need in the days to come.

He'll be hard to convince. Not the kind who likes to sit out the big show.

Frame it as an order from me if it helps.

With Feros gone I ain't too sure how he'll feel about taking orders, and my influence ain't what it was. But I'll try. When will you be able to trance again?

I'm not sure. The welcome we'll receive in the Red Tides is . . . uncertain to say the least.

Dealt with a fair few Varestians in my time. They're a practical folk above all else, and they got spies everywhere. They have to know what's been happening, or at least a good deal of it. Could be they don't need as much persuading as you think. Besides which, there's a service you could do me in Varestia.

He went on to explain about Zenida Okanas and her father's connection to whatever lay beneath the waters of Krystaline Lake. *A place called the High Wall,* Clay told her. *She says he had a pile of maps there. They'll be useful if we're gonna find this thing.*

I'll see what I can do, Lizanne replied. She paused and their shared mindscape took on a darker hue as the knowledge of what had befallen Feros struck home once again. *What will you tell your uncle?* she asked.

The truth. Think he and Lori deserve that much. Lines of deep red began to snake through the moon-dust like miniature lava floes. Grief took many forms in the trance, it seemed that in his case it burned. *Looks like we both lost an aunt, huh? And Joya. Was hoping I'd see her again one day.*

We don't fully know what happened yet, she replied. *There may yet be a chance some people escaped. The refugees were ever a resourceful lot.* It was scant comfort, something else they both knew, but it was all she had.

Where are you now? she asked, happy to alter the topic of conversation.

Saw our last iceberg two days ago, so a good lick farther north. Captain Hilemore reckons another two weeks before we sight Arradsia. Would be quicker if we weren't nurse-maiding that old Blue-hunter. They're awful scared of Jack. Makes me nervous.

The connection thrummed as Lizanne's Blue began to fade. *Guess it's time to say our farewells for now,* Clay observed.

Wait. Lizanne drew one of her whirlwinds closer and formed it into one of his shared memories, the aerostat of marvellous design he had used to escape the world below the ice. *I need more images of this. Anything you can remember. And anything that woman told you about it.*

Think you can copy it, huh? he asked, swiftly moving to comply. Nelphia's surface sprouted a new crop of memories, the dust blossoming into a panoply of image and sensation.

The drakes hold a very singular advantage over us, she replied, opening her mind to drink in all the knowledge before the Blue ran out. *If we can contest the skies, we may have a chance.*

CHAPTER 10

Hilemore

They were forced to leave the *Dreadfire* behind. Hilemore had briefly considered taking her under tow but that would have required leaving a skeleton crew on board and they had barely enough hands for the *Superior* as it was. He took possession of Captain Bledthorne's charts and log, thinking they would be a boon to any historian, especially one with deep pockets. Following a brief solo inspection to ensure every scrap of anything useful had been removed from the hold he strode across her deck for what he knew would be the last time.

"Sorry, old girl," he whispered, running a hand over her timbers before stepping onto the gang-plank. "I doubt you'd have liked the modern world, in any case. It's far too noisy."

"Sir?" Steelfine asked from the other side of the walkway.

"Nothing, Number One." Hilemore crossed to the *Superior*, gesturing for the gang-plank to be removed. "Let's get these lines cast off and see her on her way."

"Could set a fire in her belly, sir," Steelfine suggested. "Give her a decent funeral. The King of the Deep's been expecting her, after all."

"Then he'll have to wait awhile longer."

Hilemore lingered to watch the old ship slip away from the *Superior*'s port side. The prevailing currents swept southwards in the Whirls and soon the *Dreadfire* was drawn back into the channel through which she had carried them to safety. Despite her lost masts and many wounds, Hilemore thought she still retained a defiant aspect, as if all the long years in the ice and the recent fury of battle had been unable to dent her pride. "Perhaps," he commented to Steelfine, "in a century or two she'll provide a refuge for some other desperate souls."

He waited until the *Dreadfire* had vanished completely into the maze of ice before turning about and striding towards the bridge. "Weigh anchor and signal the *Farlight* to make steam and take the lead. It's only proper since they know the way out."

It transpired that Lieutenant Talmant had done an excellent job of clearing a channel through the Chokes to the open sea. The young officer had used his stock of explosives wisely, blasting a course through the obstructing ice that was narrow but straight enough to eliminate the need for any tricky manoeuvring. Hilemore had ordered Talmant and his small squad back to the *Superior*, seeing little need to maintain a supervising presence on the *Farlight* now their escape route had been secured. In fact Hilemore nursed a secret hope the Blue-hunter might decide to follow her own course once free of the Chokes, thinking Captain Tidelow and his crew more of an irksome burden than useful allies. But, upon reaching the open sea the other ship duly fell in behind the *Superior* as she set her bows due north. So far she showed little sign of shirking the warship's protection.

Scrimshine, against the odds generated by the growing pool of bets on the possibility of his demise, recovered from his gas-related illness seven days after the ships cleared the Chokes. Having been released from the sick bay on Skaggerhill's advice he stood in the bridge entrance, swaying a little as he offered Hilemore a clumsy salute. "Reporting for duty, Skip—" he began before correcting himself. "Sir."

Scrimshine's already cadaverous face had been rendered even more gaunt and his colour was pale. However, what distracted Hilemore the most was the fact that the man was wearing a Protectorate uniform for the first time since joining the ship. Furthermore, it appeared to have been cleaned and pressed.

"Skipper will do, Mr. Scrimshine," Hilemore told him. "I've grown accustomed to it." He gestured at the wheel, which had been manned by Talmant for the past week. "Relieve the lieutenant at the helm, if you please. The heading is north-north-east."

"Aye, sir."

"Mr. Talmant," Hilemore went on, "note for the log. Deck Hand Scrim-

shine hereby promoted to the rank of leading deck hand. Also, awarded a
mention in dispatches for his outstanding actions during recent operations."

"Very good, sir."

He saw Scrimshine straighten a little as he took the wheel, but the former smuggler gave no other indication he had heard. "Heavy cloud ahead,
Skipper," he said instead. "Sitting low on the horizon. Looks like we're in
for it."

"When aren't we, Mr. Scrimshine?"

This brought a restrained chuckle from the others on the bridge and a
small flare of reassurance in Hilemore's breast. *After all I put them through,*
they can still laugh, he thought. His good humour, however, evaporated
with the arrival of Claydon Torcreek some minutes later. The Blood-
blessed's face was as grim as Hilemore had seen it. Beyond him Braddon
Torcreek held his daughter in a tight embrace, tears streaming down the
young gunhand's face, which was for once rendered ugly as she strove to
contain her sorrow.

"Tranced with Miss Lethridge this morning," Clay said. "I got news."

He ordered the news shared with the crew. It may have been wiser to
spare their morale by concealing the truth, but Hilemore felt it best
to ensure they knew the reality of the situation, however grim it might be.
Many crewmen had family in Feros, it was the largest Maritime Protectorate base after all, and the knowledge of its fall left a thick pall of despair
over the ship. He kept them distracted with constant drills and much-
needed repairs. Prolonged exposure to freezing temperatures had left
many of the fittings and armaments in a poor state, in addition to causing
much of the ship's paint-work to flake off. The hold yielded a decent stock
of paint in various hues and Hilemore ordered the renewed colour scheme
to feature both Protectorate blue and Corvantine green. Although the remaining Corvantine crew were small in number, he was keen to emphasise
the fact that, despite being a ship of several different allegiances, they had
but one common purpose.

The possibility of an attack by Blues was a constant worry, albeit allevi-
ated by Clay, who spent most days on the prow in silent communion with
Jack. The huge Blue would range out ahead of the ships, his remarkable hear-

ing able to detect his drake brethren over huge distances. Consequently, they were able to avoid the danger as Clay related a series of course changes to steer them clear of trouble. However, he also provided a warning.

"He says they're hunting us," the Blood-blessed told Hilemore during the evening watch. It was Clay's habit to remain at his post until midnight before retiring for a few hours' sleep. He sipped the coffee Hilemore had brought him with a tired but grateful grin. "The White's got 'em scouring the southern seas for us. Ain't sure how it knows what we're about, but it surely does, and it don't like it."

"Can't he . . ." Hilemore fumbled for the right words. "Talk to the other Blues, somehow. Tell them to leave us alone."

"He can talk, but they ain't listening. They only got ears for the White. That's how it was centuries ago when it rose before. That's how it is now. To them Jack's just another enemy in need of killing."

Hilemore inclined his head at the crew quarters. "Has she been any more forthcoming with her intelligence?"

"Kriz? Not really. Seems right fascinated with your ship's library and charts and all. Hard to get her head out of a book just now, though it could be just a ruse to stop me asking questions. Fact is, until we get where we're going, I doubt she'll tell us anything she ain't already."

"Land in sight, Captain," Talmant related from the speaking-tube connected to the crow's nest. "Sea and sky reported clear of enemies."

"All stop," Hilemore ordered, Talmant promptly relaying the instruction to the engine room via the bridge telegraph. "Drop anchor and signal the *Farlight* to draw alongside. Tell them I also request Captain Tidelow's presence for a conference."

"I put us here," Hilemore said a short while later, tapping a compass-needle to a position on the chart laid out on the ward-room table. In addition to Captain Tidelow he had summoned Zenida, Clay, Braddon and Kriz to the conference. Braddon was the only one seated, placing himself at the far end of the table and paying scant attention as he stroked his beard, eyes brooding and distant. Hilemore hadn't heard him speak more than a few words since receiving the news about Feros and the man's bearing didn't invite conversation. By contrast, his daughter had been highly vocal in her grief.

The night after Clay had related the news that her mother was most likely dead Loriabeth had contrived to get drunk on a cask of rum purloined from the ship's diminishing stores. She spent an hour or more at the stern, raging profanities into the sea air in between blasting imaginary enemies with her twin revolvers. Hilemore had ordered her left alone until she became so insensible as to mistake one of the life-boats for a drake. It was Lieutenant Sigoral who calmed her, grabbing her about the arms and chest as she attempted to reload her guns and put another salvo of bullets into the life-boat's hull. The Corvantine held her as she twisted and spat in his arms, speaking softly into her ear until the rum in her veins finally drew her into an exhausted slump. Sigoral then carried her back to her bunk, staying by her side until morning.

"Forty miles due south of the Barnahy Firth," Tidelow said, eyes tracking a westward course over the map. "Which would make Stockcombe the nearest port."

"We're not going to Stockcombe," Hilemore said. He took a pencil and sketched out a route from their current position and into the Firth.

"The Lower Torquil." Tidelow frowned as his finger tapped the small inland sea. "That's some tricky sailing, Captain. It's a fractious stretch of water, small though it may be."

"So I've heard," Hilemore agreed. "And even trickier when we get to the Upper Torquil."

Tidelow moved back from the map, shaking his head. "The Upper Torquil is said to be richer in aquatic Greens than any other place in Arradsia. Hardly the safest course in the circumstances, sir."

"But our course nonetheless." Reading the deep uncertainty on Tidelow's face, Hilemore added, "One you are not obliged to follow, sir."

"What fine choices you give me." Tidelow let out a sardonic laugh. "Follow you into drake-infested waters or sail alone to Stockcombe in the faint hope there might be someone left alive there to reprovision us."

Hilemore turned to regard Braddon's silent bulk. "Your counsel would be welcome, Captain Torcreek. I'd hazard there are few souls who know the Arradsian Interior better than you do."

For a prolonged moment Braddon didn't respond, continuing to stare into the middle distance until Clay said softly, "Need your help here, Uncle."

The elder Torcreek gave his nephew an impassive glance then got to his feet, moving to regard the map for several seconds. "Northern flank of the Upper Torquil is mostly marshland," he said, voice flat as he swept a hand over the numerous water-ways that characterised the region. "Impassible on foot or boat except for here." His finger came to rest on a particular river at the northernmost point of the Upper Torquil. "Quilam River. Named for one of the fellas first discovered the Torquils. Current's fierce but it's the only means of making it to the plains country west of the Krystaline without going through the Coppersoles."

"I got no desire to see them again," Clay commented.

"The depth of the river?" Hilemore asked Braddon.

"Should accommodate the *Superior* for about half the way, after that we'll need a steamboat of some kind to make it the rest of the way. Oars won't do it, the current's too strong."

"I'll set Chief Bozware to the task," Hilemore said. "I'm sure he can rig something up. Been awhile since I commanded a small steam craft. I'm sure I can still remember how."

"Erm," Clay said, giving a small cough of discomfort. "Miss Lethridge had opinions on this matter, Captain. Thinks it's best you stay with the ship this time."

Hilemore stared at him, feeling an icy anger stealing over him. "She thinks that, does she?" he enquired in a low voice. "How very interesting."

"Says you now command the most advanced warship in the world," Clay went on with an apologetic shrug. "Probably, with all the Corvie ships sunk and all. You and this ship are too valuable an asset to risk. If we don't make it back from the Krystaline you should sail for Varestia and aid with the defence. Said you can regard it as an order from Exceptional Initiatives if it helps."

Hilemore's anger abruptly switched from icy to hot, and he felt a red flush creep over his cheeks as he leaned forward, meeting Clay's reluctant gaze. "Understand this, Mr. Torcreek. I do not take orders . . ."

"He's right," Zenida interrupted.

Hilemore rounded on her, rage swelling further, then paused at the hard but insistent honesty he saw in her gaze. "This crew didn't follow me," she told him. "They followed you, through battle, mutiny, drake fire, ice and deadly gas. You might think I chose to wait for you, but you're wrong. I knew if I had attempted to sail away they would have hung me from the mainmast and continued to wait until they froze. I cannot command this ship in your absence. That is the simple truth, sea-brother. You belong here."

Hilemore rested his clenched fists on the map, trying to calm the thumping in his temples. *The worst thing about being a captain,* Grandfather Racksmith told him once, *is recognising that you're the most important man on the ship. And that's a burden of responsibility few men can stand, for you no longer have the luxury of pride.* "How will we know if you're successful?" he said, his hard, grating voice breaking what he realised had been a protracted silence.

"I can trance with Captain Okanas," Clay said. "Reckon we've been in each other's company long enough for a viable connection. Anything happens to me, then Lieutenant Sigoral can trance in my stead. Anything happens to him, well, we're most likely all dead and you need to sail for Varestia."

Hilemore swallowed, feeling his rage subside into a nauseous anger. "Very well," he said. "Assuming you reach the Krystaline, what then?"

Kriz stepped forward, placing a sheaf of papers on the table. Peering closer, Hilemore saw they were mechanical designs, but the device depicted was unfamiliar. It appeared to consist of a large sealed tube attached to a frame and something that resembled an upended metal fish-bowl. "What is that?" he asked.

"A subaquatic breathing apparatus," Kriz said. "We'll need to explore the lake-bed to locate the aerostat and recover what we need."

"You can build this?"

She nodded. "There are sufficient materials on board to construct it. But I'll require education in how to operate your welding gear."

"The Chief will be busy, it seems." Hilemore straightened, breathing deep to banish his anger, though a simmering core of it remained. It was selfish, he knew. Born of a desire to see the Interior for himself. For all its many dangers his time on the ice and the wonders witnessed there had birthed a thirst for more. *Perhaps it's in the blood,* he mused. *Grandfather was an explorer after all.* But this was an active-duty warship and exploration would have to wait for more peaceful days.

"We will clear the Firth and enter the Lower Torquil by tomorrow evening," he said. "Weather and drakes permitting we should reach the mouth of the Quilam River three days later. All your mechanicals will need to be complete by then. Let's be about it."

Chief Bozware used the *Superior's* largest launch as the basis for his steam-powered river-boat. Taking his cue from the *Superior's* own radical design, he opted for a propeller-driven craft rather than paddles. "Too complex to put together in the time available, sir," he advised Hilemore during a visit to the makeshift workshop on the fore-deck. The Chief appeared tired under the usual sheen of oily grime, but the enthusiasm for his task shone through nonetheless. The shaft was a length of iron pole fashioned from a ceiling beam taken from the crew quarters. The propeller had been constructed of copper tubing from the ship's hot-water system, the pipes flattened and welded into three identical blades. "With this it's just two separate components instead of ten."

"And the engine?" Hilemore enquired.

Bozware pulled back the tarpaulin covering a bulky shape in the centre of the launch. To Hilemore's eyes the unveiled contraption resembled a greatly enlarged iron top hat sprouting from a dense nest of copper and iron tubing. "Luckily, the Corvies had a decent stock of spares for their auxiliary power plant," Bozware said. "So the gearing and pipe-work weren't too difficult. The boiler and condenser were another matter. Had to purloin a good few of cookie's pots and pans from the galley, plus some deck-plates from the hold."

He slapped a hand to the engine, a glimmer of pride evident in his besmirched features. "Reckon she'll do a good ten knots in calm waters, if she's stoked high enough."

Hilemore turned to where Braddon Torcreek stood appraising the craft in his now-habitual silence. "Will ten knots suffice, do you think, Captain?" Hilemore asked him.

Braddon shrugged and muttered, "It'll have to." With that he stalked off towards the crew quarters. Hilemore had seen men succumb to grief before, crewmates who had learned of the death of loved ones on return to port. Some would lose themselves in drink, others whores or gambling and a few could be expected to tip themselves over the side during a lonely midnight watch. In Braddon's case the man neither drank nor gambled, nor showed any inclination to suicide. Instead when not compelled to take part in a discussion he sat in his cabin repeatedly disassembling and cleaning his guns.

It's not self-pity that's snared this one, Hilemore decided, watching Braddon disappear belowdecks. *It's revenge. Which may be worse.*

The Lower Torquil soon lived up to its reputation for troublesome sailing. Captain Tidelow, having taken a vote amongst those members of his crew not incarcerated in the brig, had opted to stay with the *Superior.* Both ships sailed through the Barnahy Firth and into the Lower Torquil without incident, finding mostly calm blue waters reflecting the clear sky above. However, the wind stiffened as the day wore on and the waters soon grew choppy. By late afternoon they were regularly swept by heavy torrents of rain and the wind had whipped the inland sea into a minor storm. They were forced to reduce speed and Leading Deck Hand Scrimshine obliged to work ever harder at the wheel to maintain their heading.

"Apparently it's all due to geography, sir," Lieutenant Talmant commented to Hilemore as they steadied themselves on a pitching bridge. "The prevailing wind comes from the west at this latitude and picks up increased velocity as it passes over the Torquils. It then slams into the natural barrier of the Coppersole Mountains, producing a kind of huge, high-pressure vortex."

"Fucking fascinating that is," Scrimshine muttered as he hauled on the wheel, low enough for only Hilemore to hear.

"Steady, Mr. Scrimshine," Hilemore snapped causing the half grin to vanish from Scrimshine's face. Recently promoted and decorated he may be, but that was no excuse for a lack of respect between ranks.

He turned his attention to the prow where Clay had continued to perch himself, despite the weather. Through the squall Hilemore caught occasional glimpses of Jack's scales, glittering in the fading light as he broke the surface. The younger Torcreek reported that the beast was unnerved by his new surroundings, finding the relatively shallow waters and confines of the Torquils a marked contrast to his vast home waters. However, his senses remained sharp and so far the Blue hadn't detected any sign of another drake.

Hilemore ordered the ship to one-third speed as evening slipped into night. The weather had stolen the stars from the sky and he was unwilling to risk navigating by dead reckoning in such shallow waters. Running aground in peacetime was a career disaster for a captain, but in times like these it would mean the end of this whole enterprise.

Morning brought calmer waters and an uninterrupted progress to the narrow channel that connected the Lower Torquil to its northern twin. It was a notoriously dangerous strait that had the official name of Tormine's Cut, another feature named for one of the explorers who had first charted this region. In the habit of sailors, however, it had long since earned the name Terror's Cut thanks to the number of ships that had fallen foul of its capricious nature. During a three-moon tide it was said the waters of the Cut could reach heights equivalent to a tidal wave. Fortunately, they were in a relatively inactive lunar period and the tides were unlikely to be high. Even so, Hilemore ordered the ship to dead slow as they approached the channel. Partly to gauge the conditions and also to allow the *Farlight* to catch up, the Blue-hunter having fallen behind during the night.

"Current appears to be flowing north, Captain," Talmant reported, having trained a spy-glass on the Cut. Hilemore followed suit, tracking his own glass between the headland on either side of the channel. The terrain consisted of the kind of bare, sandy scrub typical to land regularly subjected to the three-moon tide, whilst the waters themselves seemed placid enough, though evidently fast-flowing.

Hilemore checked to ensure the *Farlight* had closed to a few hundred yards then ordered Talmant to signal the engine room. "Ahead one-third. Captain Okanas to stand by to fire the blood-burner if necessary."

"Aye, sir."

Hilemore turned his spy-glass towards the prow, watching as Jack's spines twisted through the gentle swell towards the Cut. After a moment the spines slipped below the surface as the beast swam ahead to scout their route. "Mr. Steelfine," Hilemore said, causing the Islander to snap to attention.

"Sir."

"Line and weight crew to the starboard beam. Best keep an eye on the depth. It's been awhile since these waters were properly charted."

"I'll see to it, sir." Steelfine saluted and left the bridge, voice carrying the length of the ship as he summoned a pair of crewmen.

The draught had reduced to fifty feet by the time they entered the Cut, and then to thirty when the *Superior* reached the halfway point. The current was swift but manageable, Scrimshine managing to correct for its occasional shoves to the hull.

"Don't suppose you ever did any smuggling here, eh, Mr. Scrimshine?" Hilemore enquired.

"Can't say I have, Skipper," he replied, turning the wheel three points to port to bring the prow back in line with the compass-needle. "No bugger around here to sell our wares to, see? Done plenty round Stockcombe, though. Many a cosy inlet to be found on that coast . . ."

"Sir!" Talmant broke in, Hilemore raising his gaze to see Clay abruptly straightening at the prow. He turned and sprinted for the bridge, hands waving and shouting. Hilemore heard the word "Stop!" through the bridge window.

"Is that another squall, sir?" Talmant asked, training his glass on something beyond the prow. Hilemore followed his gaze, seeing the waters of the Cut some two hundred yards ahead had begun to roil, as if stirred up by a sudden and vicious wind.

"He couldn't hear them!" Clay said, appearing in the doorway, breathless and face hard with dire warning. "They were hiding under the silt."

Hilemore turned back to view the roiling waters. He didn't need his spy-glass to discern the cause. They were breaking the surface now, verdant scales glittering in the morning sun. *Greens.* Large aquatic Greens, so many they filled the entire breadth of Terror's Cut from end to end.

CHAPTER 11

Lizanne

"Estimated maximum altitude of fifteen hundred feet," Professor Lethridge said. He strolled around the redesigned aerostat, arms clasped behind his back and listing its virtues with a pride Lizanne couldn't recall being directed at her. "Maximum speed of forty miles an hour on kerosene, eighty-three under thermoplasmic power. A significant improvement in performance thanks to the information provided by you." He favoured Lizanne with a rare smile. "The aerodynamic refinements to the envelope alone added twenty miles an hour to the top speed, and another ten thanks to the addition of an enclosed gondola."

The new aerostat was indeed a more impressive specimen than its predecessor. The balloon itself had a more robust and elongated appearance, almost shark-like in the smooth curves achieved by Tinkerer's internal copper frame. The gondola was no longer just a small boat suspended by ropes from the balloon but a narrow canoe-shaped capsule with glass windows in front and back and hinged port-holes in the side which were wide enough to accommodate a carbine or mini-Growler if the need arose. The engine was suspended from the base of the gondola on a sturdy steel frame that enabled it to be swivelled about by the pilot, facilitating a much greater range of control. Jermayah had wanted to add a second engine but there simply weren't enough materials on board to construct it. Lizanne's gaze narrowed as it fell on the ugly bulk of the caloric burner. The way it sprouted through the roof of the gondola spoilt the craft's otherwise elegant lines.

"A temporary but necessary modification," her father said, following her gaze. "With no helium or hydrogen on hand it's the only means of achieving elevation."

"I'm sure it will work perfectly, Father," she told him. She turned as Tekela appeared at her side, clad in a heavy seaman's jacket, the sleeves of which had been trimmed to accommodate her less-than-regulation proportions. She carried a second jacket in her arms and wore a thick woollen hat on her head. Lizanne considered that she might have resembled a child playing dress-up but for the shrewd appraisal she displayed in surveying the aerostat.

"No time for test flight, I suppose?" she asked Jermayah.

"We don't have the fuel," he said with a grimace of apology before handing her a leather map-case. "The course is marked and the compass heading already set. The captain advises that the winds tend to swing north over the Red Tides so be sure to account for it."

Tekela gave a tense nod then hefted the second jacket into Lizanne's arms. "It gets cold up there," she said, striding forward. "Shall we?"

Lizanne lingered a moment to exchange a few words with Makario, who had come along with Captain Trumane to see them off. Tinkerer apparently felt no compulsion towards such social niceties and was busy in the workshop improving Jermayah's mini-Growler. "Keep working on the solargraph," Lizanne told the musician. "If you should happen to discover the final tune, don't play it for Tinkerer until I return."

He nodded, forcing a smile before nodding at the aerostat. Tekela had already climbed the ladder into the gondola and started up the caloric burner with a loud whoosh, causing the craft to lift several inches off the aft deck. "Room in there for a third party?" Makario asked and she was surprised to see he was serious. "Who'll save your life when you get captured again?" he added.

"I'll just have to manage," she said, folding him into a brief embrace before turning to Captain Trumane.

"Our formal proposal," he said, holding out a sealed envelope. "I'm sure they'll find the terms generous enough to be tempting."

"Let's hope they also find them credible," Lizanne replied, taking the envelope.

Trumane gave one of his short but deep coughs, stiffening into a more formal posture. "We shall proceed to a point twenty miles west of here," he said. "The waters off Viemen's Island. An uninhabited rock of little interest, but an easy locale to find. Also, pirates tend to avoid it. Some superstition about the place's being cursed by the King of the Deep."

"If my mission succeeds I shall trance with Mrs. Griffan at the allotted hour," Lizanne told him. "Please ask Dr. Weygrand not to sedate her too heavily."

"And if you are unsuccessful?"

"Then it's doubtful a trance will be possible. I suggest you linger at Vieman's Island no longer than two weeks." She paused, discomforted by the fact that she had no alternative destination to offer.

"After two weeks," Trumane said, "we will have no option but to risk Corvantine waters."

She nodded, wishing she had more to say, and that she felt this man to be more trustworthy. But once again the course of events had conspired to present her with nothing but bad choices. "Best of luck, Captain," was all she could think to say.

He gave a salute, the twitch that marred his features marginally less pronounced today. "And to you, miss."

Lizanne went to Jermayah, took the Smoker and ammunition from him before sharing a short, wordless embrace. She then moved to where her father was crouched beneath the gondola, engaged in a last-minute inspection of the engine.

"Any problems?" she enquired.

He didn't look up, gaze fixed on some component in the engine's internals. "The plasma-ignition valve can hold only one charge at a time," he said. "The released energy will last for no more than three hours. It's ignited via a viewing tube in the gondola . . ."

"I know, Father. It's very simple." She pulled on the jacket Tekela had given her, finding a woollen hat in one of the pockets. Professor Lethridge remained crouched, working a screwdriver as he fixed an access panel in place.

"The feed tube to the condenser will freeze if the engine remains idle for too long at altitude . . ."

"I know that too, Father."

He tightened the last screw and finally raised his gaze to hers. She was shocked to find herself confronted by the pale, damp-eyed face of a very frightened man. "Your aunt . . ." he began in a strained voice, then faltered, looking away.

Lizanne crouched at his side. "Aunt Pendilla loved us both and we loved her," she said. "We were a family." She leaned forward and pressed a kiss to his temple. "We still are. Best stand back, Father. It's time for me to leave."

Tekela's small but nimble hands darted over the aerostat controls as the craft lifted off from the *Viable*. She sat at the front of the gondola with Lizanne in the rear behind the central strut that connected the engine to the main body of the craft. Tekela used a large central lever fitted with a throttle to control the angle and speed of the engine. A smaller one to the left was connected to what her father had named "ailerons," a pair of stubby wings protruding from either side of the gondola which were used to control the forward and back pitch of the craft. A pair of foot-levers directed the large rear rudder which determined the port and starboard angle. Watching Tekela engage in the complex dance of lever and pedal that sent the aerostat into the air and on the correct heading, Lizanne wondered aloud if her musical training made her such a quick student as a pilot.

"Possibly," Tekela conceded once they were clear of the ship. It was surprisingly quiet in the gondola. With the engine positioned outside its whirring buzz was reduced to a low hum, allowing for easy conversation. "When I was little Mother would stand over me with a ruler as I played my scales on the pianola. If I hit the wrong note, down came the ruler. It made for very quick hands."

If I'd ever met your mother I'd have wrung the evil bitch's neck, Lizanne thought but chose not to say.

She glanced over her shoulder, seeing the rapidly diminishing outline of the *Viable* through the rear window. As the aerostat drew higher still the rest of the fleet came into view, dozens of ships all reduced to toy-like dimensions in the space of a few moments. Although no stranger to heights Lizanne found that such a rapid ascent brought an uncomfortable lurch to the stomach and a decided sense of disorientation. She turned away, occupying herself with checking their weapons. In addition to the Smoker they had the original mini-Growler Jermayah had constructed in Feros, plus a pair of pistols and a standard-issue Silworth rifle fitted with a telescopic sight. In Lizanne's experience it always paid to have a long-range weapon close at hand, a lesson starkly underlined by her experience in Scorazin.

"It has a tendency to veer upwards," Tekela said. Lizanne looked up from the mini-Growler to see her eyes in the mirror above the forward window. "Best keep it to short bursts." Lizanne saw a shadow creep into Tekela's eyes then and she quickly lowered them to the controls. "Heading is set," she said, finger tapping the compass. "Jermayah rigged a kind of pulley system that'll keep the levers at the right angle. Still have to correct for the wind though, but it makes for a lighter work-load."

"We still haven't spoken," Lizanne said, "about what you saw in Feros. About Sirus."

Lizanne saw Tekela's slim shoulders tense beneath the bulky confines of her jacket. "I wasn't making it up," she said.

"I know. But it does raise some troubling questions." She shifted forward, speaking softly. "You said he saved you. How?"

"The Greens . . ." Tekela paused to swallow before continuing. "The Greens burned their way in and Sirus was there. Standing in the wreckage of the workshop doors. He was Spoiled, but I knew him right away. I . . . I tried to kill him. I had Jermayah's new gun and I tried to kill them all. I got all the Greens but I ran out of bullets before I could get Sirus. He just stood there looking at me, then another Spoiled came in, a woman. I didn't recognise her but she seemed to know me, and not in a friendly way. She had a pistol . . . Sirus shot her. I could tell it wasn't easy for him, but he did it. He did it to save me."

She fell silent for a while, tending to the controls with an occasional pause to wipe at her eyes. "I wanted him to come with us. I asked him to, but he said he couldn't. He told us to go."

Lizanne reached around the central strut to grip the younger woman's shoulder, feeling her shudder as she contained a sob. "He always loved you," she said.

"I suppose." Tekela gave a miserable sniff and wiped at her nose with the sleeve of her jacket. "Though Emperor knows why. I was never exactly nice to him. All that awful poetry." She drew in a hard breath, exhaling slowly. "Still, I doubt he writes anything any more."

"No, I don't expect he does. Tekela"—Lizanne's grip grew slightly firmer on her shoulder—"if he's Spoiled it means he's in thrall to the White. Which means the White may possess every memory in his head, every memory of you, me, the solargraph, all of it. If it doesn't have it now, it may well soon."

"He saved me," Tekela insisted. "He wouldn't betray us."

"Not willingly. I doubt any of the Spoiled do what they do willingly, but they do it nonetheless. Saviour or not, he's a threat to us. And I think he knows that. It's why he wouldn't go with you. Should we see him again . . ."

Tekela shifted, drawing her shoulder clear of Lizanne's grip. "I won't do that," she stated, sitting straighter in her seat. "And I don't want to talk about this any more," she added in a familiar but now rarely heard tone, rich in all the truculent stubbornness Lizanne recalled from those first days in Morsvale.

"You might as well sleep," Tekela went on, shifting the main lever as the compass-needle strayed a little from the heading. "It'll be hours before we see anything but ocean."

The weather remained kind and the aerostat made swift progress on its westward flight, aided by the wind for much of the way until the first Varestian islands came into view a day and a half later. Tekela had managed barely two hours' sleep, slumping in her seat with one hand on the control lever and the engine set to its slowest speed. Nevertheless she seemed fresh enough today, one of the advantages of youth, Lizanne supposed.

"The captain wasn't wrong about the wind," Tekela commented, grunting a little as she hauled on the controls to keep the craft on the correct heading.

Lizanne peered down at the small specks of land passing by below. These were the mostly uninhabited outer islands that formed the Sabiras Archipelago, a natural barrier on the eastern fringe of the Varestian region that served as an unofficial border between the Orethic Ocean and the Red Tides. From here on the only ships to sail these waters were Varestian, either traders or pirates. Even before the Corvantine Empire had been forced to forsake its sovereignty over the region, the Red Tides had mostly been shunned by both Imperial and corporate ships. Despite a reputation as the finest and most wide-ranging mariners in the world, the Varestians had always been hostile to intruders into their own waters.

Lizanne read through Captain Trumane's letter once more. She had felt no compunction about breaking the seal and was quite prepared to discard it should the contents prove counter-productive. In fact she found the letter's diplomatic phrasing to be elegant and effective, containing nothing their potential hosts could take offence at and striking the right balance between solicitation and conciliation. What would interest them most, she knew, was the offer of ten million in Syndicate scrip or stock of equivalent value in return for safe harbour, an offer far beyond Trumane's authority to make. *And far beyond mine for that matter,* she thought, folding the letter away. It was clear that in order to secure Varestian co-operation she would have to engage in some spectacular lies.

They saw their first Varestian vessel once they were over the larger islands a dozen miles farther west. It was a large three-paddle freighter easily identified by the broad wake it left on the ocean. Lizanne used the riflescope to scan the ship. A flag she didn't recognise flew from the mast, making it an Independent as was the case with most Varestian ships. *And pirates,* she added inwardly. She doubted that this vessel was engaged in piracy, being too large for the kind of swift manoeuvring required of that trade. It did, however, turn out to be armed.

A flash appeared on the freighter's fore-deck, followed a second or two later by the faint crump of a cannon-shot. The gunners were clearly untrained in firing at aerial targets because the shell was both wide and short, its fuse causing it to explode about fifty yards below and a hundred yards behind the aerostat. Even so, it was close enough for Tekela to open the throttle and increase the angle of the ailerons, taking them up to the craft's maximum ceiling in another gut-disturbing lurch.

"Could you warn me when you're going to do that?" Lizanne requested.

"Sorry." Tekela glanced out of the starboard port-hole at the ship below. "That wasn't very friendly, was it?"

"No." Lizanne saw several more flashes flaring on the freighter's deck as it brought all its guns into play, though none of the shells it launched came any closer than the first. "They have no idea who we are," she went on as the cluster of small black clouds left by the exploding shells drifted away and the freighter shrank into the distance. "Or any notion what this craft is. Troubled times makes for nervous hands."

"And when we get to the Seven Walls?"

Lizanne turned to Tekela, finding her doll's face tense with worry. *Easy to forget how young she is sometimes,* Lizanne chided herself. She resisted the impulse to lie, offer some bland reassurance. But a co-operative mission required trust between agents. "I don't know," she said. "They may fire on us as soon as they see us. Or they may not. They may allow us to land and immediately arrest us."

Tekela nodded, small worry lines creasing her forehead. "Or worse," she said.

"Yes. Or worse." She gestured at the small clock Jermayah had set amongst the cluster of dials in front of the pilot's station. "How much longer?"

Tekela straightened and turned, taking a firmer grip on the control lever. "In this wind, at least another ten hours."

"Which means we'll be arriving in darkness."

"I can circle through the night, begin the approach at dawn."

"No. You'll be too fatigued." Lizanne rose into a crouch and shuffled forward to the viewing tube that sat alongside the central strut. "Time to fire up the blood-burner, I think."

"The professor said it has only one charge. And once started the only way to stop it is to flush the plasma from the combustion chamber. It might be better to save it for emergencies."

"We can recharge it when we land, assuming we're allowed to take off again. If not then it won't matter." She flipped open the cover on the viewing tube and put her eye to the socket. "Besides, I should like to see just how fast this thing can go. Ready?"

"One second. Need to level the ailerons; otherwise, the slip-stream will tear them off." Lizanne heard a snick as Tekela locked one of the levers into place. "Ready."

Lizanne took her wallet from the pocket of her jacket and extracted a vial of Red, taking a small sip before returning her eye to the viewing tube. Her father had placed a little luminescent disc inside the plasma valve so it was easy to make out the small pool of viscous liquid it held. A brief flare of Red and the product immediately burst into an eye-wateringly bright fire-ball. She was about to opine that adding tinted glass to the eyepiece might be a good idea when the aerostat surged forward with enough force to send her sprawling. She heard Tekela let out a startled but delighted giggle and blinked the moisture from her eyes to see that she now had both hands on the control lever. Over her shoulder Lizanne could see the needle on the speedometer swiftly ascending to its maximum reading, where it stayed.

"Must be over a hundred miles an hour at least," Tekela said with an appreciative laugh. "Looks as if the professor underestimated his invention."

"Co-invention," Lizanne corrected, glancing through a port-hole to see the wispy cloud beyond passing by at a greatly accelerated rate. "When we get back to the ship, remind me to draft a proper patent and a contract to cover distribution of future profits."

They cleared the Sabiras Archipelago in what seemed like minutes, bringing them into the Red Tides proper. They were low enough to make out the waves passing below, the ocean surface blurring thanks to their speed. Several more ships came into view, most much smaller than the freighter, though none felt the need to fire on them. Lizanne suspected this was due more to their increased speed than any lack of hostility. In all it took just under four hours before Tekela reported land in sight. The thermoplasmic engine had exhausted its supply by then, forcing Tekela to combat the winds once more, though she proved adept at keeping the approaching land-mass firmly in the centre of the forward window.

Lizanne moved forward, leaning over Tekela's shoulder to view the landscape, her eyes tracking over the coast in search of landmarks. "Iskamir," she said, spying a broad inlet a few degrees to the north. She gave Tekela's shoulder a grateful squeeze. "We're in the right place. You better take us up, high as you can, please. No telling what reception we'll get from the locals."

The island of Iskamir was often referred to in atlases and almanacs as the "jewel" or "beating heart" of Varestia, the central hub where pirates came to sell their booty and traders to buy it. As they flew over the eastern coast Lizanne was struck by how many ports it featured, all surrounded by towns of varying proportions. It occurred to her that this might well be the most densely populated land-mass on the globe, meaning the place had to be reliant on imported cargo to feed its population, as the interior was mostly mountains or rough hill-country. *Not a place to hold out for very long in a siege,* she concluded as the aerostat drew away from the coast and into the mountains. The peaks were so tall Tekela had to slow the craft and steer a way through them, hauling on the controls with ever more energy thanks to the fractious air currents and drifting patches of mist.

"Best if we fly around this place on the way back," she said, her labour having left a sheen of sweat on her face despite the chill.

Once through the mountains they flew across a thin stretch of cultivated fields before once again finding themselves over the sea as they reached the strait that separated Iskamir from the unique construction that formed the Seven Walls. It came into view quickly, at first appearing to be a dark strangely regular notch on the horizon, but soon grew to a size that put her in mind of the mountains they had just traversed. She knew the great fortress's origin dated back at least a thousand years and was a truly ingenious design; a small central island complete with a port around which a series of seven walls had been constructed between the smaller outlying islets. The result was a self-contained port permanently shielded from the tide on all sides. However, during the days when the old Varestian League had fought the last of its wars against the encroaching Corvantine Empire it had been greatly enlarged. The walls now stood over a hundred feet high featuring a miniature fort at each intersection. Once again making use of the riflescope, Lizanne could see each fort bristling with guns and busy with ant-sized figures running to their stations. It appeared their approach had not gone unnoticed.

Within the walls lay the port itself, so crammed with buildings, wharfs and jetties Lizanne could see scant sign of vegetation save for the occasional tree. *I hope they've been stockpiling food,* she mused. The only open space was a central square surrounded by a series of grand buildings, the largest of which she assumed would house the Varestians' quasi-government.

"We'll land there," Lizanne said, pointing to the square.

"The forts?" Tekela asked in a thin voice. They were close enough now to see the gun-crews loading their pieces.

"Let's hope they have enough honour to observe traditional customs." Lizanne went to the canvas bag she had obtained from Captain Trumane.

The item it contained was large and unwieldy, taking several tiresome minutes to extract. When it was done she dragged it to the hatch in the gondola's floor.

"Hover in place for a moment," she told Tekela. "We need to make sure they see it."

She opened the hatch as Tekela duly brought the craft to a slow sideways drift, then fastened the ties attached to the corners of the item to the main strut before pushing it out. The flag unfurled to its full length thanks to the stiff winds found at these heights, revealing a design Lizanne hoped would still be recognised in these uncertain times; a white circle on a red background. Even the Varestians were reputed to respect the universal signal requesting truce and negotiation.

They drifted for several minutes as the flag fluttered and flapped below the aerostat. Lizanne kept careful watch on the closest fort, detecting a certain amount of confusion amongst the gun-crews, and no small amount of accompanying argument. She even saw a couple of men come to blows, but no cannon were fired.

"Take us in," she told Tekela. "A slow and gentle approach would be best."

She was obliged to cut the flag free once they were over the wall as it was coming perilously close to fouling the engine's propellers. They would just have to hope the Varestians didn't take this as a signal of hostile intent. People thronged the wharfs and streets as they flew over the port towards the square, most staring in wonder or suspicion, a few running in panic. There were numerous ships at anchor and many began to make steam at the sight of the aerostat. None of this gave Lizanne much confidence in a safe landing, but they couldn't turn back now.

Tekela guided the aerostat to a hover when they came to the square, then slowly reduced the heat of the caloric burner to ensure a gentle congress with the ground. One of Jermayah's design additions to the aerostat was retractable landing gear that sprouted from the gondola's underside and rather resembled a metallic eagle's claw. Tekela deployed it when they were a few feet from the square's paved surface and the aerostat settled down with only a small bump.

"Excellently done," Lizanne complimented her, peering through the window at a group of men rapidly descending the steps of the large building to their front. There were about twenty of them, and each one bore a rifle or carbine. "You had better go out and greet our hosts."

Tekela gaped at her. "Me?"

Lizanne went to the rear of the gondola and began assembling the required equipment. "I'll be along directly," she said, strapping on her Spider.

"What do I say to them?"

"'Hello' is traditional."

"I don't speak Varestian."

"Don't worry. They're almost always multilingual."

Tekela hesitated for a long, silent moment then undid the forward hatch and climbed out of the gondola. Lizanne heard the pounding of boots as the men drew near and fanned out, one of them demanding something in harsh, breathless Varestian.

"Ah," Tekela said. "Hello."

There was a short pause, during which Lizanne used the Spider to inject a small burst of Green before moving to the rear hatch.

"Who the fuck are you?" the same voice demanded in heavily accented Mandinorian. "And what the fuck is this?"

"My name is Burgravine Tekela Artonin," came the response in admirably steady tones. "And I don't see any need for profanity, sir."

"Trust me, girl," the voice went on, growing louder as its owner drew closer, "a foul tongue is the least of—"

His words were drowned out as Lizanne stepped out from under the gondola, raised the mini-Growler and let loose with a prolonged burst of fire. She found Tekela was right about the weapon's tendency to pull up when fired, it was also somewhat unwieldy thanks to the ammunition load and the miniature caloric engine required to spin the barrels. Consequently, even with the benefit of Green Lizanne's aim was not as precise as she would have liked. The mini-Growler stitched a vertical line of bullet-holes up the edifice of the largest building in the square before transforming one of the statues on its roof into a stump of shattered marble.

Lizanne removed her finger from the firing mechanism, lowering her gaze to find that the men who had come to greet them were all now lying face-down on the paving-stones. She strode forward, focusing her gaze on the upturned face of the man who had addressed Tekela. In normal circumstances he would probably have been an imposing fellow, with his weathered face and sabre-scarred cheeks. Now he was just another scared man facing death. It was an expression she had grown used to recently.

"I shall explain your choices in very simple terms," she said. "You can get up, apologise to my friend for your language and take us to see the Varestian Ruling Council. Or"—she aimed the mini-Growler's smoking barrels directly at his head—"I'll kill you and every man here, then go and find them myself."

CHAPTER 12

Clay

"Battle stations! Riflemen assemble on deck!"

Hilemore's orders rang out from the bridge as Clay turned and slid down the ladder, making for his position on the prow. The *Superior*'s forward pivot-gun fired before he could get there, the shot aimed low so that it impacted in the centre of the approaching mass of Greens in a spout of white and red. Clay went to the port rail instead, pistol drawn as he stared down at the water below. *Jack!*

He could feel the Blue's distress, an instinctive fear of greater numbers overcoming his loyalty. A brief sharing of minds revealed him to be circling frantically beneath the *Superior*'s stern, attempting to conceal himself in the silt his coils raised from the sea-bed. *Old Jack was never as mighty as Last Look,* Clay reminded himself. *Nor so crazy.*

He heard another shouted command from the bridge and saw Steelfine marshalling his riflemen. The Islander sent a squad of six to the port rail and the remaining seven to starboard. Several more riflemen appeared on the upper works, accompanied by Sigoral and Loriabeth. A glance above revealed Preacher's tall form scaling the ladder to the crow's nest, his rifle slung across his back. Clay couldn't see his uncle or Skaggerhill but knew they would be taking up station somewhere in the aft section.

The forward gun fired again, quickly followed by both the port and starboard cannon, meaning the Greens were all around them now. Clay returned his gaze to the sea, at first seeing nothing but the roiling wake rebounding from the hull, then reeling back as a Green launched itself out of the water, mouth gaping. The heat of the drake's fire was fierce enough to stun him, sending him sprawling onto the deck, smoke rising from his singed clothing. He scrabbled to extinguish the flames clinging to his sleeves then, realising he had dropped his revolver, reached for the wallet of product in his jacket. He had managed to get it open when a loud hiss dragged his gaze to the rail in time to see the Green clambering onto the deck.

Like most aquatic Greens it was considerably larger and longer of body than its land-based cousins, the head and snout narrow and spear-like, and possessed of a barbed, whip-like tail. Seeing the beast coil its tail for a strike, Clay rolled on the deck an instant before the thorny tip slammed into the boards with splintering force. Clay's mind filled with feverish curses as he fumbled for his vials, desperately trying to get one to his lips. The Green, however, saw no reason to allow him the luxury of time and lunged, jaws snapping, then fell dead as a bullet tore through its skull.

Clay gaped at the bleeding twitching body of the Green then felt hands grip him beneath the shoulders, trying to drag him upright. "Are you hurt?" Kriz asked once he was on his feet. She had obtained a revolver from somewhere and stood with her back to him, aiming at the multiple Greens now boiling over the *Superior's* rails. Rifle fire crackled continually, punctuated by more rapid pistol and carbine-shots and the hissing roar of drake flames. A scream snapped Clay's gaze to the forward gun-crew. They had abandoned the pivot-gun and were attempting to fend off a trio of Greens with sea-axes and boat-hooks. One gunner was already down, yelping as he beat at the flames consuming his legs.

Clay took three vials from his wallet, Green, Red and Black, put all three to his lips and drank half the contents. "Take all of it," he said, handing the vials to Kriz before crouching to retrieve his pistol and starting forward. "I'll do the killing. Keep them off me."

He froze one Green in place as it darted towards the burning crewman, shooting it in the head, then stunned the other two with a mixed blast of Red and Black. They skittered back, hissing in distress and rage. He used his Green-enhanced reflexes to shoot one through the eye, but the other was too quick, swiftly dodging to the side then lashing out with its tail to spear one of the gunners through the chest. Kriz shouted an enraged expletive in her own language, casting out an inexpert but effective wave of Black that pinned the Green to the side-rail long enough for Clay to put a bullet through its head.

The burnt man lay writhing in agony as the two remaining gunners used a jacket to quench the last of the flames, but Clay could tell the fellow wouldn't last long. A quick look around confirmed the fore-deck and the prow free of Greens, but the mid-deck and the upper works were thick with the beasts. Dozens had been killed, and dozens more continued to fall to the crew's desperate fusillade, but ever more were boiling out of the sea to clamber up the hull.

"You got cannister?" Clay asked one of the gunners, who could only stare at him in shock until Clay grabbed his jacket and shook him. "Cannister! You got any?"

"Just three shells," the man said, moving to the recessed compartment in the deck where the ammunition was stored. "The Corvies used most of it up at the Strait."

"Get it loaded," Clay said. "We'll keep them back."

The gunners got to work whilst Clay and Kriz positioned themselves to the rear of the gun, dispatching any Green that detached itself from the main pack to charge them. Kriz seemed to be learning with every use of product, her blasts of Red and Black becoming more accurate. Clay saw her snap the forelegs of one Green then roast its eyes as it stumbled to a halt a few yards away.

"Neat trick," he said, finishing the Green with a bullet to the skull. His last bullet. "You ready yet?" he demanded, turning back to the gun.

"Ready," one of the gunners said, snapping the breech closed before he and his comrade began swivelling the gun about. "Better get behind us if you don't want to be shredded."

Clay and Kriz moved swiftly to comply as the gunners brought the pivot-gun to bear on the upper works. "Where do we aim?" one asked.

"Starboard side," Clay said, pointing. "That's where they're thickest."

"Guard your ears," the other gunner said, reaching for the firing lanyard. Clay clamped his hands over the side of his head, nodding for Kriz to do the same. Even so, the gun's blast was enough to leave a ringing in his ears and cause an involuntary closing of the eyes. When he looked again the mass of drakes assailing the starboard flank of the upper works had been transformed into a green-and-red morass. Eviscerated and part-dismembered Greens lay about the ladders and walkways, some still twitching. Amongst it all Clay could see the dark uniform of a Protectorate sailor.

"Port side," he said, forcing his gaze away. "Hurry up."

They had to fend off another charge before the gun was ready to fire again, Clay feeling his reserves of product diminish with every slaughtered drake. Fortunately, Preacher had evidently seen their plight and chose to lend a hand. Three Greens went down in quick succession, felled by long-rifle shots from the crow's nest. Despite this, the Greens continued to come for them and by the time the gunners called out a warning their product was almost all spent. There was no time to retreat so he and Kriz threw themselves flat, hands covering their ears as the gun blasted out its hail of iron balls.

The effect of this shot was even more deadly than the first, sweeping most of the attacking Greens away in an instant, leaving behind a dozen or so thrashing wounded. Clay scanned the midships seeing no sign of any more Greens clambering out of the sea. A cacophony of shots and shouts could be heard from the stern, indicating this fight wasn't over yet.

"Come on," he told Kriz, running for a ladder. "I expect the captain's got some more product."

"**Y**our pet is a coward." Steelfine glared at Clay, tattooed features hard with accusation beneath a mask of blood. A drake claw had left a trio of parallel cuts on the crown of his shaven head, though any pain he might have felt seemed to have been subsumed by anger. "Eight good men dead and six grievously burned or gashed, whilst that monster skulks below."

They were on the aft deck where Lieutenant Talmant had charge of the clean-up crew. They were all clad in oilskins to protect against the effects of so much drake blood and used brooms to push the Green bodies, most of them in pieces, over the side. The more intact ones had been piled near the hold for harvesting later.

The fighting had been fiercest here. Having been forced back from the rails, Steelfine's riflemen had taken up a defensive position near the stern, consequently suffering the brunt of the casualties. Once the pivot-gun's cannister had cleared the upper works Hilemore and Lieutenant Sigoral, fortified by product from the ship's safe, had led the counter-attack to clear the rear of the ship. But not before the majority of the Islander's squad had been killed or wounded.

"He ain't a pet," Clay replied, keeping his voice as passive as he could.

This wasn't a time to surrender to provocation. "He's a creature from another age trapped in a body that ain't his. And he don't even understand what a coward is. He's just trying to survive."

"So he survives whilst my men die." Steelfine took a step closer, a murderous glint in his eye. "That doesn't seem a fair exchange to me . . ."

"Number One," Hilemore said. His voice was soft but commanding enough to bring Steelfine to immediate attention.

"Sir!"

"You're wounded. Report to sick bay for treatment."

Steelfine didn't move for a moment, continuing to stare at Clay with jaw clenched until he snapped off a salute, grated, "Aye, sir!" between clenched teeth and marched away.

"At least now our Green stocks should hold out for a while," Hilemore commented, clasping his arms behind his back as he surveyed the blood-drenched deck. "I'll set Mr. Skaggerhill to it when he's finished in the sick bay."

He paused to regard one particular corpse, a drake that had been caught by cannister-shot. Its lower body had been disintegrated whilst its upper half hung from a walkway, the creature's jaw fixed on an overhead beam with such force none of the crewmen had yet managed to dislodge it.

"It was well done, Mr. Torcreek," Hilemore said. "The cannister. An excellent notion."

Clay forced a half grin. "Just trying to survive too, Captain."

"You might have made a fine Protectorate officer, had things been different."

"That don't seem likely. But thank you anyways."

"Those were your uncle's doing." Hilemore gestured at a cluster of Green corpses arranged in a rough semicircle around the starboard-gun emplacement. "I saw him step up onto the gun just as it all started. Just kept loading and firing throughout the whole engagement. I don't think he missed once."

"Uncle Braddon's always been one of the finest marksmen on the continent."

"It's not his marksmanship that concerns me. It's his demeanour. Or rather his lack of it. He killed all of these and didn't once change his expression. Nor did he show any sign of seeking a safer vantage point."

"He's . . . not quite himself just now. You know why."

"Grief can lead a man to madness, if it's stoked by vengeance. I'm wondering if instead of leaving one captain behind on your expedition, it might be better to leave two."

"No." Clay gave an adamant shake of his head. "Mad with grief or not, we wouldn't last more than a few days in the Interior without him."

"We have all suffered much on this strange voyage of ours," Hilemore replied. "Lost many lives, men who trusted my judgement enough to follow me to the end of the world and back. I would not have that sacrifice be in vain, see this mission imperilled . . ."

"Captain!"

Hilemore turned at Lieutenant Talmant's urgent call. The young officer stood at the stern, pointing at the *Farlight*, which had previously been anchored some hundred yards off but was now making steam and drawing away. The Blue-hunter had been completely unscathed by the Green assault, seemingly ignored by the drakes, who focused their fury entirely on the *Superior*. However, it appeared her crew had finally seen enough.

"'Getting too hot around here,'" Talmant translated the flickering signal lamp on the *Farlight*'s bridgehouse. "'Crew won't stand it. Making for Stockcombe. Best of luck, and apologies. Tidelow.'"

"Seems your Islander's got more cowards to rant about," Clay observed.

"Yes," Hilemore agreed. "Captain Tidelow would do well to avoid him in future." He gave Clay a critical glance. "Are you sure about your uncle?"

"The one man in this world I'll always be sure of is my uncle."

"Very well. But make no mistake, Mr. Torcreek. Whether you know it or not, or like it or not, the expedition to Krystaline Lake will be under your command. Your uncle Braddon has forsaken such duty; I see it if you do not."

They cleared Terror's Cut the following morning, Hilemore having ordered the blood-burner brought on-line to ensure a swift passage. They were aided by the tide which raised the waters of the Cut into a fast-moving swell, propelling them clear of the channel without the risk of running aground on an uncharted sand-bank. Fortunately, no more Greens appeared come daylight and they made an unmolested progress into the Upper Torquil, covering much of the distance to the mouth of the

Quilam River before nightfall. The *Superior* spent a nervous night at full alert, riflemen and look-outs posted in double shifts and all guns manned and loaded. For now at least it seemed the aquatic Greens were content to leave them be.

"You sure this thing will work?" Clay asked Kriz the next morning as he helped her carry her bulky breathing apparatus to the steam-launch.

"I think so, and so does Chief Bozware," she replied. "I would have liked to conduct a proper test, but . . ." She glanced around at the becalmed, misty waters surrounding their anchorage. The Upper Torquil had so far proven to be less fractious than the Lower. In slight winds the surface took on an almost glass-like aspect, which somehow made it more ominous as it betrayed no sign of what might lie beneath.

"Yeah," Clay agreed, grunting as they heaved the apparatus into the launch. "Best to wait till we get to the lake."

He left her to check the device's various valves and tubes, joining Loriabeth and Sigoral at the rail where they were engaged in a typically acerbic discussion.

"Just take it off," his cousin told the Corvantine, reaching out to pluck at his eye-patch. "Can't keep it on forever."

"Still hurts," he said in a sullen mutter, snatching his head away. There was a tension to his bearing that told Clay his reluctance to remove the patch had little to do with any pain it might cause.

"Lori," he said. "Skaggs needs help hauling up the rest of the ammo."

She seemed about to tell him to do it himself but paused on seeing his insistent frown. "Your men think you're weird for still wearing it," she informed Sigoral before making for the hold.

"If I recall correctly," Clay said, moving to Sigoral's side, "you favour the right eye when shooting. How are you with the left?"

Sigoral gave a chagrined grimace. "When the drakes attacked, I must have fired fifty rounds. I think I managed six hits, all at close range."

"You'll do better over time. Just takes practice." He fished inside his duster and came out with a wallet. "Compliments of the captain," he said, handing it over. "Full vials of all four colours. I had a short trance with Captain Okanas this morning. Be obliged if you did the same."

Sigoral nodded, consigning the wallet to his jacket pocket. "How's her mind?"

"Surprisingly neat, and pretty. It's a ship, as you might expect, but made of jewels. Each jewel is a memory. You?"

"The cliffs on Takmarin's Land. I spent many hours there as a boy. The Cadre agent who tutored me said it was best to choose something familiar."

Sigoral fell silent, looking to the broad river mouth half a mile to the north. "You have travelled the Arradsian Interior before," he said. "Is it as bad as they say?"

"No," Clay replied. "And yes. A lot depends on your manner of travel. I knew a woman who spent near twenty years out there and never got a scratch. Though she did have a good deal of help." He gave Sigoral a sidelong glance, seeing the mottled flesh poking out from the edges of his eyepatch. "My cousin really don't care about scars and such," he said. "Just so you know."

Sigoral lowered his gaze, saying nothing. Clay slapped his hands to the rail and moved away. "Captain Hilemore says the ship will only manage a few hours' travel up the river before they have to drop us off," he said. "Be sure to do your trancing before then."

They were a good five miles into the river mouth before it began to narrow, banks thick with tall reeds closing in on both sides and drawing closer the farther north they steamed. The previously calm waters became churned with wayward currents and dark with disturbed silt. Clay stood at the stern, watching Jack's spines cut the surface as he followed the ship. The drake could sense the imminence of their separation and didn't like it, his fearful thoughts accompanied by a plaintive call that thrummed the deck beneath Clay's feet.

You can't go where I'm going, Clay told him once again, a mantra he had been obliged to repeat for the last few hours. *But I'll still be with you.*

Jack seemed to take only marginal reassurance from this, his confusion having deepened ever since the Greens attacked the ship. He had never encountered their kind before and his thoughts were tinged with a wary repugnance that could be articulated as: *smell wrong, sound wrong.*

That they do, Clay conceded. *And if they come back, you may have to fight them.*

Jack's thoughts grew warier still, an instinctive desire to avoid danger conflicting with his need to maintain their connection. Clay wondered if it might be kinder to set the beast free, as he had with Lutharon before they set off for the ice. But they still had so much to do, and who knew what use he might be in the future? *I really ain't a very nice person,* he reflected causing Jack to voice a puzzled rumble, this one thrumming the ship with sufficient force to make the rail buzz in Clay's hands.

Awful big ocean out there, Clay reminded him. *You ain't my slave, Jack. You want to go, then go.*

Jack's head rose out of the water for a moment, twin jets of flame sprouting from his nostrils as he gave what could only be called a derisive snort. His snout dipped back below the surface but his eyes remained visible, Clay sensing a certain reproach in the stare Jack levelled at him.

Guess that settles it, he conceded. *Once I'm gone this ship will return to the Torquils to wait for us. Stay close if you can, but don't starve yourself.*

Jack replied with an image, a drake's-eye view of what appeared to be a shimmering, shifting cloud that Clay soon realised was a large shoal of fish. Jack, it appeared, would not be going hungry in his absence.

The *Superior's* steam-whistle let out the four short blasts that indicated an imminent stop, Clay feeling the faint rhythmic thud of the auxiliary engine fade from the deckboards. It seemed Captain Hilemore had decided this was as far as the ship could go. *It's time,* he told Jack. *If I die . . .* he began, provoking an upsurge of fear in the drake. Clay asserted his will, forcing his thoughts through the fog of distress. *If I die you'll feel it. What you do then is up to you. Like I said, it's an awful big ocean.*

"The *Lady Malynda.*" Loriabeth read the name Chief Bozware had painted on the steam-launch's hull in finely executed letters of red and black. "Couldn't we call her something a sight more fierce?"

"It's my former wife's name," the Chief responded, rubbing his back as he straightened from tightening a bolt on the engine. He vaulted over the craft's side onto the *Superior's* deck. "And be assured, miss, she was plenty fierce enough, even after the divorce."

The engineer turned to Hilemore and touched two fingers to his forehead in a sketchy salute. Clay had noticed that the Chief was perhaps the only crew member Hilemore afforded such leeway when it came to formal discipline. "She's as ready as I can make her, sir."

"Fine work, Chief," the captain told him. "Alright, Mr. Talmant, let's get her in the water if you please."

"Aye, sir."

Under the young officer's guidance a dozen crewmen lowered the *Lady Malynda* over the side and onto the swift-flowing surface of the Quilam. Skaggerhill climbed down first followed by Kriz, the only two in their party who had a notion of how to operate the engine. It was a coal-burner and took a good half-hour to heat the boiler to the required temperature. Supplies were duly lowered, enough for at least a month's travel though Clay knew well they might have to resort to hunting for food in time.

"All I can spare," Hilemore said, handing Clay a satchel containing several flasks. "Ten of Green. One each of the other colours."

"Sure you can spare this much Red?" Clay asked, checking the satchel.

"The exigencies of the mission require it, Mr. Torcreek." Hilemore glanced down at the launch where the rest of the party waited. Uncle Braddon had taken up position on the prow and sat in now-customary silence, his rifle cradled in his lap as his gaze roamed the river with predatory keenness. "No regrets about your choices?" the captain asked. "It's not too late. Mr. Steelfine would make a fine addition to this company, and I know he would relish the challenge."

"Yeah, but he also hates my guts."

Clay offered his hand and Hilemore took it. "Captain Okanas will be expecting regular communication," he said. "As will I."

"Every three days till we get to the lake," Clay said. "After that we'll reschedule as needed, depending on how the Blue holds out." He cast his gaze towards the stern of the ship where Jack's spines could be seen tracking back and forth across the river. "If he leaves and don't come back within two days, it most likely means I'm dead. Same if Captain Okanas don't hear from me or Lieutenant Sigoral for five days. In that case it'd be best if you took off, make for Varestia like Miss Lethridge said."

"Noted." Hilemore inclined his head. "But I'd thank you to leave command decisions to me."

"O' course."

Clay moved to the rail and clambered over, descending the rope net to the *Lady Malynda*. Kriz was tending the engine whilst Skaggerhill had the tiller. Loriabeth and Sigoral were seated in the middle whilst Preacher sat close to Braddon at the prow. Clay waited for his uncle to say something, hoping he would turn and offer at least some word of command to set them on their way. Even the smallest grunt would have been welcome. But he said nothing, continuing to sit and maintain his hungry vigil over the water. Clay opened his mouth to call to Braddon but stopped when Loriabeth caught his eye and gave a stern shake of her head.

"Daylight's burning," he said instead, lowering his gaze to Kriz. "If she's ready, let's be on our way. Lori, Lieutenant, eyes on the water. Preacher, watch the sky. It's a safe bet we'll have company before long."

CHAPTER 13

Lizanne

"Ten million in Syndicate scrip, eh?" The broken-nosed man grinned at Lizanne as he lowered Trumane's letter. "Quite the offer, don't you think, Mother?" He held the letter out to the prim, neatly attired woman who stood close by. "Have a gander at the signature. I think you'll find it amusing."

The woman's handsome features remained impassive as she scanned the letter, though her lips curled a little when she got to the end. "'Your faithful correspondent, Captain Wulfcot Trumane,'" she read before raising her eyebrows at Lizanne. "Or 'Captain Noose' as he's known in these waters. I must confess, Miss Lethridge, but for the manner of your arrival I might otherwise have taken this as a rather poor joke."

"I have no jokes to offer you," Lizanne replied. "Just an honest offer in return for safe harbour, and sound intelligence I believe you will find useful."

"Your captain hung my cousin on the deck of his own ship," the broken-nosed man said, then frowned and added, "Well, second cousin, and a truly rotten bastard to be sure. But still blood of my blood. And my people are all about blood. But then so are you. After all, it's your name, isn't it? Miss Blood?"

Lizanne and Tekela had been guided to a grand room on the second floor of the building the Varestians referred to simply as "The Navigation." The title apparently derived from the building's original use as the home of the Loyal Guild of South Corvantine Cartographers and Navigational Experts. The map-makers and compass designers had long since been exiled back to their northern homelands, but the building remained, complete with its appropriate and overwhelming decor. Maps were everywhere, hanging in tapestry form on the walls, rendered in oils on huge canvases, reproduced as floor mosaics and even plasterwork reliefs on the ceilings. She assumed this particular chamber had been some kind of ball-room, the floor covered from end to end in a vast map of the world which, judging from the florid Eutherian lettering and place names, dated back to the early corporate era.

Apart from herself and Tekela, the only other occupants were the broken-nosed man, his handsome of face if somewhat severe of demeanour mother and a man of South Mandinorian origin clad in curiously archaic clothing. Lizanne had quickly judged this man to be the most salient physical threat, not least by virtue of his cutlass and pistol, but also his muscular frame and set features, tensed as if in constant expectation of combat. She also deduced from the way the broken-nosed man moved about the room that he was not to be under-estimated either.

"We know who you are, you see?" he went on. "Famed Defender of Carvenport, Hero of the Corvantine Revolution and, most importantly at this particular juncture, a thieving, murdering bitch in the employ of the Ironship Exceptional Initiatives Division." All humour faded from his face, voice dropping to a murmur. "And therefore not to be trusted."

"I know of you too," Lizanne replied, meeting his gaze squarely. "Arshav Okanas, renowned pirate and former Chief Director of the criminal enclave known as the Hive, where I believe you lost a duel to an Islander named Steelfine not so long ago. How's your nose, by the way?" She turned her gaze from his reddening face before he could reply, inclining her head at the primly attired woman. "And you are Ethilda Okanas, widow to the late founder of the Hive and, I'm told, possessed of a more rational mind than your son."

"Be assured that we speak with one mind on matters of business," Ethilda replied. She briefly read through Trumane's letter once more before tossing it onto a near by table. "This is worthless. With Arradsia lost your Syndicate's collapse is inevitable, along with much of the corporate world. What use will we have for your scrip then? It has always been nothing more than paper, after all, and we have sufficient kindling."

Lizanne took a moment to scan the opulence of the room, hoping the myriad maps might spark some stratagem. "I had hoped to address the whole council," she said, playing for time as inspiration failed to materialise. "I believe a quorum of eight is required before any decision can be reached."

She saw Arshav exchange an amused glance with his mother. "I'm afraid you'll have to be content with a quorum of two," he said. "You see, upon return to our beloved homeland there was what I believe historians refer to as a vicious power struggle. Our wise Ruling Council had taken it upon themselves to declare us dead after the Corvantine attack on the Hive, helping themselves to our family holdings in the process. It took five successive duels to put the matter right, by which time the council was short five members and the remainder had decided they preferred life at sea."

"So you see, Miss Blood," Ethilda said, "any accommodation you wish to make will require our agreement, and as yet I find myself content to let your fleet of beggars rot where it sits."

Lizanne looked down, biting on a frustrated sigh. She saw that her boot rested on the Barrier Isles north of the Arradsian continent, the toe covering the Strait, the portal through which so much wealth had once flowed, enough to transform an entire world.

"You're right," she said, raising her gaze to address Ethilda. "Without product the corporate world will fall. But what are you without the corporations? With whom will you trade when they're gone? Whose ships will you prey upon? The Corvantine Empire destroyed itself trying to maintain the illusion it could remain separate, eternal and unchanged for all time. They failed to see a basic truth: The corporate world *is* the world. If it falls so does everything else."

She lowered her gaze once more, striding across the map until her boots came to rest on Varestia. "Do you imagine you are immune here? I'm sure your spies have informed you of what befell the Barrier Isles and Feros."

"We have defences," Arshav said. "A great many ships and the best sailors in the world."

"The Corvantines had the most modern fleet in the world," Lizanne returned. "I watched it sink and burn off Carvenport. If you know as much as you claim you'll have some inkling of the force that will come against you. An army of Spoiled controlled by a single mind. And drakes, thousands of Reds, Greens and Blues, all of them filled with hate and hunger by the thing that commands them."

Ethilda exchanged another glance with her son, this one much more serious. "How will taking in a bunch of impoverished corporatists aid us?" Arshav asked. "It strikes me you will be more a burden than a blessing."

Lizanne pointed at the mini-Growler. She had been obliged to surrender it on entering the room and it lay on a table close to the entrance. "That," she said. "And many more like it, along with larger and even more powerful weapons. You also saw the craft that brought us here. Give us the means and we can make more."

Arshav went to the mini-Growler, lifting it and pursing his lips in reluctant admiration. "A nice toy," he said. "But expensive and time-consuming to manufacture, I would imagine."

"There is something else," Lizanne told him. "Something that can be fashioned in hours rather than days. I assume your men searched the aerostat. They would have found a carbine there."

Arshav raised an eyebrow at the man in the archaic clothing, who nodded. "Bring it here, please, Mr. Lockbar," the pirate told him.

"I'll need a target," Lizanne said, reaching for the Smoker when Lockbar returned with it a few minutes later. "Something you don't value."

"I think not, miss," Arshav said, taking the carbine from Lockbar. "I'd rather form my own conclusions."

He went to one of the expansive window doors lining the room's south-facing wall and opened it. Stepping out onto the veranda beyond, he gestured for Lizanne to follow and pointed at something in the lush gardens below. A tall rectangular plinth sitting amidst a circle of flower-beds.

"The monument to the fallen members of the Corvantine Navigational Guild," he said. "Kept intact due to the sentiment of my predecessors. Personally, I see no reason to honour the souls of those who once enslaved us."

He put the carbine to his shoulder, chambered a round and fired. "King of the Deep," he breathed as the top of the monument shattered. Arshav laughed, worked the lever and fired again, blasting away another chunk of the plinth. He kept on until the carbine was empty, his laughter increasing as he reduced the monument to a jagged remnant.

"After due consideration," he said, lowering the Smoker and coughing a little as he wafted the smoke away, "I believe . . ."

"Further consideration is warranted," Ethilda broke in, giving her son a glare of sufficient severity as to wipe the laughter from his face. Ethilda turned to Lizanne with a humourless smile. "In the meantime you and your lovely young companion will be our guests. Mr. Lockbar, please see these ladies to their room."

M r. Lockbar, together with a squad of five equally stern-faced guards, had escorted Lizanne and Tekela to a room on the upper floor of the Navigation. It was small with a narrow cot and a tiny window that had been nailed shut. "Servant's quarters," Tekela sniffed with snobbish disdain.

"I doubt we'll be here long," Lizanne said, sitting on the cot. Mr. Lockbar had relieved her of the vials of product in the Spider but she had had the foresight to conceal a vial of Blue in her hollow boot-heel. She had been permitted to keep her watch and waited the required forty-three minutes before commencing the trance at the scheduled hour.

"Listen at the door," she told Tekela, slotting the vial into the Spider. "If they come back try to delay letting them in until I'm done."

She found Sofiya Griffan wandering her mindscape in a black mourning-dress, her vibrant red hair the only colour to be found. Lizanne thought the woman's mindscape must have been beautiful before her grief. She imagined dappled forest-glades carpeted with wild flowers above which butterflies danced in air scented by honeysuckle. Something almost certainly taken from a picture-book read in childhood. Now it was like walking through the same scene reimagined by an illustrator in the midst of a depression. The forest was bleached of all colour, the sky above the tree-tops an ominous smear of black and grey.

Another ship took off on its own yesterday, Sofiya informed Lizanne, her thoughts as dull and uncoloured as the environment. *The second in two days.*

Tell Captain Trumane to do all he can to prevent further desertions, Lizanne told her. *I have a sense we will need to muster as large a work-force as possible, if our hosts choose to accept us that is.*

She paused, watching as Sofiya gazed at something near by. At first glance Lizanne took it for a butterfly frozen in flight, but closer inspection revealed it to be a miniature person, a lissome young girl with diaphanous wings plucking a morsel of pollen from an orchid.

The sylph-folk would visit me when I was a little girl, Sofiya recalled.

Whirl in spirals around my head as I danced. Such music they sang. Nanny said it was all in my head and spanked me for my foolishness, and in time they went away, but I never truly stopped believing. Their music was so beautiful, far beyond the mind of a child to conjure . . .

Speaking of music, Lizanne interrupted, keen to break the woman's reverie, which she suspected might go on for some time. *Has Makario made any more progress?*

With your mysterious box? Not as far as I'm aware. He plays for me sometimes, when I get sad enough to start crying again. He's very kind.

Yes, he is. And your . . . Lizanne fumbled for the right words. Her experience of pregnant women was minimal, and she had determined long ago to avoid such a mammoth complication to her own life. *Condition?* she decided finally.

I am vomiting less, thanks to Dr. Weygrand. He tells me it's far too soon for such things but I feel my son kicking sometimes. Curiously, it only happens when I think of Zakaeus. I believe he's keen to be born so he can avenge his father.

Lizanne clamped down on her own thoughts, lest the words "mad as a Blue-addled rat" leach into the shared mindscape. *We'll have to ensure that won't be necessary,* she told Sofiya. *Have you had any success in contacting Northern Fleet Headquarters?*

Yes. My contact there was clearly very harassed and seemed to regard my intelligence as more of a nuisance than anything. They had little to say other than that Captain Trumane is instructed to await further orders. I'm to trance again in five days.

Ask Professor Lethridge and Mr. Tollermine to provide you with blueprints for their weapons designs and memorise them. When you trance with the Northern Fleet again, make it very clear that their best course of action is to build as many of these devices as they can.

I had the impression no one is building anything at the moment. Apparently, a third of Ironship manufactories are on strike. There's a great deal of Voter agitation in many cities and the Protectorate is fully engaged in dealing with what my contact called "urban disturbances."

So they're rioting already, Lizanne thought, her own mindscape filling with unpleasant memories of Scorazin and the northern march of the People's Freedom Army. She was careful to confine the images within her own mind for fear of distressing Sofiya. *If ever there was a poor time to start a revolution.*

Miss Lethridge? Sofiya enquired, perturbed by the lack of communication.

Tell them also that secrecy is no protection now, Lizanne added. *They need to publicise the complete and unvarnished story of what happened in Arradsia and Feros. Only truth will unite us. Tell them that.*

"Blaska Sound." Ethilda Okanas pointed to a spot somewhere in the middle of the painted map. It stood seven feet high and occupied much of the north-facing wall in the round tower that sprouted from the Navigation's roof-top. The tower's eastern wall was dominated by a broad window facing out to sea, the room itself liberally equipped with optical devices of varying types and dimensions. Arshav occupied himself with peering through the lens of a huge telescope whilst his mother conversed with Lizanne.

The painting was a rendering of the entire Varestian region, though the style was illustrative rather than strictly cartographical. Mountain ranges and forests were depicted in elevated perspective rather than the usual lines and text. Lizanne was also grimly amused to see that the artist had chosen to populate the Red Tides with several fancifully proportioned drakes.

She stepped closer to the map, peering at the narrow coastal channel marked in elaborate Eutherian as "Blaska Sound." The mouth of the Sound stood perhaps twenty miles north of the Seven Walls and Iskamir. *Close enough for a secure supply route,* Lizanne mused. *And also an easy place in which to bottle us up should they see the need.*

"What facilities are there?" she asked, drawing a faint snicker from Arshav, who, she noticed, still had the Smoker slung over his shoulder.

"There's a coal-mine ten miles in on the northern bank of the Sound," Ethilda told her. "'Raker's Mount' they call it. It's an old Corvantine penal colony, abandoned since the Varestian Liberation. Our people have never been fond of grubbing in the dirt. The seams are still viable, so I'm told, so fuel won't be a problem."

"It's also a desolate shit-hole," Arshav added, grinning as he raised his eye from the telescope. "No roads or railways and tall mountains all around. The only way in and out is by sea."

"We'll need other materials," Lizanne said. "Iron and steel, copper too. Also chemical agents for munitions. Not to mention food."

Ethilda looked at her son, who shrugged, apparently bored with logistical details. "There'll be stocks in the Iskamir warehouses," he said. "All sorts of cargo's piled up recently since trade's been so poor."

"Make a list before you leave," Ethilda said and handed Lizanne an envelope. "Our formal counter-proposal."

Seeing that the envelope had no seal Lizanne extracted the papers within, reading over the first few paragraphs. "This is a company charter," she said, frowning.

"Indeed," Ethilda said. "This day marks the founding of the Varestian Defence Conglomerate. I and Arshav are Co-Directors in Chief. You'll note I've appointed you Director of Intelligence and Manufactory Liaison."

"Congratulations," Arshav put in.

"'The Conglomerate will retain exclusive lifetime rights to any and all novel devices manufactured on Conglomerate soil,'" Lizanne read, feeling her pulse quicken. "'Also all salvage rights over any captured belligerent vessel, including its cargo, fixtures and fittings. Plus any draconic plasma, heretoafter referred to as "product," harvested within the established borders of the Varestian region will be regarded as Conglomerate property.'"

"Entirely fair in the circumstances," Arshav said, moving away from the telescope and holding up a pen. "Wouldn't you agree?"

Lizanne stared at him, thinking it would be an easy matter to take that pen and push it through his eye and into his brain.

"You'll get your share," Ethilda said. "As a Director you will be afforded ten percent of total company stock. How you wish to distribute the dividends is up to you. Please add your signature to the final page." She angled her head, looking past Lizanne at Tekela with a fond smile. "Your delightful ward can witness the transaction."

Lizanne set her jaw and reached for the pen. "There is one other matter," Ethilda said, her son giving a pout of mock apology as he drew the pen out of reach. "My late husband's granddaughter."

"What of her?"

"You indicated a detailed knowledge of what transpired at the Hive. I wish to know how."

"I'm an Exceptional Initiatives agent. Intelligence is my business."

"Then be so kind as to share what intelligence you hold regarding the whereabouts of Akina Okanas. This is not a matter for negotiation."

Seeing the hard glint in the woman's eyes, Lizanne knew this was no bluff. She also knew it wouldn't profit her to share too much with these people. She abruptly decided to avoid any mention of Clay's mission to Krystaline Lake, despite what insights these two might offer regarding the explorations undertaken by Zenida's late father. An adage from Burgrave Artonin's translation of Selvurin folk-tales popped into her head as she took in the poorly concealed greed on the Arshavs' faces: *Feed a snake and your only thanks will be venom.*

"Captain Trumane's flagship is the *Viable Opportunity*," Lizanne said. "A vessel I believe you are familiar with. I learned the story from the crew."

Arshav took a step forward, gaze narrowing. "Is my niece aboard?" he demanded in a low, dangerous voice. "Do you have her?"

"She's no longer on the ship," Lizanne went on in a clipped uncoloured tone, the voice her tutors had drilled into her as the most effective when lying. *Poor liars always attempt a performance,* she had been told. *The truth requires no theatrics.* "The *Viable Opportunity* sailed eastward around Arradsia after departing the Hive, eventually putting in at Lossermark where Zenida Okanas contrived to escape with her daughter."

"That's a pile of dog shit," Arshav growled.

"Captain Trumane was wounded at the Battle of the Strait," Lizanne continued, ignoring him and addressing his mother. "Leaving him in a comatose state. Command of the *Viable* then fell to a Lieutenant Hilemore, with whom I believe you are also familiar. Hilemore freed Zenida Okanas from Protectorate custody and employed her as the ship's Blood-blessed. A measure that earned Captain Trumane's severe disapproval when he woke from his coma in Lossermark harbour. It was the captain's intention to return Zenida Okanas to the brig for eventual trial and likely execution. It appears Lieutenant Hilemore found such a course of action unacceptable to his honour and so he contrived to desert the ship along with Zenida, her daughter and a small number of mutineers. It seems they seized a Corvantine warship that had taken refuge in the harbour and sailed away, destination as yet unknown."

Arshav glowered and turned away, he and Ethilda retreating to a corner of the room for a whispered discussion. They spoke in Varestian, which Lizanne knew well, but using a pirate slang that made translation difficult. She did, however, hear Ethilda utter the phrases "coming here" and "determined to kill us when she does," to which Arshav replied, "I do hope so, Mother."

Eventually they seemed to reach some form of agreement and turned back to Lizanne, Arshav tossing her the pen. "Rest assured, Miss Blood," he cautioned her as she scrawled her name on the document, "we regard formal agreements just as seriously as does the corporate world, except in Varestia breach of contract is usually a fatal matter." He gave a bland smile and patted the stock of the Smoker. "Don't mind if I keep this do you?"

"Not at all." Lizanne said, handing the contract back to Ethilda. "It's customary to mark a new partnership with gifts, after all."

"Partnership." Ethilda's mouth twitched a little in suppressed amusement. "What quaint notions you have, miss." Her lips broadened into a smile as she extended the contract and pen to Tekela. "Come, my dear. Your very dainty hand is needed."

CHAPTER 14

Sirus

"Varestia," Morradin said, a sneer curling his broad lips as his gaze tracked over the pencil-line Sirus had sketched on the map. The marshal's thoughts went on to form the old Eutherian term for the region, one born of the many wars the Empire had fought there: *the Sewer of Malcontents.*

"A formidable target then?" Catheline asked, her red-and-black eyes shifting between Sirus and Morradin. The principal captains of the White's army were clustered around the navigation table on the bridge of a large freighter recently renamed the *Malign Influence*, the new flagship of their fleet. Following behind were over sixty ships of varying sizes, together with numerous towed barges laden with Spoiled. In all the army now totalled some sixty thousand formerly human souls but, from the grudging concern leaking from Morradin's thoughts, it might well prove insufficient for the task ahead.

"The Corvantine Empire was never able to fully control the region," Sirus said. "Even after it had been officially conquered. Rebellions were frequent and the attrition of Imperial forces constant. When the previous revolution broke out, the Empire was obliged to withdraw its forces to reinforce the northern provinces. Following the revolution repeated attempts to reconquer Varestia met with disaster." Sirus's gaze flicked to Morradin. "Including one led by you, I believe, Marshal."

"Fuck you, boy!" Morradin spat. Sirus didn't bother to conceal his satisfaction at the marshal's blossoming rage. "And fuck your mother," Morradin went on. "I was second in command of that expedition, as you well know. And we'd have won if that fool admiral had listened to me . . ."

Be quiet.

Morradin's teeth clacked as his mouth slammed shut in response to

Catheline's thought-command. He stood with nostrils flaring and eyes blazing as Catheline turned back to Sirus. "You were saying, General?"

"The Varestians' success in defeating the Empire was largely due to their command of the sea," Sirus went on. "And a willingness to put aside long-standing clan rivalries to pursue a common aim. Their society is famed for its supposed brutality but is in fact remarkably stable and cohesive, due in part to a strictly observed code of ethics and the practice of resolving irreconcilable disputes through duels rather than large-scale conflict. The geography of the region also presents numerous challenges. So many islands offer numerous refuges for enemy vessels and many opportunities for ambush. Then there is the question of numbers." Sirus fell silent, turning to Veilmist in expectation.

"The Ironship records seized at Feros," the Islander began in her unhesitant, precise Mandinorian, "contain a demographic analysis of the Varestian region. It was compiled five years ago when the Syndicate was considering seeking a formal arrangement with the Varestian Ruling Council regarding trading concessions. It concluded the region is home to approximately thirty million people. This is based on the availability of arable land and consumption of imported food-stuffs, a more reliable method than the Corvantine census, which is notoriously inaccurate. This means that in the event of a large-scale conflict the region could muster close to four million recruits of military age, including both men and women."

Catheline arched an elegant eyebrow at Veilmist. "Four million? That does seem rather a lot."

"This is the figure they could amass under ideal conditions," Veilmist replied. "The true figure, given the challenges of local terrain, factional conflicts and logistical difficulties, will be much lower. Perhaps as low as one million, and even then that would require several months of organisation."

"Let's say we give them"—Catheline pursed her lips in consideration—"just one month. How many are we likely to face then?"

"Given the armed citizenry already on hand, local militias and likely rate of recruitment, between two hundred to two hundred and fifty thousand."

Forest Spear spoke up, which was a rarity in these meetings as he tended to make any contributions mentally. However, since Catheline's ascension Sirus had noticed an increased tendency amongst the Spoiled to communicate verbally. He assumed she just liked it that way. "We faced more in the islands," Forest Spear said in his guttural but still-comprehensible Varsal. For some as yet unexplained reason the tribals seemed to prefer the Corvantine common tongue when speaking aloud, not that it mattered. All languages were equally understood in this army. "Warriors born and bred for battle," Forest Spear added. "And still they fell before us."

"But they didn't all possess fire-arms," Sirus pointed out. "Neither did they possess a large fleet of armed ships crewed by the best sailors in the world." He turned to Catheline, compelled by her desire for unalloyed truth. "We don't have the numbers for a successful conquest. Or the ships."

Morradin gave a pained grunt, drawing Catheline's gaze. She smiled and unlocked his mouth. "Something to add, Marshal?"

"The southern coastal ports of the Empire," he said, stubby finger jabbing at a series of successive points on the map. "Each one separated by at least fifty miles, unable to come to the other's aid should they be attacked."

"Population?" Catheline asked, turning to Veilmist.

"Five million all told," she said after a pause of only a few seconds. "But dispersed. Melkorin, the most westerly port has a population of only eighty-five thousand. Even allowing for the vagaries of the Corvantine census, it would seem a manageable objective. I estimate the recruitment yield to be close to twenty thousand Spoiled, allowing for a three to four percent casualty rate amongst our own forces."

"And when we're done there," Catheline said, a note of approval in her voice as she traced her crimson finger-nail along the coast, "we'll have yet more fruit to pluck. Excellent reasoning, my dear. You are as clever as you are beautiful."

Sirus managed to summon enough fear to mask his disgust at the warm gratification these words provoked in Veilmist's mind. Even the Spoiled, it seemed, were not immune to the flattery of a beautiful madwoman.

"Any additional concerns, General?" she asked, her gaze swivelling to Sirus as she sensed his fear.

He shook his head. "Only an observation that battle is always uncertain," he said.

She laughed, moving closer to pat his arm, her hand lingering to caress taut muscle beneath his sleeve. "But that's what makes it *so* stimulating."

Catheline stepped back, closing her eyes momentarily as she communed with the White, which had chosen to perch itself on the wide aft deck of the *Malign Influence*, along with its clutch of juveniles. After a moment she opened her eyes and favoured them all with one of her brightest smiles. "Consent is given. Please plot a course to Melkorin."

"**A**re you angry with me?" Catheline asked as they dined together. The *Malign Influence* lay at anchor a mile south of Melkorin and Sirus could see the flames rising above the harbour wall. "For keeping you from all the fun," she added, sipping her wine.

They had dined on sea-trout, expertly poached by a former head chef from one of Morsvale's more exclusive restaurants. Upon finding the fellow amongst the ranks of Spoiled Catheline had immediately appointed him as her personal cook and dined every day on lavish meals of the highest quality. She always ate dinner on the observation deck to the rear of the bridge, seated at a table complete with an ornate silver candelabra, plates of antique Dalcian porcelain and silver cutlery.

It was a week since the conference, sufficient time to plan their attack and complete the approach. At Catheline's instruction the entire affair had been left in Morradin's hands. Sirus found his own role restricted to overseeing the running of the fleet. He suspected she either wanted to stoke the rivalry between them or obtain an unvarnished example of the marshal's abilities. Perhaps both.

Morradin's plan had been characteristically straightforward, though he borrowed some of the more subtle elements from Sirus's attack on Feros. A small flotilla of ships, disguised as refugee vessels with besmirched hulls and unkempt works, approached the port in late evening, their signal pennants displaying a request for safe harbour. The Melkorin authorities, however, had staunchly refused to raise the door in their wall, gathering their garrison and militia in and around the docks. Sirus felt his sympathy for these people erode slightly when gun-batteries on the wall began casting shells at the supposed refugees.

Yes, Catheline agreed, sensing his disdain. *Yet more souls deserving of their fate. But then, they all are.*

Whilst the attention of the Melkorin defenders remained fixed on the ships outside their wall, the White's host of Reds swept over the coast to the east. They flew north for several miles before turning west as the sun began to fade, swooping low to deposit Spoiled and Greens on the port's outlying suburbs. Meanwhile, Morradin led the bulk of the fleet to land the main force of Spoiled infantry on a broad stretch of beach three miles to the west. Within hours the entire port was in chaos and the Corvantine troops and militia were unable to mount an organised defence. Resistance was still fierce, however, especially amongst the militia who were defending their homes and families. A few companies barricaded themselves into the more substantial buildings in the commercial district, holding out against repeated assaults until Morradin lost patience and asked for assistance from the Reds. Any action undertaken by the drakes that lay outside the original plan had to be approved by Catheline, their lives being regarded as so much more precious than the Spoiled.

Are you sure, Marshal? Catheline asked. *Seems a trifle excessive to me. Can't you just wait for them to run out of ammunition?*

They're blocking the main thoroughfare into the residential neighbourhoods, Morradin replied. *My scouts report a large number of people fleeing to the hill-country to the north. The longer this lot holds out the smaller our yield of recruits.*

This had been enough for Catheline to unleash the Reds, Katarias leading several dozen out of the night sky to blast the buildings with flame from top to bottom. This attack succeeded in eliminating resistance but also birthed a conflagration that soon spread to much of the port's western districts.

What a marvellous strategist you are, Marshal, Catheline observed. *I ask for recruits and you give me charred corpses.*

Morradin's response consisted of a sullen, reluctant pulse of apology which provoked a surprising laugh from Catheline. "What a simply dreadful man," she commented to Sirus. "But useful. Not as useful as you, dear General, but still worth keeping around. Don't you think?" Sirus sensed a genuine enquiry in her tone, eyebrows raised above her wine-glass as she added, "I'll kill him if you like."

He felt Morradin tense, the Spoiled of his personal guard immediately turning towards the marshal with levelled rifles. Sirus let the fear seep into his mind, masking his thoughts. Morradin was useful to the White, it was true. He was also supremely arrogant and self-interested to the point of mania, not to mention an Imperial butcher with the blood of thousands on his hands. But, more than that, he hated his enslavement just as much as Sirus did, and such hatred might suit his own ends in time.

"In land warfare he has no equal," Sirus said, reaching for his own wine-glass. He shrugged as he took a small sip. The wine was an expensive Mandinorian white of impressive vintage, part of the copious stocks looted from the Ironship stores in Feros. Sirus doubted even his father could have afforded a single bottle of the stuff. He had found since his conversion that his senses had been enhanced, including his taste-buds, and he savoured the tingle the wine left on his tongue. *Notes of apple with a hint of lemon, matured in oak for at least eighteen years.* He shared the taste with Morradin, feeling the marshal's hatred swell along with his terror.

"However," Sirus went on, lowering his glass, "his instinctive aggression can cause problems, as you've seen. Perhaps punishment would be preferable to execution. But, of course, I leave the matter in your hands."

"Do you seek to teach me restraint?" Catheline's lips pursed in mock offence. "I should hope not, sir. I was never one for moderation. But you speak sense. Punishment it is."

Sirus flinched as she blinked and sent a pulse of pure agony into Morradin's brain. The marshal stiffened and collapsed, writhing on the cobbled street as the port burned around him. Catheline held out her glass to the Spoiled waiter near by, who dutifully filled it. She had drained the glass by the time the pain faded from Morradin's mind.

I trust such lessons will not be necessary in future, she told him, all humour gone and her thoughts chilly with sincerity. *Now be about your business. Twenty thousand recruits is what I was promised, and what I expect.*

Sirus felt the marshal's thought-command spread to the rest of the army, carrying strict injunctions against any unnecessary killing. *Apart from the children, of course,* he added. *They're of no use.*

"Ah," Catheline said, brightening as a second waiter approached bearing a tray. "Dessert!"

"This is the point in the evening when most men would try to fuck me."

She had him stroll with her after dinner. Sirus had been required to dress for the occasion and wore the uniform of an Ironship Protectorate colonel of infantry, complete with several medals won by its former owner. Catheline was attired in an elegant gown of black silk embroidered with flames of red, the product of a skilled dress-maker captured and converted in Feros. She also wore a shawl about her shoulders, fine lace threaded with jewels that glittered as they caught the flickering flames from Melkorin. Sirus supposed that, but for their deformities and the dying city across the water, an ignorant observer might have thought them the image of a romantic young couple.

"Oh, I beg your pardon," she added, sensing his surprise at the coarseness of her language. "*Seduce* me."

Sirus found himself at a complete loss for words. He had experienced a great deal in a short space of time, but some things were still far beyond his abilities.

"Despite my reputation I was quite choosy, you know," Catheline went on. "Married men were always my preference, especially if their wives were one of those managerial bitches who loved to sneer at me so. I always found sex and revenge a potent mix."

They came to the prow of the ship where she paused, rearranging her shawl to reveal her shoulders. Sirus found himself momentarily distracted by the way the light of the burning city played over her flesh, smooth, unscaled and wonderfully human.

"Why thank you, sir," Catheline said, sensing his involuntary lust. "I was beginning to think such things beneath you."

She turned back to the city as a large explosion blossomed above the wall. From the scale of the blast Sirus assumed the fire had reached the garrison's arsenal. "I had them burn Feros before we left," Catheline continued, the explosion fading into a cascade of debris. "*He* hates cities, you see? The very notion of human civilisation is offensive to him. I expect this is a sight to which we'll become quite accustomed before we're done."

"What happens then?" Sirus asked. He was aware this might be dangerous, the Spoiled did not question their great White god after all. But he coloured his mind with what he hoped was a sufficient level of simple curiosity to conceal any sense of concern for the fate of the human world.

"The world will be his, and we will be his grateful servants," Catheline replied, apparently failing to detect any artifice. "For He has blessed us, has

He not? The ability to seamlessly share thoughts and experience. Think of a whole world where lies have been banished, where every mind is united in a common purpose. This will be the last war in human history. I have a yen to be a mother when this is all over. My child will be heir to a new world of eternal peace." She glanced over her perfect shoulder at him. "You fathered a child, did you not?"

Katrya's face when he shot her . . . Can we not love too? He drowned the memories in a deluge of fear and grief, but not before Catheline sensed his guilt.

"We can't keep them all alive, General," she said, a frown of sincere sympathy creasing her brow. "More's the pity. I'm sorry for your woman, and the child, but soldiers die in war. Come the morning we'll have thousands of freshly converted young women in our ranks. Choose one, if you wish."

"No thank you."

Catheline's sympathy turned to amusement and she moved to him, reaching out to take his hand, perfect unblemished fingers tracing over the callused, scaled flesh. "Still carrying a torch for your fallen lover?" she asked. "Or do I flatter myself that you worry over making me jealous?"

Nothing, he thought, his mind sliding over hers like a hand pushing at smooth, cold glass. *No clue as to her true intentions. What she really is.*

"What I am?" she asked with a laugh provoking the shocked realisation that he had failed to shield his thoughts. "Oh, don't fret," she added, squeezing his hand as the fear flooded in. "It's refreshing to find a genuinely curious mind amongst this lot." She moved closer, her perfume rendered near intoxicating by his enhanced senses. "I am the final word in his blessing of this world," she murmured, lips close to his. "He needed me, you see? Not all of me, since He got a good deal from the other bitch before she died. But, great as his mind is, it lacks . . ."

She let out an involuntary shout, her breath hot on Sirus's face as she convulsed and collapsed at his feet. Sirus started to crouch at her side but froze as another far more powerful will invaded his mind. A low, rattling growl came from above and Sirus looked up to find the White's huge head poised above them, thin tendrils of smoke leaking from both nostrils. Its gaze flicked over Sirus before locking onto Catheline. She let out a strangled scream, jerking on the deck as spittle drooled from her lips.

Punishment, Sirus thought.

A series of thuds drew his gaze to the surrounding deck and he saw the juvenile Whites had come to watch the spectacle, wings flapping in excitement, tails and necks coiling as they hissed and squawked. Sirus found he had no need to draw on his reserves of fear to mask his thoughts, the fist of terror that gripped him now was completely authentic, though he did find room amongst it all for a singular insight. *Your god does not love you back,* he decided as Catheline's choking shudders subsided into a gibbering tremble.

The White's growl trailed off and it grunted out a gust of smoke before launching itself into the air, the wind generated by its wings strong enough to force Sirus to his knees. He watched it ascend into the night air, ivory scales painted pink by the light of the burning city. It levelled out and angled its massive body towards Melkorin, its juvenile brood clustering around it, screaming in excited hunger. It had been the same after Feros. After the fall came the feast, and there were many children in this city.

He lowered his gaze to Catheline, seeing that her tremors had stopped and she now lay in an exhausted stupor. He also saw that she had contrived to besmirch her silk gown with a copious amount of urine. He wondered if the White would care if he killed her now.

Sirus crouched and gathered Catheline into his arms, lifting her easily. He stood watching the White dive down into the burning city, its dreadful brood following close behind, before lowering his gaze to the dark waters below. *Throw the mad bitch over the side. The world will thank you for it.*

Catheline let out a soft, fearful whimper, her fluttering eyelids telling of a mind beset by nightmares. She shifted in his arms, moving her head closer to his chest in an instinctive quest for comfort. Sirus turned and carried her towards the nearest hatch, making for her cabin and sending a command to the crew to bring her some clean clothes.

CHAPTER 15

Lizanne

"I didn't like the way that woman looked at me."

Lizanne glanced up at Tekela from the contract that cemented her employment in the Varestian Defence Conglomerate. She had read it several times during the return journey, finding to her annoyance that Ethilda Okanas had crafted something it would be very hard to extricate herself from later, at least legally. "You shouldn't," she muttered in agreement before glancing out the window. They had left Iskamir behind a day ago and were nearing the southern extremity of the Sabiras Archipelago, beyond which lay the hopefully secure anchorage of Viemen's Island.

"I won't have to see her again, will I?" Tekela asked. "Or that son of hers. He was almost as horrid."

Lizanne began to snap at her, irritation at the cleverness of the Okanas clan leading her to scold this girl for her weakness. *An entire world of horrid people awaits you,* she had been about to say. *Harden your sensibilities and keep a loaded revolver handy.* Instead she took a breath and recalled all the many trials Tekela had endured, concluding she was already as hardened as Lizanne wished her to be. So she said, "I'm sorry. I'll do my best to ensure you don't find yourself in their company again."

They had resisted lighting the blood-burner for the return trip, Lizanne deciding the burst of speed would be best saved for emergencies. The flight was therefore long and somewhat tedious, passed in resentful scrutiny of the contract she had been obliged to sign interspersed with fitful dozing. Her sleep had been interrupted several times by the buffeting the aerostat received from the winds at this more southerly latitude. Hours of fighting to keep the machine on course left Tekela increasingly fatigued as the journey wore on. Lizanne wanted to take over for a time but lacked the required familiarity with the controls. Besides which, manoeuvring herself into the pilot's seat in the cramped confines of the gondola seemed next to impossible.

"When we're back on the ship," she told Tekela as the first of the outlying Sabiras Isles drifted by below, "your first task will be teaching me how to fly this thing."

The fleet came into view some two hours later, the many ships clustered in a tight arc around the speck of rock Lizanne's map confirmed as Vieman's Island. Daylight was fading fast and Lizanne feared night would fall before they could settle onto the fore-deck of the *Viable Opportunity*. Fortunately, Captain Trumane evidently saw the danger and ordered all lights lit, including the frigate's powerful search-light, which was lowered to illuminate the front of the ship. Tekela was obliged to navigate a stiff crosswind to complete the approach, her hands dancing from lever to lever as she gave voice to some choice curses in Varsal Lizanne would never have suspected her of knowing.

Finally, the landing gear bumped onto the deck and Tekela closed the throttle, stilling the thrum of the engine, before slumping forward with a soft sigh. She sat with her head resting on the dials in what Lizanne suspected was a theatrical pose until she heard a very faint snore emerge from the girl's nose.

"At any other time signing this would be an unconscionable act." Trumane sighed before tossing the contract onto his desk. "One the Syndicate would most likely punish with a prison sentence. Now, however." He shrugged and sank into his seat. Lizanne had expected more resistance from him but divined that his pragmatism outweighed any ingrained corporatist abhorrence for such a patently poor deal.

"There is something else to consider," she said. "The contract makes no mention of you."

Trumane frowned at her. "So?"

"It stipulates just about every aspect of our arrangement, including my role and the role of our coterie of inventors, and the employment of the refugees, but says nothing about you, the man they refer to as Captain Noose. I believe this to be a deliberate omission. Captain, I must advise you not to accompany us into Varestian waters. Take the *Viable Opportunity* and head north, along with Mrs. Griffan. If you can make it to a Mandinorian port you can enlighten what's left of the Syndicate hierarchy on the true nature of this crisis. Such understanding appears to be sadly lacking at this juncture."

"No." Trumane gave a stiff shake of his head. "I have not led this fleet so far to abandon it . . ."

"They'll hang you," Lizanne broke in. "The Okanas family, and many of the other clans, feel they owe you a blood debt, something Varestians do not forgive."

"I have never run from pirates, Miss Lethridge," he replied in a quiet but steady voice that told her this discussion was over. "I do not intend to start now." He lowered his gaze to the charts unfurled on his desk, reaching for a pen and compass. "Now, I have a course to plot if you'll excuse me."

"The whole composition has eight distinct movements," Makario said, handing her a partially crumpled sheaf of musical notation. "It was realising this that proved the key. The Artisan certainly had a passion for the number eight."

Glancing over the papers, Lizanne found them covered in a mostly illegible scrawl of notes interspersed with comments in the musician's often-tiny script. Lifting her gaze to him, she was struck by the redness of his eyes and the jittery tremble to his hand as he ran it through a mop of unkempt hair.

"How long since you slept?" she asked.

His brow bunched in genuine bafflement. "Why would I sleep with a puzzle like this to solve? I once thought Illemont would be my sole consuming passion, but this." He turned his gaze to the solargraph and Lizanne found herself wondering about the ability of this device to capture the hearts of those cursed to study it. "The Artisan was as much a musician as he was an inventor. To have met him would have been to know greatness."

"You're sure this is all of it?" she asked, setting the pages down on the work-bench.

"I've tested it several times, out of earshot of our fellow convict, of course."

"Very well." Lizanne turned to regard Tinkerer, who stood at another bench near the starboard bulkhead. He was engaged in completing a prototype redesign of the rocket projectile that had been so useful during the march from Scorazin. This one was larger with a greatly increased range and, thanks to an internal clock-work apparatus of dizzying complexity, would possess a remarkable level of accuracy.

"We'll wait until he's finished his new toy," she said. "In the meantime, please get some rest."

Three days later she watched Tinkerer's face closely as the solargraph played the tune, deciding Makario had been right about the Artisan's musical gifts matching his inventiveness. After he tapped out the first three movements on the chimes the device began to play on its own. Cogs whirred and dials turned as it gave voice to something of such sombre precision that it couldn't help but tug at her heart. Tinkerer sat through it all with an expression of interest but no particular concern and when he was done his only reaction was to blink at her.

"Have you . . ." Lizanne ventured, "anything to tell me?"

"Yes," he said with an earnest nod that caused her to lean closer. "I need more brass for the rocket-guidance mechanism."

"About this," she grated, stabbing a finger at the solargraph. "About all of this."

"Oh," said Tinkerer. "Then no."

"It's the right tune," Makario insisted as Lizanne turned her gaze upon him.

She thought back over her interactions with Tinkerer, all mentions of the Artisan and his shared memories in the trance. The trance. "Here," she said, taking a vial of Blue from her wallet. "Play it again," she instructed Makario after she and Tinkerer had both imbibed equal portions of the product.

This time the reaction was immediate. As soon as the tune began Tinkerer's gaze took on the unfocused cast that told of an imminent trance. However, it wasn't until the fourth movement that the full effect took hold. Tinkerer's eyes closed and he slumped to the floor, limbs twitching. Lizanne began to rise from her seat to check on him . . . and found herself standing waist deep in the middle of a fast-flowing river.

She had never experienced such a seamless transition into the trance state before and found it jarring. The sudden switch in surroundings, complete with a change in temperature, sights, smells and sounds made her stagger in the water. She would have lost her footing on the loose shingle of the river-bed if a pair of hands hadn't reached out to steady her.

"Careful now," said a voice in soft, cultured Eutherian. "You really can drown in here, you know."

The woman who had hold of her arms was trimly built of average height with shrewd dark eyes peering at Lizanne from behind a pair of spectacles. She wore sturdy clothes of strong fabric, the kind worn by someone who spends a good deal of time outdoors. A heavy pack was slung over her shoulders and a short-brimmed felt hat sat on her head, tilted back to reveal a shock of close-cropped black hair. She was also, Lizanne noticed, possessed of a high-cheek-boned beauty normally reserved for the imaginary heroines found adorning the covers of cheap romance novels.

"This . . ." Lizanne closed her eyes and shook her befuddled head before taking a more fulsome look at her surroundings. *A swift river, thick jungle on both banks.* "This is the Arradsian Interior."

"It is indeed." The woman gave an apologetic smile and released Lizanne's arms from her gentle but firm grasp. "Though I have always preferred the Eutherian name for the continent. *Kilnahria*, it derives from a serpent god of the pre-Imperial era. Quite apt, wouldn't you agree, miss . . . ?"

"Lethridge," she said, straightening and extending her hand. "Lizanne Lethridge. And yes, very apposite."

"Alestine Akiv Azkarian," the woman said, shaking her hand and giving a formal bow. "I was about to stop for lunch," she went on, sloshing her way towards the far bank. "If you would care to join me."

"You are the Artisan?" Lizanne asked, voicing a rueful laugh as she laboured through the water in her wake. The trance had seen fit to attire her in a somewhat impractical skirt and jacket of archaic dimensions, making for laggardly progress. "The Artisan was a woman."

"How observant you are," Alestine remarked, clambering onto the river-bank and extending a hand as Lizanne struggled to extricate herself from the water.

"I thought you would already know my name," Lizanne said, hauling herself free of the river and keeping hold of Alestine's hand. "The Artisan having foreseen this meeting."

"The Mad Artisan," Alestine said, her smile now tinged with a mix of sadness and humour. "Isn't that what they will come to call me?"

"The appellation of madness has faded recently," Lizanne replied. "Which is strange, given that the world around us grows madder by the day."

Alestine released her hand and turned, leading her deeper into the jungle. "I did not, in fact, know your name," she told Lizanne, as they tracked along a narrow trail. "But I have foreseen this meeting, or at least a portion of it. Oddly, I remember you having darker hair, and being markedly less polite. It happens sometimes, the vision's truth proves illusory. Due, I have theorised, to the relative passage of time. The longer I have to wait for it to come true, the less true it turns out to be."

"What did we discuss in the vision?" Lizanne asked, aware that her voice betrayed a note of desperation she would normally try to conceal. The shock of actually finding herself conversing with this person after expending so much time and effort to do so made her a little giddy, even nervous.

"You said your world was burning," Alestine said, coming to a halt as the trail opened out into a broad clearing. She unslung her pack and set it down before casting around with a searching gaze. "We need fire-wood. If you wouldn't mind lending a hand."

Lizanne began to comply but found her eyes drawn to a dark shape above the tree-tops ahead, the sides jagged black teeth against the pale blue of the sky. *The temple,* she realised, recalling one of Clay's shared memories. "Are we close to Krystaline Lake?" she enquired.

"Oh, Emperor's Soul no," Alestine laughed, crouching to gather up a fallen branch. "The lake lies over three hundred miles north-east of here." She followed Lizanne's gaze to the bulky silhouette above the trees. "Seen one like it before, I see. Krystaline Lake, eh? I must confess I had no idea there were ruins there."

"A whole city in fact."

"One I'll never get to see, except through your eyes if you're willing to share."

Lizanne turned to her, finding the same half-sad, half-amused smile on her lips. It wasn't unkind, but Lizanne found there was too much knowledge behind that smile for her to like it. "So in your vision I told you my world was burning," she said. "In reality it has only just begun to smoulder, though I think the flames are about to rise very high indeed. I believe you know how to prevent that, and I would have you tell me."

Alestine's smile switched to a grimace, her face clouding in reflective sorrow. "Then I fear you may be disappointed, miss. But"—she dumped the branch she had gathered on the ground and set about searching for more—"let's discuss it over dinner, shall we? I have an excellent cut of Cerath haunch to share. It's good meat, but does require proper seasoning."

She proved deaf to further questions so Lizanne helped her build the fire and a frame with which to spit the haunch of meat. Alestine scored the layer of fat coating the flesh with a knife then rubbed it with salt before sprinkling on some wild thyme. She constructed the frame in only a few moments, crafting two sturdy bipods and a cross-beam from scavenged wood. The swift, unconscious precision with which she went about the task was enough to banish any doubts Lizanne might have as to her identity. *She looks like Tinkerer,* she realised. *Or Father when he's particularly engrossed.*

"The secret is to keep it turning," Alestine said, adjusting the haunch's position over the fire before turning to her pack. "Would you care for an aperitif?" She extracted a metal flask and two tin cups, handing one to Lizanne before pouring a pinkish liquid into it. "A local vintage," Alestine said, raising her own cup to her nose to sample the aroma. "I'm afraid the name is quite unpronounceable. I call it 'Kilnahria's Milk.'"

Lizanne sniffed the substance, finding it pleasantly fruity, before taking a sip. "Very nice," she said. "If a little strong for my tastes."

"I'm glad you like it. You didn't in the vision." She drained her own cup and poured some more. "So, how did you like the music? I assume you unlocked the solargraph; otherwise, you wouldn't be here."

"A highly accomplished tune, to be sure. The musician I employed to decipher it was suitably impressed, and he is something of an expert in the music of your era."

"And you, Miss Lethridge? Did you like it?"

There was a weight to Alestine's gaze that caused Lizanne to conclude her answer was important. *A test of some kind?* she wondered. *Did my vi-*

sion self hate the music or love it? "It was beautiful," she said, deciding honesty would be the best course. "But sad. Your musical skills appear to match your flair for things mechanical."

"I can assure you they do not. I didn't write the music, you see. I merely captured it for posterity, although it's nice to know my flair for the mechanical had some uses."

"A great many uses. So many in fact, people have killed to possess the fruits of your labour, myself included."

"Such was never my intention." Alestine took another sip from her cup and turned to the meat, asking Lizanne to help as she adjusted the spit to revolve the haunch above the flames. "Approach every task with care and diligence and you won't go far wrong," she said. "Something my mother never tired of telling me."

"If you didn't write the music," Lizanne said, stepping back to waft the thickening smoke away, "who did?"

She saw the sadness return to Alestine's face, though this time it was not accompanied by any humour. "A lady of my prior acquaintance," she said. "You remind me a little of her. So much passion and humanity bound up in a tight, controlled package. I think you two would have gotten on quite well. Although, in time she would probably have come to see you as a threat and had you executed. She was prone to such things in later life, so I'm told."

"Had me executed?" Lizanne asked. "A woman of some influence, then?"

"You could say that. They made her empress eventually, well, Emperor to be strictly accurate. Apparently the title cannot accommodate a change in gender."

A singular memory sprang to the fore of Lizanne's mind: one of the many statues adorning the miniature temples that lay outside the Corvantine Imperial Sanctum, a hawk-nosed woman rendered in marble. "The Empress Azireh," she said. "You knew her? She wrote the music?"

"She wrote a great many things, but music was her passion. And yes, I knew her, but she wasn't an empress then."

There was a rustle of disturbed vegetation as Alestine turned towards the far end of the clearing, Lizanne following her gaze to see the foliage twisting and merging to form a new tableau. A young woman sat at a pianola, playing the same tune the Artisan had captured in the solargraph. Although the surrounding jungle remained unchanged, the floor beneath the pianola was smooth chequered marble reflecting a grand, palatial interior. Despite her youth Lizanne saw clearly the resemblance to the stern, commanding woman who would later adorn the temple built in her honour.

"She was just a lonely girl then," Alestine went on as the young future empress played her beautifully sad music. "Lost in a court of privileged, scheming idiots who would quite happily have seen her dead. I've often thought divine blood was more a curse than a blessing. So much promise, so much more music to give to the world, all swallowed up by the fate her blood made for her. But, the young are ever prone to the hope, perhaps the delusion, that their fate can be changed."

Lizanne watched as a young woman emerged from the jungle and bowed to the woman at the pianola, who immediately straightened into a much more attentive posture. The younger Alestine was also easy to recognise, but in this memory she wore the white blouse, black waistcoat and skirt of a Corvantine court attendant, and a low-ranking one at that. "It's the upper c minor again, I'm afraid," Azireh said, tapping one of the pianola's keys. "A little tinny, don't you think?"

"My musical knowledge was only functional," the older Alestine told Lizanne as her younger self opened the lid of the pianola. "I knew enough to repair instruments but not play them with any skill. My primary duty in the Sanctum was fixing the various toys and automata with which the noble children amused themselves. The 'Fiddly Girl,' they called me, amongst other things." She gave a fond chuckle. "Awful brats the lot of them, apart from one."

At the young Alestine's bidding Azireh repeatedly tapped the key as she worked away at something in the pianola's innards. Lizanne was no expert but couldn't detect more than a fractional change in the pitch. "I found out later she used to loosen the strings herself," the older Alestine said. "Just so she would have a reason to talk to me."

"That seems perfect, my lady," her younger self said, closing the pianola lid and dropping into a low curtsy. "If you'll excuse me."

"Wait a moment," Azireh said. "I've been working on a little something and would so like your opinion. My lady attendants wouldn't know a decent tune if I strangled them with it."

She began to play without waiting for a response, the same composition as before but now executed with expert clarity and precision. Lizanne found it much more affecting than that recreated by the solargraph's chimes, music that seemed to reach inside her, forcing her mind to explore the most vibrant memories, good and bad. It was both an unnerving and intoxicating experience, and, judging by the changing expression on the young Alestine's face, one she shared in full measure. Up until now her face had maintained the same incurious, carefully neutral mode common to servants of long standing. Now she stared at the young woman before her with rapt fascination, a single tear tracing down her cheek.

"Love is always a surprise," the older Alestine said. "Don't you find? Whether it creeps up on you over the course of years or reaches out to snare you in an instant. The moment is always a revelation and it can happen in the space of a heart-beat, or the time it takes to play the most wondrous music a foolish young woman had ever heard."

She looked away and the memory swiftly merged back into the jungle. "I do believe it's time for another turn of the spit," she said, moving back to the fire.

"You were lovers," Lizanne said, finding the notion scarcely conceivable. *A servant and a princess trysting in the Imperial Sanctum.* "If you had been discovered . . ."

"Oh we were, make no mistake about that." Alestine gestured for Lizanne to take the other end of the spit and together they turned the meat, the fire hissing and popping as grease flowed from the cuts. "We weren't even particularly discreet. It wasn't uncommon for nobles to indulge themselves with the servants. There was an unspoken tolerance for such things, life in the Sanctum being so monumentally dull. But not for us. For what we had was not mere indulgence, and that made it dangerous. For a time we were left in peace. Azireh had me assigned as her personal attendant and we lived in happy seclusion in our own little palace. She composed her music and I designed and constructed my toys, then came the Regency Wars."

The sound of rustling plants came again and Lizanne looked round to see the entire clearing morphing into a grand ball-room. Huge chandeliers of glittering crystal hung from the ceiling above a dance floor streaked in blood from the many corpses that covered it. There were men and women, infants and elderly, all dressed in the finery befitting the various ranks of Corvantine nobility. From the pattern of the blood spatter Lizanne deduced this massacre had been carried out with the blade rather than the gun.

"The Coronation Day Purge," Alestine said, sprinkling a little salt on the roasting meat. "At least half of the upper tier of Imperial aristocracy wiped out in a single day. I won't go into the tedium of what led up to it. Suffice to say a bunch of malcontent inbreds wanted to seize power from the ruling bunch of inbreds. The result was the Regency Wars, which began with all this. Azireh survived, thanks to me. I dressed her up in servant's clothes and we managed to escape the Sanctum. We took refuge in my grandparents' house, which could have been a costly mistake, it being an obvious place to look. Luckily, her uncle found her before anyone else did. He heaved her up onto a horse and off they went. We barely had time to say good-bye and I didn't see her again for five years. When I did, this is what they had made of her."

The ball-room shimmered and shifted into an even grander room of cathedralesque proportions. Tall windows rose on each side and huge pillars supported vaulted ceilings of such height they were wreathed in mist gathered from the thousand or more people below. They were all kneeling in abject supplication, heads pressed to the floor and arms outstretched as they paid obeisance to a figure seated on a dais. Lizanne was barely able to recognise Azireh under the mask of alabaster paint that covered her face, her features bunched by the weight of the bejewelled crown atop her head. More than that was the new hardness to her eyes. These were the eyes of her statue, the eyes of a woman who had seen and done terrible things, too many to remain that same young woman who had once sabotaged her pianola just for the chance to talk to someone she thought she might love.

"Emperor Azireh I," Alestine said. "Quite impressive isn't she?"

Lizanne saw that there was one figure amongst the multitude who was not kneeling. Alestine stood at the rear of the huge vaulted chamber, clad in a plain muslin dress as she stared at the newly crowned empress that official history would record as an emperor. "This was the last time you saw her," Lizanne realised.

"Yes." Alestine didn't turn from her cookery, crouching to add some more wood to the fire. "I was surprised to receive a formal invitation to the coronation, somewhat frightened in fact. But I went, nevertheless. How could I not? And I didn't kneel, which was noticed but by then she was already so feared none would dare voice an objection. After the ceremony a chamberlain gave me an envelope. Inside was a large amount of money and notification that I had been commanded by the Emperor to undertake a research expedition to the continent of Kilnahria. There was also a note in her own hand, just one line: 'Find me treasure.'"

The coronation faded into the green wall of the jungle as Alestine took a knife and cut a portion of meat from the haunch. "I do believe this is close to done," she said, biting off a morsel before offering it to Lizanne. "Don't you think?"

Lizanne took the meat, putting the whole piece in her mouth and discovering Cerath meat to be both flavoursome and tender. "She exiled you," she said, chewing and swallowing.

"She had little choice. And I believe she thought she was being kind. I had often spoken of this place, you see. Idle talk about its many mysteries as we lay together in the small hours. It was a surprise to find she was actually listening. Ah!" She turned as fresh rustling sounded from the jungle. "It seems our guests have arrived."

"Guests?"

"I invited a few old friends. I hope you don't mind."

Lizanne's polite response died as a figure stepped out of the jungle, a tall figure carrying a spear and a war-club. His face, adorned in a black-and-white mottling of war-paint, was the distorted, scaled and hostile visage of a tribal Spoiled. Lizanne lunged for Alestine, catching her by the wrist and tearing the knife from her grip. Lizanne whirled to face the Spoiled as he dropped into a fighting crouch and charged, teeth bared in a snarl.

She side-stepped the Spoiled, lashing out with her knife in an attempt to sever the veins in its neck. It was too swift, however, dancing out of reach and countering with a fast sweep of its spear, aiming for her legs. Lizanne leapt over the weapon, rolled and cast her knife at the Spoiled's face, an expert throw that would have skewered it through the eye. Instead the knife shuddered to a halt in mid air, where it continued to hang.

"That's hardly the way to greet an honoured guest," Alestine reproached her, moving to pluck the knife from the air before turning to the Spoiled. "Tree Speaker," she said. "Good of you to come."

The Spoiled continued to glare in challenge at Lizanne for several seconds then abruptly straightened into a calmer posture, the hostility fading from its face. "Maker of Things," it greeted Alestine, speaking with such calm affability that Lizanne realised it was conforming to a pre-set sequence of events. This trance had been crafted with such care it was easy to forget the entire thing was essentially a narrative dream.

"You made yourself a pet Spoiled," Lizanne said, watching Alestine lead the tribal to the fire where she cut him a portion of meat.

"I didn't make anything," she said with a laugh. "I merely discovered some new friends."

She inclined her head at the jungle where more Spoiled had begun to appear. There were about fifty of them, male and female, all of fighting age and carrying weapons. They were clad in a similar garb of soft dark leather, albeit with a few individual embellishments. Some wore face-paint of various hues whilst others didn't. Some wore necklaces of bone or beads, whilst others were unadorned. She had had little opportunity to study the tribal Spoiled that attacked Carvenport but she did recall a rigid uniformity of appearance amongst the different tribal groups. Her experience during the final moments aboard the *Profitable Venture* had provided a partial explanation. *They share minds. It's how the White controls them.*

"There was a Gathering," Tree Speaker told Alestine with grave formality. "Your words were heard. Agreement was reached." He pointed his spear at the temple above the trees. "We will go with you to end what must be ended."

"And very decent of you it is too," Alestine replied, handing him some meat. "Best eat up. From what I recall you're going to need your strength."

Lizanne spent some time in confused contemplation, gaze roaming the assembled Spoiled as they came forward to share in the feast. "Language," she said finally, one particular realisation rising through the babble of thoughts. "Are they speaking yours or you theirs?"

"Does it matter?" Alestine asked and Lizanne realised that it didn't, at least not here. In the trance, language was thought.

"But if this is a memory you must have found a way to communicate," she persisted. "Did you . . . change them somehow?"

Alestine gave a full, hearty laugh that lasted long enough for Lizanne to find quite aggravating. "No," Alestine said when she finally sobered, shaking her head and wiping a tear from the corner of her eye. "If anything, it was the opposite. They found me not far from here, a few years before all this. I'd had the misfortune to encounter some of their less friendly cousins and was in rather dire need of medical attention. Tree Speaker's daughter found me, bleeding away and close to death." She smiled fondly at the Spoiled, who was now busily gorging himself on Cerath flesh. "He's a healer as well as a warrior. They have a remarkable knowledge of the healing properties of Green, and all manner of medicinal herbs to be found in this jungle. They usually kill our kind when they find us, the Sickened they call us. But for me they made an exception." Her face took on a more serious aspect and she turned to regard the temple. "I think because somehow they knew we would share an important task one day."

"What's in there?" Lizanne said, moving to her side. "Your empress's treasure?"

"I suppose you could call it that. The greatest treasure and the greatest danger." She raised her gaze to the sky as a rumble of thunder sounded. "It appears you're running out of Blue, Miss Lethridge. Do be sure to call again soon. Tell your musician friend to take a look at the *Follies of Cevokas*."

"Wait." Lizanne winced as a pulse of confusion went through her, the sense of dislocation that indicated the end of a trance. "You locked your memories in Tinkerer's head for a reason. You knew we would meet. I need to know why."

"You already have what you need," Alestine said, the jungle turning to mist around her as the trance neared its terminus. She gestured at the Spoiled as they transformed into vague, wisp-like ghosts. "For now, at least. I look forward to your next visit . . ."

CHAPTER 16

Clay

"They should call this place Bug-aria," Loriabeth said, slapping a hand against her neck to squash yet another fly. They hung over the water in thick swarms and would plague the *Lady Malynda* at regular intervals as she ploughed her way north along the Quilam. Lieutenant Sigoral had the best map-reading skills amongst them and reckoned it had taken two days to cover some twenty miles of river. Skaggerhill blamed the current, which had a tendency to force random shifts in the boat's course as well as impeding progress despite the efforts of her engine. As yet there had been no change in the green wall of reeds that covered both banks, if anything Clay thought they had grown taller as the miles wore on.

"Seer dammit, you little bastards!" Loriabeth cursed, slapping at her arms and neck as the *Malynda* carried them through another swarm.

"Cover up more," Sigoral told her, pulling a duster from beneath his bench. He had donned a seaman's jacket to ward off the flies, finding the sweat and discomfort caused by the humid atmosphere preferable to the attentions of the insects.

"In this heat?" Loriabeth said, more in resignation than protest, and she voiced no further objection as the lieutenant settled the heavy garment around her shoulders.

Kriz was the only member of the crew who didn't feel obliged to cover her skin as the constant pall of smoke from the *Malynda*'s engine proved a deterrent to the bugs. Chief Bozware's design was ingenious but not especially efficient, being prone to emitting a variety of unpleasant miasmas, a sooty, oil-tinged smoke being the most copious.

"We'll need fuel soon," Kriz told Clay, blinking at him above the handkerchief she used to shield her lungs from the engine's vapours. "At this rate the coal will be exhausted by tomorrow afternoon."

"She'd run on wood well enough," Skaggerhill put in from the tiller before casting a sour glance at their surroundings. "If there was any to be had round here."

"How about reducing speed?" Clay asked. "Won't she burn less then?"

"We're barely making headway as it is," Skaggerhill said. "Any slower and we'll be standing still."

"We could harvest some reeds," Sigoral suggested. "They should burn."

"Not enough . . ." Kriz frowned, evidently translating the explanation in her head. "Energy. Besides, we would need to dry them out first."

Clay turned his gaze to the prow where his uncle sat in customary, unspeaking vigilance. He had barely moved from the spot so far, except to partake of a brief meal or clean his rifle. "Any guidance to offer here, Uncle?" Clay called to him. "You know this place, right?"

He wasn't sure Braddon would answer. He hadn't said a word since setting off and even Loriabeth's attempts to elicit a response had met with either non-committal grunts or outright silence. Today, however, he seemed willing to talk. "There's an island," he said, not turning. "'Bout ten miles on where the river widens. It's got trees on it." He paused and added, "Greens too, most likely."

Clay's gaze automatically began to scan the river, as it did whenever mention of Greens was made. So far they hadn't seen a single sign of any drakes, not even a ripple in the Quilam's swift-flowing surface. Even so, the sense of being observed had lingered ever since leaving the *Superior*. *This is their place,* he reminded himself. *Even before the White I doubt they appreciated visitors.*

"Can't be helped," he said, forcing a brisk decisiveness into his tone. It was something he noticed Hilemore tended to do when things weren't going well. "There's no walking out of here. Lieutenant, how long before we make this island?"

Sigoral briefly consulted his map and compass. "It's not marked on this chart," he said. "But assuming it's to be found ten miles on, we should be there by late afternoon."

"Everyone clean and load your iron," Clay said. "Preacher, when we get there I want you at the prow with Uncle Braddon. You two'll kill any Greens on the island, the rest of us will keep them off the boat."

True to Sigoral's calculation the island came into view a few minutes past the seventeenth hour. It was formed of a narrow spit of land some two hundred yards long and about fifty wide with, Clay was relieved to see, a copse of stunted but thick-limbed trees rising from its centre.

"What d'you see?" he asked Preacher as Skaggerhill steered them towards the eastern shore of the island.

The marksman took a moment to thoroughly scan the place before replying. "Only two. Starting to stir. Looks like the engine woke them up."

"Take 'em as soon as you're sure of the shot," Clay said, pistol in one hand and vials of Red, Green and Black in the other as his gaze roved the river and the banks. Braddon fired almost immediately, the shot like a thunder-clap as it echoed across the water. His Protectorate-issue rifle had been equipped with a telescopic sight, a gift from the *Superior*'s armoury courtesy of Mr. Steelfine, enabling a clean kill even at this range. He worked the bolt and fired again after only the slightest pause, grunting, "Got both."

"Take us in," Clay told Skaggerhill then crouched to retrieve the bag of tools Chief Bozware had stowed in the lower hull. The engineer had had the foresight to include a saw and a pair of axes. "Me and the lieutenant will gather the fuel. The rest of you watch the water."

He drank a full vial of Green and nodded at Sigoral to do the same. They leapt clear of the *Malynda* as Skaggerhill grounded her on the island's sandy eastern bank, rushing into the trees in search of the most easily harvested timber. Sigoral chose a sapling and set about its trunk with the axe, hacking through it in less than a minute. Clay found a more thickly bodied tree farther in, the trunk too broad to be felled, but with a number of easily severed branches. By the time the Green wore off they had amassed a considerable pile of wood, albeit of less-than-regular proportions.

"Guess carpentry ain't your strong suit," Skaggerhill observed, eyeing the pile in amusement.

"We'll saw it up on the boat," Clay said, gathering logs into his arms. "Lend a hand here, will you?"

They had piled most of the wood onto the boat when he heard a commotion in the trees. Recognising Loriabeth's voice raised in anger and alarm, Sigoral immediately snatched up his carbine and charged into the undergrowth, Clay and the others close behind.

"Just stop it, Pa! Please!" They found Loriabeth in a small clearing, staring at her father in shocked misery, tears shining in her eyes. Braddon stood a short distance away, hefting something in his hands. Something small that wriggled and screeched as he swung it up and then down. The screeching abruptly ceased as the thing's head made contact with a boulder, the skull cracking open to spill blood and brains.

A chorus of screeches dragged Clay's gaze from the grisly sight to a pair of infant Greens. They scrabbled about in a nest surrounded by the remnants of their scorched shells, hides shifting colour in distress. *Only just hatched,* Clay realised as his uncle bent to retrieve one of the infants, grabbing it by the hind legs and swinging it up and back.

"Uncle," Clay said, wincing as the infant's head connected with the boulder, its brains mixing with that of its sibling. Loriabeth let out a sob and took an involuntary step towards her father, fists balled. Clay caught her before she could launch herself at Braddon, who barely seemed to notice.

"That's enough, Uncle," Clay said as Braddon tossed the dead infant aside and reached for the last one. He appeared deaf to Clay's words, tearing his arm away as Clay reached for him.

"Captain!" Skaggerhill had arrived at the clearing and stood staring at the scene, eyes wide and appalled.

"It's time for them to die, Skaggs," Braddon said, reaching for the final infant. "All of them."

"Contractor's code," Skaggerhill said, stepping forward to grip Braddon by the shoulders. The harvester gave a brief shake of his captain's shoulders. "Young 'uns are left be. Elst what are we gonna hunt in days to come?"

"Time for hunting's over," Braddon replied, Clay seeing a strange emptiness in his uncle's eyes as he regarded Skaggerhill. "It's time for slaughter now. Ain't no room in this world for both us and them. The thing that commands them sees it. Time we did too."

He tried to shrug off Skaggerhill's hands but the harvester held on, a certain desperate bafflement creeping into his voice as he said, "This ain't you, Captain. And it ain't us . . ."

His words were abruptly drowned out by the flat crack of a longrifle from the direction of the boat, followed soon after by a flurry of pistol shots. "Greens!" Clay said. "Get back to the *Malynda*."

Sigoral and Loriabeth immediately sprinted off, followed by Skagger-hill after a brief, hesitant glance at Braddon, who stood unmoving, gaze locked on the squalling infant drake. It had calmed now and stared up at its would-be murderer, yellow eyes blinking as it let out a series of chirps, small tail sweeping from side to side.

"Let's go, Uncle," Clay said, his voice pitched just below a shout. Braddon took a step towards the infant, boot raised. "I said, let's go!" Clay stepped between his uncle and the drake, meeting his gaze and finding the previous emptiness replaced with dark, quivering fury.

"Since when do you command me, boy?" Braddon demanded in a low voice.

Clay looked over his shoulder as another volley of shots sounded from the direction of the *Malynda*. "We ain't got time for . . ." he began, turning back to take his uncle's fist in the face. As he landed flat on his back, tasting blood and blinking away stars, he at least had the satisfaction of seeing the infant Green scamper off into the undergrowth.

"This is my company," Braddon said, advancing towards him, fist pulled back for another punch. He let out a pained grunt as Clay jack-knifed, lashing out with both boots to catch his uncle in the chest. Clay rolled to his feet and swung a punch into Braddon's jaw, hard enough to set him back a step or two.

"Not any more," Clay said, jabbing another blow at his uncle's nose, drawing blood. "Not since you gave it up to wallow in the shit of your misery." He lashed out again, catching Braddon on the chin, then followed up with a three-punch combination to the body that left the older man stooped and winded. "It's my company now." Another punch, blood flying from Braddon's lips as he reeled away. "You ain't nothing no more, old man!" A right hook to the side of the head, Braddon staggering, about to fall. "Aunt Freda would be ashamed . . ."

Braddon's arm moved in a blur as Clay's fist swung again, blocking the blow before taking hold of his arm. He delivered a punch of his own to Clay's gut, doubling him over, before hoisting him up and tossing him into the bushes. Clay groaned, clutching at his aching midriff as he tried to fill his winded lungs. After a few ragged breaths he managed to roll over and began to push himself upright, then saw his uncle striding towards him with a drawn pistol.

Shit, thought Clay. *Guess I finally made him mad enough to kill me.*

Braddon brought the pistol level with his chest and fired, left hand fanning the hammer as he loosed off a rapid salvo. Clay heard something heavy hit the ground behind him and turned to see a fully grown aquatic Green lying dead a short distance away, its hide continuing to flicker as it twitched. His gaze swung back to his uncle, now calmly but swiftly slotting cartridges into his revolver. He met Clay's eyes, sighed and stooped to offer him a hand.

"If you're gonna hit a man," he said. "Make sure you put him down with the first blow."

Clay took the proffered hand and hauled himself upright, drawing his revolver and following as his uncle set off for the boat at a run. They found it wreathed in gunsmoke with several Green corpses littering the surrounding sand-bank. Kriz had already stoked the engine to full power and Skaggerhill sat at the tiller, beckoning urgently for them to get aboard. Clay fixed his gaze on the boat and accelerated into a sprint, refusing to look back as a chorus of enraged growls erupted behind. Preacher stood at the prow of the boat, rifle at his shoulder and apparently aimed at Clay's head. He instinctively jerked to the side but Preacher had already fired, the bullet whipping past Clay's ear like an angry hornet before finding its target.

Skaggerhill had drawn the *Malynda* a few yards away from the bank to get her clear of the sand, so they were obliged to wade through the last few yards. Preacher and Sigoral kept up a steady barrage as Kriz and Loriabeth helped haul Clay and Braddon aboard. Once they lay gasping on the deck Kriz engaged the propeller, setting the boat into forward motion.

"They get you?" Loriabeth asked, her gaze switching from Clay's bloodied face to that of her father.

"Ran into a tree," Clay replied, wiping blood from his nose and getting to his feet. He looked back at the island, finding it overrun with Greens, all howling a chorus of rage in their high-pitched, almost bird-like voices. A few slipped into the water in pursuit but soon fell behind thanks to the *Malynda*'s speed, aided by the reduced current, which seemed to be less swift in this stretch of river.

"Why ain't they coming for us?" Braddon wondered, frowning in puzzlement. "Thought the White wants us dead."

"I don't think the White's got hold of them right now," Clay said, recalling the nest and the infant Greens. "They're just defending the place where their young 'uns get hatched."

He sat down, taking a canteen and tipping some of the contents over his face to wash away the rest of the blood. He had a lingering ache in his gut and a swelling below his eye but it looked like his uncle had spared him any permanent damage or lost teeth. Braddon, it turned out, hadn't been so lucky. Clay watched him take the bench opposite and open his mouth wide, reaching inside to pluck out a tooth. He gave Clay a sour glance before tossing it over the side.

Clay winced at a sudden upsurge of pain in his gut. He extracted a vial of Green from his wallet and took a quarter sip before offering it to his uncle. "Won't grow a new tooth, but it'll take away the pain and heal the hole."

Braddon shrugged and accepted the vial, taking a small sip before tipping the entire contents down his throat. He sat for a time, jaws clenched against the burn of the Green. "So . . . Captain," he said eventually. "There's still a great deal of country betwixt us and Krystaline Lake. You got any notion of what we're gonna do when we get to the end of this river?"

Clay gave a humourless grin. "Was kinda hoping you did, Captain."

Seen through the lens of a spy-glass the Cerath seemed small at first, Clay initially concluding they were of horse-like dimensions, albeit with a longer neck and more sturdy body and legs. It was only when one of them began grazing on the upper leaves of a tree that he gained a true impression of their size. "At least a third again bigger than the biggest horse I ever saw," he said, handing the spy-glass back to his uncle. "You really think we can tame these beasts?"

"Tame them, no," Braddon said. "But you can ride them."

"You sure, Pa?" Loriabeth asked, shielding her eyes to view the Cerath herd. "Seem a little rambunctious to me."

Clay surveyed the herd once more, seeing two of the larger beasts squaring up for a confrontation. They both pawed the ground with their fore-hooves, heads lowered as they bellowed out a challenge that could be heard even at this distance. After a lengthy period of bellowing and earth scraping the Cerath charged at each other, dust billowing across the plain as they met. They fought by rearing up and assailing one another with their hooves, reminding Clay of inexpert drunks fighting in a Blinds bar. The combat was brief if loud, one Cerath abruptly abandoning the fight to gallop away a short distance. Its opponent chased it for a short time then veered off, spending a few moments to call out in triumph before returning to the business of grazing on the long grass that seemed to dominate the southern plains.

"That's the bull," Braddon said. "He's the one we want."

The *Lady Malynda* had come to a grinding halt in the shallows of the upper Quilam two days before, forcing them to proceed on foot. They cut reeds to camouflage her, there being the faint possibility that a Spoiled might happen upon her in their absence. Hauling their gear and Kriz's apparatus across the marsh to the plains had been both tedious and exhausting. The spongey, bug-infested land seemed to go on forever and their feet suffered from the constant damp. By the time the marsh gave way to firm grasslands Clay had to order an extended halt just to dry out their feet. Consequently, he had welcomed his uncle's suggestion that they ride rather than walk to Krystaline Lake, but now he wasn't so sure. Still, it was an awfully long way.

"Alright," he said. "How's this done?"

"Cerath's a herd animal," Braddon said a short time later. He led Clay towards the herd with a purposeful stride, making no effort at concealment. "The bull's the leader and the rest are so loyal they'll follow him over a cliff. Curious thing about these beasts is they get all docile-like once you're on their back. Met a naturalist fella in Carvenport once, said it was to do with their size. They're so big nothing of any weight ever sits on them. Even the drakes don't land on them when they hunt the herds. Blacks'll pin them to the ground and Reds'll roast their legs so's they can't run off. So when something gets astride them they get set in a state of scared confusion. Thing is"—he paused and came to a halt, turning and handing Clay a length of coiled rope—"only ever seen this done by a Blood-blessed. Us normal folk are just too slow."

Clay looked at the bull, which by now had noticed their approach. The other Cerath were slowly gathering behind him as he stared at the two small interlopers, jaws grinding on a mouthful of grass and one foreleg stamping the ground. "That's a warning sign," Braddon said, although Clay hadn't really needed the explanation. At this remove the bull seemed much larger than his first estimation and it was hard to credit being able to control such a beast just by virtue of landing on its back.

"It has to be him, huh?" he asked Braddon, reaching for his wallet.

"Yep. Try landing on one of the smaller ones and the others'll just run off and leave it. Be sure to loop that rope around his neck soon as you can."

Clay took a vial of Green from his wallet, drank it all then, after a moment's consideration, drank another. He waited for the product to flood his system, feeling his limbs thrum with it as he focused on the bull. The animal clearly sensed an increased level of danger for it let out a bellow, head lowering and fore-hooves pawing. Clay set off at a sprint, Green-enhanced speed making the grassland blur around him as he sped towards the bull. It bellowed again and charged to meet the challenge. Time seemed to slow as Clay closed with the animal, the dust it raised from the plain ascending in gentle clouds and the huge muscles of its legs quivering. After covering the last few yards it planted both fore-hooves on the ground and spun, lashing out with its hind legs. Clay dived and rolled under the flailing hooves, coming to a halt as the bull whirled to face him.

They stared at each other for a second, separated by a distance of barely ten feet. The Cerath shook its mighty head, eyes narrowed in wary contemplation of its foe. Unwilling to allow it the time to launch another attack, Clay surged into a sprint once more, covering the distance in two strides and leaping as high as his enhanced strength would allow. He turned head over heels in mid air, twisting with an acrobat's precision to bring himself down squarely on the bull's back . . . then let out a painful grunt as the bull dodged aside and he landed hard on the ground.

The bull roared and reared above him, hooves rising for a killing stamp, then froze. The beast's roar choked off in its throat as it continued to stand there on its hind legs, immobile as a statue.

"Looked like you needed some help."

Clay looked round to see Sigoral standing a short distance away, his gaze locked on the bull with the kind of concentration that only came from use of Black.

"That's the truth." Clay got to his feet, unslinging the coiled rope from his shoulders. "Probably should've thought of this in the first place." He leapt onto the bull's back, swiftly looping the rope over its neck before the elevated angle caused him to slip off. "Alright," he told Sigoral, who nodded and withdrew his Black before wisely retreating several yards.

The bull let out a strange sound as it settled onto all four legs. It was somewhere between a sigh and a whinny and spoke of a deep, primal distress. Clay had expected it to buck or stamp, but true to his uncle's word it just stood there, its sighs becoming more shrill by the second.

"Easy, big fella," Clay said, smoothing a hand along the beast's leathery hide. The bull twitched in response, craning its head to view the thing on its back with wide, fearful eyes. Clay continued to try and soothe it without much success before it occurred to him he had no notion of how to get it to move.

"Lay the rope on the right side of his neck," Braddon said a short while later. "Gentle like, no need to whip him." Clay did as he said, the muscles of the bull's right shoulder shuddering in response as the animal shifted to the left. It came to a halt when he removed the rope from its hide. Clay tried the same trick with the left side with similar results. "Lay it on his rump to get him to walk," Braddon said. "A couple of taps and he'll run, but don't try that just yet. Gotta get the rest of them in line."

The other Cerath continued to stand a short way off, voicing sighing whinnies of distress but displaying no sign of any violent action. It was as if the immobility of the bull cast some sort of spell over them, robbing them of their will. A few grew skittish as the rest of the company approached, some shying away. At Braddon's direction Lieutenant Sigoral used Black to hold a chosen few still long enough for them to be mounted and the gear securely strapped in place.

"Compass bearing, if you please, Lieutenant," Braddon said once they had all mounted up. "East-north-east."

Sigoral rode behind Loriabeth, who had hold of the reins of their Cerath, a young male only a few inches shorter than the bull. Unlike the herd leader, however, this beast was prone to continually turning about so it took awhile for the lieutenant to get a compass bearing. "That way," he said finally, pointing towards a stretch of open plain.

"Once he starts he won't stop till he's tired," Braddon called to Clay. "And that may take a good long while so hold tight."

It took Clay a few minutes to manoeuvre the bull into position, the rest of the herd growing more agitated as he did so. Once he was reasonably sure the beast was facing the required direction Clay slapped the rope twice against his rump, whereupon the bull let out a throaty roar of alarm and spurred into a gallop.

Clay gave an involuntary laugh of exhilaration as the Cerath sped across the grasslands. Its speed far outstripped that of any horse he had ever ridden and the joy of acceleration came close to matching the feeling of riding atop Lutharon's back. A thunder of hooves caused him to look over his shoulder to be greeted by the sight of the rest of the herd following, the earth seeming to tremble as they raced to keep up with their leader. Dust rose high enough to obscure the sun so that it felt like they were galloping through a foggy void. Clay turned his gaze to the front where the plains stretched away like a yellow-green sea. Taking a firm grip on the rope coiled about the bull's neck he wondered if it might have been a good idea to drink some more Green before setting off.

CHAPTER 17

Lizanne

Lizanne blinked and found herself back in the hold, Makario retreating from her in surprise and lowering the mirror he had been holding close to her mouth. "Checking for breath," he said. "You were gone a long time."

Lizanne realised she had been placed on a bunk and concluded she must have collapsed. Usually a Blood-blessed would remain in the same seated pose whilst trancing. This one had evidently been different. Jermayah, Tekela and her father stood close by, all staring at her with worried faces. Lizanne swung her legs off the bunk, groaning a little at the lingering fog in her head. The Artisan's trance had been the deepest and most vibrant she had experienced and leaving it rather felt like stepping from one world to another.

"Are you alright?" her father asked, moving closer to place a hand on her forehead. "Your temperature's low. I'll fetch Dr. Weygrand."

"I'm fine," she said, trying to swallow and finding her mouth dry. "Some water would be nice, though."

"I'll get it," Tekela said, immediately scampering off.

Seeing Tinkerer on the next bunk Lizanne reached out to grasp his arm, giving it a gentle shake. "Do you remember anything?" she asked.

Tinkerer gave no response, continuing to lie still, eyes closed. Lizanne took his hand, finding it cold and seeing that his chest was barely moving. "I think you'd better get the doctor after all," she told her father.

"Some form of comatose state," Dr. Weygrand said a short while later. "But of a kind I've never seen before."

He had conducted a full examination of the artificer, pronouncing his condition stable but unresponsive. Attempts to wake him with smelling-salts or prods from a small but sharp needle to the soles of his feet had produced no reaction. The doctor sighed, running a hand through his thinning hair. "I'll need to transfer him to the medical bay, rig up an intravenous drip to ensure he doesn't dehydrate. I can add some stimulants to the mix which might wake him up."

"No," Lizanne said. *He's waiting,* she realised. *Or rather she's waiting. Pumping drugs into his veins could disrupt his memories.* "Thank you, Doctor," she went on. "But I believe he's best left unmedicated for now. However, I can't stress enough how important it is that he remain alive."

"It's important for me that all my patients remain alive, miss," Weygrand replied.

"Of course." She smiled and gestured for Makario to follow her to a secluded corner of the hold. "The *Follies of Cevokas*," she said. "Does it mean anything to you?"

"It's a comic opera," he said. "Dating back to the Third Imperium. Cevokas was . . ."

"A possibly fictional explorer of the Arradsian continent, I know. The tales of his exploits are classics of Corvantine literature."

"And the basis for the *Follies*. It's a fairly minor work, but highly popular in its day. It does seem a little vulgar for the Artisan's tastes. He strikes me as a more discerning fellow."

"She," Lizanne corrected. "And she made it clear that we need to study the *Follies of Cevokas*. I believe there's another movement to the composition, something that will unlock further memories from her chosen vessel."

Makario glanced back at Tinkerer, silent and pale on the bunk. "So he'll remain like this until we come up with the next movement?"

"I think so."

The musician pursed his lips, frowning deeply, presumably as archaic tunes played in his head. "I'll need to reconstruct the opera from memory. It'll take awhile."

Catching sight of her father returning to his work-bench, Lizanne started towards him. "Tekela might be able to help," she told Makario. "She does seem to have a facility for such things."

"And an equal facility for getting on my bloody nerves," he added.

"Time is a factor," she reminded him before joining her father. He was engaged in an improved version of the aerostat's blood-burner, a new feed mechanism that would enable product to be combusted in batches rather than all at once. "Tinkerer's rocket," she said. "Do you think you can finish it?"

Captain Trumane's course guided the fleet in a wide arc around Iskamir Island, keen to limit any contact with Varestian vessels during the voyage. They saw a few merchantmen over the course of the next few days but none felt the need to investigate such a large formation of foreigners. It was only when they made the westward turn towards Blaska Sound that a flotilla of fast, sloop-class ships appeared on the northern flank of their convoy. A few hours later another flotilla of similar size appeared to the south. The Varestian ships maintained a consistent distance from the fleet, making no attempt at communication.

"Making sure we don't change our minds," Trumane concluded after the second flotilla appeared. He tracked his spy-glass along the line of Varestian vessels, grunting in grim recognition. "Pirates, the lot of them. That one in the lead is the *Ironspike*. Chased her all the way around the Southern Barrier Isles a few years ago. The captain kept throwing his cargo away to increase speed. After a while we started finding the bodies of his crew. He couldn't have had more than a half dozen men left by the time a storm brewed up. Had hoped the bugger had foundered in it."

Blaska Sound came into view the next morning, a mist-shrouded estuary about three miles wide. The passage was further constricted by a series of granite reefs that prohibited any rapid manoeuvring. Trumane signalled one of the smaller ships to lead the way, a one-paddle mail packet of aged appearance but with a veteran captain renowned for his navigational skills. The *Viable Opportunity* took up station a mile to the east, circling slowly with all hands at battle stations. Trumane maintained a rigid vigilance over their Varestian escorts as the fleet made its way into the Sound, calling out the range to each ship for the ensign at his shoulder to note down. Lizanne felt there to be a certain theatre in all of this, Trumane putting on a show to bolster the nerves of his crew. However, he must have known that whilst the *Viable* was a formidable ship, if the Varestians chose to attack she would be overwhelmed in short order.

"Looks as if your employers are keeping their end of the bargain," he said, lowering the spy-glass as the last of the refugee vessels proceeded into the Sound. "For now at least. Helm, steer forty points to port. Mr. Tollver, signal the engine room to take us to one-third speed."

"What a Divinity-forsaken dump," Tekela observed as the *Viable* weighed anchor off Raker's Mount. The place consisted of a loose arrangement of dilapidated hovels clustered around a series of hill-sized slag-heaps. The mine itself was a gaping black hole gouged into the slope of the mountain that loomed over the town. An incline railway line led all the way from the mine to the docks, which were the only truly impressive feature the settlement had to offer.

Five piers jutted out from the quay, which had been constructed atop a granite shelf that became a cliff at low tide. Consequently, the piers had been built on tall supporting legs of iron, each one streaked with rust. It was a testament to the sturdiness of their original construction that the piers were still standing after so many years of neglect. The steam-driven elevators that had once conveyed cargo and crew from moored vessels to the docks were apparently rusted to uselessness. Therefore, the fleet had been obliged to wait for high tide before disembarking the refugees. They were crowding onto the quayside in increasing numbers, most standing around in groups which reflected the ship they had spent so many weeks aboard. A few had begun to drift into the town in search of shelter but it was clear to Lizanne that a great deal of organisation would be needed before these people could be called a work-force.

"You should've seen Scorazin, my dear," Makario told Tekela. "This is a genteel spa-town in comparison. Besides, I'll be happy just to feel solid ground beneath my feet again. I find myself heartily sick of a sailor's life."

"If not the sailors," Tekela muttered, earning a stern look from Lizanne.

"It looks as if I'll have need of your secretarial skills once more," she told her. "I trust you can find a note-book somewhere."

"I thought I'd take the *Firefly* up again," Tekela said. "Have a scout around."

"*Firefly?*"

"The aerostat. I decided she should have a name."

"Very nice, I'm sure." Lizanne turned and started towards the derrick where Ensign Tollver was preparing a launch to take them to shore. "But I'm afraid your aerial adventures will have to wait." She paused as an angry murmur rose from the direction of the docks. Two of the refugee groups had begun to jostle each other, voices raised as pushes and shoves soon became punches and kicks.

"Be sure to bring a revolver along with the note-book," Lizanne added. "I believe we're about to have a very trying day."

"We work or we starve."

The assembled crowd hushed as Lizanne's words swept over them. She stood atop a raised platform in what had once been a shed used to house the locomotive engines for the incline railway. It was the largest covered space in the town and therefore a useful place for a general meeting. It also benefited from a scaffold of elevated walkways where a number of riflemen from the *Viable* had been stationed. She was flanked on either side by Captain Trumane and Madame Hakugen, and had hoped that the presence of the refugee fleet's leaders, and the riflemen, might moderate any discontent. At this juncture, however, the assembly seemed unimpressed and certainly not cowed.

The hush that followed Lizanne's statement was soon replaced by a babble of discontented voices, rising in pitch and volume. "We are not slaves!" one woman near the front shouted as she and a dozen others struggled against the line of sailors positioned in front of the platform. "I have children!" shouted another. "Corporate bitch!" added someone else.

Lizanne pressed the first and third buttons on the Spider and let loose with a blast of heated air, spread wide enough to prickle the skin but not set anything alight, along with a hard shove of Black, which sent the refugees at the forefront of the mob sprawling.

"I apologise," Lizanne said, breaking the silence that followed. The crowd stared at her now, fear on most faces, but also plenty of defiance too. "Clearly I did not introduce myself properly," she went on. "My name is indeed Lizanne Lethridge and I truly am a shareholder in the Ironship Protectorate. But I have another name, one I earned at Carvenport. They called me Miss Blood, and it was not a name I came by accidentally."

She paused, scanning the crowd. She was quite prepared to send a concentrated blast of Black into the face of anyone who shouted another insult, but for now they seemed content to remain silent. "At Carvenport I organised a defence that saw thousands to safety," she said. "I did so because those people gave me their trust, as I gave them mine. So I ask you to trust me now as I set out, in clear terms, the reality of our current circumstance.

"We have been provided with this haven, ugly as it is, not because our hosts desire our company or because their hearts are swollen with compassion at our plight. We exist here because I promised them weapons. You will make those weapons. If you do not the best we can expect from our hosts is to be told to leave. I don't think you need a great deal of imagination to deduce what the worst will be."

She allowed a few seconds to let the information settle, seeing a measure of defiance slip from some faces, and the fear deepen on others. "But know that the weapons we will construct here will not just be for our hosts," she continued. "Sooner or later an army of monsters will come for us, and there will be no corner of the world left in which to hide. Running before this storm is no longer an option. I told you we work or we starve, and that is true. What is also true is that we fight or we die."

She let the subsequent silence string out, hearing a murmur of tense discussion but no more shouts. "This facility will be run in accordance with corporate law," she said, adopting a brisk, managerial tone. "With the addition of certain provisions in the Protectorate Disciplinary Code. Desertion will be punished by death. Shirking work will be punished by reduction of rations. Repeat offenders will be flogged. Every adult of fighting age will receive two hours' military training a day. Crèches and schools will be organised for the children."

She pointed to the rear of the shed where Ensign Tollver and a group of sailors had begun to set up a row of tables. "Please form orderly lines. Provide your name, age, previous work history and any useful skills. Any Blood-blessed will also make themselves known. We will be conducting a blood lot eventually so if you have the Blessing there's no point trying to hide it."

"A little to the left!" her father called from atop the scaffold. Lizanne injected an additional measure of Black and concentrated her gaze on the bulbous steel container she had manoeuvred onto the twenty-foot-tall bottle-shaped brick chimney. There were several such chimneys scattered about the town, usually found in proximity to the slag-heaps. Lizanne had initially seen little of interest in them so was surprised by her father's enthusiasm for what he called "coking ovens."

"Stop!" he called, waving his arms. Lizanne halted the flow of Black and the container settled onto the chimney-top with an ugly groan of metal on brick. "Excellent," he said, then called on his assigned group of workers to start shovelling coal into the aperture in the chimney's base. Once the oven had been filled he turned expectantly to Lizanne. "I think this would go quicker if you would . . ." he said, gesturing at the Spider.

Lizanne moved to crouch at the aperture, injecting a dose of Red before concentrating her gaze on the mass of coal. She stepped back as a deep red glow blossomed in the pile, then jerked aside as the whole thing burst into fiery life, the jet of flame coming close to singeing the sleeve of her overalls.

"Close it up," the professor commanded and a labourer came forward with a long iron pole to secure an iron door over the blazing aperture. Lizanne climbed the scaffold to peer over her father's shoulder as he stared at a dial fixed to a valve in the container's side.

"It's working," he said as the dial's indicator began to inch upwards. "We have ourselves a gas-plant."

"Coal-gas will work as well as helium?" she asked.

"It doesn't have quite the same lifting power but we can compensate for that with an expanded envelope. It does benefit from being less flammable than hydrogen. But given that we have neither helium nor hydrogen there seems little alternative in any case."

The sound of a ship's siren drew Lizanne's gaze to the docks. She could see men running to their stations on the deck of the *Viable Opportunity* whilst smoke blossomed from her stacks. The reason for the commotion soon became clear as she saw a sleek Varestian sloop approaching from the eastern stretch of the Sound. She was flying a truce flag but it seemed Captain Trumane wasn't willing to allow the *Viable* to remain at her mooring with a potential threat so close.

"Our hosts have decided to pay us a visit," she said.

"Good," her father said. "I hope they brought some copper."

"Did you know?" Arshav Okanas glared at her with dark, angry eyes. He had arrived on shore with a ten-man escort led by the perennially stern of face Mr. Lockbar. Lizanne decided to meet Arshav with a squad of riflemen under Ensign Tollver's command. The two groups eyed each other across the wharf whilst Lizanne stepped forward to offer her employer the most polite greeting she could muster. Today, however, conversational niceties didn't seem to concern him.

"Know what?" she enquired, resisting the urge to flex her fingers over the Spider's buttons. This man had a tendency to lead her towards unwise impulses.

"Melkorin," Arshav said. "It's been burned to the ground and most of its population appears to have vanished, those that aren't lying dead in the streets that is."

Melkorin, a port-town on the south Corvantine coast. The thought immediately led her to an obvious conclusion. *It followed us.*

"Strange that this should happen shortly after you arrive in our waters," Arshav went on, a snarl creeping into his voice. "Quite the coincidence, don't you agree?"

She considered dissembling, professing ignorance or confusion, but didn't see the point at this juncture. The suspicion born on the deck of the *Profitable Venture*, when the Spoiled boarding party began their co-ordinated attempt to kill her, now seemed fully borne out. "The White is desirous of my death," she said. "And the deaths of those I travel with. I did warn you its forces would be coming here."

"Not so soon you didn't." His voice had risen to a shout, causing her escort of riflemen to stir, which in turn had Arshav's pirates reaching for their weapons. "Alright," he said, waving a hand at Lockbar and making an effort to calm himself. "Why does it want you dead?" he asked in a marginally more controlled tone.

"That," Lizanne said, turning away and gesturing for him to follow, "is quite a lengthy tale, best shared over lunch."

"Krystaline Lake," Arshav said, shaking his head and reaching for the wine-bottle. "Father's mad obsessions return to plague me once more." He poured himself a generous measure and offered the bottle to Lizanne.

"No thank you."

"Captain Noose?" Arshav asked, waving the bottle at Trumane, who sat opposite him. Lizanne had organised the meal in the only dwelling in Raker's Mount that might be called grand. It was a three-storey house positioned at a decent remove from the rest of the town, proclaimed as the home of the Imperial Comptroller by the Eutherian letters carved above the lintel. The roof was mostly gone, the windows long vanished and the place smelled strongly of rot, but it did feature a dining-table complete with chairs.

"No," Trumane replied, returning the enmity in Arshav's gaze in full measure.

"Suit yourself." Arshav set the bottle down and took a deep drink from his glass. "Piss water," he said, with a grimace. "Don't you people know how to greet an honoured guest?"

"Krystaline Lake," Lizanne said.

"Oh yes, where your friends are off looking for Father's fabled treasure. It's all nonsense, you know. Ancient scribblings sold to generations of gullible fools, much of them fake, I'm sure."

"We have reason to believe otherwise. There is something at the bottom of that lake that can help us win this war. If your father told you anything . . ."

Arshav laughed and drained his glass. "I mostly remember him telling me to get out of his sight. I was as much a disappointment to him as he was to me. So no, my dear Miss Blood, I have no secrets to share. Anything of use will be at the High Wall, and I am not welcome there." His gaze darkened, fist tightening on the wine-bottle. "Even though it's mine by right."

"The High Wall is the seat of the Okanas family, is it not?" Lizanne asked. "It would seem strange that you and your mother were able to assert control over the Ruling Council, and the Seven Walls, but not your family home."

"A home stolen from me by my own kin." His gaze softened a little and he poured more wine, grimacing as he emptied the bottle before throwing it over his shoulder. "Perils of being born into a family of pirates, I suppose. The bastards'll steal the gold from your teeth if you're not careful. My dear cousin Alzar Lokaras, first-born son to my late aunt Kezia, now holds the High Wall. Supposedly in my sister's name, as if she's about to appear on the horizon anytime soon."

"Will he be amenable to negotiation? Perhaps, if I went . . ."

"He'll shoot you the moment he claps eyes on you. Hates all things corporate, y'see? Almost like a religion, really." Arshav's gaze swivelled to Trumane. "But it's not like you didn't give him plenty of reason, Captain. He lost a lot of sea-brothers to your attentions, as did I."

He drank more wine, gulping it down so that some leaked from the corners of his mouth. "Was going to kill you, y'know," he gasped when the glass was empty. "Had it all planned. Once you'd settled in here and gotten all comfortable. I'd turn up with all my ships and threaten to pound the town to pieces, just like you intended to do to the Hive. Then I was going to hang you on your own deck, you vicious fuck!" He slammed the wine-glass down on the table, hard enough to shatter it, blood leaking from his fingers as he glared at Trumane.

Lizanne found herself impressed by the captain's failure to flinch. Martinet or not he was still a veteran Protectorate officer and Arshav his long-standing enemy, fully deserving of justice. Trumane said nothing, instead reaching for a napkin to dab away the drop of wine on his cheek.

Lizanne began to speak but Arshav held up his bloodied hand, turning his baleful gaze from Trumane to her. "Your fables and doomed friends trekking through the Interior mean nothing to me. We have a war to fight and my mother and I want our weapons. How soon before you actually start producing anything?"

"We need materials . . ."

"They're being unloaded now. Everything on your list, just about, and enough food for a month. There'll be more coming by the end of the week. How long?"

"We're already making progress," Lizanne lied. In fact most of the work-force's efforts since arriving in Raker's Mount had been directed towards making the place fit for habitation. Lizanne had placed Madame Hakugen in charge of civil matters and the former Comptroller had done a great deal to smooth the ruffled nerves in the wake of Lizanne's speech. The former members of the Eastern Conglomerate Levies had been organised into a militia that also served as a constabulary, which did much to imbue the town with a sense of order. Jermayah was organising the principal manufactory in the old railway shed, but as yet no actual weapons had been produced.

"Lack of heavy plant is a problem," Lizanne said. "Especially lifting gear. We've identified only three other Blood-blessed amongst the refugees. To make maximum use of their abilities requires product, especially Black and Red."

"Product is an increasingly scarce resource," Arshav replied. "For obvious reasons, and what stocks we do have will be needed by our own Blood-blessed when the fighting starts. But"—he gave a reluctant shrug—"there are a few flasks in my ship's safe. You can have that."

"That would be greatly appreciated."

"I notice you haven't answered my question."

"A month," she said, adopting her uncoloured tone. "The first delivery of Growlers and Thumpers will be made one month from now."

"You think our enemy will give us that long?"

It was Trumane who answered, neatly folding his napkin and setting it down before addressing Arshav in a carefully modulated voice, no doubt designed to conceal his distaste. "Time in war is not given," he said. "It's bought, with blood. I command the fastest ship in these waters. Letting it sit here unused is a waste of a valuable asset."

"Want to take the fight to them, eh?" Arshav grunted. "Feel free, Captain. I'll spread the word that your ship is to remain unmolested, just don't expect any direct assistance." He looked at his bloodied hand and grimaced in annoyance. "And if you should contrive to get yourself killed in the process, all the better."

He rose from the table, fixing Lizanne with a hard stare. "One month, Miss Blood. And when I return I expect to find a fulsome level of productivity." With that he turned and stalked from the building, shouting for Lockbar and his guards to follow.

Lizanne gave Trumane a sidelong glance. "Do you really think you can accomplish anything useful with just one ship, however fast?"

"Your father was kind enough to share the specifics of his latest design," Trumane replied with a thin smile. "Provided it's ready before we set off, yes, I believe we can accomplish a great deal."

"This is foolish," her father said. "You are needed here."

Lizanne fastened the buttons on her overalls. They were the work of a seamstress from Lossermark, lined with fur to ward off the cold found at altitude, as well as featuring numerous additional pockets for tools and weapons. Jermayah had managed to produce another Smoker for her, though on this trip she would have to do without the mini-Growler.

"Madame Hakugen has things well in hand," Lizanne replied. "And the production line is nearly complete. The intelligence to be had at the High Wall is too important to ignore." She pulled on a shoulder rig for her twin revolvers. "Are you close to completing Captain Trumane's project?"

Professor Lethridge appeared unconvinced by her reasoning and less than happy with the change of subject. "Two more days," he said, face dark with reproach. "It would have taken longer but we've been fortunate in having so many skilled instrument-makers here. Lossermark was a port, after all, and sailors always need clocks and compasses."

"Excellent," Lizanne said. "When it's done please concentrate your efforts on constructing more of these." She nodded at the aerostat, bobbing gently in the wind between the two mooring poles at the end of the pier. The *Firefly* had undergone considerable modification since the last flight, with a wider gondola that would allow her to switch places with Tekela during flight and an envelope of greater size. An additional cannister of pressurised coal-gas had been fitted to the gondola should they need to replenish it. The improved feed mechanism for the blood-burner was also in place, though they had precious little product with which to fire it.

"Any we build from now on will be warcraft," she added. "Capable of carrying as much fire-power as possible."

"I've already drawn up the requisite designs," he said.

"Of course you have." She pecked a kiss to the professor's cheek before starting towards the *Firefly*, the engine's propellers starting to turn as Tekela powered up the caloric engine. "I'll return in four days."

"And if you don't?" he called after her, fighting to be heard above the growl of the engine.

"Then at least you can consider our contract with the Okanas family null and void."

II

THE BURNING SEAS

From the Journal of Miss Lewella Tythencroft—
Sanorah, 21st Vorellum, 1600 (Company Year 211)

The successful management of a revolution, it transpires, requires neither
military genius nor inspired leadership nor great rhetoric. No, if there is one
lesson I have learned over the course of the preceding weeks it is that revolu-
tions require, above all things, paper and ink as well as presses with which to
apply the latter to the former.

I have no precise figures for the number of pamphlets, posters, handbills,
one-sheet newspapers and other sundry publications produced by the Voters
Rights Alliance since this all began but it surely must run into many thou-
sands by now. The doughty old Alebond Commodities Mark II press that
had served the Voters Gazette *so well for several years eventually collapsed*
under the strain of it all. Had we not agreed on an alliance with the Print-
er's Guild during the early days of this upheaval I doubt we would have
achieved any measure of success in rousing the populace, but success, of
course, is a relative concept.

Having read the paragraph above I find my tendency to ramble has once
more come to the fore. It has been some time since I had the leisure to write
in this journal and so much has happened in the interval that it will take too
long to document every particular here. So, I am forced to summarise the
principal events.

True to my promise to Mrs. Fredabel Torcreek, the Voters Rights Alli-
ance shouldered most of the burden in housing the refugees from the Tyrell

Islands. I must confess to operating in a haze of confused emotions for much of this time. Mrs. Torcreek's news about Corrick engendered as much doubt and consternation as it did joy. It appears he has actually sailed off to the southern ice-cap in search of something glimpsed in a vision. Although, a much more thoughtful man than many in his profession, Corrick was never one given to flights of fancy and the notion that he might throw off Protectorate shackles to pursue something so ephemeral it seemed absurd to the point of impossibility.

Mrs. Torcreek, however, had at least a partial explanation: "My nephew drank the blood of White Drake, miss. Guess that makes a fella awful persuasive."

Despite the doubts and unanswerable questions that threatened to befuddle my brain, I set myself to the task of aiding the refugees with all the energy I could muster. The minority who belonged to the managerial class were usually able to find relatives or friends to take them in which left the much-less-fortunate majority homeless without a scrip to their name. Many Voter families volunteered to provide foster homes for the distressingly high number of orphans, whilst others gave over spare rooms and attics to the few intact families to disembark the ships. Even so, the Alliance was forced to rent warehouse space to house the remainder. Wild speculation in the markets has had a strange effect on the warehouse district. Some remain full to capacity with unwanted luxury goods whilst those usually given over to agricultural produce and other necessities are increasingly empty. Consequently, finding a suitable location at a reasonable price was not difficult.

The large number of sick and wounded presented a far greater problem. All but a few independent hospitals in Sanorah are under corporate control and, since none of the refugees could provide an insurance certificate, their doors remained firmly closed to us. As might be expected many of the refugees with sick or injured relatives reacted badly to this, especially those hailing from Carvenport who, on the whole, display only a small regard for corporate authority. A minor riot erupted at the gates of the Ironship General

Hospital, which degenerated into an ugly free-for-all when the constabulary arrived. More trouble might have broken out if aid hadn't come from an unexpected quarter.

The day after the riot my father arrived at the Gazette offices with a letter of credit amounting to some one hundred thousand in exchange notes. Thanks to this donation the Alliance was able to secure all the required beds in the independent Sanorah hospitals. I will confess to a few private tears following this incident, my emotions being so aggravatingly variable at this juncture. The fact that my father's intervention had been completely unsolicited, and I am aware that accumulating such a sum would have required him to liquidate a large portion of his personal assets, still brings a certain moistness to the eye.

In all over seven thousand people were successfully provided with shelter, food and medical care within two days of arrival in this port. I should record that all this was achieved without any assistance whatsoever from the Ironship Syndicate. The few managerial representatives with whom I secured a meeting provided only empty platitudes and reminders of the wider crisis facing the entire globe. If anything, their demeanour was mostly one of irritation, as if the need to provide succour to thousands of dispossessed souls was a mere diversion from the real issue.

Over the years the Voters Rights Alliance has maintained contacts with various sympathetic persons employed within the corporate structure. I wouldn't go so far as to describe them as "covert agents," more a small number of individuals disenchanted with their employers and occasionally willing to part with relevant information. Once such person, who I shall name only as "X," met with me in the aftermath of yet another fruitless approach to the interim Board to impart a singular and important fact.

"The Ironship Syndicate is bankrupt," X told me. I had chosen a quiet corner in a secluded tavern for our meeting and was obliged to lean across the table to hear, the words being so softly spoken.

"Bankrupt?" I asked, finding myself suddenly lacking comprehension. I knew the meaning of the word but placing it in conjunction with the wealth-

iest single entity in the world was momentarily disorientating. "What exactly do you mean?"

"I mean they have no money." X is not a character given to overt emotion so it was disconcerting to take note of a tremulous voice and twitching hands. "The company reserves are exhausted. There is no money to pay the workers in the manufactories. No money to pay the Protectorate soldiers. No money to pay the managers, executives or clerks. They've been printing scrip by the bucketload but it's only a matter of time before a finance house attempts to convert a substantial amount of scrip into exchange notes or gold and discovers they hold nothing more than a pile of worthless paper."

I must confess to a certain hesitation before asking my next question. Although I had spent much of my adult years longing for the fall of the Ironship Syndicate, the apparent reality of just such an outcome was sobering to say the least. The Alliance had always campaigned for a peaceful transition to representative government and regulated markets, but the sudden collapse of the world's greatest corporation would herald an era likely to be anything but peaceful. In all honesty, I wasn't sure I wanted it to be true. Nevertheless I buttressed my resolve and asked the question anyway: "You have proof of this?"

In response X handed over a weighty stack of financial ledgers, all marked "Secret—Board Eyes Only" and all showing a zero in the total column.

"How could this happen?" I asked.

"Product." X let out a laugh at this point, somewhat shrill and rich in despair. "It was all built on product. Take that away and what is Ironship? Just a collection of offices, ships and manufactories, all soon to stand empty. And it's not just the Syndicate. The Chairman of the Alebond Commodities Board committed suicide two days ago after being presented with a summation of the company accounts. Yesterday, South Seas Maritime issued an order forbidding any of its ships from leaving port, for the simple reason that they have no funds to buy coal or Red to fire the engines."

X gave another near-hysterical laugh, which soon faded, their features sagging into the pallid mask of a defeated soul. "Now, if you'll excuse me," X said, rising from the table. "I need to go home, dismiss all my servants and tell my spouse they are married to a pauper. After which, I suspect I shall get very drunk indeed."

I made a slow return to the offices of the Gazette, clutching the ledgers tight and gazing around at all the people passing by. Despite recent troubles there was still an air of normalcy to Sanorah then. Stall holders still hawked their wares, boys still ran around delivering the Intelligencer and constables still strolled the thoroughfares, every one of them blithely unaware of the calamity that had already befallen their comfortable world. Upon returning to my office I ignored the many calls for my attention, locking the door and spending several hours in silent contemplation of the stack of ledgers on my desk. The decision before me was stark and, I decided in a fit of cowardice, not one I was prepared to make without counsel.

Regardless of our short acquaintance, Mrs. Torcreek had proven herself to be one of the most level-headed and basically sensible individuals I had yet to meet. Also, her recent experience gave her a depth of insight beyond that of my immediate colleagues in the Alliance. Father knows more about corporate finance than anyone of my acquaintance, and was therefore far better attuned to the consequences of the act I was now forced to consider. Having answered my invitation they both stood in silence as I related the news. Mrs. Torcreek reacted with a stoic lack of surprise and a sympathetic shrug. "Trouble's gonna find everyone sooner or later," she said. "That's the nature of the world right now."

My father was notably less phlegmatic, removing his jacket to roll up his sleeves before spending over an hour in feverish examination of the ledgers. "Seer save us all," he breathed, closing the final one with a snap, resting his elbows on my desk as he rubbed at his temples. "It's true. Ironship is ruined."

I should like to relate that I immediately rose to my feet with a suitably impressive declaration regarding the duty of the press and the rights of the populace to be informed of such disastrous news. However, in actuality I continued to sit behind my desk, staring at my father's stricken features as I asked in a small, frightened voice, "What do I do?"

He stared at me for some time, long enough for me to take shocked notice of the tears welling in his eyes. "Once . . ." he began in a choked quaver then paused, taking out a handkerchief and wiping his eyes. He coughed before continuing in a voice that actually sounded like my father. "Once I would have implored you to wait, give me time to liquidise the family holdings. And I'm sure you would have had many ugly things to say about my greed and selfishness, and perhaps you would have been right. Now . . ." He rested a hand on the ledgers, shaking his head. "Now it doesn't matter. A disaster of this scale will take us all down with it, regardless of any action I take. Publish today or publish tomorrow, but publish. The world should know what's coming."

"Your pa's right, miss," Mrs. Torcreek put in. "People got a right to know, and it's your job to tell them, elst what are you doing here?"

"Well quite," I said, voice still small and hatefully weak. Taking a very deep breath, I rose to my feet, thanked them both for their advice and opened my office door, calling loudly for an urgent editorial meeting.

The following day the headline of the Voters Gazette read: "IRON-SHIP BANKRUPT," rendered in the largest lettering our print set would allow. The story beneath contained a detailed summation, compiled with my father's assistance, of the information in the ledgers provided by X. A battalion of Alliance volunteers spent several hours making copies of the ledgers which were sent to the editor of the Intelligencer and every other periodical in Sanorah. Copies were also dispatched via one of the few mail packets still operating to every major port in northern Mandinor.

Although the Gazette's circulation has never been huge, the fact that this particular issue had been distributed for free guaranteed an initial readership of thousands. Our vendors were quick to demand more copies and our available presses were soon producing issues as fast as could be managed. By the evening of that day lengthy queues had appeared outside *all of the major Sanorah banks as depositors demanded withdrawal of their funds. The fact that all but the first few dozen were turned away was all the proof the populace required to validate the Gazette's claim. The previously orderly crowds outside the banks soon became considerably less so. These were not the agitators and campaigners often dismissed as extremists and malcontents by the corporations. These were ordinary people of many trades and occupations, all suddenly finding themselves impoverished through no fault of their own. Windows were broken, the doors to the banks battered down and bank tellers forced to open vaults which were found to be mostly empty.*

Ironship's reaction was swift but unfortunately predictable. A night-time curfew was declared, the Sanorah garrison was turned out with orders to assist the constabulary in clearing the streets. They also made the singular mistake of sending a company of Protectorate soldiers to arrest my good self and close the Gazette. The refugees, having been roused by Mrs. Torcreek, were more than happy to assist in establishing barricades in the surrounding streets. There are many stalwart souls amongst the refugees, some of them former Contractors hardened by numerous sojourns through the Arradsian Interior. Others are products of the notorious Carvenport slums and therefore habituated to use of weapons. Many of these people had contrived to retain ownership of their fire-arms, or found ways to purchase replacements since their arrival. Also, they were all unified, thanks to Mrs. Torcreek and the work I had done on their behalf, in a determination not to allow me to fall into Protectorate hands.

Consequently, the commander of the Protectorate force bearing my arrest warrant found himself confronted by a series of fortified streets bristling with guns wielded by persons well acquainted with their use. Our defences were also augmented by a significant number of Voters Rights Alliance volunteers, veterans of many a protest who had armed themselves with clubs and piles of displaced cobble-stones for use as projectiles.

The Protectorate captain, a resolute fellow, ordered his men to remain in ranks and approached our largest barricade alone, calling out a demand for my immediate surrender and a list of pertinent charges. "Corporate libel. Theft of Syndicate property. Conspiracy to disrupt public order . . ." This litany of misdeeds ended abruptly when one Molly Pins, the clown-faced woman I had first met at the docks, fired a single pistol shot that shattered a cobble-stone barely an inch from the captain's foot.

"Get the f—— out of here, y'Syndicate p——!" Miss Pins advised to loud acclaim from her fellow defenders. "And take those limp d——s with you, lessen y'wanna see 'em all dead!"

The captain, now somewhat white of face, barked an order that had his soldiers unslinging their rifles, although some began to hesitate when Mrs. Torcreek added her own voice to the proceedings. "They ain't paying you enough to die, boys!" she called out, standing tall on the barricade. "Fact is, they ain't paying you at all!"

Peering through a small gap in the barricade, I saw a few of the soldiers exchanging uncertain glances, whilst a number of others had failed to respond to their captain's order. Apart from the sergeants they were all young, eighteen or nineteen for the most part, conscripts from the outlying holdings drafted only weeks or days before. However, most were dutifully bringing their rifles to port arms as their sergeants barked out their commands. It was clear that any chance to avoid this ending in violence was fast disappearing and I had no desire to see anyone die on my account.

"Stop this!" I said, scrambling up to stand alongside Mrs. Torcreek.

"What're you doing, miss?" she asked.

"I'm sorry. I can't let this happen."

I turned to the captain, raising my arms above my head. He stared up at me in grim satisfaction as I opened my mouth to surrender, then saw his body crumple when one of his men shot him in the back.

For perhaps three full seconds nothing happened. The captain lay bleeding on the street. The soldier who had shot him stood frozen with smoke leaking from the muzzle of his rifle. The other soldiers all gaped at him or the captain's corpse. Then one of the sergeants raised his rifle and shot the soldier in the head. After that, everything happened very quickly.

"Geddown!" Molly Pins hissed, she and Mrs. Torcreek forcing me back behind the barricade as gun-fire exploded all around. The crack and snap of splintering wood accompanied the multitude of discharging fire-arms as bullets tore at the piled furniture that formed the barricade.

"Stop shooting, Seer dammit!" Mrs. Torcreek yelled, her voice possessed of enough volume and authority to cause the surrounding refugees to cease their fusillade. "They're fighting each other."

A quick glance above the barricade confirmed her judgement. The Protectorate company had split into two factions, both rapidly backing away from one another as they exchanged rifle-shots, often tripping over the bodies of their comrades in the process. In the confusion it was impossible to tell which group might harbour sympathy for our cause, although I did note that one was about two-thirds the size of the other. Also, the smaller group seemed to contain a number of sergeants whilst the larger had none.

After a few frantic minutes the smaller group seemed to have fled, whilst the others remained, having taken cover in near by doorways and alleys. A half-dozen soldiers lay on the cobbles, most unmoving, a couple twitching as they groaned.

The renegade soldiers emerged from cover shortly after, led by a scrawny, hook-nosed youth with the broad vowels of the Marsh Wold. "Not been paid for weeks," he said. "Nor fed much the last few days. Not like we volunteered either. Most of us only got called up cos our folk've got land-hold contracts with Ironship."

He went on to describe the widespread discontent amongst the ranks of the Sanorah garrison and alluded to the possibility that he could persuade more of his comrades to join.

"Join what?" I asked, a question I have since recognised as singularly foolish.

"Why, the revolution o'course, miss," the scrawny youth told me. "That's you, ain't it?"

CHAPTER 18

Hilemore

"They're safely on the plains," Zenida said. "Mr. Torcreek thinks another three days until they reach the lake."

"So soon?" Hilemore asked in puzzlement. His examination of the charts relating to southern Arradsia left him with no illusions as to the distances involved.

"Apparently a stampeding Cerath herd can cover a hundred miles a day," she said. "Seems a hazardous form of travel to me, but there you have it."

They were in his cabin, Zenida having just emerged from the regularly scheduled trance. Every time she did this Hilemore would sit in tense expectation of her awakening with nothing to report. "He also said to tell you that his uncle's mood seems to have improved a little," she added.

"Well that's something at least."

Hilemore rose from his desk, pacing to the window to gaze at the placid waters outside. They were anchored off the southern shore of the Upper Torquil. Unwilling to sit idle whilst awaiting the Longrifles' return, Hilemore had undertaken an ad hoc mapping operation of this inland sea. It was clear that the charts of this region held by both the Maritime Protectorate and the Corvantine Imperial Navy were badly outdated and in sore need of revision. Besides which, he preferred to occupy the crew with something beyond yet more painting of the hull or another scrubbing of the bilge tanks.

"I thought I'd take a launch to shore tomorrow," Zenida said, joining him at the port-hole. "Akina hasn't set foot on dry land for months. Even for a Varestian, it's not good to lose touch with the earth. With your permission of course."

Hilemore surveyed the shore, which was much more picturesque than the marshlands that surrounded the Quilam. Small rocky islands topped by trees proliferated amongst the many inlets and creeks, though any scenic appreciation was offset by the knowledge of what lay beyond. "If you wish," he said. "I'll send Mr. Talmant along with an escort."

"Why not come yourself? Take a little time away from your charts. I know Akina would like that."

"All she ever does is make fun of me, when she's not cursing me in pirate slang."

"That's why she would like it. And so would I."

Hilemore turned towards her, finding a wary but definite smile on her lips. They were conversing half in Varestian and half Mandinorian, as they often did when alone, which reminded him that she hadn't referred to him as "sea-brother" for several days now. In Varestian culture the absence of such formality between crewmates could have significant implications. The thought immediately summoned Lewella's face to mind and he looked away.

You have no obligations, he reminded himself. *A broken engagement is just that; the absence of obligation.*

"I . . ." he began, unsure as he spoke what his answer would be, then stopped as a palpable vibration thrummed through the deck beneath his feet. The sensation was accompanied by a loud keening sound that seemed to be coming from beneath the ship.

He frowned at Zenida. "Is that . . . ?"

"It's Jack," she said. "And I believe that's a warning cry."

"Twenty points off the starboard bow, sir," Talmant said, handing Hilemore a spy-glass as he and Zenida rushed onto the bridge. "About two miles out. Another to stern, similar distance. Chief Bozware has the auxiliary engine on-line and the blood-burner is standing by. Anchors are being raised."

Hilemore settled the spy-glass on a patch of sea two miles beyond the bows, finding a familiar roiling to the Torquil's surface he had hoped never to see again. A quick check of the stern confirmed it. *Greens, and a damn sight more than we faced in the Cut.*

"Well done, Mr. Talmant," he said, lowering the glass and speaking swiftly but calmly. "Signal the Chief to bring us to one-third auxiliary power. Mr. Scrimshine, steer due west, if you please." He pulled the set of keys from the chain around his neck and handed it to Zenida, lowering his voice. "Take every vial and report to the engine room. Tell the Chief to pack the blood-burner with as much product as he thinks she can take. Wait for my signal before firing it."

She reached out to take the key, her hand closing over his and lingering for a second. "You owe me a trip to shore," she said before swiftly exiting the bridge.

"Sound battle stations, Mr. Talmant," Hilemore said, drawing his revolver and checking the cylinder. "Riflemen to the rail. All guns to load cannister."

After the near-fatal confrontation in the Cut he had ordered Steelfine to see to the conversion of half their remaining standard shells to cannister. The armour-piercing warheads had been pried off and replaced with modified food cans filled with rifle bullets and whatever scrap-metal they could find. Such munitions were unlikely to prove as effective as true cannister-shot from an Ironship manufactory, but Hilemore expected them to prove their worth if the range was short enough.

He went out on the walkway tracking his spy-glass between the two approaching Green packs. It seemed to him that perhaps every aquatic Green in the Upper Torquil had been mustered by the White's unseen but undeniable hand. *Perhaps that's why it took them so long to return,* he mused. *Gathering forces to make sure of us the next time.*

"Take us to full auxiliary power, Mr. Talmant," he called over his shoulder as the *Superior* settled to midships, shifting his glass to the western horizon, finding it mercifully clear of enemies. Hilemore returned to the bridge to plot their position on the map table. They were fast approaching the point where the Upper Torquil narrowed north of the Cut, meaning their overall speed would be reduced as they ran headlong into the morning tidal surge. The realisation raised the uncomfortable suspicion that the timing of this attack might not be coincidental.

"Signal the engine room," he told Talmant. "Fire the blood-burner."

"Aye, sir."

Hilemore moved to stand at Scrimshine's shoulder, peering through the bridge window. The blood-burner came on-line an instant later, the choppier waters of the narrows suddenly seeming to speed towards them as they surged to thirty knots then beyond. "Got some more tight manoeuvring for you, Leading Deck Hand," Hilemore told Scrimshine. "Though I doubt it'll be quite as bad as the Shelf. Think you're up to it?"

"Beg pardon, sir," Scrimshine said. "But there ain't another hand on this tub I'd trust the job to."

Hilemore didn't feel inclined to argue the point, the helmsman was probably right. "You know the course from here," he said. "On through the narrows to the Cut. Once there don't wait for orders, take us straight through."

"It'll be heavy going, sir," Scrimshine warned. "Tide's likely to be fierce at this hour. Even with the blood-burner going."

"If it's hard for us it's hard for the Greens," Hilemore said, turning away. "Mr. Talmant, you have the bridge. Mr. Scrimshine's position is to be protected at all costs. I'll send two riflemen to assist."

Talmant saluted and drew his revolver. "Very good, sir."

"Mr. Steelfine!" Hilemore called as he descended the ladder to the deck, drawing up short as the Islander's bulky form materialised at his shoulder almost immediately. "Muster all spare hands into a working party," Hilemore ordered. "Shift the port and starboard batteries to the stern, and stack up the cannister for rapid loading."

"Aye, sir."

The lieutenant strode off shouting orders as Hilemore went aft, ordering two riflemen to the bridge and the rest to position themselves on the upper works. "No firing until they're at the rails," he cautioned as they scrambled up the ladders.

Moving to the stern he trained his glass on the sea beyond the *Superior*'s frothing wake, seeing the two groups of Greens beginning to converge two miles off. "They're within range, sir," the aft battery's lead gunner pointed out. "Could throw out a salvo of steel-heads, get a few at least."

Hilemore shook his head. "Waste of powder. Save it for the cannister."

It took over a quarter hour to man-handle the port and starboard guns to the stern. When it was done they had five muzzle-loading thirteen-pound cannon lined up side by side, each with a stack of twenty cannister shells.

"When the time comes forget about accuracy," Hilemore told the gunners, all kneeling in readiness. "Rate of fire is more important just now. The *Undaunted* was my grandfather's favourite ship, and he was given to boasting that she had the best gunners in Protectorate history. Four shots a minute in close action, he said. I always swore I'd beat that if I ever got the chance. Don't make me a liar, lads."

"Aye, sir!" Steelfine barked, the others joining in with the enthusiasm of men facing death and keen for any source of encouragement. The fact that Hilemore's grandfather, the legendary Commodore Racksmith, had never said any such thing was immaterial at this point.

The *Superior* lurched as Scrimshine altered the angle of the rudder to centre the bows on the fast-approaching Cut. There was a noticeable drop in forward speed once the ship completed the turn, her wake broadening as the engine laboured against the tide. Hilemore reckoned their speed to have reduced by at least a third. As ever in the moments before combat time became distorted, the agony of anticipation stretching seconds into minutes. Hilemore heard one of the gunners let out a gasp of relief as the roiling waters beyond the wake began to dissipate.

"Bastards are giving up," the man breathed, sagging a little then straightening as Steelfine barked out a rebuke.

"I'm afraid the bastards are being clever," Hilemore said after scanning the water with his glass. The Greens had divided, splitting off into two narrow groups, keeping close to the edge of the channel where the current was weakest. They were near enough now for him to see that they were slip-streaming, one Green leading the way, making the going easier for those behind. After several minutes the lead Green would fall back to be immediately replaced by another. *Clever bastards indeed*, Hilemore thought.

They entered the Cut proper soon after, whereupon the *Superior* slowed to the equivalent of one-third auxiliary speed. The Greens once again proved their cunning by veering away from the banks and into the ship's wake. With the frigate acting as a breakwater they were soon able to close on the stern, approaching in a dense pack that stretched away for at least three hundred yards.

"Range fifty yards, sir," the lead gunner reported, Hilemore noting how the man's hand shook on his gun's firing lanyard.

"Wait for the order," Hilemore instructed, moving without particular haste to stand at the aft rail, hands clasped behind his back as he watched the Greens draw closer still. He waited until he could see the sunlight glinting on their scales and shook his head, possessed by a curious sense of regret for what was about to unfold. *Such foolish things the White makes you do,* he thought, turning away and nodding at Steelfine. "Sequential order, Number One. Port to starboard. Fire when ready."

The gun on the far right fired even before Steelfine had finished shouting the command. The other four followed suit in quick succession. Hilemore moved to the left to gauge the effect of the shot as the crews feverishly began to reload. He could see a patch of red amongst the froth of the *Superior*'s wake, but the Greens were still coming on apace. The next salvo raised five identical waterspouts amongst the heart of the pack, Hilemore taking satisfaction from the sight of tumbling and torn Green bodies raining down in the aftermath.

"Got a dozen at least with that one, lads!" he called to the gunners. "Keep it up!"

He wasn't sure the gun-crews did in fact manage four shots a minute in the time it took them to expend two-thirds of their cannister, but if not it was certainly close. The *Superior* left a pinkish stain the length of the Cut. Dead and dying Greens rolled and twisted in the current, some calling out plaintive cries before slipping beneath the water. None came within twenty yards of the ship's stern and the survivors seemed to have abandoned their pursuit, milling about in the centre of the Cut as the *Superior* drew away.

The guns fired once more before Hilemore called out a cease-fire order, the cannister launched at too great a range to have any effect but the crews let out a triumphant cheer anyway. "A good day's work, sir," Steelfine commented as they surveyed the carnage churning in their wake.

"Actually, no, Number One, it isn't," Hilemore replied. "We appear to have been expelled from the Upper Torquil, making our mission markedly more difficult. We'll have to find another location to retrieve the expedition . . ."

"Sir!" He trailed off as one of the riflemen he had assigned to the bridge approached at a run, coming to a halt and offering a quick salute. "Mr. Talmant's compliments, sir. He requests your presence on the bridge." The man's shoulders slumped a little, face grim as he added, "There are more of them ahead, sir. Hundreds of the buggers sealing the far end of the Cut."

*C*hased us right into a trap, and I fell for it.
Hilemore's hands bunched into fists at the small of his back as he sought to keep the combined anger and self-reproach from his features. He had ordered the *Superior* to one-half auxiliary power, which, thanks to the inrushing tidal surge, kept them in a stationary position a half mile from the southern mouth of the Cut. He stood at the *Superior*'s prow along with Steelfine and Zenida, surveying the mass of Greens that filled the exit from the channel. There were so many it seemed as if they formed a solid barrier of drake flesh, far too thick to blast their way through with the ammunition they had left.

"We could wait for the tide to shift," Zenida suggested. "Fire up the blood-burner when it does and charge them."

"They'll swarm the ship," Hilemore said.

"We can fortify the upper works, sir," Steelfine said. "Seal all the hatches and shift the cannon to the walkways." The Islander's features were rigid, but Hilemore saw the truth in his eyes clearly; a desperate ploy, but better than nothing. One thing was clear: They couldn't just sit here and wait to run out of fuel.

"Very well," he said. "Form parties to gather anything we can use as a barricade . . ."

He fell silent as a roar sounded from the mouth of the Cut, turning in time to see a column of flame erupt from the centre of the Green barrier. The drakes let out an immediate, shrill chorus of alarm as a very large blue shape burst through their ranks. Jack continued to belch out fire as he rose amongst them, turning the sea to steam and boiling the Greens who thrashed around him. Then, as the flames died, he arched his massive body and brought his tail up and down in a blow that shook the ship as he whipped it into the mass of flailing drakes.

"Get to the engine room," Hilemore told Zenida, who was already running for the hatch. "Full power to the blood-burner!" he called after her before turning to Steelfine. "Take charge of the pivot-gun. Fire as she bears."

Hilemore sprinted for the bridge, hauling himself up the ladder in a rapid scramble. The order he was about to give Scrimshine proved unnecessary as the ship lurched into forward motion and the helmsman spun the wheel to aim her at the opening Jack had torn in the cordon of Greens.

"Thought the bastard was a coward," he said as Hilemore moved to his side.

"Not today it seems."

Flames rose again as they sped forward, Jack casting the jet of fire all around him. The death cries of the Greens rose to ear-piercing levels as the *Superior* charged into the remnants of their barrier. A stream of fire flashed over the fore-deck, blinding Hilemore for a second. He blinked and wiped at his eyes, looking again to see Jack's head rising to port with a pair of struggling Greens clamped in his jaws. The Blue bit down and shook his head, the Greens coming apart in an explosion of blood and shredded flesh. Jack opened his mouth wide, sword-length teeth gleaming red and white as he dived down in search of fresh prey.

Flames licked at the *Superior*'s flanks as she exited the mouth of the Cut, a last desperate attempt by the drakes to bar their escape that did little damage. Only one Green appeared on the fore-deck, a burnt, ragged thing that struggled over the rail to stagger about, coughing flame in all directions until a blast of cannister from the pivot-gun tore it to pieces. Then they were through, the smoke and billowing steam clearing to reveal the welcome sight of the Lower Torquil.

"Maintain speed and heading," Hilemore said before going out onto the walkway and turning to the stern. He could see Jack still assailing the Greens but now they were fighting back, dozens of them leaping clear of the water to belch fire at his head whilst others clamped themselves onto his coils, biting furiously at his scales. The great Blue let out a roar of pain and rage, his flames incinerating a half-dozen Greens as he thrashed his massive body, but there were more boiling out of the sea. Within moments Jack was covered in them, clinging like leeches to his hide. The weight of so much flesh inevitably began to bear him down, though he fought and bit and roasted his enemies to the end. Hilemore closed his eyes as Jack's head disappeared beneath the surface in a cloud of steam, his last roar swallowed by a sea stained dark with drake blood.

"Report from the crow's nest, sir," Talmant called from the bridge. "More Greens to the east."

Hilemore tore his gaze from the scene of Jack's demise, training his glass on the eastern horizon. The Green pack was a good way off, four miles or more, even larger than those they had already encountered and approaching fast. *Every aquatic Green in the Torquils,* he thought, returning to the bridge. Defeat was not a pleasant sensation but to deny it would make him a poor excuse for a captain.

"Mr. Scrimshine," he said, "steer due south. We're quitting the Torquils."

CHAPTER 19

Lizanne

"I can see where it got its name," Tekela commented, pulling back on the control lever so the *Firefly* ascended into a bank of cloud, the tall spike of the High Wall fading from view beneath.

The Okanas family had chosen to construct its seat in the crater of a long-extinct volcano. The narrow peak rose from the sea to a height of well over two hundred feet. The entire south-facing slope appeared to either have been shorn away by the elements or deliberately removed to be replaced by a wall of smooth granite. A massive iron door lay at the base of the wall, presumably to allow for the comings and goings of the family's ships. Before the cloud closed in Lizanne had used a spy-glass to survey the cluster of buildings nestling in the volcano's crater, marking the largest as a possible barracks and the more narrow but taller structure opposite as the Okanas mansion.

There was no sign of alarm in the crater or any indication they had been seen. Lizanne had ordered Tekela to stay as high as possible during the approach and make full use of the fortuitously plentiful cloud-cover. Also, the hour was late and the gathering gloom would make them harder still to spot, especially by look-outs accustomed to scanning the sea for likely enemies.

"The island three miles west," Lizanne said, pointing at a stretch of sea visible through a gap in the cloud. "It's flat enough for a landing. Wait until . . ."

". . . dawn tomorrow before picking you up," Tekela finished. "I know."

"Steer north," Lizanne said, reasoning there might be fewer sentries facing away from the most likely seaward approach. "Circle until it gets dark."

The cloud-cover thinned as evening slipped into night, the two moons casting a long shadow from the High Wall and scattering glitter over the sea. "Are you sure this is the best idea?" Tekela asked, not for the first time. "It's a tricky piece of flying."

Lizanne rose from her seat, crouching to open the hatch in the floor of the gondola. "I have every confidence in your abilities," she said, pulling on a harness. It was constructed from strong, heavily stitched leather with two additional straps above her shoulders that were joined by a steel ring. Once she had buckled the harness into place Lizanne reached for a twenty-yard-long coil of steel cable. One end of the cable was a standard eye hook whilst the other was something Jermayah had quickly put together before they set off. She buckled this device onto the harness's steel ring before leaning down to reach outside and attach the other end to the half-ring on the gondola's underside.

"Ready," she told Tekela, swinging her legs into the opening and using the Spider to inject a large dose of Green.

"Engine off," Tekela said, closing the throttle then taking a firmer hold of the central control lever. "Descending now."

Lizanne jumped as Tekela put the aerostat into a steep dive, the force of the wind instantly whipping her back as the cable extended. The Green limited the effect of the jarring impact when the cable reached its limit, Lizanne feeling her vertebrae strain with the jolting instant deceleration. The cable scraped over the engine mounting as she swung behind the plummeting *Firefly*, and would have fouled the propellers if they hadn't had the foresight to kill the power.

The aerostat continued to dive for about thirty seconds whereupon Tekela pulled back on the control lever and it came to a stop, the *Firefly* rearing backwards. Lizanne continued to plummet, the cable tightening to swing her beneath the gondola at near-terminal velocity. The High Wall loomed before her as she neared the apex of the swing, the fortified edge of the crater no more than fifty yards away.

Lizanne reached up and hit the catch on Jermayah's hook, detaching herself from the cable. The momentum was sufficient to carry her across the edge of the crater and the parapet beyond. As she passed over it she could see only one sentry, face lit by a glow as he touched a match to his cigarillo, completely oblivious to anything that might be happening above.

She landed on the roof of the barracks, displacing several tiles in the process, then sliding to the edge of the roof. Lizanne twisted about and caught hold of the gutter, hanging there in rigid silence. She heard a few raised voices and the rapid tread of boots on cobbles, no doubt drawn by the cascade of falling tiles. Her Green-enhanced ears caught much of the subsequent conversation.

"Could be gulls again . . ."

"Too many fallen slates for that. Better take a look."

"Do we tell him?"

"Fuck no . . ."

Lizanne waited for the tread of boot leather to fade then hauled herself back up onto the roof. It was overlooked by the parapet and she knew she had only moments before the inquisitive and overly conscientious guard climbed up and raised the alarm. The barracks were separated from the Okanas mansion by a twenty-foot gap, a relatively easy jump for a Blood-blessed stoked with Green, but requiring a decent run up and yet more fallen tiles. Instead Lizanne opted for the shorter jump to the crater wall to the rear of the barracks. It was a rough-hewn cliff-face with hand- and footholds aplenty, enabling her to latch on and descend rapidly into the shadows below.

Upon reaching the ground she immediately sprinted towards the mansion, disappearing into the refuge of the house's shadowed rear in the space of a few heart-beats. Given the lack of alarm she had successfully avoided the attentions of the inquisitive guard.

Scanning the rear edifice of the mansion, she saw lights in the ground-level windows, but none in the floors above. Intelligence on this place had been meagre, garnered from the few sailors and refugees she could find with some familiarity of Varestian waters. Only one, a former Blue-hunter hand recently recruited into Madame Hakugen's militia, had actually been to the High Wall but never reached these lofty heights. "They're a right suspicious bunch to be sure, miss," the man had said. "Don't let visiting sailors wander from their docks. Though there's rumours of all manner of treasure in the upper reaches of that mountain."

Lizanne, of course, wasn't interested in treasure tonight, merely maps and documents which experience told her would most likely be found on the first floor. The mansion was a close copy of a larger-than-average Mandinorian country-house, the kind purchased by the upper middle rank of the corporate managerial class desirous of a refuge from the odorous bustle of city life. She had had occasion to burgle such places before and the study would normally be found opposite the stairwell on the first-floor landing. Quickly identifying the correct window, she moved to the mansion wall and launched herself upwards, the Green ensuring she gained purchase on the window-sill some twelve feet off the ground. Hoisting herself up, she was gratified to find only a basic latch on the window, easily opened after a fractional injection of Black. She used the remaining Black to draw the window up and swiftly swung herself inside, crouching to survey the room with her enhanced vision. After a few seconds of squinting at brooms, buckets and a variety of mops she realised she had chosen the wrong access point after all.

Getting rusty, she chided herself, moving to press her ear to the door of what was plainly a closet. She could hear a faint murmur of voices from the lower floor, two or three, all male. The words were indistinct but the pitch was casual, lacking in urgency. Lizanne found the door unlocked and eased it open, seeing an empty landing and two stairwells, one leading up, the other down. Spotting another door opposite the cupboard, she stole out onto the landing, moving in a slow crouch, her feet testing each floorboard before putting her full weight on it. She found the other door secured by a heavy Alebond Commodities double-mortise lock, indicating something of value might well lie on the other side. Another injection of Black and some careful probing later and she was in, closing the door softly behind her.

The room was fully dark and the windows shuttered so even with Green in her veins it took a moment to confirm she had in fact found the study this time. However, it was more of a library-cum–map room, the walls lined with book-laden shelves from floor to ceiling whilst a number of chart-bearing easels were arranged around a large central map table.

Not so rusty after all. Lizanne allowed herself a small compliment as she went to the map table. Laid out on its surface beneath a thick sheet of glass was the largest complete map of the Arradsian continent she had ever seen. It was clearly several decades old from the foxing that discoloured the edges of the paper, but it also appeared to be remarkably accurate, albeit also heavily modified. Annotations in dense Varestian script had been scribbled all around the coast and at some places in the mostly blank Interior. Lizanne's interest piqued, however, as her gaze tracked across the chart to Krystaline Lake where the annotations became a jumbled, overlapping frenzy.

"Mrreaaoow?"

Lizanne's gaze snapped to the underside of the table, finding a pair of green eyes blinking up at her from the gloom. The cat slinked out of the shadows and wound itself around her legs, tail swishing. Lizanne ignored it and returned to the map, peering closer at the cloud of scribbles around the lake. Her spoken Varestian was perfect but her understanding of the written form less so. It was a curious mode of text in that it mixed pictography with phonetics, making rapid translation difficult.

"Current becomes . . . a vortex here," she murmured, her finger tapping a notation next to a series of circular arrows. It was marked with several cruciform squiggles she knew to be the equivalent of a Mandinorian exclamation mark.

The cat let out another plaintive miaow then purred as it prodded her calf with its head. Keen to quiet the animal, Lizanne crouched and gathered it up, stroking it as she continued to examine the map. Large as it was the depiction of Krystaline Lake still lacked sufficient detail for her to identify a precise location. She gauged the swirl of arrows as about sixty miles south of the falls that fed the lake, and at least three miles from shore, but doubted that would be enough for Clay and his Contractors to pin-point it.

She stepped back from the map, turning her attention to the easels that surrounded it. She carried the cat to the closest one, the furry bundle purring as she scratched under its chin. The map was a detailed scientific study of the lake marked with the crest of the Consolidated Research Company. Various depths were depicted and coded in different colours and likely concentrations of "draconic activity" outlined in green ink, but the map itself gave no clues as to the location of what had so obsessed the late patriarch of the Okanas clan.

She examined each of the easels in turn, finding them all detailed renderings of various regions of Krystaline Lake, until she came to one that was plainly an enlarged version of the region with the swirling currents. The arrows depicting the vortex were drawn with more care, some rendered in black, others red and often marked with the Varestian equivalent of a question mark. However, what drew most of her attention was the large "X" in the centre of the vortex. The notation next to it was unusual in that it wasn't written in Varestian, but something that resembled the flowing elegance of Dalcian. *Ancient Dalcian,* she decided, recalling what Clay had told her about the original legend regarding the treasure of Krystaline Lake. She didn't know this script and therefore couldn't translate it, but was sure if she had it would have read "a vessel of wonder, unbound by earth or sea, come to rest with precious cargo 'neath the silver waters."

"I do believe," Lizanne said, giving the cat a hug, "I may have found what I came for."

The cat squirmed in her arms, suddenly agitated. A flicker of movement drew Lizanne's gaze to a near by bookcase, finding another cat perched atop it. Unlike the grey tabby she held, this one was black, and considerably larger. Also, judging by the white teeth it bared at Lizanne as it hissed, much less desirous of petting.

"Don't do that," Lizanne said, patting the cat she held on the head. "See? I'm nice."

The black cat, however, seemed unimpressed, its hiss becoming louder still as it lowered itself for a pounce. The cat in Lizanne's arms let out a frightened growl and tore itself free, bounding off into the gloomy recesses of the study, swiftly pursued by its darker cousin. Soon came the sound of tumbled books and furniture as the cats raced around the room, letting out a chorus of shrieks and hisses as they did so. From the sound of raised voices from below, it was evident the commotion hadn't been missed.

Lizanne snapped her gaze back to the map on the easel, trained eyes drinking in every detail in the space of a few seconds. Hearing keys rattling in the door's lock she ran to the nearest window. The shutters were locked so she injected Black and tore them away before shattering the window itself. She leapt through just as the door to the study burst open. A pistol shot boomed behind her as she tumbled into space, followed by a stern rebuke in Varestian: "No firing, shit-brain! I need her alive!"

Lizanne landed amidst a cluster of rose-bushes in the mansion's small garden. Tearing herself free and ignoring the sting of thorns, she refreshed her Green and ran for a stairwell carved into the surrounding crater wall. As she scaled the steps a man leapt down from above to land in front of her, swinging the butt of a carbine at her head, then finding himself tumbling through the air as she blasted him aside with Black. Below light flooded the crater as torches and lanterns sprang to life accompanied by a chorus of shouts and orders. Loudest amongst the babble of voices was one calling for "Morva! Get up here, you lazy bitch!"

Messy, Lizanne reproached herself as she neared the top of the stairwell. *Next time just throttle any cats.*

A five-strong squad of sentries charged at her when she got to the parapet, arms locked and grouped together in a tight bunch in the hope it might protect them. They were wrong. She swept their legs away with a wave of Black, sending them all sprawling face-first onto the parapet. Lizanne leapt the struggling quintet, landing atop the battlement and pausing to gauge the distance to the crashing waves below. It would be the highest dive she had ever attempted, but survivable with sufficient Green in her veins and Black to part the water as she came down.

Lizanne leapt, her form perfect, legs straight and toes pointed, arms outstretched then pulled forward and hands clasped together . . .

The air rushed out of her lungs as an invisible fist closed about her chest, holding her in mid air for a second before dragging her backwards. She managed to cushion the impact with Black, sending out a pulse just before she collided with the cobbled surface of the courtyard to the front of the mansion. She rolled as she landed, jerking to the side as a wave of heated air told of a near miss with Red. Lizanne whirled and dodged, gaze roaming the courtyard for her assailant, taking in the onlooking cordon of Varestians. They were all carrying weapons and many were in a state of undress, having just been roused from their beds. The Blood-blessed wasn't hard to find, a tall slim figure standing apart from the others, female with a scarlet headscarf. She stood with her arms crossed and head tilted in a way that put Lizanne in mind of the cat that had just undone her mission. It didn't improve her mood.

She sent a contained blast of her own Black straight at the woman's face then followed it with one to the chest as she dodged aside, Lizanne experiencing the satisfaction of watching her opponent spun into an untidy pirouette by the force of the blow. The woman let out a frustrated yelp, bounding upright in an impressive display of agility and letting loose with a stream of Red. It was an undisciplined riposte, one Lizanne easily evaded with a Green-enhanced leap that brought her to a height of twenty feet, whereupon she pinned the woman to the cobbles with a stream of Black. Lizanne drew both her revolvers and landed astride the woman's prostrate form, levelling one pistol at her forehead as she tracked the other across the surrounding Varestians.

They all raised their own weapons with a metallic rattle of drawn hammers and chambered rounds. They held a mix of carbines and pistols along with the occasional shotgun. Lizanne knew in an instant the chances of evading so many projectiles at once were non-existent, and given the confident anticipation on their faces, so did they.

"Kill her if you want," said one of the Varestians, a bearded fellow of broad stature who stepped from the cordon with a long-barrelled pistol in hand. He cast a withering glance at the woman on the ground, who returned it with a resentful frown. "My niece has never really earned her salt," he said, sliding the pistol into a shoulder holster. "So you would in fact be doing me a great favour."

Lizanne cast a final glance around at the ring of armed men and women, then slowly raised both pistols above her head. "My name is Lizanne Lethridge . . ." she began.

"Miss Blood herself?" the bearded man cut in, eyebrows raised in apparent awe. However, the awe disappeared almost instantly and he began to voice a laugh that was soon shared by his compatriots, the sound of their humour echoing through the crater. "I did rather think it might be," he added once the laughter had faded, inclining his head in a grudging gesture of respect. "Alzar Lokaras, Custodian of the High Wall. And before I hang your worthless corporate hide from said wall, I should very much like to know what you're doing here."

Lizanne replied with an affable nod, smiling to distract him before dropping the pistol in her right hand and pressing the fourth button on the Spider. Alzar Lokaras swore and lunged towards her as she collapsed, Blue flooding her veins and dragging her into the deepest trance.

CHAPTER 20

Clay

"Thank the Seer for that," Skaggerhill groaned, slipping from the back of the female Cerath he had been riding. The animal immediately cantered away to cluster with its kin as the Harvester rubbed at the small of his back. "One more mile would have done for me, I reckon."

"I believe we're close enough to walk the rest of the way," Lieutenant Sigoral said, looking up from his map. "Just over twelve miles due east should bring us to the lake's western shore."

Clay leaned forward then back to relieve his own aching muscles, casting his gaze over the darkening blue of the sky, broken by Nelphia's pale crescent rising over the eastern horizon. "It's late," he said. "We'll rest up. Same watch order as last night, lest anyone's got any objections."

Since taking on the primary burden of leadership he had also assumed the post-midnight watch, generally considered the least desirable, something his uncle had tended to do during their search for the White. He wasn't sure if the absence of argument was due to an acceptance of his leadership or a desire for uninterrupted sleep.

"Would never light a fire out here before," Braddon said later, tossing a few sticks into the small but healthy blaze in the centre of the camp. "Woulda drawn Spoiled by the dozen." He paused to scan the surrounding plains, the grass whispering faintly beneath a starlit sky. "Now, there's no fresh sign of their passing for miles around. Used to be six different tribes on the plains, that we knew of anyways."

"All gone off to fight the White's war," Clay said. "Those that ain't dead already."

"Makes you wonder," Skaggerhill said. "If they got any notion of what they're fighting for. Or any say in the matter."

"'Those that serve the drake's will surrender their own,'" Preacher said, causing the usual stir of surprise at breaking his customary silence.

"Forgive my ignorance," Sigoral said. "But did the Seer predict any of this? His writings have long been banned in the Empire."

"He tried to warn the world of what was to come," Preacher replied. "Though there were few who listened."

"I have read all the Seer's words, more than once," Braddon said. "Don't recall mention of anything that resembles what's happening right now."

Preacher fixed Braddon with a bright-eyed stare of the kind Clay had last seen during their previous visit to Krystaline Lake. "Then you should have read deeper, Captain," the marksman said in a low, intent voice. "For it's all there. The Travail is at last upon us and are we not seven in number?"

Braddon gave no reply causing Loriabeth to pipe up. "What's that gotta do with anything?"

"The Seven Penitents," Braddon said. "The Seer claimed that when the forces of darkness rise up during the Travail they'll be opposed by Seven Penitents."

"Seven Righteous Penitents," Preacher said, the volume of his voice climbing a notch. "Chosen from amongst the great throng of sinners to stand against the ravaging tide." He paused, gaze unfocused but gleaming. "I see it now. Though I hid from it for many years. Though I sundered myself from the church and sought death in the Interior. Though I have revelled in slaughter of drake and Spoiled and sullied my soul in the revelling, ever has the truth of the Seer's word pursued me, until now, at last it finds me."

He stood, raising his arms, hands outstretched, fingers spread wide. "Will you pray with me, brothers and sisters?" he said, head lowered. "Give thanks to the Seer for his guidance and seek his blessing for the task ahead."

Loriabeth exchanged a brief glance with Clay and her father before getting to her feet, lip curled in distaste. "Fuck off," she said wearily before going to her bedroll.

"Wait a second, cuz," Clay said, bringing her to an uncertain pause. He rose to his feet and went to clasp Preacher's outstretched hand. The marksman gripped it with all the fierceness of a man clinging to wreckage in a stormy sea. "Thank you, brother," he breathed, head still lowered.

"Well, why not?" Clay said, looking at each of them in turn and holding out his own hand. "Reckon we'll be needing all the help we can get before long."

It was Kriz who took his hand, albeit with a bemused smile. Braddon moved to clasp Preacher's other hand, extending his own to Skaggerhill, who took it after a moment's hesitation.

"Lieutenant?" Kriz said, holding her hand out to Sigoral.

The Corvantine frowned in rueful resignation before joining his hand to hers, muttering, "A man would find himself hung for this in the Empire." He turned, hand raised expectantly to Loriabeth. The distaste still lingered on her face, though the sneer had disappeared now.

"Ma never had no truck with such nonsense," she said, crossing her arms. "Neither do I."

"Please, Lori," Braddon said. "It's just for a second."

Loriabeth raised her face to the sky, breath misting a little in the chill night air as she let out a soft curse. "As long as he don't take all night about it," she said, moving to join hands with Sigoral and Skaggerhill, closing the circle.

"The final resting place of the Seer is unknown to this day," Preacher said, raising his face, eyes still lit by the same glow of conviction. "For that was his wish. 'Make no idols of me,' he said. 'My words are my temple and my testament.' The Seer offered no false promises, no empty lies, that those who followed his words would earn an eternal place in another world or riches in this one. His message was simple: The Travail is coming. And now it is here. Of the Seven Penitents he said only this: 'When the storm winds born of the Travail blow hardest, when the flames reach highest, when the screams of the damned grow loudest, then will the Seven Righteous Penitents rise. Long will they travel and much will they suffer, but it is they who will quench the flames and silence the screams, though it cost them all.'"

"Well, that's cheery," Loriabeth muttered.

"We are Seven!" Preacher said, Clay wincing a little as his grip tightened. "Joined in purpose and now joined in faith. I know the Seer blesses our endeavour." He lowered his gaze once more, saying, "Heed the words of the Seer."

"Heed the words of the Seer," Braddon repeated, Clay and the others doing the same.

Silence reigned for a time as they stood there, holding hands in silent contemplation until, from somewhere out on the darkened plain, there came the shrill cry of a drake.

"Shit!" Loriabeth drew both pistols and threw herself flat, the circle breaking apart as the rest of them armed themselves and hunkered down. "Sounded a mite too high-pitched for a Green," she said.

"Plains Green," Skaggerhill said, drawing back the hammers on his shotgun. "Little smaller than jungle Greens, but a good deal more cunning. They move in packs of six or more and hunt at night. Most likely caught the scent of the Cerath we rode here on. Be after the young 'uns."

"And if they ain't?" Clay asked.

Skaggerhill sighed and reached for his pack, placing it in front of him and laying the shotgun on top. "Then we're in for a very long night."

Either through blind luck or disinterest they spent a nervous night untroubled by any Greens. Clay eventually ordered the resumption of the watch rota and each of them managed a few hours' sleep before dawn. They set off after a short breakfast of canned sea rations washed down with a larger-than-usual quota of coffee to stave off the lingering fatigue. It took two of them to carry Kriz's apparatus, the bulky device lashed into a tarpaulin suspended between two poles. Clay had been taking his turn lugging the apparatus when they came upon the body of a juvenile Cerath.

Flies buzzed in greedy swarms around the empty cavity of the animal's stomach and the many wounds that scored its hide. "Like I said," Skaggerhill commented, "after the young 'uns."

"Got a dead Green over here," Braddon said, pointing to something in the long grass near by. "Looks like its head got stoved in. Guess momma Cerath got herself some vengeance."

"You wanna stop and harvest it?" Skaggerhill said. "Won't take too long."

"No," Clay said. He grunted and settled the poles on his shoulders before resuming the trek. "The lake's only a coupla miles away, and we already got us a decent stock of Green."

Krystaline Lake came into view just after noon, the plains suddenly descending in a gentle slope towards the shore that stretched away on either side. The water was as blue and deceptively inviting as Clay remembered, and at this latitude so broad that the jungle covering the eastern shore was lost to view.

"We're gonna need another boat," Braddon said. "Or at least a raft."

"Need some notion of where to look first," Clay said as he and Sigoral set the apparatus down. "I'll trance with Miss Lethridge toni—"

The rush of fear hit him like a punch, sending him to his knees, a pain-filled yell escaping his clenched teeth as thoughts that were not his own flooded his head: *A great host of aquatic Greens, seen from below, sediment billowing, Jack's huge heart hammering in alarm as he let out a plaintive warning cry.*

"Clay?" his uncle was at his side, holding him as he convulsed, Jack's need for reassurance dominating his thoughts.

STOP!

Clay forced the command through Jack's terrorised babble, reaching into the core of his mind to crush the worst of his fear. Jack calmed, his huge body ceasing its desperate coiling as he sought to conceal himself in a cloud of raised sediment. Clay had Jack cast his gaze upwards once more, seeing that the Green pack had passed overhead now. They were clustering together on the surface a short way off, forming some kind of barrier. Clay turned Jack about, seeing the narrow hull of the *Superior* cutting the surface towards them, its wake diminishing as it came to a halt. Jack's incredible hearing was full of the massed clicking and chirping of the Greens directly to the *Superior*'s front and keen enough to detect a similar cacophony of another pack behind. From the way the sound echoed around he was also able to deduce they were in a narrow channel.

Got themselves trapped in the Cut, Clay realised. *Bet the captain's pissed about that.*

He centred Jack's gaze on the twisting coil of the Green barrier, several yards thick and growing thicker as more drakes swam to join it. *It's time to fight, Jack,* Clay told the Blue, which caused an immediate resurgence of his fear. Clay tried to calm him again but this time the terror couldn't be stemmed. *I'm sorry,* Clay said, guilt and resignation mingling in his heart. *But I need Last Look for this.*

He dived deep into the Blue's memories, pulling together all the messy remnants of Jack's life, forming them into an ugly ball that throbbed with violence. Clay pushed himself into the ball, fighting nausea at the blood-lust he found. Rummaging through the shifting mass of slaughter and madness felt like sinking his hands into a charnel-house trough. Finally, he found what he was looking for, the still-living core that had been Last Look Jack. It was a dark, twisted thing, denuded of much of its being but still holding on to all that useful hatred.

See them? Clay asked it, focusing the Blue's gaze on the Greens once more. *They ain't drakes, they're men.* He took an image of one of the Greens and remoulded it, shrinking the tail and growing the limbs, sculpting the head into a ball rather than a spear. Jack's hunger swelled at the sight, then blossomed further as Clay spread the remade image of the Green to its brethren. Within seconds what had been a mass of drake flesh had become a mass of men, and Jack required no further encouragement.

The shared awareness began to fragment as Jack surged upwards into the Greens, flame erupting from his mouth. Clay felt himself convulse as the subsequent kaleidoscope of horrors played out, man after man roasted or snapped into bloody remnants, except they weren't men. Even at his worst Jack had never experienced such an ecstasy of vengeance. His mind exulted with it, as if this were the pinnacle of his quest to rid the seas of humankind.

Clay was vaguely aware of the *Superior* passing by, but Jack was too preoccupied with his feast to pay the ship much mind. Soon, however, he began to feel pain amongst the fury, Clay's hands scrabbling at his body as he felt the Greens tear at his hide. He started to choke and gasp as the weight of them bore him down, Greens worrying their way past his scales to the flesh beneath whilst flames licked at Jack's eyes. Clay let out a groan as ever more of the Blue's blood seeped into the sea and his mind became a distant, withered remnant.

I'm sorry, Jack. He sent the thought after the Blue as his mind flickered in the depths, flared bright for one last second and then died. *I'm so sorry.*

He didn't wake until the next morning, blinking the blur from his gaze to find a ring of concerned faces staring down at him. "Told you he weren't dying," Loriabeth said, poking Sigoral in the ribs.

"Fever's gone," Kriz said, crouching to press a hand to his forehead. "Your temperature was a little alarming for a while."

Clay shook his head, finding he had only the most dim recollection of the previous few hours. There had been dreams, he knew that, but he had a sense of being fortunate not to remember them.

"What was that?" Kriz asked. "Has it happened to you before?"

"Jack died," Clay said, climbing to his feet. "The ship ain't waiting for us in the Torquils no more. We'll have to find another way back to it."

He shrugged away their helping hands and turned his gaze to the lake. Jack's demise kept replaying in his head, provoking a sick, guilty jab at his gut with every repetition. "Uncle's right," he said. "We need a raft. Time to find some trees."

Constructing a raft of sufficient dimensions took two full days, much of the time spent harvesting the necessary wood from the infrequent trees found on the lake's western shore. Kriz oversaw the design whilst Skaggerhill and Sigoral did the bulk of the construction, they being the most familiar with water-craft. When it was done they had a square platform some twelve feet wide complete with four oars for steering. They carried it to the shore for a test launch, which confirmed it could actually float and bear the weight of Kriz's apparatus.

"Now we just need somewhere to look," Braddon said.

That night Clay drank Blue and sank into the trance, his relief surging at finding Lizanne waiting for him though he was surprised to find her usually neat whirlwinds a roiling mess.

I don't have long, she told him, mind curt and urgent. *Here.*

One of the whirlwinds swept towards him and unfolded into what at first appeared to be a confused, vaguely circular jumble of scribbled text. *Co-ordinates,* Lizanne added, pushing a set of numbers into his mind with an uncharacteristic clumsiness.

Ow! Clay protested, the intrusion sending a pulse of discomfort through his mindscape. *What—?*

No time.

And she was gone, leaving him dazed on Nelphia's dusty plains.

"Five miles north along the coast," Sigoral said after plotting the co-ordinates onto his map. "Just under three miles from shore."

"Three miles is a lot," Skaggerhill said. "'Specially on a lake as rich in Greens as this one."

"Can't be helped," Clay said. "We'll go out only in daylight, for just a few hours at a time. Me and the lieutenant will accompany every trip." He pulled on his pack and moved to take one of the ropes securing the raft to the shore. "Best get to towing this thing whilst there's still daylight."

They reached the required stretch of coast by midafternoon, towing the raft along the shore-line until Sigoral confirmed they were in the right place.

"You don't want to wait for tomorrow?" Clay asked Kriz as she prepared her breathing apparatus.

"There's plenty of daylight left," she said, fixing a pipe onto the pump then connecting the other end to the helmet she would wear whilst underwater.

"Seems pretty simple," Clay went on. "Maybe I should . . ."

"It's not," she said. "And you shouldn't."

They launched the raft a short while later, Clay and Sigoral imbibing Green and manning the oars to ensure a swift transit, whilst Braddon and Preacher kept a close watch on the surrounding waters. Kriz took charge of the tiller, keeping an eye on Sigoral's compass as she steered them towards the required spot. After a quarter hour of rowing the raft took on a wayward spin, Clay noticing that the lake's surface had become much more lively.

"I think this is it," Sigoral said. "The chart you drew indicated a circular current surrounding the site."

They pressed on for a short distance until the water became calm again. They had crafted a makeshift anchor by gathering up as many boulders as they could and wrapping them in a tarpaulin bound with rope. Clay pushed it over the side and the raft slowly came to a halt.

"Depth one hundred and thirty-five feet," Sigoral reported after checking the markers whitewashed onto the anchor rope.

Kriz nodded and adjusted a valve on her apparatus before donning a leather belt which had been fitted with several lead weights. "Green and Black," Clay said, handing her two vials. "Drink all of it now." When she had done so he slipped a vial of Blue into the top pocket of her overalls. "Just in case," he said.

Kriz sat on the edge of the raft as Clay readied the helmet. Even with Green in his veins it was a weighty item fashioned from some old boiler plate with the assistance of Chief Bozware. The plate had been hammered into two half-spheres and riveted together, a hole then cut through one side and a sealed glass window fitted.

"You see any Greens come straight back up," he told Kriz, who replied with an impatient nod, gesturing for him to get on with it. Clay placed the helmet over her head and settled it onto the padded-leather collar about her neck before moving to the pump. It was a simple hand-powered device that would have benefited from an engine, but there hadn't been time to construct one before leaving the *Superior*. However, Kriz had concluded that a Blood-blessed with sufficient Green would easily provide the required amount of air.

Clay refreshed his Green before taking hold of the pump-handle, the lever it was attached to blurring as he started to turn it. Sigoral moved to tie a rope around Kriz's waist after which she took a few breaths before slipping into the water, sinking down immediately in a cloud of bubbles. Clay kept turning the pump-handle, his gaze fixed on the patch of disturbed water as Sigoral played out the rope.

"That's it," he said as the rope stilled in his grip. "She's on the bottom."

Minutes ticked by with grating slowness, Clay never faltering at the pump, his eyes tracking the bubbles as they moved away from the raft and more and more of the air-line was drawn over the side. *This was a bad idea.* The words kept repeating in his head with every turn of the pump-handle, the growing certainty fed by his still-raw guilt over Jack's death. *This was a bad idea. This was . . .*

"Two tugs," Sigoral said, the rope jerking in his hands. "She's coming back up."

It seemed to take an age for her to reappear, bobbing to the surface a few yards from the raft. Sigoral and Braddon hauled her closer before removing the helmet. Kriz hung onto the side of the raft, breathing heavily but her sweat-beaded face flushed with excitement. "I found it," she told Clay, pointing. "One hundred yards that way."

"No Greens?" he asked.

Kriz laughed, shaking her head. "Not one." She raised her arms and he and Sigoral hauled her on board. "Let's go," she said, nodding at the oars.

"Getting late," Braddon said, eyes narrowed as he surveyed the sky. "Better to wait for tomorrow."

"It won't take more than an hour," Kriz insisted. "We should take the chance while there are no drakes in the vicinity." She met Clay's gaze, an insistent plea in her eyes. "We're so close," she added in her own language.

"Captain's call," Braddon told Clay, keeping his tone neutral, though Clay could see the shrewd appraisal in his uncle's gaze.

"She's right," Clay said, his desire to get this hazardous enterprise out of the way overcoming his caution. "The more days we spend around here the more likely the Greens will catch our scent." He moved to take up his oar, gesturing for Sigoral to do the same. "Let's get it done."

Her next dive was considerably longer, so much so that Clay used up a full dose of Green at the pump and was forced to change places with Sigoral. Clay's growing agitation was made worse by an inability to perceive much of anything below the lake's surface. However, this didn't stop him continually attempting to do so as he stood at the edge of the raft, staring fixedly into the depths.

"Just gone past the hour," his uncle said, holding up his pocket-watch. "Reckon it'll be dark before long."

Clay didn't need any further persuasion. "I'm calling her back," he said, reaching for the rope and giving it two hard tugs. He waited, the rope twisting a little in his grip but failing to slacken. He muttered a curse and began to tug again, but stopped when Preacher spoke a single terse word: "Green."

Braddon instantly brought his rifle to his shoulder, moving to stand beside Preacher's kneeling form. The marksman had his rifle trained on what seemed to Clay to be an empty stretch of water to the south, but he had learned by now to trust the man's eyes.

"How many?" he asked.

"One. Just over a hundred yards out."

"There'll be more," Braddon said, sweeping his own rifle from left to right.

Clay tugged on the rope once more then fell back as it lost all tension. "Shit!" He began to draw it up, hands moving in a rapid blur until the ragged end of the rope emerged from the water.

"Mr. Torcreek," Sigoral said, nodding at something twenty yards away, Clay seeing a great mass of bubbles rising to the surface. A split-second later the air-line began to twist and coil like an elongated snake. Clay immediately began to haul it up, knowing he would also find it severed even before he got it out of the water.

"Sliced through," his uncle said. He stepped closer, putting a hand on Clay's shoulder, though any commiseration he was about to offer was drowned out by the boom of Preacher's longrifle. Clay turned in time to see a long tail whipping the surface fifty yards to the south, the water flashing both red and white.

"She's gone, Clay," Braddon said, tugging his shoulder.

Clay returned his gaze to the water, staring hard into the depths. *No . . . Blue, I gave her Blue.* He reached for the vial in his wallet, raising it to his lips then stopping as an image blossomed in his head . . . Greens, a pack of them, gliding through the misty depths, their shapes rendered vague and distorted, as if he were seeing them through scratched glass . . .

It was as clear and real as any trance he had experienced, made more so by the near panic that accompanied the image. He looked at the vial in his hand, still full. *I tranced with her,* he realised, astonishment momentarily freezing him in place. *I didn't drink but I still tranced.*

"We gotta go," Braddon said, shaking him now as Preacher's rifle boomed again. "You and the lieutenant get on the oars. Me and Preacher'll hold them . . ."

Clay wasn't listening, kicking off his boots and shrugging free of his duster before drinking down full vials of Green, Red and Black. "Don't!" his uncle shouted, reaching for Clay as he launched himself clear of the raft, plunging into the lake and diving deep.

CHAPTER 21

Sirus

Like many older Corvantine cities the port of Sairvek had once been enclosed within a defensive wall, long since fallen into disuse as the conurbation grew in size and the Empire became more unified. It was still discernible amidst the maze of streets and houses as an irregular semicircle snaking from the coast through the outlying suburbs, but the days when troops had patrolled its battlements were long gone. Its principal aid to the defence of the city now lay in the fortified gatehouses which served as both police stations and barracks for Imperial soldiery. Two nights before Sirus had flown over the port on Katarias's back and discovered there were twelve of these strong points in all. Eliminating them simultaneously would be the key to seizing the city.

He chose mostly tribal Spoiled and former Islanders for the initial assault, they being the most attuned to the stealth required for such a task. Each squad was small, only ten fighters apiece, but in an operation of this nature surprise would offset any disadvantage in numbers. They had been dropped by Reds at various locations in the surrounding country-side, Sirus choosing a moonless night to maximise the concealing power of the dark. He decided to lead one of the squads himself, something that had provoked concern from an unlikely source.

"Who will I eat dinner with if you get yourself killed?" Catheline asked, her apparent flippancy diluted somewhat by the tic of genuine worry he saw in her red-black eyes.

"The operation will be dynamic," he said. "Requiring swift modification. First hand experience of the conditions . . ."

"Oh, don't be boring," she chided, pulling her shawl tighter around her shoulders. Her demeanour had remained largely unchanged since suffering the White's punishment outside Melkorin, though any impulse she might have felt towards confiding in him had vanished in the aftermath. "No unwise heroics," she said, stepping closer to press a kiss to his cheek. Her lips felt soft and warm on his scaled flesh. "We need our general."

They steered clear of roads or marked paths during the approach to the city, moving in a loose formation at a steady run. Sirus called a halt when the lights of the outlying western quarter came into view. Veilmist had advised that this was one of the wealthiest districts, which meant a lack of people on the streets at night and, hopefully, fewer patrolling members of the Corvantine Constabulary.

Report, he commanded the other squads as his keen inhuman eyes surveyed broad, neatly kept streets lined with cherry-blossom and acacia. There was no sign of a living soul beyond the lights in the windows. The other squads all reported an untroubled approach, apart from Forest Spear pausing to dispatch a farmer who chose an inopportune moment to visit his outhouse.

A trap? the tribal warrior wondered, sharing his own view of the narrow but empty streets of the much poorer northern quarter. *They must know what happened to Melkorin.*

More likely a curfew, Sirus replied. *It's probably been in place since Corvus fell to the rebels.*

So the garrison is on guard.

Against their own people, not us. We're likely to encounter patrols the deeper we go. Keep to the roof-tops, kill any sentries you find. Otherwise, proceed as planned.

He led his squad forward, increasing the pace as they entered the first streets, then scrambling up the wall of one of the larger houses to reach the roof. Spoiled hands were perfect for climbing, the claws hard enough to dig into the brickwork as the muscles of their remade limbs carried them upwards. The squad covered the distance to their objective in little under ten minutes, leaping from roof-top to roof-top. A few attic windows blazed into life as their boots sent some slates clattering to the streets below, but they had moved on by the time any curious eyes came to investigate.

The squad encountered the first sentry only when the gatehouse came into view, a youthful and bored-looking conscript fiddling with the rear-sight of his rifle. He was perched on the roof of a shop opposite the gatehouse, Sirus taking note of his unkempt uniform and unsoldierly disregard for his surroundings. A Spoiled Islander used his short-bow to sink an arrow into the base of the boy's skull as Sirus quickly scanned the vicinity for more look-outs. There were two atop the gatehouse itself but none in the street or enclosing roof-tops.

Whoever has charge of this place deserves a court martial, he decided, sending the squad into their prearranged assault plan.

His two marksmen took up position close by, rifles aimed at the sentries on the gatehouse roof, whilst Sirus and the rest of the squad descended to a shadowed alley. He paused for a moment as they prepared their munitions, confirming that the other squads were all in position, then struck a match and touched it to the fuse of the grenade in his hand.

The two marksmen fired as they charged across the street, Sirus glancing up to see the two sentries falling back from the parapet. When they were close enough he threw his grenade, the smoke from the fuse describing an elegant arc as it flew through the narrow gun-port in the gatehouse's upper floor. The rest of the squad followed suit, save for one who sprinted forward to lay his grenade against the building's heavy door. The multiple explosions cast an instant pall of dust and smoke over the entire street, Sirus leading his squad through it to hurdle the remnants of the door and charge inside.

A Corvantine sergeant came stumbling down a spiral staircase to Sirus's left, hands clutching at a bloodied face, then falling dead as one of the tribals slammed the spike of her war-club into his back. The other soldiers on the ground floor were dispatched with similar swiftness, each of them too stunned to offer resistance. Sirus led the squad up the stairs, lighting another grenade then casting it ahead of him. They crouched in the stairwell, waiting for the explosion and when it came charged into the resultant carnage to cut down any survivors. They repeated the process until they reached the roof, finding both sentries dead, each with a bullet-hole through the forehead. The entire assault had taken less than ten minutes.

Sirus checked on the other squads, finding all had met with similar success apart from one who had the misfortune to encounter a Blood Cadre agent in the dock-side gatehouse. The woman clearly had a good deal of experience from the way she set about killing his Spoiled, crushing the skulls of three in quick succession before lighting the rest on fire. Despite this Sirus considered the assault a success, since the agent had done them the service of setting light to the gatehouse before making good her escape.

It's done, he told Catheline as she watched the distant port from the deck of the *Malign Influence. Send them.*

You see, Marshal, she said, casting her thoughts wide so as to encompass Morradin's mind. *This is how it should be done.*

She shoved Morradin's dark, envious thoughts aside to share her vision with Sirus, his mind filling with the sight of the army's entire contingent of Reds alighting from the decks of the fleet, each one carrying Greens in their talons. *They'll spare the docks and the harbour,* she said. *Just as you asked. We do need more ships, after all.*

Veilmist had calculated a carefully co-ordinated sequence in which the fires would be set. Sirus expressed doubts that the drakes would be capable of keeping to such a complex plan but Catheline assured him it wouldn't be an issue. Even so, he noticed she had spent several hours in silent communion with the White before giving the final assent to his stratagem. *It needed something from me . . .* the words for which she had been punished replaying in his head as he watched her entwine herself about the beast's forelegs, both she and the White barely seeming to breathe as their minds touched.

In the event, the drakes kept rigidly to their allotted schedule, first setting fire to the market square near the docks, then the houses to the east and west. There was no repeat of the mass, uncontrolled conflagration that had consumed Melkorin, instead the fires advanced across the city from south to north in a steady progression that had the population fleeing before it. Streets became choked with people, some clutching bundles of hastily gathered belongings, others herding screaming children. Those who attempted to flee to the east or west found themselves menaced by packs of Greens and forced into an unco-ordinated horde which by morning had begun to straggle in loose order along the region's principal road. This highway led into a shallow river valley to the north where Marshal Morradin waited with seventy thousand Spoiled. The first conversions began by the end of the day.

Sporadic resistance had flared up in the city as remnants of the Sairvek garrison mounted a few desperate and easily contained counter-attacks. The Blood Cadre agent made a reappearance as the fire reached the grand square at the centre of the city. She proceeded to put on a spectacular display of Blood-blessed abilities that left a dozen Spoiled dead along with several Greens. Her valiant stand came to an end when Katarias descended from the sky to bathe the woman in a torrent of fire, leaving her a pile of smoking ash on the square's cobbled surface. Sirus made a well-concealed mental note to learn her name if he ever got the chance.

"Four thousand two hundred and seventy conversions already," Veilmist reported to the conference of captains two days later after they gathered aboard the *Malign Influence*. "The overall yield is projected to exceed fifty thousand by the end of the week. There are numerous villages in the region which are adding to the total."

"Over twice the yield at Melkorin," Catheline observed, arching an eyebrow at Morradin. "Quite impressive, wouldn't you agree, Marshal?"

Morradin's eyes flicked to Sirus before he replied in a colourless mutter, "Yes, an impressive victory won against minimal opposition."

Catheline's expression darkened a fraction and might have led to more punishment if Sirus hadn't added, "The Marshal is correct. Opposition was weak here, and poorly organised. From the intelligence we have gleaned it seems the city authorities had been rendered into a state of disarray by the revolution. Some wanted to send envoys to the rebels, but the majority held loyalist sympathies. In the face of mounting discord the garrison commander declared martial law some weeks ago, apparently at the behest of the local Cadre representative."

"That heroic bitch you were so impressed by, you mean?" Catheline said, Sirus detecting a faint trickle of jealousy leaking from her thoughts.

"Yes," he said, seeing little point in subterfuge. She always saw more than he suspected and considered himself fortunate she hadn't yet uncovered his hidden machinations. "The point is we can't expect opposition to be so ineffective in future. Word of what happened here will already be spreading. Fear will breed unity."

Catheline lowered her gaze to the map of the region, finger tapping at the port of Subarisk some sixty miles westward. "Our next source of recruits. It's the largest port on the coast, is it not?"

"Over two million inhabitants," Veilmist said. "Defended by a full division of Imperial troops and a seven-strong flotilla of warships."

"The harbour wall is formidable," Sirus added. "Gun batteries on the wall itself and a series of island forts defending the approaches."

"But we have lots of lovely new ships," Catheline said. "Do we not?"

"We captured thirty-three merchant vessels in Melkorin harbour," Sirus confirmed. "But only one warship, an aged customs cutter with only three guns."

"You're saying we can't take this port?" she asked, voice pitched into a soft, intent murmur as she surveyed each Spoiled at the table. "But, you see, that can't be right. For I want it, and *He* wants it." She fixed Sirus with as cold a stare as she had ever shown him. "Find a way, General," she said before sweeping from the room, Sirus quelling the surge of self-annoyance for enjoying the perfume she left in her wake.

"An overland march will take too long." Morradin sucked deeply on a short, sweet-smelling cigarillo, the tip glowing in the dusky gloom. "By the time we advance within striking distance they'll have had plenty of time to fortify their inland defences. Plus we don't have anywhere near enough artillery for a siege."

After a week of fruitless pondering Sirus had called him to the roof of the dock-side gatehouse for a discussion. Any enjoyment of the marshal's resentment at being summoned by someone he still considered an inferior was diminished somewhat by their shared dilemma. This meeting could have been conducted mentally but the marshal had developed an ability to shield his thoughts almost as well-honed as Sirus's own. Whereas he used fear, Morradin's mental walls were forged from anger. Sirus could feel it now, though outwardly the marshal seemed oddly affable as he puffed away on his cigarillo, stubby claws scratching at his spines in gloomy contemplation, betraying no indication of the constantly stoked rage within.

"So it has to be a sea-borne assault," Sirus said. They shared a memorised image of the map detailing the port of Subarisk and the six island forts that guarded the coastal approaches.

"The fortifications were designed a century ago by the great military architect Zevaris Lek Akiv Torlak," Morradin said. "Clearly a man who knew his business. We'd need at least a thousand troops to take each one, and they'll be attacking under fire and in daylight, since the landing sites are only accessible with the morning tide."

"We augment the attack with Reds," Sirus said. "Assault them from the air and the sea at the same time."

Morradin summoned another image, a pen-and-ink diagram of something that resembled a brick sculpture of a legless tortoise. "These aren't ordinary fortifications, boy," he said. "Domed roofs to deflect plunging shot, walls ten feet thick and a battery of twenty-pounders, which means they have enough range to provide fire support to the neighbouring forts. And even if we do manage to subdue the outer defences, we still have the harbour wall to contend with. As I said, Torlak knew his business."

"Are you saying the place is impregnable?"

Morradin's eyes narrowed behind the smoke as he took another deep drag. "Nowhere's impregnable, boy," he said, "if you're prepared to spill enough blood. Your stealthy tricks won't help us at Sairvek. This is my kind of battle. Something I think you already know, else why would you bring me here?"

Sirus stiffened a little as the barb struck home, finding himself irked by how the truth jabbed at his pride. *Pride in slaughter,* he thought, letting the fear rise to mask the self-disgust. On impulse he reached out to Morradin mentally, colouring the thought with mingled images of the White and Catheline's red-black eyes. Any eavesdropping mind would hopefully mistake what followed for a shared terror of the consequences of failure.

Do you like this life, Marshal? he asked Morradin, watching his eyes narrow further as the emotionless question slipped through the torrent of fear.

You are full of tricks, aren't you? Morradin returned, taking the cue to stoke his own fears along with a fresh bout of anger. *You sure she can't hear us?*

No, but we'll find out very soon if she can. Do you have an answer for me?

This life? Morradin let smoke seep from his nostrils before raising his hand and stubbing the cigarillo's burning tip out on the palm. *Can barely feel this,* he commented. *And by tomorrow it'll have healed. Can't deny the gifts we've been given.*

Or the lives we've taken, the children now being hunted in the hills by the monsters we serve. We leave nothing but ash and grief in our wake.

As armies have always done. And I never before had command of an army like this.

Except you don't. I do.

Morradin's anger rose again, this time coloured by some authentic heat, and he revealed elongated teeth in a grin. *For now. She'll tire of you soon enough. I know the type. Beauty and privilege were ever a toxic combination. And let's not forget the fact that she's completely fucking insane.*

I know. Something which doesn't bode well for any of us.

Morradin's grin subsided into a glower. *You ask if I like this life. Of course I don't. I hate it. I was not born to be a slave.*

Nor was anyone. But what if there was a way to free us. All of us?

Sirus felt a sour, despairing note creep into Morradin's mind. *To date I have tried to shoot myself six times,* the marshal told him, playing out a series of memories. A room in Morsvale, Morradin staring at his Spoiled visage in the mirror, a pistol pressed to his temple. He pulled the trigger and the hammer clicked on an empty chamber. Another memory, this time in the Barrier Isles, the cold metal of the pistol's barrel sliding over his tongue, pressing against the roof of his mouth. Another pull of the trigger, another dry click from the hammer. Then again during the voyage to Feros, then again during the hill-country campaign . . .

I did load the pistol, Morradin went on as the final fruitless suicide attempt played out, this one only yesterday. *Or rather I remember loading the pistol, but each time when I looked again it was empty. Somehow the White knew and changed my thoughts accordingly. If you ever try it, you'll probably discover the same thing. So, how exactly do you intend to free us from a nightmare crafted by a being that knows our thoughts?*

I don't know yet, Sirus confessed. *But I do know it can only happen if we act as one. Not just you and me, all of us.*

There are Spoiled in this army who love their new lives. What for us is torment is paradise to them.

Unity of purpose is the only thing that will free us. We'll have to ensure there are less of them to pollute our thoughts, and we have a very costly engagement to plan, do we not?

He withdrew his thoughts, speaking aloud after a silence that had lasted only a few seconds. "Your plan, Marshal?"

Morradin was wise enough to colour his mind with a sense of triumph before replying. Catheline, should she be listening, would expect no less. "Tell me," he said. "Have you ever heard of a Protectorate naval hero named Racksmith?"

CHAPTER 22

Lizanne

It was only as the Blue began to dissipate in her veins that Clay chose to appear in the trance, leaving barely a few seconds for her to share the information she had obtained. The trance evaporated before she could be sure he had acquired the shared memory, or learn anything about his current circumstances.

Lizanne blinked into full consciousness, finding herself lying on the stone floor of a narrow cell. The walls were windowless rough-hewn rock and a heavy, iron-bracketed door barred the exit. The Spider was gone from her wrist and her feet were bare and numb with cold. Her captors had evidently been thorough enough to rob her of the product concealed in the heels of her boots.

She rose into a sitting position, rubbing her benumbed feet and replaying the unsuccessful mission in her head. Failure was not a sensation she enjoyed but rigorous and objective self-examination were a core part of her training. *Too long playing the politician,* she thought, grimacing as a vestige of feeling returned to her feet. *And overconfidence,* she admitted after further reflection. *It's unhealthy to believe one's own legend.*

There was a snicking sound from the door and she looked up to see a pair of dark, hostile eyes regarding her through a small slat. The eyes were female and it took Lizanne a moment to recognise the Blood-blessed woman she had come close to killing the night before.

"You were lucky," the woman said, breaking a lengthy silence.

"No," Lizanne said, returning the stare, face impassive. "I was better."

The eyes narrowed and the slat slid shut with a loud clatter followed shortly after by the rattle of a lock and key. The door swung open on squealing hinges, revealing the Blood-blessed woman standing with a pistol in hand. Two burly pirates stood on either side of her, both bearing shotguns.

"Get up," the woman said, gesturing with the pistol. "He wants to see you."

Lizanne was surprised to find herself unmanacled as the woman led her along a cramped tunnel, the two shotgun-carrying guards at her back. *They assume I'm no threat without product,* she surmised, watching how the Varestian woman moved with an air of studied nonchalance. *A foolish miscalculation.*

Throughout the subsequent journey she identified three separate occasions when it would have been a relatively simple matter to subdue the woman, take her pistol and kill the two guards. But that would have left her isolated in an unfamiliar locale and, unless the woman had indulged the additional misjudgement of carrying product on her person, with no practical means of escaping this rock.

The tunnel eventually opened out into a broad platform set into the wall of a huge, wind-gusted chasm. Looking to her right, Lizanne saw that a complete section of the chasm was formed of a massive, smooth edifice and realised she was viewing the High Wall from the inside. Glancing down, she could see a placid lagoon and a wharf where half a dozen ships were moored. Despite her circumstances she couldn't help but be impressed by the scale of this place and the ambition of its construction.

"Even your Protectorate couldn't take it," the woman said, reading Lizanne's expression. "They tried once, you know. Or rather they hired a bunch've mercenary scum to try it. My great-grandfather saw them off then pursued them all around the world so that every pirate who dared challenge the Okanas clan was sent to serve the King of the Deep." She stepped closer, looming over Lizanne. "So it is with all our enemies."

Lizanne pursed her lips and nodded before placing a puzzled frown on her brow. "Except, these days you are your own enemy, are you not? Your cousin Arshav seems to think this place is his by right . . ."

The woman snarled and lashed out with her empty hand, which met only air as Lizanne ducked under it, delivered a hard punch to the woman's solar plexus then stepped close to snare her other limb in an arm-lock. She forced the woman to her knees and twisted the pistol from her grip, pressing it to the back of her head. She looked up to see the two guards raising their shotguns, though not with the sense of urgency she expected.

"That's very unwise," the larger of the two advised, speaking in an unruffled tone that told Lizanne a great deal. The Blood-blessed woman wasn't in charge of this escort, he was, and he didn't care if Lizanne killed her.

She grunted and released the woman, tossing the pistol over the side of the platform. "A weapon only has value if you have the knowledge and intent to use it," Lizanne told her, quoting a favourite line from one of her tutors.

The woman let out another snarl, hand flashing to the knife tucked into the top of her boot.

"Morva," the larger guard said as the woman crouched for a lunge. She came to a halt, features quivering with rage. The guard stepped between them, jerking his head at Lizanne. "Enough of this. He's waiting."

She was carried up the chasm wall in an elevating contraption. It was formed of a cage attached to a cable driven by some sort of counterweight mechanism she was sure her father would have found fascinating. Lizanne noticed that the two guards became markedly more attentive as they neared the top, the larger one pointing his shotgun at her head whilst the other levelled his at the small of her back. When the cage came to a jerky halt at the top of the chasm the two guards kept pace with Lizanne as she stepped out. Their weapons never strayed from their target as Morva led them through the courtyard and up the stairway to the parapet.

Alzar Lokaras stood atop a raised turret on the western flank of the crater lip, playing a hand along the back of a large black cat sitting on the battlement beside him. The cat hissed as it caught sight of Lizanne, she instantly recognising it as the author of her current misfortune.

"Don't mind Sherva," Alzar said as the guards brought her to a halt a few feet away. "She's bred to dislike strangers." He gave the cat's chin a scratch then beckoned Lizanne closer. "I found myself greeted by a curious sight during my morning stroll," he said, pointing to something out at sea. "Perhaps you can enlighten me as to what it might be."

Lizanne moved closer, aware of the increased tension of the guards as she did so. Their indifference to Morva's well-being clearly didn't apply here. She followed Alzar's finger to a small, flat-topped island some three miles away. The *Firefly* hovered above it at a height of about fifty feet, Tekela pointing the aerostat into the prevailing wind so that it bobbed up and down continually, but showed no sign of leaving.

"It's been there since first light," Alzar said. "My crew are very keen to sail out and capture it. Should I let them do so, do you think? Or maybe just have my gunners blast it out of the sky."

"You'll miss," Lizanne said. "And then it'll just fly away."

Alzar grunted out a short laugh. "I'm not too sure about that. I suspect whoever has charge of that thing is possessed of an unreasoning loyalty; otherwise, they'd have departed as soon as it became clear your mission here had failed." He turned, resting his back against the battlement, regarding Lizanne with careful scrutiny. "I think if I tie a rope around your legs and dangle you over the side of this rock they might well decide to deliver that marvellous contraption to me. Am I wrong?"

I hope so, Lizanne thought, suspecting the opposite to be true. "What makes you think I failed?" she asked instead.

Alzar's scrutiny faded, replaced by a cold calculation. "You tranced," he said. "So it's safe to assume your corporate masters have whatever information you came for. Therefore, I find it curious that the more interesting documents in my uncle's library remain undisturbed. Nothing appears to have been taken or destroyed." He jerked his head at the guards, who stepped closer, shotgun barrels pressing into Lizanne's head and back.

"I am not some Imperial Cadre fool," Alzar said, voice terse with harsh sincerity. "I will not play your games or entertain your bargains. Tell me what you came here for and why or I'll show your friend over there what we do to spies at the High Wall."

Lizanne replied quickly. Experience taught her how to spot a bluff, and this wasn't one. "It's quite simple, really," she said. "Zenida sent me."

"Quite a story you weave," Alzar said a few hours later. After a hasty explanation on the parapet he had her brought to the mansion for a more fulsome account. Lizanne sat in a chair in the library, the larger of the two guards at her back and Morva stalking about on the edge of her vision. Alzar remained standing throughout, his gaze occupied by the huge table map of Arradsia. "What makes you think I believe a word of it?" he added.

"The fact that you haven't killed me," Lizanne replied. "And how else would I know the details of your feud with Arshav and his mother?"

"Ironship spies know a great many things, and they've always been overly interested in my family."

"Indeed. In fact they were interested enough to employ Zenida as a privateer. She did the Syndicate some valuable service over the years."

"What?" Morva said, stepping into view and addressing the question to her uncle. "What did she say?"

"Mind your place!" Alzar snapped, jaws bunching and shooting Lizanne a glare. "My cousin's choices did not always meet with my approval," he said as Morva retreated with a sullen scowl. "But she is truly of this clan, in blood and spirit, unlike her corrupted wretch of a brother and his bitch mother."

"Who now hold sway over the Seven Walls and the Ruling Council," Lizanne pointed out.

"Council." Alzar grated out a laugh rich in contempt. "There never really was a Ruling Council. Just a bunch've puffed-up bilge rats playing politics, and failing for the most part. The High Wall had no truck with their empty prattle. Arshav and his mother can preen and pronounce all they want, Varestia has never truly had a government, nor has it needed one."

"Until now. You do know what's coming, I assume? A clan with so many ships at its command will surely have some notion of the threat this region faces."

Alzar turned back to the map, saying nothing, though Lizanne discerned from his deeply furrowed brow her words had struck home.

"Melkorin has been destroyed," she pressed on. "Other towns and cities will follow. Our enemy swells in number with every conquest and when it has sufficient strength it will be coming to lay waste to the Red Tides."

He kept his gaze on the map, his expression that of a man forced into hateful consideration. "When I was a boy," he said after a lengthy silence, "I would watch my uncle stare at this map for hours. There was something about this land that had once captured his soul and never let go for the rest of his life, right up until it killed him. Now, you tell me the key to saving us all rests at the very heart of his greatest obsession." He gave a very small, humourless laugh. "And Zenida thought it all just an old man's delusion."

Alzar moved away from the map to sit in the chair opposite Lizanne's. "I would like it remembered," he said in a hard, resigned tone, "that, at any other time, your corpse would now be decorating our wall."

"Duly noted," Lizanne said.

"Take a message to Arshav and Ethilda. I'll join our ships with theirs. We'll fight for the Red Tides, but this changes nothing between us. He is still a bastard and a faithless cutthroat who sullies our name and she is still a scheming whore my uncle should have strangled when he had the chance. When this war is done and Zenida resumes her rightful place here, there will be a reckoning."

"I'll tell them."

"I have three further conditions," he went on. "Firstly, any prize captured by our ships belongs to the High Wall and not your absurd company. Secondly, we receive equal amounts of any weapons produced by your manufactory. And, thirdly." He turned his gaze to Morva standing in sulky silence in the corner of the library. "I require a tutor for a wayward youth."

"What's she doing?" Tekela asked as Morva climbed into the gondola.

"We have a passenger," Lizanne said. "This is Morva, my . . . student."

"Student . . . ? Don't touch that!" Tekela snapped as Morva's hand strayed towards the control panel.

The Blood-blessed woman stared at her for a second, face dark. "This one's a Corvantine," she muttered, voice laden with menace. "I kill Corvantines."

"I think we both know you've never actually killed anyone," Lizanne said. "But Tekela has, so watch your tongue. Go and sit in the back."

Lizanne settled herself into the seat alongside Tekela, buckling on the straps. "I'll explain later," she said. "For now, please let's get out of here."

She looked through the side-window as Tekela opened a valve to add more gas to the envelope, seeing Alzar standing in the High Wall's courtyard. His gaze tracked the *Firefly* as it ascended, face hard with resentment at the necessary bargain he had struck. However, despite his evident detestation of the corporate world she still found him a preferable business partner to Arshav and Ethilda.

She heard Morva issue a small sound as the High Wall shrank beneath them and Tekela angled the aerostat towards the north. Glancing back Lizanne saw the Varestian woman sitting with her eyes closed tight, knuckles white as they gripped her seat.

"Don't worry," Lizanne told her. "You get used to it."

Morva muttered something in barely articulate and profanity-laden Varestian, Lizanne detecting the words "corporate devilry" amongst the torrent.

"Headwind's pretty strong today," Tekela advised. "It'll take at least five hours to reach the Sound."

This drew another whimper from Morva, which Lizanne ignored. "We're not going to the Sound," she said. "Set course for the Seven Walls."

"You had no authority to negotiate on behalf of this Conglomerate," Ethilda Okanas said in a surprisingly placid tone. Unlike her in-law at the High Wall she possessed the ability to keep her voice and face free of emotion, though she couldn't quite keep the glint of anger from her eyes. "Agreement will require a vote of the Board . . ."

"The Okanas family has direct command of thirty ships," Lizanne broke in. "They also have clan affiliations with most of the families in southern Varestia, the majority of whom, I'm reliably informed, would rather see you and your son dead than answer any call to battle you might issue. Like it or not we'll need them if we're to have any hope of defending this region."

Ethilda's eyes strayed to the *Firefly*, hovering above the docks of the Seven Walls. Lizanne had descended to the quayside via rope and told the harbour-master who came to greet her to fetch either Ethilda or her son, refusing his request to follow him to the Navigation. Ethilda had arrived along with an escort under the command of the inevitable Mr. Lockbar.

"Burgravine Artonin isn't joining us?" Ethilda asked.

"We won't be staying long," Lizanne replied. "Too many landings deplete the gas reserves."

"Such a pity. I am so starved of well-spoken company . . ." Ethilda trailed off, eyes narrowing. "So," she said. "Alzar off-loaded the little bitch on you, did he?"

Lizanne looked over her shoulder, seeing Morva's face in the aerostat's open hatchway. "He felt his niece would benefit from some education,"

Lizanne replied. In fact Alzar had said, *She's no use as she is. Like a child with a loaded gun but no notion of how to aim it.*

"Niece?" Ethilda asked. "That's what he's calling her now? You should know she's not a true Okanas, just some Blessed orphan he purchased from the hold of a Dalcian reaver. With Zenida off on her privateering adventures he felt the clan needed a new Blood-blessed. She's always been trouble, causing discord and being far too free with her body. Varestians are not a prudish people but daughters of the major clans are expected to display some decorum, if not discernment. Legacy of whatever those reavers did to her, I suppose. Ruin a girl young and she'll stay ruined." Ethilda shrugged. "Leave her here, if you like. We'll find a use for her."

Lizanne wondered whether it would matter all that much if she killed this woman this very moment. *Only if her son still lives.* "We need more Blood-blessed at the Sound," she said, fingers twitching on the Spider as she added, "Is Arshav here?"

"Gone to the peninsular to gather more ships and fighters." Ethilda nodded at the harbour, which now held at least double the number of vessels than Lizanne had seen during her first visit. "We've been doing fairly well so far. Especially since the news about Sairvek broke."

"Sairvek?"

"Burned, just like Melkorin. Although our enemies have remained in port for now. We lost three fast ships to Blue attacks just to find that out."

Sairvek. They're getting closer with every attack. "The total size of our fleet?" Lizanne asked.

"Thirty ships here and another two hundred in the Iskamir ports. Only a handful could truly be called warships." She settled a steady gaze on Lizanne. "We assured the captains who answered the call they would receive mighty and ingenious weapons. They're already getting impatient."

"I promised the first delivery in a month," Lizanne said, turning and striding back towards the rope dangling from the *Firefly*. "And I meant it. Don't waste any more ships on reconnaissance. We'll take care of that."

"It's impossible."

Jermayah blinked tired eyes at her, voice barely audible above the constant clatter of the manufactory. Lizanne had been impressed by the progress made in her absence, the place now resembled an Ironship facility with its long rows of assembly tables attended by numerous workers. The town had also undergone a swift transformation, whitewash covering many of its previously drab walls and about half the houses now had roofs and shutters on the windows. However, it transpired all this effort had yet to result in any actual output.

"You have materials . . ." Lizanne began only to be waved to silence by Jermayah.

"Materials have to be converted into components and components assembled into finished products. All of this requires organisation, skills and the time to learn them. At the moment we have perhaps one-third of the components we need for a production run of fifty Growlers and half that number of Thumpers. At the current rate they'll be ready in seven weeks."

He paused, running a hand through his shaggy, unkempt hair. Lizanne knew she had pushed him close to exhaustion already, and dearly wanted to order him to rest, but the situation required a harder heart. "What's the biggest obstacle to rapid production?" she asked.

Jermayah thought for a moment. "Moulding, I suppose. Copper, brass and steel all has to be melted and poured into moulds and the components finished by hand before assembly. We have plenty of fuel but the forging facilities here are primitive and minimal, designed for repairing locomotives rather than large-scale manufacture."

"Can't the Blood-blessed help with the melting?" Lizanne asked.

"We've been trying to husband what product we have. Madame Hakugen has a supply of Eastern Conglomerate stocks from Lossermark but guards it fiercely. Says we'll need it for defence when the time comes."

"I'll speak to her." Lizanne turned and started for the exit, pausing to add, "And drink some Green. You look terrible."

"Too much," Lizanne said, stepping back and raising an arm to shield herself from the sparks fountaining from the bulky granite flask.

"Want it melted, don't you?" Morva replied.

"Yes, melted, not exploded. Watch." Lizanne concentrated her gaze on the next flask and the three copper ingots it contained. "Think of the Red as a pool and you the stream that flows from it," she said, the air shimmering as she sent a steady, narrow wave of Red into the flask. The copper took on a glow before the ingots started to sublime into one another. After a few minutes the flask was full of steaming liquid metal.

Lizanne nodded to the team of workers, all clad head to toe in thick leather. Two of them stepped forward to clamp the flask with iron poles before lifting and tilting it to pour the contents into the prearranged row of moulds.

"Try again," Lizanne told Morva pointing to another flask, this one full of brass.

Thanks to Madame Hakugen's reluctantly surrendered product and Lizanne's employing all the settlement's Blood-blessed in the forge, they had quadrupled the output of components in a single day. The woman's warning that such profligate use would soon exhaust their supply was undoubtedly correct but Lizanne argued the need to produce finished weapons outweighed any concerns about defence. "One thing I have learned, madame," she said. "In war moderation is not a virtue but an impediment."

Using so much product so quickly also gave her the chance to fulfil her educational obligation, though Morva was a frequently recalcitrant student. After completing a shift at the forge Lizanne had her assist with moving the moulded components to the assembly line. The Varestian woman's first attempt had an entire row of workers ducking for cover when she propelled a crate full of components across the manufactory with all the force of a cannon-shot.

"Only ever used it to throw things," she said with a shrug of what Lizanne discerned to be studied indifference. "The Okanas family needs a Blood-blessed that can fight, not push things around like a glorified cart-horse."

"I've seen you fight," Lizanne returned. "And you're no better a cart-horse than you are a fighter."

That earned a glaring sneer, Morva turning on her heel to stalk from the manufactory, then freezing in place as Lizanne's Black closed around her. She held her still for a second then slowly lifted her off the ground, turning her around and setting her down close to the stack of crated components. She could feel the woman struggling in her grip, lashing out with her own Black in a series of undisciplined blasts that were too unfocused to have any effect. Lizanne maintained her grip until Morva exhausted her reserves, then released her after a final squeeze to empty her lungs.

"Ethilda says you're not really an Okanas," Lizanne said, moving to stand over Morva as she knelt, clutching her chest and gasping. "Is that true?"

"That ... whore is ... no Okanas either," Morva rasped, raising her gaze to glare at Lizanne.

"She says they bought you." Lizanne went to her haunches, bringing her face level with Morva's. "Why are you so loyal to a family that sees you as just a useful slave?"

Morva gritted her teeth and looked away. "Uncle Alzar always told me I was free to go ..."

"Go? A lone child in the Red Tides. Where exactly would you go?"

"You don't understand. The High Wall, it's my home."

A child taken from a life of bondage and abuse, given a home, told she had a family. Even if it was all just a contrivance to win her loyalty, clearly it worked. "Your home will burn," Lizanne said. "Along with everything else if we don't win this war. Make no mistake, I have seen the face of our enemy and it is all too real. This is the first battle." She inclined her head at the busy lines of workers. "Every minute spent here is another step to victory. Every bolt, screw and lever we make is worth a thousand bullets."

She took a fresh vial of Black from the pocket of her overalls and held it out. "Let's try again, shall we? Shift me five tons by the end of the day and I'll show you how to shatter a knee-cap with just a drop of Black."

The first Growler came off the production line a week later, followed by the first Thumper two days after that. Jermayah had given manufacture of the Smokers over to the small band of gunsmiths and armourers who had escaped Lossermark. Their progress was slow and they shared a tendency to ignore entreaties to forsake long-ingrained perfectionism for speedy production. However, after another week of cajoling and a liberal ration of Green to stave off fatigue the gunsmiths' workshop was producing the new carbines at a rate of five a day.

With the assembly lines running at reasonable efficiency Jermayah focused his efforts on ammunition, Lizanne and the other Blood-blessed exhausting all but a small amount of their Red to once again kick-start the process. The shell casings and projectiles were soon coming off the lines in decent quantities but the propellant needed to fill them required a more prolonged and hazardous process.

"The Varestians only gave us black powder," Jermayah said. He had established a separate workshop to manufacture the ammunition, an old warehouse situated at a decent remove from the town. The mostly female work-force had been hand-picked for their dexterity and many were former seamstresses or print-setters. They all wore overalls fastened with laces rather than buttons, Jermayah having forbidden the smallest scrap of metal in the place.

"Works fine for cannon but it'll foul the workings of the Growlers and Thumpers," he went on. "We need to add flakes of nitrate and grind it into a fine dust."

"As long as it works," Lizanne said. Watching his head sag a little as he nodded, she said, "Get some sleep. You've done more than enough for now."

"This lot needs watching . . ."

"Then send them home." A faint smile formed on her lips as an idea occurred to her. "Tomorrow will be a holiday," she said. "I think these people deserve a small celebration." The smile slipped from her lips as she turned away, knowing that for many whatever festivities she organised could well be the last they ever saw.

CHAPTER 23

Clay

It was only thanks to the Green in his veins that he was able to make out much of anything below the surface. The undulating lake-bed stretched away beneath him, featureless but for a sand-covered hump almost directly below. He angled his body towards the hump and kicked with all the enhanced strength his body would allow. His objective became clearer as he descended, resolving into something vaguely boat-shaped. It was almost entirely covered by silt but for one section near its narrow prow that appeared to have been scraped away.

A gondola, he realised as he swam closer, the sight of a hatch resolving through the murk, an open hatch. *An aerostat's gondola.*

Clay's lungs began to burn as he forced his body lower, coming to a thrashing halt a good forty feet short. *Got too much air in me,* he knew as a renewed bout of kicking failed to push him any lower. He stopped moving, focusing his gaze on the half-open hatch and reaching out with Black. It took two hard tugs before the hatch came free revealing something round and shiny in the gloom within. *Kriz,* Clay thought, recognising the helmet and using Black to draw her out of the gondola. His vision was already beginning to blur thanks to the lack of air and there was no time for finesse. Kriz's helmet thumped against the side of the hatchway as he dragged her clear, opening his arms to catch her as she shot upwards.

She sagged in his grasp, limp and unmoving but he could feel the faint beat of her heart as his hands pressed against her chest. Clay's hands fumbled at the weighted belt about her waist for a few agonising seconds before it came free. He began to kick for the surface when something fast and large streaked out of the gloom directly ahead, Clay having time to register the sight of two triangular rows of teeth before instinctively unleashing his

Black. The Green recoiled as if it had charged into a brick wall, blood seeping like crimson smoke from its nostrils as it twisted and vanished into the gloom, tail whipping.

Clay twisted about, seeing a sleek narrow shape cut through the murk a short distance away, quickly followed by another moving in the opposite direction. *They're circling,* he realised, head swivelling left and right. His body spasmed then as the product in his veins started to thin in earnest, lungs now like fire, the Greens coming closer with every circle. He knew with awful certainty that the attack would come soon and all at once, the whole pack rending and tearing at the hated intruders in a frenzy. It was as if they knew his product was fading and all they had to do was wait.

Panic rising he lashed out with Red at the closest drake, leaving a lightning-fork-like trail of bubbles through the water. The Green veered away, more in confusion than distress as Clay could see no apparent damage to the beast. *Stupid,* he thought, skin prickling in the suddenly warm water. *Boil them and you boil yourself.* Which left only the Black, and there were too many to push away.

He convulsed again, clamping his mouth shut against his body's instinctive need to gasp. A strange, reflective calm overtook him then, the panic vanishing as the imminence of death became a certainty. A last serene notion slipped into his head as he felt Kriz begin to slip from his arms. *Too many to push . . . Then don't push, pull . . . Pull the water.*

Water. More substantial than air, which could be affected by Black but only in the most unfocused way. Water was different, water could be pulled.

Clay used the last vestiges of his reason to marshal his Black, focusing his attention on the space separating them from the drakes, then expending it all at once to draw the water towards them. The effect was immediate and dramatic, the pressure of so much water compressing at once shooting the pair of them to the surface.

They broke through into a cacophony of sound and beautiful, sweet-tasting air. Clay heard his uncle call out before they plunged down. He kicked for the surface and dragged more air into his lungs as they bobbed back up. He could see the raft a little over ten yards away, which suddenly seemed a great distance in light of what lurked beneath. Uncle Braddon and Preacher were both kneeling, rifles pointed in his direction whilst Sigoral stood to the side, tipping a vial of product down his throat. Clay began to call out for a rope but the yell died as Sigoral cast the vial aside and focused his gaze. Clay felt the invisible hand of Black close around him and a heart-beat later he and Kriz were being dragged through the water at a considerable rate of knots.

Braddon and Preacher fired several shots in the time it took for them to reach the raft, Sigoral lifting them clear of the lake at the last instant to deposit them in the centre of the raft. Clay was forced to spend some time gasping for breath before he began to get the helmet off Kriz's head.

"I got it," Braddon said, crouching to pull the helmet clear, revealing Kriz's slack, unresponsive features. Braddon held a hand to her mouth then, muttering a curse, lay her flat on her back and delivered several hard shoves to her sternum with both hands. Clay's gaze was dragged away by a sudden commotion, turning to see a Green frozen in mid-leap close to the edge of the raft. Sigoral held the beast in place long enough to aim his carbine and put a bullet through its skull. The lieutenant cast the Green's corpse away and Clay turned back, watching his uncle pumping Kriz's chest.

"Must've had some air left in the helmet," Clay said, knowing it was a desperate notion. "I felt her heart-beat, Uncle."

Braddon said nothing, continuing his rhythmic shoves, Kriz's head lolling in response with not even a flicker to her eyelids. He kept at it until Preacher's rifle fell silent a minute or so later. Braddon sat back on his haunches, turning to Clay with a grim shake of his head. "I . . ."

All four of them started as Kriz jerked, a gout of water erupting from her mouth. She spent some time convulsing, breath coming in deep, saw-like rasps, eventually choking into a bout of violent coughing. Clay moved to clasp her hand as she continued to cough, finding it closed into a tight fist.

"I . . . I found them," she said when the coughing had subsided, meeting Clay's gaze with a bright smile. She opened her fist to reveal two objects. One was a small crystal shard, little bigger than an arrow-head, and the other a glass vial. Clay initially took it for product but the colour was strange, possessed of a rainbow-like sheen as it caught the light.

"What are they?" he asked.

Kriz's smile broadened and she reached out with her other hand to caress his face. "The keys . . . to convergence."

"Seems we came an awful long way for such small things." Loriabeth peered at the two objects in Kriz's palm with a dubious gaze.

"Density is relative and often deceptive," Kriz replied. "Everything you can see or touch is made up of mostly empty space." She sat huddled close to the camp-fire, a blanket about her shoulders. They had retreated a good distance from the lake-shore before making camp, Kriz having to be carried most of the way. She had shivered continually during the trip and even now spoke with a pronounced tremor to her voice. "I need Black," she said, looking at Clay.

He frowned, concerned by her wan face and red, over-bright eyes. "You don't want to wait awhile . . . ?"

"Black." She held out her free hand, continuing in her own language, "As you know, I have waited a very long time for this and find myself out of patience."

Clay duly handed over a vial of Black, Kriz drinking a quarter of the contents before focusing her gaze on the crystal sitting in her palm. It floated free and drifted away from her then seemed to shimmer as it began to vibrate, Clay detecting a familiar tinkling sound he had last heard in their trance in the hidden enclave. The rest of the company let out a mingling of gasps and surprised profanity as the crystal abruptly unfolded. Narrow spikes lanced out from the core, catching the fire-light as it spun under Kriz's manipulation, eventually slowing to hang serenely in the air, resembling a star in the way it glittered. Clay stepped closer to it, memory racing with recognition. The trance in which Kriz had shown him the cavern where Zembi had created the first White, the four crystals, Red, Green, Blue . . . *and one so dark it seemed to swallow the light.*

"The Black crystal," he said, reaching out to press a tentative finger to one of the spikes. "We actually Seer-damn found it."

"Kinda begs the question of what we do with it," Braddon said, moving closer to peer at the crystal.

"It will enable communication," Kriz said. "Between drake and human, specifically Black drakes and humans."

"Clay can already do that," Skaggerhill said.

"Only with Lutharon," Clay said. "And that was thanks to Miss Ethelynne. If he'd stayed with us any longer things would've gone bad sooner or later, for us and him." He turned to Kriz. "We can command them with this, right? Make them join us?"

She shook her head. "Of all the pure-bred species the Blacks were always the hardest to control, more intelligent than the others and more aggressive towards humans. This was partially why Father was never able to successfully cross-breed them. The White contains blood lines from all drake species, except the Black."

"Guess that's why they didn't join its war," Clay said. "And why they fought him when he rose before, fought alongside the people who lived here to bring him down."

"That I can't explain," Kriz replied. "It's clear that the world my people built fell, and the civilisation that grew in its place was able to achieve some kind of symbiosis with the drakes."

"Heart-blood." Clay remembered the mosaic from the hidden city that lay on the far side of the lake. "Their queen would drink heart-blood and bond with a Black. That's what bound them together. With this"—he nodded at the crystal—"we won't have to."

He heard his uncle let out a faint groan and turned to find him frowning in grim realisation.

"Captain?" Skaggerhill asked.

"He means we're gonna have to go find us some Blacks," Braddon said, "to make friends with."

"That's what you need?" Clay asked later, nodding at the glass vial in Kriz's hand. The others were all sleeping, Clay and Kriz having taken the first watch. She had returned the Black crystal to its original state and now sat regarding the vial in one hand and the blade-shaped shard in the other. "You drink that and you can unlock the memories Zembi put in there?" he went on.

"Yes," she said, her eyes tracking from the shard to the vial but making no move to drink it.

"Is it dangerous?" he asked, sensing her reluctance and switching to her language.

"All knowledge is dangerous, but all knowledge is precious. The contradiction at the heart of everything the Philos Caste studied or created."

"Convergence," Clay said. "What is it?"

Kriz was silent for a time, turning the vial over in her fingers, face rapt. "Does this look like drake blood to you?" she asked, holding the vial out to him. He took it, holding it up so the fire-light illuminated the contents.

"Kinda," he said, handing it back. "Looks a little like one of the more expensive Ironship dilutions. Colour's different, though."

"Then it might surprise you to know that no part of what is in this vial came from a drake, except the knowledge of how to make it. This is what your people call product, Clay. It will do everything Blue will do, but it was not syphoned from the corpse of some unfortunate beast. It was made.

"Zembi believed that the abilities of the Blood-blessed lay dormant in all of us. What else could explain the random nature of the Blessing? If only a small proportion of the population developed the ability during early adolescence, an ability they clearly didn't inherit, then the same potential rested in all of us. If the right formula could be found, it could unlock that potential. Think of it, Clay, a whole world of people able to share their thoughts, craft wonders, walk this earth without fear. This is what we were working for all those years under the ice. This is the key to convergence. This"—she held up the vial once more—"is synthetic product. Anyone can drink it and harness the power it holds. Not just the Blessed. Anyone."

"The White," Clay said. "You needed it to make this?"

She lowered her gaze, Clay seeing a mirror of the shame he had seen on the face of her younger self in the trance. *It's unfair of me to despise you so,* she had told the sickly White as it glared at her from the pit. *Like you, it appears I should never have been born.* "There is more than just drake blood in the White," she said.

It took him a moment to realise the import of what she had said, a chilly fist closing around his heart as the implications struck home. "People," he said in a slow, hard rasp. "You used people to make that thing."

"Not people. Human tissue, mostly unfertilised eggs and plasma. Zembi had developed a method of blending organic material at the microscopic level. Another barely understood gift from the crystals. It took years, there were many failures." Kriz's head lowered farther still, voice dropping to nearly a whisper. "Many . . . things were brought into this world, things we are fortunate did not live for more than a few minutes after hatching. Then came the first White, and Zembi thought he had his discovery, the ultimate triumph of the Philos Caste. Its blood was unique, much easier to study than the other breeds. It gave us clues as to how to formulate synthetic compounds, clues we would never have had if it hadn't been born."

"But it got out, while you slept it got out, turned him into a Spoiled and somehow made it to Arradsia."

"All knowledge is dangerous, all knowledge is precious." Kriz looked again at the shard in her hand. "At least now we have a chance to discover how it got out."

"Could be he only had that thing because the White allowed it. Maybe it wanted him to give it to you. For all we know you'll drop down dead the moment you enter the trance."

Kriz jerked her chin at Preacher's sleeping form on the other side of the camp-fire. "Your friend gave us a lesson in faith the other day. Maybe it's one we should heed."

"Faithful he surely is, but he's also crazy." Clay reached out, placing his hand over hers to cover the vial and the shard. "Don't. At least not here, not now. Wait till we're back on the ship, or at least somewhere that could be called civilised. We got what we came for."

She gave a small grin, slipping back into her accented Mandinorian to ask, "That an order, Captain?"

"If you like. We got a long way to go and a better chance of surviving this trip with three Blood-blessed 'stead of two."

She gently pushed his hand away and looked again at the items in her hand before nodding and consigning them to the pocket of her jacket. "As you wish. I wouldn't want anyone calling me a mutineer."

In the morning he woke in time for his trance with Zenida Okanas, spending several minutes in contemplation of the vial in his hand. *It did happen,* he thought, replaying the events at the lake in his head. *I tranced without drinking. But how?* There was only one explanation that made any sense. *Heart-blood.* He had been able to maintain a mental connection with Jack from the moment he drank Blue heart-blood, and what else could that be called but a kind of trance? If he could trance with a drake, why not a human?

Checking his watch to confirm the moment had arrived, he shrugged and returned the Blue vial to his wallet. *One way to find out.*

Closing his eyes he concentrated on Zenida's face, reasoning it would summon enough memories of her to establish the connection. Nothing happened. He tried to recall every interaction with the Varestian woman, discovering they were few in number, just enough in fact to forge enough of a connection for the Blue-facilitated trance. *Looks like I need something more for this one,* he decided, pondering that moment on the raft again. The trance with Kriz had seemed to occur naturally, without any conscious decision, as if his fear for her had reached down to the bottom of the lake and forced its way into her mind. *Fear . . . Fear is an emotion.* When they first met, Lizanne had tutored him on the basics of the trance, explaining that mental communication required some form of emotional connection between the two parties. *It's how we remember one another in the real world,* she said. *Not through faces but feelings, however slight. Think of all the people you must have met in your life. Now ask yourself how many you remember. Comparatively few, I imagine. You remember those who made you laugh, those who made you cry, and, especially in your case, Mr. Torcreek, apparently those who made you angry most of all.*

Anger, another emotion. Zenida had never made him angry, nor had she made him laugh, except during those times she directed her occasionally caustic observations at Captain Hilemore . . . An image blossomed in his mind then, Hilemore's face, rendered in much more detail than Clay could have recalled. The captain, it transpired, had a small mole on his chin Clay had never noticed. *But she did,* he realised. *This ain't my memory. It's hers. Hilemore's our connection.*

He summoned his much more plentiful supply of Hilemore-related memories, all shot through with the conflicting range of emotions the captain always birthed in him, from grudging admiration to consternation to, most of all, anger.

Zenida's mindscape arrived with disorienting swiftness, the jewel-encrusted ship filling his vision in a flash and Clay stumbling as he felt its boards beneath his boots. He let out a delighted laugh at the sight of Zenida herself, standing near the prow and regarding him with a half-baffled, half-amused expression.

Are you alright? she asked. *The captain will be dismayed to discover the Interior has driven you mad.*

We wouldn't want that, Clay replied. *I know how you'd hate to disappoint him, and all.*

Zenida's expression hardened into something that reminded Clay this was a very dangerous woman if the mood took her, and this was her mind.

Just a bad joke, he said, raising his hands. *I got some interesting news to share, if you're ready.*

"The Carnstadt Mountains," Braddon said, gloved finger tapping the map. The mountains lay south-west of the Torquils, a considerable distance from their current location.

"That's an awful long way, Uncle," Clay pointed out.

"You want Blacks, that's where you'll find 'em. Largest concentration anywhere on the continent. There are pockets in the Coppersoles and the Cragmines on the far western coast, but this is the only place you're guaranteed a Black kill."

"'Cept we ain't going to kill 'em," Loriabeth put in. "We're going to make nice and ask them to join up to fight the White, iffen you can believe it. Not sure I do, so the Seer's ass knows what they'll think of it." Seeing Preacher stiffen at the blasphemy she added, "Sorry," in a low mumble.

"They're a rambunctious lot to be sure," Skaggerhill said. "Blacks grow big and mean in those mountains. Cunning too. Longrifles took a pass through the foot-hills a few years back. Lost a marksman and a gunhand with only two kills to show for it."

"Still a profitable trip by my recollection," Braddon said, a faint note of annoyance in his voice. "Good news is," he continued, turning back to Clay, "we don't have no Spoiled to worry about twixt here and there. Just a whole lotta Cerath wrangling and walking in between." He lowered his voice to add, "Skaggs is right, though. Next to the Red Sands it's just about the worst country I ever contracted in. Had hoped never to set eyes on the place again."

Clay looked at the map. The distance was dismaying but if they were to make this expedition count for something he couldn't see any other option. "I tranced with Captain Okanas this morning," he said. "The *Superior*'s making for Stockcombe." He tapped the dot a hundred miles or so south of the Carnstadts. "So we have to get there and the route leads us past the mountains in any case."

He clapped his uncle's shoulder and moved away, eyes roaming the surrounding plain. "Looks like we got some mounts to find. Lieutenant, I believe it's your turn to tame the bull."

CHAPTER 24

Hilemore

Hilemore tracked his spy-glass over the bodies hanging from the Stockcombe-harbour wall, counting twenty in all. Curiously, the row of suspended corpses was confined to the right-hand side of the wall, halting at the huge copper-and-wood edifice of the harbour door. Each corpse had a noose around its neck and some kind of sign fixed to its chest, but the distance was too great to make out any words. *I doubt it's a welcome in any case*, he decided, lowering the glass and nodding to Talmant. "Ahead dead slow, Lieutenant."

"Ahead dead slow, aye sir."

Hilemore had ordered the *Superior* to battle stations upon commencing their approach to the port, although the truce pennant fluttered from her mast and her signal lamp flashed a repeated request for safe harbour. So far, however, no one had appeared atop the harbour wall to issue either a welcome or a warning. Stockcombe's wall was unusual in that it was more of a dam than a simple barrier against the tide. It curved out from the steep slopes forming the apex of the channel where the port lay. It was famed for the unique geographical feature of a waterfall that cascaded into a lake at the base of a huge crater within which the port had grown. The lake was kept at a constant depth by a series of huge outlet tunnels. Consequently, the waters around the wall were in a permanent state of frothy turmoil save for a narrow stretch of calm water directly in front of the door. This ensured a nervous approach as any evasive manoeuvres the *Superior* might make would see her floundering in the churn.

"All stop," Hilemore ordered as the door loomed larger. He was close enough now to read the signs adorning the hanging bodies, finding them each bearing the same message painted in red Mandinorian letters: **CORPORATE MURDERER**.

Perhaps coming here wasn't the best idea, Hilemore concluded. He was about to order Talmant to signal the engine room to reverse the propeller, drawing them away in preparation for turning about, when the harbour door let out a loud squeal of grinding metal and began to ascend.

"Pretty sight, ain't it, Skipper?" Scrimshine commented as the port was revealed. The famous Stockcombe falls cascaded from atop a tall narrow promontory extending from the crater wall. The falls birthed a plume of misty vapour as it met the lake below, producing a small rainbow as it caught the sun. This pleasing spectacle was contrasted by the sight of the town itself. It stretched away on either side of the falls, covering the banks of the lake and ascending up the steep flanks of the crater. Denied building space, the residents of Stockcombe had built up rather than out, the place featuring some of the tallest buildings Hilemore had seen, some rising six storeys or more. The architecture varied in style, from high-angled roofed colonial mansions to Corvantine-influenced official buildings complete with classical pillars and statuary. The taller structures all conformed to modern standards, reflecting the clean, uncluttered lines favoured by the corporate world.

This would all have made for an aesthetically varied and interesting view if Hilemore's practised eye hadn't noticed the signature signs of cannon-shot on many walls, accompanied by the blackening and vanished roofs that told of extensive burning. The damage was worse close to the docks where many buildings had been completely burned out and others reduced to rubble. Hilemore's initial assumption that the port had been attacked in much the same manner as Carvenport was proven mistaken as he took in the sight of the numerous flags flying over the buildings on either side of the falls. The flags on the western side were all the black square emblazoned with a silver ship pennant of the South Seas Maritime Company, whilst those on the eastern side consisted of a simpler design; white with an uneven red X within a square. Thanks to his prior engagement Hilemore was fairly familiar with this symbol and was obliged to contain a dismayed groan at the sight of it.

"Buggers've been fighting each other, Skipper," Scrimshine observed.

Even with his new-found regard for military manners he still had difficulty in restraining his tongue. "Don't recognise that flag, though. One of those new East Mandinorian syndicates, maybe?"

"It's not a company flag," Hilemore said. "It appears the Voters Rights Alliance has a significant presence here."

He could see numerous vessels in the harbour, none of them warships. Only one was in motion, an old Blue-hunter Hilemore soon recognised. The *Farlight*'s signal lamp blinked out a message as she approached, moving at dead slow and drifting to a halt some fifty yards short of the door.

"'Half the town v. pleased to see you,'" Talmant related the message. "'Steer to port or the other half will fire on you.'"

Hilemore was tempted to follow his first impulse to turn the *Superior* about and make for open water. This place was clearly riven with internal strife and he had no desire to embroil his command in a conflict that might impede their mission. But the *Superior* was down to less than one-fifth of her coal reserves. Added to that was their rapidly diminishing food stocks and all the ammunition they had expended in the Torquils. Without a substantial resupply the chances of recovering the Longrifles and making use of their discovery were slight at best.

"Ahead dead slow," Hilemore told Talmant. "Mr. Scrimshine, take her in and steer immediately to port."

"Ethany Kulvetch." The young woman in the ill-fitting and besmirched uniform greeted Hilemore with a salute. "Acting Colonel, South Seas Maritime Defence and Security Force."

Given her youth and diminutive size Hilemore might have found Kulvetch's appearance almost comical but for the recently stitched cut above her left eye and the carbine slung over her shoulder. The fact that she had the weapon slung barrel down and wore a half-empty bandolier across her chest indicated she had plenty of practice in using it. She had been waiting on the quayside along with a squad of similarly dishevelled but well-armed South Seas Maritime Marines. He took note of the way her gaze continually strayed to the eastern regions of the port across the harbour, as if expecting a cannon shell to come sailing over at any second.

"Corrick Hilemore," he replied with a salute of his own. "Captain of the IPV *Superior.*"

"Welcome, Captain. Captain Tidelow of the *Farlight* vouched for your conduct but was somewhat reluctant to elaborate as to your mission here."

"Resupply. Assuming South Seas Maritime is still open for business."

Kulvetch's gaze darkened with disappointment. "I had hoped you might have been subcontracted to assist us in our . . . local difficulty. We tranced requests for reinforcement with Head Office until our Blood-blessed fell victim to a sniper's bullet. That was two weeks ago."

"Sadly, I knew nothing of the situation here until we caught sight of your wall. Unfortunate business."

The colonel's eyes grew darker still as she settled her gaze on the eastern districts. "They hung all our senior managers on the first day of their so-called uprising. Held a trial and so on, to give it the appearance of actual justice."

"The signs proclaim them as murderers."

"There had been a good deal of trouble since the other ports went silent and ships started arriving with all manner of mad rumours. Management's attempts to quell the disorder may have been . . . excessive but they certainly didn't deserve to be slaughtered at the hands of a slum-born mob." A shudder ran through Kulvetch then and she lowered her gaze, Hilemore realising she was even younger than she first appeared. "Forgive me," she said, straightening her back. "My father was amongst the slain. He had command of Defence and Security here."

"I see. My condolences. And your position in this port, Colonel?"

"When the uprising began I was a junior executive in the Customs Enforcement Division. Two days later I was the most senior official left. It took some hard fighting but with good and loyal soldiers"—she inclined her head at the squad of Marines—"and the support of the corporate populace, we won back half the city."

"Would I be correct in assuming, therefore, that you are the only figure in authority on this side of the harbour?"

"You would. If you wish to purchase supplies you will negotiate with me. As a corporate officer I'm sure you'll understand that prices will reflect prevailing circumstances."

Hilemore's hand went to his breast pocket and emerged with a gold Dalcian sovereign, one of the stack taken from the wreck of the *Windqueen*. Hilemore had fortuitously liberated the coins and other sundry valuables from the *Viable Opportunity*'s safe before seizing the *Superior*. "I'm sure we can agree on a mutually beneficial price," he said, handing over the coin.

Kulvetch glanced at the sovereign, betraying scant interest before handing it back. "You mistake me, Captain," she said. "It is not money I require, but your service. Vile insurrection has sundered this port in two. I require your assistance in uniting it and"—she fixed him with a steely, implacable gaze, voice taking on a hungry tremor—"ensuring justice is meted out to every last Voter bastard we can lay our hands on."

"It's been a stalemate for the better part of a month." Kulvetch had escorted him to the roof of South Seas Maritime headquarters in Stockcombe, the tallest structure in the port, affording a fine view of the whole city. "As you can see the falls create a natural and impassible barrier between the eastern and western districts. Meaning the only avenues of advance are via the harbour or the wall. The Voters attempted a charge across the wall the day after we secured control of this side. A few massed rifle volleys were enough to see them off. They tried a night attack in boats next. Fortunately, most of the ships in the harbour chose to ally with us and they didn't even make it to the wharf. Since then they've been content to stay in their hovels and cast the occasional shell at us."

"They have artillery then?" Hilemore asked.

"Two batteries of six-pounders and one eighteen-pounder long-barrelled cannon, whilst we have only four heavy guns. That's the main reason I haven't yet ordered an attack of our own, plus lack of numbers. All told I have less than three hundred soldiers under arms, plus just over seven hundred volunteers from the townsfolk. They're low on training and weapons but keen as a blade."

"The Voter numbers?"

"The neighbourhoods east of the falls are more populous than on our side, plenty of slum rats over there to recruit to their deluded cause. I'd estimate at least three thousand under arms."

Hilemore let out a sigh of grim amusement. "I have faced long odds before, Colonel, but never impossible ones. What exactly do you expect a single warship to do against such numerous shore-based opposition?"

"Destroy that damn artillery of theirs," Kulvetch returned, her tone heating appreciably. She pulled a folded map from the pocket of her tunic and began to unfurl it. "Through careful observation we have pin-pointed most of their guns . . ."

"No."

She fell silent, clearly taken aback by the flat, uncompromising tone of his refusal. "This plan is sound . . ."

"Colonel." Hilemore's voice was pitched just below a shout and he took a moment to calm his rising frustration before continuing. "Do you have any notion of what is happening in the rest of the world?"

She stared at him, confusion and anger adding a red tinge to her face. "Some kind of emergency," she said. "Drakes and Spoiled running amok. Once the combined might of the corporate world is brought to bear on the savages and beasts . . ."

"Carvenport has fallen to those savages and beasts," Hilemore broke in. "Morsvale has fallen. Feros has fallen and I daresay other cities have since shared their fate. The might of the corporate world has already been brought to bear and found wanting. And while the world burns this city tears itself apart without a drake in sight. I'll have no part of your petty war. And if you are unwilling to sell me supplies, perhaps your friends across the water will be more amenable."

Kulvetch's face twisted into a snarl, her hands twitching, and Hilemore knew she was resisting the impulse to reach for her carbine. "You would treat with those scum?"

"To fulfil my mission I would treat with all the demons of the Travail." Hilemore stood to attention and spoke in formal tones. "I am impressed with your achievements here, but you have no hope of victory. I am willing to mediate . . ."

"Piss on your mediation!" Kulvetch's nostrils flared as she glared at him, breath becoming ragged in her fury. "I should shoot you . . ."

"Then you'll have my ship's guns to contend with alongside the Voters' artillery." Hilemore gave a salute, which she failed to return, and started towards the stairwell.

Instead of a single authority figure, the Voters presented him with a committee of six. Hilemore was depressed to find them all much the same age as Colonel Kulvetch, with a similarly steely look in their eyes which told him he was in for a very taxing meeting.

He had made his way to the eastern docks in the ship's launch, standing at the prow with a truce flag in hand. He found the wharf abandoned, though the flicker of movement behind the windows of the surrounding houses indicated his arrival had been noticed. After an interval of several minutes a lone, stocky young man in a Contractor's duster emerged from a shadowed alley with a revolver in hand. On the sleeve of his duster was an arm-band bearing the cross-and-square emblem of the Voters Rights Alliance. The young man lurked in a crouch at the corner of the alley, wary eyes tracking from Hilemore to the western side of the city. After some further scrutiny he pointed to the launch, scowling at Hilemore.

"Send 'em back," he said.

Hilemore nodded and called out an order for the launch to return to the ship. The crew were clearly reluctant to leave him in such uncertain company but dutifully dipped their oars and began to row away.

"C'mere," the stocky man said, gesturing with his revolver before disappearing back into the alley. Hilemore followed him through a short maze of cramped streets until he rounded a corner to find himself confronted by a dozen or so young men and women, all levelling fire-arms at him.

"Search him," the man in the duster ordered. Hilemore was then subjected to a few minutes' rough handling at the hands of a trio of rebels, which came to an abrupt end when he jabbed his elbow into the face of a skinny youth who tried to take his pocket-watch.

"Are you Voters or thieves?" he asked as they tensed around him.

"Corprate bastud!" the skinny youth said, lying on the cobbles and clutching a broken nose. "Shood 'im, Coll!"

"Shut it!" the duster-clad man said. "Freeman Towl's got unfortunate habits," he told Hilemore. "Comes from growing up living off the scraps allowed us by corporate slavers."

Hilemore brushed the blood from the sleeve of his tunic and said nothing.

"I'm Freeman Coll and this is the Wash Lane Defence Volunteers," the young man said, gesturing to the other youths. "Don't mistake us,

Mr. Protectorate Man, you don't get a second chance." He slowly lowered his revolver and jerked his head to the left. "This way. Towl, you're on guard duty tonight. Told you before 'bout thieving."

Coll led Hilemore to a cobbled square formed by the intersection of several streets. Sitting in the centre of the square was an inn of such antique, slant-walled appearance that Hilemore concluded it must have stood there since the earliest days of the city. An armed guard hauled the door open as they approached, Hilemore following Coll into the gloomy, candle-lit interior. After squinting for several seconds to adjust his sight Hilemore saw Coll taking a seat at a long table alongside five other people of similar age.

There were two men besides Coll and three women, all staring at Hilemore in expectant silence. The inn was clearly a headquarters of some kind. Maps and documents littered the tables and the walls were covered in leaflets and radical propaganda including, Hilemore was both amused and dismayed to see, numerous pages from the *Voters Gazette*.

Seeing little need to stand on ceremony he took a stool from one of the tables, dragging it across the tiled floor to sit down. "Lieutenant Corrick Hilemore," he introduced himself. "Commander of the Ironship Protectorate Vessel *Superior*. Might I know to whom I am speaking?"

"Free men and free women," one of the six replied, a girl of about nineteen by Hilemore's reckoning. From the sunken state of her eyes and sallow skin she appeared not to have slept for several days. Despite her fatigue the defiance in her voice and bearing was palpable as she added, "Who will not be cowed by corporate threats."

"I haven't made any threats," Hilemore pointed out.

"How many ships in your fleet?" another of the six demanded, a red-haired and freckle-faced lad with a bandage covering one ear.

"My fleet?" Hilemore enquired.

"Don't play with us," Coll growled. "We know Ironship's been hired to retake this place for South Seas Maritime."

"Then you know more than I do," Hilemore told him. "I have no fleet. For that matter, the Ironship Syndicate no longer has a fleet, not in these waters at least."

"South Seas Maritime agents met in Sanorah with the Interim Ironship Board three weeks ago," the hollow-eyed girl said. "You presume to tell us you are not here as a result?"

Hilemore gave no immediate reply, gaze narrowing as it tracked over each of them. *So young and guileless despite all the blood they've spilled.* "So, you're in trance communication with Sanorah," he said.

This heralded a silence during which the girl lowered her head as her red-haired colleague shot her a glare of reproach.

"I have had no contact with Ironship senior management for quite some time now," Hilemore went on. "My ship is here on business unconnected with your insurrection. I wish to purchase supplies and I have gold to pay for it. That is all."

"He's lying!" the red-haired youth rasped. "Corporatists lie. It's what they do. Remember Red Lomansday."

Another silence as they exchanged glances, both fierce and uncertain.

"Red Lomansday?" Hilemore asked.

"The spark that lit the tinder," Coll replied. "Colonel Kulvetch, the first one, invited our leaders to a meeting. He told them their concerns would be addressed. Told them a new government would be established for this port, a joint government he said. When they turned up he had them stripped naked, flogged, paraded through the streets then shot in the head." He gave a thin smile. "Hung the bastard myself from the wall and laughed as he dangled and kicked, looked a little like the clown from that circus marionette show they put on for the kiddies. So you see." His smile faded as he reclined in his seat. "We ain't too trusting of corporate types these days."

Hilemore nodded and rose from his stool. He went to the wall, scanning the many pages pinned to it until he found something familiar and ripped it free.

"'The Shared Guilt of the Corporate Age,'" he read aloud. "'How the greed and corruption of the modern economy shames us all.'" He moved to the table, placing the page in front of Coll. "By Lewella Tythencroft, Acting Editor of the *Voters Gazette*. I was actually in her office when she wrote this." He grimaced, huffing out a small, regretful sigh. "We had quite the argument about it, as I recall."

"You know Lewella Tythencroft?" the hollow-eyed girl asked, gaze narrowed in doubt.

"I should," Hilemore replied. "We were engaged to be married until very recently."

The hollow-eyed girl's name was Jillett and it transpired that she was the only Blood-blessed left in Stockcombe. After Hilemore's revelation the committee had him escorted outside before spending the next hour in discussion, some of it quite heated judging by the shouts emerging from the inn. Eventually the voices fell silent and Hilemore was obliged to spend another hour wandering the square, closely watched by the Wash Lane Defence Volunteers.

"You been in battles then?" one of them asked, a hefty boy no more than sixteen years old who seemed intrigued by the medal ribbons on Hilemore's tunic.

"I have," he replied.

"Who with?"

"Dalcians, pirates, Corvantines and, most recently, drakes."

The boy's features bunched in surprise. "So it's true then? They've risen up, like the Seer said."

"I'm not sure the Seer foresaw all of this, but yes, the drakes are now making war on us, with the help of the Spoiled."

"How come they ain't come for us then?"

Hilemore cast a gaze at the sky and the surrounding cliffs. The lip of the enclosing crater was crowned with a series of defensive forts joined by a wall. To Hilemore's eyes it seemed too insubstantial and dilapidated to offer much defence in the event of a serious attack. "I don't know," he replied. "But I'm sure they'll get to it eventually."

"You're wanted," Coll called from the inn's doorway.

"Your first ship," Jillett said once Hilemore had made his way back inside. She stood reading from a sheet of paper, suspicion still evident in her face.

"The IPV *Company Pride*," Hilemore replied.

"Your youngest brother's name and occupation."

"Starrick, he's a schoolmaster."

"Where and when did you first meet Lewella Tythencroft?"

"During a riot in Sanorah, four years ago."

"Her dog's name."

"She's never had a dog, preferring cats. Her last cat, Mr. Mewsly, died shortly before I left for Dalcia. He was very old."

Jillett lowered the sheet and nodded to Coll. "It's him."

"Couldn't they just have shown you a photostat?" Hilemore asked.

Jillett's lips formed a faint smile. "Apparently Free Woman Tythencroft advised our Blood-blessed contact that she no longer possesses any photostats of you."

"I see." Hilemore coughed. "I assume, nevertheless, that she also advised that my word can be trusted."

"No, she didn't. Not yet anyway." Jillett pointed to a table where a stack of blank paper sheets had been placed alongside a pen and ink-well. "Free Woman Tythencroft insists on a full report of your activities and whereabouts for the past year. You will write it, I will memorise it and, once she has been fully apprised of its contents, she will advise us how best to proceed."

"Advise or command?" Hilemore asked. "It seems Free Woman Tythencroft enjoys considerable authority here."

"Not just here." Jillett exchanged a glance with Coll, apparently unsure of how much information to share.

"Thought it was just Stockcombe, did you?" the stocky youth asked. "This revolution ain't local, Captain. Half of Sanorah is now under Voter control, along with two complete cities in northern Mandinor."

"You're telling me Mandinor is now in a state of civil war?"

"There's been fighting, but no battles as such from what we're told. Protectorate ain't got enough troops to do more than hold what they already got. Free Woman Tythencroft is the guiding light at the heart of it all, calming tempers so things don't slip out of control like they did here. She wants a peaceful end to the corporate world. Myself, I ain't too fussed about that." He nodded at the stack of pages. "She's waiting. Best get to it."

Hilemore moved to the table and sat down, unbuttoning his tunic. "Might I have some coffee?" he asked, reaching for the pen. "This will take quite some time. I'll also write a note for you to take to my ship; otherwise, my First Officer is likely to come ashore to look for me, and you really don't want that."

CHAPTER 25

Sirus

"It's always been one of my favourite examples of military pragmatism," Morradin commented as they watched the ships approach the Subarisk defences. "Given the apparently impossible task of destroying the great fortress of Aben Mael, and thereby ending the siege of Redways Station, Commodore Racksmith chose to regard the ships in his fleet no differently than any other military asset, and all military assets must be expendable; otherwise, what use are they?"

The *Malign Influence* lay at anchor beyond the range of the many guns in the Subarisk island forts. On either side of the flagship the entire fleet waited, merchant ships crammed with Spoiled towing similarly laden barges. It was some minutes past dawn, which meant the defenders of this port would by now have been fully aware of the size of the armada they faced, not that this appeared to concern Marshal Morradin. "Surprise is not our object here," he said when Sirus had queried the allotted hour for the attack. "But shock. I want every soldier in that city to see what's about to happen and know themselves doomed when they do."

Sirus used a spy-glass to track the progress of the ships they had sent into the approaches. There were twelve in all, two for each of the forts. The force had been split into pairs consisting of a freighter and a warship. Catheline had been reluctant to commit their few military vessels to a mission of this nature but the combined faith of Morradin and Sirus convinced her to grant assent, albeit with a dark warning, "Lose me this battle and I won't punish you," she said. "*He* will."

Sirus could sense the hungry anticipation of the Spoiled on the ships. They had all been selected for their enjoyment of their new lives and unreasoning loyalty to the White. Many had barely been sane before their conversion and some driven mad by the horrors witnessed since, revelling in slaughter and destruction with a sadistic glee that was painful to share. The need to use such fanatical soldiers was easily explained to Catheline, Sirus managing to conceal his gratification at removing so many maddened souls from the army.

Hearing the echoing boom of cannon, Sirus shifted the spy-glass to one of the forts, seeing several horizontal plumes of smoke erupting from its gun-ports. He tracked the fall of shot, watching the shells raise waterspouts in front of their ships but falling far too short to score any hits.

"Firing too soon," Morradin grunted with a note of satisfaction. "Nervous. All to the good. The Corvantine commander at Aben Mael made a similar error, wasting much of his ammunition before Racksmith's stratagem began to play out."

The ships maintained formation as they drew closer to the forts, the warships limiting their speed to enable the freighters to keep up. They began to return fire as soon as the forts came within range, firing smoke shells rather than explosives. Soon each of the island forts was wreathed in a grey blanket of smoke, but not before their gunners had managed to take a toll on the attackers. One of the warships, the *Null and Void*, took a direct hit to the bridge, which killed most of the Spoiled in the upper works. This would have been critical damage for a ship with a human crew but not the *Null and Void*, which continued to steam a true course towards its objective. Guided by the look-outs in the *Malign Influence*'s crow's nest, the Spoiled belowdecks steered the tiller by hand, whilst the undaunted gunners on the upper decks kept up a steady barrage.

Two hundred yards east of the *Null and Void*, the *Fatal Indulgence* was less fortunate. An expertly aimed Corvantine salvo wrecked her forward gun and port paddle, sending her into an untidy spin. Sirus ordered the starboard paddle halted and set the crew rushing to conduct rapid repairs. But such a conspicuously maimed target soon drew fire from every fort in range and a concentrated barrage tore her apart minutes later.

"Couldn't be helped," Morradin sniffed. "Did her job anyway, the freighter's almost there."

Sirus felt the marshal's anticipation swell as the freighter steamed through the smoking debris left by the demise of her escort, making straight for the fort beyond. Shells struck her repeatedly as she swept forward, laying waste to her upper deck and holing her hull in several places, but scoring only one hit below the water-line. Despite the sudden inrush of water, the freighter possessed enough momentum to bring her crashing into the island fort's rocky shore-line. She settled as her lower decks flooded, shuddering like a great dying monster as the fort's cannon fired into her at point-blank range.

"I see little point in any delay, do you?" Morradin said.

Sirus nodded and sent a mental command to the five Spoiled in the freighter's hold, who immediately set about lighting the fuses connected to the massed barrels of powder. The arsenals at Feros, Melkorin and Sairvek had yielded an impressive tonnage of explosive but comparatively few cannon with which to fire it. Morradin's greatly expanded version of the plan so famously used by Commodore Racksmith provided a fine opportunity to use this surplus. Fully four-fifths of their entire powder stocks had been crammed onto the freighters. The fuses were set for thirty seconds, giving the Spoiled allotted the task of lighting them an opportunity to escape. Even when dealing with deluded monsters such as these the human instinct against suicide could be a barrier to obedience so Sirus was careful to allow them the hope of survival, however illusory.

In the event not a single Spoiled escaped the freighter before it exploded, Sirus feeling their confused, oddly gleeful minds blink out as the ship disappeared in a massive ball of fire. The shock wave reached them before the sound, Catheline letting out an exultant laugh as she staggered in the gale of displaced air. The roar of the blast came next, loud enough to pain the ears sufficiently for Catheline's laughter to transform into a painful wince.

The fire-ball ascended to at least two hundred feet, dissipating into a thick column of black smoke that towered over the island. Debris fell in a thick rain that made the surrounding water roil until the smoke started to clear and reveal the damage. The freighter had disintegrated completely and for a brief second Sirus concluded the fort had somehow survived the blast, its south-facing wall seeming to be mostly intact. Then he saw the rubble covering the west side of the island and registered the absence of the structure's domed roof. Flames rose from within the blackened ruin and soon there came the crump of exploding powder as they reached the fort's magazine.

"Satisfactory," Morradin concluded, peering through his spy-glass at the carnage. "Though I believe Racksmith managed to destroy Aben Mael completely. Of course, he had only one to contend with." He shifted his spy-glass to the right where a pair of ships were bearing down on another fort. "I do believe I am about to outdo him by a factor of five."

"Twenty-five thousand, eight hundred and ninety-six Spoiled confirmed dead," Veilmist reported with her customary precision. "Six thousand one hundred and thirty-two wounded, of whom approximately half are expected to survive."

"Approximately?" Catheline asked her, one eyebrow arched in mock surprise.

"It's impossible to provide an accurate figure for recovery rates . . ." Veilmist trailed off into puzzled silence as Catheline laughed and pressed a kiss to her scaled forehead.

"Don't worry, my dear," she said. "Approximately will do perfectly well."

From the centre of the square came a familiar scream, rich in terror but mercifully brief. Sirus glanced over to see the juvenile Whites squabbling over the remains of a captured Blood-blessed, another Cadre agent who proved a stark contrast to the heroic woman at Sairvek. The portly fellow had been dragged from an attic hideaway during the post-conquest search and taken to the White for what had become a grim ritual. The administrative district of Subarisk was dominated by a broad plaza of fountains and statues commemorating various Imperial heroes, the largest of which was a recently completed marble rendition of Emperor Caranis himself. It lay in several pieces at the base of the tall column rising from the centre of the square, having been toppled by the White, which had chosen to perch its massive form in the emperor's place.

The Blood Cadre agent begged and pleaded as he was dragged through the surrounding ranks of Spoiled and captives. When confronted with the White he collapsed, gibbering on the paving-slabs and soiling himself. Judging by the satisfaction leaking from the minds of recently converted captives Sirus concluded this man had been something of a terror in the city, both before and after the revolution. His grisly and frenzied demise was therefore greeted with much less horror and dismay than might otherwise have been expected.

Beyond the squabbling juvenile Whites a continual line of captives were being paraded in front of the Blue crystal. The conversion wouldn't take long, just a moment or two and the terrified prisoner would fall into a dead faint and be carried away, their features already showing the deformities to come. The Blue crystal would occasionally flicker, its light becoming dim whereupon the White would lean down from its perch to bathe it in an intense stream of fire.

Energy, Sirus had concluded when first witnessing this spectacle back in Morsvale. *It needs energy to work, like any machine.*

"A stiff price to pay for victory, Marshal," he heard Catheline say, turning back to see Morradin meeting her critical gaze with an expression that wasn't exactly defiant, but neither was it contrite.

"Our casualties were only marginally greater than the estimate," he replied. "And the capture rate means our losses will be made good within the day."

Catheline turned a questioning glance to Veilmist, who nodded. "We currently have over eighty thousand captives," the Island girl said. "Given the success of our sweeps in the outlying districts and surrounding country-side the army should exceed two hundred thousand within six days."

"Enough to take Varestia, wouldn't you say, General?" Catheline enquired of Sirus.

"Given the ships we captured, yes," he replied. "We were fortunate the city authorities had forbidden the harbour doors to be opened since the fall of Corvus."

The harbour had yielded sixty-three ships in all, together with three Imperial warships, all captured during the massed rush of Spoiled following the destruction of the island forts. True to Morradin's prediction the sight of so much destruction had unnerved the defenders. When thousands of Spoiled came streaming up the ropes from the barges and ships clustered along the length of the wall, resistance had been patchy. Some Imperial units fought with dogged determination whilst others fled almost immediately. Securing the wall took an hour of hard fighting by which time the waters both within and without the harbour were stained red and littered with bobbing corpses.

Resistance grew fiercer once they had swept over the docks and into the town itself. The garrison commander here was evidently a more able officer than his counterpart in Sairvek. Having correctly deduced that efforts to hold the harbour wall would prove fruitless, he drew his remaining forces back into a series of defensive lines, barricading interlocking streets and making good use of his remaining cannon to blast apart the repeated assaults Morradin launched against them. Sirus felt the man must have known the city would fall and the desperate struggle put up by his soldiers was intended to buy time for the residents to flee. Consequently, he had advised Catheline to forbid further assaults on the barricades, allowing the defenders the illusion of success. Thousands of people fled into the hills to the north, only to be confronted by packs of Greens and Reds who herded them back into the suburbs. Meanwhile Morradin led ten thousand Spoiled in a flanking move through the city's outskirts, cutting the defending soldiers off from the refugees. It took another two days of vicious fighting to subdue organised resistance, and even now occasional reports would come in of Spoiled patrols being ambushed in the more constricted streets. Despite this the city effectively now belonged to the White.

"How long before we can strike south?" Catheline asked Sirus. "He wishes this matter resolved."

"We'll need at least two weeks to prepare the ships," he replied. "The Varestians will prove fearsome opponents at sea and the more arms and armour we can add to our own vessels the better. Luckily, this port has excellent facilities and a skilled work-force to draw upon."

"Very good. And where do we strike first?"

Sirus exchanged a barely perceptible glance with Morradin. They had expected this question and knew the answer would be a key factor in any design aimed at breaking the White's control. "The Seven Walls," he said, allowing a modicum of heightened concern to colour his thoughts. She would expect some degree of uncertainty. "The Varestian Ruling Council resides there, and it's the most important port in the region. Varestian resistance will be most likely to concentrate there and around the neighbouring Iskamir Island, meaning we will be able to destroy the bulk of their forces in the first engagement."

"Destroying their forces is a secondary concern," she said. "Finding and killing Lizanne Lethridge is our priority, along with anyone she has been in close contact with. Gear all your efforts towards that end."

Sirus and the other Spoiled present replied with a thought-pulse of subservient agreement, which brought a smile to her lips. "See to your fleet, General," she told Sirus, moving closer to brush his hand with hers before she strode off towards the White. "I shall expect you for dinner tonight."

"You take too many risks for my liking," she told him, tracing a finger along the recently healed scar on his cheek. He had earned it leading a charge atop the harbour wall. It was the legacy of a final bayonet thrust from a wounded Corvantine regular, the needle-pointed triangular blade having come within a fraction of piercing Sirus's eye and skewering his brain. Forest Spear pushed him aside at the last instant, saving his life and dispatching the doughty regular with a blow from his war-club.

"A commander unwilling to share the risks of his soldiers will lose their respect," he replied. "Even in this army."

This was true, at least to a certain extent. He sensed a definite warm regard for him amongst many of the other Spoiled, especially amongst the Islanders and, for reasons he hadn't been able to divine, the Arradsian tribals. When the time came to move against the White he suspected such a depth of feeling might be useful.

"Morradin takes risks too," Catheline pointed out, her hand broadening into a caress. "And they all hate him."

They were in the sitting-room on the upper floor of the palatial mansion she had taken over. It had belonged to the city's richest merchant family, all now vanished into the ranks of the Spoiled or slaughtered as being of no use. They ate dinner in a capacious, echoing ball-room of gleaming chandeliers and tall paintings. Throughout the meal Catheline allowed him to share a taste of her thoughts and he was surprised at the deep well of contempt she held for her surroundings. *Frippery, luxury, empty art for empty souls. Just like those managerial bastards.*

There was a discomfiting heat to these thoughts, a genuine hatred simmering beneath the contempt. Sirus was tempted to ask her about this, seek answers to the mystery of why she so detested her own class, but suspected that such enquiry might well be pointless. It was possible there were no reasons, none that made any rational sense given that she was an essentially irrational soul. He maintained a pall of fear to conceal all this contemplation of her nature, something she seemed to enjoy as she led him from the ball-room to her sitting-room.

"You wonder what I want of you," she said, baring her elongated canines in a smile, hand smoothing over his scaled face. Sinking down next to him on the couch, she leaned close, letting her perfume assail him with all its terrible allure. "What does any woman want of a man she finds so interesting?"

"I am not a man," Sirus pointed out. "Even before I . . . became this, most would have called me just a boy . . ."

"Before doesn't matter." She leaned closer still, Sirus feeling her breath flutter over his remade skin, the heat of it mingling with the effects of her scent to produce something intoxicating. He turned his face to hers so that their lips almost touched. "Now," she breathed, "is all that matters . . ."

They both let out a pained gasp as a new thought invaded their minds, Sirus forced to his knees by the pain of it. *Punishment?* he thought, wondering if the White might harbour some dislike for such intimacy between its servants. But then he recognised the dark, alien stain of Katarias's thoughts and realised it was a shared memory.

Another aerostat, he thought, seeing the elongated oval shape slipping through a darkened sky. It grew in size as Katarias soared towards it, the beast's excited hunger swelling at the sight of the figure leaning out of the gondola beneath the bulbous air-bag. Drake eyesight was far keener than any human's or Spoiled's and, despite the goggles the woman wore, Katarias recognised her instantly.

Lizanne Lethridge! Catheline exulted, Sirus finding himself choking down a retch at the depth of her blood-lust. *KILL HER!*

CHAPTER 26

Lizanne

Hyran, it transpired, had company when Lizanne slipped into his mind-scape, finding it merged with another. At the mid-point of the spice-shop the cabinets and cases sublimed into a stretch of rocky shore-line, dotted with many pools. She could see him wandering a shingle beach close by, a smaller and more slender figure at his side. Lizanne moved to one of the rock-pools, seeing a swirl of colours in the water, vague shapes forming and breaking apart in what one of her tutors had called "the dance of memory."

Miss Blood?

Lizanne turned to see Hyran standing close by. At his side was a young woman Lizanne had last seen killing Corvantine Imperial troops at the Sanctum. It was the young woman who had addressed her, this being her mindscape.

Jelna, Lizanne greeted her. *Good to see you, and please pardon the interruption.*

I suppose I should be grateful you didn't turn up ten minutes ago, Jelna replied, provoking a blossom of embarrassment from Hyran. *I'm guessing you're here for him, not me,* she added.

I am.

Jelna nodded, Lizanne seeing the colour bleach from the surrounding mindscape as she prepared to leave the trance. *They still talk about you,* she said. *Some of us have been arguing for a statue in your honour.*

Then please stop.

Jelna let out a pulse of warm amusement before her mindscape vanished completely, leaving her alone with Hyran in the spice-shop. *When I met her in Corvus, she was of a . . . fiercer disposition,* Lizanne recalled.

She's still fierce enough, he responded. *When the need arises. Do your respective organisations approve? One of the Co-respondent Brotherhood dallying with a member of Republic First.*

It has become clear to many of us that holding fast to old allegiances is not in the best interests of our new republic.

Although evidently glad to see his former comrade and informal mentor again, Hyran's thoughts were tinged with a wary suspicion. Lizanne suppressed a small pulse of pride at this, glad to see her lessons during the long march to Corvus hadn't been wasted. A good Blood-blessed agent should always suspect everyone, even their friends.

I did wonder if I would ever see you again, Hyran went on.

And now you wonder what on earth I could want?

Quite.

She summoned one of her whirlwinds, opening it out to display a recent memory. It was the view of a ruined port city captured from far above during a reconnaissance flight in the *Firefly* the day before. Blackened buildings stretched away from the docks, smoke still lingering in some places. A few Red drakes glided over the town and a pack of Blues could be seen breaking the surface of the sea beyond the harbour wall. Lizanne magnified the image to bring the many bodies littering the streets into focus, sensing Hyran's distress at the sight of so many slaughtered children.

They take the adults and kill the young, Lizanne explained.

Where is this? he asked.

Sairvek, what's left of it. I take it neither the general nor the Electress know about this?

Rumours have been flying lately, but the southern coast is a long way from Corvus and all the Blood-blessed there are Cadre loyalists. Besides, we've had plenty to keep us busy in the north.

So not every Corvantine is enamoured with the revolution?

It was glorious at first. General Arberus led one army west and the Electress another north. Jelna went with her, I went with the general. Village after village, town after town all welcomed us, young people flocked to our ranks . . . Then it began to change. Not every region of the Empire suffered under the Regnarchy's yoke, and some of the most prosperous lands lie in the west. Often the people there had no urge to offer their loyalty to those they saw as traitors and usurpers of the ancient and divine order. There were battles. We lost troops winning them and many in our ranks felt the need to take vengeance on those we had vanquished. The general did his best to stem the worst of it but . . . Things got uglier the farther west we marched. By the time we reached the coast they were calling it "Arberus's Red March to the Sea."

I'd wager he didn't like that.

No. He didn't.

Where are you now?

Torivek, the largest port on the western coast. Unlike the others it fell without a shot. People are a lot poorer here.

The Electress?

Besieging Merivus in Northern Kestria along with Varkash.

Varkash, the former Varestian pirate and leader of the Verdigris gang in Scorazin, who once said he couldn't give a sea-dog's cock for the revolution. *I thought he would have sailed for home by now,* she commented.

He agreed lucrative terms with the Electress, one-third of the value of any noble property seized. Plus she made him an admiral, which pandered to his vanity. She advanced up the coast roads and he kept her supplied en route with what's left of the Imperial fleet. It worked well until she got to Merivus. She's been at it for a good few weeks now. Jelna says her captains keep advising her to by-pass it but she stubbornly refuses to move on. There are rumours she has scores to settle with some of the townsfolk.

Lizanne recalled Electress Atalina's tale of how she came to end up in Scorazin and felt a brief pang of pity for any Imperial officials she managed to capture alive when Merivus fell. Lizanne also concluded the Electress would be too preoccupied in pursuing her vengeance to have much regard for crises elsewhere, but it couldn't hurt to try.

Share the memory of Sairvek with Jelna, she told Hyran. *Tell her to bring it to the Electress's attention. You do the same with the general.*

I will, he promised. *But that doesn't mean they'll send any aid. Without the presence of the revolutionary armies this entire country may fall into anarchy.*

If the White triumphs in Varestia your revolution will be worth nothing.

Feeling her Blue begin to thin, Lizanne prepared to exit the trance, pausing as another notion occurred to her. *Make sure Jelna also shares what she knows with Varkash, it's his homeland after all.*

"I'm pregnant, not crippled," Sofiya Griffan told Captain Trumane, ignoring his further protestations and ascending the gangway to the deck of the *Viable Opportunity.*

Flustered, Trumane turned to Lizanne. "Couldn't you . . . ?"

"She's an experienced Maritime Protectorate Blood-blessed," Lizanne replied. "And I have a trance connection with her. Besides, I suspect within a few weeks she'll be as safe aboard your ship as anywhere else."

She switched her gaze to the *Viable*, taking in the sight of the newly manufactured Growlers on the upper works and the four Thumpers mounted on the rails. Situated on the fore-deck in front of the pivot-gun was a large canvas-covered object standing over fifteen feet high. At this angle it somewhat resembled an abstract sculpture awaiting an unveiling. She could see her father's long-coated form moving about as he made adjustments to the revolving circular frame on which the object was mounted. He had wanted to go on this mission but, unlike Sofiya, Lizanne firmly asserted he was needed at the Mount Works, as the inhabitants were now calling it. Instead, a trio of the more mechanically adept workers had been recruited to operate the professor's latest device.

"You're confident this will work?" Lizanne asked Trumane. This mission had been his notion, conceived after being advised of the new invention's capabilities.

"It would have been preferable to do a proper test," Trumane replied. "But in time of war thorough preparation is a luxury. I trust your father's engineering above all others. With continual reconnaissance during the approach there's every reason to expect success."

"And you're certain they'll strike next at Subarisk?"

"It's the most logical choice, if the enemy's object is to gather strength. Given their evident efficiency the port may already have fallen."

Lizanne nodded, discomforted by the grim military logic of this plan, which required Subarisk to be in enemy hands for it to work. "Your new recruits are shaping up, I trust?" she asked. Trumane's crew had been brought to full strength by a number of former sailors from the refugee fleet. It hadn't been necessary to draft any recruits as the captain had been swamped with volunteers keen to escape the monotony of the manufactory.

"Only a few have military experience," Trumane replied. "But they know their way around a ship, which is the main thing. I'll whip them into shape soon enough."

Lizanne didn't like the emphasis he put on the word "whip," but resisted the urge to voice any concerns. Trumane's competence had become clear over the preceding weeks, forcing her to overlook his other less admirable qualities.

"As planned, we will conduct the first aerial reconnaissance in four days," she said. "Advising any course changes to Mrs. Griffan."

Recent flights had revealed that Blue drakes were surprisingly easy to spot from the air. Even at night the patrolling packs left a tell-tale series of white tracks across the ocean surface. This meant she would be able to guide the *Viable* around any concentrations of Blues during the voyage to Subarisk. A timetable had been drawn up for frequent trance communication between Lizanne and Sofiya. It made for an inflexible approach but that wouldn't matter once the *Viable* was in position and could make full use of her remarkable speed.

"Four days then," he said, surprising her with a salute before he strode up the gangway.

She waited for her father to disembark and together they watched the *Viable* sail away, following the course of Blaska Sound east to the sea. "I called it the *Tinkerer Mark I*," he said once the ship had rounded a bend and disappeared from view. "Didn't feel right naming it for myself. Since it's not really mine."

"Very generous of you, Father."

They made their way back to the manufactory via the town, which at this hour was mainly occupied by children liberated from their morning lessons. Lizanne thought them an oddly well behaved lot, given to prolonged silence, little mischief and an absence of laughter, even when they played. *They all saw too much at too young an age,* Lizanne concluded, feeling for perhaps the first time in her life that her own childhood had been one of comparative ease and security.

"No sign of Tinkerer waking from his coma, I suppose?" the professor asked.

"None," Lizanne replied. "And Makario's made little progress with the next movement."

"Pity. A fellow of many uses, even with his irksome manners."

"I don't think he has much say over his manners. It's just how he's made."

They paused at the entrance to his workshop, a large warehouse with a canvas awning where its roof had been. Lizanne glanced through the open doors, trying to gauge the nature of the machine taking shape within.

"There's still work to do," her father said, moving to block her view.

"It's not a Year's End present, Father," she said. "You don't need to surprise me."

"I would prefer an unvarnished opinion of the finished machine," he said. "Free of any insights into the narrative of its construction."

Lizanne gave a bemused shrug and clasped his arm before moving on. "As you wish."

"I need thicker steel wire," he called after her. "The coils you gave me were too flimsy."

She waved her assent in response and went to find Morva for her afternoon lesson.

What do you think she meant? Clay asked after Lizanne had finished sharing the memories recovered from Tinkerer's mind. The trance connection between them felt different now, the clarity of his mindscape sharper and the exchange of thoughts more rapid. When he had revealed the fact that he could now trance without the aid of product she had been sceptical, but a few seconds of communication had banished any doubts.

The Artisan's greatest discovery was a tribe of Spoiled? he went on.

No ordinary tribe, Lizanne pointed out. *They saved her, and they seemed different to the others. Using spoken language and dressing as individuals.*

Never met a friendly Spoiled, to be sure, Clay conceded. *But it all happened centuries ago, right? What use is this now?*

A question to be answered if I can unlock more memories.

She turned her attention to the images he had shared, particularly the

Black crystal and the vial of what the ancient woman called "convergence." *Synthetic product.* She allowed her conflicted emotions to colour the shared trance. The very idea of such a thing was both tantalising and incredible, if not ominous in its implications.

You saw what her people built, Clay responded. *What they were able to do with the crystals, even though they never really understood them.*

If they had they might never have bred the White, for which we would all have been grateful.

She plucked the vial from the mound of moon-dust where he had placed it, turning it over to watch the viscous contents slosh about. An amusing notion sent a disordered twitch through her whirlwinds, provoking a pulse of curiosity from Clay.

Just thinking, she told him. *About Madame Bondersil and her obsession with the White. She said its blood promised more than all the other variants combined. But, if this can do what your friend claims, all the blood we might drain from the White's corpse would be worth only a fraction of the price we could command for this.*

Can't argue with that. As for the White's blood, seeing the future's sorely overrated. When we kill it the best thing we could do with its corpse is burn it.

Let's hope we get the chance. What is your current location?

Lieutenant Sigoral puts us about seventy miles north-east of the Carn-stadts. We're doing a lot more walking the last few days. Getting harder to find Cerath to ride. Skaggerhill says the herds start to thin the closer you get to Black country, those that do graze here are a sight more jittery.

Tomorrow I'll be flying north where I expect to find another city fallen to the White. Meaning it won't be long before it has sufficient strength to invade Varestia. Urgency is required, Mr. Torcreek.

I'm aware. As for the White's gathering strength, I've been thinking about that. It uses a Blue crystal to change folk into Spoiled. Destroy or steal that and its army ain't growing any bigger.

Meaning it's sure to be well-guarded.

Didn't say it would be easy.

Point taken. Trance again when you reach the mountains. And if you should feel the urge to try this convergence product, make sure your ancient friend drinks it first.

Mr. Lockbar arrived the next day aboard a bulky freighter with instructions to take delivery of the first consignment of weapons. The hard mask of his face betrayed little emotion when Lizanne met him on the wharf to advise two ships would be required to carry the full load. "You have ships at anchor here," he said. "Assign one of them."

"Ships require crews," Lizanne replied. "And that would denude our work-force."

"Then tell the rest to work harder. If they need any encouragement we can always cut the food supplies." He didn't wait for an answer, instead producing a sealed envelope and handing it to her. "The Board has convened a council of war at the Seven Walls. It meets in twelve days. Your attendance is requested."

"Requested?"

Lockbar met her gaze, blinked once and turned away. "I'll expect the second ship to be fully loaded and ready to sail with the morning tide."

"They're going to kill you, you know," Morva said.

Lizanne glanced back from the control panel with a raised eyebrow. "Really?"

"Yes, really," Morva insisted. "Arshav and Ethilda don't share. Now your people are delivering weapons they'll see it as the perfect time to get rid of you. When you go to this war council of theirs they'll either come up with a convenient lie justifying your execution, or they'll arrange an accident. Then the Mount Works and all the weapons will be theirs."

"How shocking," Lizanne observed, turning back to the control panel. She eased the pitch lever to port as a gust of wind pushed the *Firefly*'s nose a few points east of due north. "What terrible people your relatives are."

"You knew," Morva said after a short silence.

"I suspected. I find when dealing with people like your cousins it's best to maintain a healthy paranoia."

"Oh. Will you kill them first then?"

"One of the first lessons I was taught regarding strategy, and your lesson for the day: Never tell anyone your thoughts."

Tekela stirred in the right-hand pilot's seat, coming awake with a groan.

"You let me sleep too long," she muttered, frowning in groggy discomfort as she tapped the clock, which showed four hours past midnight.

"You needed to rest," Lizanne said, relinquishing control of the aerostat as Tekela gripped the lever and settled her feet onto the pedals. Her natural affinity for piloting this machine was evident in the way it seemed to calm at her touch like a horse responding to a familiar rider. The buffeting that had made the gondola thrum faded into a faint vibration and the slight see-saw action of the compass-needle was replaced by a near-perfect stability.

"We're ten miles due south of Subarisk," Lizanne said. She unbuckled from the pilot's seat and moved to the rear of the gondola to peer at the glass viewport Jermayah had set into the floor. Depressing the second button on the Spider, she scanned the ocean passing below, seeing no sign of any patrolling Blue packs.

"Green," she instructed Morva. "I need you to be our eyes whilst I'm in the trance."

Morva nodded and pressed the appropriate button on her own Spider. Jermayah had made new devices for all the Blood-blessed at the Mount Works, an improved design which cut down on the weight and added a quick-release catch for swift removal. Lizanne injected a small amount of Blue, sinking into the trance where Sofiya waited in her fairy-tale forest.

The starting point is clear, Lizanne reported. *We'll hover here then track your progress when the* Viable *commences the attack.*

Acknowledged, Sofiya responded. The trance connection faded almost immediately but not before Lizanne had the opportunity to note that the sky above the forest had taken on a strangely reddish hue, the clouds frozen like a painting of sunset. Lizanne found herself unable to decide if this was a good or a bad sign regarding Sofiya's mental stability. *Sunset means the onset of night,* she thought. *But also the promise of a new day.*

She blinked and found herself back in the gondola, finding to her annoyance that Morva was peering through the starboard port-hole rather than observing the sea below. Her rebuke died, however, when Morva said, "There's something out there."

Lizanne moved swiftly to her side, peering at the darkened sky beyond the port-hole. The cloud-cover was intermittent at this height, slipping by like wisps of powdered silver and growing into an obscuring fog farther out. A short scan of the sky with her Green-enhanced sight revealed nothing.

"Drake?" she asked Morva.

"It was hard to make out, and gone in an instant. It *was* there," she added in response to Lizanne's frown.

"Stand by at the ignition tube," she said, reaching to retrieve her Smoker before returning her gaze to the port-hole. "Light the blood-burner on my order. Tekela, increase height by five hundred feet then begin to circle."

Lizanne levered a round into the Smoker's chamber then opened the starboard hatch. She was obliged to don a pair of welder's goggles before leaning out into the icy chill, eyes roaming the sky. The clouds thinned as Tekela brought the *Firefly* higher, becoming a patchy blanket through which she could see the light of two moons glittering on the ocean. The aerostat tilted as Tekela began to turn, Lizanne gripping the handhold above the hatch and leaning out yet farther, still finding no sign . . .

It was the snap of the beast's wings that saved her, reaching her ears barely a second before it attacked and giving her enough time to lurch back from the hatch. The Red's jaws thrust through the opening and came together less than six inches from Lizanne's flailing foot. The *Firefly* shuddered and went into a spiralling descent as the Red latched its claws onto the gondola's hull. Lizanne had time to register the fact that it was the largest Red she had ever seen, matching the size of an adult Black. Its eyes were bright with hate above the snout, jaws widening and throat rattling as it summoned its flames.

The continuing spin forced Lizanne to clamp a hand to the support strut as she aimed the Smoker one-handed at the beast's eyes and fired. Blood and scales erupted as the explosive round impacted, the snout vanishing from the hatch. From outside came a shrieking roar of pain and rage, followed by a chorus of answering shrieks. *There's more than one,* Lizanne concluded.

Hearing a pained exclamation from the pilot's seat, she rushed forward, finding Tekela clamping a gloved hand on her neck. "Let me see," she said, pulling the hand away to reveal the blackish, reddened welt of un-Blessed skin subjected to undiluted drake blood. Lizanne reached for the satchel containing their reserves of product, extracting a vial of Green and emptying the contents over the burn. Tekela let out a strangled yell, shuddering in her seat.

"Can you still fly this thing?" Lizanne asked her.

Tekela took in a series of ragged breaths before straightening, flexing her fingers to banish the shudder then gripping the control lever. "I can fly," she said, voice hoarse but steady.

"Due south," Lizanne told her, moving back to the hatch and chambering another round. Peering out she saw that the huge Red's attack had forced them back down into the clouds, making observation difficult. As the *Firefly* angled itself southwards a glance to the rear revealed at least six dark shapes, wings sweeping in rapid beats as they drew closer.

"Light the blood-burner," she told Morva, turning to find her clutching the ignition tube with both hands, eyes wide and unseeing and face a frozen pale mask. She stirred when Lizanne reached out to deliver a hard shove to the side of her head, blinking and looking around as if waking from a nightmare. "Light the blood-burner," Lizanne repeated in emphatic and deliberate tones.

Morva stared at her for a second then nodded and put her eye to the tube, depressing the forefinger button on her Spider. The thermoplasmic engine came on-line a split-second later, Lizanne bracing herself in the hatch against the sudden acceleration. Turning her gaze to the rear once more, she saw that one of the pursuing drakes had drawn close enough for her to make out the bloody, smoking wound on the side of its head. As the *Firefly* began to draw away, the drake worked its wings with furious energy to match their speed, spewing flame in copious blasts that fell just short of the aerostat's tail rudder. The huge Red let out another shrieking roar as the *Firefly*'s speed increased, leaving it behind to be swallowed by the clouds, although Lizanne could still hear its roar for what seemed a very long time.

"One hundred and thirty miles an hour," Tekela reported from the pilot's seat, voice strained with forced humour. "A record."

Lizanne closed the hatch and made her way forward, extracting another vial of Green from the satchel. "Drink this," she said, handing it to Tekela, whose face was now grey with suppressed pain. She didn't argue, tipping the entire contents of the vial down her throat and letting out a groan of relief. Lizanne checked her burn, finding the blackening gone but a raw, puckered scar some three inches long remained that no amount of Green could banish.

"It's alright," Tekela said with a weary smile. "I'm sure I've seen worse."

Lizanne squeezed her shoulder and returned to Morva, pushing the Smoker into her trembling hands. "Take this," Lizanne said. "Keep watch. I need to trance again."

"I . . ." Morva said. "I never saw one . . . Not a real one . . ."

"It's always a bracing experience," Lizanne agreed. "Inject some Green. It'll steady your hands."

She settled back into the rear seat and injected Blue, slipping instantly into the trance. Sofiya's mindscape took a few minutes to appear, Lizanne noting that the redness of the sky had deepened considerably.

Captain Trumane has just ordered the attack run, Sofiya informed Lizanne, an oddly serene smile on her lips.

We were intercepted, Lizanne told her. *Reds. Tell the captain to abort the mission.*

Sofiya pursed her lips in momentary consideration, then shook her head. *No, I don't think I'll do that.*

The White will be alerted. Lizanne added a forceful, commanding resonance to her thoughts. *And we can no longer provide warning of any Blues. Abort the mission, Sofiya.*

The other woman replied with a small, apologetic smile. *I'm sorry, Miss Lethridge, but I don't recall signing a contract with you. My contract is with the Ironship Maritime Protectorate, a body which, to all intents and purposes, no longer exists. I believe that makes me effectively a free agent. Excuse me, but I must bid you farewell for now. I really don't want to miss the show.*

SOFIYA!

But she was gone, Lizanne's shouted thoughts vanishing into the void left by her absent mindscape. "Seer damn her to the Travail!" she fumed upon exiting the trance.

"Something wrong?" Morva asked. She stood at the rear port-hole, Lizanne taking some comfort from the fact that the woman's hands no longer shook as she held the carbine.

Lizanne looked through the rear portal at the vortex of disturbed vapour coiling in the *Firefly*'s slip-stream. Turning back to resume the fight with the Reds was the courageous thing to do, another chapter to add to the legend of Miss Blood, a legend she had already made the mistake of believing. "Yes," she said. "But nothing we can do anything about."

CHAPTER 27

Sirus

"Seer damn that bitch!" Catheline's fury chased him all the way to the docks, her seething frustration at the Lethridge woman's escape a constant ache in his head. "She must be here for something. Find out what it is."

Any consideration of shared intimacy had vanished and Sirus had been swiftly dispatched to the harbour to put their defences on alert whilst the White sent every Red in its thrall to scour the skies for the aerostat. Despite the continuing ache of Catheline's anger, Sirus had carefully examined Katarias's shared memory, fixating on one particular image: a young woman seated at the front of the gondola, doll-like face turned to regard the sight of the drake as it attempted to flood the craft with flame. It was no more than a glimpse captured in the instant before a bright flash of agony had seen the Red cast out from the aerostat, thrashing in rage and smelling the stench of its own burnt flesh.

Tekela. She's still alive. He cloaked the knowledge with a flare of genuine fear. The thought of what Catheline might do should she discover these particular memories was truly terrifying.

The security contingent atop the harbour wall was at full strength by the time he arrived, Sirus having already roused the near by garrisons with a thought-command. Forest Spear had charge of the contingent and Sirus joined him on the roof of the old lighthouse that stood to the left of the harbour door.

"Anything?" Sirus asked, speaking in Varsal in deference to the tribal's linguistic preferences.

"Nothing," Forest Spear replied. "But the Blues seem agitated."

It was a two-moon night and the tide was high, the sea only a dozen feet from the top of the wall. The water displayed deceptive calm apart from a disturbance a few hundred yards out, Sirus recognising the signature splashes of a Blue pack. He sent out queries to the look-outs they had posted amongst the ruins of the island forts and received successive negative responses until the most southerly fort reported a ship on the horizon.

Just one vessel, Sirus told Catheline, conveying the image of the fast-moving frigate. *A warship, and a blood-burner.*

Why would they send only one ship? she asked.

Reconnaissance most likely. If it doesn't turn away it will be in range of our cannon in four minutes. Or the Blues could deal with it.

There's no point risking them for only one ship. Blast it out of the water then return to me. I should like a distraction from this most irksome night.

Sirus sent a pulse of agreement and raised a spy-glass. The frigate was close enough for him to make it out now, the white crest below the prow broadening on either side as the paddles churned the sea. Sirus had seen fast blood-burners before but this one was the most impressive, coming on at a rate of knots beyond his experience. Also, she showed no sign of veering off. He began to send a command to the cannon batteries atop the wall to prepare to fire, then saw a bright orange plume erupt on the frigate's fore-deck.

"She's firing," Forest Spear said.

"Pointless at this range," Sirus mused, puzzled by the bright flaming track the projectile painted across the darkened sky. Cannon shells often left a trail of smoke to describe their trajectory but it was only discernible after the shell had impacted on its target. By contrast Sirus was able to track the progress of this shell, if that's what it was, as it ascended to at least a thousand feet in height before commencing a downward plunge. The fiery trail died as it descended but not before Sirus was able to make out a long, pointed shape plummeting down with arrow-like straightness towards the harbour door.

The warning he sent out to the Spoiled on either side of the door came too late, every one within twenty feet of the impact died instantly. The explosion sent Sirus and Forest Spear flying from the lighthouse roof. As he careened through the air Sirus managed to take in the sight of the huge spout of water just in front of the western side of the door, resembling an inverted waterfall as it rose high above. He landed amid a hard rain of falling sea-water, Forest Spear grunting as he came down a few feet away.

They both scrambled to their feet and rushed towards the door, then reared back as the walkway to the left of the lighthouse crumbled and collapsed into a white torrent of water. The western casement holding the harbour door in place had vanished and the door itself blasted aside. The force of the two-moon tide soon tore the door away completely before sweeping on into the harbour.

The ships . . . Sirus thought, watching the harbour waters rise, taking the vessels with them as they deluged the quayside and the warehouses beyond. The inrushing tide didn't stop there, swallowing the mercantile district north of the docks, the ships it carried adding to the destruction as their iron hulls tore buildings into flotsam. He could see bodies amongst the surging fury of the flood, thousands of bodies, all Spoiled and all screaming in confusion in his mind before they blinked into the void.

"I'm sorry," Catheline said, red-black eyes downcast and face tense with genuine regret. Then she sent a bolt of purest agony into Sirus's mind.

He was no stranger to torture and had considered the torments visited upon him by the Imperial Cadre to be the worst pain he was ever likely to endure. He had been wrong. His body bent taut like a bow, jaws clamped together so tight he couldn't even scream as he convulsed. His mind fragmented under the weight of agony, rationality disappearing into a jumbled haze of discordant memory, glimpsed only for an instant before the pain took them away. There was one image he managed to hold on to longer than the others. *Tekela's face* . . . The scorn she had shown him in Morsvale, the pity in Feros and the fear as she looked upon Katarias. Her face became his saviour, like the wreckage he had clung to after the battle with the Ironship cruiser, a single point of comfort in the storm of pain.

When it ended he found himself lying on the floor of Catheline's ballroom, one-half of his face damp from the drool that had gushed from his lips. The relief was almost like pain in itself, being such a jarring contrast to what he had just endured, and he found he had to choke down a scream.

"Even if we could refloat the ships," he heard Morradin say, "without a working harbour Subarisk is useless as a port."

"Tell me, at least, that you caught that fucking ship," Catheline said.

"The Blues gave chase but she was so confounded fast." Morradin's voice was controlled but possessed of a wary tone, as if expecting his own bout of punishment at any second. "The Blues tracked it south for a time but it seems they can't swim faster than a blood-burner, at least not this one."

Catheline let out a sigh of exasperation. "How can just one shell from one ship destroy an entire city?"

"It wasn't a shell," Sirus said, grimacing as he got to his feet. "It was a rocket."

The council of war were standing a few feet away, each one maintaining a carefully neutral visage, except for Catheline, who offered him a brief, relieved smile.

He wanted to feed you to his brood, she said in his mind. *I persuaded him otherwise, told him you were still our best hope for victory. Don't prove me a liar, General.*

"A rocket?" Morradin said, heavy brows bunched in doubt. "Never seen one with that kind of range or that kind of punch."

"Clearly, this one is something new," Sirus replied, straightening his tunic and moving to Catheline's side. "Launched out of range of our guns during a two-moon tide. And not aimed at the harbour door itself but the sea just in front of it. Water has a strange effect on explosions, at depth the pressure greatly magnifies their power. Even a comparatively small amount of explosive would have achieved the same result provided it was placed with sufficient accuracy." He paused, scaled brows raised in reluctant admiration. "Miss Lethridge is either very clever or has some very clever friends."

He turned his gaze to Veilmist. "Casualties?"

"Twenty thousand, six hundred and forty-two Spoiled dead," she replied, prompt as ever. "Plus five thousand two hundred captives who hadn't yet been converted. Also"—she shot a guarded look at Catheline—"two hundred and twenty-three Greens and eighteen Reds."

So few? Sirus thought, masking his regret with fear. "The fleet?" he asked instead.

"We have five ships in working order, only one a warship."

Sirus looked at Morradin, who kept his face rigid although their shared minds reached the same conclusion. "So, an invasion of Varestia is now impossible," Catheline said, reading their thoughts.

"Not for several months," Sirus replied. "At least not by sea. There is one alternative."

"A land invasion," Morradin elaborated. "We march overland to the Varestian Peninsular. There are numerous towns and villages en route where more recruits can be harvested."

"What's to stop our enemies simply sailing away?" Catheline enquired.

"We can assume the Varestians will stay and defend their homeland," Sirus said. "And since it seems clear that Miss Lethridge is now allied with them, so will she."

"You assume a great deal, General."

"With Varestia in our hands we will have all the ships we'll need. Enough ships to carry this army to every corner of the world."

Catheline fell silent, her face taking on the unfocused blankness that told of communion with the White. From outside came a roar, rich in frustration and loud enough to shake the windows. Catheline began to tremble as the roar descended into a low growl that persisted for some time. Eventually it faded and she let out a gasp, falling to her knees, shuddering. Sirus crouched at her side, placing a tentative hand on her shoulder, feeling the flesh tremble beneath her shawl.

"We . . ." she began, voice faltering into a cough. Catheline swallowed and spoke on, "We have leave to march on Varestia, but He wishes to educate our army first."

Sirus's gaze snapped to Morradin as the marshal let out a strangled yell and collapsed to the floor, swiftly followed by Veilmist, Forest Spear and the other Spoiled present. Only Sirus and Catheline remained immune. From beyond the windows came a strange murmuration, the massed discordant chorus of thousands of souls thrashing in pain but unable to scream. Sirus moved to the window, knowing what he would see. He could feel their pain and confusion, his entire army lying amidst the ruined streets of Subarisk, convulsing beneath the weight of the White's punishment.

"He promises so much," Catheline said, moving to join him at the window. Sirus felt her hand slip into his, grasping it tight. "But great works require great sacrifice."

CHAPTER 28

Clay

The Carnstadt Mountains were less tall than the Coppersoles but somehow more threatening in appearance. They rose in sheer-sided monoliths from a thick blanket of encroaching jungle, flanks shrouded in drifting mist. The company had already spotted their first Black the day before, a youthful female according to Skaggerhill's experienced opinion. They had dismounted from their final Cerath ride the previous morning and spent the next two days trekking through the increasingly verdant plains north of the mountains. The Black appeared at noon, a dark silhouette in the sky that circled them well out of longrifle range before flying off to the south.

"Guess they know we're coming," Clay said, watching the drake fade into the distance.

"Think she's gonna go tell her folks they got visitors?" Skaggerhill said, a note of humour in his voice that faded when he saw Clay's expression.

"Yeah," Clay told him. "That's exactly what I think she's gonna do."

"They're still animals," Skaggerhill insisted, a certain stubborn sullenness creasing his brow. "It's a mistake to imagine they think like us, talk like us."

"These ain't the dumb beasts you imagined them to be all these years," Clay replied. "You gotta know that after everything we seen. And no, they don't think like us, or talk like us. But they do think." He turned his gaze to the south once more, the Black now no more than a speck above the mountains cresting the horizon. "And they do talk."

The plains gave way to sparse forest as they neared the mountains, which soon grew into thick jungle. Clay called a halt with the onset of evening and they settled down to eat a meal of roasted Cerath meat. Whilst the others talked over their options Clay sat in silent contemplation of the map Hilemore had given him.

"Climbing the first mountain we come to seems like the best bet," his uncle said. "Find us a nesting drake and Miss Kriz can do what she does with the crystal. Females don't fly when they're nesting."

"You think they'll let us get anywhere near a nest, Captain?" Skaggerhill said. "Nesting female will be sure to have a big mean male close by who's likely to roast us before we manage to scale more than a few feet. I say we do what we did last time, 'cept we try for a capture 'stead of a kill. Preacher'll shoot us some game and we leave the carcass out in a clearing. Black'll come along sooner or later, most likely a young 'un as they're less wary than the adults, be easier to rope up too since they're smaller. After that the lady can do her thing and . . ." Skaggerhill shrugged. "I guess we'll see iffen it works."

"Worth a try, I guess," Braddon said after some thought. "Be right tricky, though. Might end up killing any beast we catch, given how they can be . . ."

"No," Clay interrupted, looking up from his map. "We ain't doing any of that."

"Then what d'you suggest, cuz?" Loriabeth asked. "We all just go strolling on in there and wait for one to come say hello?"

"Not all." Clay scanned them with a steady gaze, making sure they all understood his next words to be sincere and not subject to argument. "Just me and Kriz. The rest of you are gonna skirt the mountains and make for the coast. I'll trance with the lieutenant along the way to let you know how we're doing. If I don't trance for three days straight, head for Stockcombe."

Loriabeth let out a disparaging laugh, quickly echoed by his uncle. "Clay, if you think I'm gonna let you walk in there on your own . . ."

"They remember!"

Braddon fell silent, his laughter fading as Clay's shout echoed through the jungle.

"Drakes ain't like us, like I said," Clay went on, voice lowered. "One thing that makes 'em different is their memory. It don't die with them, they carry it. Every Black holds the memory of its parents, and its grandparents, and their grandparents, going all the way back for thousands of years.

You've been here before so they know your scent and they know what you did. They'll kill you."

"I ain't been here before," Loriabeth said. "I should come too."

"You carry your pa's scent, cuz," Clay said, shaking his head. "I ain't risking it." Braddon began to say something more but Clay cut him off. "It's settled, Uncle. You made me captain, well, I'm giving orders. You head for the coast." He turned to Kriz. "We'll set off in the morning, if you're willing."

He detected a slight hesitation before she replied with a nod and a forced smile. "Of course. There was a city here in my time. I'm keen to see if there's anything left of it."

They parted the next morning after a brief farewell that saw Loriabeth fighting tears and Braddon make a last and fruitless attempt to persuade Clay to another course of action.

"Course is set, Uncle," he replied, turning to walk away before pausing for a second to add, "And don't try tracking after us."

To be certain, he called a halt after he and Kriz had covered the first few miles and waited, hearing and seeing no sign that they were being followed. "Is it true?" Kriz whispered as they crouched in the undergrowth.

"What?" Clay asked.

"About drake memory. It's not just something you told them to spare them danger?"

"'Course not." He turned to her, frowning in realisation. "You didn't know?"

Her face took on a sheepish grimace. "Clearly we had much left to discover."

"Seems to me the more I find out about your people, the more dumb they seem. You didn't know how the crystals work but you used them anyway. You didn't know what the White was capable of but that didn't stop you breeding the damn thing. Also, turns out you barely know shit about the animals you spent years studying."

"All knowledge is . . ."

"Precious and dangerous. Yeah, I remember." Clay waited for a few moments more and, satisfied they were in fact travelling alone, rose and resumed the southward trek towards the nearest mountain. He stopped when he realised Kriz wasn't following, turning back to find her standing with her gaze averted, hands fidgeting on the straps of her back.

"What?" he asked her.

"Thousands of years," she said. "Their memory goes back thousands of years."

"So?"

"So . . ." She raised her gaze, eyes wary with reluctant admission. "So, they might well remember me. Remember what I did, all those years ago."

Clay took a step towards her, finding his voice had hardened when he spoke on. "What you did?"

"Experiments." She closed her eyes and let out a heavy sigh. "Dissections."

Clay came to a halt and they stared at each other for a time, Kriz forcing herself to meet his eyes, Clay realising the depth of his ignorance about this woman.

"As you said," she went on, breaking a lengthy silence, "we barely knew shit about them."

"We can still find the others," he said in a flat weary voice, starting back down the trail. "You'll go with them . . ."

"No." She was emphatic, unmoving. "No. You need me to activate the crystal. If they remember . . . then we'll just have to hope the crystal conveys sufficient understanding for them to hear a heart-felt apology."

"Do we climb?" Kriz asked, her voice betraying an ill-concealed reluctance as she gazed up at the granite flanks of the mountain. A thick mist concealed the summit and, although the cliff-face before them featured numerous ledges and cracks, Clay found the prospect of climbing it distinctly unappealing.

He glanced around at the jungle canopy surrounding the low, grassy hill where they stood. Once clear of the jungle the air took on a clammy chill adding to the sense of exposure. The clouds that seemed to linger constantly over the mountains could conceal any manner of threats and Clay was beset by a persistent sense that a dark-winged shape would come swooping out of the white sky at any moment.

"No," he said, unslinging his pack. "We'll camp here tonight. Keep moving south come the morning."

"There's no cover," she pointed out, casting a hand at the sky.

"That's kinda the point. We want to be found, remember?" He set his pack down, resting a hand on the bulbous shape within. *Come a long way, young 'un,* he thought, smoothing his palm over the egg's grainy shell. *Hope your kin are pleased to see you.*

They took turns on watch through the night, which proved uneventful if somewhat tense. Like all jungles this one generated a nerve-straining chorus of combined animal chatter and creaking branches. The only potential sign of a drake came during Clay's watch in the small hours when the night was blackest. The clouds parted for a short time allowing a patch of moonlight to play over the jungle. Clay gazed at the pale blue light playing on the tree-tops, making them glitter as it caught the innumerable leaves, then started as a swift shadow swept across the scene. His gaze jerked upwards, honed instincts making one hand reach for his revolver whilst the other went to his wallet of product. He checked himself and forced his hands back into his lap, eyes roving the sky as the clouds closed in again. He heard no drake call, nor flap of wings but the feeling of being observed raised a prickle to his skin.

"I know you're up there," he whispered, hearing the quaver in his voice. "Why not come say hello?"

His hand went to the vials around his neck, the fruits of his sojourn in the enclave beneath the ice. White blood and Black heart-blood, the existence of which he had chosen to keep from Captain Hilemore. He hadn't explicitly told Lizanne either but, given her facility for trance communication, it was possible she already knew. Once again, the notion of drinking White played through his mind.

It might show me where to go, he thought. *Where to find them.* The vial's contents were dark, catching only a marginal gleam from the camp-fire. With no plasmologist dilutions to preserve it the blood had congealed, making it appear a thick, oily sludge he knew would be the foulest thing he had ever tasted. *Only when everything else has failed,* he decided, letting it fall from his grasp and turning his gaze on the vial of heart-blood.

It was similarly congealed but even darker. The pain of drinking the Blue heart-blood still lingered in his mind. Also, he knew now the connection was not inevitable. This was not a magic potion from some fable that would cast a spell over any drake he chose. It allowed the joining of minds and his control over Jack had been possible only because the drake's mind had been fractured and susceptible to remoulding. Miss Ethelynne had forged a connection with Lutharon but he had been an infant at the time. Somehow he doubted a sane adult Black would present an easier prospect.

Another last resort, he concluded, concealing the vials beneath his shirt and looking at his pack and the round shape within. *Looks like it'll be down to you, young 'un.*

They moved on come the morning, Clay following a course that would lead them into the heart of the Carnstadts. The jungle was similar to the country east of Krystaline Lake, though the trees were less tall and the ground-level vegetation thicker. He was wary at first, recognising this as perfect Green country and walking with his revolver drawn. He holstered it after trekking for several hours during which he saw no claw tracks on the jungle floor or any of the markings Greens habitually left on tree-trunks to mark their territory. *Not Green country,* he thought, peering up at the sky through the canopy. *They steer well clear of this place. This is Black country.*

"So, what was it called?" he asked Kriz when they paused in a clearing some miles on. "The city that used to sit here?"

"Devos Eluzica," she said, speaking in her own language as they both did most of the time now. "It means 'The Divine Tree.'" She gave a wistful sigh as she gazed around at the enclosing wall of jungle. "It was beautiful, Clay. An entire city built by a subsect of the Devos Caste. They chose to build without the aid of any crystals, in fact shunning their use entirely, believing the Benefactors had sent them as a test rather than a gift."

"A test?" Clay asked. "Of what?"

"It's all a little confused," she said, drinking from her canteen and frowning in remembrance. "But then I always had trouble comprehending the vagaries of the Devos. It had something to do with our worthiness, our value as a species. They felt we had lessened ourselves by using the crystals, become as pampered children in the eyes of the Benefactors. Only by re-building our civilisation with our own hands could we win back their favour; otherwise, they were sure to punish us with a great cataclysm of some kind."

"Maybe they had a point, given what was coming and all."

"They were hypocrites. The city they built here was small at first. Just a series of interlinked houses crafted to sit amongst the tree-tops in supposed harmony with nature. But as time went on it grew taller, coming to resemble a great tree itself, adorned with glowing baubles when night fell. But they would never have been able to build it without the engineering knowledge acquired since the dawn of the crystal age. And, as the decades passed, successive generations crafted convenient sophistry to enable them to use crystals, eventually forgetting their heresy altogether, and the great tree grew ever taller. In my time, it rose higher than some of the mountains." She paused, voice becoming sombre and her fond smile fading. "It must have been quite a sight when it fell."

Clay was about to ask more then stopped when his gaze alighted on something in the gloom beyond Kriz's shoulder: the fire-light playing on the outline of a crouched figure. He scrambled to his feet, drawing his revolver, Kriz doing the same. "What is it?" she whispered, moving to his side.

"Company." Clay trained his revolver on the outline, eyes flicking left and right for any sign of another intruder, seeing only darkened jungle. After several long seconds in which nothing happened he began to discern the unnatural stillness of the crouched figure. *Even a Spoiled couldn't sit still for that long,* he decided, nevertheless keeping the revolver aimed at the figure as he crept closer.

"Seer-damn statue," he muttered in relief as the figure came fully into view. The statue was cracked and mostly covered with vines. However, enough of its original form remained to make out the shape of a kneeling man, hands clasped together but head raised to stare directly ahead.

"Spoiled," Clay said, running a hand over the statue's scaled features, feeling the stunted spines on its forehead. He was no scholar of the arts but there was something familiar about the way the stone had been worked, the sharp angles and blockiness of the statue putting him in mind of the hidden city near Krystaline Lake. But there were also subtle differences, a more curved line than he had seen before and, as a quick inspection of the statue's base confirmed, it had been decorated with a markedly different form of writing. The characters adorning the statues in the hidden city had a flowing, almost organic quality whilst these were much more regular and dense, almost like words in a printed book.

"Miss Ethy might've been able to read it," he murmured, running a hand over the inscription.

"Who?" Kriz asked.

"Friend of mine. She died. And I was too dumb to look at her notebooks when I had the chance."

"Oh." She reached out to smooth a hand over the statue's upper arm. "Finely worked. Whoever made this was very skilled. But there was nothing like it in my time."

"Yeah, I guessed it didn't come from your holy tree city."

Clay straightened as something occurred to him. *Where there's one there'll be more.* He extracted a vial of Green from his wallet and drank a small amount, casting his gaze about at the revealed jungle. "There," he said, pointing as his enhanced gaze picked out another crouching figure some twenty yards away. A brief inspection revealed it to be mostly identical to the first one, albeit with a greater level of damage. Further investigation revealed another two statues farther on, each spaced at what seemed to be precisely the same distance.

"And there's another one," Clay said, nodding to the next figure in what was clearly a long line of statues. "Looks like we got a trail to follow come the morning."

They counted over two hundred statues by the time the trail ended in a broad clearing about three miles from where they had camped. They changed in form as the trail continued, the kneeling figures rising to a crouch, then standing, then with arms stretched out in front. Clay began to suspect they were in fact looking at a sequence depicting the same Spoiled captured at different stages in some kind of ritual. The final statue was the most damaged of all. The head was gone and half the figure's vine-enmeshed torso had tumbled into dust long ago. One outstretched arm remained, however, the hand closed into a fist with a stunted finger extended.

The Artisan's memory, he realised, following the direction of the pointed finger. They were in the same clearing from the memory Lizanne had shared with him, but instead of the statue pointing to a jagged outline above the tree-tops, it pointed only at empty sky. "Must've fallen to ruin since," he murmured.

"What must have?" Kriz asked.

"A temple," he said, starting forward. "This way . . ."

He staggered as a gust of wind swept down from above, raising enough dust to blind him whilst his ears were assailed by the roar of an enraged drake. A shudder ran through the ground as a large Black descended directly to his front, wings spread wide and mouth open. More shudders followed in quick succession, Clay whirling to see two more Blacks landing to their rear.

"The crystal," Clay said and Kriz immediately reached into her pocket. The Black to their front let out a squawk of alarm at this, lowering itself into a crouch, smoke rising from its nostrils.

"Hey!" Clay raised both arms, presenting his empty hands to the Black, hoping to buy time for Kriz to activate the crystal. "We're friends! See, no weapons! And we brought a gift."

He unshouldered his pack, swiftly undoing the ties and extracting what was inside. "Peace offering," he said, setting the egg down in front of the Black. Its aggressive posture didn't change, though it did lower its gaze a fraction to take in the sight of the egg. Letting out a suspicious grunt, the Black dipped its head to sniff the egg, huffing in what Clay took for recognition. "Young 'un needs a new home," he said. "Brung him a long way to find it."

The Black's eyes narrowed, a low, guttural rumble sounding from its throat as it enclosed the egg in its claw, dragging it back as it hissed in warning. Clay watched as the beast's gaze tracked from him to Kriz where it lingered, narrowed further then flared into a deep angry recognition. *Shit!* he thought, turning and dragging Kriz into a protective huddle as the Black roared and unleashed its flames.

CHAPTER 29

Lizanne

"You were right," Lizanne told Captain Trumane. "Mrs. Griffan is not suited to service aboard your ship."

Trumane glanced to where Sofiya was fussing over some of the children, her face showing a rare animation and joy. "The mission was a success," he said. "I believe she acquitted herself well."

"She should have passed on my order to abort," Lizanne insisted. "We were compromised."

"War-time operations are not intelligence missions, Miss Lethridge." Trumane's tone was mild but his gaze betrayed a twitch of resentment she realised came from her use of the word "order." "They cannot be abandoned due to mere compromise," Trumane went on. "War is an exercise in the management and acceptance of risk. If Mrs. Griffan had passed on your *order* I may well have discounted it in any case, considering the advantage we stood to gain. A sea-borne invasion of the Red Tides is now impossible, at least for some considerable time. In short, the risk was worth it."

Is it pride, Lizanne wondered, trying not to let her burgeoning anger show on her face, *that makes me dislike this man so? Do I hunger for power? Like Countess Sefka, or the Electress.*

Despite her resentment she knew there was merit in his judgement. It was two days since the *Viable Opportunity* had returned from its mission, during which time Tekela and Lizanne had made a brief reconnaissance flight. They flew in daylight with Morva and a volunteer from the militia, both armed with mini-Growlers. They kept a wary eye on the surrounding sky as the aerostat drew close enough to Subarisk to confirm it mostly ruined by flooding and the White's fleet wrecked, save for a few vessels seen floating in the harbour. More disturbingly, there was no sign of any drakes or, as they drifted lower, no Spoiled either.

Lizanne had decided to risk an inland flight, having Morva stand by to ignite the blood-burner as they flew north. The tail end of the White's army came into view some ten miles beyond the city, the huge host raising a pall of brownish dust as it snaked away across the landscape. The sight of dark-winged specks flying above the horde was enough to convince Lizanne to turn back. The conclusion was obvious: The White had abandoned Subarisk and commenced an overland march. Its eventual destination was not hard to divine. They had won victory and precious time, but this war was very far from over.

"Ah," Trumane said, turning towards her father's workshop as a sudden upsurge in noise rose from beneath the awning. "I believe we are about to be treated to an unveiling."

The work-force had been granted the afternoon off to witness this event, a reward for exceeding their production targets and also a pragmatic measure intended to obviate the exhaustion of many. The patch of bare ground that lay in front of the workshop had been converted into a park of sorts complete with benches and gravel paths. Some former gardeners from Lossermark had even planted flower-beds, though it would be some weeks before they blossomed. It was mainly used as a playground, carpenters and metal-workers having used their infrequent spare time to construct swings and a climbing frame for the children. Today the park was crowded with off-duty workers, mostly clad in their overalls, though Lizanne saw some who had taken the time to change into finer garb somehow salvaged from their previous lives. Despite the tiredness evident on most faces, there was a distinct sense of celebration in the air, as if the unveiling of the professor's latest marvel might even be a cause for optimism.

The noise from the workshop rose to a greater pitch, sounding to Lizanne like the buzzing of a thousand giant hornets. Ripples spread across the awning and it began to snap with increasing energy before the ties holding it in place were either deliberately undone or it was torn away by the gale raging beneath. As the awning peeled back from the workshop's roof a large curved shape began to rise drawing an awed gasp from the onlooking crowd. Lizanne had expected the Mark II aerostat to be larger than the *Firefly*, but this was on another scale entirely.

The gas envelope that rose from the workshop was at least four times the size of the *Firefly* and different in shape. Instead of an elongated egg it put Lizanne in mind of a headless whale, being flatter and wider. Also, its smooth surface was broken by a cupola on its topside. She instantly recognised her father's tall form standing in the cupola, giving a hesitant wave as a cheer rose from the crowd at the sight of him. Four rudders protruded from the stern, two vertical and two horizontal, swivelling in response to Tekela's touch on the controls.

The aerostat rose higher, the source of the great buzzing noise soon revealed as two propelling engines fitted to either side of the gondola that seemed to sprout like some organic growth from the craft's underside. The engines were angled so that the propellers pointed at the ground, blurred to invisibility as they pushed the aerostat higher still, drawing it clear of the workshop. It slowed to a hover some fifty feet off the ground at which point the spectators all burst into applause.

"Impressive," Captain Trumane said, Lizanne turning to see a corner of his mouth curling in an infrequently seen expression of pleasure, or perhaps anticipation. "I wonder if it can lift a rocket."

"It looks like a whale," Morva said. "That's what we should call it, the *Flying Whale*."

"We're not calling her that," Tekela insisted. "She's the *Typhoon*. I'm the pilot so I get to name her." She turned to Lizanne with an expectant smile. "Isn't that so?"

"I couldn't care less if you call her the *Flying Turd*," Lizanne said. "As long as she performs as expected."

Her gaze tracked over the interior of the gondola. After a brief circuit of the Mount the new aerostat had been tethered to one of the taller chimneys. Lizanne, Morva and Trumane had climbed a rope ladder for an inspection. She estimated the compartment was sufficiently spacious for at least a dozen crew with wide hatches in the hull to which gun mountings had already been fitted.

"She can carry two Thumpers or five Growlers," Professor Lethridge said, descending a ladder which extended from the centre of the floor into an opening in the ceiling. "Or a mix of the two. Plus another Growler in the upper observation point."

"A clever modification, Father," she complimented him. "Drakes do like to attack from above."

"It might not be entirely necessary," Captain Trumane put in, glancing up from an inspection of the control panel at the front of the gondola. "Is this altitude indicator's maximum level accurate, Graysen?"

"A reasonable estimation based on the lifting capacity," the professor replied. "There will be variations depending on atmospheric conditions, of course."

"Ten thousand feet," Captain Trumane said, tapping one of the dials. "I'm no drake-ologist but I believe no Red has ever been observed to fly higher than six thousand feet. Something to do with the thinness of the air, I believe."

"Speed?" Lizanne asked her father, although it was Tekela who answered.

"On standard power we think she might get up to eighty miles per hour," she said. "Two engines, you see? Once the blood-burners are lit, however . . ." She smiled. "Well, I'm very keen to find out just how fast she'll go."

"So," Lizanne mused, moving to one of the gun mountings, "we have the advantage of height, speed and fire-power."

"Whilst they possess greater numbers," Trumane pointed out. "One ship doesn't make a fleet."

"With the materials already on hand," Professor Lethridge said after a moment's mental calculation, "we could produce perhaps two a month."

"That won't be enough," Lizanne said. "Destroying the White's ships has bought us time, but we can expect its army to reach the Varestian Peninsular within four to five weeks." *Growing larger with every village and town it destroys along the way,* she added to herself.

"It's a matter of labour rather than resources," her father said. "With an expanded work-force . . ."

"You'll have it," she promised. "It'll mean reduced production of weapons but that can't be helped. Without more of these I doubt we have a chance." She turned to Tekela. "I'm appointing you Chief Pilot. Your first task is to identify and train others in how to fly this thing."

Tekela's face took on a puzzled frown. "How do I do that?"

"Find people with relevant experience. Former helmsmen, locomotive-drivers and the like. Madame Hakugen should be able to help. Failing that just ask people to volunteer. I'm sure there are many keen to get out of the manufactory." She turned to her father. "Captain Trumane voiced a pertinent question earlier," she said, "regarding rockets."

Ethilda and Arshav convened their war council in the observation tower crowning the Navigation. Lizanne had arrived alone in the *Firefly* an hour before, piloting it herself to land on the building's expansive front lawn. Mr. Lockbar and his gang duly arrived, failing to deliver a formal greeting of any kind before conducting a thorough and ungentle search of her person for product and weapons. He then escorted her to the meeting where Lizanne was surprised to find Alzar Lokaras in attendance along with a half dozen captains of varying clan allegiances.

Ethilda hadn't bothered to introduce any of the captains, though a few possessed sufficient manners to make themselves known to Lizanne before the meeting began. The most courteous was a trim woman clad in a long, waxed-canvas jacket and sea-boots, the least expensive garb of any other captain present. She was about Lizanne's height and build and would have seemed much the same age but for her hair and lined face.

"Mirram Kashiel," she said, removing her broad-brimmed hat and performing a low bow. "Captain of the *Sunrider* and Chief of Clan Kashiel."

"Lizanne Lethridge . . ."

"Oh, I know who you are. They call you Miss Blood." The woman straightened with a grin. "But I won't. Bit of a silly name, don't you think?"

"Extremely. I didn't choose it."

"Got our first delivery of your marvellous guns yesterday. Very impressive, 'specially the big ones. Could do with a lot more, though."

"They're on their way," Lizanne assured her.

"If you're finished with your chatter," Arshav broke in, eyes hard and face set in as serious an expression as Lizanne had yet seen. "We have a war to plan." He turned to Ethilda as the room fell silent. "Mother?"

Ethilda moved to stand next to the oil painting depicting the Varestian region. She held a thin ivory baton and wore a dress which had been adorned with various military accoutrements, including shoulder epaulets and a yellow sash of the kind worn by marshals of the late Mandinorian Imperium. Lizanne somehow knew Ethilda was already imagining the portrait of her in this dress that would one day adorn the halls of this building.

"Subarisk," Ethilda said, tapping the tip of the baton to the relevant section of the painting. "Fallen to our enemy and since abandoned, thanks to an unsanctioned action by our supposed ally." She fixed Lizanne with a glare before moving the baton westward. "Denied ships, the enemy is now marching towards the peninsular."

"Where they will no doubt visit all manner of vile havoc on every Varestian they get they claws on," Arshav added. Unlike his mother he didn't glare, though Lizanne recognised the set of his features, having seen the face of many a man set on murder.

Subarisk, Lizanne decided, recalling Morva's words. *That will be their pretext.*

"With ships they would have invaded the Red Tides within days," she pointed out, keeping her tone mild. "Now we have weeks to prepare."

"For a land campaign," Ethilda said. "Varestians are not accustomed to fighting on land. At sea we would have had a much better chance of victory, especially with the new weapons."

A small murmur of agreement came from the other captains, though by no means all. "Many ships aren't yet armed," Alzar Lokaras said, voice flat, though his animosity to his cousins shone in his eyes clearly enough. "And there are only a few hundred of the new carbines. I also note my cousin Arshav has barely managed to gather more than ten thousand fighters."

"I can't be held accountable for the cowardice of others," Arshav said, a snarl creeping into his voice.

"It isn't cowardice, cousin," Alzar replied. "It's you. No true Varestian wants the stain on their honour that comes from serving under your flag."

"Careful, cousin," Arshav returned, his hand straying towards the hilt of his sabre. "Challenges may be forbidden in time of war, but don't imagine that will protect you."

Alzar met Arshav's gaze squarely, a sneer forming on his lips. "From what?"

"Enough!" Ethilda barked as Arshav's fist closed on the sabre hilt. "This avails us nothing." She focused her gaze on Lizanne. "We have a disloyal ally to deal with."

Lizanne had prepared an initial response to this trap, a short but effective speech highlighting Arshav's and Ethilda's many and obvious faults in both character and judgement. It was designed to stoke the pre-existing resentments of the other captains, perhaps even to the point where they might be tempted to stage a coup. But the Okanas's clumsy intrigues were proving sufficiently tiresome for her to proceed directly to the alternative option.

"I take it Mr. Lockbar is outside awaiting some form of signal," she said, arching a quizzical eyebrow at Ethilda. "Soon he'll come bursting in to arrest me for breach of contract whereupon I'll be marched off to some dungeon, perhaps making a doomed and fatal escape attempt along the way."

Ethilda stared at her with an expression that mingled poorly hidden surprise with unconcealed animosity, her eyes flicking towards Arshav as they exchanged an uncertain glance. Lizanne gave a disgusted sigh and strode towards the large telescope opposite the huge oil-painted map. She swivelled the tube on the tripod to point it towards the large window, setting the correct angle before checking the focus through the eyepiece.

"Please," she said, stepping back and gesturing at the telescope. "I should like you to see my father's latest invention," she added as mother and son exchanged another glance. They continued to stand in rigid and enraged immobility so Alzar stepped forward.

"What is that?" he asked, brows creasing as he squinted through the eyepiece.

"She's called the *Typhoon*," Lizanne replied. "A Mark II aerostat, currently hovering at a height of six thousand feet, well outside the range of any current artillery piece. Please note the object below the gondola."

"I see it," Alzar said after some more squinting.

"We call that the Tinkerer Mark I rocket. It's identical to the one that destroyed the harbour door at Subarisk. You will also note it is aimed directly at this building. Should I fail to fly away from the Seven Walls within the hour it will be fired, and please harbour no illusions that it will miss its target."

She turned to Ethilda and Arshav, speaking in clear, precise tones to ensure there would be no mistaking her intent. "Our contract is hereby voided on grounds of corporate duplicity and negotiations undertaken in bad faith. Should you make any attempt to reassert the provisions of said contract the *Typhoon* will return and destroy this building. It will then destroy every ship your family owns. The Mount Works Manufacturing Company is of this moment a separate entity and free to negotiate its own contracts. Your business, however, is not welcome and your authority over the Varestian region is no longer recognised."

She stepped away from the telescope and bowed to the other attendees. "Captains, should you wish to engage in serious discussions regarding the defence of the Red Tides you can find me at Blaska Sound. All munitions will be supplied free of charge to any who choose to ally with us." She bowed again and moved to the door. "Good day."

CHAPTER 30

Hilemore

"I'm sorry, Corrick. But you can expect no help."

Hilemore reread the last line of the communique several times, it being the only sentence to convey any sense of intimacy. The rest of the missive contained a brief and depressing summary of recent events in Mandinor and assurances that she had advised the Voters Rights Alliance in this city to render assistance to him *"subject to a reciprocal arrangement compatible with your honour."* This was followed shortly after by an observation he felt had been intended as much for his hosts' eyes as his: *"I'm sure all parties will benefit from your advice and calm counsel."*

"So you see," Coll said after Hilemore had finished. "You want our help, you help us win this city back."

"That," Hilemore replied, "is not her intent."

"Reads that way to me," the stocky youth replied to a murmur of agreement from the other committee members. "We got supplies, you want 'em. So take your boat across the harbour and pound that bitch Kulvetch's headquarters to rubble . . ."

"That's not going to happen," Hilemore interrupted, glancing over the communique once more before consigning it to his pocket. Lacking intimacy or not, it was the only correspondence he had received from Lewella in many months and he found himself unwilling to part with it. "You forget that I know Free Woman Tythencroft far better than any of you. Her intention, misguided though I believe it to be, is for me to negotiate a ceasefire between the Voters Rights Alliance and corporate forces, and subsequently to assume leadership of this city."

Hilemore rose from his stool, scanning each of the young, angry faces before him and feeling far older than his twenty-eight years. *Twenty-nine,* he reminded himself, recalling his uncelebrated birthday on the ice. "Clearly," he said, "had she met Colonel Kulvetch or any of you lot, she would have known this to be a hopeless prospect, as is any further negotiation with me."

"Wait!" Jillett said as he started towards the door. Hilemore turned back to find her on her feet exchanging hard glares with her fellow committee members. She snatched her arm away as Coll reached out to restrain her. "We need to know," she hissed at him.

"Know what?" Hilemore enquired.

"Your report to Free Woman Tythencroft," she said. "How much of it is true?"

Hilemore had been circumspect in revealing full details of his eventful life since boarding the *Viable Opportunity* all those months ago, but saw little point in being overly secretive. His account had omitted the exact nature of the Longrifles' mission to the Interior but confirmed its importance in resolving what he had termed "the current emergency." "Every word," he said.

"So there's really an army of drakes and Spoiled rampaging across the world," Jillett persisted.

"Indeed there is."

"We ain't seen 'em," Coll said. "How do we know this ain't all a pile of horse shit?"

"There is an entire fleet of merchant ships in your harbour terrified of putting to sea," Hilemore pointed out. "Also, how long has it been since a Contractor crew, or anyone else for that matter, turned up at the gates?"

More exchanging of glances, though much of the previous hostility had given way to uncertainty.

"The world is in chaos," Hilemore went on, "whilst you sit here indulging your petty squabbles and childish politics. I don't know why you've been spared so far, but sooner or later they will be coming for you. Still"—he straightened his tunic and turned to leave once more—"on the bright side you may well have slaughtered each other before they get here."

"Kulvetch won't sell to you 'less you fight for her!" Coll called after him. "Where you gonna get your supplies?"

Hilemore had to admit it was a good question. Although, as he made his way back to the wharf and the crowded harbour came into view, it occurred to him that there was in fact a third party in this port who might be open to more rational negotiation.

"You want to sail away from the only safe port left on this continent?" Captain Tidelow asked, weathered brow creasing in doubt. "So's we can go off and fight in a war all the way across the ocean?"

"I do," Hilemore replied, voice raised so that all the other captains present could hear it. It appeared the master of every vessel in the harbour had come in answer to his invitation, so many in fact that he had been obliged to hold this conference on the *Superior's* fore-deck. This had the added benefit of ensuring that both Colonel Kulvetch and the Voter rebels would be made fully aware of the proceedings. The captains were a mixed lot, North and South Mandinorian, Dalcian and Varestian, even a few Corvantines. Some had charge of company vessels but most were independents and habitually inclined to resent corporate authority.

"On whose say-so?" one of the other captains asked, a Dalcian woman of diminutive height but with the bearing and the scars that told of a piratical past.

"I am issuing no orders," Hilemore said. "Merely appealing to reason and common sense."

"Sailing off to fight a horde of drakes and Spoiled doesn't sound particularly sensible," one of the Corvantine captains observed in accented but precisely spoken Mandinorian. He was a tall man with a studious look, though his salt-reddened cheeks bespoke many years at sea. "It took weeks of hard perilous sailing to find a refuge for my ship and my crew," the Corvantine went on. "One it will not be easy to persuade them to give up."

"This is not a refuge," Hilemore told him. "It's a trap, and you are snared here by your own delusions. Do you really wish to be caught between these hate-filled children when they start fighting again? Because they will. And even if they don't you are anchored in what may be the last occupied human settlement in Arradsia. Any time you spend here is borrowed time."

He allowed a moment to let his words sink in, knowing each skipper present had their own epic of survival to ponder and that he was asking a great deal. "I make no promises and offer no reassurances," he continued. "Only a chance to join a fight that needs fighting."

"How're we s'posed to get there?" the Dalcian woman asked. "My coal bunker's barely a third full."

"I don't have the reserves to make it out of the harbour," the Corvantine added.

"We pool our resources," Hilemore told them. "Gather together all the coal we have and decide how many bunkers we can fill."

"Meaning you intend some ships to be abandoned," the Corvantine concluded.

Hilemore faced them, replying in a tone he hoped was both confident and regretful. "Yes." This provoked an instant growl of protest but he continued, voice loud enough to override the grumbling. "There are ships at anchor here in such poor repair they'll never sail again. You all know this. Others are too frail and slow for any kind of war-service. Their crews will be allocated to other ships, no sailor will be left behind."

"Pox on this," the Dalcian woman said, casting a dismissive hand at Hilemore and stomping towards the rail. She added something in her own tongue as she swung a leg over the side and began to scale the rope netting to her boat. Hilemore's Dalcian was rusty and imperfect but this phrase was one he had heard often enough to translate: *"Corporate swine are always selling you shit and telling you it's gold."*

Hilemore resisted the urge to plead with them as other captains quickly followed the Dalcian woman's example. He had neither the authority nor the power to compel them, and his conscience forbade making any false promises as to the likelihood of victory or any rich rewards. Had the situation been reversed he had to admit that he might well have taken the same course. Therefore, it was surprising to find about half the captains still standing on the fore-deck when the exodus had ended. The Corvantine had remained, as had Captain Tidelow.

"Not all my crew will come," the Blue-hunter skipper mused, fingers playing through his lengthy beard. "But I reckon I can talk maybe two-thirds of them round."

"My crew will follow my orders," the Corvantine asserted. "They're all former sailors in the Imperial Navy, as am I. And we're very tired of running."

The subsequent discussion with the other skippers confirmed similar sentiments, although with one important proviso. "We can't fight without weapons," the Corvantine said. He had introduced himself as Captain Gurkan of the merchant vessel *Holloway*, a swift three-paddle clipper built for the tea trade. Although not a blood-burner Hilemore knew she would make perhaps the most valuable addition to his makeshift flotilla.

"Weapons are being produced in a manufactory in Varestia," he assured them. "New weapons of far greater power and accuracy than anything we have."

"Lots of sea 'twixt here and there," Tidelow pointed out. "Blues too, I'd reckon. And we don't have your pet monster to guide us any more."

"I'm reliably informed the Blues are concentrated in Varestian and Corvantine waters. Meaning we should have an unmolested journey, at least until we arrive."

Hilemore clasped his hands together, briskly moving on before Tidelow asked him to elaborate. In actuality he had no such intelligence regarding the whereabouts of any Blue drakes but a lack of certainty was an obstacle just now, and a modicum of dishonesty a necessity. "I shall require full manifests of all cargo, crew and supplies for each of your ships. My chief engineer will conduct a thorough inspection of all vessels and will have the final word on what sails and what doesn't."

In all, Chief Bozware advised that some eighteen vessels out of a total of twenty-two were in a sufficient state of repair to make an ocean voyage to Varestia. Unfortunately, the parlous state of the combined fuel stocks meant they had only enough coal for a dozen vessels.

"Twelve's better than one, Chief," Hilemore said.

"Turns out there's a jewel in the dung pile," Bozware went on, handing Hilemore one of the manifests. The name ECT *Endeavour* was scrawled at the top of the sheet in laboured Mandinorian above a crew list of only six names and a cargo schedule containing mostly worthless sundries but one item of considerable importance.

"One full flask of Red," Hilemore read.

"She's a blood-burner," the chief confirmed. "Fast Eastern Conglomerate Mail Packet working the route between Dalcia and Arradsia. Crew told me all about their misfortunes when I went to look her over. Turns out a Blue gave them a terrible mauling south of the Razor Sea, lost their skipper, company Blood-blessed and most of their mates. Somehow they managed to sail her all the way here. The upper works are a mess but the hull and the mechanicals are sound."

"She'll need crew," Hilemore said. "A Blood-blessed . . . and a captain."

"W hat do you think?" he asked Zenida a short while later. They had taken a boat to the *Endeavour*, the sparse crew welcoming them aboard with a refreshing display of relief and gratitude.

"Thought we was gonna just rot here," the bosun said, apparently the only senior sailor left on board. He was a burly fellow but young for his rank, Hilemore suspecting he had earned it mostly through physical strength and, judging by the way the other crewmen avoided his eye, no small amount of intimidation. Still, he had managed to salvage his ship and sail it for hundreds of miles to a safe harbour, which indicated at least some facility for leadership.

"Nothing some decent carpentry and a lick of paint wouldn't fix," Zenida said, voice rich in irony as she surveyed the scorched and partly shattered wheel-house.

"I'll assign you a work crew," Hilemore told her.

"Me?" She stared at him in bafflement for a second, then frowned as realisation dawned. "A new command," she mused, a mix of wariness and anticipation playing over her features as she once again looked the ship over. "Who will fire the *Viable*'s engine?"

"Lieutenant Sigoral, or Mr. Torcreek."

"Assuming either of them actually survives to make it here."

"There is at least one other Blood-blessed in this port. In extremis, I'm sure I can persuade her to join us."

"Persuade or kidnap?"

"I did say, in extremis."

"You always were a ruthless man, Captain." She let out a soft laugh as she scanned the ugly mess of the vessel's upper deck. The *Endeavour* was a one-stack, two-paddle ship with a narrow hull. *Built for speed not comfort,* Hilemore's grandfather would have said.

"I had such fine hopes for my next ship," Zenida commented. "I even had the plans drawn up. She would have been called the *Flameheart*, fastest ship afloat, and one day Akina would have been her captain."

"That can all still happen," Hilemore said. "When this war's over."

"Perhaps." Zenida gave a wistful laugh. "The plans would need to be redone. I suspect all future ships will be propeller-driven like the *Superior*. We stand at the dawn of a new age, Captain. Let's hope we live to see it, eh?"

"We will," Hilemore said, voice flat with a certainty they both knew to be false.

Zenida nodded and cast a final glance over the ship. "I accept my new commission," she said. "But with one condition."

"**I** am not staying here!"

Hilemore ducked to let the spanner Akina had thrown sail over his head, making a loud clang as it collided with the engine-room bulkhead. The girl's grease-besmirched face was bunched in fury as she reached into her tool-box for another missile.

"Akina!" Zenida said, voice hard with a rarely used parental authority. She stepped between her daughter and Hilemore, snaring the girl's wrist in a tight grip as she drew her arm back for another throw. "This is my wish, not his," she said in quietly spoken Varestian. "Are you my daughter?" She tugged Akina's arm, the wrench in her grasp falling to the deck. "Are you my crew?"

Akina stared up at her mother, the fury vanished from her face to be replaced with naked fear. "I should be with you," she said in a hoarse whisper. "Don't leave me here, please, Mama."

Zenida released Akina's arm, Hilemore seeing how she resisted the impulse to pull her close. "Daughters obey their mothers," she said. "Crew obey their captains. You are ordered to stay here and follow our sea-brother's instructions. You are his crew now."

Akina pressed herself to her mother, arms enclosing her waist, the only sob Hilemore had ever heard from her escaping her lips and she clung on tight. Feeling like an intruder, he turned away, moving to the hatchway then pausing as a low whistle sounded from the speaking-tube.

"Signal from the crow's nest, sir," Talmant's tinny voice reported. "Drake in sight overhead."

"It's definitely a Red, sir," Steelfine said, spy-glass raised high as he tracked the winged silhouette across the sky. "Just one, though."

"That'll change soon enough," Hilemore heard Scrimshine mutter at his back.

He scanned the surrounding ships, seeing the multitude of sailors crowding the decks, faces all turned skyward.

"It's just out of rifle-range," Steelfine went on. "That mad Contractor marksman might've been able to take it down. The rest of us would just be wasting ammunition. We could try a shot with the pivot-gun."

"Also a waste of ammunition, Number One," Hilemore said. "It's already seen us in any case." From his conversations with Clay he was well aware that what one drake saw, so did the White. *It knows this ship,* he thought. *And now it knows where we are.*

"Signal lamp, sir," Talmant said, pointing to a blinking light on one of the neighbouring ships. It was a broad-beamed one-paddle freighter with Dalcian lettering on the hull. Hilemore could see the diminutive pirate captain at the lamp, signalling in plain code: *I changed my mind.*

Within minutes more lamps began blinking on other ships and soon it appeared every vessel in the harbour was sending out variations of the same message. "It appears," Hilemore said, "we have a fleet after all."

CHAPTER 31

Clay

He pulled Kriz close, trying to cover them both with his duster. A blast of heat prickled his skin as the Black's flames swept over the Green leather. Then the heat abruptly vanished and the ground shuddered as something heavy came to earth near by, Clay grimacing as a drake's roar filled his ears. It was different from the challenging screech of the Black that had just tried to roast them. This was the deep, throaty roar of a mature male, and he had heard it before.

He drew the duster back to find himself bathed in shadow. A large claw scraped the earth close to his head and a glance upwards revealed a massive scaled rib-cage that swelled and contracted as the beast above let out another roar. It was answered by a chorus of screeches from the other drakes, the huge shape shifting above Clay and Kriz, the air whooshing as its tail whipped and its wings flared. Clay saw the other two Blacks spread their own wings, but in obvious supplication rather than challenge. They lowered their heads and backed away, emitting small, low-pitched grunts as they retreated. The third Black, however, was not so easily cowed.

Clay ducked as another blast of flame rushed between the male Black's rear legs. The duster protected them from the worst of it but not all, Clay letting out a shout as fire licked at the back of his left hand, scorching the flesh. The shadow and the claw disappeared as the male Black leapt, the ground trembling when it landed a split-second later.

Clay looked up from his scorched hand to see the two drakes locked in a fierce if brief struggle. The larger male had the smaller female pinned beneath his forelegs, jaws clamped on her throat. She let out a defiant roar, earning a fierce, punishing shake of the head from the male. He held her there for several seconds, jaws slowly tightening until she grew still and let out a low-pitched grunt.

The male released her, folding his wings and settling into a resting crouch, tail twisting placidly. He didn't look at the female as she rose and darted forward to retrieve the egg she had been offered. Clutching the prize in her jaws, she cast a final glance of deepest antipathy at Clay and Kriz, then turned about and launched herself into the air after a short sprint. Clay turned at the snap of wings, seeing the other two drakes following suit.

"Here," Kriz said, taking out a vial of Green and tipping half the contents over his hand. Clay took a moment to let the product banish his pain before approaching the male, having motioned for Kriz to stay put.

He moved into the beast's eye-line, extending a tentative hand to smooth the scales of his foreleg. Lutharon let out a low rumble as the human skin met his own, the muscle shuddering much as it had done back on the *Superior* the night Clay sent him away. "Hello again, big fella," Clay said. "I gotta say, it's awful nice to be remembered."

Lutharon lowered his head, letting out a rumble of greeting that took on a much more ominous tone when his gaze flicked to Kriz. She stood at a decent remove, the Black crystal hovering before her and producing a familiar tinkle as it expanded.

"What are you doing?" Clay asked.

"What we came here for," she said, gaze locked on Lutharon. Clay saw that she held a vial of Red in her hand. "It needs energy to activate," she said.

"Be better if I did it," Clay said, moving towards her. "He knows me."

"And hates me." Kriz's eyes were wide, features the rigid mask of one who has recently escaped death. "All of them do. If I do this, perhaps they won't . . ."

Her words were drowned out as Lutharon let out another roar, wings flaring once more as he sank into a threat stance. Clay noted how the drake's eyes were focused on the now fully expanded crystal. It revolved slowly, resembling some kind of hole in space in the way it exuded no light save for a small glimmer on the tips of its spikes.

"Stop," Clay said. "He doesn't like it."

"He doesn't have to . . ."

Lutharon gave a sudden intake of breath followed by the throaty rattle that told of disgorging combustible gas. Clay lunged towards Kriz, dragging her aside. Lutharon let out a fierce and sustained jet of flame, aimed not at Kriz but at the crystal. With Kriz's focus distracted the stream of Black keeping it in the air vanished and it fell to the ground, a dark smudge amidst the torrent of flame.

Lutharon's fire died, leaving a sizable blaze in its wake. Clay squinted through the flames to make out the jagged shape of the crystal. It seemed to be completely undamaged, the centre of it still as dark as before but the spikes glowing brighter. Lutharon evidently found this unacceptable and began to take another large breath.

"Don't!" Clay shouted, moving to stand in front of the Black, arms raised.

"Clay . . ." Kriz said. "It's active."

"What?" He turned, blinking in confusion at the sight that confronted him.

The crystal hung in the air once more, risen from the flames. Its jagged spikes now glowed with a fierce white light, though its centre retained the same absolute darkness.

"You doing this?" he asked Kriz.

"No. The fire. Energy, remember?"

Clay took a step back as the crystal drifted closer, finding himself backing into Lutharon. The Black didn't move, Clay glancing up to see that the drake's gaze was now fixed on the crystal, not with rage, but rapt fascination.

"How do we shut it down . . ." Clay's voice trailed off as his gaze returned to the crystal, finding it snared by the dark, light swallowing void at the centre. *Like a hole in the world,* he thought before he fainted. *Something you can fall into . . .*

"You look older."

Clay blinked, finding his eyes filled with bright sunlight and his head buzzing with disorientation. He staggered a little, steadying as a hand gripped his elbow. "Quite a trick you've pulled this time, Claydon," a young female voice said. "Making your way in here. You must tell me how you did it."

He blinked again and his vision cleared to reveal the small, oval face of a diminutive woman about his own age. Despite her youth he knew her instantly. It was the eyes, as bright, open and inquisitive as he remembered, and the half smile playing on her lips. It held a hint of mockery but betrayed mostly the simple affection of greeting a valued friend.

"Miss Ethy," he said, the name emerging in a laugh as he drew her into an embrace.

"Just Ethelynne will do," she said, voice muffled against his shoulder. "As I told you before."

She drew back, eyes searching his face as a frown put a single line in her otherwise smooth forehead. "How long has it been since . . . ?" She grimaced and shrugged. "Well, you know."

"Months," he said, his joy muted by the knowledge that this was a trance. *Another ghost,* he thought. *Like Silverpin.*

He looked around seeing a tall mountain range. It wasn't the grim majesty of the Coppersoles or the jungle giants of the Carnstadts. Here the air was far colder, and the peaks not as tall and placed closer together to create a maze of deeply weathered stone. The landscape had a gnarled, twisted appearance conveying an impression of ruin, even though there was no sign of civilisation.

"Only months?" Ethelynne asked, gaze still roaming his face. "You really need to take better care of yourself."

"A lot happened after you . . . left."

"And not for the good, I assume?"

He shook his head and gestured at their surroundings. "I've never been here," he said. "Wherever it is. How can I craft a trance from somewhere I've never seen?"

Her smile returned, the mockery more in evidence now. "You haven't. This isn't your mind, it's Lutharon's."

Clay took another survey of the mountain range, finding it as perfect a mindscape as he had ever seen. Even Lizanne would have had trouble matching the precision of detail, the slight variation in the chilled air. But he saw no vestige of drake perception in it. His trances with Jack and the drake memories Ethelynne had shared gave him an understanding of how they perceived the world, and it wasn't like this.

"No drake saw this," he said. "This is a human memory."

"Quite right. How perceptive you've become."

She turned, moving to the edge of the broad summit on which they stood. "The Cragmines of western Arradsia," she said, spreading her arms wide. "As captured by my very own eyes quite some time ago, when I was still spry enough to climb all the way up here. Fascinating geography, don't you think? No one's really all that sure how they formed. There is evidence of glaciation but that's only a partial explanation."

"I got a new friend who might be able to help with that," he muttered, fighting a sudden lurch in his chest as he watched her take in the view. She seemed so real, so alive it inevitably summoned memories of her death, a death he hadn't been able to prevent. *A ghost,* he reminded himself. *Living in Lutharon's mind like Silverpin lived in mine.*

"The White . . ." he began but she waved him to silence.

"I do seem to recall your doing your damnedest to ensure I didn't follow you," she said.

"If you hadn't maybe you'd be talking to my ghost just now."

"Ghost?" She pursed her lips. "A name that fits, I suppose. Though I would hate to think Lutharon feels he's being haunted."

"It was you. You kept him by me after the White rose."

"Not entirely. I merely encouraged an impulse that was already there. He does seem to like you, you know. Thank you for making him leave, by the way. He would certainly have perished on the ice."

"Least I could do." He looked around at the mountains once more. "Was it the heart-blood? Is that what kept you here?"

"Lutharon and I shared minds for many years. I suppose I am the echo of that connection." She beckoned to him and started to descend the steep, rocky slope below the summit. "Come on. I would like you to see something."

Clay followed her, traversing a series of narrow ledges and granite boulders protruding from the mountain side. Ethelynne appeared almost childlike as she hopped from ledge to boulder with all the sure-footed skill of someone who had followed this course many times. Clay was markedly more careful, forcing her to loiter with amused impatience as he navigated the often-damp rock.

"You never did like heights, as I recall," she observed. "It does rather make one wonder, though. I mean, would it make any difference if you fell?

We are both just a collection of memories. It's not like we have any bones to break."

"Feel free to try it," Clay replied, inching his way along a ledge. "I ain't too keen on finding out."

"No, me either." She leapt nimbly onto a granite outcrop and paused to peer down. "But it's strange that it hasn't occurred to me before. All the time spent in this place and I've never been tempted to just jump and see if I go splat."

"Maybe Lutharon won't let you. It's his head. Guess he makes the rules."

A ten-minute descent brought them to a narrow crevice where the flank of the mountain levelled out. An infant Black crouched at the edge of the fissure, small wings and tail twitching as it peered into the depths, a series of soft plaintive grunts issuing from its snout.

"This is where I found him," Ethelynne said, moving to crouch a short distance from the keening infant. "All those years ago."

The infant whirled at her approach, a warning hiss emerging from its mouth. It seemed to have no awareness of Clay, its gaze fixed on Ethelynne, jaws snapping as she extended a hand holding a morsel of meat. Clay moved to the edge of the crevice, looking down to see the large, crumpled form of an adult Black far below.

"He was barely two days old when the Contractors killed her," Ethelynne said. "I couldn't just leave him to perish. But there was only one way to save him. And it scared me."

"Heart-blood," Clay said, eyes lingering on the drake corpse. "I had my own taste not long ago. Ain't got any plans to repeat it anytime soon."

"You drank heart-blood?" Ethelynne straightened, a mix of sympathy and fascination on her face. "What species?"

"Blue. A great and fearsome Blue of terrible reputation . . . He died."

"I'm sorry."

Clay nodded, casting a final glance at the dead drake and moving away. "We got things to talk about," he said. "Plans to make."

"Plans?"

"Yeah. War plans. The White's got itself an army now, and they're killing a lotta people. Those they don't kill they turn into Spoiled. We're fighting it, but things ain't going so well."

"And you want Lutharon to join your war?"

"Not just him. The Blacks. All of them. They fought it before, we know that. We need them to fight it again, and finish it this time."

Ethelynne folded her arms, her head tilting and lips pursing in an expression he knew indicated her fearsome mind was hard at work. "Just how did you get in here, Claydon?" she asked. "You still haven't told me."

He looked down, exerting his own will in a brief experiment as he wasn't sure he possessed any power here. The rock beneath his feet obligingly turned to moon-dust, a portion of which he raised and moulded into the Black crystal.

"What is that?" Ethelynne asked, moving closer to extend a finger to one of the glowing spikes. Clay assumed it had been quite some time since she had seen something so completely unfamiliar.

"Be easier to show you," he said, expanding his will further. The surrounding mountains transformed into the forest that greeted him when he first stepped into the strange world beneath the ice. "Welcome to the last enclave of the Philos Caste . . ."

"Incredible." Ethelynne let out a small laugh as the enclave faded around them, shifting back into the Cragmines. He had shown her all of it, every scrap of memory he could summon regarding the enclave, every morsel of information he had acquired.

"All those years in the Interior," Ethelynne went on, shaking her head. "I had no idea, no clue whatsoever. I thought the temple builders must have been the first people to walk this continent. But all the wonders they crafted were just an echo of something greater." She paused, summoning the vision of the Black crystal he had shared. Ethelynne's gaze darkened as she stared at the glowing spikes revolving around the void. "Or perhaps," she said, "it was something worse. Something best consigned to the past."

"We need it," Clay insisted. "We need it to ally with the Blacks . . ."

"Ally? Or enslave? The ancients did remarkable things, but committed the most vile acts in the process. There are memories in here, deep and very old. So nightmarish and confused it's hard to make sense of them, and they're so painful I only tried once. Were I to delve deeper would I find your friend there, scalpel in hand?"

Clay saw little point in denial. "Yeah," he said. "She'd be there. But she ain't what she used to be. None of us are. And it don't change the fact that we got a war to fight. When the White's done with us you know it'll come for them. It remembers and it don't forgive. Lutharon and all his kin will have to fight it anyways. With us they got a better chance."

The rock beneath their feet began to shudder and the sky darkened from misty grey to red-tinged black. A cacophony of fracturing rock assailed Clay's ears as the mountains began to twist and grow. Cliff-faces became wings and boulders claws. What had been a jagged ridge slowly revealed itself as the spiny neck of a huge drake. They rose all around, wings spreading, tails and necks uncoiling. The crescendo of shattered stone subsided into a low murmur, reminding Clay of distant thunder as the host of giant drakes lowered their heads to regard him, eyes shining with a bright red glow.

"It's not me you need to convince, Claydon," Ethelynne told him. "It's them."

CHAPTER 32

Lizanne

"Remarkable," Alzar Lokaras said, looking at the photostats arrayed on the *Viable*'s ward-room table. They had been taken by a nervous young man who had emerged from the ranks of the Mount Works employees some days before, camera in hand, to offer his services. He was an apprentice photostatist who increasingly found the life of a manufactory worker less than pleasant. It had been Captain Trumane's notion to pack him onto the *Typhoon* for a reconnaissance flight to the north. The aerostat was able to hover in place long enough for an exposure of decent length and Jermayah provided the required chemicals and equipment to develop the plates. The result was a visual record of northern Varestia far more accurate than any map, Imperial cartographers having neglected the area through fear of banditry for many years.

"You can see the passes clearly," Alzar went on, finger tapping three points on a series of photostats that had been aligned to produce a continuous image. It captured the central span of the mountain range dominating the region the Varestians referred to as "the Neck." There were three channels through the mountains, each separated by a ten-mile gap with the largest and most easily traversed one in the centre. This was known as the Grand Cut, whilst the eastern pass was the Small Cut and the western the Little Cut.

"The gateways to the peninsular," Alzar went on. "They used to be fortified but the defences were destroyed by the Corvantines during the occupation. No one's bothered to repair them since."

"Meaning the enemy's line of advance is wide open," Trumane said.

There were only three of them in the ward-room, Alzar acting as the sole representative for the host of Varestian captains who had deserted

Ethilda and Arshav's authority. A dozen pirate vessels and armed freighters had arrived in Blaska Sound that morning. Alzar duly came ashore with a delegation to inform Lizanne that he was now Admiral of the Varestian Defence League before enquiring as to the progress of his niece's education.

"She does very well," Lizanne assured him, gesturing to where Morva waited near by. "Feel free to ask her yourself."

"Business comes first," he said after the briefest glance in Morva's direction. "Here," he went on, handing Lizanne a folded document. "I know how you corporate types like your contracts."

The contract terms were sparse and simple: The Mount Works Manufacturing Company would supply weapons and personnel to assist in the defence of the Varestian Peninsular in return for continued safe harbour within Blaska Sound and provision of food and medical supplies guaranteed by the Varestian Defence League. There was no mention of patents, shares or allocation of future profits. Lizanne thought it a clumsily worded document but, as she doubted it would ever require scrutiny before an arbitration court in any case, was happy to sign it there on the wharf.

"Not necessarily," she told Trumane now, sliding another photostat across the table showing a magnified view of the Grand Cut. The image had been captured at a slight angle, giving an impression of the steepness of the cliffs rising on either side of the track that snaked through the pass. "Even without fortifications, the terrain would seem to offer a singular opportunity to a defender."

"With your aerial contraption we could shift some cannon onto the cliff-tops," Alzar agreed after a moment's consideration. "And your newfangled guns. Any army that tries to make it through will suffer a fearful toll."

"You forget their command of the air," Trumane said. "We know the enemy is far from stupid. They'll send drakes to secure the cliff-tops before marching through." His gaze narrowed as he turned it on Lizanne. "I believe Miss Lethridge has another stratagem in mind."

"I do," Lizanne said, playing a hand across the three passes. "We use explosive to block the Small and Little Cuts, leaving the Grand Cut open." She pointed to the northern end of the pass. "We will still have to mount a meaningful defence, but it will take the form of a fighting withdrawal so as to draw the White's forces in, and we'll need all the Blood-blessed in our ranks and all the product we can gather to make it work."

"I brought twenty-three Blood-blessed," Alzar said. "But only half can be spared. The rest are needed to power the few blood-burners we possess. As for product." He grimaced and shrugged. "Stocks are thinner by the day and those that hold them loath to sell except at extortionate prices."

"Write promissory notes," Lizanne advised. "Make the Mount Works Manufactory the guarantor if you like. If that fails the stocks will just have to be seized. The time for observing the legal niceties of trade is over."

She turned back to the photostats, her finger tracing to a point two-thirds of the way along the Grand Cut. "The pass is at its narrowest here," she said. "And overlooked by a promontory. I propose that we prepare the promontory with explosives and once the bulk of the White's army reaches this point we bring it down. All three passes will be blocked and we will have killed a large number of enemy troops."

"It won't stop them," Trumane said. "The passes can still be cleared. And the White will be sure to gather more strength to clear the rubble."

"It will buy us time," Lizanne replied. "As for the White's ability to gather strength, I have an idea about that."

She watched Tinkerer's face closely as Makario lifted his hands from the pianola and the last note faded. The *Follies of Cevokas*, according to the musician's judgement, was as inane and trite a piece of musical doggerel as he had ever heard. However, once he had reproduced the entire score on paper close examination of the text revealed one short melody of interest in the third act. It was hidden in a lyrically dense song known as "Cevokas the Genius," in which the ever-pompous titular character reeled off a list of his intellectual achievements accompanied by a jaunty high-tempo tune. Once the tempo was slowed something far more elegant and familiar began to emerge.

"It's definitely her," Makario reported. "Empress Azireh's handiwork concealed within a comic operetta of little distinction. It's rather like finding a pearl in a pile of turds."

"A shared joke, perhaps," Lizanne mused, her gaze still lingering on Tinkerer, his face as pale and immobile as before. "A secret between lovers." She imagined Azireh playing the tune for Alestine, first at the original speed then faster, perhaps improvising the lyrics. *How they must have giggled together,* she thought. *Another secret shared between the princess and the Fiddly Girl.*

"When this is over," she said to Makario, "you might want to examine some other operettas of the period. I suspect Azireh penned quite a few. Doctor," she went on, glancing at Dr. Weygrand, "if you would, please."

Madame Hakugen had given over a large two-storey building for use as the settlement's clinic, though it had required considerable repair and cleaning before Dr. Weygrand consented to occupy it. Tinkerer had been placed in an upstairs room along with a pianola where Makario laboured to craft the music that might wake him. However, the artificer remained as immobile as ever, forcing Lizanne to conclude that another trance was required.

The doctor betrayed some hesitation before moving to the bottle suspended from a metal stand at Tinkerer's bedside. The bottle contained a mix of saline and powdered nutrients needed to keep the comatose patient alive these past weeks. A rubber tube trailed from it, ending in a needle inserted into the vein in Tinkerer's forearm. Despite the attentions of Dr. Weygrand and his small staff of orderlies, Tinkerer had grown ever more thin and pale as the days went by and Lizanne didn't need any expert advice to deduce he didn't have many more left.

"The last trance didn't do him much good," Weygrand pointed out. He had prepared a syringe of Blue, high-quality Ironship product provided by Alzar Lokaras, but seemed reluctant to push the needle into the cork seal at the base of the bottle. "Who's to say the next one won't kill him?"

"He's already dying," Lizanne said. "And we need him. Please proceed, Doctor."

Weygrand nodded, swallowing a sigh as he depressed the plunger on the syringe, sending a cloud of amber fluid into the bottle. Lizanne waited until the product had faded, indicating it was all now running through Tinkerer's veins, then gestured for Makario to play the tune once more. She unstoppered her own vial of Blue and kept careful watch on Tinkerer's face as the melody filled the room. At first there was no reaction, then she saw the faint circular shadow on his closed lids as his eyes began to move—a clear signal of a dream state.

"This may take some time," she said, raising the vial to her lips.

"I'm not going anywhere," Makario promised, which made her smile just as the room disappeared and she found herself in darkness.

At first she thought she had been cast into a void, some blank vacuum left by Tinkerer's vanished mind, but then she saw a burst of yellow flame directly ahead. It was bright enough to illuminate the uneven walls of the tunnel in which she stood, at the same time filling it with a roar of pain and rage of sufficient volume to force her to clamp her hands over her ears. The flame faded along with the roar, although this time the darkness wasn't so absolute. The flames had evidently found a target judging by the flickering glow rising from a dark shape lying at what she recognised as the end of this tunnel.

Lizanne started forward then stopped as her foot came close to tripping over something. Looking down she saw the disordered and scaled features of a Spoiled, slackened in death. *Alestine's friend from the clearing,* she realised, recognising the monochrome war-paint on the Spoiled's face. *Tree Speaker.*

Another gout of flame snapped her gaze to the end of the tunnel, although the roar that accompanied it was far weaker now. As the flames faded she heard a ragged rasp of indrawn breath followed by a high-pitched rattle that told of a drake in immense pain. Remembering Alestine's warning about the real risk of injury in this trance, she waited until the rattle had died away before starting forward again. Sinking to her haunches at the end of the tunnel, she crouched close to the wall and peered out at a huge cavern, the floor of which featured a tower of some kind.

Bone tower, she surmised, recalling Clay's shared memories of the White's lair and Arberus's tale of his expeditions to the Interior. The tower rose from the centre of a scorched circle on the cavern floor. Slumped against its base was a White Drake, blood seeping in a thick stream from the large iron spike protruding from its rib-cage. It let out a plaintive moan as Lizanne stepped out from the tunnel, but seemed to show no sign of noticing her presence, tail coiling in twitches of diminishing intensity. Lizanne judged its size as perhaps half that of the beast Clay had found beneath the Coppersoles, which still made it larger than an adult Red and comparable to a youthful Black. The only light came from the flaming corpse lying a few yards within the scorched circle. The flames had consumed it so completely it was impossible to tell if it had been human or Spoiled.

Lizanne gave a start as a cascade of dust descended from above, along with a shower of displaced stones. Her gaze jerked upwards to the roof of the cavern, her ears detecting the sound of claws frantically skittering on stone.

"We thought there would only be one."

Lizanne spun in alarm as Alestine stepped into the light, offering a grin of welcome that seemed impossibly broad, too many teeth gleaming in the glow of the fire. *Burned,* Lizanne realised as Alestine turned her gaze upward. Much of the flesh around her lower jaw and upper neck had been seared, along with her left ear. The impossible grin was in fact the result of half her lips having been burned away.

"Actually, there were two," Alestine went on, speaking in a wet rasp. "A male and a female, and she was pregnant. I had hoped her wounds were fatal." She pointed at a stream of blood visible in the continuing cascade of dust and stone. "That she would crawl away and die somewhere along with the egg growing in her womb. But in my heart I knew it could never be that simple." Her gaze settled on the dying male White. "I had to know. Excuse me a moment."

Alestine abruptly collapsed onto her hands and knees and began a slow painful crawl towards the dying White. It lay almost immobile now, chest rising and falling in ever-slower and more laboured breaths. But its eyes were still bright, Lizanne recognising the hate in its gaze as Alestine crawled near.

"One of my last inventions," she said upon reaching the beast's side, her voice free of the pain that made her arm tremble as she raised it to grip the iron spike protruding from the rib-cage. "Or rediscoveries to be fully accurate. The ancients had an alloy that could pierce anything if fashioned into a point and projected with sufficient force. I had enough Black for a killing thrust, but we only had one spear."

She gripped the spike tighter and jerked it, provoking a convulsive thrash from the White. Blood steamed in the heat blossoming from its maw as it raised its head, neck coiling in a final attempt to roast its tormentor. Alestine raised herself up, grunting with the effort of twisting the spike then driving it deeper. The White's last flames subsided into smoke, its head thudding onto the stone floor. The tail and the wings continued to twitch but the dull, empty gleam of its eyes told the tale clearly.

"Tree Speaker's people carried the old stories," Alestine said, slumping against the dead drake's flank. "Treasured them throughout the ages. At first, I could scarcely believe what they told me. The White was real, and once it came close to burning this continent to ash, perhaps the rest of the world into the bargain. So great was its malice that it twisted the people here, made them into deformed two-legged versions of itself, a whole continent of willing slaves. But there were those who resisted, kept the kernel of humanity burning within themselves, and in time they fought back, with the help of the Blacks."

"How?" Lizanne said, moving closer to crouch at the Artisan's side. "How did they beat it?"

"The White could control all drakes but the Blacks. It could control humans it Spoiled, but not the Blood-blessed. It needed something to match them, match their abilities, but it never found it. Through battle and guile and courage the Blood-blessed freed enough Spoiled to ally with the Blacks and bring it down, though by the time the war was won their civilisation that once flourished here had fallen to rubble. The enslaved Spoiled, maddened by the loss of their god, hunted their free enemies mercilessly. After decades and centuries of persecution, only Tree Speaker and his tribe were left."

Alestine cast a stricken, wet-eyed glance at the burning corpse lying close by. "Meeting me sealed their fate. When I told them I had deciphered writings telling of an ancient White sleeping in the caverns beneath this temple they had no choice but to follow me. Every warrior they sent died here, meaning their young will be defenceless. The other Spoiled will destroy them now. But what else could I do?" She turned to Lizanne, tears streaming from her eyes into her ruined flesh. "It couldn't be allowed to rise again. They knew that."

She held Lizanne's gaze, beseeching some kind of absolution. But Lizanne was not a priest.

"What did it need?" she said, seeing the distress on Alestine's face dissipate at the hardness of her tone. "You said it needed something to match the Blood-blessed. What was it?"

"What else could it be?" the Artisan said with a shrug. "A Blood-blessed of its own of course. One with the right kind of mind."

"What kind of mind?"

Alestine blinked and turned away, grunting in pain as she shifted closer to the rivulet of blood still flowing from the wound the iron spike had torn in the White's hide. "Madness is a common trait amongst humans," she said. "But the non-Blessed are many and we are few. And it needed to be the right pitch of madness, coloured with enough cruelty, envy and resentment to see what it intended for the world as right and just. All those centuries ago it never found the right mind. In your time, it would be more fortunate."

She leaned closer to the stream of blood, face tense in expectation and fear.

"You drank," Lizanne said. "You drank and saw that it would rise again."

"I saw . . ." Alestine lifted a trembling hand and touched her fingers to the blood, wincing as the tips turned white in the flow. "Many things, Lizanne. Terrible and beautiful, cruel and kind. For that is life, and I saw it all. But there was a greater gift to be had here."

She reached into her pocket and drew out a flask, drinking down the contents in a few gulps before tossing it aside. Lizanne saw the strength flood Alestine's body as the Green took hold, the woman rising to her feet and taking a firmer grip on the iron spike with both hands. A few hard tugs and she had drawn it out, raising it to let the diminishing flames play on the dark, near-black substance on the spear-point tip.

"The heart-blood of a White," she said. "For someone who had spent much of her life seeking knowledge, how could I resist it?"

Alestine pressed her ruined mouth to the spear-point, jerking in agony as the blood made its way past her exposed teeth and down her throat. The cavern disappeared, leaving them floating in what Lizanne at first took for some kind of giant fish-bowl. Forms swirled around them, some indistinct, others vibrant and shimmering with colour. They were constantly shifting, a formless misty swirl one second then a human face or a fully realised body, sometimes naked, sometimes clothed. There were men and women, infants and elderly. Lizanne realised she could hear them, a thousand voices babbling at once. *Not voices,* she realised. *Thoughts. These are minds.*

"Indeed they are," Alestine said. She floated close by, whole and beautiful once again, a mix of wonder and dismay on her face as she surveyed the swirling minds. "Every Blood-blessed drawing breath at the moment I drank the White's blood. And they were all mine. All I had to do was reach out and take one."

One of the shimmering minds veered towards them, Lizanne recognising the face of a woman in the misty shape. "Curious thing about heart-blood," Alestine mused. "The abilities it conveys never fade. They are seared into your being, an eternal gift . . . or a curse. And one that can be shared." She flicked her hand and the woman's mind flew away, soon lost amongst the multitude.

"This is how you called the first one to you in Scorazin," Lizanne said. "And how he called the next."

"Yes. A great and unforgivable sin. But one I had to commit if this world was to survive. There wasn't just heart-blood on the spear. I saw what was coming, and I saw you and I saw the clever boy and knew it was my role to bring you together."

The huge fish-bowl turned into a grey mist, which soon coalesced into something familiar. Lizanne found herself regarding walls of uneven stone lit by the light of an oil-lamp. She turned at the sound of scraping chalk and saw Tinkerer at the smooth patch of wall he used as a blackboard. The flat surface was covered in an incomprehensible mélange of numbers and formulae, some of it so dense the stone was completely covered in chalk. He gave no sign of having noticed Lizanne's presence, his hand moving in a blur as it added yet more wisdom to the wall.

"It wasn't like this when I lived here," Alestine said in a croak, appearing at Lizanne's side. "The others must've enlarged it over the years." Her form had recovered its wounds, though the burns appeared much older now, the scars pink and mottled rather than puckered and blackish red. Lizanne could see wrinkles on her undamaged skin and she stood with a pronounced stoop, grey hair hanging over her ruined face in slack, unwashed tendrils.

"How did you come to be here?" Lizanne asked.

"I wrote a letter to an old friend when I returned to the Empire." Alestine moved to peer at Tinkerer's wall, frowning in bafflement. "And I thought I was clever," she muttered.

"Azireh," Lizanne said. "She put you here."

"It was what I asked for, somewhere to hide and remain hidden for all time. A reward for all the marvellous trinkets I brought back from Arradsia. She was effusive in her thanks and prompt in granting my request, but never came for a visit, not that I blame her. No doubt the Imperial agents who escorted me here gave her a fulsome report on my appearance. Hey, boy!" She snapped her fingers beside Tinkerer's ear. "Not polite to ignore your guests, you know."

Tinkerer's chalk kept moving and he betrayed no indication of having heard her. "Always knew he'd be a rude bugger," Alestine said, aiming a cuff at the back of Tinkerer's head but her fingers passed through. "Not my mind, y'see," she told Lizanne. "This is all his. Doesn't want to see me so he doesn't." She leaned closer to Tinkerer, shouting into his ear. "Can't stay in here forever though, can you?"

Lizanne went to stand at Tinkerer's shoulder, looking closely at his face, which displayed the habitual blankness that overtook him when he lost himself in a task. *Perhaps he doesn't want to come back,* she thought, turning her gaze on the mass of calculus. *Perhaps this is all he wants.* She fought down an upswell of guilt as she raised her hand and placed it over his, stopping the chalk in its tracks. *What he wants doesn't matter. Alestine had a task and so do I.*

"Looks like he's happy to see you," Alestine said, moving away. "Time for me to go, I think."

"Wait," Lizanne said. "You said the ancient Blood-blessed freed some of the Spoiled. How?"

"I don't know. Tree Speaker's people had no tale to tell on that score. The White's blood showed me a battle, great and terrible, Spoiled and human and drake locked in a struggle to the death. You were there, Lizanne, fighting and bleeding."

"Do we win?"

Alestine's aged and stooped form slipped away and she was once again the same woman Lizanne had met in the clearing, beautiful and brave but now with a vast weight of guilt behind her eyes.

"I saw nothing beyond this," she told Lizanne. "This song is played out and now will end, as all songs must." She cast a final, unreadable glance at

Tinkerer and stepped away, disappearing into the wall and leaving them alone.

Lizanne turned back to Tinkerer, finding herself shocked by his wide and fearful eyes. "I . . ." he began, faltering over the words in a halting rasp. "I have been here a very long time. Months, I think. Perhaps years. Perhaps longer. I couldn't count the minutes, or the hours or the days. It was . . . disturbing."

"I'm sorry," Lizanne said. "But we can leave now."

He frowned at her, utterly baffled. "How?"

"She's gone. This is your mind and your trance. Just decide to wake up."

Tinkerer's brow smoothed, eyes sliding from her face as he lost himself in momentary calculation. "Oh," he said. "Very well."

Lizanne blinked and found herself in darkness once again, though the moonlight streaming through the window revealed her to be back in Tinkerer's infirmary room. The lack of light was puzzling, however, as was the chill in the air which she assumed resulted from the fact that the window was open. She saw Makario slumped at the pianola and began to speak his name, then stopped when she saw something dark dripping over the keys. Tearing her gaze away she scanned the room, coming to a halt at the sight of Dr. Weygrand's body lying close to the door.

"Awake at last," Mr. Lockbar said, rising from the shadows beneath the window, his knife gleaming bright in the moonlight. "They wanted you to know," he explained before leaping towards her, blade outstretched.

CHAPTER 33

Sirus

A cluster of old people huddled together beneath the tower of their village temple. It was an old Oracular church long since converted to the Imperial cult, the tower crowned by a bronze bust of Emperor Caranis. The elderly villagers, about twenty in all, displayed mixed reactions to their imminent fate. Some kept their gaze firmly on the rain-muddied ground. Others stared at Sirus and the other Spoiled in unabashed defiance whilst a few cast repeated glances at the bust of the recently dead Emperor above, as if even now he possessed some divine power of deliverance.

"This is all?" Sirus asked Forest Spear.

"Every house is empty," the tribal reported. "We found cart-tracks leading to the west, but they're a few days old. Just like the others."

It had been the same for the past week. The White's host had enjoyed a period of success early in the march, capturing a string of towns and villages and swelling their ranks in the process. Veilmist calculated the daily recruitment tally at over eight thousand and Catheline communicated the White's satisfaction to the entire army. But it hadn't lasted.

The farther south they marched the farther news of their coming travelled. At first the villages were only half-deserted, the inhabitants caught in the midst of their panicked flight. Later they found a large town empty of all but the sick and the old but, with the aid of the Reds, had managed to pursue and capture the bulk of the populace a few miles to the south-west. It had been a messy business, the yield of recruits limited thanks to the Reds, who had been permitted a bout of indulgent slaughter. By the time the first Spoiled battalions arrived fully half the adults and most of the children were dead, the corpses scattered about the country-side in ugly, half-eaten mounds as the Reds squawked and gorged themselves.

They require rewards too, Catheline explained in response to Sirus's frustrated query. *For a drake, flesh is the spoil of victory.*

Since then every village had been like this one, the people fled so far and fast that any attempt to capture them would entail an unacceptable delay. All that remained were those too old or infirm to run.

"Leave them for the drakes?" Forest Spear asked, flicking his war-club at the huddle of old people.

Kinder to kill them, Sirus thought. *One bullet each to the head.* Left alive the Greens would most likely claim them, or worse, the White's hideous brood of juveniles might see them as a source of amusement.

He began to issue the order then stopped as one of the old people stepped forward, a tall man in threadbare clothing but possessed of a sturdy bearing despite his age. Sirus suspected the man had once been a soldier, probably a sergeant judging by the volume in his voice as he cried out, "Monsters!" before bending to retrieve a stone from the muddy ground. "Filthy, demon monsters!" he yelled, wrinkled face red with fury as he threw the stone at Sirus. He ducked and it sailed harmlessly overhead, the old man immediately crouching to search the ground for another missile.

Don't, Sirus commanded as Forest Spear unslung his rifle.

Unable to find a stone, the old man settled for a handful of mud, casting it at Sirus with impressive aim. It struck him squarely on the breast of the Corvantine general's tunic Catheline insisted he wear. The old man straightened from the throw, gnarled fists bunched as he glowered in defiance. It was clear that he expected a swift death. Sirus returned his stare, unmoving and expressionless. The old soldier let out a snarl and quickly bent to fill both his fists with more mud, hurling it at Sirus then immediately crouching for more ammunition. Sirus allowed the missiles to strike him on the head and shoulder, doing and saying nothing.

Apparently emboldened by this display, and the lack of reaction from Sirus or the other Spoiled, a few of the old man's companions began to join in his assault. Two old women, one so bent and crook-legged she had to hobble forward with the aid of a stick, scraped mud and stones from the ground and hurled it at the impassive monsters, accompanied by a torrent of colourful insults.

"Demon shit-eaters!"

"Cock-sucking freaks!"

Soon what had been a cowed and miserable huddle had become an enraged mob, the air filled with arcing mud and stones that rained down on the immobile Spoiled. Sirus held them in place, forbidding retaliation as the barrage continued. He felt a range of emotions from his fellow Spoiled, from anger and frustration to cruel amusement. But there was also grudging admiration, even from Forest Spear and a few of the other tribals. Normally they viewed the un-Spoiled with a mixture of contempt and indifference, now it appeared they were capable of more feeling than he suspected.

He allowed the assault to continue, wondering how long it might take for these old folk to exhaust themselves as his uniform became increasingly caked in mud. The question proved moot, however, when a dark-winged shadow swept over the village. The barrage instantly stopped, the mob's defiance vanished as all eyes turned upwards, wide and bright with terror. All eyes except those of the old soldier.

"Kill me, you fucker!" he raged as the shadow swept over them once again, both fists raised to the sky. "Go on kill me, if you got the balls!"

Catheline's half-amused, half-baffled query slipped into Sirus's mind. *What is this?* He looked up to see her perched on the back of Katarias, the Red's wings blurring as he hovered fifty yards above.

An oddly irrational display, he replied. *You know I can't help but be curious.*

Be curious later.

Katarias stilled his wings and went into a dive, streaking down to unleash a torrent of fire that consumed first the old soldier and then his terrified companions. The fire was so swift and intense none had a chance to run and soon a pile of twisted, blackened corpses lay beneath the temple tower.

Come, Catheline ordered as Katarias bore her towards the edge of the village. *I have something to show you.*

It was a drake memory and therefore not instantly comprehensible. Soon, however, Sirus's mind shifted to accommodate the difference in perception and what had been a blur of smudged colours became a jungle viewed from above.

Arradsia, he concluded, recognising some of the trees as unique to the continent.

Yes, Catheline responded, her thoughts tinged with impatience. *This is from this morning. Watch . . . There at the edge of the trees.*

Sirus concentrated on the required portion of the view, soon picking out the sight of a pair of human figures emerging from the jungle into a region of sparse bush-country. The height of the drake that had seen this was too great to make out any details.

Spoiled? he asked, so far failing to perceive the significance of this memory.

No. Catheline's mind had darkened considerably, rich in the same rage as when she shared visions of the Lethridge woman. The image magnified as the drake focused on the two figures, Sirus making out the features of a man and a woman, both young and of South Mandinorian heritage. They wore the garb typical of the corporate Contractors who, until recently, had roamed the Interior in search of drakes.

So a few Contractors are still alive, he thought. *Hardly surprising. It's a big land-mass.*

These aren't just Contractors. Her rage blossomed to new heights, possessed of the kind of intensity he knew could only be compelled by the White. *They are as dangerous as that Lethridge bitch, perhaps even more so.*

The memory shifted again as the Red that had captured it began a descent, gaze fixed on the pair below. They grew in size as it streaked down, Sirus feeling the beast's killing urge and the heat of the gases rising from belly to throat. It never got a chance to ignite its flames. The vision turned completely red and Sirus felt something hard and sharp clamp onto the Red's neck. After that the memory fragmented into a discordant series of images and brief flashes of agony that told of a furious struggle, and a losing one at that. Catheline froze it just as the Red coiled its neck for a final snap at its assailant, Sirus finding himself confronted by the sight of a very large Black drake, the lower jaw partially obscured by the thick stream of fire it had called forth.

"They were saved by a Black," he said as Catheline withdrew her mind.

She paced back and forth on a patch of muddy ground a short distance from the village. Lately she had taken to wearing a Corvantine cavalry officer's uniform, complete with short jacket, sword, riding britches and knee-high boots. Of course it had been tailored to fit her pleasing proportions making for what would normally be a striking appearance. But today her boots and britches were stained with mud and the continuing drizzle had disordered her hair. The frantic expression she struggled to keep from her face, and the way she kept her arms tightly crossed, made this the least attractive impression she had yet made on him. He found he didn't enjoy seeing her like this. For all her red-black eyes and fearsome abilities, now she appeared merely human, and he preferred her a monster. *A monster will be easier to kill when the time comes.*

He concealed the thought with a suitable degree of fear but Catheline barely seemed to notice.

"You know what this means," she said, inhuman eyes flashing at him from behind a damp veil of displaced hair.

"Actually, I don't," he replied honestly.

"The Blacks!" She bared elongated teeth in a snarl. "The Blacks will be coming against us." Her voice subsided into a murmur, gaze becoming distant. "Just like before. He thought with their allies destroyed they would keep themselves removed, to be dealt with later. But somehow . . ." Her lips twitched, brows furrowed in fury. "Somehow these two have formed an alliance with them. They will be coming."

"There's a great deal of ocean between Arradsia and Varestia," Sirus pointed out.

"And many ships here." She pushed another memory into his head, a top-down view of a crater situated on a stretch of coast-line and resembling a huge bite mark, within which lay a harbour city Sirus had only ever seen in books.

"Stockcombe," he said, noting the fleet in the harbour. His attention was immediately drawn to the only warship present, an unusual design in that it lacked paddles. The Red capturing the image evidently sensed a similar significance in the warship for its gaze focused on the upper decks. Sirus saw a tall man standing there, spy-glass raised as he returned the drake's scrutiny.

"Many ships can carry many Blacks," Catheline said. Sirus could sense a desperate need for guidance in her, powerful enough to birth a compulsion to cooperate that no amount of fear or inner resolve could dispel.

"There are still drakes left in Arradsia," he said. "Are there not?"

"Thousands," she replied. "Those that couldn't be gathered for the crusade. But they're scattered."

"Gather them now," he advised. "Send all you can to Stockcombe. Without a fleet the Blacks won't be going anywhere."

"But the Blacks might get there first. The harbour could be empty by the time an assault could be made."

"As I said, there's a great deal of ocean separating this continent from that one. And we have a means of commanding the ocean, do we not? A means not required for our current campaign."

The Blues were dispatched that evening, each of them filled with the desire to make for southern Arradsia and sink any ship they found. Previously they had been engaged in blockading the Red Tides in order to prevent the Varestians acquiring supplies or reinforcements from elsewhere. Marshal Morradin had contested the move, arguing that limiting the enemy's sea-borne communications would have a crucial effect on the land campaign. Sirus considered the marshal had been lucky that Catheline's punishment for dissent amounted to only a five-minute bout of agony, her mood being so fraught and intolerant of argument.

She's frightened, he knew. *Or rather, she is the vessel of the White's fear. The Blacks, those Contractors, Lizanne Lethridge. He fears them all.*

The next two days brought an unexpected increase in numbers when they encountered a town where the inhabitants had taken the admirable if unwise decision to defend their homes rather than flee. They had made strenuous efforts to fortify the place with a line of trench works and an impressive array of cannon, the place being home to an Imperial armaments works.

"A grand battery of cannon and a host of new recruits," Morradin said with grim relish as he reordered his columns for an assault. "What a generous gift they have made for us."

Whilst the town had many with the skills to manufacture cannon, it transpired they had few skilled in using them. Morradin spent the day surrounding the place and sending small forays towards the defensive lines to entice the town's gunners into revealing their positions, which many obligingly proceeded to do before nightfall. In the small hours of the morning Reds were used to drop parties of Spoiled on all the pin-pointed batteries. They were all swiftly seized and the captured cannon duly turned on the defenders. Informed by one party of raiders of a stretch of line which had suffered the most casualties, Morradin sent forward twenty thousand Spoiled in a massed attack. At the same time he assailed the rest of the line with small-scale attacks to prevent the defenders switching forces to contest the main assault.

It was over before dawn save for some street skirmishes in the town itself. By the afternoon Veilmist reported another twenty-five thousand additions to their ranks for the cost of less than two thousand casualties. For once Morradin was happy to share his thoughts. *Neatest and most complete victory I ever won,* he told Sirus as they toured the southern fringes of the town. The marshal's mind seemed to shine with satisfaction at his own tactical acumen. Sirus found it distasteful to share in such self-regard but also recognised that Morradin was at his core a man who relished command in battle. Expecting him not to take pride in such a victory was like expecting a carpenter not to take pride in a perfectly crafted table.

"I doubt there will be any more neat victories ahead," Sirus said aloud in Eutherian, nodding at the mountains jutting above the southern horizon. This town was the last settlement of reasonable size to be found north of the peaks marking the boundary between the Corvantine Empire proper and its lost dominion of Varestia.

"The passes," Morradin grunted, Sirus feeling his mood darken. "Where, if our enemy has any brains at all, they will seek to kill as many of us as they can, if not halt us completely."

"How would you defend them?"

Morradin's lip curled in the sardonic grin of a professional suffering the questions of an amateur. "I wouldn't. I'd block them, force us to waste time clearing them or make for the coastal route to the east. Numbers won't count for much there. Mountains on our right flank and the sea on our left with only a few miles frontage. No room for manoeuvre, for us or them. If they choose to fight us there that will be a bloody day indeed."

Sirus summoned his fear at this last statement, using it to conceal the mental communication that followed, speaking aloud as he did so. "We'll use Reds to drop Spoiled, seize the heights covering the largest pass." *Have you thought any more about my proposal?*

"We can expect some nasty surprises waiting for them." *A proposal is one thing, boy. A plan is another. As yet I see no prospect of one emerging.*

"Scouting parties will go ahead. We'll only commit to the assault when we know the way is clear." *She's afraid, so is He. Something's coming, something that will change our fortunes, I'm sure of it. But we need to buy time.*

"It might be better to avoid the passes altogether, or at least mount a feinting attack. Make them think we're heading for the mountains whilst we steal a march by immediately making for the coast." *One more failure and she could well kill one of us, or both. And you can bet it won't be quick.*

"We'll put both options to her. She can decide." *I saw something the other day.* He shared the memory of the old man inciting his fellow doomed left-behinds to engage in one last act of defiance. *A man who accepts the necessity of sacrifice need never be afraid.*

Easy to say when it's not you doing the sacrificing.

Sirus cast another glance at the distant peaks before turning away. He started back to the village where the screams of the captured children were rising into the morning air, determined to witness it all. *It will be.*

CHAPTER 34

Clay

The glowing eyes of the mountainous drakes shone like search-lights in the misted air as they converged on Clay. Then they waited, emitting a low, expectant rumble as he gaped up at them in blank-minded silence.

"Who are they?" he asked Ethelynne.

"Memory accrues over time," she replied. "Like sand washed onto a beach where the tide is unending. Over thousands of years all those countless grains of sand will come together"—she smiled, raising her arms to the rumbling giants above—"to form mountains. You might want to say something. Old as they are, they can get a little grouchy if you keep them waiting."

Clay's gaze shifted from one glowing-eyed behemoth to the other, feeling much as an ant must feel when confronted with a vast creature beyond its understanding that might crush it on a whim. "You know me," he began. "At least Lutharon does, and I'm guessing you know everything he does. So you know I'm his friend, which makes me your friend."

The rumbling rose in pitch, one of the giants giving a shake of its head that resembled a horse fidgeting in irritation.

"Getting a little too human for their liking," Ethelynne warned. "Drakes don't really understand friendship. There is enemy and non-enemy and family. That's all."

"What does that make me?"

"If you want their help, you need to be family."

Clay sighed in frustration, mind wrestling with the gulf between his needs and his knowledge. "I travelled far with Lutharon," he began again. "We saw and risked much together. He was bound to me but I let him go. To save his life I let him go. So you know you can trust me. And you know what we found beneath the mountain."

He summoned the memory of his encounter with the White in all its fiery, terrorised glory. The giants reared back from the vision of the White bathing the eggs in the waking fire, eyes blazing in distress as their rumbling became a snarl.

"You've seen this before," Clay went on. "You fought it before. Now it's back. It will remember you, and you know it won't forgive."

The giants swung their heads back and forth, eyes flickering in confusion, and Clay quickly realised forgiveness was another concept beyond drake understanding. "Your kind are still a threat to it," he said. "It will want you dead. All of you. You know this."

He summoned another image, Jack's memory of the battle at sea where Reds and Blues fought Blacks with human riders. "Once we fought together. Once there was trust between us."

The giants settled at the sight of his shared memory, their search-light eyes converging on him once more. One of them dipped its head, averting its gaze to focus the beams from its eyes on the ground close by. The light flickered and Clay saw images playing out in the beam: *an infant Black lying dead beside the corpse of its mother, both with blood leaking from bullet-holes to the head . . . passing mountains viewed from behind the thick bars of a cage . . . two-legged creatures approaching with knives and gouges and buckets . . .*

Clay winced at the pain and distress leaking from these images, but forced himself to share it, despite a certain dreadful expectation building in his breast as the memories played out. When the last sequence came he viewed it with a wrenching sense of inevitability.

. . . thrashing against the chains clamped to his limbs . . . crying out in rage as the harvester enters the vat to thrust the spile into his neck . . . pain and anguish as his blood leaks out . . . the female two-legged creature lands in front of him, clutching an infant . . . his chains are shattered . . . a glory of vengeance as he tears the harvesters apart, demolishes walls and houses, feeling his life seep away but determined to visit all the pain he can on his tormentors before it's gone . . . assailing ships in the harbour until something freezes him in place, holds him tighter than the chains until a sudden final jolt and blackness.

Clay let out a gasp and sank to his knees as the memory ended. "It was you," he breathed. "One of you . . . all of you." The rage was unjustified, irrational, but he couldn't help it. "You bastards killed my mother. You know that?" He looked up at them, teeth bared in fury and loss. "You killed my mother! Do you know what you did to me?"

"You lost a mother, Clay," Ethelynne said. "But Lutharon lost his father that day. He was only half-grown when he felt it, his father's memories slipping into his, all that rage. He came close to killing me, and I had raised him. But he didn't, for our minds were linked and he saw my guilt and my grief."

Clay looked again at the giants staring down at him with their search-light eyes. *Grief*, he thought, trying to quell the myriad memories of his mother summoned by the vision of the rampaging Black. *They don't know forgiveness but they do know grief, and we gave them a whole lot to grieve over.*

"It'll end," he said, getting to his feet. "Fight with us and it'll end, we won't hunt you no more. There'll be no need. We found something, y'see? A new kind of product. Fight with us and we'll leave you in peace."

He meant it, with every ounce of his being. There were no lies in the trance and he knew they saw all of him now. But that also meant they saw the small kernel of doubt, the awareness that whatever offer he made here might well be ignored in the aftermath of victory.

"My promise is all I can give," he said. "But it's something. And you know you'll only get death from the White. It's got human blood as well as drake, which means it hates what it can't control. Fight with us, like you did before. I know you still hold those memories, you still remember the time when human and drake lived in peace. Together you fought the White and you freed the Spoiled. Come with me and free them again."

The beam focused on the ground flickered, Clay seeing new images appear in the light. The beam grew in size, the light swallowing Clay so that he stood in the shared memory. *Another city*, he realised, gazing round at the temples and buildings, noting how many were scorched and dam-aged, rubble littering the streets along with numerous corpses. Dead Greens and Reds lay alongside human and Spoiled, smoke rising above the carnage. Here and there he could see the body of a Black. However, there was still life in this city, people crouching beside the fallen, others wander-ing in a daze. Close by he could see a group of people standing in a circle.

A large male Black stood outside the circle, neck coiled as it peered at what lay inside it.

Moving closer Clay heard voices raised. Two people amongst those gathered, a man and a woman were engaged in a bitter argument. She wore a long blue robe whilst he was clearly a warrior judging by the spear he carried. He was evidently fresh from the battle that had raged here, Clay noting the livid burn mark on the bronze skin of his shoulder and the dark blood that covered the head of his spear. The woman was uninjured but her face was stained with a mix of soot and blood, meaning she hadn't been idle in the conflict either. He realised there was something familiar about her clothing, her robe and her head-dress of feathers stirring his memory of the mosaic in the hidden city.

"Blood-blessed," he said. "A priestess."

"One who has drunk heart-blood," Ethelynne said, appearing at his side, nodding to the male Black.

"Can you tell what they're saying?" Clay asked as the man and the woman continued to argue, their words meaningless to him.

"Only a small part of it. Lutharon's kind have a fractional understanding of human language. I've often delved into his more ancient memories, trying to learn more about the vanished civilisation I spent so many years searching for. Some words and phrases have become clear but . . ." She paused, grimacing in consternation. "Without my note-books translation is ever a frustrating task." Her gaze narrowed as she noticed something beyond the warrior and the priestess. "However, I suspect their discussion has much to do with him."

There was a Spoiled within the circle, tightly bound with rope that had been secured with pegs thrust into the earth, keeping him on his knees. He looked around at his captors with no sign of fear, his deformed face betraying nothing beyond mild curiosity. Even when the priestess ended the argument with a shout and a hard slash of her hand, the Spoiled barely reacted as she strode towards him and sank to her haunches. She stared directly into his eyes, gaze unwavering, commanding whilst the Spoiled blinked in response and spoke a short few words in a dull monotone.

"Any notion of what that was?" Clay asked Ethelynne.

"He's speaking the same language," she said, frowning in concentration as she tried to translate. "'Soon . . . you and I . . . walk mirror . . .' No. Not walk mirror." Ethelynne gave a huff of self-annoyance. "'Become as one. Soon you and I will become as one.'"

Clay turned back as the woman replied, Ethelynne providing a halting translation. "'No . . . soon you . . . will fly, no, ascend . . . to life.' I think they use the words 'life' and 'freedom' interchangeably."

Clay watched the priestess reach for something around her neck, seeing her remove the stopper from a small copper vial. She kept her gaze locked onto the Spoiled's as she drank, then took on the stillness that indicated a trance state. The Spoiled suddenly jerked, straining against his bonds, elongated teeth bared in a grimace as he tried vainly to tear himself free, then he stopped. All expression left the Spoiled's face as his struggles ceased and he took on the same stillness as the priestess.

"She's trancing with him," Clay concluded. "But how? He didn't drink."

"I don't think he's even Blessed," Ethelynne said, then let out a short laugh of realisation. "We know they communicate mentally, and the only known means of doing that is via a trance state. Meaning the Spoiled must be in a permanent trance state from the moment of their conversion. It's how the White controls them. Any Blood-blessed could trance with a Spoiled if they form a connection."

The trance continued for some time, priestess and Spoiled remaining in absolute stillness. The surrounding circle of people grew restless, the warrior the priestess had argued with pacing back and forth with his spear clutched in readiness. Seeing the way he looked at the crouching woman Clay realised the man's opposition to this attempt had been based on concern rather than suspicion. Was he her lover? Husband perhaps? Did she even know he loved her? All questions he knew would never be answered.

Finally, the priestess opened her eyes and stood up. As she did so the Spoiled collapsed, all strength seeming to seep out of him as he lay, head nuzzling the dirt. He seemed to be twitching but then Clay heard the soft sounds coming from his throat and realised he was weeping. A shadow of guilt passed over the priestess's face as she looked down at the Spoiled before she straightened, putting a commanding expression on her face as she turned and issued a curt command to the warrior. He approached the Spoiled with a wary reluctance, peering down at the sobbing deformed face with a mixture of disgust and bafflement.

The woman spoke again, flicking a hand impatiently as Ethelynne translated. "'Life . . . is given . . . Freedom is given. He is free.'"

Clay was about to ask a question but the warrior voiced it for him. "'How?'"

"'Freedom lives . . . exists in all . . . head, minds . . . Allowed him . . . memory . . . remember.'"

"He remembered being free," Clay said. "And now he is. Can it be that simple?"

Ethelynne's gaze clouded with sympathy as she looked at the Spoiled who continued to lie on the ground sobbing even after the warrior had cut away his bonds. "I doubt that, for him, anything was ever simple again. It seems you can free a mind from bondage, but not the memory of crimes committed in that bondage."

The scene became dark, the tableau of the freed, guilt-wracked Spoiled lying between the warrior and the priestess faded into shadow. When the light returned they were back on the mountain side with the giant drakes looming above. Their eye-beams slowly shifted to converge on Ethelynne, the giants issuing a loud inquisitive rumble.

"I trust him," she told them. "The gift you have given is gratefully received. But he is one, and the White has many in its thrall, and he tells the truth of it; if the White lives, we will perish."

The giants' rumbling became a discordant rattle that sounded like an avalanche. They reared back from Clay and Ethelynne, eye-beams lancing into the darkened sky as they let out a roar. Clay staggered under the weight of the sound, feeling as if it were tearing into him, pulling him apart. The surrounding vision shattered and swirled into a maelstrom of gravel, Clay feeling the sting of it in his skin, a sting that soon grew into a sharp continuous pain.

"A drake's mind laid bare," Ethelynne told him, standing placidly amidst the swirl. "Not something a human mind can stand for long, but he has to do this to call to them."

She moved to Clay, reaching out to take his hands, which, he saw, were bleeding from a thousand or more tiny cuts. "Good-bye, Claydon," she said with a warm smile. "It's probably best if you don't visit again. Not for a long time anyway. But, if you ever get the chance, do see if you can recover my note-books."

He tried to reply but his mouth filled with gravel that burned like a swarm of tiny bees. Ethelynne gave a sympathetic wince and leaned forward to press a kiss to his cheek.

He blinked awake to find his gaze immediately assaulted by a bright beam of sunlight streaming through the jungle canopy. Letting out a grunt of pain he sat up, blinking watery eyes until Kriz's concerned face came into focus. "How long?" he asked.

"A day," she said. "And a night."

Time moves differently in the trance, he remembered.

The tread of clawed feet on soft ground drew his gaze to Lutharon as he turned about, sinking to his haunches and angling his back towards them. Clay felt a faint sensation of impatience which he quickly realised wasn't his own. Before his connection with Lutharon had been a vague thing, often feeling like he was trying to communicate through a thick fog. Now the drake's mind was a clear and constant presence in his own. It was similar to his connection to Jack, but somehow felt deeper, Lutharon's mind stronger and more coherent than the often-confused and scared soul Clay had poured into the fractured mess of Jack's mind.

"Looks like we're going somewhere," he said, getting to his feet.

"We're going to ride it?" Kriz asked with a doubtful pitch to her voice he knew had once coloured his own when presented with the same option.

"Him," Clay corrected. "And it's easy once you know how. Ain't no skill to it. Just a matter of holding on and letting him take you where he wants to go."

He moved to retrieve the Black crystal, which lay a few feet away, now shrunk once again into a small shard. Unsure whether it would be needed again but certain it would be a bad idea to leave it behind, he consigned it to his pack and strode towards the waiting drake.

Kriz took some coaxing to climb up behind him. Lutharon seemed to have abandoned his previous antipathy towards her and barely shuddered when she tentatively grasped one of his spines, but she retained an understandable nervousness.

"He hasn't forgotten, has he?" she asked having finally settled herself onto Lutharon's back.

"I don't think they can forget," Clay said. "But they do recognise more pressing concerns. Hold on," he added as Lutharon flared his wings, "and if you throw up, don't do it on me."

A short loping sprint and they were air-borne, Lutharon pushing them higher with a few beats of his wings. The jungle fell away into a vast green blanket broken by the mist-shrouded, wedge-shaped bulk of the mountains. Clay let out a laugh at the familiar thrill of flying, something it turned out he had missed greatly, although he had forgotten how chilled the air could get only a few hundred feet off the ground.

Lutharon angled his wings and flew south, gliding for a time as he let out a long, loud call. It was different than the other calls Clay had heard him make, pitched higher than a roar but with a sustained volume that ensured it would carry for miles. The mountains and the jungle slipped beneath them for the length of several miles before he saw it, another winged shape gliding through the sparse mist below. Lutharon let out another call, identical to the first, and this time there was an answer. The other drake repeated the call as it rose to fly level with Lutharon. It was a young male perhaps two-thirds Lutharon's size, coiling its neck to take in the sight of Clay and Kriz but displaying no sign of aggression.

Lutharon banked and began to fly in a wide circle, he and the other male continuing to call out. Another reply sounded to the rear and Clay looked over his shoulder to see two more Blacks rising to follow, with three more behind. Within the space of an hour the sky around them became filled with drakes, Clay losing count at twenty as it became impossible to keep track of them all as the ever-growing flock swirled around. The sound of their calls was extraordinary, a vast chorus of greeting and agreement that thrummed the air for miles around.

Clay leaned over Lutharon's side to peer down at the mountains below, seeing drake after drake rise from the broad summits. He also saw that not all the Blacks were answering the call. Some looked up at the huge whirlwind of drakes in obvious agitation but showed no inclination to join it.

Guess they ain't your kin, huh? he thought, running a hand over the scaly patch at the base of Lutharon's neck.

It went on for over an hour by which time they were flying in shadow, so great were the number of wings obscuring the sun. Lutharon let out a final call, longer and louder than the others, and the great flock of Blacks answered with a vast cry of their own, so loud Clay's ears throbbed with it.

Lutharon levelled out, the jungle seeming to blur beneath them as he beat his wings, a thousand or more Black drakes following as he flew south.

They found the Longrifles trekking through the bush-country south of the jungle, keeping close to the tall cliffs that marked this stretch of the southern Arradsian coast. Clay obtained their location from Sigoral via the Blue-less trance, the Corvantine's thoughts betraying a mounting but tightly controlled alarm at the sight of so many Blacks filling the sky. Lutharon set down a few yards from the company, all formed into a defensive knot with weapons at the ready. Contractor habits were hard to break.

Clay dismounted and went to greet his uncle, receiving a warm but distracted embrace in response as Braddon's gaze roved constantly over the Blacks as they circled overhead or folded their wings to descend to the clifftop.

"Seer damn me if you didn't actually do it, Clay," he said, fingers twitching on the stock of his rifle.

"Best if you keep that slung, Uncle," Clay told him. "You really don't wanna stir up any unpleasant recollections amongst our present company."

Braddon nodded and slung his rifle over his shoulder, barrel down as marksmen always did, motioning for the others to do the same.

"Seems like you brought every Black in Arradsia," Loriabeth said, coming forward to hug him.

"Not quite." Clay raised his eyes to the host above. "Just hope it's enough."

"Reckon we'll find out soon enough," Braddon said. "Great many Reds flew over three days gone. We hunkered down in a fissure in one of the cliffs so they didn't see. Next day we saw more Greens than I have in my life, all moving in one great pack."

"Where to?" Clay asked.

"Same as the Reds, south."

"Stockcombe." He moved to the cliff edge, shielding his eyes to peer at the distant flank of the peninsular which led to the port. *The White*, he thought. *Should've known it'd keep looking.*

"Mount up," he said, turning about and striding towards Lutharon. "We got a lotta distance to cover."

"To where?" asked Braddon.

"Mount what?" asked Loriabeth.

"Stockcombe, where else?" Clay climbed onto Lutharon's back, quickly followed by Kriz, who seemed to have lost her reluctance during the flight from the mountains. He grinned at Loriabeth and pointed at one of the drakes perched at the cliff edge. "And what else?"

III

THE RED TIDES

From the Journal of Miss Lewella Tythencroft—
Sanorah, 32nd Vorellum, 1600 (Company Year 211)

That the sad, ugly but mercifully brief affair that sparked the revolution has since earned the name "The Battle of the Barricade" says much for the scale of the fighting that followed. There had been some rioting following the mob assault on the banks, but this died down when it became apparent that the Protectorate was prepared to use lethal force to guard its principal installations. However, for the most part the Ironship military stayed in barracks, probably due to the sudden spike in desertions which robbed it of more than half its strength within a week. Sporadic gun-battles erupted between the constabulary and more radical anti-corporate elements, but the latter lacked sufficient numbers to be more than a nuisance. By far the most important thing to happen in the aftermath of what has, to my mortification, also occasionally been dubbed "Free Woman Tythencroft's defiant stand" was the walk-out and subsequent strike by the vast majority of corporate employees in Sanorah.

Within two days every company office and manufactory in the city and outlying districts lay silent and empty, the strikers forming delegations which duly turned up at the offices of the Gazette in search of acknowledgment and guidance. My days soon became an often-trying mix of meetings, speeches, correspondence and yet more meetings. Those queueing up outside my door were a varied lot indeed, ranging from soldiers and sailors representing what has become known as "The Free Protectorate," to civic *and company bureaucrats who suddenly find themselves bereft of higher authority.*

Rumours began to circulate following the brief spate of strife after the Battle of the Barricade that the interim Board had effectively ceased functioning, its principal members either fled to country estates or taken to secluding themselves in their town houses. It was a company of infantry from the Free Protectorate who confirmed this to be truth rather than rumour, barging into the Sanorah Ironship headquarters to find the upper floors largely empty. The senior management of the largest corporate entity in the world had, it appears, simply given up and gone home.

It was at this juncture that I realised my ad hoc approach to organisation was no longer practical and I began appointing deputies, assuring my fellow Voters that all such appointments would be confirmed by electoral sanction when the situation became less fraught. I have to admit to a palpable sense of the bizarre as I went about the business of building what is essentially a dictatorship, some might even call it a dynasty given that, lacking another qualified and trustworthy figure to fill the role, I was obliged to appoint my father to the position of City Treasurer.

The most pressing issue proved to be the most complex, despite its simple urgency: The city needed to be fed. The large corporate-owned farms surrounding Sanorah had stopped supplying food to the markets during the riots, and continued to withhold produce in the aftermath. Swiftly deposing their managers when wages stopped being paid, the farm labourers declared themselves a confederation of independents. They subsequently agreed to resume supplying food-stuffs only on condition that all outstanding debts would be paid, along with assurances that future debts would be honoured. It required several hours of persuasion to calm the more hot-headed elements of my nascent administration, who argued the Free Protectorate should be sent to seize the farms.

"Farms with dead labourers and ruined buildings won't grow anything," I pointed out, deciding on a more conciliatory approach. The main obstacle was the fact that, at the dawn of a new age in which corporate scrip had be-

come worthless, how was it possible to pay anyone for anything? Fortunately, our new treasurer came up with a novel solution in the form of Liquidation Notes. These were essentially promissory notes issued by the Free Sanorah Republic guaranteeing the bearer an allotted share of assets resulting from the impending liquidation of the Ironship Syndicate and others. Whilst Ironship no longer possessed any financial wealth its warehouses and manufactories still held considerable stocks of goods of all description. Wealth, it transpires, is what those in authority deem it to be.

"But it's just paper," I protested when my father first proposed the measure. The prototype note he had given me consisted of a rectangle bearing a date stamp and two signatures, mine appearing above his.

"Of course it is, Lewella," he told me in mild irritation. "That's all money has ever been."

Despite my misgivings the Liquidation Notes gained a surprisingly rapid level of acceptance amongst the populace, including the newly independent farmers, who soon resumed food shipments. I ascribed some of this to the prevailing mood of uncertainty; the appearance of something, however nebulous, that indicated a return to normalcy proving highly welcome.

In addition to local concerns there was also the continual distraction of events elsewhere. The Voters Rights Alliance has long made use of sympathetic Blood-blessed and they proved invaluable in keeping us up to date with developments from far and wide, the most important from my perspective being the communications from the Arradsian port of Stockcombe, not least because the event brought news I had begun to suspect I might never hear.

"Captain Corrick Hilemore," the young Blood-blessed told me during one of our semi-regular meetings. He looked tired, having responsibility for maintaining communications with numerous locations despite a rapidly dwindling supply of product. "He says he knows you. I think they're hoping you'll tell them he's lying so they can seize his ship."

"I do indeed know him," I replied, finding a genuine smile on my lips for the first time in many days. "And any attempt to seize his ship will be highly ill-advised."

34th Vorellum

I have just concluded a highly taxing meeting with Mrs. Torcreek. Whilst I value this woman's insights greatly, of late her brusque manners and increasingly unreasonable demands have been a distraction I could well do without.

I write these next words some minutes after penning the above paragraph, having partaken of a calming measure of tea. Mrs. Torcreek is more than just my friend, she is in many ways as crucial to the initial success of this project as I am. Without her, and the support of the Carvenport refugees, the barricade may well have fallen and I would be writing this journal in the seclusion of a Protectorate prison cell. So I will continue to attest my deep regard and respect for Mrs. Torcreek and hope our friendship continues. However, the simple matter remains that I cannot give her what she wants.

"The Protectorate's still got ships," she pointed out to me. "And soldiers. And I got plenty of folks willing to shoulder arms and join this fight."

"The Free Protectorate's maritime forces are in a state of considerable disarray," I replied, forcing as much patient sympathy into my tone as I could. We had discussed this matter several times and I have always detested repetition. "Desertion has robbed the Northern Fleet of at least half its strength," I went on. "Whilst the rest are scattered throughout Mandinor and elsewhere. Not all regions are sympathetic to our cause, nor all officers. As for our soldiers, given that the success we have enjoyed stemmed in no small part from the unwillingness of the rank and file to fight, I have few illusions they would be willing to sail across an ocean to do so in a war many regard as just a fanciful rumour."

"Convince them otherwise," Fredabel said bluntly. "You're awful persuasive."

"No amount of persuasion can overcome hard realities. This nascent republic of ours hangs by the slimmest thread. I regard it as nothing short of a miracle that we have avoided outright civil war. Sending the bulk of our military strength off on an expedition from which it seems unlikely they will return is unwise to the point of folly, and I will not do it."

Seeing a glint of anger spark in Mrs. Torcreek's eye, I realised my tone had become more strident than I intended. "I am fully aware of and sympathetic to your concerns, Fredabel," I said, striving to adopt a more sedate tone. "And, thanks to my recent communication with Captain Hilemore, I know how dire the situation in Varestia is. It pains me to say this, but in all likelihood the peninsular is already lost. This monstrous army will assuredly visit itself on the former Corvantine Empire before turning its gaze towards Mandinor. When that happens we will need to be ready to meet it, with all the weapons at our disposal."

She stared at me with an expression it pained me to see on her face: deep, sorrowful disappointment. "Won your great victory over the corporate world," she said. "Now you don't want to risk it. If the White takes Varestia there'll be no stopping it. The battle is there."

I closed my eyes, sighing heavily and knowing our friendship was now in peril, but the burden of duty sometimes permits no recourse to sentiment. Power, I have learned, can be a lonely business. "I have made my decision, Mrs. Torcreek," I said. "Thank you for coming."

35th Vorellum

The man who came to see me this afternoon was slight of build, his suit neat and nondescript, as was his face, neither especially handsome nor especially ugly. In short, he was the kind of man it would be easy to miss. It quickly transpired that this lack of notability was far from accidental.

The nondescript man had taken his place amongst the multitude of those who daily come in search of a meeting with Free Woman Tythencroft. The only noteworthy aspect to him was his willingness to wait patiently and without complaint. In recent days I have taken up residence in the formerly vacated Ironship headquarters, it seeming to me somewhat perverse and self-defeating to eschew use of eminently suitable accommodation for reasons of anti-corporate prejudice. It also benefited from a large and unheated lobby devoid of seating of any kind, meaning only the hardiest and most persistent souls will consent to wait out the hours required to gain access to my presence. Most can be diverted to my deputies and sundry officials, but others are not so easily palmed off. The nondescript man offered a card to the receptionist which stated his name, an alias I won't bother to record, and business: Trans Global Export Consultant. His stated reason for seeking an audience related to "valuable information concerning the state of affairs in Varestia."

I had him brought in immediately. My brief but highly significant communication with Corrick had left me in little doubt as to the importance of events unfolding on the far side of the Orethic Ocean and I was keen to obtain all the accurate intelligence I could.

"This . . . army," I said, "of deformed and enslaved people . . ."

"And drakes," the nondescript man put in with a polite smile.

"And drakes. They are now advancing into the peninsular itself?"

"That is my understanding. It is estimated that they will, unless faced with considerable resistance, complete the conquest of Varestia within a maximum of two months. After that we expect them to strike north into the Corvantine Empire proper, or is it Republic these days? So hard to keep track, don't you find?"

"We?" I enquired. "Your company seems well informed, sir."

The nondescript man remained silent for a brief moment before speaking two words: "Exceptional Initiatives."

My initial impulse was to reach for the small bell on my desk and summon the two Free Protectorate soldiers stationed outside my door. For one who has devoted years to the Voter cause, these two words cannot fail to provoke alarm.

"There is no longer an Ironship Protectorate," I pointed out, silently commending myself for the steadiness of my voice. "Therefore, there is no longer an Exceptional Initiatives Division."

The nondescript man replied with a short laugh, but otherwise said nothing, continuing to sit in patient expectation of my next words.

"What do you want?" I asked, choosing the obvious route as I was suddenly in no mood for any cryptic obfuscation.

The nondescript man cast a glance around the room before replying. "We want in. It's cold outside."

"You expect me to find a place for your vile organisation within this administration? I think you mistake the nature of what we are building here."

"On the contrary, we understand it very well. Power, Miss Tythencroft. You are building power, and for that to succeed you need us." His hand went into the inner lining of his suit and emerged with a sheet of paper, which he unfolded before placing it on my desk. I saw it to be a diagram of some kind, though the long cylindrical device it depicted was unfamiliar.

"This," the nondescript man said, "is a blueprint for a weapon of unprecedented destructive power and accuracy. It is currently being produced at a secluded location on the Varestian Peninsular, ostensibly as a defence against the invaders in the north. Should that defence succeed, exclusive rights to and use of this weapon will then fall to whomsoever has authority over the region. Unless I misjudge your character, I assume you fully appreciate the significance of this intelligence."

I sat back in my chair, keeping my features expressionless. "You have a Blood-blessed agent on the peninsular," I said. "Presumably located at the very place where this weapon is being produced."

The nondescript man returned my gaze, saying nothing until it became clear that I had no intention of speaking until he did. "There are . . . sympathetic elements amongst those gathered to defend Varestia," he said. "Some of them keen to exploit old contacts for personal reasons."

"Personal reasons?"

"We are not the only former Ironship employees keen to find a place in your new world."

I looked again at the diagram. It had long been my hope that, should the day ever arrive when the Voters Rights Alliance gained sufficient power to effect change in the world, we would aspire to something better than the greed and endless conflict of the Corporate Age. But then, none of us had ever envisaged the old world's fall to happen so completely nor so swiftly. My

days as unelected leader of this nascent government had left me with few illusions about the realities of wielding power, especially when my hold on it
was so fragile.

"Can this device be replicated?" I asked.

"It can," he assured me. "If the appropriate labour and resources are
provided. However, I must point out that this device is the product of a very
singular and unusual mind. Who can say what such a mind might produce
in the future?"

I could have refused him, of course. I could have rung my little bell and
had him thrown out, or even killed since there are many in the Free Protectorate perfectly willing to undertake such tasks. But I didn't. Instead I
clasped my hands together, conjured a brisk, businesslike smile to my lips
and asked, "I assume you have a course of action to propose?"

CHAPTER 35

Hilemore

Colonel Kulvetch arrived late, marching along the outer-wall battlement in company with a full squad of South Seas Maritime Marines. Hilemore assumed her tardiness was the result of a careful surveillance of the wall to ensure the Voter rebels hadn't prepared a treacherous ambush. Coll and Jillett had come to represent the Voters Committee along with a half-dozen fighters from the Wash Lane Defence Volunteers. Hilemore had arranged for the parley to take place atop the bridge that spanned the river flowing through the wall and over the falls. He thought it a rather marvellous piece of construction, an elegant stone arch some thirty yards long with a defensive tower at each end. The towers were unique amongst Stockcombe's outer defences in that they hadn't fallen into disuse. Although they now featured a pocked and cracked appearance thanks to the rival groups occupying them continuing to exchange fire throughout the crisis. Coll said the otherwise well-maintained appearance of the towers resulted from the corporate regime's desire to police the main access point between the two halves of the city.

"You had to pay a three-scrip toll to walk from east to west," he said. "They always did their best to keep the scum out."

Kulvetch motioned for her escort to remain at the far end of the bridge and proceeded alone, ascending the curving incline and coming to a halt a few feet away. She gave Coll and Jillett a glance of cursory hatred before focusing her gaze on Hilemore, face rigid and voice clipped as she uttered a curt "What is it?"

"You saw the drake, I assume?" he asked.

"We did."

"Then I also assume you know what it portends."

"I know it means there are still Reds living on this continent. Beyond that, I know nothing."

Jillett let out a disgusted snort but fell silent at Hilemore's sharp glance. Persuading the Voters to agree to a parley hadn't been easy, but at least they fully recognised the danger this city now faced. Kulvetch, he knew, would be even more reluctant to set aside her hatred and lust for revenge.

"I have sound intelligence," Hilemore said, turning back to Kulvetch, "that a large host of Green and Red drakes is advancing towards this city. We estimate they will arrive in less than two days."

Kulvetch managed to keep her reaction to a few rapid blinks of her eyes, but Hilemore saw how her throat bunched a little above the starched collar of her tunic. "What sound intelligence?" she asked. "Or am I to simply trust the word of a corporate officer who so willingly surrenders his honour to throw in with these murderous fanatics?"

"Your father was the murderer," Coll shot back. "Where were you on Lomansday when he flogged and slaughtered innocent people? Busy at home playing with your dolls?"

"Enough!" Hilemore barked, seeing Kulvetch's face redden with fury, her hand inching towards the side-arm on her belt. "I have thrown in with no one," he told her. "I come here in search of common cause, for without it we may all be doomed."

He paused, pondering his next words and coming to the conclusion that there was no longer much value in secrecy. "As for the source of my intelligence, the Blood-blessed on my ship is in trance communication with a Contractor company in the Interior. You wondered why we came here, well, they are why. Their mission is vital, and I must recover them."

"So," Coll said, "you want us to fight the drakes off long enough for them to get here."

"I don't need to stay here to recover them," Hilemore replied, once again deciding honesty was the best tactic. "But I do need the ships in this port. Most are now willing to sail to Varestia where there is a struggle of far greater import than your feud."

"What assurance do I have that any of this is true?" Kulvetch asked.

"Wait two days and find out, you silly bitch," Jillett advised with a bland smile.

Kulvetch flushed a little with suppressed rage and addressed her next question to Hilemore. "You propose we evacuate?"

He shook his head. "There aren't enough ships to accommodate more than a quarter of your population. You questioned my honour, but it's my honour that keeps me here rather than leaving you to your fate. I have formulated a plan which may succeed in ensuring this city's survival, but to survive you'll have to fight, and fight together. If you can't do that, tell me now and we will be on our way."

Kulvetch and the two Voters continued to stare at each other during the lengthy silence that followed. Hilemore felt as if the air separating them had somehow become heated with their mutual enmity. He had begun to wonder if this hadn't been a fool's errand when Coll spoke up, speaking directly to Kulvetch, "It's a truce. That's all. We ain't forgiving or forgetting nothing. When it's over there'll be an accounting."

"A day I hunger for," Kulvetch replied before turning to Hilemore. "Your plan, Captain?"

They didn't like it, nor had he expected them to, but at least grudgingly agreed to put it to their respective populations. Hilemore spent the rest of the day overseeing the redistribution of crew and fuel amongst his new fleet, all the while expecting both sides to respond with a firm no. However, such worries were overthrown by the reappearance of the Red that afternoon.

It flew lower this time, descending to a height that proved irresistible to marksmen throughout the divided city and the fleet, who let loose with a furious barrage of rifle fire. The Red twisted and turned in the sky above the harbour, the hail of bullets thrumming the air around it without scoring a hit. Hilemore detected, or perhaps imagined, a taunting note in the screech the Red let out before flying off to the north, chased by yet more ineffectual rifle fire. Despite the waste of ammunition the drake's visit had the beneficial effect of focusing minds on both sides of the falls and Hilemore received the agreement of both factions by nightfall.

Via a trance with Zenida, Clay had confirmed that the Greens appeared to be keeping to the western bank of the river. Greens were renowned as good swimmers but at this latitude the river was too fast-flowing even for them, meaning their assault would fall on that side of the city. Colonel

Kulvetch seemed to enjoy almost absolute authority over the western side for the bulk of the populace obediently decamped for an orderly transfer to the other side of the falls. Many made their way over the bridge but most were moved by the ships in the harbour.

At Kulvetch's insistence an entire quarter of the eastern side had been cleared to make way for the new inhabitants. The civilians were preceded by a large contingent of Marines, who cordoned off the allocated streets. There were complaints, of course, few west-siders relished the prospect of taking up residence in what one middle-aged manager referred to as "the hovels of the uncontracted." But the mood for the most part was one of fear rather than defiance. At least for the time being the citizens of Stockcombe were willing to forgo their bitter little war for the sake of survival.

It took over thirty hours to fully clear the west side, save for a few die-hards who refused to leave their homes. They were mostly former senior management types, those who had survived the initial bout of conflict but then found themselves side-lined in the days that followed, their skills and prior authority suddenly rendered meaningless. Colonel Kulvetch displayed an unsuspected sentimentality in not having the heart to compel obedience from these impotent luminaries. Hilemore, finding the issue a distracting nuisance, didn't press the matter when she refused his offer to have the stubborn old buggers forced into boats at gunpoint.

With the transfer complete he arrayed the ships into a defensive line across the harbour, starboard hulls facing the other side. Every cannon, rifle and harpoon in the fleet was arrayed along the starboard rails and west-facing upper works. Unsurprisingly, the Dalcian vessels proved to contain the most armaments, piracy being a time-honoured hobby amongst those who plied the merchant trade. Altogether, Steelfine reported a total of seventeen cannon and three hundred rifles, plus the harpoons of the Blue-hunters. It was less than the combined fire-power of a single Protectorate flotilla but it would have to do.

Hilemore put more faith in the mines with which they had seeded the harbour waters. The value of such devices had been made clear to him amidst the southern ice and he had the survivors from that travail to thank for the rapidity with which the mines had been manufactured. Furthermore, a number of nasty surprises had been prepared in the streets of the west side. Hilemore knew this would all take a fearful toll on the Greens, but the Reds were another matter.

He had Kulvetch and the Voters place all the armed personnel under their command on the roof-tops of the east side. There were a few Contractors amongst the Voters with experience in killing drakes, but the bulk of the defenders had been told to aim for the wings rather than waste ammunition in vain attempts to achieve a head-shot. Positioned at various points in the streets were numerous fire-fighting squads armed with buckets and pump hoses. It was a measure of Hilemore's assessment of their ability to defeat the coming assault that the fire-fighters outnumbered the armed defenders by two to one.

Time, he reminded himself as he made his way to the crest of the arched bridge. Night was coming on fast and his gaze was fixed on the northern horizon beyond the moonlit waters of the river. *We just have to buy enough time.*

He had left Steelfine in command of the *Superior* in favour of occupying a vantage point atop the east-side bridge tower. He had complete faith in the Islander's ability to command in combat, besides which the plan allowed little scope for improvisation when set in motion. In fact there was only one decision to be taken dependent on the outcome of events. Mothers with children had been secluded in the cellars closest to the docks, ready to be rushed to the ships for a swift evacuation should the coming battle turn into a disaster. It would entail raising the harbour door on a one-moon night, meaning the lower portion of the city would be lost along with many of the townsfolk, but he considered this preferable to the alternative.

Hilemore had asked for only one volunteer to accompany him, Lieutenant Talmant stepping forward immediately. Hilemore's first impulse had been to inform him that he belonged on the ship, being technically third in command. But faced with the young man's stern, almost demanding expression the words died on Hilemore's tongue. *The lad's earned the right to stand where he likes tonight,* he thought, clapping the lieutenant on the shoulder and ordering him to draw a rifle.

Besides Talmant, he had been joined by the Wash Lane Defence Volunteers, there on Coll's order with instructions to "keep the corporate bastard alive." Hilemore thought them a strangely cheerful lot in the circumstances, clustering round a flaming brazier as the night drew on and engaging in banter rich in mutual ridicule and lacking any mention of the impending danger. He detected a forced tone to much of their profane humour and knew it to be a refuge from fear, one he didn't begrudge them.

The company included one additional recruit, there at Hilemore's insistence and provisioned with as much product as he felt able to spare. Jillett had objected to being placed under his command, expressing a desire to stand alongside her Voter comrades in a speech that was rich in indignation but, to Hilemore's ears, lacking in conviction. He could see the palpable fear in her eyes as she stood amongst the Volunteers. As the Voters' only Blood-blessed she had been shielded during the conflict and tonight would be her first true taste of battle. He had wanted to place her aboard the *Superior* as added insurance in case the ships were forced to flee, but knew that Coll and the rest of the committee would never have stood for it.

The time before battle was usually a trial of jangled nerves and unnaturally long minutes, so he felt a pang of paradoxical gratitude when the drakes chose not to keep them waiting. "Sir," Talmant said, handing him a spy-glass and pointing to the north. It didn't take Hilemore long to find them, Nelphia's light shimmering as it played over the mass of Greens on the western bank of the river. They were moving at a steady loping trot rather than a mad rush, presumably to conserve energy for a charge when they drew closer. He quelled an upsurge of dismay, realising it indicated some kind of reasoning intelligence behind this attack.

"We could just go," Zenida had said before he took his leave an hour earlier. "This lot are intent on killing each other in any case. What do we owe them?"

"There are children here," he said. "And others who took no part in this bloody farce. I can't just abandon them."

She hadn't pursued the issue, merely shaking her head with a weary grin as she said, "You would have made a terrible pirate."

"Send the signal," Hilemore said. He raised the spy-glass to the sky finding it a starlit, partially clouded spectacle free of any drakes. *They're up there,* he knew. *Too high to see, probably.*

The night was split by the flat crump of an exploding rocket as Talmant let the fleet and the city know the enemy was in sight. The message was answered with a prearranged chorus of sirens and steam-whistles from the ships, intended to wake any drowsing defenders on the roof-tops. Hilemore lowered the glass to gauge the progress of the Greens. They were keeping close to the edge of the river, those in front increasing their speed, mouths gaping as they let out their challenge calls. It grew in volume as the mass drew nearer, the screeching barks combining to produce something that resembled the burgeoning growl of a hungry monster.

"Oh fuck me," he heard a Wash Lane Volunteer mutter then curse as one of his fellows cuffed him to silence.

Hilemore tracked the leading Greens until they reached the base of the wall on the far side of the river. They boiled over the partially ruined structure in a leaping, snarling torrent, some charging directly into the town whilst others scrambled onto the battlement and sprinted towards the bridge.

Hilemore closed the spy-glass with a brisk snap and handed it back to Talmant before descending the tower steps at a measured walk. He moved to the box positioned at the point where the bridge met the eastern wall. One of the Volunteers barked out a command and they moved to position themselves alongside him in two ranks, kneeling in front, rifles and carbines levelled.

"Save your rounds," Hilemore advised, turning the locking switch on the box and elevating the handle. Chief Bozware had rigged this some hours earlier, Hilemore unwilling to trust the task to anyone else. "Once the lock's off just push it forward, sir," he said. "There's a one-second delay, give you a chance to put your hands over your ears."

He told the Volunteers to do this now, but, receiving only puzzled glances in response, shrugged and turned his attention back to the bridge. The first Green crested the span almost immediately, flames already blooming in its maw. The Volunteers all fired as one, peppering the bridge with bullets and scoring hits on the beast's forelegs and shoulders but failing to stop its charge. Seeing another two Greens behind it Hilemore decided further delay would be unwise and pushed the handle on the detonator before clamping his hands over his ears.

The blast wave was sufficient to send Hilemore and the Volunteers sprawling, blinking rapidly against the instant pall of dust then huddling or dodging to avoid the falling cascade of debris. Hilemore shook his head to clear the ringing from his ears, rubbing at his eyes and wafting smoke. When it cleared he was rewarded with the sight of a dozen or more Greens tumbling into the space where the central span of the bridge had been. They fell screeching into the fast-flowing torrent below to be instantly swept over the falls. The momentum of the Greens' charge was such that the cascade of falling drakes continued for several minutes, much to the amusement of the Volunteers.

"That's it, drown, you scaly fucks!" a thin-faced girl yelled across the divide where a dense throng of Greens milled about the end of the stunted bridge, shrieking in rage and coughing out flames. "Try and eat us now!"

Hilemore shifted his gaze from the enraged Greens to the west-side streets below the wall, seeing them packed with a tide of onrushing drakes. The first booby trap went off a few seconds later, the explosion destroying the fountain in one of the palatial squares in the administrative district. Hilemore saw at least ten Greens tumbling amidst flame and debris. The remaining traps exploded in quick succession, each blast seemingly bigger than the one before.

Despite the carnage the Greens charged undaunted through the streets towards the harbour. The bulk of the booby traps had been placed in and around the harbour side, explosives strapped to the piers and wharfs in the expectation the Greens would be drawn there, and so it proved. The entire water-front seemed to instantaneously erupt into a wall of flame. Numerous mansion houses were transformed into rubble by the multiple blasts, which birthed a series of raging fires.

Hilemore called for Talmant to toss him the spy-glass and trained it on the water-front, seeing a mass of drifting smoke and rising flame. For one brief moment he entertained the notion that they had stopped the Greens completely, perhaps destroyed them all, but a brief scan of the neighbourhoods beyond the inferno revealed ever more Greens thronging the streets. Undeterred they charged through the raging fires and into the harbour waters, churning them white with multiple overlapping wakes as they swam towards the western side of the harbour.

Hilemore was impressed by the discipline of the merchantmen who, as instructed, held their fire, waiting for the moment when the *Superior* let loose with her broadside. The first mine erupted when the Greens were a third of the way across the harbour, producing a sixty-foot-high spout of water along with several dismembered drakes. The remaining mines exploded in quick succession with similarly grisly results. For a brief time it seemed the harbour waters were boiling, such was the energy released in so short a time. Water lapped over the east-side wharfs like waves in a storm-tossed sea and the line of ships heaved in the swell.

"Did we get all the bastards, Cap?" one of the Volunteers asked, the hefty lad who had shown an interest in Hilemore's medals.

"It's Captain," Hilemore replied, watching the displaced water subside back into the harbour in a miniature rain-storm. "And I very much doubt it."

An instant later a Green shot from the water barely ten yards from the hull of a Blue-hunter and latched itself onto the forward anchor chain. It managed to scramble halfway to the prow of the ship before a fusillade of rifle-shots from the crew sent it flailing back into the water. Small-arms fire erupted as Green after Green shot through the surface, reminding Hilemore of a huge shoal of salmon making their way up-stream. Most were cut down in mid air but some managed to gain purchase on the rails, casting their flames across the decks and roasting several crewmen before being shot down. Hilemore saw with dismay the numerous white flashes close to the *Superior* and knew the mind overseeing this attack had recognised the greatest threat and concentrated its forces accordingly.

Thankfully, under Steelfine's command the *Superior* proved equal to the task. The cannon arrayed along the starboard rail fired successive blasts of cannister as the Greens rose into their sights, blasting most to pieces. The few who did manage to clamber up the hull were swiftly cut down by experienced marksmen on the upper works.

Taking the sound of the *Superior*'s cannon as their cue the other ships opened fire with their heavy ordnance. At Hilemore's insistence they had all been loaded with cannister or, in many cases, a collection of any hard metal that could be found. The deadly rain lashed the harbour, killing Greens still attempting to swim across from the west side and catching many as they leapt clear of the water.

The cannon fell silent and Hilemore knew this to be the moment of greatest danger as the gun-crews frantically began reloading their pieces.

The burden of holding off the Greens now fell on the riflemen and those merchant crew with small-arms. The crackle of rifle- and carbine-shots sounded the length of the ships, the marksmen moving to the rail and firing down at the Greens below. The drakes seemed to have abandoned their tactic of leaping for the rails in favour of climbing up the hull with the aid of their iron-hard claws. Several ships began to take on a serious list as the weight of drake flesh dragged them down. Hilemore bit down a curse at the sight of drakes swarming over the side of a small steam-packet. The potentially disastrous loss was averted when the next ship in line, the freighter commanded by the Dalcian pirate woman, turned its freshly loaded cannon on its neighbour and raked it with cannister-shot. Blasted free of drakes, the steam-packet righted itself but there was no sign of life, either drake or human, on its deck.

The Greens seemed to vanish when the rest of the fleet resumed fire with their cannon, those attempting to haul themselves up the hulls slipping back into the water. Hilemore could see numerous drake corpses bobbing on the surface and knew that in daylight the entire harbour would now be stained a deep crimson. *It would probably burn to the touch too,* he thought, pondering the grimly amusing notion that, with product now so scarce, he had inadvertently created a vast pool of wealth.

"Sir," Talmant called from the tower, Hilemore looking up to see him pointing to the eastern rim of the crater. "Some sort of commotion."

Hilemore raised his glass, blinking in alarm as a bright plume of flame occluded the eyepiece. When he looked again he was confronted with the sight of a Red drake clambering down from the ruined wall. It launched itself forward and landed amidst a group of defenders on a near by rooftop, jaw snapping and tail lashing as it cut them to pieces in a matter of seconds. Flames flooded the view once more and Hilemore lowered the glass to see dozens of dark shapes crawling down from the wall and into the town, fire erupting every time one reached the outer houses.

They were supposed to attack from the air, he thought, a hard ball of guilt-ridden despair building in his gut, fed by the certain knowledge of being outgeneralled. *The Greens were just a distraction.*

"Mr. Talmant!" he called up to the tower. "Get to the *Superior* and tell Mr. Steelfine to load standard shell and concentrate fire on the eastern rim of the crater. Spread the word to the other ships to do the same."

"Aye, sir!" Talmant snapped off a salute and swiftly descended the tower steps before sprinting off along the battlement.

Hilemore drew his pistol, casting his gaze around at the Wash Lane Volunteers before it fell on Jillett. "I believe, miss," he said, "it's time for you to drink some product."

CHAPTER 36

Lizanne

There is no such thing as a fair fight, one of Lizanne's instructors had told her years ago. *Just the fight you win and the fight you lose.*

Given that he hadn't taken advantage of the opportunity to tie her up or maim her whilst in the trance Mr. Lockbar, she assumed for reasons of professional pride, had apparently decided he wanted a fair fight. It was a singular miscalculation.

She side-stepped his blade, ducking as she did so and feeling the sting of its edge nick her ear. She stiffened the fingers of her left hand into a spear-point and jabbed it into his wrist before he could draw the knife back, hitting the nerve required to loosen his grip and allow the weapon to fall. The momentary distraction would have been enough to dodge away, perhaps make it to the window, but the image of Makario slumped over the pianola's dripping keys banished such considerations. Instead she pressed herself to him, wrapping her legs about his waist and one arm around his neck in a strange parody of a lover's passionate embrace. But she had no love to offer Mr. Lockbar.

He tried to choke down his scream as she drew back her free arm and jammed her thumb into his eye, digging deep whilst simultaneously clamping her teeth onto his nose. She worried at it with terrier-like energy, blood flooding her mouth, her thumb digging ever deeper. They careened about the room in a mad waltz, Lockbar's scream finally escaping his throat. He hammered at her, fists like balls of iron as they pummelled her back and head. Lizanne barely felt it, putting all her strength into her limbs and her jaw, feeling a fierce exultant satisfaction as her teeth met and her thumb made a wet pop as it sank deeper into his eye-socket.

Lockbar howled in mingled rage and pain, charging forward to slam her into the wall, once then twice. With Green in her veins she might have been able to withstand it, but not now. Her legs lost their grip with the third slam, Lockbar tearing himself free of her. Too stunned to stand she could only slide down the wall and watch him stagger about, clutching his ruined face.

"Bitch," he cursed in a high-pitched gasp, sounding like a child nursing a playground injury. The notion made Lizanne laugh, something to which Mr. Lockbar took understandable exception. "Dead . . ." he gasped, casting about with his one good eye until it alighted on his knife. "Fucking kill you . . ." He snatched the weapon from the floor, turning back to Lizanne. "Make you eat your own guts . . ."

Lizanne tried to get up but found her limbs unwilling to co-operate. Things might have gone very badly if Tinkerer hadn't sat up in bed, unhooked himself from his saline bottle and thrown it at Lockbar. It was a well-aimed throw, the bottle shattering on the side of Lockbar's head and making him stagger in confusion as blood seeped into his remaining eye. Lizanne willed all the strength she could into her limbs, bracing her back against the wall as she pushed herself upright. Seeing Lockbar scrape the blood from his eye she dived onto Tinkerer, grasping him tight and rolling both of them clear of the bed just before Lockbar's knife sank into the mattress.

"Fucking kill you!" he roared, heaving the bed aside as they scrambled away. He lowered himself in preparation for a final, murderous charge, then the door exploded.

Lockbar whirled amidst a shower of shattered wood, lashing out with his knife as he shielded his face, but the knife met only air as he continued to slash . . . then froze. He stood there in mid-slash, pierced all over with splinters and blood streaming from his vanished nose and empty eye-socket.

"What do you want done?" Morva asked Lizanne, stepping through the remnants of the shattered door.

Lizanne disentangled herself from Tinkerer, helping him to his feet before turning her attention to Makario. The musician's head lay on the pianola's keyboard at an angle, almost as if he were resting. His eyes were open and Lizanne found his skin icy as she reached out to lay a hand on his cheek. The cut to his neck was deep and even now blood was still dripping onto the keys.

"Don't kill him," she told Morva, turning and moving to stand close to Mr. Lockbar. She peered into his remaining eye, wide and wet. "We still have a great deal to talk about."

She didn't ask questions, lacking the inclination and the skills for a proper interrogation which was a task best left in expert hands. Instead she had the iron works cleared, giving the workers a much-needed morning off, whilst Mr. Lockbar was suspended in chains above the huge smelting bowl filled with ingots which in turn sat above the sliding doors on top of the furnace.

Morva had offered to help but Lizanne sent her away, stoking the furnace herself, taking her time as she shovelled coke into the oven and ignited the kerosene-fuelled engine that worked the bellows. Lockbar hung in silence for the first ten minutes, blood leaking through the bandages on his face, applied none too gently by one of Dr. Weygrand's orderlies. Lizanne was keen to ensure he didn't bleed to death.

After a quarter of an hour Lockbar began to fidget, chains jangling as he jerked his body, but still refused to speak. Lizanne checked the temperature on the smelter's gauge, and, finding it at the required level, opened the furnace doors. Lockbar's fidgeting turned into desperate struggles at the sudden blast of heat, the first words emerging from his bandaged face as Lizanne climbed the scaffold to watch the smoke rising from the ingots in the bowl.

"We . . ." he said in his strange nasal rasp. "We are in the same business."

Lizanne angled her head, watching the ingots on top shift as those on the bottom began to melt. Despite the heat she somehow contrived to feel cold, her face frozen and her hands numb as they settled onto the scaffolding. Makario's music played in her head, or rather the music he had spent his life rediscovering. She made a mental note to ensure all his papers were properly catalogued and secured then closed her eyes, remembering that first time she had heard him play back in the Miner's Repose. Even in the midst of the worst place on earth, there had been something magical about it. A jarring note interrupted her reverie and she realised Lockbar was speaking again.

". . . not so different." She opened her eyes to find him attempting to angle his body towards her, striving to meet her gaze. "We are guilty of similar sins, I suspect." He grunted the words out, Lizanne seeing sweat bathing his skin as more smoke rose from the bowl. She could see the first flecks of molten metal bubbling up between the as yet unmelted ingots at the top. "So, I ask you," Lockbar went on, "would you consider this a fitting end? Would you not deserve some courtesy?"

He had managed to contort himself sufficiently to meet her gaze, his one good eye gleaming amidst the mask of bandages. Lizanne felt no reluctance in meeting his gaze, nor any in looking away. She said nothing, watching the iron melt and realising with a pang of deep regret that she had never learned Makario's full name. She could hear Lockbar continuing to babble out entreaties but none of it captured her attention until he began to bargain.

"I bribed a bosun on one of the pirate ships to smuggle me here," he said, his eye flicking between her and the now-almost-melted contents of the bowl. "I can give you his name."

Seeing the last ingot subside into the bright orange soup, Lizanne moved to the length of chain hanging near by. It ran through a series of pulleys from which Lockbar had been suspended and required only minimal exertion to shift him about.

"Arshav and Ethilda!" Lockbar went on, shouting now. "I know where they are. They left the Seven Walls! As you must have guessed. But I know where they went."

Lizanne hauled on the chain, tilting Lockbar's body so that his feet pointed towards the bubbling contents of the bowl.

"North!" Lockbar screamed, legs flailing as a splash of molten iron escaped the bowl. "They went north, intending to treat with the Corvantine rebels. I was to join them in Corvus."

Lizanne's hands paused on the chain, lips pursed as she considered the information. "Yes," she said, "I thought they might." Then she began to haul on the chain once more, lowering him towards the bowl.

"Lizanne!" Her father stood at the top of the ladder, breathless from the run that had brought him here and staring at her in appalled dismay. "What are you doing?"

"The ironworkers tell me it won't spoil the output," she said, continuing to haul on the chain.

"Stop that!" He rushed from the ladder, reaching out to grasp her hands. She grimaced in annoyance and tried to jerk her hands free but he held on. "This is not justice," he said. "Justice requires a court and judge."

"I'm not sure the world has a use for such things any more, Father," she said, inclining her head at Lockbar. "Now there are only people like him, and me."

He gazed down at her with the expression of a man seeing a baffling stranger for the first time. "What did they do to you?" he murmured, releasing her hands to cup her face. "What did they turn you into?"

"What did you think they would make of me, Father?" she asked. "When you let them take me, what did you think I would become? You must have known I was Blessed even before the Blood-lot. A clever man like you would have made sure to discover his daughter's true nature, would he not?"

Professor Lethridge lowered his gaze, giving a fractional nod.

"And yet you let them take me."

"It was the law." She saw him wince in the knowledge that he had spoken a lie. A clever man like him could have hidden her, perhaps even taken her far away, where the Syndicate would never find her. "I thought it for the best," he said, meeting her gaze once more. "Academy-educated Blood-blessed enjoy great privilege, have rewarding careers. What could I offer you? A lifetime tinkering with novelties with barely a scrip to rub together. I didn't know . . ." His hands gripped her face more tightly and he leaned closer, whispering, "I didn't know what they would do to you. If I had I would never have allowed it."

She felt her purpose slip away then, her body seeming to sag as the need for retribution faded into simple grief and loss. "I am such a disappointment then?" she asked him.

"No." He pulled her close. "No, you are what you have always been. A very frightening but wonderful surprise."

And Lizanne Lethridge held her father tight and wept for the first time in many years.

Mr. Lockbar was executed by firing squad the next morning. His trial had been brief but as thorough as they could make it. Madame Hakugen sat as judge whilst Captain Trumane acted as prosecuting counsel. Ensign Tollver took on the role of defending counsel and displayed an impressive gift for inventive argument. Employing a fine set of rhetorical skills, the young officer contended that Mr. Lockbar's actions, terrible as they were, had been committed in a location lacking anything that could be called established legal process, or even a canon of recognised law. Therefore, they were not technically illegal. Madame Hakugen, however, ruled in favour of Captain Trumane's argument that the charter of the Mount Works Manufacturing Company had been constituted on the same basis as Ironship Syndicate law, a law that prohibited murder and mandated the death penalty for convicted offenders.

The firing squad consisted of riflemen from the *Viable Opportunity*, though there had been numerous volunteers from the ranks of the workers. Dr. Weygrand had been popular and many had also appreciated the nights when Makario would consent to play a tune or two once the shifts had ended. Lockbar was marched to the end of a pier at high tide whereupon he refused a blindfold and faced his executioners as they levelled their rifles in response to Trumane's order. Lizanne had heard how it was common for a few shots to go astray on such occasions, thanks to the natural human aversion to killing. If so, it was not the case with Mr. Lockbar. Every bullet fired slammed home into his chest, sending him tumbling from the pier into the waters of Blaska Sound.

"Too bad about Arshav and Ethilda," Alzar Lokaras said as Lizanne accompanied him back to his ship. "They're probably a hundred miles away by now. And forget what Lockbar told you about their heading north, too many Blues. My guess is they'll head for the Cape of Souls and then make their way up the east Corvantine coast. Either that or strike out for Dalcia, if they've got the fuel. You could send your flying contraptions after them . . ."

"We have a war to fight," Lizanne interrupted. "Other concerns will have to wait. The *Firefly* made a reconnaissance flight yesterday, it seems the White forces are less than twenty miles from the passes."

He nodded and they halted at the foot of the gangway to his ship. "The

Blood-blessed will be put ashore this evening, those that were willing. Seems the Blessing isn't a cure for cowardice."

Cowardice? Lizanne wondered. *Or wisdom? In times like these perhaps there's no difference.* "This operation is only a delaying tactic," she told him. "Even if every aspect succeeds the main battles are still to come. We need fighters, as many as you can gather and transport to the peninsular in the time remaining."

He gave a small nod, a frown of consternation on his brow. "Wish they'd obliged us with a sea battle. Ethilda wasn't right about much, but she was about Varestians never being fond of fighting on land. It's how the Corvantines beat us."

"A clever enemy never does what you expect. And our enemy is aggravatingly clever." She gave him a formal nod and turned to go.

"My niece," he said, making her pause. "You'll be taking her with you?"

"Of course," Lizanne told him.

There was a guardedness to his gaze, his voice clipped to ensure it betrayed no emotion. "Be smart to have a few Blood-blessed in reserve, wouldn't it?"

"Not if this is going to work. And I doubt I could make her stay behind if I wanted to."

Alzar gritted his teeth as he went on, eyes averted. "She's the last Blood-blessed left to the Lokaras line, even though she's not truly of our blood."

"The Blessing might not be a cure for cowardice," Lizanne told him, "but apparently being part of your line is." Alzar nodded but didn't move, Lizanne swallowing a weary sigh at the sight of him struggling to find a way of asking for a favour in a manner that didn't chafe his pride. "She'll remain on the *Typhoon*," she told him. "As a rear guard. With any luck she'll be clear of danger for much of the operation."

Alzar let out a grunt of apparent satisfaction, still not looking at her as he turned and made his way up the gang-plank without a word of farewell.

She returned to the town, making her way to the administrative building and forcing herself to return the greetings she received along the way. Grief should have been a familiar sensation by now, and she had hoped such familiarity would have calloused her heart against fresh pain. But it transpired that she had no such callous and the pain, fresh and very raw, made her less inclined towards conventional civility. Even so, she maintained as friendly a demeanour as she could when greeting her employees, though she was thankful that their apparently genuine respect was coloured by a certain wariness, even fear. *They saw what I did to Mr. Lockbar,* she knew. *And what I wanted to do to him.*

"I don't mind waiting if she's busy," she told Madame Hakugen's secretary upon entering the outer foyer of her office. The girl immediately blanched and scurried to the office door, opening it wide after a whispered enquiry with the occupant.

"Miss Lethridge." Madame Hakugen rose as Lizanne entered.

"Madame." Lizanne gestured at the chair in front of the director's desk. "May I?"

"Of course. Dissel," she said, turning to her secretary, "please fetch us some tea."

"Tea?" Lizanne enquired, sinking into the chair with a raised eyebrow as the girl bustled out.

"Sovereign Black no less," Madame said, also taking a seat. "A gift from Captain Kashiel. We were acquainted before in Lossermark. She always did appreciate the social aspect of business."

"I trust you shared it with your staff." Lizanne gave her a bland smile. "I am hoping to foster a more egalitarian approach to management in this company. Individual privilege would appear to negate that."

"I have never been one to hoard luxuries, in truth we are about to enjoy the last of the supply." She paused for a moment, eyes narrowing a fraction. "Am I to take it then that the Mount Works will adopt a radical approach to commerce? Your intention seems more in line with that of a Corvantine revolutionary than the traditional corporate ethos."

"The traditions of the corporate world seem to have availed us little of late. I think it's time we tried something different." She reached inside the pocket of the seaman's jacket she wore over her overalls, producing a sheaf of papers. "It's all in here," she said, setting the papers on the desk. "Proposed management structure and remuneration protocols."

Madame unfolded the papers and began to read, her eyes narrowing all the while. She read in silence, scouring the pages with a scrutiny of sufficient length that Dissel had returned bearing a tea-tray by the time she finished.

"The difference between salaries for management and worker is hardly considerable," Madame Hakugen observed after the girl had made her exit.

"Indeed it isn't," Lizanne agreed, taking a sip from the steaming cup Dissel placed in front of her. Sovereign Black had never been her favourite but, after so long without the taste of tea it was quite wonderful.

"And all employees are automatically made shareholders," Madame went on.

"Yes, with current workers and managers all holding an equal number of shares. New workers, assuming we ever have the opportunity to employ any, will receive one share upon joining to be increased by a share a year until they achieve parity with their colleagues."

"A co-operative," Madame said, setting the papers down and reaching for her own tea-cup.

"Quite so. A company where everyone shares in the profits and is thereby incentivised to generate more. And I should like you to run it."

"A novel proposal, and one I'll certainly consider. But I find it odd you would put this forward now, with the continuing emergency . . ."

"I put it forward because of the continuing emergency. You'll find another document at the end of the bundle. I ask that you witness it."

Madame leafed through the papers until she found it, her brows knitting in puzzlement as she read the opening paragraph. "You appear to have written a will," she said.

"I have. There was a pre-existing will stored at Exceptional Initiatives headquarters, but I suspect it's ash by now. In any case, my wishes have changed since then. The list of beneficiaries is short and I trust you will ensure they all receive the allotted bequests in due course."

"One typically puts one's affairs in order in the expectation of an imminent demise."

Lizanne pursed her lips in agreement. "One does."

Madame Hakugen sat back in her chair, eyeing Lizanne closely. "The fact that you prepared a will indicates you expect the beneficiaries to survive, but you do not. Am I wrong?"

"Rarely, I suspect."

The director let out a soft humourless laugh, shaking her head. "It is my contention that you are far too valuable . . ."

"Just sign it."

Madame's gaze snapped up at the hardness in Lizanne's voice. She met the older woman's eyes, making sure she understood her resolve. After a moment, Madame reached for a pen, dabbed the nib in an inkpot and added her signature to the document.

"Thank you," Lizanne said, taking a moment to drain her tea-cup. "I have one more request before I go, regarding personnel."

"Personnel?"

"Yes. I know you have compiled copious records regarding the prior occupations of our employees. I require one with a special set of skills."

"All those with military experience have been identified . . ."

"Not military experience," Lizanne broke in. "Theatrical."

The Little Cut was too far away to hear the explosion but the cloudless morning sky gave Lizanne a clear view of it. She watched through the front window of the *Typhoon*'s gondola as a brief flash of white blazed in the centre of the pass before a vaguely mushroom-shaped cloud began to rise above the mountains of the Neck. The charges laid in the Small Cut exploded shortly after and soon there were two tall mushrooms rising to east and west. The demolition crews, all experienced miners or road-builders, had been dropped by aerostat three days before, working with feverish energy to complete the task in the time available. Lizanne had yet to catch sight of any Reds but knew their enemy must have seen the explosions.

They know the only quick route now lies in the Grand Cut, she thought. *But will they take the bait?* It was possible the White could steer its army towards the coast road to the west, buying the Defence League valuable time in the process, but she had a sense it would try for the pass despite the obvious risks. *What does it care about risks? It can always make more Spoiled, at least for now.*

She held on to the central support strut as Tekela put the *Typhoon* into a steep descent. The other Blood-blessed, ten in all including Morva, were crowded together in various states of white-faced nausea. For most it was their first trip in an aerostat, and three of the Blood-blessed from the Mount Works had never seen any kind of combat before. They all carried Smoker carbines and each had a Spider on their wrist, fully loaded with product. In addition they carried full flasks of Red, Green and Black with an emergency vial of Blue. It occurred to Lizanne that with all the product on their person those drafted into this mission might well be, albeit briefly, the richest group of individuals on the planet.

"Get ready," Lizanne told them as the *Typhoon* levelled out. She peered through the rear window at the *Tempest*, the *Typhoon*'s recently constructed sister ship into which another thirteen Blood-blessed had been crammed. The *Tempest* bristled with armaments, two Thumpers on either side of the gondola with a Growler at the rear and another two in a fixed position at the front which could be triggered by the pilot. The look-out in the upper gondola also had a mini-Growler to ward off attacks from above. The *Typhoon* was armed only with Growlers thanks to the heavy object hanging beneath her gondola, which limited the weight she could bear and still manoeuvre.

"Check your watch," Lizanne told Morva, who obligingly extended her wrist to display her timepiece. Lizanne placed her own watch alongside to ensure they were synchronised. "Start the trance . . ."

"In exactly two hours," Morva finished. "Remain in the trance until you contact me or the product runs out. I know."

Lizanne nodded in satisfaction and started towards the front of the gondola, pausing when Morva said, "It was my uncle, wasn't it? He made you leave me behind." There was no heat to her words, just careful observation.

"My trance connection with you is stronger than with the others," Lizanne replied.

"Mrs. Griffan could have taken on the role."

"Mrs. Griffan is insane. She's better off remaining on the *Viable*." She met Morva's gaze. "You have this role because I trust no one else to do it."

She returned to Tekela's side, watching the approaching mountains. The morning winds were stiff but she had been advised by Varestians familiar with the region they would grow fierce as the day wore on. The Grand Cut came into view as they flew over the southern foot-hills. Lizanne found its appearance somewhat at odds with its name, a narrow, cliff-sided track tracing the contours between the flanks of two mountains. She took some solace from the photostats that showed the pass to be considerably wider to the north and, therefore, hopefully a more tempting option for whoever had command of the White's forces today.

Tekela, having made this trip several times over the preceding days, steered the *Typhoon* towards a broad ledge jutting from a point a hundred feet or so up the eastern mountain. Reconnaissance had revealed this as the optimum landing site as there was a similarly proportioned ledge on the opposite side of the pass. Tekela brought the aerostat closer, deft hands correcting their course as the fractious mountain air-currents buffeted the craft. After a few minutes of careful handling the *Typhoon* hovered over the ledge at a height of twenty feet.

"Remember," she told Tekela, "not until Morva gives the order. No matter what else might happen."

Tekela looked up at her, the tension evident in her set features. "And if there is no order?" she asked.

"The mission will be over. Fly back to the Mount." She paused before moving to the hatch in the floor. "And be sure to meet with Madame Hakugen as soon as you return."

CHAPTER 37

Clay

It seemed as if half of Stockcombe was already alight by the time Lutharon swept over the outer wall. Fires raged on both sides of the falls and he could see people running through the streets on the eastern side. At first it appeared to be the chaotic end of another city fallen to the White's malice, but then he saw smoke-plumes rising from the cannon on the ships in the harbour. To Clay's bemusement they were firing into the eastern districts of the city, the shells falling amidst the houses closest to the rim of the crater. As Lutharon flew closer, however, he saw Reds leaping from one roof-top to another, belching flame at the people running in the streets below. He saw one Red blasted in half by a direct hit from a cannon shell, but there were dozens, perhaps hundreds more still scrambling over the lip of the crater. Fortunately, it appeared none had noticed Lutharon's arrival.

Clay had already filled his fist with vials of Red, Green and Black. He drank them all now then glanced over his shoulder to ensure Kriz was doing the same. He leaned forward, placing a hand on Lutharon's neck with the intent of guiding his attack but the Black needed no instruction tonight. Folding his wings, Lutharon angled his body in a near-vertical dive, Clay finding himself thankful for the Green he had imbibed as the slip-stream might otherwise have torn his grip from the neck spines. Lutharon flared his wings and tilted back as they neared the roof-tops, claws stabbing down to pierce the hide of an unsuspecting Red. It struggled frantically, tail lashing at Lutharon's hide, close enough for Clay to reel away from a whip-crack an inch from his ear. Lutharon clamped his jaws on the Red's neck and snapped it with a swift wrenching jerk.

Rearing back from the kill, Lutharon raised his head to the sky and let out a loud, summoning roar. The great host of Blacks circling above responded without hesitation, streaking out of the gloom in a dark torrent. To Clay's eyes it seemed as if the night sky were reaching down to pour a shadow over the city. Red after Red was crushed under the weight of the assault, some tried vainly to take to the skies only to be caught and dragged back into the tearing, rending maelstrom.

The rain of Black drakes swept over the upper districts, swallowing Reds as it did so, then spilling over the lip of the crater to assail those still charging across the plain beyond. The mind controlling the drake assault evidently realised the danger at that point for the sky beyond the edge of the crater suddenly became filled with Reds as they abandoned their ground assault. The Blacks began to take off in response, leaving behind a host of slaughtered drakes.

Clay communicated to Lutharon the need to wait as he and Kriz slipped from his back and hurried to a safe distance. "They're all yours, big fella," Clay told him as Lutharon crouched then launched himself upwards, his wings birthing a gale as he climbed into the darkness.

"Come on," Clay told Kriz. "We gotta find the captain."

They leapt from one building to another, sailing over streets thronged with panicked people, Clay constantly searching for someone in authority. He soon happened upon a crew of fire-fighters attempting to contain a blaze raging in a two-storey tenement. "Hilemore?" he said, leaping down to shout into the ear of the youth who seemed to be in charge.

"That way," the youngster shouted in response, pointing to another blaze burning a few streets ahead. Clay and Kriz ran on, dodging past fleeing townsfolk who as yet failed to recognise the fact that their deliverance had arrived.

They rounded a corner into a small square where Clay's gaze immediately alighted on Hilemore's unmistakable form. The captain stood over a large Red, surrounded by bodies in various states of burnt dismemberment. A girl of about eighteen knelt close by, face frozen and expressionless despite the tears streaming from her eyes. As he drew closer, Clay saw that the Red was still alive despite the numerous bullet-holes in its hide. Its wings flapped feebly and its claws dug into the cobbles as it sought to raise itself, and might have done so had Hilemore not raised a revolver and put a bullet through its skull.

"Captain," Clay called out, running to his side.

Hilemore's face was grim as he glanced at Clay and offered a muttered greeting. "Mr. Torcreek. I had hoped to see you earlier in the evening."

"Blacks can only fly so fast." Watching Hilemore's gaze track over the surrounding corpses, rich in guilt, he asked, "Friends of yours, huh?"

"The Wash Lane Defence Volunteers," Hilemore replied. He went to the kneeling girl, crouching to gently pull her to her feet, murmuring, "It's done, Jillett. We won."

The girl closed her eyes and stepped away from him, hugging herself tight. "What did they win?" she asked in a sob, jerking her head at the bodies. Hilemore had no answer for her and she sagged a little in mingled sorrow and exhaustion.

"Here," Kriz said, coming forward to take hold of the girl, offering a vial of Green. "This will help."

Jillett made a faint effort to shrug her off, but allowed herself to be guided to a near by bench where she drank down the Green.

"We killed the first one we found easily enough," Hilemore was saying in a faint distant voice, his gaze now fixed on the Red he had shot. "This one was different. Jillett tried to hold it with Black but it was just too fast, too strong . . ."

Clay coughed, finding he didn't particularly care for this version of the captain. Much as they grated on each other the man's unerring will and discipline had long been a source of reassurance.

Hilemore blinked and straightened, turning back to him. "There are still Greens on the other side of the falls and in the harbour," he said, holstering his revolver. "They'll need to be dealt with."

"Our friends'll take care of it," Clay assured him. "Gonna need you to make sure the folks here don't shoot at them. Think you can do that?"

Hilemore's expression hardened into a gratifyingly familiar frown. "Of course," he snapped and marched off, heading south to the harbour. "We'll need help fighting these fires," he added over his shoulder. "If you don't mind."

The battle between Red and Black raged in the skies over Stockcombe for nearly an hour, swift moonlit shapes soaring and diving against a back-drop of stars. Occasionally the struggle would be illuminated by a concordance of flame. Human spectators were briefly presented with the sight of a dozen or more drakes assailing each other in a whirling knot of lashing tails and stabbing claws, before the flames died and all became confusion once more. Drakes fell into the harbour throughout it all, trailing smoke as they plummeted down. Most were dead but a few struggled on the surface for a time, screaming out distress calls until the water pulled them down.

By dawn all the Reds appeared to have either fled or fallen and the Blacks turned their attention to the Greens still prowling the western side of the city. They swooped down in successive relays, plucking Greens from the streets, crushing them with claws and teeth before casting the bodies away and diving down for more. When sunlight crested the edge of the crater Clay saw a steady stream of Greens fleeing over the western wall. Apparently the unseen hand that commanded them had finally allowed a retreat.

In the aftermath Stockcombe lay silent under a pall of smoke. The ships sat in harbour waters painted a dull red in the meagre light. There was no celebration amongst the townsfolk, no upsurge of joy in victory. Many stood or huddled together, soot-stained faces blank with shock whilst others wandered aimlessly, staring at the blackened ruins of homes or businesses. The children were an exception, clustering around the many drake corpses and chattering in excitement as they poked them with sticks, sometimes scurrying back in delighted alarm when they twitched in response.

The Blacks continued to patrol the skies above the city, drawing many a concerned and wary eye. Clay had communicated to Lutharon the need to keep out of rifle-range along with a stern warning against perching in the city itself. Instead the Blacks came to rest on the walls along the crater rim, bodies turned towards the rising sun and wings spread to catch the warmth.

Captain Hilemore, seemingly immune to fatigue, organised working parties from the *Superior* and the merchant ships to assist in clearing the worst of the rubble from the streets and extinguishing the few remaining fires. He also enlisted the large number of harvesters in the port to extract product from the bountiful supply of corpses littering the streets and the surrounding country, raising a somewhat problematic question in the process.

"We'll need it," Hilemore said. "This war isn't over, Mr. Torcreek. As you well know."

Clay looked at the corpse of the Black lying on the eastern quayside. It was an adult female some twenty feet long, congealed blood covering the wounds in her hide from numerous Red tail strikes. There were others to be found in the city and the harbour waters, a valuable resource to Hilemore's eyes.

In truth Clay wasn't sure how the Blacks would react to the harvesting of their dead. Whilst he was well aware of their capacity for grief, unlike humans they didn't seem inclined to keen over the corpses of their kin. *Perhaps they don't need to,* he thought. *The memories get passed on, leaving the flesh behind, empty and dead.* Lutharon seemed indifferent to the matter, his mind preoccupied with scouring the surrounding country for more enemies. Even so, Clay thought it best not to risk antagonising their allies unnecessarily.

"Do it under cover," he told Hilemore. "And tonight, lessen the chance of their seeing."

Hilemore called a conference aboard the *Superior* that evening where he gave a reckoning of the losses suffered and damage done. Altogether, over four hundred people had perished in the fighting with double that number injured, most of the casualties having been inflicted by the Reds. Although Hilemore spoke with his usual brisk authority, Clay could see the guilt behind his eyes.

"Could've been a lot worse, Captain," he told him, heralding a murmur of muted agreement from the others present. Captain Okanas had come, along with Captain Tidelow, as representative of the merchant fleet. There was also the Blood-blessed girl from the square, still somewhat pale of face, and a chunky youth in a Contractor's duster Clay doubted he had any right to wear. These two represented the Voter rebels who had apparently been engaged in a minor civil war with the young woman in a partially scorched military uniform facing them across the ward-room table. To Clay's eyes it didn't appear that the previous night's events had done much to heal the rift betwixt the two groups.

"With the danger averted," the young woman, Kulvetch, said when Hilemore fell silent, "my people are keen to return to their homes."

"Who says it's averted?" Coll, the chunky youth, returned. "Plenty of drakes still out there."

"This city now enjoys a very special form of protection," Kulvetch replied, casting a meaningful glance at Clay.

"This fleet will be sailing for Varestia once the harvesting is complete," Hilemore said. "Whatever dispositions you wish to make after that are a matter for you."

"You just gonna leave us?" Coll asked.

"I have discussed the matter with Mr. Torcreek," Hilemore replied. "He will . . . consult with our allies, requesting that they leave a third of their number here to ward off future attacks."

"There are those of us," Jillett said, "who don't want to stay here any more. What about them?"

"What?" Coll demanded but she ignored him, keeping her gaze on Hilemore.

"We can't take children," he said. "Or anyone not of fighting age. We're sailing into battle, after all."

"Then I want to volunteer," she said, continuing to ignore the glowering reaction of her fellow Voter. "And there are plenty more who think like me. The real war needs fighting, and it isn't here."

"Very well," Hilemore said, turning to Kulvetch. "Colonel? Any volunteers from your side of the falls?"

"Forget it, Captain," Coll said as Kulvetch hesitated. "She's just itching for you to leave with our best fighters so she can finally take the whole city."

Kulvetch's indecision faded abruptly and she straightened into a military bearing. "*I* will volunteer. Also, I've little doubt my Marines will follow me."

"And they would be very welcome," Hilemore said, turning back to Coll. "As for those who remain I recommend concentrating your forces in the east side and doing everything you can to fortify the outer wall." He stepped back from the table. "Harvesting is expected to be complete within two days. Please be prepared to sail by then." He nodded and started towards the door.

"You think we're just gonna let you sail off with our best fighters?" Coll demanded, moving to stand in his way. "Our committee answers to the Voters Rights Alli—"

He fell silent as Hilemore's fist slammed into the centre of his face. Coll's head snapped back and he fell to all fours, blood streaming from a broken nose. "I have had enough of your infantile politics," Hilemore said, very precisely. "After all your people suffered last night you still seek to play your games. Were you a member of my crew I would have you shot. In fact . . ." Clay stepped forward as Hilemore's hand went to his revolver.

"I think that's meeting adjourned, folks," Clay said cheerfully, crouching to drag Coll to his feet and pushing him towards the door. "Nice coat," he said as he hustled him from the room. "Where'd you get it?"

"Here," Clay said, entering the cabin Kriz shared with Loriabeth. He hadn't knocked but she didn't seem to mind. "Gotcha a present." He set the duster alongside her on the bunk. She had been sitting with her knees drawn up in silent contemplation of the vial of synthetic product. His cousin wasn't present, which he didn't find surprising. She and Lieutenant Sigoral hadn't been seen much since they returned to the ship.

"It's got blood on it," Kriz observed, casting a brief glance over the duster. "Fresh blood."

"Nobody died, don't worry. And it'll wash."

"I thought only members of your . . . profession wore these."

"Fella who had it before didn't deserve it. Reckon you've earned it."

He sat himself on the bunk and rested his back against the bulkhead, suddenly weary. It occurred to him that neither of them had slept for close on two days.

"I'm honoured," Kriz said, her tone vague but genuine. She turned her gaze back to the vial, her other hand gripping the crystal shard about her neck.

"Still tempted, huh?" Clay asked her.

"I have to know, Clay," she said, slipping into her own language. "Given what we're about to sail into, there might not be another chance."

"We already know a lot of it," he pointed out. "One of the Whites you bred got free somehow. Zembi got Spoiled and Hezkhi flew off to Arradsia in the aerostat."

"He wanted me to know," she insisted, holding up the crystal so the light from the port-hole caught its myriad facets. "There's knowledge in here, important knowledge."

"Or a trap. He was Spoiled, remember? And he did try to kill you."

"Part of him was still there, deep inside. I know it. Perhaps"—she gripped the crystal tighter—"in here, also."

She's already decided, he realised, seeing the resolve on her face. Short of tying her up there wasn't much he could do to stop her. "Well, if you have to," he said, shifting to face her. "But we do this together. You ain't going in there on your own."

Kriz seemed about to argue but then swallowed a sigh and nodded. They sat facing each other on the bunk, Clay seeing how she had to still the tremble in her fingers before she could remove the stopper from the vial. She unhooked the crystal from the chain about her neck and set it down on the bunk between them. "Ready?" she asked, vial poised before her lips.

"No, but as you're gonna do it anyway . . ."

A smile ghosted across her lips and she drank, taking in perhaps a third of the vial's contents. The reaction was immediate, Kriz stiffening with a sharp intake of breath. The vial slipped from her fingers and Clay's hand darted forward to catch it before it spilled.

"Kriz?" he asked, receiving no response. She sat in rigid silence, eyes wide open but he knew they saw nothing. Clay blinked as something flashed. Looking down he saw the crystal shard pulsing with light, slow at first but the rhythm building rapidly until it emitted a constant bluish light. Clay returned the stopper to the vial and focused his gaze on Kriz's blank face, finding the focus needed to summon the Blue-less trance.

It was different than before, Clay finding himself floating in a place without sensation. There was no ground beneath his feet and no air on his skin. The images he saw seemed to play out at a remove, like watching a play. Kriz stood in the chamber where they had found the ruined stone eggs, the place that had become the tomb of her fellow ancient Blood-blessed. When Clay had come here it had been a dark, dust-covered mess of rubble but now it was brightly lit by the crystal floating above the sleeping chambers. He watched Kriz move to each of the chambers, her hand playing over the stone surfaces.

"All the kids are still asleep, I guess," he said, receiving no response. He called out to her but she didn't seem to hear as she continued her inspection of the giant eggs. Repeated attempts proved similarly fruitless forcing him to conclude he would have to resign himself to the role of spectator rather than participant.

He saw Kriz start as the crystal flickered, stepping back from the chambers at the sound of grinding stone. The egg-shaped mass to her left began to come apart, leaking fluid over the floor. A naked figure tumbled out as the object became fully segmented. It was a young man, tall and lean, the light from the crystal gleaming on his athletic frame as he slowly rose to his feet

"Hezkhi," Kriz said, involuntarily reaching out to him. However, this memory appeared both deaf and blind to her presence. His face, a handsome adult version of the boy she had once tutored in the Philos Enclave, was set in a preoccupied frown, his eyes constantly blinking and lips moving in a silent mutter. After a slight pause he returned to the segmented chamber and retrieved a set of sodden clothes, dressing rapidly, then bent to recover a belt holding four flasks. Donning the belt Hezkhi moved to the exit, then stopped, shaking his head as if in confusion. Then, slowly, he turned back and raised his gaze to the crystal hanging above the sleeping chambers.

"Don't," Clay heard Kriz say in a gasp, but of course, Hezkhi couldn't hear her. Taking one of the flasks from his belt he took a hefty gulp and concentrated his gaze on the crystal. It began to emit the tinkling that told of being subjected to Black, but instead of being refashioned into a sculpture it spun violently in the air and let out a loud crack. The light bathing the stone eggs flickered and died, the crystal tumbling to the floor along with the chambers, each one birthing a loud boom as they toppled and rolled.

Clay heard Kriz let out a sob, rich in the kind of despair and grief he remembered from his last visit here. Then she had seen proof of the deaths of her companions, now she had been forced to witness their murder. He wanted to say something to her, reach through the invisible veil separating them to offer comfort. Even the most empty, awkward expression of consolation would have been preferable to impotently witnessing her anguish. But, try as he might, the veil proved impenetrable and he could only watch her stagger, sobbing after Hezkhi as he made his way from the chamber.

The memory blurred and accelerated then, Clay catching only glimpses of the rapid mélange of images that followed; Hezkhi making his way through the mountains to the cliff-face covered in wooden scaffolding . . . taking two eggs from the terraces at the base of the cavernous chamber within . . . drinking more product, Red this time, and bathing both eggs in heat before retreating to a safe distance.

The memory slowed when the eggs hatched, bursting apart like bombs. When the smoke cleared two infant White Drakes sat amidst the shattered shells, chirping as they nuzzled each other. Hezkhi approached to crouch near by and they leapt into his arms, wings flapping in excitement. Seeing how Hezkhi nodded in response, Clay realised he had seen his expression before. *Silverpin,* he thought. *He's their Silverpin. They were able to call to him even from within the egg.*

Hezkhi gave another nod and set the two infants down before moving to the row of crystals, drinking from one of his flasks as he did so. A short pause and then the Blue crystal began to glow, growing brighter as it rose from the chamber floor. Hezkhi spread his arms out wide as the crystal emitted a pulse of light bright enough to swamp the vision. When the light faded Hezkhi had collapsed to his knees, shuddering. Seeing the light play over the scales on his back Clay knew what he would see before Hezkhi raised his face, the yellow eyes, the ridged brows, the spines. *The first ever Spoiled,* he thought.

The memory blurred again, the images racing by with dizzying speed too fast for Clay to catch. When it slowed again Hezkhi stood over the wet, naked form of an old man. Beyond them a segmented sleeping chamber hovered in the air below a glowing crystal. The two infant Whites snapped at the old man as he slowly heaved himself up, raising his gaze to regard Hezkhi's deformed visage.

"I grew tired of your prison, Father," Hezkhi told him. "I have been offered freedom, and a whole world to play in."

Zembi's gaze went to the two drakes. They hissed in response, one lashing out with its tail to score a cut into the old man's arm. "The eggs," Zembi groaned, his head sagging. "We should have destroyed the eggs."

"Yes," Hezkhi agreed. "But you didn't. They called to me for centuries, Father. Though I fought them, tried to resist their enticements, the many dreams they planted in my mind. When the promises didn't work they made their dreams into nightmares, but a free mind can wake from a nightmare, and I was not free. For year after year I suffered, and then a very important question occurred to me: Why?" Hezkhi crouched in front of the old man, speaking softly. "Why suffer so much for a man who gave me so little?"

"You're insane," Zembi told him. "They drove you mad."

"They set me free," Hezkhi corrected in a chiding tone. "Guided me to the facet within the crystal that would unlock the sarcophagus. No longer would I live according to your whim, or Krizelle's."

Zembi's head snapped up at this, eyes bright with alarm and anger.

"Oh don't worry," Hezkhi told him. "I intend to leave her very much alive. One day she'll wake." He rose and stood back, gesturing at the Blue crystal which floated close by. "And find you waiting for her."

The Blue crystal flared into life, Zembi letting out a short pain-filled cry that soon choked into a strangled gurgle. When the light faded the old man remained on the floor, convulsing. To Clay it appeared as if the scales on his back were only partially formed, his hands twisting into claws then back again. *He's fighting it,* Clay realised.

"A parting gift," Hezkhi went on, moving to the Blue crystal. He drank from one of his flasks and focused his gaze. A tinkling sound rose as one of the crystal's spikes separated from the core and floated into Hezkhi's hand. He stared at the shard for a moment of intense concentration, a faint light flaring then fading within.

"Perhaps you'll kill her," he went on, returning to Zembi. "Or she'll kill you. In which case, I should very much like her to know. She can think about it for however long it takes her to grow old and die down here."

He opened his hand, offering the shard to Zembi. The old man's face was contorting now, ridges swelling on his forehead, gritted teeth elongating. It would only be seconds before the transformation was complete.

Clay heard Kriz let out a surprised yelp as Zembi's hand shot out to grasp the shard then stab it into Hezkhi's chest. The younger man shouted in pain and shock, reeling away, the shard falling free as he did so. He staggered back, blood leaking from the wound. The two infant Whites set upon Zembi, biting at his flesh in a fury, then stopping abruptly and scurrying back.

Zembi slowly rose to his full height, remade features now firmly in place, a fully converted Spoiled.

"You vicious old bastard!" Hezkhi railed at him, hand clutched over his bleeding chest. But the insults were wasted now, for Zembi replied with only an incurious glance. Hezkhi let out a grunt of impotent fury then reached for another flask, drinking the entire contents in a few urgent gulps.

"It's not healing right," he said in an aggrieved whimper, casting a desperate gaze at the two Whites. "The bleeding stopped but it's not healed. I can feel it."

The two infants let out an identical hiss and his mouth clamped shut. Hezkhi stood frozen in place as the Whites turned their gaze on Zembi. He blinked and turned back to the sleeping chamber, climbing inside whereupon it closed around him once more. The Whites issued a brief squawk and Hezkhi shuddered. The memory faded into a grey void as he started towards the rear of the chamber in an agonised stumble with the Whites scurrying close behind.

"You were right."

Clay blinked and found himself back in the cabin. Kriz sat before him, face downcast and tears falling onto the blankets.

"It was a trap," she went on in a whisper. "I should have left it be."

"We learned some things we didn't know before," Clay said, reaching out to cup her face, thumbing the tears away. "Hezkhi flew them to Arradsia, but his wound must've killed him on the way and the aerostat crashed in Krystaline Lake. Sad to say the Whites didn't drown with him. Somehow they made it out, made their way to the enclave and started making eggs. In time they had a big enough brood to start their war."

"It doesn't help us," she said. "There was nothing there beyond malice, my brother's need to hurt me."

"Not true," Clay said, pulling her closer. "You saw Zembi fight it. We know from Miss Lethridge there were once free Spoiled here. If they can be freed . . ."

His words died as she kissed him. It was long kiss after which she drew back and glanced at the door. "Your cousin isn't coming back soon, is she?"

"I doubt it."

Kriz turned back to him, hands moving to unbutton her shirt. "Good."

CHAPTER 38

Sirus

He could feel Catheline's mingled terror and anger as he made the suggestion that the surviving Greens and Reds should scatter. She had called him to her command tent to oversee the assault on Stockcombe. Given that it was an all-drake affair she would act as conduit whilst Sirus supplied the tactical direction. Linking minds with her was always a disconcerting experience, like sinking into a constantly shifting swamp of muted emotion whilst beneath it all the vast will of the White rumbled and smoked like a fractious volcano.

Sirus couldn't help a perverse pride in both the conception and execution of his plan, making him ponder the unwelcome notion that he might have absorbed some of Morradin's characteristics. His opponent at Stockcombe had evidently been a capable commander, the booby traps and the mines in the harbour were an unpleasant and costly surprise, as was the fierce resistance of the ships. But he had learned by now that it was always a sound strategy to subvert the expectations of one's enemy. In compelling the Reds to mount a ground assault rather than attack from the air, he had done exactly that. Victory would undoubtedly have been his had not the Blacks arrived.

After hours of hopeless resistance, during which Catheline's mind continued to communicate the death agonies of hundreds of drakes, Sirus had been forced to withdraw from their shared connection. "We can't win this," he said simply. "If He wishes to preserve their lives, they should scatter."

Her red-black eyes bore into him with such intensity he wondered if she had suddenly decided to hate him. But then she reached out to capture his mind once more and he realised her expression was born of concern rather than hatred. For the first time he was able to fully experience her communion with the White. There were no words, no shared images, just an exchange of emotion so rapid it sent a jolt of pain through his mind. Somehow, despite the pain, he was able to discern the essence of this communication:

Failure.

Reproach.

Contrition.

Anger.

Deeper contrition.

Need to punish.

Acceptance . . . and supplication.

For a brief moment he managed to make out a coherent thought as Catheline ensured her message was unambiguous. *He is still needed. My failure. My punishment.* There was no pause before the White responded: *Concurrence.*

Sirus let out a groan as Catheline released her mental hold, seeing her offer him a sad smile and a shrug. "This time He would have killed you," she said.

Abruptly she stiffened, arching like a bow, limbs shuddering as her head snapped back. Her body was so rigid she couldn't even fall from her chair. Sirus forced himself to watch as she convulsed, blood spouting from her mouth and streaming from her nose. The sudden appearance of more blood beneath her chair indicating she was bleeding from all orifices. It continued for what seemed an age, so long in fact that her finely tailored cavalry uniform became drenched in blood and Sirus felt certain she would soon have no more left to give. The notion raised an important question: *If she dies, what then?*

But she didn't die. Finally, when her skin had taken on an alabaster hue and the blood had begun to pool on the carpet, she collapsed. Sirus leapt forward to catch her as she fell, lifting her easily in his remade arms. Catheline's eyelids fluttered as she shivered in his grasp, her lips forming a smile as she raised a hand to caress his scaled cheek. "My hero," she whispered before fainting.

There were few foot-hills north of the pass known as the Grand Cut, the mountains rearing up out of the grassy plains in sudden, sheer-sided majesty. The pass itself was a broad canyon that narrowed considerably as it proceeded deeper into the range of peaks dominating the region the Varestians called "the Neck." Reconnaissance flights by Reds the day before had confirmed the smaller passes to the east and west closed by rubble. The Grand Cut, however, remained open.

"An obvious trap," Morradin growled, squinting at the pass and the clouds lingering over the cliffs that formed its flanks. "Expected better of them."

"You're sure?" Catheline asked. She had recovered quickly from the previous night's punishment, colour having returned to her face and her bearing displaying scant sign of fatigue. Sirus detected a new wariness in her, however. In place of her ruined uniform she wore a simple muslin dress, a thick woollen shawl about her shoulders, which were slightly hunched. He also noted the tightness of her grip on the shawl, the knuckles bone-white.

"We go in there, we'll pay for it," Morradin asserted. "In blood."

Catheline raised an eyebrow at Sirus, letting out an exasperated hiss when he gave a nod of confirmation. "Very well," she said, turning away. "The scenic route it is . . ."

She trailed off as a loud boom sounded from the Grand Cut. Turning back Sirus saw a large grey cloud rising above the mountain mist, followed a second later by a thick pall of dust issuing from the mouth of the pass.

"What was that?" Catheline demanded.

Morradin's brows knitted in bemusement as he raised a spy-glass to scan the pass. "Looks as if they've blocked it anyway," he said when the dust had cleared. He continued to peer through the glass then straightened in surprise. "Or at least tried to. Bloody thing's still open."

Sirus extended his own glass and trained it on the Grand Cut. Morradin was right, there was a good deal of rubble littering the floor of the pass but it was far from blocked.

"Miscalculated their charge, perhaps?" Morradin said as he and Sirus exchanged glances. "Or blew themselves up trying to rig it."

"It could still be a trap," Sirus said. "Bait to lure us in."

"The Reds will find out soon enough," Catheline said. A trio of Reds flew overhead a few seconds later, wings sweeping in broad arcs as they climbed into the mist. Catheline shared the view through the eyes of the lead Red as it flew over the pass. *As I thought,* Morradin commented in satisfaction at the sight of numerous armed figures dotting the rocky terrain atop the cliffs. Sirus estimated their number at three hundred at most. Hardly the kind of force he would have expected if their enemy intended to inflict serious harm.

Unless they want the pass to do it for them, Morradin mused, reading his thoughts. *Wait until we march in then bring the mountains down on top of us.* A pulse of grim amusement. *Looks like they pissed on their own breakfast with this one.*

It could still . . . Sirus began but his thought was swallowed by a sudden upsurge of excitement from Catheline.

She's here!

The Red's vision of the pass sprang into more vivid life, focusing on a particular figure standing at the cliff-edge. Thanks to the power of drake sight they were soon confronted with a close-up view of the figure's features. Lizanne Lethridge stared back at them through the Red's eyes, a smile of grim mockery on her lips. She moved slightly and the image refocused, drawing back to reveal the sight of her raising a carbine to her shoulder. The muzzle flared in a bright orange plume and the vision went black. The absence of the usual confusion and pain indicated the Red had died instantly.

"Bitch," Catheline breathed in a tone of hungry malice. Her gaze flashed at Sirus and Morradin, the red pupils seeming to glow like coals. "Get in there! Send all of them!"

Her will was implacable and shot through with the White's irresistible blood-lust. Every Red leapt into the sky as the Spoiled battalions started forward. The Greens charged in two huge packs on the flanks, every mind, Spoiled and drake, filled with a single purpose: KILL HER!

CHAPTER 39

Lizanne

The Smoker jerked against her shoulder as she unleashed the Redball. It impacted at the base of the Red's neck, the explosion instantly severing it from the body. The rest of the fighters, all armed with Smokers, opened fire on the other Reds. The hail of explosive bullets felled one immediately, but it took several more shots before they brought down the other, the bullets chasing it across the sky until one of the Varestians managed a hit on its chest.

Lizanne watched the stricken creature spiral down into the misty depths of the Grand Cut then turned her gaze to the north. She found that the fog, mingled with the drifting smoke from their intentionally abortive attempt to block the pass, made it difficult to gauge the reaction of the White's army. She injected a small amount of product to enhance her vision and was soon rewarded with the sight of a multitude of Green drakes streaming towards the Cut. Following close behind were the Spoiled, their previously neat ranks forgotten now as they charged across the plain in a disorderly mob thousands strong. Shifting her gaze upwards, she saw the fast-approaching shapes of more Reds than could easily be counted.

In addition to the Blood-blessed contingent there were about two hundred Varestian fighters, mostly of a piratical nature judging by their clothing and abundance of knives. They were all volunteers who had been dropped on the lower south-facing slopes by aerostat the day before.

"They're coming," she told them. "Remember your orders, fire and retreat. We need to draw them in."

The Varestians immediately ran off to occupy their positions deeper in the pass, the group on the other side of the dividing chasm following suit, leaving the Blood-blessed to face the first rush of Reds. Lizanne injected a short burst of Blue and slipped into the trance where Morva was waiting on the deck of the antique sailing-ship that formed her mindscape.

"It worked," Lizanne told her. "Tell Tekela to commence her run."

She ended the trance without waiting for a reply and moved back from the cliff-edge. "Product!" Lizanne ordered the other Blood-blessed, depressing the first three buttons on her Spider. "Full doses! No need to skimp here. Every one we kill today is one we don't have to kill tomorrow."

She moved to crouch behind a near by boulder, the other Blood-blessed also finding cover in the surrounding rocks. Lizanne rested the Smoker's forestock on the top of the boulder, pointing it at the sky, and slotted another Redball into the glass receptacle atop the chamber. She waited, veins thrumming with product and eyes fixed on the Smoker's sights. She heard the Reds before she saw them, their shrill cries echoing up the mountain side in a hungry chorus. She lit the Redball the instant a dark silhouette slipped into her sights, blasting it apart as a cacophony of carbine fire erupted all around.

Lizanne stood up, seeing a dozen Reds falling out of the sky as the explosive rounds took their toll. Seeing a Red twisting amidst the barrage she tracked it with the Smoker, sights aimed just in front of its nose to compensate for the distance, and fired three rounds in quick succession, the carbine's lever blurring as she worked it. Mortally wounded by the trio of large holes punched into its hide, the Red let out a stream of impotent flame before slamming into the cliff-face below.

A warning shout from one of her fellow Blood-blessed had Lizanne leaping away, Green-enhanced limbs carrying her wide of the stream of fire cast at her by a diving Red. It reared back, wings fanning the air and neck coiling for another try. A salvo of rounds from the surrounding Blood-blessed tore one of its wings away and left a gaping hole in its chest, leaving it a bloody tangle clinging feebly to the cliff-edge before sliding into the Grand Cut.

Casting a glance skyward, Lizanne saw that the Reds had been forced higher by the fire of the Smokers and were now circling in a huge spiral. Seeing them begin to cluster together in groups of five or more, Lizanne knew that the defenders were about to be subjected to a massed onslaught from above. No amount of explosive bullets could hope to stem such a weight of drake flesh.

"Pull back!" she shouted, moving across the rocky ground in an unnaturally fast, leaping sprint.

Seeing their prey attempting an escape, the Reds let out a collective scream of fury and gave chase. Hearing the beat of large wings at her back, Lizanne leapt and pivoted in midair, aiming the Smoker one-handed at the head of the pursuing Red. Thanks to the reflex-enhancing effects of Green she was able to put a bullet in its eye before whirling about for a landing.

She didn't pause as her boots met rock, propelling herself on and refreshing her diminishing Green with the Spider. A scream sounded behind her, human rather than drake, brief and full of agony before it choked off. Lizanne didn't turn to see the inevitable grisly spectacle. She had entertained a faint hope of completing this mission without casualties, but knew it to be an indulgent self-delusion designed to assuage the guilt of commanding others in battle.

Upon reaching a point halfway along the pass she leapt atop a tall boulder and came to a halt, turning to face the Reds. The other Blood-blessed all rushed to pre-chosen spots and did the same, all Smokers raised and aimed as the Reds closed. Here the pass constricted to its narrowest point and was overlooked by ledges on the mountains rising on both sides, ledges where their pirate allies now waited, Smokers tracking the Reds streaming into their sights.

Over two hundred carbines began firing at once, blasting at least thirty Reds out of the sky. Lizanne aimed at the densest concentration of drakes and emptied her Smoker, hand once again blurring on the lever and cartridges spinning away in a brass cascade. The Blood-blessed had all been trained in the same technique, meaning the Reds found themselves charging into an impassible wall of bullets. The mass of drakes reared back from the fusillade, resembling a huge swarm of hornets retreating from a flaming torch.

"Reload!" Lizanne ordered, jumping down from the boulder and slotting fresh bullets into her Smoker from the bandolier about her chest. Her gaze was fixed on the southern end of the pass, the sun now risen high enough to burn off much of the mist. For a second she thought Morva had failed to pass on the order but then saw the curved wedge of the *Typhoon*'s envelope cresting the mountain side. She rose swiftly with the *Tempest* close alongside, the two aerostats drifting forward as they ascended. They stalled their ascent about eight hundred feet above, the *Tempest* letting loose with her Thumpers whilst the *Typhoon* unleashed a hail of bullets from her Growlers.

Assailed from above and below, the swarm of Reds split apart, one group banking away to the east whilst the other furiously beat their wings to gain more height, desperate to get at the aircraft. Lizanne concentrated on the other group, watching it split apart twice more, each subdivision banking away. *Trying to disperse our fire*, she realised. *Come at us from all sides at once.* They had only a few moments' respite before the storm descended.

"It's time!" she called out, rising to her feet and pointing at the southern end of the pass. "Make for the pick-up point!"

Most needed no encouragement, the Blood-blessed immediately refreshing their Green to sprint and leap away with the pirates following as fast as they could. But a few stayed, mostly Varestians but also a couple of Blood-blessed. "Miss Blood?" one of them asked, a middle-aged man who cast repeated nervous glances at the sky.

Lizanne resisted the urge to snap, "Don't call me that!" and forced a smile instead. "Rear guard," she told him, gesturing towards the south. "I'll be along. Now go!"

She watched them flee then turned back to gauge the progress of the White's army. The Grand Cut was thick with Greens and Spoiled all the way to the promontory where she stood, the promontory which their explosives had deliberately failed to send tumbling into the pass. However, the as yet unexploded second batch contained more than enough firepower to bring it down. Lizanne quickly spotted the detonator positioned in a shallow crevice near by and started towards it, then stopped at a challenging squawk from above. Seeing a Red separate from the main pack to dive towards her, she swiftly slotted a Redball into the Smoker and blew it out of the sky at a distance of fifty yards.

Turning back to the detonator she rushed towards it and crouched in the shadowed confines of the crevice. Reaching into the pocket of her overalls she extracted the item so carefully crafted by Madame Hakugen's theatrically experienced employee. Fashioned mostly from congealed glue and rubber Lizanne, with her extensive experience of disguises, had initially been sceptical of its efficacy. But, upon trying it out she had been reassured by Tekela's assertion that she looked "utterly ghastly." Pressing it to her face, she took a bottle of pig's blood from her other pocket and emptied it over her head. It was thick with coagulants and possessed of a truly appalling smell, but she needed it to complete the disguise.

A fresh chorus of drake screams told her she was out of time and she reached for the detonator, one hand on the lever whilst the other pressed the second button on the Spider to flood her veins with all the remaining Green. She pushed the detonator's lever then clamped her hands over her ears, shutting her eyes tight. A bare second later the explosives went off, Lizanne finding herself lifted clear of the mountain side by the blast. She spread her limbs to stabilise herself as she tumbled, grit-filled air whipping past as she plummeted into the pass.

She didn't need to feign unconsciousness. Her attempt to slide down the flank of the dislodged promontory to the floor of the pass went well at first, but the huge slab of rock contrived to break apart upon connecting with the ground, leaving her tumbling in a cloud of dust. Something hard slammed into her back, possessed of enough force to cause serious injury if not for the copious Green in her system. Lizanne attempted to angle her feet towards the ground, intending to roll with the impact and hopefully prevent any fractures, but another something cracked against the side of her head and she found herself falling into a vast pool of utter blackness.

She came to atop a pile of corpses, blinking into the dull-eyed stare of a dead Green only inches from her face. It lay across an equally dead Spoiled, a woman about Lizanne's own age with her neck twisted at an impossible angle. Looking around through bleary eyes Lizanne saw that the bodies were all stacked against the newly created wall of rock spanning the width of the Grand Cut. Those not buried by the avalanche had evidently piled up in front of it, crushing themselves to death in the process.

Lizanne tried to raise herself, which had the effect of dislodging many of the bodies, causing the pile to collapse. She rolled with the slack, lifeless forms, coming to rest on the floor of the pass where she lay, drawing in slow even breaths in an attempt to recover her senses.

It took several minutes to get to her feet, the world seeming to tilt and spin around her. When she finally stood up she found herself confronted by a Spoiled, a tall male in a ragged Protectorate uniform regarding her with his scaled brows formed into a curious frown. She hoped he saw a fellow Spoiled, albeit one with a mass of blood concealing her deformed features, not all of it pig's blood judging by the warm trickle tracing from the back of her head. Lizanne just stared back at the Spoiled for a brief interval then staggered away in apparent confusion. She could feel his eyes on her and could only hope he put her failure to communicate down to her head injury.

The pass was full of Spoiled soldiery, and some drakes, many injured and all stumbling around in a directionless stupor. Unsure of how long this helpful state of confusion might last, Lizanne kept staggering towards the northern end of the Cut, her pace deliberately slow. She fell several times during the journey, not always of her own volition as her befuddled brain saw fit to randomly deny her control of her legs. If any of the other Spoiled afforded her an unduly long gaze she would fall and remain immobile until they lost interest.

The Spoiled began to regain a sense of order once she came to the mouth of the pass, their confusion slipping away as they stiffened into a semblance of military bearing and began to form companies. Hoping her grievous wound would explain her immunity to this resurgence of discipline, Lizanne continued to stumble and collapse her way clear of the Grand Cut, pausing at the sight of the huge camp only a few hundred yards away.

Where would it be? she wondered, gaze tracking over the neat rows of tents. The answer proved obvious and unmistakable. Rising in the centre of the camp was a very large winged shape, pale in the fading pall of dust. *The White.* She had only seen it before in Clay's shared memories and found the experience of viewing it in the flesh both unnerving and irresistible. *It's right there. Well within range.*

The temptation to slip back into the trance was strong. *Tell Tekela to launch now. Finish this.* But she held off. *It could just fly away. You came for the crystal. Stick to the mission.*

She staggered on, joining a thin stream of wounded Spoiled making a slow progress to the camp. They were all dazed and bleeding like her and thankfully in no condition to attempt communication. She kept to the rear of the group, head lowered as she moved in a stumbling shuffle. The fuzz-iness in her head finally started to fade as they entered the camp. It was mostly deserted apart from a few Spoiled, all of whom were rushing to form companies and paid the group of wounded no attention.

She had expected the wounded to report to some kind of medical tent but they all began to peel off from the group. She saw one Spoiled, a large man wearing a Corvantine constable's hat and cradling an obviously bro-ken arm, stagger into one of the tents and lay down on the bedroll within. Before moving on she saw him close his eyes and fall asleep. One by one the other Spoiled followed suit until she found herself alone but for two others.

Lizanne began to drop back, intending to find an empty tent to hide in until they moved on, but the pair came to a sudden halt and turned to face her, eyes narrowed in suspicious scrutiny. They were both female, one with a spectacular head injury deep enough for Lizanne to make out the white bone of her skull through the gore. The other appeared to have only a bro-ken wrist and was consequently much more alert. From the way their brows twitched she realised they were attempting to communicate and knew she had only seconds to act.

There was still a great deal of Green in her system, meaning she was able to close the distance in a heart-beat. The knife concealed in her wrist sheath came free in a blur, gleaming as it slashed left then right. The two Spoiled fell in unison, blood leaking from the gaping wounds in their throats. Lizanne gave a short vertical jump, bringing both boots down hard on the heads of the fallen Spoiled, crushing their skulls and hopefully preventing any alarming thoughts spreading to their comrades.

She moved on swiftly, unwilling to wait for any possible reaction and knowing her time was fast running short. The White was still ahead of her, wings spread wide and head raised. A large swirling pack of Reds had be-gun to assemble in the sky above it and she realised it must be summoning them back, which boded well for the fate of the Blood-blessed and the pi-rates. The *Tempest* had orders to guard the pirates until they mounted the horses tethered at the southern end of the pass and galloped off towards the south. The Blood-blessed were to be picked up and carried away at speed thanks to the aerostat's blood-burner. The *Typhoon*, on the other hand, had different orders.

The number of Spoiled increased as she drew nearer to the White, although they all seemed to be moving towards it, meaning she managed to avoid their line of sight. However, it was clear that a more stealthy approach was now needed. Slipping into a tent, she waited for a moment to ensure she hadn't been noticed, then slit open the rear of it and moved to the next in line. It was a laborious but necessary business, eventually bringing her to the point where the line of tents ended. She cut a small slit in the tent wall and peered out at what lay beyond.

The White occupied a broad circular patch of empty ground, wings folded now as it prowled back and forth. Lizanne started in shock at the sight of a number of smaller infants scurrying about the White as it prowled. *There are more?* This was something no one had expected and the knowledge banished any doubts she might have about the need for this mission.

Standing at a short remove from the White were three figures. One was a Spoiled of youthful appearance wearing a Corvantine general's uniform. Thanks to the Green Lizanne was able to focus on his face. His features were heavily modified by his deformity but somehow his profile retained an echo of the earnest youth she had met in Morsvale. *Sirus,* she realised with a note of dismay, deciding Tekela would never know of his presence here. *Not that I'll be in a position to tell her,* she added, finding it strange that she was still capable of humour even now.

The second figure was also one she knew, although they had never actually met. Grand Marshal Morradin was even more imposing as a Spoiled. Lizanne thought that his brutish features were actually enhanced by the spines and the scales, considering it a more accurate reflection of the soul behind the face.

The third figure was odd in that she appeared at first glance to be entirely human. A slender golden-haired woman in a muslin dress with a shawl about her shoulders, she stood at the forefront of the trio, her gaze fixed on the prowling White. When she turned Lizanne was struck by another sense of recognition. She had definitely seen this woman somewhere but apparently her memory hadn't ascribed enough significance to the experience to retain her name. *Not human after all,* she decided, noting the woman's eyes. She seemed to be in silent communication with Sirus from the way her gaze concentrated on him to the exclusion of Morradin.

Unable to discern the content of their conversation Lizanne turned away, searching until she found what she was looking for. A cart was positioned not far from the White, a cart in which lay four crystals. It was hard to make out the hues in the mid morning sun but she was certain she had found her target.

Depressing the fourth button on the Spider, she slipped into the trance, finding Morva waiting once more. It was clear she was close to the limits of her Blue from the way the old sailing-ship pitched and yawed on a fractious, partially invisible sea.

"Are you alright?" Morva asked.

"We don't have time," Lizanne told her curtly. "Here." She summoned one of her whirlwinds, quickly forming it into a reconstruction of the camp then added a glowing aura around the location of the cart. "The White's close," she said. "With any luck we'll get it too. Launch immediately then light the blood-burner and return to the Mount."

"What about you? Tinkerer said the blast radius . . ."

"I'm aware of the blast radius. Just get it done."

She severed the connection and exited the trance before Morva could argue further. Blinking and returning her gaze to the rent she had sliced in the side of the tent, she realised in shock that the three of them—Sirus, Morradin and the familiar but as yet unnamed woman—were all looking directly at her.

Turning, she found the reason staring at her through the tent flap. The wounded Spoiled leaked blood from the ruin of his face, which appeared to have been partially crushed. Sadly, this didn't appear to have affected his mental faculties. He glared at her in fierce animosity, a strangled growl escaping his mangled face as he crouched for a charge. Lizanne pressed a button on the Spider and broke his neck with a well-placed surge of Black.

She quickly returned her attention to the rent in the tent wall, finding her gaze momentarily snared by the slender woman's red-black eyes as recognition finally dawned. *Famed society beauty Catheline Dewsmine*, she thought, recalling a news-sheet headline as the woman opened her mouth to scream.

"KILL HER!" She started towards Lizanne in a frantic charge, eyes alive with hatred, still screaming. "KILL THE BITCH!"

Lizanne had time to catch sight of the White whirling about with an inquisitive roar, before she tore her gaze away and fled the tent, fingers pressing hard on the Spider to flood her system with Red and Black.

Outside a Spoiled jabbed at her with a bayonet-tipped rifle, Lizanne side-stepping the blow, sending him flying with a hard shove of Black. She ran as rifles cracked all around, bullets snapping the air. Thanks to the Green she was able to leap over knots of Spoiled as they attempted to block her path, blasting others aside with Black when they came too close.

"Launch!" she begged in a fierce whisper, casting occasional glances at the sky as she dodged and fought. Of course the *Typhoon* was hovering at too great an altitude to be seen from the ground, but she did hope to catch the flare of the rocket's engine as it streaked down.

The distraction nearly proved fatal. A burly Spoiled tackled her, strong arms encircling her waist and bearing her to the ground. Lizanne rolled with the impact and slashed her knife across the Spoiled's eyes, wrestling free of his grip then unleashing Red to incinerate the upper torso of another levelling a rifle at her. Lizanne continued the stream of Red as she ran, setting light to every tent she passed in the hope the smoke and the flames would provide enough cover, and buy time.

Nearing the edge of camp, she began to entertain the previously unsuspected notion that she might actually survive this mission. *It seems I wasted Madame Hakugen's time,* she thought, then came to a mid-air halt as an invisible rope caught her about the neck.

Black, she realised, legs kicking as she hung there. *They have a Blood-blessed.*

She fought back with her own Black, sending a wave towards the ground to push her free, but only succeeding in spinning herself about. The hold on her neck tightened, starving her lungs of air. Lizanne's vision began to dim, greying around the edges as her pulse throbbed in her temples. However, she was able to make out the sight of the woman, Catheline Dewsmine, doyen of the society pages, pelting towards her amongst the charging horde of Spoiled.

How on earth did she get here?

The question lost all significance when her ears became filled with a shrieking whoosh followed by a blinding flash beyond the oncoming mob. The grip on her neck instantly disappeared and Lizanne found herself once again tumbling in a blast wave. She used the last of her Green to turn into the blast and dig her boots in the earth, sliding to a crouching halt amidst the maelstrom. Looking up she saw the ground to her front littered with the unconscious or dead bodies of dozens of Spoiled. Beyond them a huge fireball rose from where the White had been only moments before.

Lizanne's initial wave of joyful triumph plummeted into despair when she saw the beast rising through the roiling fire, flames licking at its wings but showing no obvious injury. Her sense of defeat increased as her eyes picked out something else. Four glowing orbs floated in the swirling dust above the wreckage of the cart. *The crystals,* she thought. *It didn't work.*

Lizanne sank to her knees, head slumping as the product thinned in her veins. Hearing the shuffling of multiple boots she half-raised her head to see a group of Spoiled moving towards her, still partially stunned by the blast but retaining enough comprehension to aim their rifles at her. Wearily she took a firmer grip on her knife and tried to rise. But, finding she hadn't the strength to do so, she reversed her grip on the handle and pressed it to her neck, the edge positioned precisely where it would sever the jugular.

A harsh, rattling growl came from above and she saw the upright Spoiled nearest to her slammed into the ground in several different pieces. Earth fountained as the growl came again, the other Spoiled falling in quick succession. Lizanne turned her gaze to the sky as a shadow fell over her, finding the broad curving shape of the *Typhoon* some fifty yards above. It was dark against the sky and she couldn't see the face of her rescuer in the gondola's lower hatch, though the invisible hand that reached down to pluck her from the earth was clue enough.

"Morva," she muttered, her vision fading away as exhaustion claimed her. "I thought I told you to leave . . ."

CHAPTER 40

Hilemore

The fleet departed with the morning tide, witnessed by a mostly silent crowd. Parents waved and wept for the sons and daughters Hilemore was carrying away to war, children called to fathers and siblings, but there was no cheering. In the few days since the drake assault Stockcombe had resumed its prior state of division. The west-siders returned to their homes and the east side remained under the control of the Voters Committee, although their authority had waned considerably. Without a Blood-blessed to act as a conduit for the guidance of wiser heads Hilemore had serious doubts the status quo would continue for much longer. Coll, now sporting a bandaged nose and shorn of his Contractor's duster, had become increasingly intolerant of dissent, forcing some of the committee members to resign and making most decisions without recourse to discussion. Factions were already forming around the former committee members and there were reports of protests which quickly degenerated into brawls.

Hilemore found he had to resist the compulsion to stay and provide some form of government for the city he had fought to defend, even if it amounted to little more than a military dictatorship. But he couldn't allow Stockcombe to become his concern, something starkly underlined by Clay once they cleared the harbour.

"Who is Catheline Dewsmine?" Hilemore asked, the name meaning nothing to him.

"Wondered that myself," Clay admitted. They were on the walkway outside the bridge, Clay having emerged from a lengthy and apparently sobering trance with the eminent Miss Blood. "According to Miss Lethridge she was kind of famous. Guess her fame never reached Arradsia though."

"Catheline Dewsmine is the eldest child of the wealthy Dewsmine family," an unexpected voice said, making them turn. Akina had been engaged in cleaning the bridgehouse windows and now stood regarding them with the smug air that came from possessing superior knowledge. "Despite being Blood-blessed she was exempt from Corporate service," Akina went on in her accented but precise Mandinorian. "Upon entering managerial society she quickly became a sensation thanks to her beauty and charm. She was romantically linked with a number of actors, musicians and senior managers before succumbing to an unexplained nervous condition which required an extensive period of isolation." Akina shrugged and flicked her wash-cloth before adding in Varestian, "She went over the rail and her family stuck her in a madhouse."

"And how might you know this?" Hilemore enquired.

"Mr. Tottleborn," she replied, referring to the one-time Blood-blessed of the *Viable Opportunity* who had met his untimely end at the Battle of the Strait. "He liked his periodicals. Catheline Dewsmine regularly featured in one called *Scandal Monthly*. He had a lot of those."

"Thank you, sea-sister," Hilemore said. He gestured for her to get back to work, which she did after a typically disdainful scowl.

"So," he said to Clay, "a mad Blood-blessed is now leading the White's forces."

"Lead ain't really the right word. It's more like she's the means by which the White leads." Clay's expression darkened and he let out a heavy sigh. "Silverpin warned me the next one would be worse. According to Miss Lethridge, she wasn't wrong."

"So, if I understand the military situation, the attempt to destroy this all-important Blue crystal was a failure but the blocking of the passes into Varestia was a success?"

"Seems about the size of it, yeah."

"At least they bought us time. I know the Varestian region well and it'll take weeks for an army of any reasonable size to proceed in force along the eastern coast of the peninsular."

"A human army," Clay pointed out. "This lot could well be different. You think we'll be able to get this whole fleet across the ocean in time for it to matter?"

"What choice do we have? The deciding battle of this war will be fought there. We have to proceed with all the force we can bring to bear."

Clay nodded but Hilemore saw a lingering uncertainty on his face. "You have an alternative suggestion?" Hilemore asked.

"Maybe, I ain't sure yet. Let me think on it awhile." Clay moved to Akina, taking the wash-cloth from her and tossing it into the bucket. "Let's take a walk, kiddo," he said, guiding her away. "What else can you tell me about Catheline Dewsmine?"

The Blacks flew overhead for much of the first day, descending to their ship-borne perches come nightfall. There were fifty of them in all, the fleet being incapable of carrying more, not least because several captains had flatly refused to have any drakes aboard their ships, citing protests from mutinous crews. Those vessels that did carry the beasts had their holds loaded with freshly hunted Cerath meat and all the livestock Stockcombe could provide. At Clay's urging Hilemore issued stern instructions that the sailors make no attempt to communicate with the Blacks. "Just feed 'em and leave 'em be," Clay said. "And in the name of the Seer's ass, don't try and touch 'em."

The sea proved uncooperative over the next few days. A heavy swell and stiff easterly winds confounded Hilemore's hopes for a swift voyage to the Green Cape, the point at the southern tip of the Barrier Isles where the Myrdin and Orethic Oceans came together. His careful organisation of the fleet into two columns, the *Superior* leading one and Captain Okanas in the *Endeavour* leading the other, was also disrupted by the weather. Consequently, by the time they entered calmer waters the fleet was spread out over several miles and required half a day before the formation could be reassembled.

"I'd wager Grandfather never had this trouble," he grumbled to himself during the evening watch, spy-glass trained on the line of ships following in the *Superior*'s wake.

He turned at the sound of boots, finding Lieutenant Talmant approaching. "Crow's nest reports land in sight, sir," he said, saluting. "An island. Thirty degrees to port and a dozen miles off."

"So we're finally at the Isles," Hilemore said. He was tempted to press on, but the Green Cape was a notoriously fractious stretch of ocean and attempting to navigate it at night highly inadvisable.

"Signal the *Endeavour*," he told Talmant. "Thirty-degree turn to port, then signal the fleet to follow. We'll anchor in the lee of the island, make for the Cape at first light."

"Aye, sir."

He was woken from a dream in which a large parrot had taken it upon itself to perch on his shoulder and ask a series of unwelcome questions. *Why did Lewella reject you?* it demanded amongst other things, each question followed by a loud squawk.

Why do you pretend not to lust after Captain Okanas? Squawk!

Do you think they'll give you a court martial before they hang you for mutiny? Squawk!

Why did you let all those youngsters die in Stockcombe? Squawk!

It was this last question that woke him, summoning memories that even his slumbering mind couldn't face. Curiously, however, as his eyes opened on a darkened cabin the parrot kept squawking even louder than before. "Right," he said, reaching for his revolver intending to shoot the bloody thing, then stopped as he came fully awake and realised the noise wasn't coming from a parrot, but a drake. One of the sailors from the midnight watch had already begun pounding on his door by the time he opened it.

"Mr. Torcreek, sir," the sailor said. "He says they're all in a right state about something."

"Sound battle stations," Hilemore ordered, pulling on his tunic. "Fire rockets to alert the fleet."

"Aye, sir."

He found Clay on the fore-deck with Lutharon, the huge beast repeatedly calling out, wings spread and tail coiling in alarm. The two other drakes on the aft deck replied with equal volume, as did every other Black in the fleet. A signal rocket streamed into the night sky and exploded, quickly followed by two more, although Hilemore doubted there was a soul aboard any of the surrounding ships not already awake.

"What is it?" he demanded, striding towards Clay.

"He smells something. I'm doubtful it's good." Clay stared at the agitated drake in intense concentration then let out a sharp exhalation. "Blues," he told Hilemore.

"How far?"

"Close, that's all I can say. They don't judge distance the way we do. There's just near and far."

Hilemore turned towards the bridge, cupping his hands about his mouth. "Battle stations! Weigh anchor and start engines! Signal the fleet to prepare for action!"

He turned back to Clay, intending to ask about the Blues' direction of attack, but the question died as the Black abruptly sprinted towards the stern and launched itself into the air. From the sudden commotion on the other ships it was clear that the other drakes were following suit. It was a two-moon night so they could see the Blacks forming into a dense flock before flying south.

"They'll do what they can," Clay explained. "But there's a lot heading this way. Gotta reckon on some getting past them."

"You have product?" Hilemore asked him.

"More'n I need."

"Then I trust you to choose your own spot and put it to good use."

He ran to the bridge, finding Steelfine and Talmant present with Scrimshine at the helm. "Riflemen to the upper works, Number One," he told Steelfine. "Mining party to stand to at the stern and deploy on the turn. Guns to load with cannister and fire at low elevations only. Be best if we avoided hitting our allies, don't you think?"

"Aye, sir!" Steelfine saluted and swiftly departed the bridge.

"Mr. Talmant, go up top and take charge of the search-light. Keep it moving until you spot a target."

"Sir!"

Hilemore moved to the speaking-tube. "Engine room."

"Engine room reporting, sir," came Chief Bozware's tinny reply.

"Ahead dead slow, Chief. And have Miss Jillett stand by the blood-burner." He waited to feel the thrum of the auxiliary engine through the deckboards before nodding at Scrimshine. "Due south, helm."

"Due south, sir."

Hilemore stepped out onto the walkway to check on the rest of the fleet. They were slowly arranging themselves into a circular formation in accordance with the plan he set out in the event of being attacked at anchor. The intention was to create an impenetrable defensive ring whilst the Superior conducted a more aggressive defence. He found the response of most of the merchantmen sluggish compared to what he would have expected from a Protectorate ship, but at least they were moving. He turned his gaze to the bow, watching the search-light beam cut through the gloom. Lieutenant Talmant was energetic in swinging the huge light about, playing the circle of bright luminescence over the gentle swell in regular, broad arcs.

Hilemore's gaze snapped to a point a few degrees to starboard as a plume of flame erupted close to the surface. He caught a brief glimpse of two shapes entwined, one winged, the other long and snake-like, then the flames died and it was gone. The sound of the struggle reached them a second later, harsh shrieks of challenge and distress echoing through the sea air.

"How far away are they?"

Hilemore glanced over his shoulder finding Kriz climbing the ladder to the walkway. She carried a carbine and wore her Contractor's duster.

"Hard to say," he replied. "Mr. Torcreek sent you, I assume?"

"He thought you might need added protection."

"Let's hope he's wrong."

They witnessed another dozen flame-illuminated contests over the course of the next few minutes, each one closer than the other. In one instance the flames continued for some time, Hilemore recognising Lutharon by virtue of his size as the Black dragged a struggling Blue from the water. The two drakes skimmed the waves as they fought, the Blue casting repeated gouts of flame at Lutharon who replied with his own, his claws latched firmly on his opponent's coils. It finally ended when Lutharon briefly released his opponent to clamp his talons onto its jaws, prising them apart to send a jet of fire directly into its throat. He let out a brief squawk of triumph before releasing the Blue's body and beating his wings to push himself skyward. Watching the Blue corpse roll in the waves, Hilemore realised with dismay it was at most sixty yards away.

"Target ten degrees to port!" Lieutenant Talmant called. Hilemore tracked the search-light beam to the Blue rearing up in the white circle barely thirty yards off the port bow. The pivot-gun fired immediately, the Blue disappearing in a haze of red and white as the cannister-shot lashed the sea.

Hilemore returned to the bridgehouse. "Ahead two-thirds," he barked into the speaking-tube before turning to Scrimshine. "Helm, hard a-port."

From outside came the crackle of rifle fire, the marksmen no doubt finding another target illuminated by the search-light. The starboard cannon also opened up, Hilemore hoping they managed to do some damage. He glanced through the rear window of the bridgehouse, taking satisfaction from the sight of the mining party casting their devices from the stern. These were improved versions of the mines that had served them so well in Stockcombe harbour. Each had been fitted with varying amounts of ballast to ensure they lay beneath the surface at different depths. They had also been packed with twice the amount of explosive.

"Five degrees to port," he told Scrimshine, repeating the order two minutes later to ensure the *Superior* seeded her mines in a wide arc along the southern flank of the fleet. Once every mine had been deployed he told the engine room to reverse revolutions and had Scrimshine bring the ship hard-about. Even in a gentle swell it was a tricky manoeuvre, taking several minutes and causing the deck to tilt at an acute angle.

The first mine exploded before they completed the turn, one of the deeper ones judging by the height of the waterspout. Hilemore saw some debris churning in the mass of bubbles boiling to the surface and hoped it was drake flesh.

"Ahead one-third," he told the engine room as Scrimshine brought the tiller to midships and the *Superior* levelled out. "Port guns look lively!" Hilemore called through the window, the last word being drowned out by the near-simultaneous explosion of three mines. This time there was no ambiguity about the damage inflicted, Hilemore hearing a cheer from the crew at the sight of what may have been as many as five Blue corpses twisting amidst the falling spume and froth.

Hilemore went out onto the walkway to watch the still-twitching bodies pass by, expecting another explosion at any instant. Instead there was silence. The struggle between Blacks and Blues seemed to have ended and the *Superior* steamed through quiet waters. "Scared the bastards off, eh, Skipper?" Scrimshine asked.

The answer came before Hilemore could reply. A thunderous cacoph-

ony of cannon fire from the fleet had Hilemore rushing through the bridge
to the starboard walkway. He had expected to find the sea around the circle of ships wreathed in smoke but instead saw a thick pall rising within
the formation. He could hear a continuous rattle of small-arms fire as the
gun-crews no doubt scrambled to reload their cannon, then saw ships silhouetted against multiple gouts of flame. It appeared as if the drakes had
learned to concentrate their fire, Hilemore cursing in dismay at the sight
of a freighter being entirely enveloped in flame. The fires soon found the
powder stocks and the ship's upper works disintegrated in a series of rapid
explosions. Secondary blasts boomed within her hull a heart-beat later and
she broke in two, each section forming a dark V against the flames as they
sank below.

"Hard a-starboard!" Hilemore shouted to Scrimshine, returning to the
bridge. "There," Hilemore said, pointing through the window at the gap
created by the freighter's demise. He resisted the urge to order an increase
in speed. They were so close to the formation that there wouldn't be sufficient time to slow their approach. It made for several agonising minutes as
the *Superior* closed with the fleet, Hilemore seeing another huge explosion
rise above the masts.

"Reverse revolutions," he called into the speaking-tube as the *Superior*'s
prow edged into the gap. "Helm, full right rudder. Miss," he said, nodding
at Kriz and drawing his revolver. "If you would care to join me."

She followed as he went outside, sliding down the ladder to the deck
and calling for Steelfine. "Sir!" the Islander said, appearing at his side with
the usual alacrity.

"Shift all guns and riflemen to port," Hilemore instructed. "Have more
mines brought up . . ."

He was interrupted by a hard shove that propelled him across the deck,
his skin prickling at the suddenly heated air. Scrambling upright he was
confronted by the sight of Steelfine beating out flames on his sleeve whilst
a few feet beyond him Kriz stared up at the immobile form of a Blue that
had reared up over the rail. Its head was frozen in place whilst the rest of
its body coiled with a desperate energy, whipping the sea into a froth. It
seemed as if every rifle, carbine and pistol on board fired at once, including
Hilemore's though he couldn't remember aiming. He fired until the hammer clicked, the Blue's head disappeared into a red cloud as the hail of

bullets struck home, tearing most of the flesh away and laying bare the skull beneath. This too was soon blasted into powder and the Blue's body immediately slackened, the beast hanging limp in Kriz's grip. She released it, letting the corpse sink below the rail, and moved to help Hilemore to his feet.

"My apologies," she said. "I didn't hurt you, did I?"

"You are entirely forgiven, miss," Hilemore assured her.

He rushed to the rail, looking out on the fleet, which now resembled something from an illustrated folio of the Travail. Three ships were fully alight with fires raging on most of the others. The sea within the confines of the circle roiled with drakes, Blues repeatedly rearing up to belch flame at the surrounding vessels, then slipping below the waves to evade the subsequent mass of rifle fire. The *Superior*'s starboard cannon commenced fire and Hilemore saw Steelfine urgently organising the relocation of the other guns. *It won't be enough,* he knew, watching the cannister lash at the drakes. With most of the heavy ordnance in the fleet now silenced it was clear they didn't possess sufficient fire-power to prevail. But there were other weapons to call on.

"Miss," he said, turning to Kriz. "I should be grateful if you would fetch Mr. Torcreek, Lieutenant Sigoral and Miss Jillett."

He busied himself with organising the mines on the fore-deck, having the crew remove the floats and the ballast before arming the fuses.

"Captain?" Clay asked, running to his side flanked by his fellow Blood-blessed.

"They need to be evenly spread," Hilemore said, pointing at the mines then the flaming chaos beyond the starboard rail.

Clay understood immediately, drinking down a full flask of Black and nodding at the others to do the same. Hilemore had the fore-deck cleared of crew and retreated to the bridge walkway before shouting out the order for the Blood-blessed to proceed. Clay went first, lifting the closest mine and gently guiding it out and over the starboard side of the ship then propelling it at speed into the seething mass of Blues. By Hilemore's reckoning the explosion killed at least two drakes, and distracted several more. He saw a cluster of snake-like forms speeding towards the *Superior*. Fortunately, Lieutenant Sigoral saw it too and dropped the next mine directly in their path.

The mines flew in a steady arcing torrent after that, the sea within the circle of ships becoming a cauldron of waterspouts, tumbling drake flesh and reflected flame. The amount of explosive released so quickly in such a confined space inevitably caused the surrounding cordon to widen, making Hilemore worry the multiple shock waves might buckle the *Superior*'s hull plating. It continued until every mine had been thrown, the water displaced by the final explosion falling in a brief rain-storm and heralding a prolonged silence.

To Hilemore it seemed as if they must have killed every drake sent against them, the mass of dead and dying Blues bobbing on the surface was so thick he could probably have walked across it. Then he saw the snouts of more Blues pushing their way up through the carnage and knew they weren't yet done. He prepared to call out an order for Steelfine to ready the cannon, but stopped at the sight of Clay urgently waving his arms above his head. The reason became clear a heart-beat later when Lutharon swooped out of the sky in company with a half dozen Blacks. Together they plunged their talons into the gory sea, dragging an uninjured Blue clear of the water. Its screams and flames of protest were cut short as the Blacks bore it high and tore it to pieces, the remnants cascading over the *Superior* in a grisly red rain that had the crew running for cover lest the blood find their skin.

More Blacks followed, diving down in groups to snare a Blue and carry it off to be slaughtered. The screeching and rending spectacle continued for nigh on a half-hour, by which time any triumph Hilemore might have felt had faded into a guilty recognition of the cost incurred by the night's events. Several ships were still burning and he saw another had capsized, the sea boiling around her flanks as it slowly claimed her. He couldn't hear the screams of those trapped within her hull, but they still sang in his head, loud and clear.

CHAPTER 41

Lizanne

She had no memory of the flight from the Grand Cut, nor any recollection of the two days that followed. Her exhaustion was so complete that her slumber remained free of dreams, something for which she would always be grateful. On waking to find herself in Tinkerer's former clinic room, body aching in numerous places, she was confronted with a sight that forced her to conclude she was dreaming after all.

"So," Arberus said, rising from a chair at the side of her bed. He regarded her with an expression full of concern but also not lacking in judgement. "Still addicted to risk, I see."

"Go away," Lizanne groaned, pushing her head deeper into her pillow. "I've no tolerance for dreams just now."

"Lizanne," he said, tone hardening a little. She looked at him again, blinking in surprise at the fact that he was still there. He wore the same cavalry officer's uniform he had worn throughout the revolution, though it now lacked any regimental badges or insignia of rank. His face was as blockishly handsome as ever, though he had picked up another scar. It looked to her like a sabre-cut, tracing along the line of his neck to his collar.

"Oh," she said. "You're really here."

"Yes. I really am."

She tried to push herself into a sitting position but her arms seemed to have been sapped of strength and he had to help her, easing her onto the pillow he propped behind her back. He began to smooth the hair back from her forehead but she stopped him, catching his hand and gently but firmly pushing it away. That time was past.

He gave a tight smile before dragging his chair closer and sitting down. "You've been busy, from what I hear."

"As have you, from what *I* hear. I take it your presence means you left the Electress in charge?"

"She finally took Merivus, showing a surprising capacity for mercy when they sued for peace. Only allowed herself one execution, some cousin of the Emperor's who wasn't particularly popular anyway. After that the other cities in the northern Empire fell into line. There's some localised resistance here and there but the war is effectively over and the Corvantine Republic now a reality."

"Don't expect it to be there when you get back." Her voice rasped over the last word and she gave a cough, finding her throat dry. Arberus poured her a cup of water, which she drank in a few gulps. "You'll be bowing to Empress Atalina I before long."

"I won't be bowing to anyone," he said. "Though I must say the pressures of leadership seem to have mellowed her somewhat, and she has agreed to organise elections."

"If there's more than one candidate, I'll be very surprised."

"There will be. But I believe we have more pressing concerns at present."

"We do. I trust you brought some troops with you."

"I did. And some old friends. One of whom brought you a present."

A rshav's milk-white eyes stared up at her from the confines of the sack. His head had been severed with a single blow which had frozen his features in an expression somewhere between surprise and disdain. His end had come some days before and the flesh was stiffened into something that resembled dried paper.

"Wanted to make a deal," Varkash said in his deep nasal voice. The wharf was covered in a light drizzle this morning and a beading of moisture clung to his pyrite nose. "An alliance between the new Corvantine Republic and the Varestian League. Made the mistake of naming you his enemy. Didn't realise the esteem Miss Blood enjoys amongst those who fought the revolution. When the Electress told him to get fucked him and his mother turned to me. When I told him to get fucked he got angry, challenged me." Varkash shrugged his broad shoulders. He still wore much the same garb as he had in Scorazin, though the waistcoat he wore was fashioned from fine material and expertly tailored to fit his muscular frame. "Over-confidence is death in a duel."

"His mother?" Lizanne asked.

"She went mad. The Electress seized her ships, gave them to me. I set the mean old bitch adrift in a row-boat."

"Lockbar hadn't lied after all," Lizanne murmured. It had taken most of the day, and some Green, to recover enough strength to come here and receive Varkash's present, so the kick she delivered to Arshav's head was weak by her usual standards. Nevertheless it possessed enough force to propel the object over the edge of the wharf and into the waters below.

"Thank you for coming," she told Varkash, glancing beyond him to the ships moored in the Sound. There were twenty in all, armed merchantmen and the rest all former Imperial Navy frigates and sloops. Apparently, this was all that remained of the Corvantine fleet. They carried a force of ten thousand volunteers, many of them expatriate Varestians come home to fight for the heartland. "We have much for you to do."

K inda dark in here, Clay observed, eyeing her whirlwinds, which, she realised, had taken on a much gloomier hue lately.

You have a report? she enquired. The fatigue that still plagued her in the real world had seen fit to follow her here. This was their second trance in three days and it transpired he hadn't brought good news.

Four ships sunk, he told her after describing the Blue attack the night before. *Another five too badly damaged to attempt the crossing. We also lost a lot of sailors.*

Hardly a mighty armada, she replied. *But it's something.* Her whirlwinds coiled in response to her frustration. It seemed their enemy had a worrying ability to anticipate their moves, which didn't bode well for the next phase of the campaign. *Morradin,* she thought, forming a vortex into an image of the marshal alongside a slim figure in a general's uniform. *And Sirus. They both stand high in the White's counsel, along with the Dewsmine woman. I assume most of its tactical acumen comes from them.*

They might be dead, Clay pointed out. *Was an awful big firework you hit them with.*

Not big enough. The White still lives. That's all that matters.

I'm not so sure. Remember what you saw in the Artisan's memories, and what Silverpin told me. It needs that woman, needs a human mind to make it complete. Take her away and maybe we have a chance.

How do you intend to do that? I very much doubt I, or any other Blood-blessed, will be able to get as close again.

We don't have to get close, or leastways I don't. He went on to outline his plan, which Lizanne found scarcely more likely to succeed than her attempt to destroy the Blue crystal. *Worth a shot, ain't it?* he asked, feeling her doubt. *Better than just fighting more and more battles till everyone's dead or Spoiled.*

She gave a grudging pulse of agreement at this, though muted somewhat by the recognition that they were fast running short of alternatives. *Will Captain Hilemore agree?* she asked.

He'll take some persuading, Clay admitted. *Though I can tell that all the people we lost is playing on his mind, so he might be more agreeable than you think.*

We'll trance at the same time tomorrow. Please ensure you impress upon the captain the lateness of the hour. Delay may be fatal.

"We simply don't have the strength to defeat them in the field," Arberus said. "Our best estimate is that they have over two hundred thousand troops, disciplined troops at that, plus the drakes. We have less than half that number."

Lizanne had convened a council of war aboard the *Viable Opportunity*, Varkash and Arberus on one side of the map table with Captain Trumane, Madame Hakugen and Alzar Lokaras on the other. Lizanne stood at the head of the table, unacknowledged but undoubtedly accepted as the ultimate authority in the room.

"Your forget the difference in fire-power," Trumane pointed out. "With the new carbines, repeating guns and the rockets we enjoy a considerable advantage in weight of gunnery. Professor Lethridge has given us another aerostat this week alone. Not to mention the fact that we now have command of the sea. If our forces are properly combined and organised it could well negate their advantage in numbers."

"Superior fire-power is only effective if it can be brought to bear en masse," Arberus returned. "The enemy has to be placed, or place themselves in a position where it can do most damage." His finger traced along the eastern coast of the Varestian Peninsular. "I can see only one place where that could happen."

"The Jet Sands," Varkash said, peering at the map.

Arberus nodded, his finger tracing across a short stretch of land close to a shallow bay. "The Sands extend from the shore to the river four miles inland. The river is too deep and fast-flowing to be forded so they'll have to advance across the dunes, and sand makes for slow marching. We concentrate our forces on the southern fringe of the dunes, giving the appearance of a thinly held stretch of line close to shore to tempt them to attack there. If they take the bait we bring the fleet's guns to bear and all our land-based fire-power."

"Also, if they've massed for an assault," Trumane added with a note of approval, "the aerostats can take a fearful toll with the rockets."

Lizanne's gaze strayed from the map table when she saw Tekela enter the room bearing a number of recently developed photostats. "It seems our latest reconnaissance is here," she said.

"Uncle," Tekela greeted Arberus briefly before spreading the photostats out on the table. "They've stopped," she said, pointing to an image showing the terrain around the eastern part of the Neck. It showed a camp more or less identical to the one where Lizanne had so nearly met her death a week before. "Or at least most of them have."

Tekela placed another photostat in the centre of the table. The image was slightly unfocused and it took Lizanne a moment to make out the sight of a column of infantry moving north in skirmish order. "There were more columns to the north-west," Tekela added. "Each one has a large number of Reds flying overhead and Greens scouting the flanks."

"They're drawing back?" Varkash asked in bemusement.

"No," Lizanne said. She turned her eyes to the map, tracing the most likely line of march for each of the columns. They all led to a region where the White's forces hadn't marched before, regions now rich in unconquered towns and villages swollen with refugees. "They're gathering strength," she went on. "Either we dealt them a heavier blow than we thought or they intend to offset our advantage in fire-power with sheer weight of numbers. My guess is the latter."

"In any case they've been forced to delay their advance," Trumane mused. "All to the good."

"Not if you happen to live in one of these regions," Tekela said. "They're within range of the aerostats. We can . . ."

"No," Lizanne cut in, Clay's plan at the forefront of her mind. "The aerostats can't be risked. The captain's right. The more time they spend north of the Neck the better. Every day they give us means more weapons, more ammunition and the chance of reinforcement."

"But the people . . ." Tekela protested.

"Will have to flee or see to their own defence." Seeing the surprised hurt on Tekela's face, Lizanne realised her tone had been sharper than she intended. "This is war," she went on, moderating her voice a little. "Difficult choices have to be made."

She turned to Alzar Lokaras. "Our situation would be greatly improved if we had more fighters," she said.

"Not so easy mustering an army in Varestia," he replied. "Our people have never taken well to being told what to do. Even the Corvantines never tried to introduce conscription here, with good reason. On top of that we have the clans to contend with. Half of them still have unresolved feuds with the other half. Many refuse outright to fight alongside each other . . ."

"They won't refuse me," Varkash said softly. Lizanne had intuited that Alzar was not a man to willingly tolerate an interruption and took note of the fact that he did so now, albeit with an angry clench to his jaw. "Not when I've spoken to them," Varkash went on, addressing his words to Lizanne. "Give me one ship and ten days, I'll bring you another thirty thousand fighters."

"Take them," she told him. "In the meantime General Arberus has graciously consented to take command of our land forces. Training will begin as soon as possible, but we require a base of operations within reasonable marching distance of the Jet Sands. The Mount is too small and isolated."

"Here," Alzar said, pointing to a small isthmus about seventy miles north of Blaska Sound.

"Gadara's Redoubt," Varkash said. "As good a place as any, if a little ill-omened."

"Ill-omened?" Arberus asked.

"It's a hill-fort," Alzar replied. "Long out of use. Built three hundred years ago by the pirate queen Gadara Slavas, considered by many to be the last monarch of Varestia. She made her final stand against the Corvantines at the Redoubt. The walls are in a state of disrepair but much of the fort itself was hewn out of solid rock and remains habitable. It also has wells for freshwater and overlooks a plain large enough to encamp an army."

"Sounds acceptable," Arberus said.

"Tekela will fly you there today," Lizanne said. "Captain Alzar, please have your fleet begin ferrying troops to the Redoubt. I'll join you in a few days. There are things to see to here."

"A mile?" Lizanne squinted at the calculations on Tinkerer's blackboard, finding little meaning in any of it.

"If the device is constructed according to specifications," he told her. "There may be some variation in the blast radius according to variable weather conditions, but a mile is a reasonable estimation in most instances."

She gave a slight shake of her head, more in wonder than doubt. "How?"

"Using a kerosene-gelatine mix in place of a standard fuel, an oxidiser-based explosive will generate a more energetic and sustained blast wave." He blinked at her blank expression and added, "It will work. Trust me."

"And it can be carried by an aerostat?"

"As long as crew numbers and additional weight are kept to a minimum."

She stared at the board for a moment longer, pondering the implications of unleashing such a device upon the world. It was only one of several notions Tinkerer had proposed since emerging from his coma. The time spent imprisoned in his own mind had evidently generated a great deal of inventive energy, much of it of a worryingly destructive nature. *If he can make this,* she thought, *what else can he make?*

"Manufacturing time?" she asked.

Tinkerer turned to her father who had been summoned from the aerostat shed for an engineering opinion. "It will require transferring labour from other tasks," he said. "Meaning no more rockets. And I'll have to conduct some experimentation with materials . . ."

"How long, Father?" Lizanne insisted.

"Ten days, to make one device. And I'll need a thousand workers to do it."

"I'll give you double the work-force," she said, "to make two."

G adara's Redoubt was in fact a chain of forts rather than a single hold-fast. They were linked by a series of walls that followed the line of a ridge dominating the interior of the isthmus in an inverted U. The elevated position afforded clear views of the landward approaches. The Redoubt's main keep consisted of a huge rocky mound which had been honeycombed over the course of succeeding decades to accommodate a number of chambers of varying sizes, providing enough space to house several battalions of troops. The mound was crowned by a narrow tower in a poor state of repair, though enough of the steps remained to allow Lizanne to climb to the top. She found Arberus there, binoculars held to his eyes as he surveyed his troops on the plain. It was a week since the conference aboard the *Viable*, and the army encamped below had grown to over fifty thousand fighters.

"How goes the training?" she asked him as she reached the top.

"It proceeds with varying success," he said, a faintly sour note to his voice. "The Varestians excel in marksmanship and close-quarters combat, but ask them to march in line and they descend into a childlike state."

"Is it strictly necessary to march in line on a modern battlefield?"

"Military discipline requires cohesion, the ability to work as a team. Drill is a useful way of instilling such discipline. These people know how to fight, but I contend they don't yet know how to war."

"Then they'd best learn quickly."

He lowered his binoculars at the seriousness of her tone, eyebrows raised. "You have news?"

"I just tranced with Morva. The columns are returning to the main camp, with numerous captives in tow. We can expect them to march within the week. It's time, General. Please muster your forces and advance to the Jet Sands with all possible haste."

CHAPTER 42

Clay

"You're certain this will work?" Hilemore asked him.

"I ain't certain of anything much these days, Captain," Clay replied. "But I do know there's no way this fleet's gonna make it across the Orethic in the state it's in. But a blood-burner might."

Hilemore turned away from him and moved to the starboard rail. Clay could almost feel the man's guilt as his gaze tracked over the burnt and blackened fleet. In addition to the damage done the cost in lives had been heavy, as had the toll in wounded. Every ship still afloat reported sick bays full of burnt and maimed crew. Fully half their stocks of Green had already been expended in keeping the wounded alive.

"Just one battle," Clay heard Hilemore murmur to himself.

"One battle don't make a war," Clay said. "The fleet may be done but the war ain't."

"You would have me abandon them?"

"Lutharon's lost all scent of any Blues. They're either dead or fled. The fleet can make its way back to Stockcombe." He steeled himself for what he had to say next, aware of the likely reaction but also knowing it had to be said. "They did what we needed, anyways. If we'd tried to sail alone the Blues would've done for us."

He refused to look away as the captain rounded on him, a dangerous glint in his eye. Since meeting Hilemore Clay had thought him incapable of breaking, a man so bound up in duty and the need to do what was right it was impossible for him to waver. Now he saw just a man like any other. Braver than most to be sure, and expert in fighting at sea, but still just a man who could be borne down by guilt. At another time it might have stirred Clay's empathy. But today, with so much at stake, it just made him angry.

"If you ain't gonna do it," he went on, voice hardening, "give us the *Endeavour* and me and the Longrifles will sail on alone. You can run on back to Stockcombe and take a nice big bath in your self-pity."

Hilemore's fists bunched as he started towards Clay, his face the rigid mask of a man intent on violence.

"Sea-brother," another voice said. It was softly spoken but still managed to bring Hilemore to a halt. Zenida stood close by, Akina at her side. "He's right," Zenida said, casting a sombre glance at the fleet. "They fought bravely but they're done. Time to send them home. But we still have work to do."

Evidently the Varestian's word carried more weight than Clay's, Hilemore's aggression leeching away as he straightened, nodding stiffly. "The *Endeavour* will go with the fleet . . ." he began.

"No," Zenida broke in. "Two blood-burners stand a better chance than one." She sighed and turned to her daughter who, Clay saw, had begun scowling again, this time with even more ferocity than usual. "Though I would ask that you request Captain Tidelow find a spare berth."

Steelfine had to carry Akina across the gangway to the *Farlight*, kicking and screaming all the way whilst her mother looked on in stern-faced silence. The girl had twisted away when her mother tried to embrace her, spitting curses in Varestian until Steelfine stepped forward to hoist her onto his shoulder.

As Akina was being forcibly disembarked others were coming aboard. Colonel Kulvetch and thirty of her Marines arrived by boat. Another twenty volunteers from amongst the ranks of the Voters were embarking the *Endeavour*. In addition to the increase in crew each ship was being loaded with extra cannon donated by the other ships. Some captains, the Dalcian pirate woman and Captain Gurkan chief amongst them, had also offered to have their ships towed by the blood-burners but Hilemore forbade it as impractical.

Every ounce of Red remaining to the fleet had been divided equally between the two blood-burners, meaning they would be able to sail on thermoplasmic power all the way to Varestia. A great deal depended on the weather but Hilemore estimated they would reach the Red Tides within ten days. The only issue remaining was the question of what to do with their allies.

"Just Lutharon," Clay said. "The others will fly home."

"We have room for two more aboard the *Superior*," Hilemore said. The usefulness of the drakes during their battle with the Blues had evidently made a deep impression on his military mind. "And the *Endeavour* could carry one."

"Just Lutharon," Clay insisted. "We only need him."

He went to the fore-deck to communicate the decision to Lutharon, who proved surprisingly resistant. He still roiled with excitement after the fight with the Blues, the fresh scars on his flanks seemingly doing little to deter his ardour. *It's my belief,* Clay thought, laying a hand on the Black's snout to send a flow of calming images into his mind, *your kin have risked enough on our account already. Time to send them home.*

Lutharon let out an aggrieved huff, twin smoke-plumes rising from his nostrils as he pulled his head away. He turned about and launched himself from the ship's prow, climbing into the sky and wheeling about, mouth gaping as he let out a summoning call. It was soon answered by the other Blacks, all rising from the ships to join him in a swirling flock. Clay could feel some of the conflicting emotions leaking from Lutharon and sense the reluctance amongst the other Blacks. Their cries became discordant and the circling flock took on a confused, disordered appearance, some drakes colliding and snapping at each other in apparent disagreement. Eventually Lutharon let out a huge roar that drowned out all other cries and the discord abruptly ceased. They continued to circle in silence for a short while, then began to peel away, flying north to the Isles in a loose formation one by one until Lutharon was left alone in the sky.

He descended in a wide arc, skimming the sea before flaring his wings and coming to rest on the *Superior*'s prow. He let out a low rumble as Clay came forward to run a hand along his flank. "Sorry, big fella," he said. "But I'm fast becoming resigned to the notion that there's only one way to win this war, and when the time comes it'll just be you and me."

Hilemore ordered the blood-burner lit once they cleared the Green Cape. The *Superior* with her larger engine and lack of paddles soon pulled ahead of the *Endeavour*, though the smaller ship's comparative lack of weight meant she was able to keep station a hundred yards off the frigate's bow.

Clay spent much of the first three days pondering every scrap of information he had been able to glean about Catheline Dewsmine. In addition to what Akina could tell him, an appeal to the rest of the fleet for any pertinent information had yielded a number of periodicals, including some copies of *Scandal Monthly* so beloved by the late Mr. Tottleborn. The details of the woman's life were so alien to his own that it was hard to find anything to empathise with, something he knew would be important if his scheme was to work. *Born rich and kinda nasty with it,* was his main conclusion upon reading the various accounts of Catheline's life. *Maybe that's why the White chose her.*

Eventually he was forced to conclude that the most useful aspect of the periodicals lay in the drawings and photostats depicting his subject, albeit with varying levels of accuracy. The drawings were mostly advertorials, a typical example exhorting readers to "Try Daulton's Skin Cleansing Cream," above a serene image of Catheline reposing on a couch, perfect profile raised towards the lips of a handsome admirer. Below the drawing was the legend "'All women deserve to feel special.'—Catheline Dewsmine."

"She doesn't look insane," Kriz commented one evening as they lay together in his bunk. He had previously shared the cabin with Lieutenant Sigoral, who now spent his nights with Loriabeth whilst Kriz spent hers with Clay. There had been no prior discussion of the arrangement, the change taking place in an unspoken atmosphere of inevitability. If Braddon had an opinion about his daughter taking up with a Corvantine Blood-blessed, he had seen fit to keep it quiet, although Clay had perceived a certain frowning disapproval whenever his uncle saw the two of them together.

"Maybe she wasn't," Clay replied. "Not then at least. Looks a mite different in this one, though."

He reached for one of the news-sheets, the front page showing a photostat of Catheline stepping into a carriage outside a large mansion house in Sanorah. "Who Did She Kiss Goodnight?" asked the headline above the photostat. The story beneath related how "Famed society beauty Catheline Dewsmine appears to be keeping late hours these days. Here she is exiting the home of Senior Ironship Manager Rence Cozgrave just after midnight.

According to neighbours Mrs. Cozgrave is currently visiting relatives in South Mandinor so perhaps Miss Dewsmine was just making sure Mr. Cozgrave didn't get too lonely." It was the expression on Catheline's face that he found most interesting. In other photostats she was always smiling, in this her slightly blurred features stared into the camera with naked, unabashed hatred.

"I reckon whoever took this was lucky she didn't have any product on her," Clay said. "Anyways, whoever she was before, she's a monster now."

"Just like Hezkhi," Kriz said, shifting to rest her head on his chest. "I never knew how much he must have hated Father. In the end, after all those years imprisoned in the Enclave, we all resented him, myself perhaps most of all. But I could never hate him. If I had it might have been me they called to whilst we slept. I wonder if madness isn't all the White needs to claim us. Maybe it needs hate too."

Hate, Clay thought, looking at the photostat again and the steady-eyed fury of the woman it depicted. *Now that's something I do know about.*

CHAPTER 43

Sirus

He didn't so much wake from unconsciousness as be dragged from it. *Get up!* Catheline's voice in his head, curt and undeniable in its authority, banishing the vague images that had begun to coalesce into a dream. Despite the immediate plethora of pain that greeted his awakened body, he was still grateful she had spared him the dream, Katrya's face having been at the forefront of it.

He sat up slowly, displacing the soil that covered him and taking in his surroundings. The soles of his boots were only a few inches away from the edge of a large crater some twenty feet across. Hovering above the crater were the four crystals, glowing bright at first but then beginning to flicker. As Sirus watched, the flicker increased whilst their glow diminished. They fell when the glow faded, landing on the partially scorched earth near by to be swiftly scooped up by a number of Spoiled.

"I hope you kept his memories," he heard Catheline say and turned to see her standing over a corpse. Morradin hadn't been as fortunate as Sirus. The upper half of his body lay outside the crater but what remained of the lower half lay within it, reduced to little more than a smear of ash shot through with patches of red. For a moment Sirus entertained the impossible notion that there might be some vestige of the marshal still lingering in his mind and reached out to try and find it. Of course there was only the cold silence of death. Grand Marshal Morradin, perhaps the finest military mind of his age, a singularly horrible human being and a worse Spoiled, was truly dead.

An enemy and ally both, Sirus thought amidst the welter of fear that followed. *What must be done will be done by me alone.*

"Didn't know you two were so close," Catheline commented, moving nearer and offering her hand.

"We weren't," he said, taking her hand and getting to his feet. "But his talents will be missed."

Catheline's gaze became guarded, red-black eyes downcast as she nodded to the crater. "I think we have a far greater loss to mourn."

The White lay in the centre of the crater, body curled around three mangled forms. The infant Whites were mostly whole but clearly dead, thick gore leaking from slack and open mouths as the White nuzzled them, letting out a sound Sirus hadn't heard from it before. It was somewhere between a whine and a rumble, the pitch of it sharp enough to pain the ears. More than the sound he could feel it seeping into his own thoughts; the raw pain of a grieving parent. The two surviving infants crouched near by, tails twitching and eyes darting nervously about.

"She got away, you know," Catheline said. "The Lethridge bitch. A Blood-blessed in one of their flying contraptions picked her up."

"She failed," Sirus said, nodding at the White.

"This time. We can take no more chances, General. We must end this. In the past I have allowed my emotions to guide us. That was my error, for which I expect I'll soon be punished. You will formulate a plan to ensure our victory beyond any doubt and I will implement it regardless of how long it might take. This army is now yours."

The calamity in the Grand Cut and the rocket attack had cost the army twelve thousand Spoiled and two thousand drakes. The Greens bore the brunt of the losses thanks to the speed with which they had charged into the pass, but the Reds had also suffered greatly, losing close to a third of their number. It was a stark illustration to Sirus that the drakes were a finite resource. They had been the key to victory in so many engagements but every battle reduced their strength. *And when they're all gone*, he mused amidst a carefully modulated pall of fear, *all He will have is an army of Spoiled. An army led by me.*

Veilmist reported that, even after such a setback, the overall strength of the army stood at close to one hundred and eighty thousand. However, Sirus found it an easy matter to convince Catheline they needed to increase their strength yet further. "Our enemy is clearly more resourceful than we could ever have expected," he told her. "Every time we meet them they reveal a new and more deadly novelty. We have no ships that fly in the air, no rockets of unfeasible accuracy, nor can I find a mind in our ranks capable of producing them. Perhaps the most important lesson I learned from Marshal Morradin was the importance of numbers. We need to overwhelm our enemy. Attack in such strength no amount of invention can save them."

The three columns set off the following day, making for regions Veilmist identified as possessing the most-developed agriculture. "Thousands fled our advance," Sirus explained to Catheline. "People have to eat. It stands to reason they would flee to where they expect to find food."

Each of the columns was led by a contingent of tribal Spoiled as they possessed the most honed tracking skills. They were under orders to avoid large-scale engagements and kill only when necessary. Their success was rapid and surprising even to Sirus. It appeared that, having avoided the passage of the White's army, many refugees had naïvely assumed they were gone for good. Several large groups were captured in the open as they attempted to return to their homes. Reds also prowled the skies, scouting the locations of refugee camps in the hills. These would then be set upon from the air and the fleeing people herded by pursuing Greens into the arms of the Spoiled. The most fruitful area of recruitment lay in the farmland north-east of the Neck. Here most people lived on plantations rather than villages, meaning they were too small and sparsely occupied to be easily fortified. With their farm buildings and crops set alight the people had no option but to flee, once again continually harassed by Greens into following a pre-chosen route.

Once a decent number of captives had been harvested Sirus would take the Blue crystal and climb onto Katarias's back. Escorting a large contingent of unwilling captives across miles of country was a troublesome business. It was far more preferable to fly to the column's location and convert them in place. Once all the recruits were converted they would begin the orderly march south to join the main body of the army.

Sirus had persuaded Catheline to limit the drakes' habitual liking for hunting down the children and elderly left over after a large-scale capture, arguing that it was a waste of time and made the unconverted prisoners harder to handle. This had the result of littering the country-side with large numbers of orphans and old people. Usually the children would flee whilst the oldsters stood around in helpless shock. On a few rare occasions the children would linger in the vicinity, crying out to their converted parents as they marched away, deaf to their tearful pleading.

After three weeks Veilmist reported a total of thirty-eight thousand fresh recruits, more than sufficient to make good their losses and swell the ranks for the advance. *Will it be enough?* Catheline asked, her new-found caution at the forefront of the thought she pushed into Sirus's mind. *We can send the columns farther north if necessary.*

Marching north will increase the risk of encountering large-scale opposition, Sirus replied. *There are a number of port-towns on the Varestian Peninsular. They will undoubtedly have been evacuated by now but there are sure to be more recruits in the outlying villages. Veilmist estimates a further yield of ten to fifteen thousand. Thanks to the Imperial arsenal we captured we have weapons enough for all. If employed correctly, an army of this size and discipline can have no equal.*

She gave a faint pulse of amusement. *Is that eagerness, General? I thought Morradin was the bloodthirsty one.*

He didn't need to summon any fear to mask the intent behind his reply, it being entirely sincere. *I should hate to leave this task undone.*

As expected the first port they came to was empty. It was more of a large fishing village than a port, its streets silent and small harbour devoid of ships. The Varestians had seen fit to raise the harbour door and disable its mechanism, ensuring the docks were subsequently inundated by the tide and rendered useless. An extensive search revealed hardly a scrap of food or ammunition, the only living inhabitants a few cats, dogs and a far larger number of rats. Catheline, in an increasingly rare display of pique, ordered the place burned to the ground and the army marched on beneath skies darkened by a tall column of black smoke.

For once Veilmist's calculations proved to be substantially wide of the mark for the Varestians had been efficient, even ruthless in clearing the outlying villages of inhabitants. Scouting parties reported a number of corpses amongst the empty houses and farms, each one with their throat slit or a single bullet through the head.

"They know us now," Sirus concluded when Catheline expressed her puzzlement at the murders. "Every living adult who refuses to leave is a potential recruit, so they are determined not to leave any."

Another thousand additional recruits were rooted out of the small farms in the hill-country to the west, but Sirus judged most were too scattered to justify the time and effort needed to capture them all. The army moved on, the neat ranks of Spoiled following the coast south in a single huge column with Greens on the flanks and Reds above and scouting ahead. Their line of march took them past yet more empty villages and another two abandoned ports. The last one appeared to have been evacuated in haste, the Varestians leaving the harbour doors undamaged and a large amount of stores in the dock-side warehouses, including food and a quantity of small-arms ammunition. A Spoiled working party several hundred strong had begun to prepare the supplies for transport when the entire warehouse district erupted in a series of explosions.

"Sneaky bastards," Catheline commented as they stood together on the town walls watching the fires rage in the dockside. There wasn't much heat to her words, just sour observation. "It appears everything I heard about Varestians was true."

"Casualties could have been worse," Sirus said, turning away to scan the country to the south. "I'm more concerned by the lack of serious opposition. They must surely have organised a defence by now. But the Reds report nothing to the south for another hundred miles." He switched his gaze to the sea, eyes tracking along the empty horizon. "The lack of seaborne attacks is also odd. For such renowned seafarers the Varestians seemed strangely reluctant to risk their ships, especially given the absence of the Blues."

"Conserving their strength," Catheline concluded. "Intending to meet us in one great battle. How pleasingly dramatic."

"Morradin said it would be a bloody day when our forces met theirs."

Catheline moved closer, pressing a kiss to his scaled cheek, whispering, "The bloodier the better, dearest General. He hungers for it, you see. We now serve a vengeful god."

Three days' march brought them into sight of a stretch of black sand that extended from the shore-line to the fast-flowing river four miles to the west. Beyond the river the steep and equally black slopes of a mountain ensured there was no easy route around this barrier. Sirus was therefore unsurprised when the Reds flew over and discovered the enemy present in impressive strength on the southern fringe of the Sands.

"I once had a lover," Catheline said as she and Sirus strolled along the edge of the Sands, "an artist, who contended that all nature was beautiful. If he had seen this place I suspect he might have formed a different opinion."

Sirus crouched to scoop up a handful of black grains, finding it rich in the small gleaming stones that gave this place its name. Unlike Catheline he found the way the Sands contrasted so starkly with the landscape fascinating. "Mount Alkus," he said, nodding at the peak to the west. "An occasionally active volcano. Every hundred years or so it coughs up a good deal of lava and ash, the Jet Sands are the result." He rose, letting the sand fall from his hand as he surveyed the undulating ground ahead. The dunes were over ten feet tall in places, robbing an attacker of a forward view whilst providing a defender an easy target when they came to the top. Plus, the looseness of the footing ensured any infantry attack would be a highly sluggish affair.

"Whoever Miss Lethridge has commanding her forces clearly knows their business," Sirus said. "They couldn't have chosen better ground for a defensive engagement."

"Another trap then?" Catheline asked.

"Very much so." He shared the image of the enemy line the Reds had captured earlier. They had been forced to fly high due to the storm of fire from the repeating guns, one falling victim to the barrage before it could gain sufficient height. The image showed at most six battalions of infantry and several batteries of cannon at the eastern end of the Sands whilst more could be seen marching up from the south. The enemy line grew thicker the farther west it went, bristling with cannon and repeating guns.

"A decent-sized force," Catheline commented. "But they're not yet fully in position."

"It's a ruse," Sirus said, shaking his head. "They want us to attack close to the shore. As soon as we do I expect their ships will suddenly appear on the horizon whilst their airships assail us from above."

"Then avoid it. Attack elsewhere."

"On this ground, any point we attack will result in considerable losses."

"Really?" He felt a murmur of scorn from her, and detected a tinge of acid to her tone when she asked, "What would Morradin have done?"

"He was a commander who never shied from the butcher's bill, to be sure. And I suspect he would have been of the opinion that once you spring a trap, it can't be sprung again."

"You're suggesting we simply do what the enemy expects?" Catheline gave a derisive laugh. "Even one with my meagre military knowledge knows that to be a mistake."

"I do indeed suggest we do just that," Sirus replied, stepping forward to press his boot into the sand. It sank into the soft surface to a depth of three inches. *Bad ground for a human,* he concluded. *But not a drake.* "Then," he went on, turning to her with a smile, "I suggest we do something else entirely. I believe it's time our army had a cavalry arm."

He waited for dusk before launching the assault, reasoning that the enemy would surely have suspected something if he had attacked in full daylight. The lead battalions advanced across the dunes in a slow steady march behind a screen of skirmishers, kept in step by their mental connection, which allowed for two continuous unbroken lines of nearly a half mile in length. There were over forty thousand Spoiled in the first wave, with more lined up behind in a densely packed, well-ordered mass. As the advance progressed Sirus sent his cannon forward, teams of Spoiled man-handling the guns over the dunes to form a large single battery on the right flank. In accordance with their orders they began to fire on the enemy line immediately, concentrating their shells on the supposedly thinly held section of the opposing line close to the shore. They were firing at the limit of the guns' range and their accuracy was therefore poor, but Sirus hoped this would at least convince the enemy commander of his intent.

Above the dunes the Reds patrolled in a dense swarm, Sirus deliberately holding them back as insurance against the appearance of the airships. Although few in number, the fire-power of these novel contraptions had been amply demonstrated at the Grand Cut. The Greens, having the most crucial role to play, he kept well to rear, awaiting the critical moment.

As expected, a line of Varestian ships appeared on the horizon as the Spoiled advance reached the halfway point to their objective. The enemy fleet approached in two divisions, steaming towards the coast at high speed then performing a sharp turn either north or south to present their broadsides to the shore. Sirus was surprised to see a number of Corvantine Imperial frigates amongst them, displaying an impressive accuracy and rapidity of fire as they unleashed their guns at the advancing Spoiled. Added to this was the fire of the enemy cannon arrayed along the southern side of the Sands. Wisely ignoring Sirus's grand battery, they concentrated their fire on the infantry assault to devastating effect.

All along the ranks of Spoiled black sand blossomed in huge gouts as the shells struck home, Sirus feeling at least four of his soldiers die with every blast. But still the two lines advanced, shrinking in the process as the Spoiled reordered themselves to fill the gaps in their ranks. The enemy's repeating guns began firing shortly after. Via the eyes of a Red, Sirus saw the human infantry casting aside earth-covered tarpaulins to spring up from previously unseen trenches, quickly manoeuvring the multibarrelled weapons into position. Their fire was rapid and accurate. The mass of bullets and cannon shells cut through the first rank of Spoiled like a huge invisible scythe. In response to Sirus's mental command, the survivors, barely two thousand strong, commenced a charge towards the enemy line. They sprinted the remaining distance to their objective with all the speed their remade bodies would permit, falling by the dozen with every few yards covered. Only about a hundred reached the enemy trenches, all of whom were swiftly cut or shot down in the brief close-quarters fight that followed. Sirus ordered the second line to charge shortly after, with similar results, then noted with satisfaction that the light was fading fast.

He ordered another ten battalions forward, sending half of them around the battery in the centre of the dunes with orders to make for the extreme left of the enemy line. He hoped this would lead the enemy commander to assume he had learned his mistake and was attempting to probe for weaknesses elsewhere. As the second wave passed by the battery, suffering only marginally fewer casualties than the first from the enemy ships and cannon, he summoned the Greens forward. They had been kept a mile to the rear and well inland, beyond the sight of any reconnaissance. Sirus turned to watch them loping past his vantage point atop a hill a few hundred yards from the Sands. Every Green in the White's thrall had been enlisted in this attack and they streamed past in a huge pack, every one carrying a Spoiled on its back.

Once the Greens were on the Sands Sirus ordered the Spoiled to the left of the battery into a dense formation ten ranks deep and sent them charging full pelt towards the enemy trenches. Rifle fire and repeating guns tore the first four ranks to pieces in short order, the Spoiled behind leaping their comrades' bodies and keeping on, bayonet-tipped rifles gleaming in the two-moon night. The charge was doomed, of course, only the last rank of Spoiled reaching the trenches where they all fell in a brief but savage hand-to-hand struggle, a struggle that prevented the human defenders from noticing the huge pack of Spoiled-mounted Greens boiling across the dunes.

Some repeating guns managed to loose a hail of bullets into the on-rushing mass of drakes, cutting down dozens in a matter of seconds, but the momentum of the charge proved unstoppable. The drakes tore through the trenches in a welter of fire, tooth and claw, the Spoiled on their backs leaping away as soon as they were clear of the Sands. They quickly formed into companies and launched an immediate attack on human defenders to their left. They had been ordered to concentrate on silencing the repeating guns and moved from trench to trench in relays, putting rifle and bayonet to murderously efficient use.

Gauging the moment had come, Sirus set the remaining battalions in motion, over one hundred thousand Spoiled starting forward at the run. A few battalions were sent into the teeth of the ship guns and cannon directly to their front, Sirus being keen to ensure the enemy commander didn't have the chance to shift any forces. The bulk of the army veered to the west, keeping close to the river as they charged for the gap the Green cavalry had torn in the enemy line.

Wonderful. Catheline's exultation and triumph sang in his head along with a not-inconsiderable measure of lust. *How could I ever have doubted you?*

The images captured by the thousands of eyes in the army played through their conjoined minds with nightmarish clarity. *A Varestian continuing to swing his sabre despite the six bayonets that pinned him to the earth. A woman stumbling across the sand with her intestines trailing from a gaping stomach wound. A knot of defenders clustered around a repeating cannon, continuing to fire until the Greens closed in and bathed them in fire.*

It was hard to make sense of the situation amidst so much horror but

Sirus soon divined that the enemy had been engaged all along the line and the stocks of ammunition and reserves to their rear were also under attack.

Send the Reds, Catheline commanded, her thoughts riven with so much eagerness for the slaughter Sirus winced in pain. *And the reserves. Finish it!*

Not yet, he insisted. *Resistance is still fierce. The Reds must be preserved for the pursuit.*

He felt her gathering her will to override his objection, fed by the White's vast need for vengeance, but the argument was rendered irrelevant when a blinding white light blossomed in the sky.

It hung in the air trailing sparks, casting its glow across the dunes. *Flare,* Sirus realised, his Spoiled eyes piercing the haze of light to make out the shape of the parachute above the blazing pyrotechnic. Two more blazed into light a split-second later, bathing the entire battlefield in a glow bright enough to banish all shadows. Sirus shielded his eyes, squinting as he focused on the black space beyond the flares, and was soon rewarded with the sight of a large, curved shape descending from the gloom.

The enemy's airships had finally arrived.

CHAPTER 44

Lizanne

"Our lot are running," Morva shouted, hair whipping in the wind as she leaned out of the *Typhoon*'s side hatch, peering through her goggles at the battlefield below. "Greens are everywhere."

"Reds?" Lizanne shouted back.

"Not that I can see."

Lizanne moved forward, making her way to Tekela's side and telling the gunners manning the Growlers in the side hatches to get ready. "Give me one minute then take us lower," she said. "Below two thousand feet."

"That's well within the ceiling for a Red," Tekela pointed out.

"I know. But we need to make sure we drop in the right place."

Lizanne injected a burst of Blue and quickly tranced with the Blood-blessed in the *Tempest* and the newly constructed *Hurricane* and *Whirlwind*, ordering them to follow the *Typhoon*. Slipping out of the trance, she gripped a handhold as Tekela put the aerostat into a steep dive.

"Reds ahead!" she called from the pilot's seat, her voice soon drowned out by the roar of the Growlers. Lizanne moved to a window to watch the tracer bullets streaming into the gloom, the arcing streams soon bisected by the larger shells from the Thumpers carried by the *Hurricane* and the *Whirlwind*. These featured a new modification from Jermayah, a fuse that would cause them to explode after a distance of four hundred yards. Consequently, the sky surrounding the aerostats soon began to resemble a firework display. Lizanne saw Reds illuminated by the exploding shells, brief, frozen glimpses of the beasts banking and coughing flame, none of which came close to the aerostats. She had the satisfaction of counting four caught in the act of being blasted out of the sky before Tekela hauled back on the control lever and called out, "Nineteen hundred feet!"

"Slow and level!" Lizanne called back, moving to the apparatus newly fitted to the floor of the gondola. It was an uncomplicated contraption consisting of a telescope positioned vertically within a frame to which a small lever had been attached. The lever was connected to a taut steel cable that descended through the base of the gondola to the release mechanism below. Lizanne injected a one-second burst of Green and pressed her eye to the telescope, placing one hand on the lever. She tried to blot out the continuing roar of the guns, punctuated by a rich stream of profane fear and exhilaration from the gunners. The view through the telescope was chaotic at first, drifting smoke shrouding a landscape of numerous fires and the ant-like forms of running people. However, thanks to the Green she was able to ascertain that they were about to fly over the southern fringe of the Jet Sands.

Where are they? she thought as the landscape slid beneath, her concentration soon broken by a shout from Morva.

"The *Tempest* is on fire!"

Cursing, Lizanne removed her eye from the telescope, moving to the hatch where Morva crouched with her mini-Growler in hand. She fired just as Lizanne came to her side, sending a stream of bullets into the belly of a Red as it swooped by, flames jetting from its mouth. It let out a screech and tumbled in the air, plummeting towards the earth in a tangle of wings and tail.

Lizanne tore her gaze away and concentrated on the *Tempest*, seeing the fire licking at the rear of her envelope. The aerostat was still keeping pace with them but her course was becoming more wayward, the craft heaving up and down as the fire spread. Lizanne switched her gaze on the large, barrel-shaped object hanging beneath the craft's gondola. *Not yet,* she implored. *Just a little longer.*

Her eyes jerked upwards at a burst of fire from the gunner in the cupola atop the *Tempest*'s envelope. The gunner had her mini-Growler raised high and unleashed a stream of bullets at a large Red streaking down towards the aerostat in a vertical dive. The beast's head was shredded by the concentrated fire but its dive continued, the corpse slamming into the aerostat and causing it to lose height. Lizanne managed to catch sight of the barrel-shaped object detaching from the gondola before a dozen Reds swooped down to bathe the *Tempest* in fire. Her envelope exploded, leaving only a cloud of wreckage trailing flame as it streamed towards the ground.

"Hold on!" Lizanne ordered, moving back from the hatch and taking a firm hold on the central beam.

The explosion was everything Tinkerer promised and more. The gondola's windows glowed orange as a massive gust of superheated air pushed the *Typhoon* up, tilting her at an acute angle as Tekela fought to keep control. The aerostat veered to the west, Tekela pushing the engines to their highest speed to take her clear of the turbulent air. When they levelled out Lizanne went to the rear window, finding that the *Hurricane* and the *Whirlwind* were now several hundred yards away, meaning the *Typhoon* would have to rely on her own guns for protection.

"Turn us around," she ordered Tekela, moving to return her eye to the telescope. She found that the *Typhoon* had been pushed clear of the Jet Sands and was now over the river. The ground pivoted as Tekela killed power to the starboard engine before reversing its propeller, turning them around in a swift pirouette. An unforeseen advantage of the *Tempest*'s demise and premature release of its device was that the skies around *Typhoon* were now clear of Reds. Consequently, they flew unmolested for several minutes as Lizanne watched the river pass by below and the ground transform into a frozen seascape of black dunes. She blinked in surprise as a dense formation of infantry trooped by directly below, thousands of Spoiled moving in a rapid march no doubt intending to turn the night's defeat into a disastrous rout.

"Stop!" she shouted, keeping her eye pressed to the telescope. She placed her hand on the release lever, waiting until the vanguard of the White's army had passed beneath the *Typhoon*. *Not yet . . . not yet.* She forced herself to count to ten then pressed the lever.

The *Typhoon* instantly began to rise as the huge weight of the device fell away, ascending at least three hundred feet in the time it took for the barrel-shaped silhouette to shrink into a speck, whereupon the view through the telescope instantly turned white. Lizanne let out a pained gasp at the brightness of it, snapping her head away, eye streaming. The shock wave hit them a heart-beat later, far more powerful than the first. Lizanne found herself careening around the gondola as the aerostat bucked and heaved in the artificial storm. When it finally settled Lizanne pressed her undazzled eye to the telescope, finding much of the western edge of the Jet

Sands had been transformed into something that resembled a huge scratched mirror.

"Reds!" one of the gunners shouted, his Growler blasting out a hail of bullets a second later.

"Due south," Lizanne told Tekela. She injected a burst of Red and moved to the blood-burner's ignition tube, hitting the switch to flood the combustion chamber with product. All the *Typhoon*'s guns were firing by the time she lit the engine, the acceleration sending her onto her back as the aerostat sped away from the pursuing Reds.

They stayed aloft for as long as their ammunition lasted, re-forming with the *Hurricane* and the *Whirlwind* to launch repeated attacks on the pursuing Reds as the Varestian army retreated along the coast. The two massive detonations on the Jet Sands appeared to have halted the White's ground forces, at least for now, but the Reds continued to harass the defenders as they fled south. Lizanne tranced with the Blood-blessed in the other aerostats to co-ordinate their efforts, attacking the mass of drakes in relays. The *Typhoon* would streak through the whirling pack on thermoplasmic power, all guns blazing, moving too fast for the drakes to catch. As the Reds recovered, the *Hurricane* and the *Whirlwind* would light their blood-burners and fly through the flock in opposite directions. This succeeded in disrupting the drakes' pursuit long enough for Arberus to establish a rear-guard position atop some high ground ten miles to the south.

The Reds' assaults on the rear guard were beaten back by massed fire from all the Growlers and Thumpers remaining in the army. With the advent of daylight the Reds no longer enjoyed the protection of darkness and, with no support on the ground, were much more vulnerable to the repeating guns. Arberus later reported that over a hundred had been hacked out of the sky by the time they abandoned their attacks. The general had been quick to get his remaining forces moving south, sadly without many of their Thumpers, which had to be destroyed in place for want of transport.

As the army retreated the Varestian fleet kept pace with them, staying close to the shore in order to bring a mass of gunnery down on any pursuing forces should it be needed. However, Lizanne's subsequent reconnaissance flights revealed that the White's army had encamped a few miles south of the Sands. Their commander had evidently taken full notice of the events of the previous night, setting out the camp in a series of small widely spaced enclosures beneath skies constantly patrolled by Reds. Even so, Lizanne felt that if she had another five such devices they could have wiped out the Spoiled for good. Sadly they didn't. Word from the Mount related that a lack of crucial chemical agents meant they could only produce one more device, and that would take at least another week. Lizanne sent instructions for them to concentrate all efforts on finishing the device whilst any spare labour would be required to work multiple shifts to make good the losses in Thumpers.

It took five days for the army to make a full withdrawal to Gadara's Redoubt. Much of their food had been left behind at the Sands meaning they had to be constantly resupplied by the fleet whilst the aerostats made repeated flights to evacuate the worst of the wounded. Arberus maintained a harsh pace throughout the retreat, something that did little to endear him to the troops, whose morale had already suffered in the aftermath of defeat. Desertion reached alarming proportions, some ten thousand troops disappearing over the course of two days. However, many soon returned after coming to the realisation that, in a land denuded of most of its population where the few crops had been destroyed, there was nowhere to go. Consequently, it was a bedraggled and none-too-happy army that limped into camp below the Redoubt. Some units stayed firm, particularly the companies formed of pirates and the volunteers who had followed Varkash to defend their homeland. Others were far less resolute and many soon began agitating for immediate evacuation from the peninsular.

"Pick out the biggest loudmouths and put them in front of a firing squad," Varkash suggested at the council of war Lizanne convened at the Redoubt. "Or hang them if you'd rather save the ammunition."

"That will set the whole army to riot," Arberus said. "A few days of rest and decent food will do much to restore their discipline."

"If the Spoiled will give us that long," Alzar said. "Besides which, cowards they may be but it doesn't make them wrong. If we couldn't stand against the monsters at the Sands, how can we stand against them here?"

Arberus began to reply but Lizanne caught his eye and shook her head. "We can't," she told them. "Not indefinitely. But General Arberus assures me that we can hold out for several days, perhaps longer. And it is important that we do so."

"Why?" Alzar asked. "We can transport the army to Iskamir, gather more strength."

"Leaving the White to advance into the heart of the peninsular," Lizanne said. "Where there are far more people than we could ever hope to evacuate. Once there the White can gather an army so great there will be no force in this world that can stop it. We have to hold here, for as long as we can." She paused, unsure of how to explain her reasoning. She was asking a great deal of these people, many would die if they continued to follow her lead. But many more might live. "A man is coming here," she said. "A Blood-blessed, bearing a new weapon found in the Arradsian Interior. Something that can kill the White."

"What kind of weapon?" Alzar demanded. "And why haven't we heard of this before?"

"Because the White knows the secrets of every human it makes into a monster," Lizanne replied. "Which is why I will not tell you the nature of this weapon. Suffice to say that if we can keep the White's attention on us for the next month, we have a chance to end this."

"We wounded them badly at the Sands," Arberus added. "They'll be more wary of us now, more cautious, and a cautious enemy is a slow enemy."

Alzar's doubts were plain but he gave a slow nod. "Very well. I'll take a tour of the camp, speak to these malcontents. See if I can't harden a few hearts."

"My lot will happily form the firing squad if you can't," Varkash offered.

"Good to see time has done a lot to mellow your soul," Alzar observed dryly.

Lizanne expected Varkash to bridle at this but he just laughed. "What use is a mellow soul in an age such as this?"

CHAPTER 45

Sirus

The glass crunched under his boots as he strode to the centre of the near-perfect circle blasted into the Jet Sands. *Hotter than a furnace,* he concluded, crouching to retrieve a shard of the glass produced by the heat of the explosion. He found the way it caught the light oddly beautiful, resembling obsidian in its lack of transparency. Casting his gaze around, he could find no corpses within this circle, despite Veilmist's estimate that over three thousand Spoiled had died at this very spot. The blast and the heat had been so powerful they had simply been vaporised. The first explosion hadn't been so well placed, claiming only about two thousand Spoiled, but together they had sown enough disruption in the advance to make his victory a flawed one.

Morradin would have been spitting bile, he thought with a grim smile, tossing the shard of glass away and rising as Catheline spoke in his head.

He's ready, she told him. *Best if you hurry. I've no idea how long he'll last.*

The captive was the only survivor of the airship the Reds had brought down, plucked from the Sands with near-fatal burns, multiple broken bones and crushed organs. Reasoning that a small experiment would cost nothing, Sirus had him taken to the Blue crystal. After the conversion many of his injuries remained beyond repair, but his brain was still intact.

Where are the airships made? Sirus enquired, staring down at the lopsided face of the newly fashioned Spoiled. The fall had robbed him of a cheek-bone and one of his eyes in addition to shattering his jaw, but Sirus didn't need to hear him talk.

Aerostats, the Spoiled corrected, his thoughts possessed of a surprising coherence. A brief rummage through the man's memories revealed him to be a former locomotive-driver with a level of technical understanding Sirus would be sorry to lose. *They are manufactured at a place called the Mount Works,* the Spoiled went on. *Along with many other weapons.*

Sirus felt a flare of excitement from Catheline, one he couldn't help but share. He summoned a mental map of the Varestian Peninsular and pushed it into the Spoiled's mind along with a question. *Where is it?*

"You shouldn't be risking yourself like this," Catheline had said as he climbed onto Katarias's back. She reached out to him as he settled between the spines, one hand clutching her shawl about her shoulders whilst she grasped his forearm. He supposed that to an ignorant observer they might have made a romantic tableau, the hero being sent off to war by his beautiful, golden-haired paramour. But he wasn't a hero, he was a monster and Catheline, in any way that mattered, was far from beautiful.

"The mission is crucial," he replied. "The outcome must be certain. I need to lead in person."

She didn't object, the White's approval overriding any objections she might harbour though Sirus was struck by the anguish evident in her face. "If you don't come back . . ." she began, then faltered before continuing. "It will be . . . difficult."

"Veilmist will make an adequate replacement," he said.

She looked up, meeting his gaze, red-black eyes wide and expression devoid of the arch cynicism he had come to expect. "That's not what I meant."

Katarias banked steeply to avoid a thick patch of cloud, bringing Sirus back to the present with a jolt. Looking down, he could see the two moons reflected on a calm sea, meaning they had crossed the coast-line north of Blaska Sound. He had opted to cover much of the distance in an overland flight, avoiding the many eyes of the Varestian fleet whilst also affording the Reds the opportunity to rest along the way. Even a drake couldn't stay aloft indefinitely. After flying from midnight to noon, Sirus had the formation set down where the mountains rose some fifty miles north-west of their objective. There were thirty Reds in all, each carrying a veteran Spoiled. Hardly a mighty force but it was important their approach not be noticed. Sirus also calculated that the intelligence provided by the aerostat pilot before his inevitable death would more than compensate for a lack of numbers.

He waited for nightfall before setting off again, skirting the northern flank of the mountains and making for the coast whereupon the Reds made a sharp turn into the Sound. They flew low over the placid waters, wary of being silhouetted against the two moons. The Mount Works soon came into view, Sirus quickly confirming that the description of the defences matched the mental image supplied by the pilot. Lizanne Lethridge clearly hadn't taken the settlement's security for granted. There were a dozen gun emplacements surrounding the town and the manufactory, with another six within, all manned day and night by the town militia. However, it was the manufactory that captured most of his interest, a large building with light streaming from its windows and open main doors, illuminating the copious steam and smoke rising from its vents.

That must burn tonight, he told Forest Spear and the other Spoiled. *Everything else is secondary.*

The Spoiled slipped from the backs of the Reds as they neared the wharf, Sirus tumbling from Katarias's back into the chill embrace of the Sound. It was a three-hundred-yard swim to the docks, an easy feat for a Spoiled. The hour corresponded with the turn of the two-moon tide so the current was friendly, allowing a swift approach. He kept beneath the surface for most of the journey, pausing occasionally to rise and poke his nose out of the water and draw in some air before slipping below, leaving barely a ripple on the surface. A number of ships were moored at the wharf, freighters waiting to take the munitions manufactured here to the army in the north. Sirus and the other Spoiled dived down and swam beneath the hulls, rising on the other side to conceal themselves in the matrix of girders beneath the wharf. With the tide high it was a short climb, Sirus dividing the Spoiled into two groups and leading one to the eastern side of the docks whilst the other went west.

Sirus scaled the girders to the edge of the platform, slowly hauling himself up to peer at what lay above and finding himself instantly greeted by a pair of guards. They were frozen in the act of sharing a match, cigarillos dangling from their mouths as they gaped at him. Sirus swung his body and vaulted over the edge, knife coming free of the sheath on his belt as he rolled towards the guards. One managed a half-shout before the blade slashed across his throat whilst the other continued to gape in shock even as Sirus stabbed him under the chin, driving the knife up into his brain.

He moved on without pause, the Spoiled following close behind. There were many crates stacked up around the docks, providing valuable cover as they slipped from one shadow to another. Upon clearing the docks pairs of Spoiled peeled off, moving swiftly to the gun-positions they had been ordered to silence. Sirus and Forest Spear, in company with four others, made for the manufactory.

As expected, there were no people in the streets, the converted pilot having informed them of the strict curfew observed at the Mount. Those not working a shift were to be afforded an uninterrupted sleep, though Sirus wondered how that was possible with the noise produced by the manufactory. A continual clatter of metal on metal rose in volume as they approached, still keeping to the shadows and avoiding the notice of the cordon of guards surrounding the works.

They paused as Sirus checked the progress of the Spoiled he had sent against the gun emplacements. Four positions had already been silenced, the gunners cut down with knife and war-club before they could raise the alarm. Another seven were wiped out in the space of a few minutes but then one of the gunners, a young woman with impressive reflexes, managed to draw her revolver in time to shoot down the two attacking Spoiled. Within seconds the piercing shriek of a siren cut through the noise of the manufactory and lights began to flare in the windows of the houses.

Sirus sent a mental command to Katarias, calling the Reds down from their circling vigil several hundred feet above. He had known the chances of achieving complete surprise were slim, but the damage already done to the Mount's defences ensured at least half the Reds would make it through the barrage.

Tracer bullets were already arcing into the air when he led the Spoiled from cover, drawing his revolver and making straight for the cordon in front of the manufactory's huge open doors. The Spoiled spread out on either side as he ran, firing their revolvers on the run and cutting down ten guards. Their comrades responded swiftly with rifle and carbines, Sirus and the other Spoiled throwing themselves flat as the bullets snapped the air around them. He took the time to reload his revolver, glancing up at the familiar hiss and roar of drake fire.

Katarias swooped down out of the night sky to blast the remaining cordon of guards with his flames. He landed directly in front of the manufactory doors, two more drakes coming to earth on either side. As one they turned and charged into the manufactory, the noise of labour soon becoming drowned by the cacophony of many people screaming in terror.

Sirus got to his feet and led the Spoiled on, leaping to the side to avoid the falling corpse of a Red that landed in his path, its hide pierced all over by cannon fire. Inside the manufactory everything was chaos, charred or mutilated corpses littered the rows of work-benches and burning people ran in all directions. Katarias and his two fellow drakes were halfway along the cavernous space, belching repeated gouts of flame at the mass of people fleeing to the rear of the building. Those running for the side exits were cut down by tail strikes or bullets from the Spoiled as Sirus led them forward in a skirmish-line.

He levelled his revolver at a fleeing man, putting a bullet through his head from thirty paces, then instinctively jerked away as the chest of the Spoiled to his right exploded. Sirus took cover beneath a work-bench, seeing another Spoiled fall, the impact of the shot that killed him powerful enough to remove his head from his shoulders. The other Spoiled raised their pistols to a higher angle and returned fire, Sirus slipping from cover to track their aim to a walkway above. A man was crouched behind some steel plating, sparks flying as the Spoiled's bullets struck home. Sirus could make out the shiny crown of the man's bald head and the barrel of the carbine he held, jerking as he reloaded. Raising his revolver, Sirus centred the sights on the man's head, then stopped as a small round object was tossed over the steel plating, trailing smoke as it arced down to land a few feet away.

Sirus leapt with all the strength his remade limbs allowed; even so, the grenade came close to killing him. Shrapnel buzzed the air as the blast sent him careening into a girder, Sirus feeling the snap of breaking ribs as his chest connected with the iron pillar. He lay stunned at the foot of the girder, pain flaring in his chest with every breath. The snick of a carbine lever drew his gaze upwards, finding the man with the carbine staring down at him from the walkway. He was a stocky fellow in soot-covered overalls, and Sirus felt a faint pulse of amusement as he scanned the man's broad features, recognising him as one of the duo that had flown away from Feros with Tekela.

"Hello," he said, though the words were probably meaningless, garbled by the blood leaking from his mouth. "A friend of Tekela's, are you not?"

Whether the man heard or even understood him, Sirus couldn't know. In either case being greeted by a Spoiled didn't seem to stir any merciful impulse. The man swiftly brought the carbine to his shoulder, eyes dark and purposeful behind the sights as he trained them on Sirus.

Forest Spear's knife came spinning out of the grenade smoke, sinking into the bald man's neck up to the hilt. The carbine swung wide as his finger gave a final convulsive twitch on the trigger, the bullet missing Sirus by a few inches, though the explosion of sparks as it impacted the girder sent flakes of molten steel into his face.

He felt Forest Spear pulling him upright and wiped the blood from his eyes, glancing around to see the other Spoiled lying dead. The interior of the manufactory was now so filled with smoke and heat it was hard even for his unnatural gaze to discern the scale of the destruction. However, a bright blaze was burning at the rear of the building, the roar of the flames punctuated by exploding munitions. Sirus was able to make out the slumped forms of two drakes, meaning they had encountered some fierce resistance during their rampage. A sudden drop in temperature made the view clearer, Sirus catching sight of a Red tearing a large rent in the manufactory's roof. He was able to recognise Katarias as the huge drake clawed his way out.

Another round of explosions sounded deep in the manufactory, shaking the ground and convincing Sirus they had done all the damage they could. He and Forest Spear rushed outside, finding the sky above the town criss-crossed by arcing lines of tracer from the surviving gun emplacements. Their fire was augmented by numerous repeating guns on the ships moored at the wharf. Sirus saw a Red fold up in mid air, caught by two converging bursts of cannon fire that sent it plummeting into the streets. Another Red swooped down, spewing flame at a squad of militia, then fell dead as their carbines sent a fusillade of exploding bullets into its chest.

A mental survey revealed to Sirus that he and Forest Spear were the only Spoiled to survive the attack, a distinction that wouldn't last long judging by the large number of militia streaming towards them from the town.

There was a brief rumbling cry from above followed by a gust of wind as Katarias came to earth near by. Sirus and Forest Spear scrambled onto his back, ducking as bullets zipped around them and the beast sprinted forward before launching himself skyward. Katarias twisted and turned as cannon shells and bullets chased them across the sky, swooping low and banking to soar to the north end of the town where the rising smoke and flame from the manufactory masked their escape.

The drake let out a loud roar as they flew away, wings sweeping as he bore them towards the mountains. Whether it was an expression of triumph or grief for his lost kin, Sirus couldn't tell.

CHAPTER 46

Lizanne

She jumped from the *Typhoon*'s gondola before it came to earth, landing hard and sprinting towards the smoking ruin of the manufactory. Some of the townsfolk called out to her but she tore past them, only vaguely registering the corpses, drake and human, that marked her path. Several long rows of covered bodies had been placed on the flat ground before the manufactory and teams of workers were busy carrying more from the blackened structure. Lizanne's gaze swung wildly from face to face, finally alighting on one she knew.

"My father?" she said, rushing to grab Madame Hakugen's arm. The woman stared at her for a moment, eyes uncomprehending in her soot-stained face, then gave a helpless shake of her head.

"I don't know," she said in a thin whisper. "I haven't seen him."

Lizanne left her, running to the ruin to be greeted by the dreadful carnage that lay within. Her strength seeped away and she slowed to a stumble, moving in a daze as she took in one horror after another. A group of workers, melted together by drake fire into an obscene parody of a sculpture, clawed, stump-fingered hands reaching up to her, teeth gleaming in the charred remnants of their faces. A young assembly worker, remarkably untouched by the flames and lacking any obvious injury, lying dead beneath her work-bench, face frozen in a wide-eyed mask of terror. She found the worst of it at the rear of the building. Hundreds had died here, crammed together amongst the heavy machinery as they tried to flee only to be roasted alive. The stench of death seemed to claw its way into her being, choking nose and throat before sinking an acidic claw into her guts.

The world went away for a time, everything becoming hazy and distant, when she came back to herself she was retching air past a dry throat, staring at a pool of her own vomit. A sound came to her then, soft but easily heard in the eerie quiet. Someone was sobbing. Lizanne got unsteadily to her feet and followed the sound to the walkway above the manufactory floor, climbing up to find Tekela weeping over the body of Jermayah Tollermine.

"It was him," she said, raising a tear-streaked face to stare at Lizanne. "A Spoiled in a general's uniform, they said. Sirus did this. He did this because I failed to kill him."

Lizanne found she had no words for her, finding that all sensation seemed to have fled her body. She could only stand and stare in dumb fascination at the knife handle jutting from Jermayah's neck. It was a curious design, one she hadn't seen before. An intricately carved piece of bone, its elegant curve oddly pleasing to the eye.

"Lizanne."

Professor Graysen Lethridge stepped cautiously onto the walkway, tattered lab coat besmirched with soot and blood, though not his own as far as she could tell. He looked at Jermayah's body, face sagging in grim resignation. Lizanne's first thought was that he must be a product of her imagination, something conjured to prevent her slipping into madness. But then her father's arms enfolded her and the freezing numbness transformed into an instant blaze of relief that had her convulsing in hard, wracking sobs as she clung to him.

"Over eight hundred killed," Madame Hakugen reported. "Three times that number wounded. About sixty percent of the machinery is damaged beyond repair. Fully half the stocks of recently completed munitions destroyed."

"The new explosives?" Lizanne asked, turning to her father.

"I'm sorry," he said, shaking his head. "We just completed the casing, it's mostly still intact, even salvageable. But the chemicals needed to achieve the correct explosive mix were consumed in the fire."

"And," Tinkerer added, "the precision instruments required to manufacture the detonator."

Lizanne had found him wandering the ashen remains of what had been his workshop, expressionlessly rummaging through the detritus as he gathered various components and scraps of charred paper. Apart from a faint grimace when Lizanne enquired as to his well-being, he hadn't betrayed any particular reaction to the disaster, although she noticed he was blinking more than usual. Looking at him, she found she had to suppress a guilt-riven and unpleasant inner question: *Why couldn't it have been him instead of Jermayah?*

She went to the window of Madame Hakugen's office, looking out at the ships in the Sound. Five freighters had arrived that morning to collect the latest shipment of weapons and were now destined to leave half-empty. "Madame," she said, "I require an honest and unvarnished opinion; how long will it take before this facility can resume production?"

"There are many variables involved . . ." Madame began then fell silent as Lizanne glanced over her shoulder, gaze steady and demanding. "At this juncture," Madame continued in a subdued tone, "too long to make any difference to the outcome of this war."

"Thank you." Lizanne returned her gaze to the window and was surprised to find children at play in the park, running and laughing, seemingly oblivious to the pall of smoke that still hung in the air over the Mount. *Just another horror witnessed in their short lives,* she thought. *One of many. Perhaps all this has rendered them immune to fear.* It occurred to her that, win or lose, the children who would grow up in the aftermath of this war were already spoiled, in mind if not body. *What kind of world will they build? But then, they could hardly do worse than we have.*

"Please call a general meeting of the work-force," she said, turning to face them. "The Mount Works Militia will sail to Gadara's Redoubt together with any adult who wishes to volunteer for military service. Lone parents with children are excluded."

"And those left behind?" Madame asked.

"Sufficient shipping will remain to carry them away should the need arise, though in the event of our defeat, I can't imagine a safe place where they might go."

"You intend to just abandon this place?" her father asked. "A place so many have laboured to exhaustion to build?"

"There is no purpose to it now. No further contribution it can make."

"There are the new rockets," Tinkerer said.

Lizanne frowned at him in bemusement. "What new rockets?"

They were lined up in a narrow brick shelter which had been constructed well away from the other buildings. Exactly three hundred in all, looking to Lizanne's eyes like a miniature version of the rockets that had served them so well at the Grand Cut. Each was about a yard long and ten inches in diameter. They had a smooth bullet-shaped steel warhead and a pair of aerofoils positioned halfway along their length with another larger pair at the base.

"It occurred to me that one of the Red drakes' advantages is their ability to attack in a massed formation," Tinkerer explained. "Rather like a swarm of bees overwhelming a larger threat. It seemed reasonable to combat one swarm with another."

"'Swarmers,'" Tekela said, sinking to her haunches and running a hand along the smooth casing of the nearest rocket. "That's what we'll call them." Lizanne detected an unfamiliar tone to Tekela's voice. It had a low, hungry note to it Lizanne didn't like. Nor did she like the sight of the bone-handle knife Tekela now wore strapped to her calf.

"Appropriate," Tinkerer said with a small shrug. "Each rocket contains a mechanism that compels it to follow a random course towards its target. When fired in a group they can be set to explode at slightly different intervals."

"So," Tekela said, smiling a little, "they might dodge one but the next one gets them."

"Quite so," Tinkerer confirmed. "The materials and components required to construct another five hundred have been set aside. It's just a matter of assembly."

"How long?" Lizanne asked.

"Two days with sufficient hands."

"I'll see to it. Have them loaded when ready. These"—she gestured at the completed Swarmers—"will be fitted to the aerostats and made ready to fire immediately."

Viewed from the air the plain below Gadara's Redoubt resembled one-half of a huge dartboard. Three continuous lines of trenches curved around the northern flank of the ridge from one end of the isthmus to the other. Dust rose in thick clouds from the people at labour on the plain, Lizanne seeing the rise and fall of many shovels as she landed the *Firefly* within the arc of the third trench line, the other larger aerostats coming to earth a short distance away.

"It worked at Carvenport," Arberus explained after Lizanne had climbed down from the gondola.

"Against the Corvantines," she said. "Not the drakes and the Spoiled."

"It might have if we'd had the numbers. This is an excellent defensive position. We can place the bulk of our muzzle-loading cannon along the walls of the Redoubt itself. From there they can reach any part of the battlefield. Plus, the whole trench network is within range of the fleet's guns. I wouldn't even consider an attack here given the likely butcher's bill."

"Morradin would," Lizanne pointed out. "And I doubt the White cares about casualties amongst its troops."

Arberus gave a short nod of agreement. "True, but in any case I thought our object was to hold them, not defeat them."

"At this juncture, I'd be happy with any outcome that didn't involve our utter destruction." She went on to relate the full scale of the calamity at the Mount, noting how he managed to keep any reaction from his features as he took in the news. It wouldn't do for an onlooking soldier to see their general succumb to despair.

"No more munitions," he said, speaking softly and pasting a bland smile on his face.

"The final consignment is on its way. Another thirty Thumpers and fifty Growlers, plus a hundred of the new carbines. The Mount Works Militia and a volunteer contingent will accompany the consignment, five thousand strong."

"All very welcome. But it's not enough."

"I know."

She noticed Tekela standing a short way off, eyes fixed on the plain beyond the trenches. They had given Jermayah as much of a funeral as they could before leaving the Mount. The headland east of the town had become an impromptu graveyard, marked with numerous freshly excavated graves. Tinkerer and Professor Lethridge came to help dig Jermayah's resting-place. Together they laid his canvas-shrouded body in the earth and covered him over. A few of the artificers who had worked under Jermayah's direction came to offer their respects but the crowd was not large, there being so many funerals that day. Tinkerer marked the grave with a wooden post onto which the words "Jermayah Tollermine—Technologist" had been etched in precise letters. Professor Lethridge then gave a halting, awkward eulogy, listing his colleague's many technical achievements and thanking him for his many hours of tireless labour in service to humankind. Throughout it all Tekela had said nothing, staring fixedly at the mound of earth, eyes red in the pale mask of her face. She pulled her hand away when Lizanne tried to take it and had maintained much the same demeanour since.

"It was a long flight," Lizanne said, moving to her side. "You should get some rest."

Tekela ignored her, turning to Arberus. "How long until they get here?"

He paused a moment before replying, frowning as if not quite recognising the face of a girl he had known since infancy. "Two days, at most," he replied. "The Spoiled march with an annoying swiftness."

"We should attack now," Tekela said, her gaze switching to Lizanne. "With the aerostats. We can test out the Swarmers. Might slow them down a bit."

"We need to conserve our resources," Arberus said.

"Sirus is their leader, isn't he?" Tekela persisted. "If we can find him . . ."

"Your uncle's right," Lizanne said, her tone leaving no room for argument. "The Swarmers will have more effect if they come as a surprise."

There was a faint echo of the old pout in Tekela's expression then, but what had once been the frustration of a spoilt child was now something far more disconcerting. "He needs to die," she whispered, voice rich in both sincerity and certainty. "And I need to kill him." She turned and stalked away, muttering, "And *he's* not my fucking uncle," at Arberus.

"She feels guilty," Lizanne explained. "About Jermayah."

"There's plenty of guilt to go around," he said. "If the history of this crisis is ever written I suspect it might well be called 'The Guilty Age.' The corporations, the Empire . . . the revolution. No one in this world has clean hands any more. Perhaps that's why it falls to us to save it."

True to Arberus's prediction the White's army appeared on the northern horizon by the evening of the following day. At first it was just a rising cloud of dust, the dark specks of patrolling Reds wheeling above, but the neat ranks of advancing Spoiled soon resolved into focus through the lens of Lizanne's spy-glass. The army proceeded along a southerly route parallel to the trench works, stringing out in a line a mile long before coming to an abrupt simultaneous halt and turning to face the Redoubt.

"A good two hundred yards out of range," Arberus muttered in frustration, tracking his binoculars along the enemy line.

They stood atop the tower, Lizanne's Spider loaded with one of her few remaining vials of Blue. Whereas they had decent but not copious stocks of the other colours, especially Red thanks to the assault on the Mount, Blue was a fast-diminishing resource. Those Blood-blessed not allocated to one of the aerostats were seeded throughout the trench works and the fleet. They had been instructed to imbibe Blue the moment the enemy began to advance, enabling Lizanne to relay the orders which would co-ordinate the defence.

The battle plan consisted of a staged withdrawal, timed to commence when Arberus had judged each successive line of trenches to have inflicted the maximum casualties on the enemy. Upon receipt of the signal the defenders would withdraw to the next line under cover of the combined weight of gunnery from the cannon on the Redoubt and the ships waiting a few hundred yards off shore. He estimated they could hold out for three days, perhaps four with a modicum of luck. Lizanne's last trance with Clay indicated he needed at least another four days to reach them, so it appeared they would have to make their own luck.

"They'll wait for darkness," Arberus concluded as the Spoiled army continued to stand immobile. "Take advantage of their freakish night-vision. Best spread the word for our lot to get what rest they can."

Lizanne nodded and began to press the fourth button on her Spider, then stopped as Arberus raised a hand. "Wait. They're moving."

"An attack?" she asked, returning her eye to her own glass and blinking in surprise at what she saw. Instead of commencing a march towards the trenches the Spoiled were clustering into three large divisions, each one resembling a disturbingly well-co-ordinated group of ants in the way they reordered themselves into narrow columns. Lizanne suspected they intended to assault the defences in three places at once, hoping the narrowness of their formation would negate the effects of the fire-power they faced. But then she saw the first rank of Spoiled sink to their knees and begin to dig. Most had shovels, but others clawed at the ground with their inhuman hands, tearing up clods of earth and grass with a fierce, near-frantic energy.

"What are they doing?" she wondered.

"Sapping," Arberus replied, a faint note of admiration in his otherwise grim tone. "Sirus always did know his history."

Apparently it was a tactic from the early days of the gunpowder age, favoured by armies besieging fortifications in an effort to spare their soldiers the fire of defending cannon. It had fallen out of favour with the advent of faster-firing modern artillery and repeating small-arms, but Sirus had evidently found a use for it now. The three trenches progressed across the plain with remarkable swiftness. The Spoiled worked in a ceaseless relay, clawing or digging at the earth until exhaustion set in, whereupon they staggered to the rear and were immediately replaced by fresh labour. Consequently, the trenches were each close to fifty yards in length before nightfall and the Spoiled didn't show any signs of resting for the night.

"They'll be in range of our cannon come morning," Lizanne pointed out. "A sustained barrage should impede their progress."

"It should," Arberus admitted. "But every shell we fire can no longer be replaced. And something tells me Sirus is too clever to simply dig his way into our sights."

He was proven correct come first light, the rising sun revealing that the forward progress of the enemy trenches had halted. Instead they were now digging laterally, new trenches branching out from the terminus of the three already dug. By late afternoon the White's army had a trench network of its own, whereupon all activity apparently ceased.

"I'd wager a sack of gold that Morradin no longer has a say over this campaign," Arberus noted with grudging respect. "Sirus has spared his troops a good two hundred yards of open ground. Even at extreme range our cannon would have taken a fearful toll when they advanced. Plus we would have had ample warning of the moment they decided to attack."

Arberus ordered a few of the more powerful cannon in the Redoubt to try their luck at the enemy trenches, scoring a few hits. However, most of the shells went wide and the damage inflicted was minimal. There was no answering fire from the Spoiled; in fact most sat in their trenches in placid quietude. Tekela made several offers to attack in the *Typhoon*, arguing that it would be a simple matter to rake the trenches from end to end with Growler fire. Lizanne forbade it, unwilling to risk an aerostat in the massed Red assault that would inevitably follow.

Arberus had the army stand on full alert throughout the night. Rocket flares supplied by the fleet were prepared all along the Redoubt, ready to bathe the battlefield in artificial light when the attack came, except it didn't.

"What are they waiting for?" Arberus wondered aloud come the morning as he and Lizanne looked out at the Spoiled still sitting quietly in the trenches.

"As long as they keep waiting," Lizanne said, "I shall consider myself satisfied."

"We can't become complacent. There must be a strategy at work here. Something we're missing. Just like the Jet Sands."

Noting the tension in his unshaven jaws, Lizanne saw for the first time how deep the sting of defeat had wounded him. *Pride,* she thought, reaching out to grasp his forearm, *the disease of generals and revolutionaries alike.* "Get some rest," she told him. "I'll be sure to wake you should anything happen."

*G*ot hit by a storm last night, Clay told her. *Lost sight of the* Endeavour *till morning. The captain had to take the blood-burner off-line. He reckons it'll be another two days sailing.*

Lizanne replied with a pulse of acknowledgment, momentarily distracted by the clarity of the shared trance. Before his new-found ability Clay's mindscape had been somewhat basic in construction, Nelphia's surface a uniform grey and the black sky above lacking a rendition of the planet they called home. Now it hung above them in majestic, blue-and-green glory against an endless spectacle of stars.

Kriz helped me with it, he explained, sensing her curiosity. *Ain't had much else to do during the voyage.*

Somehow I doubt that, she replied, enjoying the momentary thrum of embarrassment that ran through the dust.

Is there a secret in my head you don't know? he asked.

Thousands, I'm sure. It's not your thoughts that betray you, but your feelings. Something they used to drill into us in the Academy.

She gave a final glance at the planet filling the sky above, resisting the urge to lose herself in the beauty of it, even for a short time. *I have to go,* she told him. *Our Blue stocks are low. Please reiterate the need for urgency to Captain Hilemore.*

I do that one more time he's like to shoot me . . . Clay trailed off, his gaze drawn to something beyond her. *Who's she?*

Lizanne turned, seeing a sailing-ship approaching across the mind-scape, the moon-dust parting like a wave before the bows. Morva was perched on the figure-head below the prow, hands cupped around her mouth as she called to Lizanne: *You have to come! It's started!*

CHAPTER 47

Sirus

Light the fuses.

Sirus watched through Forest Spear's eyes as he touched a match to the tip of the fuse wire, igniting a ball of sparks, then tracked its fiery dance into the depths of the tunnel. He checked to ensure the fuses laid in the other two tunnels had also been lit then returned to his own eyes, peering down from Katarias's back at the enemy trench works below.

The captives they had taken at the Jet Sands had confirmed the identity of his opponent and Sirus would very much have liked to see Arberus's face at the instant he realised his efforts had all been for nothing. He had never particularly cared for the major, finding his attitude to Tekela disconcertingly opposite to his own. Though she called him "Uncle," at her father's insistence, Sirus had long perceived a lack of warmth between the two. The fact that Arberus was half a foot taller and much admired by the female nobility of Morsvale hadn't done much to endear him to Sirus either.

Such adolescent notions you cling to, General, Catheline's thought popped into his head, amused and judgemental in equal measure. *Sometimes I forget how young you were.*

As do I, Sirus admitted. *It all seems so far away. Like a dream of someone else's life.*

As it should. We all have new lives now, for which we should be grateful.

The first mine exploded directly beneath the first line of Varestian trenches, bathing the darkened plain in yellow-orange light, Sirus watching the debris and bodies tumble in the rising ball of flame. The size of the crater was as Veilmist had predicted, leaving a hole thirty feet wide. It had taken the Spoiled a total of sixty hours to dig the three tunnels and pack them with explosives. Arberus had presumably expected a massed night-time assault, which he would shortly receive, but only after the mines had done their work in piercing the outer defences.

The next two mines exploded barely two seconds later, with similarly gratifying results, the glow revealing ten battalions of Spoiled rising from their own trenches and advancing across the plain at the run. A dozen rocket flares streamed into the sky from the fortified ridge-line above the trenches, banishing the dark and heralding a barrage from the guns along the walls. Shells tore into the ranks of the attacking Spoiled, felling dozens at a time. Casualties increased as a few repeating guns opened fire from the undamaged sections of the enemy trench, inflicting heavy losses, but none of it was enough to stop the tide.

The Spoiled boiled over the outer trench, Sirus feeling the pain, joy and death of close-quarters combat as they battled the human defenders. Glimpsing the struggle through Forest Spear's eyes, he was struck by the savagery of the Varestians, most of them eschewing fire-arms to fight with swords and knives, seemingly without any regard for their own survival.

Pirate scum, Catheline surmised, taking the measure of the Varestians' clothing.

Pirate scum with an inconvenient amount of courage, Sirus replied, noting the continued fighting all along the trench. Frenzied mêlées were raging in each of the craters and the trench itself was choked with Spoiled and humans locked in desperate combat. As yet, he could see no evidence of the hoped-for flight to the second trench line. The fiercest resistance came wherever the enemy had placed a Blood-blessed, the Varestians clustering around them as they blasted the attackers with Red and Black. Some leading desperate countercharges with sword or clubbed rifle in hand, the Green in their veins making them more than a match for any Spoiled.

A swift survey of minds revealed a spot close to where the first mine had exploded which appeared to be free of Blood-blessed. Sirus immediately ordered another four battalions into the attack, aiming them at this point. They streamed across the plain, covering the distance with a speed no human could match, but that didn't spare them the attentions of the Varestian gunners or their fleet.

The cannon on the Redoubt kept up a steady fire but the most damaging barrage came from the ships off shore. Shells arced down in a continuous torrent, aimed with expert precision to explode above rather than amongst the advancing Spoiled. The lead battalion was cut to pieces in the barrage, only about a fifth of them managing to press home their attack, whilst the battalions following behind fared little better. However, the sudden arrival of additional numbers at the crucial point finally told and soon Spoiled were spilling through into the flat ground beyond the trench.

A plethora of bugle calls and shouted orders ran the length of the trench, evidently the signal for the defenders to withdraw. In an obviously pre-rehearsed manoeuvre the humans abandoned the struggle and immediately sprinted towards the second line whilst the Varestian ships lowered their sights to rake the conquered trench in shell-fire. The Spoiled who had broken through on the left pelted towards the second line only to be met by a hail of fire from well-positioned repeating guns. None of them managed to get within twenty yards of the trench and Sirus ordered the survivors to withdraw to the first line.

The ship-borne fire continued, Sirus feeling the death or maiming of multiple Spoiled with every exploding shell. It petered out as the flares guttered and died, leaving the battlefield mostly in darkness save for Nelphia's glow. Small-arms fire continued to crackle as sharpshooters in the second trench and the Redoubt trained their longrifles on the first trench, though they scored only a few hits.

A good start, don't you think? Catheline asked.

I had hoped to take the second trench in the first assault, Sirus replied. *We need to do something about those ships.*

A singular paradox of being in proximity to the White was that he didn't need to engage with the increasingly difficult task of summoning fear to mask his thoughts. Being close enough to smell the sulphurous breath of the beast, and see the awful, knowing gleam of its eyes, birthed all the terror he could ever need. As before he felt the communication between Catheline and the White rather than heard it as thought-speech. The deep lust for vengeance that had characterised its thoughts ever since the loss of the infants at the Grand Cut was still present in full force, but the intervening time had also seen a resurgence of the beast's innate cunning.

It responded with a disconcerting rumble as Catheline communicated the essence of Sirus's plan. Whilst it never balked at casualties amongst the Spoiled, risking the lives of so many drakes was another matter. Smoke streamed from the White's nostrils as it turned about, pacing back and forth. It had established itself on the summit of a hill-top, the only high ground to be found on the plain. It offered an uninterrupted view of the fortified isthmus a mile away where its quarry waited. The two surviving infants were at work close by on one of their bone towers, squawking in apparent contentment as they fused the remains together with regurgitated bile. Sirus assumed the bones had been supplied by the other drakes, fruits of their labour at the Jet Sands.

Necessity, Catheline emoted, receiving a pulse of angry reluctance in response as the White turned its baleful gaze on them, Sirus noting the small sparks amidst the smoke rising from his nostrils.

He had never before sought to intervene in a communication between Catheline and the White, but did so now. Summoning all the memories he could of Lizanne Lethridge, he entwined them with the image of the dead infant Whites, condensing it all into a dark ball of sensation before offering it to Catheline.

Revenge, she thought, accepting Sirus's gift, breaking the ball of memory apart so it expanded in the White's mind. For the briefest moment Sirus was able to share the link between them, experiencing it as an image of a dark roiling sea of fire shot through with veins of light. Wherever the light touched the fire the flames calmed, became placid, taking on a semblance of order.

That's what he needs her for, he realised. *She calms the storm of his mind, allowing true intelligence to blossom.*

The White gave a grunt of annoyance at the intrusion and Sirus found himself shut out. The jarring sense of disconnection was accompanied by a bolt of punishing agony that sent him to his knees, teeth clenched. The pain lingered for a time, preventing him from following the rest of the communication. When it faded he felt Catheline's hands on his face, fingers wiping the pain-induced tears from his scaled skin. She smiled and pressed a kiss to his forehead, speaking softly, "He said yes."

CHAPTER 48

Hilemore

"Land in sight, sir. Dead ahead."

"Thank you, Mr. Talmant. Tell the Chief to take the Blood-burner off-line and signal the *Endeavour* to follow suit."

"Aye, sir."

Hilemore went outside and trained his glass to westward, making out the misted slopes of an island cresting the horizon. If his calculations were correct this was the most easterly islet of the Sabiras chain. Navigating the channel through the islands to the Red Tides was not a task that could be performed at speed, necessitating another delay. The storm that had swept across their path three days before had been mild by the standards of the Orethic but the seas it produced were sufficiently steep to force a reduction in speed. Since then Hilemore found his mood veering between frustration at the lack of progress and a small, barely acknowledged kernel of relief he knew stemmed from the battle off the Green Cape.

Steelfine insisted on recording the engagement as a victory in the ship's log, one the rest of the crew seemed to consider the equal of anything won by Hilemore's grandfather. He knew differently. *No admiral who loses his fleet can be counted a victor of anything.* If the *Superior* didn't reach Gadara's Redoubt in time for Clay to attempt his plan, a plan Hilemore still didn't fully understand, he might well consider it a reprieve rather than a failure. He had already studied the charts of the northern Orethic in preparation for a voyage to Sanorah, where he felt sure Free Woman Tythencroft would offer refuge to the valiant crew of the *Superior*.

And then what? he asked himself. *Sit and wait for the White's army to appear, however long it takes, all the time knowing yourself to be a miserable coward.*

He closed his spy-glass with a hard snap and returned to the bridge-house. "Ever sail the Red Tides, Mr. Scrimshine?" he enquired of the helmsman.

"A few times, Skipper." The former smuggler gave a small, wary smile. "Didn't find it the friendliest place, truth be told. Varestians love to steal but hate to be stolen from. Kind've hypocritical of them, if you ask me."

"Indeed so. I'll trust you to choose the best approach to the channel. I require a swift but safe navigation to the Red Tides. Mr. Talmant, ask Chief Bozware to join me in the hold. You have the bridge."

"Don't seem big enough to do much damage," Clay said, squinting at the apple-sized object the chief placed on the work-bench.

"Got enough of a charge to kill a drake of any size," Bozware replied, his oily brows forming a piqued frown. "Gun-cotton laced with lamp oil around a core of black powder. Made the casing deliberately brittle so's it'll shatter into sharp pieces when it goes off. Jagged iron'll cut through anything if it's travelling fast enough."

"What are these?" Kriz asked, extending a finger to one of the blunt spikes protruding from the device's casing.

"Contact points," the chief said. "Got the notion from those mines the captain had us make. Sets it off the instant they touch anything. Don't worry, missy," he added as Kriz swiftly withdrew her finger, "won't do nothing until you arm it." He pointed to a metal ring in the top of the device. "Yank this out before you throw the bomb, just make sure anything you chuck it at is at least twenty yards off."

"Excellent," Lieutenant Sigoral said, giving the chief a nod of respectful approval. "It's certainly preferable to trying to get a bead on a drake's head in the midst of a battle."

"Long as you've got Black in your veins," Clay said. "Don't relish the prospect of throwing one of these by hand."

"We only had sufficient materials to construct forty in total," Hilemore said, addressing himself to Clay. "How many do you think you'll need?"

"Hard to say. I'll take ten, I guess. You can share the rest out amongst the others."

"Very well. We'll relight the blood-burner upon clearing the Sabiras Islands, which means we should reach our objective shortly after first light tomorrow. I suggest you get what rest you can in the meantime." Hilemore watched them leave, all but Jillett whose gaze lingered on the grenade, face even paler than usual.

"I'll require you to remain in the engine room," he told her. "Your job is to fire the blood-burner."

"Guess you weren't impressed, huh?" she said with a faint grin. "By my fighting skills, I mean. Can't say I blame you."

"You fought bravely and well. What happened at Stockcombe was not your fault."

She moved her slim shoulders in a shrug. "They were a bunch've rotten bastards, y'know. The Wash Lane Bully Boys was their real name before the revolt. When I was little, my ma used to give me a fresh piece of fruit every day to take to school. An apple usually, even an orange sometimes, though it must've cost her plenty. And every day those Wash Lane fuckers'd corner me and steal it, till I realised what I was. Scrounged up enough scrip to buy just a smidge of Black." Her grin broadened. "They didn't steal from me after that."

She reached out to the bomb, fingers playing tentatively over the contact points before picking it up. "I'll take this one, if you don't mind," she said. "Just in case."

They passed the first ship shortly after Scrimshine steered the *Superior* through the islands and into the Red Tides. An aged one-stack clipper steamed by a mile off the starboard bow, sails raised to augment her paddles. She sat low in the water, a crowd of close-packed people thronging her deck fore and aft. The crow's nest related a signal that had been rapidly hauled to the top of her mainmast: *Turn back. No safe harbour ahead.*

Hilemore ordered the signaller to reply via the lamp, advising the clipper to make for the east Corvantine coast, but the *Superior* was moving too fast to catch any reply. They saw four more ships before nightfall, all heavily laden with refugees and steaming towards different points of the compass. One, a broad-beamed freighter, altered course to approach the *Superior*, her signal pennants displaying a request for medical assistance. Hilemore had the battle flag raised to warn them off, maintaining their speed and heading until the freighter was far to their rear.

When night fell he had the blood-burner taken off-line briefly to allow the *Endeavour* to draw alongside then ordered the ship to battle stations. Steelfine mustered the riflemen and had cannister stacked alongside the gun-crews. Braddon Torcreek and Preacher climbed the mast to the crow's nest, rifles strapped across their backs. Kriz took up station with Clay and Lutharon on the fore-deck whilst Sigoral and the few remaining Corvantines from the original crew stationed themselves aft. Hilemore had Colonel Kulvetch position her Marines on the upper works, each squad supplied with full water buckets and sandbags to combat the inevitable fires.

"Got room for two more?" Loriabeth asked, appearing in the bridge hatchway with Skaggerhill at her back. Steelfine had already assigned a squad of riflemen to the captain's guard, but additional guns couldn't hurt.

"Of course, miss," Hilemore told her. "You're very welcome."

He went outside to check on the *Endeavour*, finding the Voter volunteers lining her rails, crews standing ready at her cannon, a half-dozen four-pounders and two rifled six-pound pivot-guns. It was poor armament for what they were about to face but ordering Zenida to remain on station would have been pointless. Hilemore climbed up to the bridgehouse roof, taking the signal lamp and flashing out a brief message: *Will proceed at full speed. Follow as best you can.*

Zenida appeared at the door of the *Endeavour*'s wheel-house, silhouetted in the light from within as she raised her own signal lamp to respond: *Try losing me, sea-brother.*

Hilemore allowed himself a brief smile before handing back the signal lamp and climbing down to the bridge. "Mr. Talmant!"

"Sir!"

"Signal the engine room. Three vials to the blood-burner."

"Aye, sir."

"Mr. Scrimshine . . ."

"I know the way, Skipper." Hilemore saw Scrimshine's hands shake a little before he took a tight grip on the tiller, eyes locked on the dark sea beyond the prow. "Dead west it is."

They heard it before they saw it. The flat crump of cannon carried through the morning mist that hung on the horizon. The sea was calm and the *Superior* steamed westward with the needle of the speed indicator dial pushed well past its maximum. By sunrise the *Endeavour* had fallen at least a mile behind causing Hilemore to entertain the faint hope the whole affair might be over before she could join the battle.

"Five miles until landfall, sir," Talmant reported, glancing up from the map table, ruler in hand.

Hilemore swallowed a curse at the lingering mist. At her current speed the *Superior* would run aground before she could slow enough for a turn, and they had yet to catch sight of a target. "Switch to auxiliary power," he said, sending Talmant rushing to the speaking-tube. "Tell the Chief to let her drift for one minute before engaging the engine. Ahead one-third."

"Aye, sir."

Hilemore saw flashes in the mist as they drew closer, then the first dim outlines of ships. He made out the shape of a Corvantine sloop and an armed Varestian freighter, both steaming in parallel to the as yet unseen shore, guns firing in relays along their port sides. More and more ships resolved into view as they drew closer and the sound of cannon fire became thunderous. There were so many ships steaming back and forth Hilemore at first had difficulty in making out the shore, but then he saw the imposing silhouette of the Redoubt rising above a narrow beach.

"Receiving multiple hails, sir," Talmant said as a plethora of flags ascended the masts of the nearest ships, accompanied by the flicker of numerous signal lamps.

"Send the response in plain," Hilemore said. "Here to assist. Blood-blessed aboard."

Hilemore scanned the ships for their response then found his attention captured by a whispered mutter from Scrimshine, spoken in a strained reverential tone he hadn't used since their first encounter with Last Look Jack. "Honoured ancestors accept the soul of this miserable wretch."

The helmsman was staring through the forward window, eyes wide and wet, hands shaking again. Hilemore followed his gaze, spying what he initially took for a large dark cloud to the right of the Redoubt. Scrimshine evidently had keener eyes, however, for the cloud soon expanded to fill the sky above the shore-line, Hilemore making out the winged shapes amongst the mass.

"That's . . ." he heard Loriabeth say in a tone eerily similar to Scrimshine's. "That's a whole lotta Reds."

Hilemore's gaze snapped to the fore-deck, seeing Clay share a brief embrace with Kriz before moving to climb up onto Lutharon's back. "Don't!" Hilemore shouted, rushing outside, cupping his hands around his mouth as he leaned over the walkway. "There are too many!"

Clay turned to him as Lutharon clambered up onto the prow. Hilemore saw him offer a grin of farewell before he raised his hand, drinking down the three vials it held in a few gulps before tossing them away. Hilemore's protestations died on his lips as the drake launched itself from the ship, mighty wings raising vapour from the sea and tail whipping as he climbed into the air.

CHAPTER 49

Lizanne

"Get them all up!" Lizanne shouted as she sprinted towards the *Typhoon*, the other aerostat crews all running across the Redoubt's courtyard to where their craft waited. Tekela was already strapping herself into the pilot's seat when Lizanne clambered inside. Morva and the three gunners followed in short order. The top gunner climbed the ladder to her station in the upper cupola as the others prepared their guns and Tekela tilted the engines toward the ground, simultaneously opening the throttles to take off.

Lizanne slotted one of her three remaining Redballs into the chamber of her Smoker, positioning herself at the rear port hatch, gaze fixed on the top of the Redoubt wall as the *Typhoon* rose, expecting the Reds to appear at any moment. Instead they ascended into an empty sky, the reason becoming obvious as the walls fell away beneath them. The Red swarm was streaming by a half-mile distant, keeping out of range of the repeating guns as they flew over the coast and banked towards the Varestian fleet in a dense crimson mass.

"They're going for the ships!" she called to Tekela, moving to the blood-burner's ignition tube. "Take us east. Maximum speed. Morva, trance with the *Hurricane* and the *Whirlwind*, tell them to form up alongside."

She waited until she could see the two aerostats through the port and starboard windows then injected Red and put her eye to the ignition tube, lighting the thermoplasmic engine. She managed to catch hold of the central support beam before the instant acceleration sent her flying and hauled herself forward to stand at Tekela's shoulder.

She could see the ships already firing at the oncoming Reds, the diminishing space between them lined with criss-crossing tracer and exploding cannon shells. White splashes pock-marked the sea beneath the swarm as drake after drake fell to the guns, but it was clear no amount of fire-power would stem their charge, there were just too many. The ships closest to shore were blotted from view as the horde of Reds swept over them, Lizanne seeing others diving onto the neighbouring ships, talons opening to deposit Greens on their decks. Within seconds the entire fleet was obscured by the multitude of drakes, Lizanne catching sight of explosions blossoming beneath as ships began to fall victim to the assault.

"There," Lizanne said, pointing to the densest part of the drake horde. "Take us straight through."

"Swarmers?" Tekela asked, hand poised to trigger the firing mechanism for the rockets. There were four switches, one for each row of ten Swarmers fitted to the underside of the gondola.

"Not yet," she said. "Let's see if we can get some to follow us. We need to take the pressure off the fleet."

A trio of Reds spotted the aerostats as they approached, peeling away from the flock to fly directly into their path. Tekela pulled the switch fitted to the top of the main control lever, triggering the forward guns and blasting the lead Red from the sky. The stream of bullets tore the wing of another, sending it spiralling down into the sea, but the third dodged aside, banking hard to assail them from the side only to be cut in two by a burst from the starboard gunner.

All guns aboard began firing as they tore into the central mass of the swarm, the hull resounding with the thud of colliding drakes and the windscreen becoming so spattered with blood Tekela had to engage the mechanical wipers. Lizanne rushed back to the rear port hatch, rapid firing her Smoker at the drakes flashing by the opening. Then they were through, the windows showing clear sky.

Lizanne turned to the rear window, letting out a relieved sigh at the sight of the *Hurricane* and *Whirlwind* following close behind. The *Hurricane* appeared undamaged but she could see smoke streaming from the *Whirlwind*'s port engine. Beyond them she was gratified to see a large number of Reds, wings blurring as they laboured in pursuit.

"Blood-burner off," she told Tekela. "Turn us around and make ready to fire the Swarmers."

The *Typhoon* slowed then tilted as Tekela killed their forward speed and reversed the propeller on the starboard engine, spinning them around. Lizanne saw the *Hurricane* and *Whirlwind* following suit, forming up on either side as Tekela put the *Typhoon* into a hover. Lizanne went forward, peering through the blood-streaked window at the fast-approaching pack of Reds. It was hard to judge the distance but she had little doubt they were now in range.

"Fire half only," she told Tekela who lost no time in flicking two of the switches on the firing mechanism. There was no recoil from the rockets, the *Typhoon* rising a little due to the reduced weight as the Swarmers shot from underneath the gondola, smoke trails overlapping to describe a complex pattern in the sky. Seeing the danger, the formation of pursuing Reds began to break apart but were unable to avoid the unpredictable trajectory of the Swarmers. Multiple explosions ripped through the drakes, sending dozens plummeting down. The survivors veered left and right only to fly into the rockets launched by the *Hurricane* and the *Whirlwind*. Within seconds the sky to the front of the *Typhoon* was clear of drakes.

"Well," Tekela said, "that worked."

Lizanne lowered her gaze to the battle raging below. She counted five ships alight and apparently adrift whilst battles seemed to be raging on several more as the crews fought the Greens that had been dropped onto their decks. However, most vessels appeared undamaged and were maintaining a blizzard of Growler and Thumper fire at the Reds, the waters around them dotted with numerous dead or dying drakes. Satisfying as this was, Lizanne also took note of the fact that whilst the battle raged, no ship was firing its main guns towards the shore.

"Take us up," she ordered.

Tekela angled the engines to ninety degrees, putting the *Typhoon* into a rapid ascent, Lizanne watching in dismay as the Redoubt came fully into view. Cannon were firing all along the fortified ridge, shells trailing smoke as they slammed into the mass of Greens and Spoiled assaulting the second trench line. The attacking army resembled a dark tide on a stormy two-moon night as it washed against a harbour wall, the waves inching closer to overwhelming the barrier with every passing heave.

"Re-engage the blood-burner," she told Tekela. "Head for the Redoubt."

She turned, intending to tell Morva to trance with the Blood-blessed in the other aerostats, but finding her distracted, frowning as she squinted at something to the east.

"He's a big bastard," she said, hefting her mini-Growler. "Think I might be able to get him from here."

Lizanne went to her side, tracking the direction of the Growler's multiple barrels to see a very large drake flying towards the fleet. In the haze beyond she could make out the outline of a ship. It was an unusual design, her hull lacking paddles and leaving a broad wake as she headed towards the shore.

"Don't!" she said, pushing Morva's mini-Growler aside and sending the stream of tracer arcing into the sea. She could see him now, a figure perched on the drake's back, a drake with black scales instead of red.

"Tekela!" she called out. "Change of course!"

CHAPTER 50

Clay

No way around, over or under, Clay mused as he looked upon a sky filled with Reds. As Lutharon flew closer to the embattled fleet the surrounding air whined with wayward bullets and shrapnel from exploding cannon shells. The drakes seemed entirely preoccupied with the ships, but he doubted that would last once they caught sight of a Black. *Looks like we'll just have to fight our way through, big fella.*

Lutharon let out a low, rumbling growl in response, broadening his wings to send them higher into the air. As expected, Clay saw a half dozen Reds separate from the main flock and fly towards them, their challenge cries audible even above the cacophony of gun-fire below. Lutharon replied with a roar, deep and hungry, angling his body to take them straight towards the nearest Red. Clay focused his gaze on the Red's left wing, waiting until it closed to within twenty yards then letting loose with a concentrated burst of Black. The drake's wing-bone snapped at the upper joint, sending the beast into an untidy forward plummet that abruptly ended when Lutharon reared back and lanced out with his talons, piercing the Red's chest with a swift, tearing slash before casting it away.

Lutharon folded his wings and corkscrewed, Clay feeling a blast of heat from the other Reds before the Black levelled out. Craning his neck, Clay saw the Reds wheeling and coming about, wings sweeping in frenzied arcs as they scrambled to pursue. He could sense Lutharon's instinctive need to turn and meet the threat but urged him to ignore it and increase his forward speed. *Got more important things to do today.*

The Reds, however, proved capable of matching Lutharon's speed. Being lighter, they were able to close half the intervening distance in short order. Clay reached into the satchel slung over his shoulder and withdrew one of Chief Bozware's grenades. He jerked the pin loose and twisted about, using his Green-enhanced sight to aim a burst of Black towards the head of the leading Red, the invisible force wave carrying the grenade along with it. The drake tried to dodge the missile but it was too swift, catching it on the shoulder and tearing much of its upper body apart in an ugly explosion of black smoke and crimson gore. The surviving Reds let out a screech of rage as the corpse fell away, sweeping upwards then diving down, moving too fast and coming too close for the grenades. Their mouths gaped as they dived, ready to belch out their flames, then the two in the lead blew apart as a line of cannon shells streamed down from above.

A shadow fell over the remaining Reds as they broke formation, proving too slow to avoid the hail of bullets and cannon shells that soon sent them plunging in pieces towards the waves. Clay looked up as the aerostats passed overhead, engines roaring. There were three of them, their size and speed more impressive in reality than the images he had seen in the trance. They descended to take up position directly to Lutharon's front, Clay spotting a slim figure leaning out of the rear hatch of the craft in the centre. She wore goggles and, although it seemed like a great deal of time had passed since he had last seen her in the flesh, he recognised her instantly.

Lizanne began to lift her hand in a wave then abruptly pivoted, bringing a carbine to her shoulder as a Red came screaming in from the side. Whatever manner of bullet she had loaded into the carbine was clearly something special, leaving a trail of flame in its wake as it impacted on the Red's torso. There was a blinding flash and the Red had mostly disappeared, save for a few chunks of flesh tumbling in the aerostat's slip-stream.

The sky suddenly grew dark and Clay realised they were now surrounded by Reds. A glance at the sea below Lutharon's wings revealed that the ships were no longer under attack. *Looks like we been recognised*, he thought.

The guns of the three aerostats all began firing at once, sending streams of tracer in all directions. Clay held Lutharon on a steady course as he continually scanned the sky for threats, sending one Red tumbling away with a blast of Black and searing the eyes of another with a fulsome torrent of Red. The loud, bone-jarring thump of a blast wave snapped his gaze back to the aerostats, finding the one on the right had lost an engine. Clay could see the blackened corpse of a Red falling away in a cloud of shattered, smoking mechanicals. The aerostat began to spin out of control, losing height and drawing away from the others. Sensing a kill, the Reds mobbed the stricken craft, uncaring of any danger as they streaked in from all sides to slam themselves into the envelope, many falling victim to the craft's guns, which continued to fire without pause. More and more drakes flung themselves onto the aerostat, tearing at it with claw and tooth, others belching fire at the gondola until it was a mass of flame. The aerostat's descent accelerated, its nose tipping forward as it went into a dive and exploded before hitting the sea.

Clay tore his gaze away from the dreadful spectacle in time to see a large Red slip through the gap between the two remaining aerostats, flaring its wings as it reared back, talons flashing. Lutharon coughed out a brief but intense stream of fire, the force and the heat of it sufficient to cast the attacking Red aside, leaving it a smoking tangle in their wake.

Lizanne reappeared in the aerostat's rear hatch, urgently pointing a finger at her head. Understanding the signal Clay closed his eyes, trying to shut out the screams of a thousand drakes as he slipped into the Blue-less trance. Lizanne took a second to appear, her whirlwinds more disordered than he had ever seen them and he was appalled to find a glimmer of panic in her gaze.

Thank you for coming, she said, forcing a smile.

Said I would.

She nodded, the misty vortices beginning to break apart as her mindscape darkened and Clay realised he was trancing with a woman who expected to die very soon. *They're forming up above the shore-line,* she told him. *Follow us closely. We'll make a hole. There's a hill a mile to the west. You'll find her there.*

Clay began to reply but she was gone, leaving him alone on Nelphia's surface. He ended the trance, blinking tears in the rushing chill. When his vision cleared he saw multiple smoke streams blossoming from the base of the aerostat's gondolas. *Rockets,* he realised, watching several small cylindrical forms detach from the craft and streak away. The rockets flew in spirals of varying widths, hurtling towards the wheeling barrier of drakes in a concentrated swarm. Their impact resembled a short but impressive firework display, except every flash and boom meant the death of at least three drakes. When it faded there was a large rent in the flock of Reds through which Clay could see a broad plain beneath a cloudless blue sky.

The two aerostats immediately accelerated towards the gap, guns blazing as they fought to keep it open. Clay sent all the urgent thoughts he could to Lutharon but the drake needed no encouragement. He surged forward with a growl, sail-sized wings sweeping faster than Clay ever thought possible. He kept his gaze on the plain beyond the gap, refusing to be distracted by the roaring gun-fire and screaming drakes on either side.

She's intending to die here, he knew, hating the knowledge and hating himself for the determination not to turn away and save her. *Make it mean something.*

Lutharon went into a steep dive as they cleared the gap, increasing his speed yet further. Clay quickly found the hill-top, the White an unmistakable landmark. Its wings were spread wide, head thrown back and mouth gaping. Even above the rushing wind Clay could hear its challenging roar.

Remember me, huh? he asked it, surprised to find a grim smile playing across his lips. He tore his gaze from the White, Green-boosted eyes scanning the hill until he found her, a slender figure standing alongside a Spoiled wearing some kind of uniform. Her features became clearer as they flew closer, eyes of red and black staring back at him, her face a porcelain mask of disconcerting beauty.

Catheline, he thought, slipping into the Blue-less trance state, summoning all the images he had memorised, all the stories from the periodicals and the scandal sheets, reaching out. There was no response, the trance felt like sinking his hands into tepid water. *Hate,* he reminded himself. *You know hate, and so does she.*

He summoned his own memories to join with hers, everything he tried to keep locked away in dark crevices of his mind. *The first time he saw his father beat his mother . . . His father's head jerking as the bullet slammed home, blood and brains on the cards . . . Dozens of vicious back-alley struggles in the Blinds . . . Keyvine's blade at his neck . . . Silverpin, the red wings blossoming across the glass floor . . . And the White.* He hated it. Hated it for all it had wrought upon the world. But more, he hated it for what it made him do. *Silverpin as the longrifle bullet tore through her . . . All those good people lost on ice and in the battles since . . . Lizanne, accepting her own death just to get him here.*

The hate burned at the core of him, filling the trance with the purity of its heat and finding a mirror in the soul of Catheline Dewsmine.

A moment of complete emptiness. He felt nothing. Not the beating of his heart. Not the air on his skin. His eyes saw nothing. There were only his thoughts, roiling in panic as he pondered if this is what it meant to die. Then he saw a single point of light, no larger than a raindrop, but growing steadily, expanding into a ball that filled his gaze and soon enveloped him.

He stood in a garden of some kind, neat hedgerows and flower-beds surrounding a vast lawn at the centre of which stood a three-storey mansion house. The sky was darkened by clouds pregnant with rain, the air chilled almost to the same degree as the southern ice. Trees dotted the garden, their bare branches sagging with a macabre fruit.

Bodies, Clay realised, gaze snapping from one tree to another. Men and women, boys and girls, old and young. They all hung from the trees, grey faces bloated and hollow eyes empty as they twisted in the stiff breeze.

I don't recall inviting you in.

He turned, finding Catheline standing close to the shore of an ornamental lake. She was human now, her eyes a pale blue, though her beauty remained undimmed, even enhanced. No human skin had ever been so luminous and no hair so golden. Her vanity, it seemed, extended deep into her consciousness. But no amount of visual artifice could mask her emotions. He could feel her outrage at his intrusion, it hung in the air as a simmering electric thrum that reminded him of the moments before a storm.

You didn't, he replied. *Yet here I am.*

You're the one. Her mouth twisted in a smile, self-satisfied and very knowing. *He remembers you.*

I remember him.

You killed her. Her smile broadened as she sensed his discomfort. *The one who came before me. I suppose I should be thanking you.*

You should, he agreed. *I'm here to set you free.*

Really? She raised her elegant eyebrows in mock contrition. *You are here to rescue me? I do crave your pardon, sir. I had assumed you were here to kill me. How remiss of me to mistake our respective roles in this drama.*

Apparently, you are the brave hero come to vanquish the monster and I the helpless princess. Tell me, how exactly do you intend to accomplish this mighty feat?

Clay looked around at the nightmarish garden with its dangling corpses and storm-dark sky. He saw that the mansion house was shifting in appearance. One second it was a fine whitewashed example of the classic style favoured by the upper echelons of the managerial class, the next it was a ruin, the windows empty of glass, the walls streaked with soot and the roof a mess of blackened timbers.

Well, I ain't gonna appeal to your kindly nature, he replied, turning back to her. *What is this place? Your home? Where you grew up, maybe?*

Mind your own fucking business, you gutter-scraping bastard. The thought was accompanied by a sweet smile, rich in sincerity.

Clay ignored her and moved towards the nearest tree, looking up at one of the corpses dangling from the branches. It was a woman of hefty proportions clad in an unadorned black dress. Her eyeless, blue-lipped face possessed a stern aspect even in death.

Who's this? Clay asked.

Catheline crossed her arms, tilting her head and remaining silent as they matched stares. After a few seconds of mutual antipathy she shrugged. *Miss Pendlecost,* she told him. *My governess. She used to twist my fingers if I got my calculus wrong, only when my parents weren't looking of course.*

Clay inclined his head at the corpse. *Is this what you did to her, or what you wanted to do to her?*

What difference does it make? Now or when I return to Mandinor, she's still dead.

Clay moved on to the next corpse, a bewhiskered man of middling years, his pot-belly poking out above a pair of half-fallen trousers. *And him?*

My mother's second cousin, Erdwin. He tried to fuck me when I was thirteen. She gave a fond smile as she looked up at the dead man. *Him I did kill. Paid a short visit to his house in Sanorah before I took ship to Feros. It was strange, but I almost pitied him. Just a sad little man living a sad little life with only his cats and his very specialised library for company. When I burned them he cried and cried so I broke his neck. Just in case you imagined mercy to be beyond me.*

Clay shifted his gaze from the tree to the house on the far side of the expansive lawn. *That seems a mite strange,* he said, noting again how its appearance continued to shift from whole to ruined. *Can't decide how you want it to look?*

What are you talking about? she demanded. *It's my parents' country residence a few miles east of Sanorah. I spent most of my childhood here.*

You don't see it, do you? he asked, finding no note of subterfuge in her thoughts.

She replied with a bemused frown, though Clay saw how her lips twitched a little as she asked, *See what?*

Not afraid of it, are you? he pressed, sensing her growing unease. *Something in there you don't want to remember?*

It's just a house. She pulled her shawl tight about her shoulders and turned away.

Then I guess you won't mind if I take a look.

He managed only a few steps before a geyser of dark earth erupted directly in his path. A Green clambered from the hole, eyes glowing and flame blossoming in its maw. *This is my head,* Catheline informed him as more Greens began to claw their way up through the lawn. *And I don't want you here.*

Clay drew the revolver from his belt, holding it out as he fused it with fresh memories. The revolver doubled in size, growing multiple barrels and a large chamber. It was a reasonable facsimile of a repeating gun, not entirely accurate but it would serve his needs well enough. He levelled the barrels on the nearest Green and pulled the trigger, the drake transforming into bloody pieces in the torrent of bullets. Clay advanced across the lawn, working the repeating gun like a scythe, sweeping the whirring barrels left and right as he reaped a harvest of dismembered Greens.

Sorry, ma'am, he called to Catheline over his shoulder as he reached the house. *You're stuck with me for a while yet.*

He turned the repeating gun on the large double door at the front of the house and blew it into splinters, stepping inside and returning the revolver to its original size. The shifting nature of the house's exterior was matched by its interior. The marble-floored lobby with its fine curving staircase and chandelier transformed every few seconds into a scorched, soot-blackened wreck. There were more bodies here, not hanging this time but lying about the chequerboard floor. Clay took them for servants from their clothing, maids and footmen either burned to death or broken by the kind of injuries that only Black could inflict.

I haven't been here in years. Catheline stood in the shattered doorway, arms crossed tight about her chest. Clay could feel the depth of her reluctance to step inside, her pale blue eyes guarded as they darted about the lobby with its many corpses. *I have no use for childhood concerns,* she insisted. *There's nothing of interest here.*

Clay saw that, although her eyes roved about, they were conspicuous in avoiding the hallway to the left. *What's back there?* he enquired, gesturing with his revolver.

Nothing. The word was spoken in a whisper, Catheline's gaze abruptly frozen, staring straight ahead. *There's nothing there. That wing of the house was long out of use, even when I was a girl.*

For someone who's done so much bad, you're a really terrible liar, Clay observed, starting down the hallway.

There's nothing there! she insisted, rushing after him. *You're wasting your time.*

He found a door at the end of the hall, locked when he tried the handle. He turned the revolver into a replica of Skaggerhill's shotgun and blew the lock to pieces, kicking the door open. The room he stepped into wasn't like the others, no continual shift from one state to another. Here everything was in a permanent state of disorder. Clay deduced it had been a study from the blackened remnant of the desk in one corner and the charred books on the shelves. The room wasn't completely burned out, however, one section near the fire-place remained intact.

A couch sat on a fine Dalcian carpet in front of the fire-place, and on the couch were two bodies, a man and a woman. They were undoubtedly dead judging by their bleached skin and open but unseeing eyes, but they sat upright, hands resting in their laps. The man was somewhere in his fifties and wore a well-tailored suit that only the most senior managers could afford. The woman was a few years younger, wearing a plain but elegant dress that would have done much to enhance her figure, had her form not been so completely drained of life. Her hair was a shade darker than Catheline's, but Clay saw the similarity in their features.

This . . . Catheline began, entering the room on unsteady feet. *This is just how I remember them . . .*

They're dead, Clay pointed out. *You remember your parents as dead folk?*

They were very dull people. She let out a short shrill laugh, her wide eyes fixed on the face of her mother. *So very very dull.*

Clay moved closer to the bodies, peering into their eyes and finding the whites threaded with a dense mesh of burst veins. It was something he had seen before. *How'd you learn that trick?* he wondered, shaking his head. *Only ever knew one Blood-blessed who could do it.*

I did nothing, she whispered, her voice taking on an accusatory tone. *You did this. This is all just theatre of your making.*

No. Clay retreated from the corpses, turning to face her. *I didn't. You did it. You broke out of the madhouse and you came here.*

No. No, I . . .

You killed all the servants and then you sat your parents down . . .

No . . .

And you used Black to squeeze the vessels in their brain so they died in agony, but they couldn't scream. Just had to sit there whilst their own daughter tortured them . . .

NO!

A rumble of thunder came from outside as Catheline collapsed to her knees, folding in on herself, tears streaming from her tight-closed eyes. *My parents loved me,* she sobbed. *They wanted to keep me safe. I would never hurt them, never, never . . .*

Clay watched her subside into her grief, face veiled by her hair as she shuddered on the floor. *I guess that's true,* he told her, turning back to the corpses of the late Mr. and Mrs. Dewsmine. *They tried to keep you safe but there was one thing they couldn't hide you from.* He crouched at her side, speaking softly. *It ain't too late. You still got a chance to put this right. End this war.*

The thunder sounded again, the room growing dark as the clouds thickened in the sky.

Yes, he heard her say in a small, scared voice. *Yes. We will end it.*

The loud echoing thud of colliding metal snapped Clay's gaze to the door, finding oak-wood had been replaced by iron and, instead of standing open with a shattered lock, the door was now firmly closed. Also, he couldn't see any sign of a lock. More metallic thuds echoed around the room, Clay turning in time to see iron shutters slamming closed on the windows, leaving the room in darkness apart from the blaze that had suddenly appeared in the fire. Clay reeled back as the fire-place blasted out a brief torrent of flame, some of it catching the sleeve of his duster. As he beat the flames out he noted that the fire-place now resembled the mouth of a large drake.

The thunder came again, far louder now, persisting until it slowly revealed itself as a growl. One Clay had heard before. It shook the room, dislodging the pictures from atop the mantelpiece. Catheline was still sobbing behind the veil of her hair, except the sobs had taken on a higher pitch. As her hair parted the glow from the fire played on a smiling face and he realised she wasn't sobbing at all.

Did you think I was alone here? she asked, getting to her feet. *That I was alone when I did this?* She cast a dismissive hand at her dead parents. *He has been with me for every step and the journey has been glorious.*

He watched her enjoy the shock on his face, blinking her pale blue eyes as they slowly transformed back into red-black orbs. *What lengths you have gone to,* Catheline observed, raising her hands to the surrounding room, now rapidly transforming into a cube of bare iron walls. *All those miles travelled and battles fought, just to place your mind in a prison.*

Clay raised his revolver, aim swift and true, the sights centred on her forehead. She moved as he fired, blurring with speed. A hard, jarring impact to his chest and he found himself slammed into the iron wall. Pain was often muted in the trance, the mental shields creating a barrier against a mostly physical sensation, but not here. Clay shouted with the shock of his spine shattering against the wall, the revolver flying from his grasp as he slid to the floor.

It isn't too late, Catheline told him, eyebrows raised in sympathy as she crouched at his side. *You still have a chance to put this right.* She lifted a finger. *You can get in here. But I can't get in there.* She pushed the finger hard into the side of his head. *Let me in and I won't make you watch when I cut your friends open.*

Guh . . . Clay coughed, jerking with pain. *Guh fuh* . . .

I do beg your pardon, Catheline inched closer, cocking her head. *Didn't quite catch that.*

Clay dragged in a slow ragged breath, speaking very deliberately. *Go . . . fuck . . . yourself.*

Catheline rolled her eyes at him. *Well, that's charming.* She glanced over her shoulder at what had been the fire-place but was now the widening maw of the White. *He just wants to eat you, in body and in mind. He doesn't really have an imagination, you see?* She extended a hand, flattening it out as the fingers grew, her nails becoming claws which she slowly pressed into his chest, provoking another shout of pain. *But then, he has me for that . . .*

She stopped talking, all emotion draining from her face, which had taken on an aspect of shocked surprise. *No,* she breathed in a voice laden with genuine fear. The claws withdrew from Clay's chest and she whirled away, blinking out of existence to leave him alone and crippled in his prison.

CHAPTER 51

Sirus

He's here! Sirus could feel Catheline's hungry exultation as she shared the image of the man riding on the back of a Black drake. Her excitement was mirrored by the White, the beast letting out a long, rumbling growl that seemed to shake the ground. Sirus watched in dismay as the great flock of Reds began to abandon their attack on the enemy fleet, rising and wheeling away towards the approaching drake and rider.

"Their mission is not complete . . ." he began, abruptly falling silent as his jaw clamped shut at a glance from Catheline.

"Their mission is what I say it is, dear General," she said. "The second line of trenches is about to fall. Concentrate your efforts there."

Sirus withdrew as much of his mind from hers as he could, worried his sudden rage might lead her to some unfortunate conclusions. Turning his attention to the assault on the trenches, he took some satisfaction from the fact that the fighting had progressed beyond the second trench line. The defending humans once again clustered around their Blood-blessed, loosing off volleys of rifle fire as the encroaching Greens and Spoiled attempted to fight their way past invisible walls of Black and scorching waves of Red. He searched for a point of weakness, somewhere to concentrate his reserve battalions, but this time the defenders appeared to be equally resolute all along their line, even pushing back in some places thanks to the Blood-blessed.

It all hinges on them, he decided, quickly conducting a mental search for the keenest marksmen in his army. He picked out a hundred in all, ordering their fellow Spoiled to hoist them up above the attacking throng, one simple command filling their heads: *Kill the Blood-blessed.*

The first fell within seconds, her head blown to pieces by five expertly aimed shots. Another two fell in quick succession, Sirus swiftly sending his lead battalions against these points in the line and ordering the reserves forward. Seeing the danger the defenders immediately clustered around the remaining Blood-blessed, shielding them with their bodies as they beat a hasty retreat to the third trench. The enemy defence collapsed soon after, the humans turning and running towards the only remaining refuge.

Sirus attempted to launch a rapid pursuit, hoping to use the momentum of the advance to overrun the third line, but found the effort frustrated by a sudden loss of discipline amongst the Greens. Combat and the overpowering scent of blood stoked their hunger beyond the point of resistance. They began a feeding frenzy, creating a series of obstacles as they gathered in thrashing mobs around the bodies littering the ground, human and Spoiled. This soon created a gap between fleeing defenders and attackers.

Arberus, evidently not one to forsake an opportunity, had the cannon on the Redoubt lower their sights and begin a rapid barrage. The attackers were close enough to the wall to bring them into range of cannister-shot, the rain of iron balls and metal shards tearing holes in the Spoiled battalions stalled around the feasting Greens. They were also now in range of the repeating guns positioned along the Redoubt. Sirus felt the minds of over two hundred Spoiled blink out of existence in the space of ten seconds as cannon shells and tracer bullets lashed the army.

Pull back to the second line, he ordered in resignation. *Bring up the artillery.* It would be a costly difficult business, but he would use his own cannon to suppress the fire from the walls, hopefully providing sufficient cover for the final assault.

He turned to Catheline, intending to ask that she impose some order on the Greens, but found her staring fixedly at the sky to the east. Following her gaze he saw that the Reds had formed a broad, swirling barrier over the shore-line, a barrier that appeared to have just had a hole punched through it. He could see two aerostats, tracer flickering around them as they fought to keep the hole open, and between them a lone drake.

The White let out a sudden, deafening roar, Sirus looking up to see it rearing, wings spread wide and head raised as it bellowed out a challenge. Sirus looked again at Catheline, hoping for an explanation as to what might be happening. She began to turn to him, then froze, all light seeming to fade from her eyes as she collapsed.

A pain shot through Sirus's head, sharp enough to make him stagger, vision blurring as confusion reigned in his mind. Memories churned in a rapid visual soup. *Katrya . . . Morradin . . . Greens feasting on the corpses of children . . . Feros burning . . .*

When it cleared he found himself on his knees, hands clasped to the side of his head. The pain slowly ebbed, and as it receded he realised something was different. *She's gone.* He looked at Catheline lying next him, eyes vacant and body limp, feeling not the slightest touch of her thoughts. Catheline's mind was gone.

Furthermore, his mental connection to the White was greatly diminished. He could still feel the Spoiled, the link with them was as strong as ever, but the White's thoughts were muted now, like distant thunder, and that distance brought a single thought to the forefront of his mind.

I have slaughtered thousands.

He looked at his hands, clawed, scaled, powerful enough to rip a man apart if he chose, and in the midst of battle he had. His plan had been a delusion, he saw that now. A hopeless lie he told himself to preserve some vestige of sanity. Win the war in the hope the Spoiled's loyalty to him would overcome their enslavement to the White. *We are its creatures. That will never change.* It occurred to him that perhaps he had been permitted this delusion, that Catheline had known all along. It had made him so useful after all. Forging a bond with Morradin as they conspired together, unifying them in the need to win freedom through victory. All just another link in his invisible slave chain.

"You knew," he said, staring at Catheline's perfect, unresponsive face. "Didn't you? All this time. All that affection. How much you must have enjoyed the game."

Anger. Another lesson he had learned from Morradin. Anger could mask his thoughts just as well as fear. He let the anger surge into a hot, all-consuming rage, feeding it with the countless horrors in his head, feeling the connection to the White shrivel in its flames. It didn't break, not completely, but for one brief instant it burned down to little more than a thread of purpose, the White's dominance lifted enough to allow his own will to blossom.

He got to his feet, moving swiftly for fear that any delay would allow the White to reassert control. Drawing his revolver, he thumbed back the hammer as he trained it on Catheline's forehead. He began to squeeze the trigger but was momentarily distracted by the sudden appearance of something in his eye-line. It resembled a spear-point, catching the light as it turned, Sirus seeing blood dripping from its sharp point down to the scaled skin that formed its base.

A soft hiss came from above and he looked up into the White's eyes. Sirus began to form a thought, something he might say, even though no human ears would ever hear it, but all thought fled as the pain arrived, and he screamed instead. The White blinked and tore its tail spike free of Sirus's body. He fell, still screaming, feeling his blood leak away in a warm torrent. A chill descended, numbing him enough to banish much of the pain.

"No."

He looked up to find Catheline standing over him, fully awake now, tears shining in her inhuman eyes. "My dear General," she said, hands cupping his face, lips pressing against his. "We had so much still to do. If that bastard hadn't snared me in the trance . . ."

"You . . ." The word emerged in a cloud of blood, staining her face though she barely seemed to feel it. "You . . . knew."

"Your mind was unique," she said, tears falling over her lips which now formed a fond smile. "Far too bright and interesting to waste, regardless of whatever little schemes you came up with over the years ahead. I was greatly looking forward to it all."

Her face bunched and she stifled a sob, raising her face to the White. For once there was no awe or reverence in her eyes, just hard, judgemental reproach. "You didn't have to," she whispered. "I locked the gutter-born bastard's mind away. It's done. You didn't have to . . ."

The White flicked its tail, spattering her face with Sirus's blood before letting out an impatient growl. Catheline's eyes clamped shut and she shuddered in pain, Sirus realising she was being subjected to more punishment. When it ended she let out a low, rasping moan, taking a few seconds to master herself before once again fixing her gaze on Sirus, the red coals of her eyes now dimmed with grief.

"I will miss you, dearest General," she said, pressing another kiss to his lips before rising and moving away. Dust rose and Sirus felt a hard gust of wind, seeing the White ascend into the sky with Catheline on its back.

When they flew out of sight he continued to stare into an empty blue sky. He could feel the battle raging, share the sight of so many Spoiled compelled by the White to renew their assault and realised in a flare of guilt that he would actually miss being a general.

An inquisitive squawk caused him to slowly turn his head and he found himself looking into the eyes of a juvenile White, tongue darting over its bared teeth. It gave another squawk and hopped closer.

CHAPTER 52

Lizanne

The *Hurricane* exploded as they headed back to the Redoubt. There was no warning and it had been several minutes since a Red had even come close. A sudden burst of flame in the upper rear portion of her envelope followed by a booming thud as the whole structure blew apart, then she was gone, just more flaming debris falling into the sea.

"A Red must have lit a small fire earlier on," Morva opined, face grim as she regarded the fast-fading wreckage. "Took awhile to spread."

Lizanne refused to let her gaze linger on the sight, moving to the rear hatch as they neared the Redoubt. A quick survey of the battlefield made for unwelcome news. The second line of trenches had fallen and Spoiled and Green were mounting a fresh assault on the third. They were met by a blizzard of Growler and Thumper fire, the ground midway between the second and third trench lines becoming marked by a growing mound of dead. Lizanne discerned a lack of cohesion in the White's forces now. The discipline and tactical organisation that had marked their previous assaults had been replaced by a seemingly desperate desire to charge straight at the human defenders, regardless of any weight of fire-power they now faced. However, Lizanne took only small comfort from the mounting enemy casualties. A brief glance to the west revealed substantial reinforcements trooping across the plain.

We must have killed close to half by now, she reasoned. *But they have the blood to spend. We don't.*

At her order the *Typhoon's* gunners expended what little ammunition they had left as they flew over the battlefield, aiming for the Spoiled rushing to join in the assault. It might buy the defenders some small respite.

Tekela closed the throttles as they passed over the walls of the Redoubt, turning the aerostat around in preparation for landing.

"It's flying," she said, hands pausing on the controls as she peered through the front window.

Lizanne moved to her side, seeing the White ascending from the hilltop where it had perched for most of the battle. She turned her gaze to the sky, finding the large Black wheeling about over the plain. She quickly injected Blue and slipped into the trance, found no sign of Clay and slipped out again. *What are you doing?* she thought, eyes fixed on the Black as it continued a seemingly placid circular glide, apparently oblivious of the White now dragging itself into the sky with broad sweeps of its huge wings.

"Get us down," she told Tekela. "We need to rearm."

Upon landing she ordered fresh Swarmers loaded and went to find Arberus. He was engaged in directing the fire of cannon on the western end of the walls, attempting to impede the advance of the mass of Spoiled closing in on the outer trench line. The cannon scored hits with every shell fired, it being impossible to miss, but the Spoiled swept on below undaunted. Lizanne noticed again how all order had apparently been forgotten and they appeared possessed by nothing more than an unreasoning desire to throw themselves at the human line.

"Can you hold them?" she asked, coming to Arberus's side.

One look at the grim resignation on his face was sufficient answer. "When the ships resumed their bombardment, I thought we might have a chance," he said, nodding at the sea. "But now . . ."

Lizanne turned, seeing that the Reds had resumed their attack on the fleet. Their strength had been eroded in the first assault but, judging from the number of burning ships, they were still capable of inflicting substantial damage.

"Is there anything you can do?" she said. They both knew evacuation was now impossible, and there was no line of retreat from this place.

"I can pull what's left into the Redoubt," he said. "Since the enemy seems to have abandoned all rational tactics, it might buy us time."

Lizanne shifted her gaze to the sky above the plain. The White was still flying towards the gently circling Black. *At least I know where it's going,* she thought. "Do it," she said, turning and running back towards the courtyard. She drew up short, however, at the sight of the *Firefly* taking off. The small aerostat drifted towards the walls before revving up its engines and flying away. Lizanne stared after it, quickly discerning that it was headed for the hill-top where the White had perched. Turning back to the court-yard, she saw Morva raising her arms in a helpless shrug.

"She took off before I could stop her!" she called up to Lizanne.

Tekela! Lizanne realised, gaze snapping back to the *Firefly* as it flew an unerring course towards the hill-top. *Gone to keep her promise.*

"Get on board!" she shouted, running to the *Typhoon* and clambering into the gondola. She flung herself into the pilot's seat, restarting the engines and pulling back the levers to angle them towards the ground.

"We've only loaded half the Swarmers," Morva protested as they took off. "And the gunners aren't aboard."

"No time," Lizanne told her. "Stand ready at the ignition tube."

She brought the *Typhoon* to three hundred feet, angling the prow at the now-distant silhouette of the *Firefly* before calling out for Morva to ignite the blood-burner. The ground blurred below as the *Typhoon* shot forward, Lizanne opening the throttle as wide as it would go. They had closed half the distance to the other aerostat when she saw a trio of Reds diving to-wards it. Lizanne looked out of the port window, seeing the White pass by in the opposite direction. Craning her neck farther she saw the huge Black finally respond to the danger, abandoning its serene glide to angle itself towards the White.

You already made your choice, Lizanne told herself, turning back to the *Firefly.* There was nothing she could do to prevent whatever was about to befall Claydon Torcreek, but she could still save Tekela.

The three Reds were less than fifty yards from the *Firefly* now. Tekela had evidently spotted the danger and put the aerostat into a sharp turn. As the drakes veered towards it they passed directly in front of the *Typhoon.* The range was fast diminishing thanks to their speed, bringing the Reds close enough for Lizanne to try her luck with the forward-facing guns. The first two flew through the bullet stream unscathed but she had the satisfac-tion of seeing the third twist in a spiral of blood, wings flailing as it plum-meted down.

"Hold on!" she called out, hitting the switch that took the blood-burner off-line then reversing the angle of the port engine. The *Typhoon* hadn't been designed for such sharp manoeuvring, the entire craft letting out a metallic howl of protest and shuddering as she wheeled about, bringing the Reds back into Lizanne's sights. She blew the second Red out of the sky with a concentrated burst, then adjusted the craft's angle to take aim at the third. It was considerably larger than the average Red and made an easy target. Lizanne let the *Typhoon* settle and pulled the trigger. Nothing happened.

"Didn't have time to reload those either," Morva called out by way of explanation.

Lizanne gave voice to some rarely spoken profanity and slammed the port engine back into a vertical angle before reopening the throttles. She drew back the main control lever as the *Typhoon* lurched forward, angling the craft to the left so Morva could fire at the Red with her mini-Growler. This drake, however, proved far more wily than most, folding its wings and slipping beneath the *Typhoon*, the stream of tracer missing by inches. Morva kept firing, tracking the drake as it passed underneath, then letting out a shout of surprise as the beast turned on its back and stabbed its talons into the hull. The mini-Growler was jerked from Morva's grasp by the impact, the weapon tumbling from the hatch into empty space. She came close to following it, managing to grasp a handhold as her legs swung outside, then screamed as flame enveloped the gondola's exterior.

Lizanne injected Black and used it to drag Morva inside, setting the automatic controls before leaping from the pilot's seat. She let out another blast of Black to banish the flames licking at Morva's legs, then lifted her from the gondola's floor as the Red's talons stabbed through the thin hull once more. Metal screamed as the talons tore at the hull, slicing open a large rent. Lizanne looked down, finding herself matching gazes with the Red and realising she had seen it before. An impressive scar marred the scales around its eye, left there by Lizanne's exploding bullet. The beast's gaze narrowed in obvious recognition and it renewed its efforts to tear open the hull, snout poking through and jaws widening. Lizanne threw Morva to the rear of the gondola, cast her gaze around until it alighted on her Smoker and used Black to pull it into her hands.

She unleashed all her Red as she trained the carbine on the Red's gaping maw, scorching its eyes and jamming the barrel deep into its throat as the Redball ignited. The bullet must have met the onrushing combustible gas from the beast's gut as it detonated, the explosion sending Lizanne into the gondola's ceiling whilst filling the interior with a thick crimson vapour. Lizanne landed hard next to the rent in the floor, watching the Red's talons lose their grip as it tumbled headless towards the earth.

Finding it hard to breathe and feeling the onset of unconsciousness, Lizanne pressed her Spider's second button, flooding her veins with all her remaining Green. A certain grogginess still lingered as she regained her footing and clumsily leapt over the gaping hole in the floor to check on Morva. She was unconscious but still breathing; the burns visible through the scorched gaps in her overalls were bad but survivable. *She might even walk again,* Lizanne thought in bitter self-reproach. Going after Tekela without properly rearming had been a mistake driven by sentiment, not something any of them could afford at this juncture. She positioned Morva on her side and used the Spider on the woman's wrist to inject a full dose of Green.

Making her way forward, she struggled into the pilot's seat, resuming control and killing their forward speed. Both engines were smoking but somehow still operational, though she had no notion of how long they might last. She could see the *Firefly* several hundred yards off now, angling towards the hill-top. Turning her gaze south, Lizanne saw the Black and the White finally come together, both drakes spewing fire at each other as they closed so the subsequent struggle began in a nova of flame.

Lizanne pointed the *Typhoon* at the ball of flame and opened the throttles.

CHAPTER 53

Hilemore

The revolver jerked in his fist, sending a bullet into the head of the Green drake charging towards him. It didn't die, however, falling onto its side and continuing to scrabble towards him, claws skittering on the deckboards until Steelfine stepped forward to bring a fire axe down on the beast's neck, the blow sufficiently powerful to sever the head from the body. The Islander reeled back from the explosion of drake blood, teeth gritted in pain as he wiped it from his hands and neck.

A challenging hiss snapped Hilemore's gaze to the left in time to see another Green charging towards him across the aft deck. He raised his revolver, finger repeatedly squeezing the trigger only to hear the dry click of the hammer on an empty chamber. A flurry of shots came from his right, scoring hits on the drake's forelegs and shoulders, sending it into a thrashing halt. Loriabeth stepped past Hilemore, stamping a boot to the back of the Green's neck, pressing it to the boards before putting her last bullet through its head.

A shout of triumph came from the stern where Lieutenant Sigoral was casting the bodies of two more Greens into the sea with the aid of Black, his Corvantine shipmates raising their weapons in celebration.

"Reckon that's the last of them, Captain," Loriabeth said, glancing up from reloading her revolvers. The *Superior*'s decks and upper works were liberally spattered with blood, most of it drake but they had suffered casualties of their own. Three of Colonel Kulvetch's Marines had been roasted in the first Red assault and one of the gun-crews had fallen victim to the Greens dropped into their midst. Looking up at the many Reds still wheeling about the sky, Hilemore deduced their troubles were far from over.

"Mr. Steelfine," he said.

Steelfine paused in the task of dousing his blood burns with water from a canteen and snapped to attention. "Sir?"

"Get any wounded below and remuster the riflemen. Have additional ammunition brought up for the guns. I'll be on the bridge."

"Very good, sir."

Loriabeth followed him as he made his way to the bridgehouse, finding Skaggerhill and two of the riflemen carefully man-handling a Green corpse over the walkway railing. "Whatever else happens, Captain," the harvester grunted as they heaved the beast over, "all the product soaked into this ship today is sure to make you a wealthy man."

"Everyone will get equal shares in any prize money, Mr. Skaggerhill," Hilemore assured him, extending his glass and training it on the shoreline. They were only two miles off but the amount of smoke from so many burning ships made it difficult to gauge the progress of the battle. He could make out numerous flashes indicating a sustained artillery barrage and even from this distance the shouts of thousands of people engaged in combat were audible. As to who might be winning he had no notion at all.

"Drakes ahead, sir!" Talmant called out. Hilemore found them an instant later, a pack of a dozen or more Reds swooping low out of a smoke bank to skim across the waves, heading for the *Superior*'s prow.

"Hard a-starboard!" he barked, Scrimshine spinning the wheel in response. The forward pivot-gun fired as the ship heaved to the right, cutting the lead Red out of the air with a well-aimed cannister shell. The remaining Reds split into two groups, wheeling about to assault the *Superior* from two sides. Hilemore saw the head of one drake jerk as it banked towards the port bow, the beast raising a curtain of water as it tumbled into the sea.

"That's another one for the Preacher, I reckon," Skaggerhill said. He slotted shells into his shotgun and snapped the breech closed before moving to stand ready in the hatch. Loriabeth took up position at the opposite hatch as the riflemen on the upper works commenced firing. The tactic of aiming at the wings paid dividends, two drakes plunging down with shredded wings before they could come close enough to cast their flames at the ship. The cannon on both sides accounted for three more, leaving four who managed to close the distance.

Hilemore saw the pivot-gun crew run for cover as a Red fanned its wing to hover over the fore-deck, fire jetting from its mouth. It managed to send one crewman over the rail in flames before a dark blur streaked into its chest and exploded. Hilemore saw Kriz crouched amidst the smoking debris, another grenade clutched in her hand should she need it. But the drake was unmistakably dead, its open chest cavity leaking gore as it lay across the prow. Hilemore saw Kriz cast the body away, then look up and dive to the side just before a wall of flame covered the bridgehouse windows. Glass shattered and fire momentarily filled the bridge, leaving Hilemore on the deck coughing smoke. He heard the double blast of Skaggerhill's shotgun followed by a chorus of pain-filled profanity.

Hilemore wafted smoke and got to his feet, finding Scrimshine frantically beating out the flames on Talmant's jacket. "Stand aside," Hilemore ordered, hefting a full water bucket and dousing the lieutenant with the contents. "Get back on the wheel."

Hilemore turned to find Loriabeth covering Skaggerhill's broad torso with her duster, smoke seeping from beneath the garment as she pressed it down. Hilemore fought down a rising gorge at the stink of charred flesh. The harvester's face was mostly untouched but, as Loriabeth drew the duster away, it became clear those parts of his chest not covered by green leather had received a bone-deep burn. It extended in a ghastly line from his collar to his belly, blackened flesh leaking blood amongst the rising smoke.

"Got . . ." he breathed, voice pitched high with suppressed pain, "the fucker." He made a vague, jerky gesture with the shotgun still clasped in his hands. Hilemore's gaze went to the head of the Red dangling in the hatchway, leaking copious blood onto the deck, its body lying atop the bridgehouse roof.

"Get that thing over the side," Hilemore called out, sending the riflemen of the captain's guard hurrying to comply. He then instructed two of the South Seas Maritime Marines to take Skaggerhill below and administer a full dose of Green. He began to suggest Loriabeth go with him and oversee his care but one glance at her part-stricken, part-furious visage convinced him to still his tongue.

He went out onto the walkway, drawing up short at the sight of a body lying across the railing. Preacher's tall form was bent like a bow, his upturned face staring up at Hilemore, as blank in death as it had been in life. Hilemore could see no burns on the marksman's body but the blood seeping in a thick torrent from his torso indicated he had fallen victim to a tail strike.

"Preacher."

Hilemore turned to see Braddon Torcreek climbing down from the mainmast. Together he and Hilemore lifted Preacher's body from the railing, laying him down on the walkway. "It was coming for me," the Contractor captain said, crouching at Preacher's side and staring into his empty eyes. "He stepped in front of me . . ." He shook his head, touching a hand to Preacher's bloody chest. "Crazy old bastard. Guess he really wanted it to come true."

"Wanted what?" Hilemore asked.

"The Seven Penitents," Braddon said. "The Seer wrote that the most faithful would be the first to die in the Travail." He shifted his gaze to Preacher's longrifle, which lay on the walkway close by. "If you'll excuse me, Captain," he said, moving to retrieve the weapon and jerking the lever to chamber a round. He slung the rifle over his shoulder, went to the ladder and began to climb. "I got business up top."

Hilemore gave Preacher's corpse a final glance then descended to the main deck, calling for reports. All the Reds had been accounted for and the fires they birthed contained, though the attack had cost them another five casualties besides Preacher, three fatal and two wounded along with Skaggerhill. One consolation was that the *Superior* had now drawn close enough to shore for him to gain an appreciation of the course of the battle. He could see cannon and repeating guns firing all along the length of the Redoubt, providing cover for a large number of defenders retreating through the main gates close to the beach. The trenches appeared to be completely in the hands of the White's army, Spoiled and Greens continuing to advance in the face of the intense fire from the walls. In places they were only yards from the retreating humans, some of whom were fighting a valiant rear-guard action. *Blood-blessed,* Hilemore concluded, seeing how the Greens and Spoiled were cast into the air or blasted with heat as they charged at these knots of resistance. Despite their courage it was clear to him they were about to be overrun. Sheer weight of numbers would tell before long.

"Ship approaching off the starboard bow, sir," Talmant reported.

Hilemore looked to the north, seeing the smoke part to reveal a familiar shape. The *Viable Opportunity* steamed to their front, paddles churning at full auxiliary power, her signal lamp blinking a message in standard Protectorate code. "Fall in astern," Hilemore read, quickly recognising the author's hand in what followed. "All guns fire to shore. Report for court martial at close of hostilities."

"So time hasn't improved his temperament," Hilemore muttered to himself before returning to the bridge. "Signal the engine room, ahead full auxiliary power. Mr. Scrimshine, follow that ship."

Under Scrimshine's deft handling the *Superior* took up position twenty yards to the stern of the *Viable*. Hilemore descended to the deck and directed the transfer of guns from the port rail to starboard, he and Steelfine man-handling one of the pieces into position before hearing an eruption of repeating gun-fire from the *Viable*. The Reds had evidently noticed their approach and determined to prevent it, descending in a dense stream straight for the lead ship. Her repeating guns were putting up a hail of fire, concentrated so that the tracer converged on the leading Reds, blasting drake after drake out of the sky.

"Load explosive shells!" Hilemore ordered the gunners, tearing his gaze from the unfolding spectacle in the sky. Their mission was to save the army on shore and the *Viable* was buying them the time to do it. "Fuses set for air-burst."

He focused his gaze on the Redoubt, seeing the rear guards breaking in the face of overwhelming odds, the defenders streaming for the gates which were now in the process of closing. "Aim at the base of the ridge," he told the gunners, glancing left and right to ensure all guns were loaded and lanyards ready to be pulled. "Fire at will!"

The cannons fired almost as one, all eight guns arrayed on the starboard rail and the forward pivot-gun. They were close enough to the shore for Hilemore to judge the fall of shot without use of a glass. Most of the shells were on target, exploding in a line along the steep lower slopes of the ridge to send their deadly rain down on the Spoiled and Greens now charging towards the Redoubt gates. The effect was immediate, the enemy so close-packed that Hilemore estimated a hundred at least had been felled by the first broadside.

"Keep firing!" he called out. "Pour it on, lads!"

A loud screech from the direction of the fore-deck drew his gaze in time to see Kriz send another grenade into the midst of a trio of attacking Reds. Two were killed outright and the third landed on the prow, managing to cough out some flames before Kriz snapped its neck with Black. Hilemore raised his gaze to the *Viable*, blinking in shock at the sight of her upper works being mobbed by drakes. They latched themselves onto the railing and superstructure, snapping at the crew or spewing flame into the hatchways. Many of the Viable's fittings were alight and she began to fall out of line as a loud boom sounded within her hull, a tall column of dark smoke shooting from her stacks a second later.

He started forward, intending to order the pivot-gun to rake the *Viable*'s deck with cannister, but forced himself to a halt. *Not my mission,* he told himself, teeth gritted as he tore his gaze away, turning it to the shore. The *Superior* fired three more broadsides as they passed by the Redoubt, each one seeming to cut down more drakes and Spoiled than the one before. They lay in mounds beneath the walls and the gates, which Hilemore noted in relief were now firmly shut. Only when satisfied that the attack had been stemmed did he turn his attention back to the *Viable*.

She was listing badly now, one paddle turning feebly whilst the other churned the sea white. Fires raged across her decks and Hilemore was treated to the dreadful sight of a crewman being torn apart by Reds, three of the beasts rending the screaming figure into pieces which they then cast into the sea, squawking in triumph. Above the screeching drakes and roaring flames he could hear the crackle of rifle fire and the growl of at least one repeating gun. *They're still fighting,* he realised.

His mission was clear. He should turn the *Superior* about and conduct another barrage of the shore-line to prevent the enemy massing at the gates. *But they're still fighting!*

For one of the very few instances in his life Hilemore was seized by an unwelcome and very palpable sense of indecision. The *Viable Opportunity*, the ship he had commanded from the Battle of the Strait through all the many travails that led them to Lossermark, was dying before his eyes, and he found he simply couldn't allow it.

"Mr. Steelfine!" he called out. "Ask Lieutenant Sigoral to join us on the fore-deck and be sure to bring his grenades. Tell all guns to load cannister, and prepare a boarding party."

"Aye, sir!"

The Islander turned and began to shout out the requisite orders, then fell silent when Hilemore, seeing a new shape resolving through the smoke a quarter-mile off the port bow, said, "Belay that, Number One."

"Sir?"

The *Endeavour* emerged from the haze on full blood-burner power, her prow knifing through the sea as she steamed towards the *Viable*. The two guns on the *Endeavour*'s bows blasted out cannister as she closed the distance, Hilemore seeing several Reds fall from the stricken ship as the metal hail struck home. When she was less than a hundred yards off, the *Endeavour* halted then reversed her paddles, the sea seeming to boil about her hull as she slowed. It was a manoeuvre that no sane captain would usually contemplate, but this day was far from usual. Shattered and splintered wood emerged in a cloud from the *Endeavour*'s paddle casements as the force of the water fought the power of the blood-burner. In seconds the paddles were in tatters, capable of making only about a third of their normal purchase on the sea, but that was more than enough for her captain to perform a rapid turn, presenting her port-side guns to the *Viable*. They fired in quick succession, raking the other ship's upper works with cannister and sweeping away at least half the Reds still tormenting her. The surviving drakes on the far side of the *Viable* rose as one to meet the new threat, wings blurring as they sought the sky.

Hilemore barked out a rapid series of orders to the pivot-gun crew. Within seconds they had loaded cannister and trained the gun on the space between the *Viable* and the *Endeavour*. "Fire!" Hilemore ordered as the first Reds began to sweep towards the smaller ship, blasting several out of the air. By then the *Endeavour* had completed another full turn, bringing to bear the as yet unfired guns on her starboard side. Water rose in tall spouts as drakes careened into the sea, cut down by the broadside, but a dozen or more remained to press home the attack on the *Endeavour*.

"Twenty degrees to port!" Hilemore shouted towards the bridge, pointing frantically towards the *Endeavour*. Scrimshine had apparently anticipated the order given the speed with which the *Superior* altered course. A pall of smoke had already blossomed around the *Endeavour*, though Hilemore could hear a cacophony of small-arms fire and drake cries. Kriz ran towards the prow, her satchel of grenades over her shoulder. At Hilemore's call Sigoral soon joined her and the two Blood-blessed waited, grenades in hand.

The smoke cleared as the *Superior* closed on the *Endeavour*'s position, revealing a ship bathed in fire from stern to bow. Reds were still hovering over her, casting their flames down to add to the inferno. Kriz and Sigoral let fly with their grenades, launching them with Black so fast that they blurred. Within moments the Reds had been blasted out of the air, leaving the *Endeavour* a flaming wreck.

"Hoses to the port rail!" Hilemore ordered, though he could see it was pointless. The fires had begun to merge, forming one great conflagration that completely covered the *Endeavour* above the water-line. Within seconds the inevitable happened and her ammunition exploded, tearing her in two. Steam rose as the divided hull capsized, the two sections slipping beneath the roiling sea before the *Superior*'s prow cut through the scene of her demise.

Sea-sister . . . He stared at the flotsam passing by the hull, flames still licking at some of it, hearing a distant voice call to him but suddenly finding himself too weary to respond.

"Captain!" Steelfine's large hand gripped his shoulder, the Islander pointing to something off the port beam. Assuming they were about to face another onslaught of Reds, Hilemore straightened his back and raised his gaze. A cluster of figures were struggling in the water twenty yards away, Zenida easily recognisable in the midst of them by virtue of her voice, loud enough to reach his ears, "Are you just going to let us drown?"

Unwilling to stop the ship unless in absolute necessity, Hilemore had Kriz and Sigoral haul the survivors aboard, plucking them from the sea with Black and depositing them on the fore-deck.

"Clever," he said as Zenida shook the salt water from her hair. "Abandoning ship the moment they pressed home their attack. Lost your ship but saved your crew."

"Not all," she said, face grim. "Left ten behind to burn."

"Victory demands a blood price," he told her in Varestian. It was an old saying, one he knew to be beloved of pirates, and was gratified to see it bring a faint smile to her lips.

"I would like to make a statement," she said.

"And that is?"

She moved close, pressing a kiss to his lips, brief but far from chaste. "I need to find some product," she said, moving away. "I trust you have some left."

Hilemore cast a brief glance around the deck, but it seemed the crew were too preoccupied with hosing away the copious amounts of drake blood from the boards to have noticed. He proceeded swiftly to the bridge, ordering the engines to dead slow and instructing Scrimshine to bring them about. He had the deck-hands play their hoses over the *Viable* as they passed by, although a good portion of the fires seemed to have already been extinguished. Despite this it was evident the ship was out of this fight, smoke leaking in a dense black cloud from her stacks and her paddles idled in the water. Seeing a signal lamp blinking atop her bridge Hilemore recognised the rigid form of Captain Trumane, working the lamp with one hand whilst pointing to the shore with the other. "See to your duty," the message read.

"Send an acknowledgment, Mr. Talmant," Hilemore said. "Then signal the engine room to increase speed to one-third."

His briefly uplifted spirits plummeted upon clearing the wallowing hulk of the *Viable* and it was a struggle to keep the dismay from his features as the situation ashore stood revealed. The White's army were boiling up the slopes of the ridge, resembling a huge swarm of ants as they clambered over one another, the bodies forming together to create a ladder of flesh. They fell by the hundred to the defenders on the walls above, massed rifle and repeating guns reaping a terrible toll, but the tide of drake and Spoiled continued to rise inexorably.

Hilemore called down to Steelfine to rig the shells to detonate on impact and have the guns fire into the base of the massed bodies. Their first pass succeeded in reducing the height of the mass by several yards, blasting grisly red holes into it that seemed to be healed almost instantly. The *Superior* circled around for another pass, achieving less impressive results. The shells evidently killed a large number of Spoiled and Greens, but the mound continued to grow. Raising his spy-glass, he soon saw why. The Spoiled were gathering up the bodies and parts of those killed by the barrage and pushing them back into the mass. They were using the flesh of their fallen as building material.

Raising his glass higher, he saw that the top of the mass was now only yards away from cresting the Redoubt walls. In desperation he brought the *Superior* round again, moving at dead slow to allow a maximum number of broadsides, the guns this time ordered to aim at the top of the mass. This succeeded in reducing its height in some places, but not all, forcing Hilemore to an unwelcome conclusion. *We are only one ship, and the ammunition won't last forever.*

Their stocks of explosive shells were already down to six rounds per gun, although they did have copious stocks of cannister but the range was too great for it to be effective. He had only one more manoeuvre to try and, although the consequences were obvious, it was either this or just sail away.

"Mr. Scrimshine," he said, "prepare to steer hard a-starboard on my command. Mr. Talmant, spread the word to the crew. Load cannister and stand ready to run aground."

He saw in annoyance that Talmant wasn't listening, instead the lieutenant had his ear pressed to the crow's nest speaking-tube, eyes wide in shock. "Mr. Talmant!" Hilemore snapped, causing the young officer to snap to attention.

"Sorry, sir," he said. "It's just . . . crow's nest reports ships to the north."

"There are ships all over this particular stretch of sea, Lieutenant. Sadly, none of them seem to be in a position to assist us at present."

"Beg pardon, sir. Not Varestian ships . . ."

Talmant's voice was drowned out by a loud whooshing sound that filled the bridge as something very large passed overhead at considerable speed. He managed to catch sight of the point of impact, the explosion dwarfing the *Superior*'s efforts with a blast that exceeded all the shells they had fired that day. The detonation turned the world white and sent the ship reeling back from the shore, Hilemore feeling a hard, stinging impact to the back of his head before the whiteness turned to black.

CHAPTER 54

Clay

This is not my body . . . He repeated the thought, over and over, jerking as he fought the pain. *My body is whole. There is no pain. This is not my body, my body is whole, there is no pain. This is not my body my body is whole there is no pain!*

He let out a shout as the pain vanished, his shattered spine fusing back together, reforged by sheer effort of will. But though he could exert control over his own mental image, the prison that held him rested in the mind of Catheline Dewsmine, who at this juncture seemed unlikely to return.

Clay got to his feet, eyes roving the featureless iron cube of his cell. *Clever or not,* he thought, *she's still crazy. There has to be a crack somewhere.*

He scoured the walls, hands tracing over the rough metal, looking for some small fissure in the surface, something he could pry apart. Several minutes of searching produced nothing but, as he retreated from the walls, grunting in frustration, something scraped beneath his boot. Looking down he saw it was one of the pictures that had fallen from the mantelpiece above the fire when it transformed. The fire-place was gone now but this picture remained. Crouching, he picked it up, expecting to find an image of Catheline in her younger days, or a photostat of her unfortunate parents. Instead it was a Spoiled wearing a military uniform. *The same one from the hill-top,* Clay realised, recalling Lizanne's shared memories from recent trances. *Sirus. Guess she must like you to keep your image in her favourite memory.*

As the thought rose, rich in self-recrimination at allowing himself to be trapped, he saw the image shift in the frame. The deformed face of Sirus turned, looking out at him in clear recognition. Clay stared back, watching Sirus's lips move. He brought the picture closer, straining to hear the words.

I'm dying, Sirus told him in a strangely matter-of-fact tone. It struck

Clay as the voice of a man entirely accepting of his fate, free of fear or desperation. He almost envied him. *She kept something of me,* Sirus went on. *I suppose she wanted to be able to talk sometimes. I suspect she gets very lonely.*

Yeah, Clay said. *That's too bad. You got anything useful to share?*

I don't think so. I had a plan, you see? A grand scheme to free us all, set the Spoiled to rebellion and bring down the White. But it was just a childish folly. She knew. The Spoiled cannot be freed. Once it takes us, it binds us forever.

No, Clay told him. *That ain't right. There were free Spoiled once. They helped bring it down before.*

The picture-frame suddenly became hot in Clay's hand, the image of Sirus emitting a soft glow. *How?*

Ain't something to be said. More something to be felt. It was the gift of the Black drakes, they showed me. And I can show you.

The frame grew hotter, the glow brighter. Clay felt Sirus's thoughts lose their reflective apathy, replaced by a fierce, rage-fuelled need. *Do you have it?* he demanded.

Clay found the required memory quickly enough, but as this was not his mind the ability to form it into something he could share was limited. In his own mindscape he could have refashioned Nelphia's surface, here all he had was what he carried with him. He drew his revolver, remoulding it into a ball of gun-metal the size of his fist. Concentrating hard, he brought to mind the crystals he had seen in the Enclave, and the Black crystal Kriz retrieved from Krystaline Lake. The ball of grey metal began to change, growing spines and the hard dull surface turning to glass. With the crystal complete, Clay summoned the memory Lutharon's ancestors had shared with him. The crystal began to take on a soft glow as Clay poured in the memory.

Here, Clay told Sirus, extending the picture towards the floating crystal. The picture-frame suddenly became white-hot. He dropped it, yelping in pain. Focusing on his singed fingers, he banished the pain and returned the charred tips to their previous state. When he looked again Sirus's picture was glowing bright enough to dazzle him. Squinting, he watched as it began to melt the iron floor of the cell, the metal glowing red then white before dropping away, creating a wide hole. The picture disappeared into the hole, quickly followed by the crystal, leaving Clay standing over it in indecision.

Well, he thought, preparing to jump. Can't see any other way out of here.

The waking world returned with a jolt, Clay gasping in shock as a heavy buffeting wind came close to dislodging him from Lutharon's back. He grabbed hold of a spine and held on, ears filled with the challenging roar of a drake, but this time it wasn't a Red.

The White streaked towards them, the roar swallowed by the flames jetting from its mouth. Lutharon banked hard, Clay gripping the spine with both hands as the Black stood on a wing-tip, deftly avoiding the flames before flaring his wings and pivoting about. The White spread its own wings, wheeling around to hover some twenty yards away, Lutharon following suit. Clay saw that the White was not alone. Catheline was perched atop its back, staring at him in evident puzzlement. Thought she'd locked me away for good, Clay surmised, reaching into his satchel and drawing out a grenade, but the White attacked before he had a chance to arm it.

Lutharon folded his wings and dived as the White surged forward, Clay hearing the snap of its jaws above his head. Lutharon extended his wings and went into a tight turn, opening his jaws to blast out a stream of fire at the White, catching the larger animal in mid-turn. It let out an enraged roar, lashing out with its tail as Lutharon swept closer, the spear-point leaving an ugly red scar on the Black's neck. Lutharon coughed flame directly into the White's face, momentarily blinding it before rearing back to lash out with its talons, tearing into the scaled flesh of its opponent. Clay could only hold on as Lutharon pressed his advantage, head stabbing forward to clamp his jaws on the White's neck, blood welling as he bit deep.

The White screamed in pain and rage, its own talons slashing at the Black, their blood mingling as they tumbled about the sky, Lutharon holding on despite the wounds scoring his hide. There was a sound like a miniature thunderclap, Lutharon's teeth tearing clear of the White's neck as he was propelled backwards. As they were pushed away Clay caught sight of Catheline, staring at them in intense concentration as she unleashed a powerful wave of Black. The force wave continued, pushing them down towards the earth. Clay glanced over his shoulder to see the plain rushing towards them and, realising he had somehow managed to keep hold of the grenade, tugged the arming pin free and used the last vestiges of his Black to propel it at Catheline.

The White moved in a blur, tail whipping to intercept the grenade before it could strike its target. The explosion broke Catheline's concentration, cutting off her stream of Black and leaving the White minus the spear-point at the end of its tail. The severed tip leaked blood as the White whirled about and went into a steep dive. Lutharon twisted and spread his wings wide, stalling their fall then sweeping back up into the sky. Clay looked down to see a fire erupting on the plain as the White chased them with its flames.

Clay armed another grenade and tossed it over his shoulder, quickly followed by two more, reasoning gravity would provide the required distance. He was rewarded with the sound of three rapid explosions, but a backwards glance revealed the dispiriting sight of the White still labouring in pursuit, albeit with one side of its face blackened and leaking blood. He could feel Lutharon's strength fading, seeing the blood streaming in thick torrents from his many wounds, but still he turned to fight.

Drawing in his wings, Lutharon turned over and streaked down to meet the White head-on. Clay met Catheline's eyes as the drakes sped towards one another, finding them full of hate but also something more. *She's afraid,* he realised, seeing how her eyes widened as the massive Black plummeted towards her. *Even the mad can learn to fear.*

He quickly drew his revolver and began to fire, managing four shots before a wave of Black blasted it out of his hand, Clay hearing the snap of breaking bones as it spun away. He ignored the flare of agony and unleashed all his remaining Red in a rapid stream. He had the satisfaction of seeing Catheline's hair take light before the two drakes collided.

The impact jarred him loose of Lutharon's back, and the surrounding air turned briefly into fire before he fell clear, trailing smoke as he tumbled towards the ground. The impact came sooner than expected, Clay careening across the earth in a cloud of raised sod before sliding to a halt, stunned and winded. He lay there, dragging air into his lungs and trying to force animation into his limbs, hearing the sweep of very large wings drawing closer.

CHAPTER 55

Sirus

He returned to his body to find his left hand clamped between the jaws of a juvenile White. He barely felt it, having lost so much blood that sensation was now just a distant thing. His hand gave an involuntary twitch as the juvenile bit down, causing it to open its jaws and hop back with an annoyed hiss. An answering squawk from the right caused Sirus to turn his head, finding the other juvenile regarding him with its head cocked, yellow eyes blinking in apparent curiosity.

"Wondering why I'm still here," he said in a guttural whisper. "So am I."

The juvenile on the right seemed to take this as some sort of challenge, flaring its wings and lowering itself to pounce, mouth opening wide. There was a sharp percussive crack and the juvenile was instantly transformed into two separate pieces. The upper half spun away from the lower, turning end over end in a bloody cart-wheel. It landed a few feet away from its twitching lower half, jaws snapping in a reflex.

The juvenile on Sirus's left leapt, wings blurring and flame jetting from its mouth, only to be swiftly blasted out of view. Sirus was curiously unsurprised by the face that looked down on him once his rescuer came into view, a face tense with hate and intent on murder.

"I . . ." Sirus began, finding the words choked by blood. He coughed, trying to clear it but Tekela didn't seem interested in any statement he might make.

"Shut up," she said, shouldering the carbine she carried and reaching down to pull a bone-handle knife from a sheath on her calf.

"I have . . ." he tried again, blood gouting from his mouth.

"Shut up, Sirus!" She stepped closer and crouched, putting the knife blade to his neck. He saw that she was crying and was pained to have grieved her so.

"I have something to do," he said, throat finally clear of blood although he could feel more rushing in. He met her damp eyes, hoping she saw some vestige of who he had once been in the monstrous visage she beheld. He managed to raise his right hand, fingers open and palm extended. "Please . . . it's very important."

Tekela let out a sob as her gaze tracked from his face to the blood welling from the hole in his chest. "You killed Jermayah," she said, taking a hard ragged breath. "You killed all those people."

"Yes," he replied, his words punctuated by sharp, rasping breaths, each one he knew bringing him closer to death. "And . . . I have done . . . far worse. Soon . . . I'll die . . . for what I've done. You can kill . . . me, if you wish. But first . . . there is something . . . I have to do. For you . . . for everyone."

Tekela closed her eyes tight, another sob escaping her as she withdrew the blade from his neck. "What?" she said, head sagging and voice laden with defeat. "What is it you have to do, Sirus?"

"Remember . . ." He extended his hand to her again. "Will you . . . help me?"

She stared at his hand, baffled and appalled in equal measure. "How?"

"I need . . . to remember . . . what it was . . . to be free."

His vision grew suddenly darker, Tekela's face becoming a vague shadow, as if veiled by a curtain of black lace. He felt her take his hand, the first time she had ever done so. It was smooth against his callused, scaled palm, small but also strong, hardly the hand of a girl. He forced himself to focus on her face, piercing the veil that covered it just for an instant, but it was enough. Once he had thought her a doll, something so beautiful as to be not quite real. Now she had a small bloody scar on her chin and another tracing across her brow into her tousled and unkempt hair. Her eyes were red with tears and dark with fatigue, lips pale and drawn back from her teeth in anguish. She was so very real and he knew she had never been a doll at all. He looked upon a face that possessed only an echo of the girl she had been, a face transforming into the woman she would be.

Sirus closed his eyes, drawing his mind back into himself. The bright shining crystal was waiting, a gift from the Contractor Catheline had imprisoned in her mind. It shone brighter as his purpose found a connection with the memories it held, blossoming out, filling him with its gift. The memory it revealed was strange, but filled with enough visual clues for his archaeologist's mind to divine that he was seeing a moment from the past, a moment which contained a vital piece of information. He watched the memory play out, and summoned Tekela's face once more, let it lead him to the moment he had first seen her. It had been some tedious ball his father forced him to attend, trussed into a suit that didn't really fit him, scratching his collar as he concealed himself in the quietest corner of the room.

When he saw her it was like everything else went away, fading into a mist with her at the centre, so bright, so utterly captivating. She moved with a peerless grace across the ball-room, gliding into a curtsy as Burgrave Artonin presented her to the Governor General. Her smile was a thing of wonder and her necklace glittered in the glow of the chandelier as she gave a delighted laugh at the governor's witticism.

But it hadn't been like that. Her smile had in fact been nervous and forced, often veering into a scowl as she scanned the other ladies present with badly concealed disdain. When she danced it was a clumsy, inelegant spectacle that drew titters from the other guests. Also her necklace, Sirus saw now, hadn't glittered very much at all. The jewels were glass set into a brass chain. Sirus discovered later that her father had sold much of her mother's jewellery to fund his expeditions to the Interior.

He had thought that the many humiliations he endured over the following months had been inevitable, that his helpless pursuit of her had been beyond his control given how completely she had captured his heart that night. He was her slave, after all. Except he wasn't. He was a foolish youth who had convinced himself he was in love with a beautiful but, on occasion, deeply unpleasant girl. He had made a choice, because a free mind can do such things and in time he had learned what it was to have no freedom at all, not in mind or body.

Until now Sirus had been shutting out the other Spoiled, the babble of their minds in the midst of battle a low, ugly murmur at the edge of his consciousness. Now he let them in, all of them, and shared the gift of long-dead drakes.

At first it was like pouring cold water on white-hot coals. Thousands of Spoiled minds snatched from the fury and chaos of battle roiled in confusion as the gift spread through the multitude. Some slipped instantly into madness, their minds breaking at the sudden intrusion of a sensation they had never suspected might return. Others fought it, raging against the separation from the all-powerful consciousness of their White god. But most welcomed it, joy filling them as the invisible shackles fell away. As the gift leapt from mind to mind like a fire let loose in a dry forest, Sirus felt more and more souls blink out of existence.

They're dying, he realised, pausing to look through the eyes of a Spoiled, seeing those around him standing still, faces drawn in wonder or shock as bullets and cannon flayed them from above. *I'm killing them.* The thought was accompanied by panic that came from an awareness of how little time he had left.

Sirus flitted from mind to mind, searching the now-silent and immobile army for a soul that might save them, finding it close to the Redoubt gates. He found Forest Spear lying only seconds from death as his life seeped out from the many bullet-holes in his chest, his mind filled with memories of his days hunting through the jungle with his brother warriors. Sirus touched minds with him, feeling a pulse of gratitude before the darkness fell. He moved on, finding Veilmist under a mound of dead and dying Spoiled. There were hundreds of them, all seemingly cut down in an instant, by what means Sirus couldn't know. Veilmist had survived the calamity but the weight of so many corpses would soon crush the air from her lungs.

Help her! Sirus commanded. The Spoiled were slow to respond, some stumbling in confusion, others taking advantage of their new-found liberty to rejoice in the novelty of refusal. *Please,* he added. *You know me. I want you to live. All of you.*

He felt a pulse of recognition run through them, shot through with a sense of trust and empathy. He had been a slave like them, and now they felt his desperate desire to preserve their lives. Several hundred Spoiled surged towards the gates, braving the continuing fire from the walls above to drag Veilmist from beneath the mound of corpses.

Get them away from the walls, Sirus told her. He found the Islander's mind warm with welcome and a seemingly endless well of gratitude.

Where are you? she asked. *We will come to you.*

It doesn't matter. Just . . . Sirus felt a growing chill creep over the fringes of his awareness, the combined vision of so many eyes rapidly eroding, shrinking to just a few images, one of which brought a fierce urgent need to cling on to life.

The White!

He could see it, mighty wings spread wide as it came to earth on the plain, the slim figure of Catheline slipping from its back. Lying near by was the body of a large Black drake.

It's there! he told them, putting every ounce of will and strength he could in the thought, the last command he would ever give to this army. *Kill it!*

The Spoiled left him then, the tumult of rage and blood-lust fading away. He blinked and found himself looking up into Tekela's eyes once more. He raised a hand, pressing it to her cheek and took joy in the affection he saw in her face, a face he found himself content to take with him into the dark.

CHAPTER 56

Clay

For a time he lay stunned, vision clouded as he sought to refill his lungs, the ominous sound of fast-approaching wings loud in his ears until it was swallowed by the roar of engines. He blinked, vision clearing to reveal Lizanne staring at him from the hatchway of her aerostat. It hovered above, engines pointed towards the ground. He lifted a hand to wave in greeting but then a loud, ragged exhalation drew his gaze and he saw Lutharon lying some twenty yards away, wings flapping and tail coiling weakly. Clay tried to stand, found he couldn't, and cursed as he reached for the product in his duster, drinking down a full flask of Green. Rising to his feet he half-stumbled to Lutharon's side, letting out a groan of dismay at the sight of his injuries.

Ragged, deep gashes had been clawed into Lutharon's hide, leaving his chest and belly a gory mess. Blood welled from a bite mark in his neck as he tried to raise his head towards Clay.

"Lie still, big fella," Clay told him, smoothing a hand over the Black's brow as he looked into his eyes. He could feel his pain and fear, and the gradually slowing beat of his heart. "It's fine, we did all we could," Clay said, exuding as much calmness as he could. "You don't have to stay on my account. They're waiting for you."

He stood and watched the light fade from Lutharon's eyes, knowing that in his dying Ethelynne would die with him, although the memory of both would live on as long as there were Black drakes to carry it.

He turned, hearing a change in the pitch of the aerostat's engine, watching as it came to earth a short distance away. Lizanne emerged from the gondola and they stood regarding each other, apparently neither having any notion of what to say. Finally, she said, "Do you have any Green? I'm running short."

"Yeah, I got another flask."

He began to reach into his duster, then his gaze jerked back to the aerostat as the air became filled with the sound of roaring flames. The White reared up from beyond the curved bulk of the aerostat, flames jetting from its mouth to bathe the craft from end to end. Clay gaped in shock as Lizanne, instead of running clear, immediately leapt back inside. He dragged his satchel round, pulling out a grenade before reaching for his product once again. He gulped down some Black and focused his gaze on the White, now in the process of crouching amidst the smoke from the burning craft. Clay raised the grenade, summoning his Black in preparation then found himself in the air, the grenade flying away to explode harmlessly well wide of its target. He landed a good fifty yards from Lutharon's body, the Green in his veins preventing serious injury, though he was obliged to spend several seconds lying stunned before managing to scramble to his feet.

"Gutter-born bastard!"

Catheline advanced through the grass towards him, weaving from side to side as if drunk, blood streaming through the fingers she had pressed to the wound in her stomach. *Guess I'm a decent shot after all,* Clay concluded. Much of Catheline's golden hair had been burned away, leaving behind a seared and smoking scalp. Her skin was marble-white from loss of blood, but her red-black eyes glowed bright, lit with a vibrant hatred.

She screamed as she sent another wave of Black towards him, Clay leaping to the side with Green-assisted speed and replying with a burst of his own. It struck her squarely in the chest, sending her flat on her back. Clay leapt high, focusing his gaze on Catheline's prone form, intending to expend all the remaining Black in crushing her into the ground until she was just a red smear on the earth.

The White's tail slammed into his midriff, sending him spinning in the opposite direction. Had the tail still possessed its spear-point tip the blow would certainly have been fatal, instead of inflicting enough agonising pain to leave Clay stunned and helpless as he rolled to a halt. He heard the White's claws scrape at the earth as it came closer, moving with unhurried intent. Looking up, Clay saw its head poised above, blackened and bleeding from his grenade but possessed of a gaze as knowing and full of malice as he remembered.

"Hate me as much as I hate you, huh?" Clay asked it in a pained grunt. "Guess that's fair. It's what we do, us folks, us people. Hate's what's worst about us, and grows worse with the hating. You were made to hate, because we made you."

The White let out a faint huff of smoke, head tilting as if in consideration. Clay had no notion of whether it understood him, or even if it cared for anything beyond its own malice. But somehow he had given it pause, and that was all he needed.

"Got something for ya," Clay said, "gonna make you hate me even more."

He snapped his gaze to the side, focusing on Catheline. She had managed to get back on her feet and resumed her stumbling walk towards him, eyes glowing bright as ever. Clay used all his Black at once, unleashing it too fast for her to deflect or evade. In one swift motion he reached out to grasp her neck with an invisible hand and snap it.

The White let out a roar as Catheline's body collapsed, rearing back from Clay, shaking its head in confusion. Clay fumbled for his satchel, clumsy hands trying and failing to grasp a grenade. By the time he had managed to drag one of the devices free of the satchel the White appeared to have recovered some of its senses, turning back to him and rearing up, a haze of heated air forming around its mouth. Then it stopped. The White stood frozen, the flames blossoming from its jaws but shooting into the air instead of at Clay. His gaze swivelled to the aerostat, now a smoking ruin, but standing in the foreground was Lizanne, staring fixedly at the White as she directed her Black at it. Slumped on her knees at Lizanne's side was a young woman Clay didn't know, but evidently also a Blood-blessed from the signature Black-fuelled focus with which she stared at the White.

Clay's gaze swung back to the beast, seeing how it shook in the invisible chains that bound it, neck slowly coiling as it fought against its bonds, its head inching closer to the point where its still-blossoming flames could be brought to bear on its victim. Clay hooked a finger into the grenade's ring and pulled, letting out a shout of pure agony when his broken digit lost purchase. Spitting curses he switched hands, sweat bathing his scalp as the heat bore down . . . then disappeared.

He looked up to see the White drowning in a dark wave. Lizanne's black had faded and it thrashed and flamed in the tide that swamped it, biting and tearing as the wave swept over it, a wave of flesh rather than water. The White continued to fight, its tail and claws leaving dozens of Spoiled rent and dying, others blasted by flame or snapped in two by its jaws. But the weight of numbers proved unstoppable. The Spoiled tore at the White with their claws, stabbed it with their bayonets or hacked at it with their war-clubs. Blood and scraps of scaled flesh rose in a cloud as they bore the beast down, thousands of them crowding in to rend at the beast in a crimson fog. Clay was struck by the fury on their faces, lacking the blank purpose he had witnessed in Lizanne's shared memories. The Spoiled, like the White, had learned to hate. Their destruction of the White took place in silence, free of shouts or screams of vengeance, the only sounds the wet tearing of the huge drake's flesh and its last few, guttural breaths.

When it was over Clay found himself surrounded by Spoiled, all standing in immobile silence. He started to rise, finding it difficult and jerking in instinctive fear when the Spoiled helped him up. Looking around, he saw that most of them regarded him with curious, even expectant faces like an audience waiting for a speech. One of them soon worked her way through the throng towards him, a diminutive female with the blonde hair typical of Island folk. She addressed him in perfect Mandinorian with a slight managerial accent, her tone formal if a little guarded.

"On behalf of those present," she said, "I offer our surrender. But we have conditions."

CHAPTER 57

Lizanne

They burned Sirus on a pyre constructed atop the hill where he died. The Spoiled lay his body on a pile of Green corpses, the plain being so lacking in trees. The bones and shredded flesh that constituted the White's remains were added to the pile, along with the bodies of the two juveniles. The body of Catheline Dewsmine had been left where it lay, none of the Spoiled showing the slightest inclination towards touching it. When it was done Lizanne injected Red whilst Clay drank a vial and together they blasted the pyre with heat, the blaze soon consuming its grisly fuel and birthing a thick, foul-smelling smoke that rose into the darkening sky.

Lizanne retreated from the fierce heat, pausing when she saw Clay lingering, something clutched in his hand as he stared into the flames. He stood with a slight stoop, his face drawn in a persistent pain large doses of Green had yet to erase and she worried what internal injuries he might have suffered. *He looks like an old man,* she thought. She ran a hand through her hair, thick with sweat and assorted grime, and it occurred to her that her own appearance was hardly any more edifying.

"What's that?" she asked him, nodding at the object in his hand.

He glanced at her, holding it up. It was a vial, the contents impossible to discern in the glow of the fire. "Just some old product," he said, tossing it into the flames. "Reckon it's gone bad."

They moved back, Lizanne going to Tekela's side and drawing her into an embrace when she saw the tears streaking her face. "I'm sorry," Tekela sobbed into her shoulder. "For flying off . . ."

"So you should be." Lizanne drew back a little, smoothing the hair away from Tekela's face. "Need to get some Green on those scars," she said, reaching to extract a vial from her Spider.

"Leave it," Tekela said, turning back to the fire and resting her head on Lizanne's shoulder. "They're not so bad."

The surrounding Spoiled, several thousand strong, stood around the hill-top in silence as they watched the fire consume their general. Lizanne could see their brows twitching and knew that however still their voices might be, the mind of every living Spoiled was joined in grief.

She had used her scant remaining Blue to trance with Sofiya Griffan, requesting that she communicate the terms of the Spoiled's surrender to Captain Trumane and the rest of the Varestian Defence League's high command. She found the woman's trance had changed, the dark forest regaining some colour, though there was a guarded feeling to it, the air shot through with an aura of tense expectation.

Something to tell me? Lizanne had asked her.

Sofiya's trance thrummed with momentary indecision before she replied, Lizanne discerning a great deal more from her thoughts than her words. *The Free Protectorate Fleet has arrived,* she said. *Captain Trumane has accepted a commission as Commodore.*

How fortuitous for him, Lizanne observed.

Their arrival was fortuitous for all of us, Sofiya returned. *Had they not, the battle might have gone against . . .*

How long have you been in contact with Exceptional Initiatives?

The sky above the forest turned a faint shade of red, Lizanne detecting both shame and defiance in Sofiya's emotions.

I recall asking you to pass on the weapons designs to the Protectorate, Lizanne continued. *I said nothing about Exceptional Initiatives. I assume the Protectorate never actually received the designs. What else have you told them, Sofiya?*

I have a child to think of, Sofiya replied, her mindscape darkening into something wind-swept and hostile. *I should like them to grow up in as safe and comfortable a place as possible.*

Was contacting Exceptional Initiatives Captain Trumane's idea or yours?

The wind grew stiffer, twisting the branches of the surrounding trees so that they resembled snakes coiling for a strike. *The captain has been a good and loyal friend in these difficult times,* Sofiya replied, Lizanne sensing a dangerous edge to her thoughts.

I am glad to find you recovered from your grief, Lizanne told her and ended the trance.

"Come on," she said, taking hold of Tekela's hand and moving to Clay's side. "The *Superior*," she said. "Have you tranced with anyone on board?"

He nodded. "Lieutenant Sigoral, says they've taken some bad knocks but she's still afloat."

"Good. We have to go." She turned, leading him towards the *Firefly*. "Now."

Morva slipped into unconsciousness during the flight to the Redoubt. Lizanne and Clay carried her to the subterranean chamber where the League had established a makeshift hospital. It was full of wounded, the air musty with stale blood and filled with the constant murmuration of hundreds of people in pain.

"Lucky we're not wanting for Green," a grey-faced doctor told Lizanne as he examined Morva. She and Clay had been obliged to remove a recently expired Varestian pirate in order to provide an empty bed. "Plenty of drakes piled up outside. The harvesters are working flat out to refine it." The doctor lifted the lid of Morva's right eye, grunting in satisfaction. "She's still with us," he said. "And her pulse is strong." His expression grew more severe as he turned his gaze to Morva's burn-covered legs. "As for these . . ."

"Use any amount of Green necessary," Lizanne instructed.

Seeing the implacable glint in her eye, he nodded. "It'll repair much of the tissue damage, but the scars . . ."

"A Lokaras is always proud of their scars."

Lizanne turned to find a bedraggled Alzar Lokaras striding towards them, his gaze dark as he surveyed his adopted niece. "Especially when earned in battle," he added in a more subdued tone. He jerked his head at the doctor, sending the man scurrying to fetch the product. "So," Alzar said, Lizanne seeing how his hand hovered near Morva's. "It appears we have a victory, Miss Blood."

"Won with her help," Lizanne said. "Your niece had a hand in killing the White. Is that sufficient to finally win your approval, Captain?"

She was expecting anger but he barely shrugged. "I didn't adopt her, you know," he said softly. "Not truly. I met to trade with some Dalcian reavers. She escaped from the cage they had her in and stowed away on my ship. They came after us, thinking I'd stolen her. Reavers are not easily dissuaded from battle, so we fought. I lost crew that day, including my son." Lizanne saw him extend a finger to tap the back of Morva's hand. "When it was over I wanted to throw her to the King of the Deep, but I couldn't. She was just a little girl who took a chance at freedom. So I took her back to the High Wall, but I never let her call me father. Only ever uncle."

Lizanne moved to Morva's side, smoothing back the hair from her head. "She's my best pupil," she murmured, for some reason finding the unwelcome face of Madame Bondersil coming to mind. *At least I didn't try to kill her,* she thought, pushing the image away.

"I have to go," she told Alzar. "Will you stay with her?"

"My ship burned and sank," he replied. "For the moment it seems I have nowhere else to be."

A rberus had his arm in a sling, the shoulder having been broken by a tail strike from one of the few Greens to make it over the wall at the height of the battle. He appeared even more aged than Clay, face sagging with fatigue as he cast his gaze over the mass of bodies below the Redoubt. They were thickest around the gates, piled up in a great ring around the crater, a legacy of the rocket fired by the Free Protectorate cruiser now moored off shore along with a flotilla of six frigates. As a result of all the damage and destruction wrought on the Varestian ships this small fleet now constituted the dominant maritime force on the globe.

The bodies were a mix of Spoiled and Greens, though not every drake had perished. The Greens left alive after the battle had fled into the hills to the west, followed by the few surviving Reds. However, Lizanne doubted that a population of drakes would continue for very long on Varestian territory. As they flew towards the Redoubt the *Firefly* passed over numerous sickly drakes stumbling about the plain, both Reds and Greens. Some had already slumped into lifeless immobility and Clay opined that it had only been the White's will that had sustained them so far from their birthplace.

"We're still counting," Arberus said, gaze still preoccupied by the bodies. "It could be over a hundred thousand people died here, ours and theirs."

Lizanne glanced back at the *Firefly*, waiting in the courtyard with Clay and Tekela on board. She was keen to be gone but required certain assurances first, and had little time to indulge his morbid reverie.

"General Arberus," she said, voice clipped and formal. It was enough to make him blink and turn towards her, a cautious frown on his brow.

"Back to business, is it?" he asked.

"The Spoiled," she said. "I need to know their terms will be respected."

So far the Varestians hadn't ventured closer than a mile to the hill where the Spoiled congregated. The fact that the Spoiled had kept their weapons and posted a cordon of cannon around their camp might have had a good deal to do with it.

"There are few in my command with the appetite for another battle," Arberus replied. "However, that may well change as the days pass. It's a rare heart that can resist the lure of vengeance, and this army has a great deal to avenge."

"Evacuate the Redoubt," Lizanne told him. "Hand it over to the Spoiled. At least then they'll have a strong position to defend if the Varestians turn on them. In the meantime I'll set about meeting the rest of their terms."

"You really think that's possible? After all this?"

"The corporate world may have fallen, but I suspect there are still bargains to be struck in the one that has replaced it."

A day later the *Firefly* rendezvoused with the *Superior*, resting at anchor some fifty miles south-east of Blaska Sound. Tekela skilfully steered the craft through a stiff cross-wind to set her down on the aft deck. Clay, still stooping a little but otherwise much recovered, was immediately embraced by his cousin and uncle as he stepped down from the gondola.

"How's Skaggs?" he asked them.

"He'll live," Braddon Torcreek assured him. "And got himself quite a scar to boast about for years to come."

"Sorry about Preacher, Uncle," Clay said. "Mad as a Blue-addled rat he may have been, but I reckon I'll still miss him."

"At least he ain't around to be proven wrong," Braddon replied with a sombre shrug. "All the Seven Penitents were s'posed to perish in the Travail."

"An impressive machine, miss." Lizanne turned to find herself confronted with a tall man she knew instantly but hadn't actually met. Hilemore's gaze roamed over the *Firefly* in evident fascination, his military mind no doubt imagining all manner of practical uses for such a contraption.

"We had others that were more so," she said, extending her hand. "You, I assume, are Captain Hilemore."

"And you are Miss Lethridge."

He gave a formal nod of his head as they shook hands. "I'm glad to see you recovered," she said. "I had heard you were wounded."

"Just a bump on the head. The blast from that newfangled rocket gave us a pretty hard smack. I got off lightly compared to my helmsman: broken jaw. Still, at least it's shut him up for a while."

"Thank you for doing this. I know you're risking much in undertaking this mission."

He gave a thin smile before replying, "Yesterday I received a signal from Captain Trumane to report aboard the Free Protectorate flagship as of this morning. I very much doubt he intended to offer warm congratulations and a captaincy in his new command."

"Doesn't that make you a mutineer? An outlaw perhaps?"

"Then little has changed. In any case, as far as I can ascertain, the laws that previously bound us no longer have meaning. Which would make me a private individual free to sail wherever I wish. Luckily, the bulk of my crew seems to share my sentiments, for the time being at least."

"Where will you go when this mission is complete?"

"My . . . co-captain and I will retrieve her daughter from Stockcombe. After that . . ." Hilemore's smile broadened. "I've a yen to do some exploring. My grandfather left a long shadow, one I've spent my life trying to match. But he was always more an explorer than a fighter. Perhaps that's the legacy I should be honouring from now on. Besides"—Hilemore's gaze darkened somewhat—"in a world that now has weapons like that rocket and your marvellous aerostat, the military path no longer has much appeal to me."

"Without the Protectorate how will you live? A ship needs supplies, repairs from time to time."

"There are many ports in this world, all now bursting with stockpiled goods. There are always opportunities for an honest captain to turn a profit."

Lizanne turned as Tinkerer's lanky form emerged from the *Firefly*. He stood surveying the ship and its scorched decks and damaged fittings, his usually bland features betraying a certain trepidation.

"I've never been on a boat," he explained, catching Lizanne's eye.

"This is a ship, sir," Hilemore pointed out in polite but emphatic tones.

"I'm afraid you'll have to become accustomed to your passenger's manners, Captain," Lizanne said. "Give him a cabin to himself, keep him supplied with pen, ink and paper and you'll find him mostly tolerable."

She went to Tinkerer, hesitating a moment before embracing him. His thin frame remained stiff and unresponsive except for the soft pat to her shoulder. "Are you sure about this?" she asked, drawing back. "Life in the new Mandinorian Republic might not be so bad."

"A prison is a prison, no matter how comfortable," he told her. "The memories the Artisan left me are more interesting in any case. There is a great deal still to find and study. Also, weapons are boring. They only do one thing."

Lizanne went forward, finding Clay on the fore-deck with a young woman she recognised from the trance. "You have it?" she asked after Clay made the introductions. Kriz looked him at him before replying. When he nodded she reached for a chain about her neck, detaching a small vial and handing it to Lizanne.

"The formula," Kriz added, giving Lizanne a strip of paper bearing a number of symbols. "I have tried to mirror the chemical notations used in this age," she went on. "Although a plasmologist should conduct a thorough analysis before attempting to recreate it. The crystals?"

Lizanne consigned both items to her pocket then inclined her head towards the stern. "Unloaded and awaiting your inspection. A fair trade, wouldn't you say?"

"Actually," Kriz said, moving away, "I believe I'm doing your world the greatest service by taking them where they won't be found."

Lizanne watched her leave before turning to Clay. "Trance with me when you arrive," she said. "I should also like to be updated as to your progress, if you're so minded."

"Happy to. Might take awhile to find all of Miss Ethelynne's notebooks. I'm thinking she had a lot of hidey-holes scattered about the Interior. We'll take a look at the Enclave first, make sure there are no more infant Whites scuttling about."

He met her gaze, his expression growing more serious. "You really think they'll agree to this deal of yours? I know everything's changed and all, but you're asking them to give up the very thing that made the old world what it was."

"With this," Lizanne said, patting the pocket containing Kriz's vial and formula, "I suspect I could ask for all the tea in Dalcia and there would be a long list of those willing to fight each other to give it to me."

She paused, unsure of what to say next. They had shared so much in the trance that words now seemed inadequate, clumsy even. "Good-bye, Mr. Torcreek," she said finally. "It has been . . . a very great honour."

"I doubt that," he said. "But thanks for saying it, anyways. And for saving my life, o'course. Occurs to me I hadn't said so before."

They didn't embrace, or even shake hands in farewell. It seemed strangely formal, even meaningless. Their minds would be joined for however many years they had left. Between them there would never truly be a good-bye.

Lizanne turned towards the stern at the sound of the *Firefly*'s engine revving up. She gave him a final smile and went aft, greeting Braddon Torcreek along the way. "If you're ready, Captain."

He nodded and pulled his daughter into a crushing embrace. Loriabeth blinked tears as he released her, saying, "Tell Ma I'll come see her soon."

"Come with me and I won't have to," Braddon said.

Loriabeth glanced at the Corvantine Marine lieutenant standing close by and lowered her head. "Sorry, Pa. I think it's time I found my own contracts."

Hilemore's hulking second in command barked out an order as Lizanne moved to board the *Firefly*, a line of sailors snapping to attention on the aft deck in response. The captain saluted as she climbed into the gondola, Braddon Torcreek following her after a moment's hesitation. She closed the hatch and Tekela angled the engine to take them up.

"Back to the Mount," Lizanne told Tekela. "I suspect Captain Trumane has already arrived."

Lizanne turned her gaze to the starboard port-hole and watched *Superior* shrink beneath them, Hilemore maintaining his salute until she could no longer make out his form. Soon the ship had become just a speck on a very big ocean, fading from view as they flew away.

EPILOGUE

To: Madame Lewella Tythencroft
premier elect, north mandinorian republic
sanorah

From: Lizanne Lethridge
co-director, mount works manufacturing company
blaska sound
varestia

Date: *5th Lebellum, 1601*

Subject: *Proposals Regarding Future Relations between the Mount Works Manufacturing Company and the North Mandinorian Republic.*

Dear Madame Premier,

May I be so bold as to open this missive by offering my most sincere congratulations on your recent election. As you will no doubt be aware news takes much longer to travel in these interesting times so please forgive my tardiness in not writing sooner, but word of your appointment only reached us in the last few days.

I assume that by now you will have been fulsomely briefed by Commodore Trumane on the outcome of his visit to our facility at the close of recent hostilities. I write in furtherance of the discussion begun during that meeting in the hope that its somewhat rancorous conclusion might be overturned and a more amicable basis for future co-operation established.

Before I set out what I believe to be a sound basis for future negotiations, I should first like to address the situation regarding the large number of individuals currently residing on the Varestian Peninsular commonly referred to as Spoiled. I confess to harbouring a distinct dislike for this particular term but since an alternative eludes us I shall employ it for the sake of brevity. As you will be aware the Spoiled currently occupy a fortified position on the peninsular and so far remain unmolested by their Varestian neighbours. However, as time progresses I hear ever more voices raised in objection to their continued presence and consider it only a matter of time until some form of violent confrontation becomes inevitable. Furthermore, the Spoiled themselves have no desire to remain in their current location. As stated in their original terms of surrender, it is their wish to be transported to the Arradsian continent. The situation is further complicated by the fact that the vast majority of Varestian captains refuse to entertain the prospect of having any Spoiled aboard their ships. Many are also highly disinclined to sail to Arradsian waters despite assurances that the danger of attack by Blues has now passed.

Another salient issue relates to an aspect I feel certain Commodore Trumane included at the forefront of his report to you regarding a particular substance currently in my possession. I feel certain, Madame Premier, that a personage of your insight will require little explanation as to the importance of this substance. I also feel sure that the newly installed First Citizen of the Corvantine Republic will also require similarly minimal explanation, should I feel minded to bring it to her attention. This would be a simple matter to arrange since I count General Arberus, Commander-in-Chief of the Corvantine People's Freedom Army, as a personal friend.

As to the nature of the substance itself, our own plasmologists have confirmed its efficacy as a synthetic substitute for the Blue variety of draconic plasma—please see the enclosed report which details their findings in full, apart from several sections which have been redacted for reasons of corporate security. You will note from the report summary that our plasmologists believe, subject to sufficient resources being made available, the knowledge gained from their analysis will in time enable production of synthetic versions of the other varieties of product (excepting White, of course, the chemical basis of which eludes our keenest plasmological minds).

Turning to the matter at hand, I am prepared to surrender both the substance and the formula required for its production to the North Mandinorian Republic subject to the agreement of the following contractual obligations:

1. The Arradsian continent will remain free of colonisation for perpetuity and there will be no further attempts to harvest drakes or breed them for harvesting purposes.

2. The North Mandinorian Republic will provide sufficient shipping to transport the Spoiled to Arradsia as soon as can be arranged.

Please note that these conditions are non-negotiable and my offer is subject to expiry within three months of the date of this letter.

Finally, returning to the subject of Commodore Trumane's visit, I regret I was unable to assist the commodore in his principal mission. However, I am not in a position to keep track of all my former employees. Also, I have no information regarding the true identity of the individual Commodore Trumane was so keen to meet, we only knew him as Tinkerer. It is my hope to one day resume his acquaintance, but where or when that might come to pass is impossible to say at this juncture. Neither, contrary to Commodore Trumane's oddly strenuous protestations, do I possess any knowledge regarding the whereabouts of the former Corvantine Imperial Navy ship *Superior*, nor its captain, nor any of its crew.

As to the crystals of bizarre nature known to have been in the possession of the White, I must confess my complete ignorance as to their fate. The rocket fired by the Free Protectorate at the height of the Battle of the Redoubt unleashed an inordinate amount of explosive power and I consider it highly probably the crystals were destroyed in the blast. I would request, in the interests of forging an amicable working relationship, that you no longer pursue this point, for I consider this particular matter is, and will remain forever, closed.

I await your reply with the greatest interest and look forward to many years of fruitful and mutually beneficial co-operation.

Yours,

Lizanne Lethridge
Co-Director, Mount Works Manufacturing Company
Blaska Sound
Varestia

DRAMATIS PERSONAE

IPV Superior

Corrick Hilemore—Captain of the IPV *Superior.*

Steelfine—Barrier Isles native and First Officer of the IPV *Superior.*

Dravin Talmant—Junior Lieutenant IPV *Superior.*

Naytanil Bozware—Chief Engineer IPV *Superior.*

Myratis Lek Sigoral—Junior Lieutenant of the Imperial Marines, former acting captain of the INS *Superior.*

Scrimshine—Convicted smuggler and inmate of Lossermark gaol, helmsman to the IPV *Superior.*

Claydon Torcreek—Unregistered Blood-blessed and member of the Longrifle Independent Contractor Company.

Krizelle "Kriz"—Ancient member of the Philos Caste.

Braddon Torcreek—Uncle of Claydon Torcreek. Captain and chief shareholder of the Longrifle Independent Contractor Company.

Loriabeth Torcreek—Daughter to Fredabel and Braddon, apprentice gunhand to the Longrifle Independent Contractor Company.

Cwentun Skaggerhill—Chief harvester to the Longrifle Independent Contractor Company.

Preacher—De-anointed cleric to the Church of the Seer and marksman to the Longrifle Independent Contractor Company.

Zenida Okanas—Blood-blessed and former captain of the pirate vessel *Windqueen.* Contracted Blood-blessed and navigator to the IPV *Superior.*

Akina Okanas—Daughter to Zenida.

Varestia

Lizanne Lethridge—Blood-blessed. Former covert agent of the Exceptional Initiatives Division, Ironship Trading Syndicate. Co-Director of the Mount Works Manufacturing Company.

Jermayah Tollermine—Technologist and employee of the Mount Works Manufacturing Company.

Professor Graysen Lethridge—Freelance Technologist. Son of Darus Lethridge, inventor of the microscope and co-inventor of the thermoplasmic locomotive engine. Father of Lizanne Lethridge.

Tekela Akiv Artonin—Orphaned daughter to Corvantine noble Burgrave Artonin. Lizanne's ward. Lead aerostat pilot to the Mount Works Manufacturing Company.

Madame Hakugen—Former Comptroller of the Eastern Conglomerate Port of Lossermark. Later Co-Director of the Mount Works Manufacturing Company.

Makario Bovosan—Composer, pianola player and former inmate of Scorazin Imperial Prison City. Friend to Lizanne.

Garrit Verricks—Captain of the IPV *Profitable Venture*.

Benric Thriftmor—Ironship Syndicate Board member and Director of Extra-Corporate Affairs.

Zakaeus Griffan—Contracted Blood-blessed of the IPV *Profitable Venture*, husband to Sofiya.

Sofiya Griffan—Contracted Blood-blessed of the IPV *Profitable Venture*, wife to Zakaeus.

Wulfcot Trumane—Captain of the IPV *Viable Opportunity*.

Ensign Tollver—Junior Officer aboard the IPV *Viable Opportunity*.

Dr. Weygrand—Medical Officer of the IPV *Viable Opportunity*.

Alzar Lokaras—Claimant to leadership of the Okanas Clan and Custodian of the High Wall.

Morva Lokaras—Blood-blessed. Adopted niece to Alzar.

Arshav Okanas—Co-Chair of the Varestian Ruling Council, claimant to leadership of the Okanas Clan and half-brother to Zenida Okanas.

Ethilda Okanas—Co-Chair of the Varestian Ruling Council, mother to Arshav.

Sanorah

Lewella Tythencroft—Acting editor of the *Voters Gazette*. Senior member of the Voters Rights Alliance.

Fredabel Torcreek—Wife to Braddon Torcreek and co-owner of the Long-rifle Independent Contractor Company. Leader of the Carvenport refugees in Sanorah.

Sigmend Talwick—Chief correspondent with the *Sanorah Intelligencer*.

Molly Pins—Former Carvenport resident.

Stockcombe

Jillett—Blood-blessed. Member of the Voters Rights Alliance and Free Stockcombe Governance Committee.

Coll—Member of the Free Stockcombe Governance Committee.

Colonel Ethany Kulvetch—Commander of corporate forces in Stockcombe.

The White Drake's Army

Catheline Dewsmine—Blood-blessed. Former Mandinorian socialite. Chosen servant of the White Drake.

Sirus Akiv Kapazin—General, former curator Morsvale Imperial Museum of Antiquities.

Henris Lek Morradin—Former Grand Marshal of Imperial Corvantine Legions. Co-general and rival to Sirus.

Veilmist—Former Island native. Chief statistician to the White's army.

Forest Spear—Arradsian tribal warrior.

Others

Arberus Lek Hakimas—General of the Corvantine People's Freedom Army.

Hyran—Blood-blessed. Aide to Arberus.

Jelna—Blood-blessed. Former revolutionary and aide to the First Citizen.

Varkash—Former pirate and inmate of Scorazin Imperial Prison City. Admiral of the Corvantine People's Freedom Navy.

Attcus Tidelow—Captain of the SSM *Farlight*.

ACKNOWLEDGMENTS

Thanks once again to my US editor, Jessica Wade; my UK editor, James Long; and my agent, Paul Lucas, for their support and guidance over the course of three long and complex books. Also, thanks to my proofreader Paul Field, who still won't let me pay him, and thanks most of all to the readers who have joined me on this journey. It's always sad to say good-bye, but every story must reach its end.

Anthony Ryan lives in London and is the *New York Times* bestselling author of the Raven's Shadow trilogy. He previously worked in a variety of roles for the UK government, but now writes full time. His interests include art, science and the unending quest for the perfect pint of real ale.

Find out more about Anthony Ryan and other Orbit authors by registering for the free monthly newsletter at www.orbitbooks.net.